Pedalers

Jack B. Sudar

Order this book online at www.trafford.com
or email orders@trafford.com

Most Trafford titles are also available at major online book retailers.

Orginal cover design by Laura Riley
Color graphichs by Josh House

Printed in the United States of America.

ISBN: 978-1-4269-4522-9 (sc)
ISBN: 978-1-4269-4523-6 (hc)
ISBN: 978-1-4269-4524-3 (e)

Library of Congress Control Number: 2010914946

Trafford rev. 12/02/2010

 www.trafford.com

North America & international
toll-free: 1 888 232 4444 (USA & Canada)
phone: 250 383 6864 ♦ fax: 812 355 4082

This book is what could happen.

I took our existing systems, and world events, plus life styles of people I have encountered, and made changes in a loving way. The rings, like circumcision, can be accepted. Self preservation will love the rings. It is going to be a drastic change in our lives.

Philosopher Aristotle said, "I count him braver who overcomes his desires than him who conquers; for the hardest victory is over self."

I have learned patience from my wife, Bernarda.

I have seen the most forgiving and unselfish, my father, Jack

I know what hard work and stress can do, my mother Ana

Prayer and meditation every day makes loving the world so much easier.

I would like to thank Jean Ayers, with Independent Clause, for the initial editing of this book. With her patience and red pen, I was able to move forward.

Thank you also to Laura Riley for the original design of the cover and to Josh House for the color graphics.

Why don't you write a book like this yourself? If never published, or you just write a few pages; you will feel that changes can be made.

When you start to write, we ask only one thing:

LOVE EVERYTHING AROUND YOU, EVEN THE BITING BUGS

Jack B. Sudar

Table of Contents

NAMES

BOT	Beginning of Tubes
The Record Keeper	Everything and anything is recorded
Orbit	Year
Rotations	Day
Moon	28 days. Four phases 1st, new, 3rd, full
Phase	Seven days
Sharer of Responsibilities	co workers
Collector of Information	Caseworkers
Enforcement Regulator	Policeman
Rings Master	Person in charge of placing the rings on every maturing male
Donor	Male, sperm donor-procreator of human offspring
Incubator	Female, incubates her egg with male sperm to give birth to an offspring
Tubes	Used by everyone and freight carts throughout the country with runners to conduct electricity made by Pedalers, and covered with solar panels.
Bounce	Similar to American football. Players have injury-free uniforms.
Fling	Person catapulted within a device that opens like a Frisbee for landing.

Everyone is named after a star

Scorpio	14 orbit youth-main character
Aires	His donor-father
Almaaz	His incubator-mother
Cepella	Female bounce player
Alcor	Space propulsion engineer
Mizor	Assistant to Alcor
Alioth	Assistant to Alcor-same incubator as Betelgeuse

Megrez	Assistant to Alcor-makes mistakes
Phecda	Trumpet musician and tube maintenance
Albiseo	Plant selector-visits the uncomfortable-seeks Phecda
Duhbe	Grade 3 scientist-seeking Aldebaran
Aldebaran	Seeking Duhbe
Struve	Scorpio's friend
Orion	Almaaz's ancestor
Betelgeuse	Nurse in birthing dwelling-same incubator as Alioth
Alnitak	Newborn female
Tau	Alnitak's incubator
Mintaka	Almaaz's ancestor
Rigel	Nurse-newborn nursery
Sirus and Castor	Old men
Alphard	Beads-female-never mated
Algol	Aires's assistant
Cetus	Scorpio's friend
Epsilon	Aires's assistant
Hydra	63 orbit female-flinger champion
Antares	Female with mental problems-tried to kidnap a female child
Norma	Alphard's incubator
Cepella	Female bounce player
Shania	Almaaz donor
Pleiades	Dietician

From a country devastated by a plague

Ivan	Very hairy
Manuel	
Fillipe	
François	

01-Too much smoke

Scorpio was soaked by water his incubator threw onto the fire he had started. "You know what? If it had gotten out of hand, kilowatts would be taken from your reserve!" "Please," Scorpio said with a firm and steady voice, "Incubator, I was just measuring the combustion time for this pile of dry wood chips. The pile had a measured amount enough to have a factor of seven. It was not out of hand. Please don't panic again with me. I believe it best to question my activities before doing what you have just done." "You should have told me before you even attempted to experiment. At your age your donor and I have total responsibility for any of your actions. The smoke from your experiment could have started a series of reactions in which all of us would have been visited by the collector of information. That visit does not come without a fee of kilowatts. You did not have a permit. The residue on your experiment shows your total disrespect for the purity of the air. I admire your excitement and knowledge in working with heat calories, but you could have just visited Calorie Experiment Results at your base. If you wish to do the same again, get a permit and the necessary heated molecule chamber. You know how important it is for us to produce as many kilowatts as we can," said his incubator with an equally firm and steady voice. "If this incident is closer to what is appropriate to your way of thought, I will give you a hug and if you feel that my actions were proper, I would just love a hug from you," she said. Scorpio smiles and quickly gives his incubator a very tight squeeze, even holding on a few seconds longer than he usually does. That was settled as it usually is.

02-Orion's panic

Scorpio was delivered by a very loving and considerate woman. She did not get that way just by accident. Her gene history does not have one account of any ancestor for eighteen generations. Her gene pool was cited recently as one that has the highest level of restraint of brain dysfunction due to spontaneous disruption. It missed the beginning of the tubes by three generations.

Third generation Donor Orion was on his last day on his third phase of the moon responsibilities as a water/waste pick up on his last route back and was completely exhausted. He decided on his own to take a land route which would have gotten him to the deposit station a few minutes earlier. The Record Keeper states that a rabbit darted in front of his bicycle and trailer, which was loaded with waste for testing by the health team. The bike's front wheel hit it at an angle causing Donor Orion to flip on its side and some of the waste packets opened and spilled their contents onto the back of his uniform. The front wheel was bent just enough to rub against the front fork but moveable. He returned to the deposit station via the land route entrance, parked the trailer, and deposited the work bicycle to the lot with all of the others, and walked to pick up the "all use" one. He was now in the area of full audio and video detection. The bicycle recovery inspector informed the waste attendant that a report was to be made for the bent wheel. He approached Orion and asked to return to the deposit station and make a report, then smelled something foul. Nothing seemed out of the ordinary other than the odor and he asked Orion if he farted or does he always smell that way? He told the attendant what happened. The attendant pushed the panic button and yelled into the microphone, "Code 4! Code 4!" That was two short of the highest alerts.

03-Donor's choice

In just a matter of minutes, three Enforcement Regulators glided out of nowhere and Donor Orion was surrounded. That wasn't upsetting, but when they smelled him they threw a body bag around him while he was seated. He struggled to free himself by clawing with his fingernails. The bag followed each of his fingers with the slightest of strain. He twisted as much as he could, placed his body across the bag, and gave one vein busting push. His effort proved successful as he was able to bust one of his feet from out of the bag. He grabbed the hole with both hands ripping it apart, growling like a mother bear protecting her cub. One tiny spray into the opening by an ER was all it took to totally immobilize the panicked prisoner. He was transported to the decontamination chamber, but was then later moved to a lonesome place for three rotations. The three ERs had to be decontaminated also, and that was another kilowatt fee that was removed from Orion's reserve. The accident would have been totally overlooked, even the bent wheel, but brain dysfunction due to any kind of spontaneous disruption is not acceptable. Orion's loss from his reserve was for replacing the bag, and the decontamination time for the three ERs, plus the spray. The Record Keeper has everyone's activities, and everyone has access to them.

Scorpio's Donor knew everything about his incubator before he accepted her offer of a union for procreation. What a romance. He programmed his DNA into The Record Keeper. Up came 429 potential females compatible to his for a sound procreation. He studied every physical attribute and learning scale number each with greater concern than his final exams as a Health Team Supervisor. The decision he makes will be with the Tubes for eternity. He wanted a stable offspring; more intelligent than even himself.

04-Swimming

A donor for today's responsibility is not a simple task. When the tubes were originated, voting gave The Record Keeper full authority to select the so-called perfect union. It was accepted because it was the craze of the time. The automatic version gave rise to a non-emotional attachment between the procreators. It did take three generations to have a complete changeover because of the fear of reverting back to the obsolete primitive culture. The fear had motivated to such a fiery tempo, the possibility of an open rebellion was very real. Free through was encouraged in all walks of life but the one; procreation.

The free flow of semen has destroyed every society that has ever existed. The separation of the sexes causes more turmoil than before the tubes.

Scorpio was most intense in his studies even at the age of 14 solar orbits. He liked soccer, bounce, swimming, and dabbled in other sports. His kilowatt hours in Reserve were normal with others his age. His incubator invited him to the beach which was 12 kilometers away. Every time he went, his generation drag was usually set low, because exertion on his sprouting joints was too painful. He tried a higher kilowatt generating number on his bike, but the exertion was too great. Off they went to the tube opening 200 meters away. Different color of body could be set by each wearer. It wasn't until five generations ago that they were all one color or another. Now, they were weird squares and stripes, and zigzags, plus many other goofy looking combinations, which had no real rhyme or reason. The beauty of free thought.

05-Pedaling Energy

The sun's radiation wasn't too great today. Solar flare session has just passed and the ozone layer was slowly recovering from abuses by the ancestors. "Scorpio, why don't you pull your R-shield over your head? Your face will take a little and no real damage will be done" pleaded Incu. He did so, and then ran across the sand, eventually being enveloped by what was the largest wave of the day. His incubator kept a sharp eye on him and was not too far away, just in case if a problem were to arise. He recognized some others he knew using the same holo-teacher. Splashing females was the best of all. Underwater tag seemed to attract the greatest number of juveniles. When the time came to close, Scorpio and Incu went to the tube entrance, picked up a bike, adjusted their seat to their own fit, and headed off to their dwelling pedaling the entire journey. Their body cover was nearly dry before they entered the tube, but was wet with sweat again a kilometer into the tube.

Incu rubbed her underarms one at a time in an upward movement which allowed the body cover to provide more body heat to be released. If need be, she would do the same wherever she felt uncomfortable. She noticed Scorpio slowing down and talked to him on his speaker phone. "What's up big boy?" asked Incu. "Nothing Incu, I'm trying to increase my generation, but the distance we have to go, I might need you to push me with my generator set to zero if I keep this number." It had happened before a few orbits ago when Scorpio was showing off to his neighborhood leader, who was in the adjacent tube. He was totally exhausted and his legs just gave out. Pride sometimes can be crushed by the simplest of actions.

06-Dwelling Color

"Incu, do you like the hues reflecting from our dwelling? They seem to have no life in them. The far right of the spectrum is great in cooler weather, but the Celsius is down" said Scorpio. "What meets your fancy today, my little kilowatt generator?" Incubator returned. "Something more in line with the others around us. OK?" "Be my guest, just not too radical, you know how Donor feels don't you?" "Incu, this was not the setting we had when we left! Someone or something moved it. I'll bet it is one of those birds perched on the control. I'm going to have to improvise some kind of cover," grunted Scorpio. "Now, you know you can't do that unless the voters approve," replied Incu. "It's no big deal. Just move the setting to where it was, and that's it" she continued. "We will only be here a few more rotations because your donor has chosen to become the leader in the recovery clinic 200 kilometers south of here. His generation rate will dramatically increase in that position. Now, you can see why our dwelling here is like everywhere, a dwelling."
The plants growing around the dwelling were in full bloom. It wouldn't be much more than 30 rotations before some of them could be harvested. Rain had not fallen for more than a moon phase and

everyone in their respective dwellings would have enough water so the plants would not suffer. Non-potable water bladders were placed at convenient locations. Covered containers for the irrigation had to be physically moved to the plants. Only the ones that would produce fruit were moistened enough for them to do what nature had intended. Plant coordinators were on the move constantly observing for drooping plants. It was their job to check the plants, water them if need be, and record the degree of damage; if any, there would be a kilowatt deduction to the dwelling occupant.

07-Medallion Color

It was late in the day when Donor Aires returned to the dwelling. He was at his chosen station at daybreak full of vigor and now had just enough energy to have the last quiet time of the day with Incu and Scorpio. It was a normal rotation. Nothing unusual. Aires popped a few pellets before spreading out his mat. They were programmed by the nutritionists. Now and then, fresh vegetables would be available and would be there to supplement the "dried stuff" as Scorpio called it.

"I'm glad to see you two at the beach today. Did you notice that gawky body cover that was under the umbrella next to yours?" Aires asked and continued, "Is there a name for that color? I looked at the color chart and it seemed it was not between any hues." "It was magenta and the reflection off the sand and the other umbrella did give it an awkward hue," said his incubator. "Now, how did you find time to get into that beach area?" Incu asked. "Now, come on mate. You were recorded leaving the tube for the beach and it only takes a moment or two to find you. With someone like your body, you stood out like a beacon," was his response. "Do I? We'll find out what your feelings are before long," she cooed. He looked at her medallion and its color was not right for them together. He knew the consequences of pregnancy. He felt fortunate that it has been fourteen solar orbits since Scorpio because of his knowing her cycle.

"Incu, acting like you are now just might make you have to use another dwelling for the night. Look at your cycle medallion. Don't tempt me again, please, please, please. The time will be here in four rotations," Donor Aires pleaded.

08-Meal Together With Pellets

Scorpio knew what his donor was going through. The agony of other ringed males was evident most everywhere. At the beach, his male associates who were a few orbits older than he would come in close contact with a female and let off a groan and be in pain. Arousal would do its normal thing, but with the ring in place, the results were such agony that it quickly dissipated. Scorpio knew that he would be having the same done to him. It was a mournful ceremony attended by anyone who was stationed in dwellings near to his.

They usually ate their food pellets at leisure, but this time they held hands around the small table together and all said, "May the originator of the universe be kind to us. May the one who taught us to love one another be with us. May the wisdom of the voters be the best for new procreation. May the Record Keeper be accurate." Each of the three released proportional amounts of the small round balls of concentrated food from its sterile dispenser. The flavor was changed for their desire by dusting whichever one they found most palatable. Water was discouraged at meals because chewing their food caused the salivary glands to work, making for easier digestion. Plus, chewing toughened the jaws and teeth roots. The small particles of the pellets would cleanse the teeth leaving them very bright. The Health Group gave notices on every monitor periodically every rotation, not only on teeth, but other necessary preventative procedures. Non-compliance would not be practical. The lunar exam at the automated examiner would notice it, and the Health Team would do a follow up. Kilowatt deductions were severe when it was administered by the Health Team.

09-Donor is Being Transferred

"How about some chess now?" asked Donor Aires. "Me first!" shouted Scorpio. The last few times Scorpio did very well. In fourteen moves he captured his donor's King. The practice with the computers did wonders. Donor Aires moved a pawn in front of the king, confusing Scorpio to no end. "What was that? The last time we went at it, you always opened a path for your bishop. What advantage would you have with that move?" he pleaded. "You know that there are all kinds of first moves, and you have to know them all. I suggest you get acquainted with First Moves in Chess. Your incubator did, and now she is unbeatable," he firmly suggested. It ended with a tie. Great for the young man to be.

"I just researched the new facility you want to move in to. We have it so much nicer in this dwelling. The beach is closer; many more boys Scorpio's age are here. Plus, all of the plants that we have will supplement our diet and we could save on kilowatts of food we need. Please give it some serious thought," Incu said. "Yes, you are right on all points. I believe we went over this before I decided for the transfer. The rate increase in itself was sufficient. The dwelling there will have plants as they are here, and the pool near the health center has a therapy pool which can be used by anyone. It is also much closer than the beach is here. Why didn't you raise any objections before now? We must keep in mind that we will not live forever and our amount in the reserve is very important. It's settled. We leave in two rotations which will be the end of my three phases. If I would have chosen the third quarter, we would be gone by now," Donor Aires firmly let his choice be known.

10-Cleaning Wand

Incubator did her best to tidy up the next two rotations. The cleaning wand was used for everything from bathing, cleaning the inside of the dwelling, top to bottom, making any edibles fit for consumption. Bath time was special for everyone. That meant removing the body cover and moving the wand over the whole body. Long hair was a challenge at times. It would block the screen cover and the vacuum would pull on the hair, especially if it was held in one place for too long. Four liters of water was the maximum that each person had for each rotation. Bathing would take one half of one liter. The residue of a bath was deposited into a proper container and was identified. It would sense the user's identification from his or her head chip. It was very important to be the closes to the user because the Health Team would call to verify that a male's estrogen levels were in error. The error did not deduct too may kilowatts the first offense.

The move would be an easy one. The tube that they were going to use had many others side by side, over and under, which meant that they could pedal at a pace that was most comfortable for Scorpio. The evening before they left, Incu cleaned all of the body covers and stored all of the information and personal discs and loaded each into three trailers. They were all the same size. A good size back pack would have been enough, but for that long of a distance, it was so much more comfortable to use the trailer. Food was the greatest burden. Donor Aires preferred the mix of his pellets form the local food supplier than he had ever before. That is one thing about being stationed here he will miss. He didn't have to use as much flavoring to make them palatable.

11-Body Cover and Generating

The body cover was worn at all times. No spare was needed because they were available everywhere. The sizes were expandable so that only a few different sizes were needed. They were worn over the body and easily pulled from top to bottom with just enough of a slit near the head to easily pull over, and then would stick together again just leaving the head out. The attached hood would cover everything but the face. A clear mask was always in the chest pocket for easy access. Its porous nature allowed for easy breathing and prevented any insects or dust on very windy days to enter.

The three left the first day of the full moon. Donor Aires first rotation until the next quarter gave him more than enough time before he had to report to duty again. Incu programmed their route and entered it into the system. Chutes would automatically open just like they would for the automated freight that used the tubes as well.

Scorpio entered the tube first, then Donor, and Incu last. The first ten kilometers went easy for them all. Scorpio had his generation set at 20, Donor 30, as was Incu. It would have been higher but the trailers did provide some drag. Conversations were say amongst the three. Their ear pieces took the boredom of the constant pedaling. "Donor, I'm going to put my generator to zero. Please," puffed Scorpio. "You keep it the same. Don't move it. Our rest exit is 2 kilometers away and the grade will be in our favor," demanded Donor.

The rest was welcome for them all. They were surprised at the number of people at that exit. It wouldn't have been, if any of the three had viewed exit activities channel. Fortunate for them, they were being entertained by Jugglers Anonymous.

12-Lonesome Place

The three made a point to make it exciting as possible. Entertainment of this kind was available on holo, life size. They had many more kilometers to pedal and this relaxing on their rolled out bed mats would make it easier. They were too close when one of the jugglers' missed batons landed next to Scorpio. One thing they had never seen before was two short batons set end to end and a chair was balanced on the top one. Holding it there for more than a minute was a real treat for the fifty or so that was watching. The show and a few food pellets, a gulp of water, and then it was back into the tube for another stint. Donor told the other two to look to either side and notice open fields with dwellings spaced about 300 meters apart. It was one of the largest gatherings of people receiving their just penalty. They were close enough to see some outside wearing a collar, and if it were to float over their heads, it would resemble a halo. This was the Lonesome Place. If greater distance was ventured by the lone person from their dwelling, a buzzing would make them aware of their boundaries. Each step further would increase the vibrations and become so severe that it would incapacitate the prisoner.

Each area had a few of them sprinkled throughout their community. The collar also monitored their voices. Singing and other vocal actions were allowed, but to only so many decibels. The buzzing and the rest was sure to bring the sounds to an acceptable level. There was no communications with anyone ever during their term of incarceration.

13-Private Place and Waste

The rule was very simple: if anyone knowingly abuses their neighbor, they will have no neighbor. They will live alone. There will be no one to abuse you verbally or physically. There were ten degrees of the amount of time to be spent in The Lonesome Place…

"Donor, why does he have a bike when he cannot go anywhere? Asked Scorpio. "If he wants his daily food, he must generate kilowatts just like the rest of us. They can never get higher than Rate 1. If you pass on land near the Lonesome Ones, you must make no gestures of any kind, even if you see no one in the Lonesome Place. It is monitored a full rotation for a whole orbit. Constantly. Sensors pick up IDs from anyone in the area," answered Donor Aires. Second degree if you do. Three days with half rations.

Incu urged that the next exit is a must for her and lucky it wasn't too far away. She sped out of the exit to nearby private place, IDed her waste container, and relieved herself. Squatting was somewhat uncomfortable because of the distance her legs had pedaled. A spray of water and a medically treated wipe and she was ready to go again. She placed the container in the pickup box which would be taken to the Health Lab for automated examination.

"Let's stay here for a good rest. The rate of 0300 to 0500 hours would have 20% bonus because the aluminum recycling plant is going to have a melt. And, if we time it right, we will be on the long downhill tube, and we all might raise our output as close to 100% as possible. Our reserve would really climb," urged Donor Aires.

14-Rest and Bounce Game

Their timing was perfect. They could barely feel the decline but it was enough for Scorpio to yell out, "62. WOW 62!. Never have I had it that high before" he screamed. A breeze from the rear with his sail out helped. Donor Aires had his to 93 with his sail out but only did that for a few kilometers. 85 satisfied him much better. Incu kept hers at 70 on the downhill grade. When they reached the bottom of the grade at 0435 and they all had to cut back on their producing numbers.

Sunrise was not too far away and Incu and Donor thought it best to have their first long stop by the 431 River. They viewed on their monitors the perfect place where their offspring would have the most enjoyment for the day. No dwellings were allowed anywhere near the water. RESERVED FOR LAYOVER signs were everywhere. Each took a pop-up one person tent from the rack and hurriedly climbed in with their mat and beautiful sleep was theirs in no time.

Incubator arose well-rested but saw that Scorpio had returned his mat and tent, and was gone. She looked at the group of pink uniformed bouncers going at it. He was in that weight bracket and that would have been what he needed before going on the next leg of the trip. She walked down to the bounce field to make sure. One of the 60 kilogram or less pink ones with a number 8 on the chest and back waved to Incu and she knew for sure it was him. His side had diagonal stripes.

15-Bounce Game

The next play #8 with the stripes was thrown the ball underhand by his teammate who was crouched sideways and a melee ensued. The play they agreed upon was he was going to run to the right. He took off in the correct direction, but did not get very far. Somehow, the opposing player in plain pink got between his front men at full speed and flung himself horizontal to the ground wrapping Scorpio around his midsection. Scorpio took a good hit. The bad part for him was that after the collision the round uniform made him roll, and the 3 or 4 quick rolls made him a bit dizzy.

It was a one meter loss. "No big deal" said an upfront man with an encouraging ring to his voice. "Let's try the same play again, but this time we let #5 in plain pink do his thing and when you get a few steps to the right, hand it to #7 who will carry the ball in the opposite direction. All of you up front bounce the other upfront ones to the right. You all got that now" he directed and they all raised up their thumbs.

It worked, and 23 meters were gained on that play. It would have been much more if it weren't for one of the speediest players Scorpio ever saw. #6 was running lead for #7 who was carrying the ball when plain #7 dove head first at full speed and that made #6 take the full impact causing him to bounce into #7, and that flattened them both real quick. Like a bolt of lightning.

16-It's A Female

Incubator noticed that Donor Aires was organizing his departure so it was time to go. It made it nice for her that two of the players from his side were being called by their incubators so they had to end the game.

Scorpio returned his bounce uniform to the rack when next to him was a female putting her #7 plain pink one there too. "It can't be. No way, no way. Impossible," he said to himself. Smiling from ear to ear she asked him, "What did you think of that last play?" "I'm nowhere near my time to be a donor, but let me tell you, if The Record Keeper would sanction our union, it would be someone just like you," Scorpio smiled as he scanned her ID and put it into his address book. "I do hope your learning number is a good one. My incubator had one of the highest. Between tutoring me and the research work she enjoys, plus all of the other incubator duties now, she can hardly wait until I get my rings and go full time. How soon do females get to know what are the best choices for productive birth? He asked. "I really don't know. I guess ever since I could walk. Sometimes it even gets boring having every incubator in the neighborhood repeat the same thing over and over again. I learned that who I choose to be my donor is totally based on The Record Keeper demands. So when the time comes and I have reached the approved age of having a mate, I hope that there are a lot of choices" was her reply.

Seventy kilometers for the first day was close to what was planned. If they did the same during the next rotation that would leave 60 for the last leg of the trip. It came out that way, and their amount of generation exceeded their expectations.

17-Medical Facility

The medical facility where Donor would be performing his duties was spread over quite a large area. Each dwelling housed a different department, color coded to a particular part of the body. Red for the head, violet for the feet with other spectrum colors with striped colors as needed. 357 was a new facility. The toxic cleanup crews did an excellent job of recovery. The half life of debris thrown out during the Old Era made many places unfit for human or animals, even plants. The facility was ideally located for residences of the area, none having to pedal any great distance for his or her medical needs.

The largest structure was for automatic waste examination. The pickup person would pull a lever and packets of human waste would be dumped onto a conveyer belt, and sorted by male and female. The female section was much larger because the testing done on theirs more intricate. They were the incubators.

Each of the tests was voted on. The experimental department was continually developing new tests and had to submit its usefulness on a ballot. Even existing tests were modified and sometimes deleted. The only ones that could vote were those in the medical field because the language used was their own.

The last vote was for procurement of an herb outside of the tube area. Was it worth the risk, plus the contamination of the tubes, structures, and other living things? That was a touchy one for the Scouts as well.

18-Scouts

Anyone leaving the defined area of the tubes was deducted kilowatts for the distance and/or the time away. Scouts had to be special people because stamina needed for their tasks was very strenuous at times. They had to return to the decontamination dwelling first. There was a case when a scout was knocked unconscious by an unfriendly protector form the Old Era and left for dead. Scouts were forbidden to exterminate any living thing. Immobilizing tools were available when needed. In this case, The Record Keeper reported that the scout was left behind because it would have been impossible to transport the body back to the tube area with the number or protectors that were pursuing the scouting crew.

The head blow was severe enough to disorient the scout, but left him with just enough reasoning to know which general direction the tube area was. Slowly, he worked his way back and avoided another and positively fatal encounter. The quad tube he saw at a distance was not familiar but in his condition he had to get to it. One and a half kilometers and he would be safe. He heard predators around. With his color changing suit, he could blend in with any surroundings. Crawling, walking in a very low crouch, sprinting at times, then into a full run to the tube. There were sounds "bang, bang" and something zinging past him which game him extra adrenaline to run and zigzag much faster. The noise attracted the perimeter guards with their longer range neutralizing devices. The Old Era humans were very protective of their area, too, and they knew exactly where to stop.

19-Decontamination and Surgery

The open wound on the scout's head was an ugly one. The swelling nearly closed his left eye. This was of little concern to the border protectors who were also trained as decontaminators. Their three meter rods with a net-like device would cover the largest of being. This was done by someone with lots of practice. It totally encased the scout and he was made prone in a very gentle procedure.

He was carted to the decontamination center and placed into a chamber along with the capturing device. It would be removed by any of the numerous arm holes that gave the medical team the ability to perform whatever they deemed as necessary to repair the damage the scout had to his body. Normally, if there were no injuries, each scout would be enclosed in a decontamination chamber for one phase of the moon. This was great for them because they could pursue any of their desired hobbies, plus be as the old sayings goes, "on the clock."

The eye of the scout was miraculously saved with micro-surgery and the wound across his eyebrow to the temple was repaired within 15 minutes. Computer surgery was advanced to where only a qualified medical worker observed on a life-size monitor the procedure. There were times when a slight modification had to be made and this was rare. The scout's bruised blood vessels caused no problem. His kilowatt generation would be the same rate as his average for the Solar Orbit until he would be released to active duty again.

20-Duty Schedule

The scout's injuries caused a lot of turmoil, not only within the scouts, but the entire tubes. What was the scout doing there? Who gave them authority to leave the tube area? Why did they venture so distant from the agreed border? All of this was brought to light and was examined by the Legal Department. They would have three rotations to research the past episodes from The Record Keeper and submit their findings.

The section that was doing the work had three associates with regular time off because of their phase of the moon relief. Their last two requests for additional personnel were denied. The workday never ends because a hobby workshop was in the vicinity of their offspring's bounce ball or other children's activities or any other family personal matters. It did not end at sunset or begin at sunrise. It was continuous the three phases of the moon. The starting and ending point of each phase was different for each rotation and it was amazing how quickly every peddler acquired the knowledge of that time. Their phase off was ever so enjoyed. Family life with no interruptions was beautiful for most. Offspring was their devotion, especially for males before they were given their Rings. Another was to adjust their sleep schedule to generate with a bonus times. They could do that while being with their offspring. For those without offspring, hobbies were in fashion.

21-Ombudsman

Their last denial reason from the Governing Board stated that their amount of effort to process the cases before them was not sufficient. It was voted upon and agreed by the other legal departments. Board members who were in the legal department knew the workload. That board informed that legal department on the standard form of rate numbers: Your generation rate will be reduced by 5 percent if your findings were not made before 62 hours. You have known that the additional ten hours were for the cushion because of unknown complications that might arise. Normally your findings were made 63 hours.

The spirit for the common good of the Tubes was lost when seeds of self destruct introduce itself in the most unusual ways. That

Legal department was the only one in the system that had that problem. Health checks were made and they all seemed normal. All the personnel at that location were given an additional automated physical examination, plus an ombudsman who was trained to listen to complaints and introduced a list of potential faults that they might knowingly have committed. That person was available the last three rotations of their third phase of duty. Ombudsmen were available at any time of the four phases, even while on their own personal phase. That person again was totally obligated to listening and counseling everyone and none of their conversations were ever entered into The Record Keeper or relayed to anyone. Nearly all were males because they analyzed their subjects subjectively without emotional feelings. Females who did have this responsibility were exceptional and rare.

22-Scientist left for dead

The findings were made about the scout's mission within a matter of hours minutes was all it took because they just voted that the herbs needed were nearby in the Old Era's domain.

Sometimes the scouts just wanted to get an adrenaline rush snooping around in areas that were well beyond their allowable limits. This was one of the cases. The scientist who knew the exact kind of plant to look for was with them. He was quite physically fit but nowhere near the least of scouts. His transfer to the scouts was not too difficult of a task. It had been done many times before. His agility was not quite sufficient to remove him from harm's way. His total focus was on the crinum x powellii. The Summer Amaryllis has some enzymes that were similar to the crocus. He had a few in his backpack and was greedily getting more for his research when a deer ran by pursued by hunters. The deer was shot at and wounded by a group that was set up in a blind. The deer reversed its direction then collapse near the scout/scientist. The lead scout gave the signal to return immediately when the first shot was fired, but one more plant was on the scout/scientist's mind and he did not heed the command.

The other scouts tried to distract both groups to follow them instead of the scientist, but the scientist goofed by being disoriented in what direction to flee. One whack across the head and down he went. The scientist was abandoned as dead while the hunters pursued the other scouts.

The whole story is recorded in The Record Keeper.

23-New dwelling

Arrival at the medical facility was late in the afternoon for the three. A dwelling took priority. Six vacant dwellings were easily identified by their drab color which was the standard color after an occupant departed. The one Incu wished she could have was the occupied one on the cliff overlooking the river.

The terrain was not too bicycle-friendly and four had little garden food. One was horrible. The last they looked at was fortunately a horticulturist's paradise. It would mean some uphill to the health center but then again the return would be great, especially when exhausted. They all agreed it would be the best, but it was up to Incu to make the final decision. She was the one who would spend most of the time there. Her desires were primary in selection of a dwelling. The other two could make suggestions or express any negative feelings and she would take them into consideration.

The walls and floor were bare. Their empty carts were returned to the cart lot by Scorpio, one at a time. Donor set the mats and screened off the private place. Incubator used the dust wand that is one of the tools always needed in all dwellings. She unrolled her monitor and programmed color selections for the dwelling's interior and exterior. Donor brought in all of the water containers and placed them just inside the opening.

As soon as Scorpio returned from his third delivery, they made a circle holding hands and said the usual, "May we love each other here. May we love our neighbors. Please let us make this world just a little better for all of us peddlers."

24-Testosterone check

The open room with a screened off private place in one corner left a lot of space for any additions. This would have to wait until the next morning. The long tube run tired them all, especially Scorpio. Growing at his rate these past few months took much out of him. The next morning all of the deposits from the private room were placed in the pickup container before the scheduled pick up time. Their daily water supply of three liters each would be delivered by the same person.

The automated testing of all of the waste containers was fool proof. If there were any suspected discrepancies, a health worker would immediately pedal to the address of the depositor. It was early afternoon when the shrill of a health worker's whistle was sounded outside of Scorpio's dwelling. Incu went out to investigate and was handed a notice for a testosterone detection number from Scorpio. "He is too young for the Ring. I haven't noticed any kind of juvenile behavior that is common in males with him. I know I have no choice in your demand but this is something new for me. I was informed a few years ago that this would happen and to accept the rule," she sadly complied.

Scorpio returned exhausted from a swim in the pool. The uphill pedal was about all he could muster. No kilowatts were generated into storage in the frame of his bike. "Why do you both look so sad? Wasn't this place to be a dwelling of joy?" Scorpio then noticed the uniformed health worker.

25-First Ring

This procedure was practiced using the holo. Without saying a word, he removed the upper part of his suit and held up his arm. The health worker placed the twenty centimeter or so disc attached by some wires to a small box just a little larger than a pedal against his rib cage just below his arm pit. The number was just below the

Rings installation number and the health worker told Incu to make an appointment with Ring Master within the next three rotations from the exact time.

Scorpio was now numbed by the notice. It was not a choice of his to refuse the procedure nor was it for his donor or incubator. It as a fact of life. The Ring was the first voted upon decision made from the inception of the Tubes. The Old Era is gone. The Rings were voted on only by males. The research in all that pertained to the Ring was intensive. It was brought about by the destructive history of the free flow of semen.

A dominate male brought chaos that was not able to be sanely controlled by even the most cruel and violent of weapons. A common enemy was what brought cooperation of the different nations of the Old Era. Some of the "common enemies" were propaganda by the greedy and powerful. Confusion within each nation brought about more violence. The environment was in total disarray.

Water was the ultimate resource. Rain water was unsafe to drink. The manmade particles in the air were prevalent. There was total disregard for the original earth man was given by Our Maker who was present in all of the eleven dimensions. Man's first instinct is self preservation. The ones in control were none the better than the lowest of the low. The poor, included in which nearly everyone had, ever so slowly, inherited the earth.

26-Why the Ring

Man's first instinct was self-preservation. The second instinct was procreation. The two were in collision from the beginning of time. The few remaining sane communicated with each other and it was decided upon that the Rings was the final answer. They were called by other names but they all had the same results. It was the male that controlled the procreation. Nothing ever should be done to the females who carry the seed to birth. No stress should ever be placed on them. It is in them the seed is developed into a beautiful offspring.

The sickly few remaining came up with some controlled way to prohibit any sexual contact between males and females. It was proven in the past that the second instinct was so powerful that no man could be trusted to take a vow of abstinence. Women had full control over males with their dominance of sexual emotions. If a man cannot control his flow of semen, the semen must be controlled by some external means.

Scorpio was soon to find out how it works. Incu made an appointment with the Rings Master for the next rotation. His donor had to be there too. All of the un-ringed males were brought into the performance dwelling to see what they would get when their testosterone numbers were "ripe". It was not a painful procedure, but very effective.

27-Scorpio gets Ringed

Scorpio removed his suit and climbed onto a long table and laid on his back. The Rings Master used a special tool to expand one of the Rings. The tools and the Rings were heated to his exterior body temperature so as not to cause him the slightest discomfort. A Ring was placed above his testicles and around his scrotum, loose enough as not to prevent any restrictions of blood flow. Pre-testosterone males could view the procedure directly or view it on their monitors. Some of the late developers saw this dozens of times. A few were bored but it was a requirement for the unringed.

The second ring was placed very loosely around Scorpio's penis. The Rings Master had to force the tiny rods from the penis ring into the matching scrotum receptacle. He sealed the union with a special adhesive and Scorpio was finished.

The Ring Master scanned each of the rings before placing them onto Scorpio. He was now entered in The Record Keeper. As Scorpio developed, or felt the slightest discomfort, he would return to the Ring Master for an adjustment..

He would now become a responsible male, not by his choosing but by the Tube voters of long ago. He would find out shortly that these Rings would cause him to moan, groan and be in such agony that he would physically try to remove them. Impossible without castrating himself. It was like a cowboy breaking in a never-saddled horse. Young males just ringed would be ignored in their antics of pain and they would happen at some of the most awkward moments.

28-Decorating the dwelling

Incu pedaled to the cart area, hooked one up then proceeded to the art dwelling. The motif she wanted was one of the works from the Old Era. The selection wasn't too great but would suffice for now. As residents shifted from one section to another maybe by chance in a phase or so something more to her liking would be returned.

The display hardware was neatly arranged in transparent drawers for easy access. She took what she needed, placed all her selection in her cart and returned home. Arranging the different pieces around the dwelling took more time than it did to procure them. Satisfied with her arrangement she lounged on her mat with great satisfaction.

Scorpio and a new friend returned home from a vigorous game of bounce and were anticipating a holo tour of "his" jungle. He introduced Cetus to Incu and they did their formal greeting. "Before you get too relaxed Scorpio, please return the cart for me, please," Incu pleaded. "I would only be too glad to," he joyfully answered. By the sound of his voice Incu felt he had some ulterior motive for being so cooperative. She knew that it wouldn't be too long after he returned pleading for some kind of liberty.

Sure as incubators intuitions were fruited, out comes Scorpio when he returned with, "Incu, Cetus would like for me to stay the night after we tour 'my' jungle here." "You will have plenty of time for camaraderie. You have just been ringed and it is best that you acclimate to some new adventures of the rings," she suggested.

29-Mona Lisa

The middle of the dwelling which was never occupied with furniture was where most of the activity took place. Scorpio and his new pal programmed the holo and everything they wanted was all around them. "Scorpio, why on earth did you ever pick such a foul smelling place? It is more than I can stand. Either you choose a pleasurable scented place to visit or my face cover has to go on," Incu said with legitimate complaint. The smell was horrible. She knew that the boys had their favorite place in common and they were greatly amused and seemed to enjoy the stench. So she pulled the face cover from her chest pack and was now oblivious to their journey.

Satisfied, they measured the wattage used and split it. It was 138 watts. They had much more with The Record Keeper and in no time it would be replaced. Cetus left and Scorpio visited the private place curtained off in one corner of the dwelling. Opening the slit in his suit he urinated into the container he IDed. He let loose with a steady stream and felt the ring at the same time. It would be his constant companion; even after he chose a mate. He could feel it because of its newness, but in time it would be "part of him" just like another part of his body.

"Incu that is the most unusual woman with all of those cracks through the whole front you put in the private place. I see it is cased in an air tight enclosure. I felt most uncomfortable because it seemed that she was looking at me when I was emptying into the kit. She looked like she had a smirk or smile at the same time, and with my new Ring it was not a place for that picture to be," Scorpio complained.

30-Scorpio's first pain

A good night's sleep without awakening gave Scorpio a lot of time for his bladder to fill up. He had no notice of the rings until it gave him a pain the likes he never had before. His bladder did some

24

messaging somewhere inside of him which gave him the beginnings of an erection. The rings were scientifically designed and voted on many generations ago. What he was experiencing was not new to all males. His yelps awakened his donor and incubator and they rushed over to comfort him.

"Scorpio, this was your first of many painful episodes. In time you will find ways so that this kind of painful episode will diminish to just a short painful notice," his donor comforted. Incu added, "Now you can see why I suggested you give yourself time to acclimate yourself to the Rings." He waddled to the private place to relieve himself and what pain he had was nearly gone before he emptied.

Researching how such a cruel mechanism could be placed in such a casual way with the tube people having nearly a unanimous vote was beyond him. The Rings were brought about by the lack of discipline of males. Venereal diseases were rampant. Deaths were eliminating nearly all of the males soon after puberty. Females were joining their mates to the grave in such large numbers that it left very young children doing manual labor long before their bodies were developed for hard work. Some of the very young were infected and perished by the craze of time. There were other devices, which proved to be ineffective in restricting sexual activity, but the sex drive was so strong, abstinence was ineffective.

31-Home schooling

Scorpio's home schooling was casual and had no real schedule. Once every other moon phase was a review on all of his past subjects. Incu did not compare his number evaluation to what she or his donor did at his age. Somehow he had an innate desire to closely watch insects. His music was superb but his singing was kind of on the raspy side. Second chair violin was the best he could do. First chair Rigel belonged to the procreation of two of the best violinists, ever.

The Mental Development Department programmed subjects and all that was pertinent to vocations that were projected needs at his graduation date. His incubator just needed to supervise his attention. She was also following her desires to physical and mental applications to lower body muscular development. Bicycles were the primary mode of transportation. Maximum generation with the minimum of effort. Incu was the first for Scorpio's questions. Second was his donor. Third and last was the holo. Holo would decide if the student's problem warranted a visit to Final Stage of Preparedness students.

Scorpio had access to browse the books and any other material stored in The Record Keeper's library. He could engage any written word in any book he desired, here in his home town or some off the beaten track. Unlimited access. Today is just for review. Tomorrow is the final.

MY DEAR READER, PLEASE TAKE A QUIET TIME. SCORPIO'S TUBERS HAVE FIVE EVERY ROTATION. LIE DOWN, CLOSE YOUR EYES, AND MEDITATE ON BEING KIND. TAKE YOUR MIND COMPLETELY OFF OF WHATEVER YOU ARE DOING FOR FIFTEEN MINUTES OR WHENEVER YOU AWAKEN.

32-Scorpio want to visit Cetus

"Incu," Scorpio asked, "I wish to visit with Cetus. In the last game of bounce, he mentioned something about a math problem he had and was having difficulties in transposing signs over the equal. That and we want to visit a cousin whose donor is researching a rare insect." "That's great. This is the first time that you have picked new friends on the first moon at a new dwelling. You will be seeing me much less now that you have been ringed. I lucked out in having a very knowledgeable male pursuing the same bacteria I am-erratic reactions to a low electric shock and magnetic field environment. Which dwelling is he in?" she asked. "Remember when we exited the tube when we first arrived here and you commented on the one overlooking the cliff. That's the one," he answered. "Please tell Cetus to ask his incubator if I could come for a visit tomorrow," Incu said while she twisted Scorpio's suit. The twists had come when he and Cetus were wrestling by the recreation dwelling after their game of bounce. He had endless energy.

33-Donor's work anxiety

Donor returned from his part of the rotation and was quite disturbed at the amount of flexibility that was allowed to the newer members of his staff. They seemed to not have any enthusiasm for their responsibilities. They were all in range one and could not be any lower so that wedge could not be forced to "get them moving." He poured it all out onto Incu and she let him empty himself of his anxieties. She knew he was finished when he asked for his health drink. It was the bitterest jug of potent stuff that anyone could ever swallow. How he ever got past the smell was beyond all comprehension. The Health Team conjured a potion of different herbs to supplement his body's needs from tests of body waste the past three moons. The correct portion was in the container delivered with his daily ration of water. Another would arrive the next rotation. The container it came in could only be opened when the recipient scanned the cap.

He was in the health field and gave no objections verbally but it was obvious that what he was ingesting was not fit for human consumption or animal for that matter. It took more than fifteen minutes before he could associate with anyone. That was some powerful stuff. Now that that was over with Incu cuddled up to him, he brought up the subject of his uncomfortable day at the health center in where he was the assistant manager.

"There is an obvious problem in reaching your goal? Is it your ego? Is it your lack of understanding human nature? Do you feel that you are more important and more knowing than the service line associates? I have a litany of related questions but that is enough for starters," she said cuddling up to him just a little tighter.

34-Donor's anxiety solution

"You know me better than that to ask me any of those questions. The complexity of the human is ever so frustrating. The spirit of life is such a fragile thing. The spirit comes from a place unknown to us mortals and what I'm having a problem with is that I try to force my spirit of life, the joy of participating and the joy of sharing with my fellow employees," Donor whispered in Incu's ear.

"The spirit is no trivial being. I'm sure you feel the spirit of life when you are with us here in this dwelling. I can feel it. Scorpio definitely does because his energy is far beyond his peers. If you think that your spirit is being forced on your associates, how best to correct your ways," she wanted to know." The previous number two man had to leave because of stress. I don't want the same for me," donor lamented. "I'm sure that all of the associates do not have the same knowledge number. If I were you I would take the top three for a mini conference or ask The Record Keeper for answers. That is for starters. Corner them together and question them about their responsibilities after you ask them why their joy of making the department more efficient is not there," she continued. "And above all give them the feeling the decisions made in quality control are from their thoughts." "Your help is great but my theory of cooperation is that I move with joy while on duty. A song is nearly always in my heart. Love of what I am doing is so obvious. Sometimes I think that I am rushing my feelings onto others when I should be patient. One moon on the job is nowhere enough time to convert my staff to be award winners," Donor said.

35-Scorpio stinks

They had just about finished discussing Donor's work feelings when Scorpio rushed in directly to the private place. The exhaust fan was not on and the chorus started right on the same beat. "Please, don't save your watts for your pleasures only. You're rotten. I've got to talk to the dietitian so your waste can be a little less aromatic," said Donor like he was in pain. Giggling from the private place, "I'm trying to get this woman with a smile to get a good laugh going so all of those cracks will get together." He motioned for the fan to go on and it IDed him for the wattage deductions. The wash wand is such a convenient clean up mechanism. The residue along with his waste was IDed and he took the container outside for the next day's pickup.

A group hug occurred every time they met. "Now is our regular quiet time," Incu said. The hustle bustle of the day was over, for now the total abandonment of activity was what rejuvenated the body and the brain. It lasted 15 minutes or more. Total rebuilding of a person could not happen unless a total blank was obtained. Each rolled out their mat and it was all quiet. It seemed automatic that they all arose at the same time. The first thing that Scorpio noticed was the pendant that Incu was wearing. "I have noticed many times. Do you change it because the color is not always the same?" he asked. "You sure are an observant one. Are you ready for a lesson on life?" and she continued. "I'll explain the highlights of why it changes color. It's best that way. Some now and some later as you develop and your knowledge of our bodies increases. I want you to look at the moon and see what phase it is in," she said.

36-Incu's medallion color change.

"I don't have to," he said adding "It's on the last rotation of the third quarter." Ever since he can remember, there were so many things that were done by it." "Females have cycles. Right now if I were to receive a sperm from your donor it would get together with the egg that is waiting for it. When it gets back to the color it is most of the time, the timing for that to happen is off and they cannot get together. Now that is enough for now on that subject." she concluded.

Incu and Donor went to visit the art dwelling for a few more choices. They could have just viewed them on their monitor but since it wasn't too distant, and they could also participate in the sing a long in the park, they walked. Donor had a beautiful voice and before long some of the singers asked him to do the lines that were solo. Eagerly he volunteered.

Time was not of essence now that he was on his phase break. He could have sung through to dusk because this is one thing that gave him great pleasure. He had a fantastic memory for so many songs. Many of the singers had to use their monitors and follow the tune and words. The music was provided by the world famous Beethoven Symphony in via Holo. The fourteen local musicians placed their seats next to fancy dressed Holo players. As they played, they could follow every movement and try to duplicate their every action. The listeners wearing head phones could not hear the missed notes of the locals. When the last tune was finished the ones without gave loud applause and shouted praises to the trumpeter next to the Cello. The park manager definitely would put this activity into The Record Keeper.

37-Musical romance

For a horn blower who just did this part time for his own pleasure, he was really good. Incu found out later by another seeker in the art building that he was tube maintenance person grade 2 which he did for many orbits. His duties were repetitious but he was never bored. There was no desire to advance himself. When his routine duties were completed he would take out his trumpet and play like it was like part of him. There were times when he would give it some loving strokes and had to be reminded that it was 'Quiet Time".

"Isn't it wonderful that we have such a variety of beautiful works from around the world? " she casually mentioned to another seeker in the art building. That started a comfortable conversation which led to the concert trumpeter Phecda. "I only go when he is there. Most of the time he is and I just get chills listening to him play. Ever so beautiful. I never tire even when the same is played day after day," she boasted. I know your monitor can locate all of the art dwellings but from what you have chosen so far, I know that you will take a few from the one two exits north. The Mona Lisa you chose would match perfectly with The Painted Lady. It is there. There was not too much demand for it but you have to be the one who makes the final decisions on what you enjoy most in your dwelling," she said. "It sure was a pleasure having met you here. We arrived two phases ago and still have not completed our settling in," Incu said. "Please come and visit at your earliest convenience. I'm on my brightest color now so my mate will be avoiding me for the next few days,"

38-Donor 4 days away

she continued. "When do you feel you will be around to getting a mate? Incu asked. "I really don't know. I had some weak desires to enter the mating pool and the joy I am having now supersedes having a mate to share my "fun" time with. My music friend that gives me the chills has not entered the pool either. He is eligible but he is possessed by that brass thing that is always with him. I have him in my address book and if it pops up in the pool, mine does too. His genes and mine are ever so compatible. My only wish is that his choice is me," and her voice felt like it was coming from one of the softest warm breezes on a cool day. "I'm leaving now and I do hope we see each other soon," Almaaz said to her and left.

Almaaz's wish was granted and sure enough the next day Albiseo pedaled to her front door and was all set for a full day of female chit chat. Aires was lounging on his mat popping a few pellets and reading a text related to Health Care Workers Responsibility. He was trying to concentrate but laughter now and then disturbed him and the guest noticed his displeasure. "Aires, Incu and I have a lot to talk about so why don't you go to my dwelling for a few days. You don't want to play with the color I'm looking at right now. I saw the bright and it's a no-no. So, I took the liberty to bring along enough pellets to last four days. Is that OK with you?" she asked. Without a word he rolled up his mat, took four days of pellets, gave Incu a warm embrace and she reminded him that the vote for the next rotation will be for lowering the mating age. "I'm for a full orbit." she added.

39-Female talk

"How long have you two been mating?" asked Albiseo.

"Aires and I have been together for 16 orbits," answered Almaaz

"You two seem refreshed and excited with each other." Albiseo then added, "I have some anxieties about the long term of total commitment. Once whomever I chose for a mate I know is forever. I'm very contented with myself in selecting plants for the planting crew plus and dwelling visits for the uncomfortable. If I choose to mate a lot of that will have to be curtailed or eliminated. Next seasons crop is very important and the attachment to a few of the uncomfortable is going to cause anxieties that I can ill afford. My feelings are in somewhat of a tizzy, and noticing the joyful atmosphere you have developed, I desire. And that desire is continually growing stronger. Please share some of our innermost feelings so that I can make a loving decision," pleaded Albiseo. Almaaz gave it a lot of thought and it was a good two minutes before she responded, "Do you know what the word submission means?" "I sure do. That is what I do for the plants and uncomfortable. I submit my whole thoughts and time to create the best results," Albiseo said.

"Those two are your participation in your occupation. Total commitment with your body is something totally unrelated. Plants and the uncomfortable share your time and you can leave for a revolution or part of one or not be there for your off phase. There may be times when you are uncomfortable and request your sharer of responsibilities to complete your duties.

40-Female talk

Total commitment with total submission of your whole body and mind can only be done if all other dreams, fantasies, past experiences and pleasures are totally released to the forgotten. Total commitment to procreating is one that you must have to have deep within yourself. The slightest of doubt is a no-no. You obviously know that what I am saying to you now is a repeat of all you have been taught when you reached puberty. Scorpio is the only thing that mattered when I chose my mate. Aires was one that I chose to be my egg donor. I spent a lot of time researching his history in The Record Keeper. I also contacted his closest of associates on the sly too. There were 434 in the male pool to choose from. It took more than 180 rotations and many sleepless nights. When my choices were dwindled down to twelve it became most difficult. Every male had so much to offer and any one of them would be the perfect donor and mate. I had to just wait for any of them to choose me. The thirty seven females were vying for them on this round. Aires was my favored of the twelve and it so happened he chose me. The next thirty rotations we became acquainted in my dwelling. It was most difficult for him because his rings caused him so much pain. That was a must for me because if he could not deliver sperm, our association would be useless. A child was all that mattered to me. Our decision to choose each other as mates produced a very special child, Scorpio. The love for each other came because we both wanted offspring that would make this world a better place. Every couple that mate want the best possible producer of kilowatts who also has a gentle way for the betterment of all living in the Tubes.

41-Female talk

Their conversation went well into the night. The questions that Albiseo had were ever so personal, every minute detail of the sex act itself. Almaaz was frank and sincere in explaining her innermost feelings. One that was most awkward was the visit from the coition instructor. She and Aires knew that at least one visit would be had by that group. During the first moon phase of their union for procreation, it was firmly enforced by that group that her color on her newly placed monitor was not in the red zone. She and Aires were free to enjoy coition as often as they wished. Her implanted pubic bone sensor was coordinated with Aires' Rings and the incision had healed.

"When I had my first Red Zone, they decided it best we wait for the next one. Aires was completely satisfied, but my erotic feelings were nowhere near what I had expected. Each time we had sex it increased for me. Aires had no problems at all. He was in his glory. How could I not have the same high finish like he did? We contacted the coition group for their expertise. We found that it was most common for new unions. We were shown the complete expectations of the couple from sunrise to sunset. What was expected to what was taboo. We were told that there are occasions in which the female will never reach a climax during coition and that a manual manipulation was necessary. It was normal and highly recommended. Complete sexual gratification was essential to a complete union. There were rare cases in which the male or the female could not complete their procreation ability. The coition group were the ones who controlled every possible aspect of coition. Their training was one of the most intensive of all of the groups. The joy of having a satisfied mate was a priority for society," rambled Almaaz. She had every detail down pat.

42-Female talk

There was plenty of occupational contacts plus recreational activities and many accidental encounters but none of them amounted to emotional feelings. There might have been a spark now and then but without knowing the male's gene pool, of what use would it be if there was not a match. Quite a few orbits ago when puberty was emotionally at its peak, I had a crush on a male much older than myself. I was totally absorbed in yielding my whole body for his use. The feeling were super. I was never so warm. So warm that every part of me needed ice to cool it. One time I had to exit my dwelling and rub by body suit to allow all of the heat to escape and that was not enough so I ran until exhustion brought me back to my senses. Oh, what a wonderful feeling, I wanted it to last forever. I wanted the male of my dreams to totally enmesh me into his arms. My donor and incubator had a difficult time trying to soothe my torturous emotions. If it were not for the tubes, I would have gone insane. Never have so many kilowatts been generated by me. It was non-stop pedaling, When desires were at their peak, I had a trailer loaded to the maximum capacity and my generator set just high enough to where I could hardly push down on the pedal,. I struggled and sweat like I never did in my life. I wasn't the only female in that ugly situation. Before that happened to me I thought I was stupid for a person to "ruin" their body in trying to generate kilowatts. It was a salvation. I'm grateful that it only lasted a few rotations a moon. As orbits went by the drives inside me subsided and I could concentrate on my vocational dreams. Now it has been three orbits since my first qualifications to enter the pool. I feel I need a boost to have the same feelings I had just ten orbits ago. Please tell me if you had the same emotions that I had," pleaded Albiseo.

QUITE TIME

43-Female talk

"The intensity varies on the amount of hormones that are generated. I was one of the fortunate ones. I had none of the wild and hairy experiences that you had. Every rotation was like the last with no mood swings. Now that you have told me yours, I strongly suggest that you search The Record Keeper for whatever you had and it is not entered with all of the females in the mate you choose. Just think if your procreation had to deal with those feelings from both sides of the mating couple. It would be pure misery especially if it was a female. Can you picture yours when it reaches puberty, it would have to pedal half way around the world before lunch. You were lucky that you chose to pedal. Some of the rebel females become totally absorbed in mating and knowing that all males are ringed, the frenzy they are in will throw themselves at one causing a chain reaction. The female is yelping and the male is moaning in severe pain caused by the Rings. What a torturous event. Enforcement Regulators cover the couple and induce a deep sleep and are carted away for therapy. Those events are kept in The Record Keeper. The male is sometimes called an innocent bystander." Almaaz went on, "Now you can see how important it is for you to study and research The Record Keeper. Your offspring is a dream that will come true. That is our only purpose in life. Our Scorpio is everything to Aires and me. We know that when he enters the mating pool that he will be one of the primary choices. It will not be too long from now that we will encounter his emotional fits. Aires did very well as did my donor plus many generations of other males. We are constantly discussing his inner feelings and he has been most cooperative. These are some of what you will be encountering with your offspring," Almaaz warned.

44-Female talk

The four rotations seemed to evaporate for Albiseo. It was not all conversation. Generation of Kilowatts was part of it, too. Almaaz and Albiseo went into the tube and set their generation rate as high as they could. Sitting and enjoying pellets did nothing but expand the waist. Albiseo wanted Almaaz to visit the art dwelling nearby. The more items she chose, the more watts would be taken from her balance. The high wire walker did some amazing acrobatics. It could be seen on everyone's monitor but being there was phenomenally exciting. How could any one even climb that high let alone sit on a chair and juggle six rings. His watt acceptor was flashing so they both gave a generous donation. It was not uncommon for acrobats to accumulate enough watts that they never have to create their own on a bike. He most likely had another profession.

Albiseo noticed that the net under this high wire walker was tighter than that of other high wire walkers was. Ten minutes on the wire doing a hand walk, the juggling, bike ride from one stand to the one on the other end of the rope, then return again with a balancing pole. His last act on the high wire was to hang by the tops of his toes and "walk" sideways to the middle of the rope juggling two rings. When he was near the middle, his foot slipped off the rope and he fell, letting out a blood curdling scream. He hit the net with the top and back of his shoulders and was lost momentarily in the cavity that he made in the net. Then he bounced nearly halfway up to the rope and he juggled the rings, which seemed like he was suspended in mid air, and back to the net he went, landing on his feet, stopping like it was a platform. When he flipped off the net onto the ground, the gathered crowd erupted. The line that formed by his wattage acceptor did show their appreciation.

45-Female talk

Albiseo was interested in the sex part of a union but her major interest now was on how to attract the trumpeter when she entered the mating pool. She knew that she was not going to unless he also entered. The gene groupings were quite large and with only having one interest, strategy in attracting a mate took some fine tuning. Almaaz told Albiseo what would happen. She could also have seen it all on her monitor many times. The number of solar orbits was the first qualification. Twenty seven was this next group. The number was getting lower for the past few orbits. A need for technicians in the magnetic electrical impulse generators was now developing into a whole new field. Many familiar with it were taken from other fields. This full moon's session would have thirty seven gene groupings. The largest group had sixteen females and nine males. The smallest had one male and no females. There were a few that had equal numbers of each and was favored by everyone but it also took away the flirting or strutting plus each side's anxiety activities were not there with full force for the side that had the fewer. The intensity was elevated but in very organized order and it was obvious who did their research in The Record Keeper.

In one group there were nine males and twelve females. It seemed that if there were more females in the group, the excitement was more electrifying and a lot more movement and interactions. The one female had four males cornering her and there was no doubt that she would be guaranteed a mate. She took the hand of one of them and asked if he would like to take a walk around the mating area. It was not final until the shock of this encounter was labeled "The best offspring".

46-Mate choosing

The other three had now to face the other females who might have felt they were the second choice. Two of the males left the mating pool area immediately because they did not research any of the other females. The fourth did not have any problems and would accept the one that would have the greatest physical attraction. He knew that the gene group would give the best procreation possible. There was little doubt in his mind that a romance would develop into a comfortable relationship. The female bonding hormone would suffice to where he would be the one for her forever.

When all of the couples were gone from the area, the remaining females were in tears, as though they were rejected by society. Not qualified for procreation. Their frustrations were obvious by their actions. It would last for a moon phase or two but they would be back into the mating pool the next full moon. Luck might be on their side and the number of males would, they hoped, would be double the number of females; A sure guarantee for a mate.

As each couple left the mate choosing area, they proceeded to the dwelling that the female had prepared for her lover. She did not have her ID disc placed so there would not be any sexual contact until the next full moon and they both accepted each other's personality and felt comfortable that they would have a life long time together and have one procreation. There were many reasons for non-compatibility. They ranged from "asking too many questions" to "Zealot in astrology." Whatever the reason, they were both free to express their desire. The real final decision for procreation would come after they both decide to have the disc implanted into the female's pubic area and programmed to the male's Rings.

47-Destructive past

There were many who never entered the mate choosing pool. Some were too absorbed in a vocation, lack of desire or even fear of having a mate. Whatever was theirs and theirs alone. No one questioned anyone because the need for unattached people was of the greatest needs. Ringed males were free to do as they wished. Females were never physically restrained. They choose a mate, have their mating chip implanted and wear their ovulation necklace.

A procreated infant requires a lot of attention and that eliminates incubators from the services that are needed for a harmonious society. Physical attraction to the opposite sex with expectations of having an offspring that would be the one that to promote total and complete utilization of the spirit to a utopian world was the supreme goal. The joy of childbirth gave way to consternation for so many that more than one was needed to fulfill their emotional needs. History did show that there was a time when it was common for a mated dwelling to have six or more. Everything depended on the ballot decision. When the tubes first started there were multiple procreations to a dwelling and the need for kilowatts was ever so great. The expansion for food hectors increased to a point were other creatures were denied their natural habitat. Where was the balance? The selected authority issued so many different rules that it was impossible for anyone lower than a legal genius to comprehend what was required. The present is as perfect as it can possibly be. Every rotation every person unrolls their monitor and in thirty three words or less, in common language with everyone is required to decide which is the most practical and loving for the greatest good of all when they vote.

48-Aires returns

When they returned that evening, Aires was waiting and had an admiring grin on his face. Aires and Almaaz rushed into a very warm embrace. The color of her cycle monitor was clear and both were knowing that love is such a beautiful thing. Albiseo held both of her palms up and Incu slid her palms side down across them very slowly. Albiseo did the same for Aires but at a faster speed. She said goodbye, took her bike from the rack and pedaled away.

"When was the last time you checked on Scorpio?" Incu asked Aires " He is at the bounce stadium and it seems like he lives there. I wish he would concentrate more on his vocation than getting jostled around in that balloon uniform. It is most difficult to identify him completely covered. I had to call the field organizer to find which number he was wearing. He told me but I couldn't see him because they all look alike. "With his appetite and the amount of energy he is expending, I expect him home in a few minutes," said Aires.

They cuddled each other and felt like one. It was the longest that they had been apart since their union. She was with him when he had the prolonged classes in health care workers communicable disease hazards. He was with her during the moon phase lectures on basic bacteria. He had infant Scorpio to care for. It was his phase off, so no watts were deducted from his amount. Aires said to himself that he was never going to let a separation be that long again. He had Scorpio to look after but a lonesome feeling lingered forever. Scorpio was ever so fortunate to have a donor and incubator in perfect harmony with themselves.

49-Scorpio gets lectured

Scorpio returned home and as usual he rushed to the lonesome place, did his business into the identified container, removed his suit and placed it into the cleaning machine. Then he bathed, removed the cleaned suit, and ran to his pellet container. It seemed like he swallowed them whole which was impossible. "You know, when I get fully developed, I'm going to be a bouncer and never have to generate watts in a tube again. The only time that will have to be done is when our team has to pedal to another location," he shouted out. "Scorpio, you will have to pedal more than you do now. The locations of the mature teams are far apart. You will be in the tubes for days at a time to reach some of the remote locations. Not only that, your vocation will require you to be on duty no matter where you participate in that violent sport," Aires corrected, "The donations that you get from the crowd might not be as rewarding as some other non-required participation." "I'll be the greatest. The coach at the field said that I show a lot of promise. Keep my nose clean and be responsible and the sky is my limit," said Scorpio.

"Now what do you call responsible?" asked Aires. "Does that only mean that you have to report to the playing field on time? Does that mean that you have to memorize all of the plays and react immediately when a play is called? Does that mean you have a proper and continuous occupation that has a higher than one generation scale? Love of the bounce game is noble and I'm sure satisfying but there is more than play." Aires added,

"Your incubator and I want you to have the fullest in life after you have chosen a vocation. Do you completely understand me?" Aires demanded.

50-Ballot-adding tubes

Scorpio laid out his mat in the far corner of the dwelling and both Incu and Donor were looking at Donor's monitor to see when Scorpio's brain waves were at the point of being sound asleep. They set the buzzer if he should awaken the slightest. These kind of moments were crucial to their enjoyment of each other.

The first thing upon arising on the next rotation was to vote. "The addition of two tubes onto the existing eight. It has been a congestion point for some time. The tube coordination committee placed it on the ballot. This gave Scorpio an opportunity to participate in how his watts were going to be directed. Anyone using this section would contact everyone they knew for a yes vote. Voting only took ten watts but the implementation of the two tubes would take a lot more. The wording of the ballot was: **Adding four (4) tubes to section eight. Cost 450,000 kWh. Redeem time 3.5 orbits. Secured within 30 rotations.** Waiting time now is seventeen minutes, twelve percent of the day. No one in their dwelling used that section very much, but the wait time to get into a tube can be very frustrating. There was more to the cost of the tube. Stationery generators were available while waiting. Musicians, clowns, orators and any other exhibitor loved a captive audience and would probably vote no. The automated freight trailers would also have an increase in their fee for using that section. Sometimes there would be a continuous flow of them two to three kilometers with no break for a peddler.

51-glucose count 207

Aires's off phase was over and he was delighted that he could be doing what he was trained for. The last day of duty before his off phase he was somewhat disappointed in Algol's attitude. She had never been mated and was well into her 40 orbits. Was it him the cause? Was he a coworker causing her upset? He had to find out. In his training, it was best that he approach the subject with great of caution. Never was it proper to bluntly degrade or point out with force the expected results of her duties. He observed her for more than an hour and all seemed to be normal this revolution. Cautiously he approached her then with a compliment, "Great work Algol. I do hope that others will proceed with their duties as you have done this morning." "Oh, I feel so much better this rotation than I have in a long time. If you would have seen my last waste report you would have known my inability to perform. My glucose count was 207 and I never had it that high. That is what I get for munching so many extra pellets at the mating rite in the dwelling next to mine. What a fool I've been. Never again. If I have caused you any consternation, please forgive me," she begged.

Aires should have checked her waste report when he first noticed that she was in a daze part of the time. Why did he not do that? That is the first step in correcting a discipline problem. Her records have showed she had been an exemplary sharer of responsibility. Had being a new arrival at this facility cause him to overlook something so obvious? Minor details that are not monitored are the usual cause for generation rate reduction. It was a good thing that he did not get into a tirade and try to force the female into compliance. He felt ever so lucky that she came forward with her recent problem.

52-Algol's medical history

Aires's first duty to himself was to get Algol's history in The Record Keeper. From infancy every, health deficiency was noted. She had no nocturnal bladder control until she was eight. First menstruation at sixteen. Her glucose count had been on the higher side since birth. Many times it was normal but, if the tendency was there, there might be a problem. One case seven generations ago the same thing happened. An overdose of sucrose caused a temporary increase in the male's glucose count. It was only 207. That might have been the reason she did not ever enter the mating pool. There might be other reasons, but he did not want to get into her personal "circle".

With that behind him, he felt relieved. The primary objective in the medical field was to get anyone who came into his facility return to generating watts. If the patient had to return for the same problem, it was not favorably looked at by the members of their department. Too many of the same would be a reflection of the inability to prescribe proper medical choices. He was a grade 2.5 and many of the medical personnel were a 3. He had to rely on their knowledge. The automated medical analyzers and the daily waste report assisted them in reaching a conclusion about what path to follow. Some of the tests had still had to be done manually and the watts needed for them were a burden to the patient.

Each orbit, new tests are added to the automated medical analyzers. It was advisable for everyone to use it one time every four phases. More often if any discomfort was noted. Thirty Kilowatt hours was not a huge amount when it could be recovered in less than one rotation. If any person used the machine more than once in that time with negative results, they were contacted by a Grade 3 medical expert.

53-Aldebaran in mating pool

The most difficult problem faced in the Health Department was follow-up on contacts. When an automated notice was sent because of a deviation in a pattern of good health and the recipient did not respond immediately, anyone in the Health Department must physically contact the person. Having a large area created some logistical problems. It wasn't too often, but when it did happen, it seemed to Aires that there were other glitches in the system.

This was the full moon phase and as always, except when the third moon starting at the beginning of another orbit, it was mate choosing time. Aldebaran was in her sixth attempt to have a male chose her. There were fourteen females and nineteen males. Sometimes none of the females were chosen, but the odds now were in favor of them all being settled. She answered the buzzer on her monitor with a "busy" beep. That was not good enough for the automated machine. After the third try, a notice was sent to Aires's section. Getting a response can be time consuming especially when one of the most important times in a person's life is in the making.

Star Algol aroused Aldebaran with a siren for a face to face on the monitors:

"Why did you not answer your buzz?"

"I'm about to finalize my mate selection."

"That is no excuse"

"Please, please, I will respond as soon as I return to my dwelling with my chosen male"

"That is not sufficient reason for this delay."

"OK, OK what is the medical problem?"

"Mucous was detected in your stool."

54-Mating pool distraction

"Can it wait until the next rotation?"

"The testing strongly recommends that you have a change in your diet."

"Can it wait until the next rotation?"

"Your dietitian must consult with you."

"Can it wait until the next rotation?"

"You will have to make the initial contact to let the dietitian schedule an appointment."

"Can it wait until the next rotation?"

"The automated notice will be sent to you now."

"Can it wait until the next rotation?"

"Yes, I will do that for you."

Aldebaran ended the conversation between Algol's o and u and turned the charm of a female in full desire for a mate.

Aldebaran told herself that Algol should have said the last line at the beginning and not wasted her time because the frenzy of the moment took priority over a tiny amount of mucous in her stool.

55-Aggressive females

Aldebaran followed the guide lines of her incubator. She made herself a little on the shy side and seemed a little passive. Inside of he a volcano waited to erupt with its full fury for any man who approached her. She did not participate in any of the clusters of females around any male that had the faintest hint of charisma. Their hormones were in full force. No holds barred.

Duhbe, a grade 3, was not in any hurry to choose this day or the past three orbits of female selection. He researched every one of his "hunts". This was to be his last.

Giddy females mostly did their female "walk" to their attraction. This event had more males than females so that only a few males had a cluster of hopefuls gathered around them. Duhbe was one of them. They all knew that he had been in the mate seeking arena numerous times before. They knew his gene pool was the one that they wanted for their offspring. He was "IT". As the formalities became informal, the dominant female gracefully wiggled herself next to Duhbe and asked him, "Why is it you are getting so much more attention than all of the others?" He gave no response then turned to the female farthest from him and asked her, "Please give me your reason for staring at me?"

56-Duhbe not liked

Somewhat stunned by such an awkward question Aldebaran responded softly with "Duhbe, we all know each other well enough in The Record Keeper so there are no secrets. I wish that you would choose me as your mate and I wish to deliver from your seed an offspring to be the best any couple could procreate. I believe that is the only reason for all of us being here."

" Isn't that a simplistic answer?" he responded then added, "Is there anything you would like to add to that?"

"You are physically attractive, your voice is masculine, and your eyes seem to penetrate deep into me. I know that I would just melt in your embrace," she responded with her eyes closed.

As she softly gave her answer, Duhbe, who towered over the females, looked in the direction of Aldebaran. "That is the one I hope asks me to her dwelling. Thank you, but I find it very difficult not to have any of you as my mate. I should gone to the one whom I have chosen before I even came here," he said. A very aggressive female came out with a loud response, "That was not very nice of you. You know perfectly well why we came here. Our spending time with you might have the other males not feel attractive enough and not respond to our advances after seeing us with you." "Males will be males and females will be females. Do not be alarmed by your time spent with me. I'm sorry but it was all of you that approached me at the entrance. I was on my way to the far side to charm Aldebaran. I noticed that there are more males than you beautiful and loving females. Be kind to yourself. After mating your bonding hormone will create a whole new attitude and all of this will be forgotten."

57-Panther

Algol's duty for the day was to contact anyone who did not enter into the system during the past rotation. Her next call was to a dwelling at the end of tube 8A. A few dwellings and were dispersed over a large area. She tried to arouse the occupant with no success. The neighbor said it was impossible to reach that dwelling because of the panther that is dominating the area. It was too dangerous. Something had to be done. The nearest medical personnel were in a dwelling more than a half hour open bike ride away and they would need armed security with tranquilizer weapons if an encounter was made with the panther.

58-Banana glider

She had to get in contact with Aires first. He was buzzed and Algol relayed the problem.
"What was the problem of the patient you could not contact?"
"Bacteria in his urine."
"Does the party have a mate or a child you could contact?"
"The mate is deceased and the child is matured.

"You say you could not arouse the patient?"

"Three times with lengthy buzzes and a siren with no response."

"I will contact security to visit the dwelling myself. Thank you for your devoted concern."

The services of security were usually very prompt. The remoteness of the dwelling that had to be visited did cause a dilemma. Not really in a sense because everyone in the tube area was five minutes from security providing their services. Aires entered the address of the dwelling that did not respond and relayed it to Exit 8 security. The nearest one. Pedaling that distance was much to long in this emergency.

Four glider crew members who were lounging in their service dwelling took off on a run to their launch tube. They were form-fitted for each glider. It was shaped like a banana that was straight and the back looked like someone took a bite from it, skin and all. The address was entered into the tube destination organizer. While this was being done, each of the four made themselves prone and pulled the last leaf of the glider over himself. This automatically propelled the sled that it was attached to fling the glider into the direction

59-No panther

of the one in need. It was like a bullet. The casing of the "banana" would open slowly above the destination. The glider could either use it as a propeller above him or move them as wings so that he could glide further than the propeller would ease him to the ground.

The propelling stations were spaced so that no area was out of their reach. Many were familiar with the joy of flying but when a need arose for some specialist who qualified for a launch whose services were needed, it took a little time for that person to be fitted with a launching suit. The only people that would have this duty were the ones that scored high in competition held in the fifth full moon of each orbit.

The four were launched and landed within a few meters of the dwelling and made as much noise as they could to frighten the panther that might be looking for some human protein. There was no sign of disturbance outside the dwelling and the first one pounded on the door with no response. The first entered and saw the man lying on his mat. They knew what the medical department's report was and whatever he had might be highly contagious. All of their face covers were in place and attached to a breathing filter. A body bag was placed over the patient and he was rolled into it and secured so that there would be no escape of any of the particles from his body.

Getting 80 kilograms of humanity to the nearest health facility was a chore in itself. The sensors inside the bag were transmitting and now the four gliders knew from that report that they did not have any time to lose. A bicycle was there and luckily the trailer could be extended to transport the patient.

60-Transporting patient

His dwelling was sealed. Pedaling was quite difficult because of the seven percent grade. That was the only bike so one of the four volunteered to be the starter. An alert notice was sent to anyone in the tube to assist him by linking their bike to his in front or using the link bar to push the trailer from behind.

The train that was going was the speed limit. Exceeding that might cause the patient more problems that he already had. The lead bicycles detached themselves leaving the glider attached to the trailer. A bunch of young bucks moved in and were showing eagerness to be helpful so much so the glider's bike moved his generating number to 130%.

The glider pedaled into the emergency entrance where medical personnel waited. The bag with the ill person was placed on a gurney and rolled into the isolation room. Everyone in that room were totally encased in clear plastic with a tube forcing in purified air.

The body bag was opened, his suit was unclasped leaving him resting naked. Sensors were attached and probes were placed in every one of his body openings. No-invasive blood test, tear moisture, plus many others, were simultaneously taken and it took less than five seconds for the results to be read.

In the anxiety of working around the patient, one of the technicians snagged the plastic of his suit on the underside of the gurney, and, like lightening, he was forced into an air tight body bag leaving only enough room for his breathing tube. That technician would now be quarantined until proven to be free of the bacteria the newly arrived patient.

61-Strange bacteria

The air in the room was processed and every living organism was destroyed. The bacteria that the patient had was extremely rare. How he contacted it was a puzzle. It could have been brought in with the fruit that was on the fruit train from overseas. Possibly it could have arrived on a bird that had migrated from another area. The puzzle was for the medical department was to seek where the last time it was isolated. The last living person that perished from that one was two generations ago.

Procedures used in that case would be tried again but in the condition that the patient was in the examiners felt that it would be useless. His vitals were at very low. Any attempt to apply any kind of medication would be futile. Their primary concern was to not have any contamination leave this room. Each person left the quarantined room through a shower of disinfectant sprayed at enough force to nearly blow them over. They removed their outer garments and walked through another shower. and naked through two more additional showers . Still naked they walked into one of the rooms in the dwelling and would be in isolation for at least one rotation.

The patient brought in was not in any serious pain and was unconscious. Encased cameras focused on him to see activities of his final demise. The research department was notified and all of the bacterial specialists were to become part that particular strain of bacteria. That was what Almaaz was specializing in. Little did she know where it would take her.

62-Bacteria vote

The director for bacterial research laboratories were notified and this rare strain was to be their primary focus. Samples of the patients' blood and body tissue would be forwarded. It had been suggested that they be propelled for quicker analysis but because of the nature of the effects of the bacteria, it would have to be voted upon.

The wording of the ballot issue was crucial to the researchers. It would be difficult to get the fear out of the vote. How could that be done? Fifteen orbits ago the same issue was brought up and defeated. Was the urgency to isolate the bacteria predominating over the safety of the people what if there was an accident with the projectile. It was discussed in the medical community with them knowing the technical facts of the case. Panic was the last thing needed now. By the time an emergency ballot was created to be voted on, the cyclers would be more than half way to their destination. Cooler heads prevailed and the encapsulated bacteria packages would be delivered by tandem cyclers.

This was a chore that few wanted. Because of the speed they were forced to travel plus the constant flashing of the trailer beacon that contained the contagious cargo. Every tube entry was closed, giving them the right of way. If they were lucky to have the vial delivered to a research center within a rotation, they could rest in a dwelling there then pedal back. The rate for delivering the package in the trailer was Rate 3. The highest. On the return trip it was back to their own rate, whatever that be. The package delivered more than a rotation away, was relayed to another set of tandem cyclers.

63-Quiet retreat

Aires, Almaaz and Scorpio were at the beach lounging. It was the beginning of the third full moon past the start of a new orbit. Everything was to be quiet for the whole duration. The youngest were not expected to comply but in time they would. This was the time of the orbit when everyone was expected to reflect on how better they could comply with the rules that were voted in. There weren't too many rules and they were simple to comprehend. The Ten Basic ones with further explanations of each. Surprisingly they were violated when a quirk would get into their heads by misinformation from a leader or procreator and not questioned as to its validity. Many times there was a misunderstanding as to what was said. The most inner reaching sessions were with the elderly who withered the storms of every rotation life for many orbits. They were seasoned with a gentle air knowing that their time for the new way of life was to be embraced.

The mystery of all life and its origin was always a main topic. Sometimes there were ones that thought that they were the center of the universe. There were times when they became so convinced of it and become so vocal that they had to be blanketed and taken to a lonesome place. Conversations about upcoming ballots were not usually brought up. The four phases were for finding each person's inner self by meditation and clearing all anxieties from their bodies.

Many second decade youngsters were restless and needed to release their oversupply of energy by running constantly as long as they didn't speak. When exhausted, they would roll out their mat and listen in any of the many circles.

64-Almaaz has an emergency

All non-essential systems were shut down and others operated at a bare minimum of personnel. The beaches were crowded with people meditating or repeating their favorite sayings over and over. Fifteen seconds, then a quiet spell then the same for the next 15 seconds. Everyone's responsibilities were abandoned and the mind was turned to total calm. The last three rotations there was to be no conversations at all. When walking, sitting or munching pellets, the mind was to be a total blank. No thoughts of any kind. Many of the children would wander aimlessly like they were in a trance.

Almaaz was in the midst of her last session of discussions when she was buzzed. It was totally unexpected. It was a shock to be disturbed when her mind and body were almost totally rejuvenated. Coming to her senses and leaving the "other world" she unrolled her monitor to see it was the director of communicable diseases. Her services were requested at the research dwelling immediately. When she questioned the reason a large NOW appeared on the face of the monitor. She found Orion in another circle deeply engrossed in some topic and reluctantly motioned him to come to her.

"I have to leave now. You can have contact with me at the research dwelling" she said in a state of total exhaustion. The buzz aroused her from a place like it was in another world. They embraced each other and she left Aires to keep watch over Scorpio.

65-Almaaz arrives at lab

Almaaz ran to the dwelling that five other groups were sharing to grab her mat and pellets. The she jumped onto her bicycle and pedaled to the tube opening for a half hour pedal to the lab. Her watt generating was set at 65 for the ride to the beach and did not pay attention to the setting until she was puffing and had a difficult time maintaining her highest speed. "What a fool I've been! UGH," grunted Almaaz. She moved the lever to 5, which was one that seemed like there no generation at all. With her speed wow where she wanted it to be, she got her wind back and pedaled like she had first jumped onto it.

Racing down the lab exit, she noticed five other bikes in the rack by the front door. What could be so important? Why now at the refresh time of the orbit? She really did not want to be here. The next third full moon in the start of the next orbit was going to be later than usual. Make the most of it she told herself. Placing her bicycle into an empty rack she left her mat and pellets with it. Briskly walking to the entrance, she tried to open as she normally did but found it sealed. Unrolling her monitor she directed her contact to the same person that informed her on this enriching time of hers. "Please pedal to the rear entrance and wait there until we respond," she said. That she did. It seemed like eternity before the red light flickered over the rear entrance and out came a totally encased lab technician carrying the same kind of suit he was wearing for Almaaz.

The technician assisted Almaaz into the encasement. When it was secure, a backpack fresh air tank was put in place. When completing his task, he told Almaaz to open her valve. A green light confirmed that there were no air leaks and they entered the dwelling.

66-Bacteria regulations

The monitor in one corner was to be her first stop of many in the next three phases. It gave a total synopsis of the suspected bacteria, and the now deceased body from many angles to show every exterior lesions. There was also MRI slabs, from the top of his head to the bottom of his feet. She read his last automated daily lab report and his past history of medical attention. A flash came across the screen showing his most recent visits. An alarm bell went off in Almaaz's head when she saw the art dwelling. " Oh no," she cried to herself. Everyone who was at the art dwelling at that time and shortly after his being there were notified to stay put and not move or touch anyone. An order was issued that the lonesome place was waiting to anyone in con-compliance. With the urgency of this deadly bacteria, time at the lonesome place would be nearly an eternity for non- compliance. She contacted her friend and told her the serious reason for her to stay put. While they were conversing the alarm was repeating the same that Almaaz just gave to Aldebaran.

It is hilarious to see a totally enclosed person pedaling a bike in a tube at full speed. Rules were rules and were to be totally complied with. His GPS directed him to the dwelling of Aldebaran. She was waiting at the entrance when the technician noticed a male lounging inside. "Is there anyone else here beside that male?" he asked. "No," she replied. He was told not to leave this location, even outside the entrance. He monitored another safety suit to be delivered to this same dwelling and sealed after their departure. Aldebaran and the technician, in full sanitary outfits pedaled to the safety of the decontamination dwelling.

67-Bacteria research

Almaaz's research for the past few orbits was unique. No one ever had done anything with the magnetic field around a bacteria. Other types of micro-organisms were out of her spectrum of expertise. There were thousands that she observed with varying charges into the nano watts. She seemed to concentrate on how they would not divide when given a certain charge. Too great of one and they would cringe and never retain their original activities. Over and over and over, she would isolate one and watch it divide again and again. Sometimes she was googol-eyed and tired observing through the telescope monitor, seeing the wiggle thing from all angles. How to de activate them and not destroy them was the task at hand. It was easy just to kill every one of them and that was the point of her interest in bacteria.

The most damaging of micro-organisms were feared because of the devastation that would follow their "visit" in humans or animals. To totally destroy an enemy of any other thing, there was a means of getting the destructive ones to modify their behavior. Almaaz knew that in every living thing there were organisms they functioned with, and in fact were needed for the living thing to exist. Some of the favored ones at times were too helpful and caused problems. It was now rest time and the lab personnel laid on the provided mats for their relaxation.

68-Bacteria splits

Upon arising Almaaz took a vial of live issue using extreme care while under the observance of the technician whose only duties were to see that Incu complied with every safety procedure in the rule book. The rule tests were taken at the beginning of each day: 100% was required every time. The wrong answers were discussed with the monitor and again the test was made. There would be no third test. Never would that party be allowed into an environment as dangerous as this one until testing was done in the next orbit.

In an sealed transparent cylinder, Incu, using robot arms, dissected a tiny section of the deceased flesh and placed it under the microscope. The sample could be enlarged thousands of times. Incu's primary objective was to have the deadly bacteria multiply at a much slower speed. Infections are devastating because of how fast the organisms can multiply. This particular one was much faster than the proverbial, "Well fed rabbits." Never had she seen them divide into three, four and once five at a time. Impossible she said to herself. No way. Something was happening in the nucleus. What? Blinded by what she called stupidity, she had to resign herself to keeping her mind on the objective.

The director of this operation had monitors of every one of the research technicians. It was impossible to see them all at the same time so he chose to put all on delay except the one that interested him. He was not on Incu's when it had the five split and she had to buzz him with the excitement of what she thought was a historic event.

69-Historic bacteria

Turning on Almaaz's monitor he said he had seen three but never five. It was historic and she was in the middle of it. How could that ever happen. The three split was a fluke and rarely occurred. It was like Quintuplets for humans at high speed. No wonder the deceased met his demise so quickly.

Now was the tricky part. Almaaz had to keep enough living tissue for the bacteria to prolong its existence in the lab. She tried different animal tissue and its multiplication decrease, then slowly stopped and vanished. It only survived on human flesh. It was the third moon of the new orbit and there was none available readily. She buzzed the manager of the operation of her need and the race was on. There were no accidents having any loss of human tissue. The dwelling of final stage was nearby and the director contacted the manager of that dwelling to procure enough for the experimenting that was being done on this new and strange bacteria. "I've seen you many times," he responded "Why don't you take some from your own posterior instead of these aged defenseless contributors of ever so many kilowatts?"

70-Guard near death

The lab director was desperate. He was a grade three producer and that left him a lot of time for his responsibilities and being sedentary. Bicycling more would have kept his waistline a little more in conforming with most everyone. He thought about doing so but was in his sanitary suit and could not escape from it. His monitor buzzed and he lucked out, that is for him. Tissue was available 5 kilometers away. A bear had attacked a security guard at the perimeter and had no chance of survival. "How much do you want?" the demise technician asked. "Could we have it all?" he pleaded. "That would take over an hour to prepare the guard and make him as comfortable as possible for the transfer," he said. "Do whatever you find that is humane. I do not want to desecrate the living just for the research even as deadly as the one we are working on now," the director pleaded again.

Three bicycles were drafted to transport the little life that was left in the guard. He was sedated and placed in a sealed bag so that none of him would be lost on the way to the research dwelling. It took a little more than an hour and the speaker from the front entrance told the three to make the delivery to the rear, unhook from the trailer and leave immediately. They complied and left not knowing that the few vials of bacteria inside could have a deadly effect on all of society.

After they departed the near death guard was placed into an airtight bag with enough air to keep him alive. A brain sensor was placed under the guards head and, much to the director's discomfort, for he was thinking to himself, "Please die now. Please."

71-Guard dies

Almaaz left her post to see the bloody mess in the clear bag. The man's intestines were strewn and many of them missing. His face did not look human: mutilated with deep claw gouges. One of the technicians was so disturbed that he vomited. Now that is a mess to clean up. It was inside his clear plastic cover and the smell inside of it activated his other stomach muscles to really constrict. He had to be assisted by his observer and go through the toxic cleanup procedure. Almaaz's hope was that the observer did not have a follow up reaction.

The man's brain waves hit a flat, and like vultures they all used remote dissectors to procure the tissue they needed before the man's cells were dead. Incu did her part in the feeding frenzy too. There was no way that any of the offending bacteria could have entered the bag that the corpse was in. Hazardous bacteria could not reproduce in a dead human. The exterior of the bag was sterilized and placed into another bag. A burial crew was summoned to put the remains underground immediately. Cremation was not a choice as it used fuel and the gasses would pollute.

Almaaz kept the guard's human tissue in more than twenty sealed containers which were placed under refrigeration and two were in liquid nitrogen. The thought of viewing the remains of the guard and the volcano vomit distracted her so much that she had to take another quiet time to reorganize her thoughts.

72-Almaaz's magnets

The dwelling that the lab was in was now secured and the usual blinking red light at each entrance was a warning that no one was to approach. An electrified five foot fence was now encircling the building with air bursts that had a weird sound that kept the birds from flying onto or near the building. It was now determined that no one was to leave the premises until all of the death causing bacteria was totally enclosed and quarantine control was positive that none of the bacteria would ever reach the outside.

The researchers had different avenues of approach in controlling the bacteria. Almaaz's electrical charge and magnetic field variations were unique. Did the bacteria have a memory? Did it have awareness of electrical or magnetic fields? At what intensity did it react? Did it respond to both? Every word that Almaaz said was recorded and coordinated with her past experiments. She had done this with other bacteria but none were as deadly as this one. Time was essential. Her monitor was shielded so Aires, Scorpio or anyone else could not contact her. If they did, the automatic response was, "Almaaz is experimenting with a deadly bacteria and will return your call as soon as possible."

The sealed building made it impossible for anyone inside to know if it was light or dark outside. The time piece used for their experiments was their friend and enemy. Total concentration took its toll. It had been one rotation and it seemed like eternity. Everyone was dedicated to isolating and controlling the bacteria. Whenever a researcher took quiet time, their refreshment was their salvation.

73-Isolation benefits

The director on this project assisted every one of the researchers and their observers. The position they achieved was not that simple. The observer must have total knowledge of the task at hand and could only hold that position to certain scientists.

The demand on their time was normal and accepted by everyone. In the case of Code 6 as this case was, there would be no phase time off nor personal accumulated leave. The longest Code 6 episode was two orbits, two moons and 3 rotations. All of those sequestered for that period returned to the normal world exhausted, depleted of any semblance of routine and their dwelling mates had to acclimate their returned "new" personalities to the norms of society. A referendum was placed on the ballot, and with everyone knowing all the facts and severity of their research, it was voted that because of the small number of humans needed for any project in Code 6, "All personnel enclosed in that code would be encapsulated until the reason for their research succeeded or failed." Failure was a no-no word. . If experiments ended in failure, at least new equipment designed and human endurance techniques were developed from their efforts. Not all was lost. Everyone on that project was advanced to grade 3 generation rate equal to the time spent in isolation. The ones that were grade 3 were thanked for their zeal.

74-Mother and Father

Almaaz knew of the record and in the third rotation she wished this one was over. She missed her offspring the most. Her mate had the same feelings. She loved being called Incu by them and others. Incubators were used as an artificial means of hatching eggs as fowl still did in the wild. Mother and father were used long ago but was gradually changed by some freak of adaptation caused by someone using the technical word over and over again. Donor seemed to fall into place replacing father soon after incubator reached its lead title.

The terms were gradually accepted and no vote was taken to make it official. Mama was now Incu. Daddy is now donor. Now and then those words were used and the younger ones had to ask for what it meant. The developing fertilized egg was the primary reason for being. It held a higher place in human existence than any other function of life. It was the future of the universe.

Incubators were given the greatest attention, even more than Grade 6 emergencies. It was sometimes annoying for a female carrying a fertilized egg constantly being observed by what it seemed by everyone. The daily waste removal was now in a special marked container and even somewhat adored by the examiners. Extra attention usually was not needed but when it came to procreation in process, nothing but love for life was in place.

75-Scorpio 16

Scorpio had the anniversary of his conception and wished that Incu could be there too. The next best sufficed. Every quiet time in the sealed dwelling she showed him what kind of gift she had for him. It might have been crude but if she wanted him to know what her duties were, how else but on his monitor. It wasn't too upsetting for him because Incu had done it many times since he was a toddler only in a more subtle way and appropriate for his age. She was hoping that he would choose something in the health field for his primary vocation.

Orion kept himself at his work place as he usually did. He would have liked to do some of the home schooling with the program that was organized by the education service. Now sixteen orbits and somewhat confused as to whatever was happening to his body, too much idle time would be devastating. He was not the one alone in this situation. There were other dwellings with males and females his age with everyone of their procreators well knowing that whatever happened to any child would someday boomerang into their own back yard.

Scorpio's dwelling was not quiet by any chance. The music generated was on the louder side with everyone dancing inside it and out. Quiet time was due it took for that to happen was a donor from the adjacent dwelling put his right index finger to his lips in the direction of the young blood, and if only one noticed him, that was enough for all to humble themselves and lie down onto their mats.

76-Male and female party

There was just enough floor space for the six youths to lie down. Procreators were never worried about having so much youth in one place unsupervised. Scorpio and the other males were ringed. The two other males were much too young and the females could do whatever they wished. The females were coached by their procreators as to what is expected of them. It was nothing unusual to have even larger gatherings of youth.

The dancing was with them since they started to walk. Music scales were taught before reading or counting. The spirit of life was for the living. The air was usually filled with all kinds of music, that was except for the third full moon after the starting of a new orbit. Night time was no exception. It was put many to sleep and when it was totally quiet, everyone awake was suspect as to "what is wrong".

The dances males did alone or with other males was quite physical. They danced combinations from slow circling rhythm with females having their eyes closed to Jump the Bar with the beat of drums which was saved for the last. Never was there a shortage of musicians. Everyone could do something with whatever was available: slapping two boards together, strumming guitar or using a variety of keyboards. Each area had a dwelling filled with instruments and maintained by the Music Service. Music was life. They were encouraged to incorporate it into all other studies.

History subjects were always related to the time of a certain kind of music. Since music was the joy of life, it overflowed into all subjects. Math used logarithms for the vibrations of sounds. Almaaz's first experiment as a very young offspring was to see reactions of different kinds of music. He learned that singing is twice as powerful as speaking.

77-Scorpio ill

When quiet time was over, five of the six arose to find an adult sitting in a lounge chair by the one exit. Castor motioned them to come by him. Miming them to unroll their monitors, each of them knew what was expected. Scorpio was still asleep and that was very unusual for him. The others were reading their monitors and taking notes while Scorpio slept on.

Castor, the neighbor, assisted the others when needed and was not aware that Scorpio was having a real problem until he rolled over and let out a soft moan. Uncovering his face shield, his face flushed red. The neighbor unrolled Scorpio's monitor and entered his body temperature. He was too hot! 40.1C.

In a panic, Castor pressed Code 6 which set off alarms to all the Medical Team nearby. In less than two minutes one bicycled to the entrance. Quickly he attached his body monitor for Scorpio's vital signs, unwrapped his clothing, leaving him naked. With all of this activity, Scorpio barely roused. Aires was notified and told to report to the Unknown Disease Dwelling immediately. Aires relayed all the immediate needs to his assistant and ran to the nearby building arriving just before the bicycle-drawn cart. He could not assist the medical team in any of their procedures because of the unknown reason for the high temperature rising in such a short time. Scorpio had acted normal before the quiet time.

78-Mosquito bite

Scorpio was placed into a quarantine tent with numerous tubes placed into all of his body openings. Two on his neck which allowed his blood to flow into the monitoring mechanism and he had a skull cap censoring device. The results took less than five minutes: Encephalitis. How could that happen when none of this was ever recorded at this time of the orbit

Medication prescribed by the automated testing control device. was injected through Scorpio's blood testing tube. The Grade 3 medical technicians standing by also took results from all of the tests and entered them into their personal hand held devices. Six of them working together wrapped Scorpio into the refrigeration blanket to get his temperature down quickly.

The brain fever was not contagious, so Aires was allowed to stand nearby in deep meditation for his offspring's quick recovery. Deep in thought with his eyes closed, he was alarmed when a hand was placed on his shoulder. It was Almaaz in tears. "It happened when we were at the beach; a mosquito bite he had on his cheek. If only he had worn his face cover this would not have happened." Almaaz blamed herself for what had happened. "There were hundreds on the beach dear, is ours the only one to contract this horrible disease? There is no fault to be placed on anyone," said Aires trying to comfort her. "Is your quarantine over?" he asks. "My research into that bacteria is not a panic thing. My specimens are secured but I will have the inconvenience of decontaminating every time I peek at the tiny rascals," she said.

79-Scorpio recovers

Scorpio was still shock with the high temperature. The time it took for it to drop was alarmingly long. There was a cooler on the blood that was drawn from his neck and returned. The doctors were questioning themselves as to the amount of sedative given. The mainframe computer was doing all of the prescribing. The input was done many years ago with much debate from all the medical field. Debate about the sedative was one of the most crucial. It was voted in and out at least three times. The lead doctor had a patient just like this one a few years ago and told the others not to panic. "Surprisingly the brain is ever so resilient," he said.

Sure enough, it wasn't but a few minutes that Scorpio opened one eye then the other, sheepishly looked around then closed them again. A good sign commented one of the dissenters. Almaaz held her face close to his and put herself into a quiet time trance. It was good for her to be calm when the love of her life aroused from his deep sleep. Aires was standing at her side with a tear rolling down his cheek. A few minutes later his near- dead boy opened both eyes, saw his incubator and grabbed her with both arms. Aires was now sobbing. Tears of joy flowed heavily. He could use a cup to catch all the liquid that was dropping from his chin. When the hug was over Scorpio wanted to sit up and was encouraged by the doctor.

80 Scorpio healed

When he was helped off the gurney, his first steps were a little on the wobbly side. Holding onto his procreators he walked around the gurney and other testing equipment with the greatest ease. "Since you both are in the medical field and aware of the problems that might arise, I'm releasing your most prized possession to your dwelling care. I doubt if any problem should arise but in case, use this syringe and inject a subcutaneous dose of this medication immediately and we will make an emergency dwelling visit," the technician said.

Donor had his offspring lie on the trailer that he was going to pedal and have Almaaz follow closely and observe him. The ride was only 15 minutes with most of it in the tubes so it was no real stress on Scorpio.

Arriving at their dwelling, Scorpio was himself again. His procreators marveled at such a speedy recovery. He said he felt like he could engage in a vigorous game of bounce but both of them came out simultaneously with a big "NO". Chess is all we are going to let you do for the next phase. "We want you to visit your monitor for what extended activities you can participate in. Do it now so we can make sure we are all on the same wave length," Almaaz demanded.

That he did. Sure enough everything he just heard was there for him to follow. His energy level was overflowing partly by the length of his inactivity and the other part was due to the medication that was administered. "Chess anyone?" he shouted. "Since there are three of us, Cribbage is more in line."

81-Researcher infected

Almaaz buzzed the sealed lab and was curious if any results were finalized in their probe into the unknown. The director of the project informed them that there was contact by one of the researchers to the deadly bacteria and now she was in the same predicament.

Her observer was grilled over and over by the staff in the dwelling, plus director of containment. They were brutal and demanding. Another life was going to be needlessly lost due to incompetence. The video of the affected researcher was run only once because of the amount of time that was spent in the sealed dwelling. No discrepancies in operations were observed. What went wrong was the main question.

It was Almaaz's turn to panic. If the bacteria escaped the most secure procedures, could she have brought it to her dwelling? Her anxiety was overwhelming. "Please play chess. I will not be able to participate in anything other that quiet time," she said. She tried to calm herself by reciting the same words over and over again and it did not work. Was she going to medicate herself? She told herself that she should not to let any of the three out of their dwelling for the next three days. She contacting the research director about this issue and he concurred. Three days of waiting could be devastating. Not only did her offspring make a remarkable recovery but with his body being in a weakened state, the slightest new monster to enter his body would kill him.

82-Tunnel vote

The ballot for the day was to cut a tunnel through the hill Number 17. It would be 8.5 kilometers and would require a lot of manual labor. Projects longer than this one were accomplished generations ago. There were always enough workers for the task. An over-abundance of free hands was what caused commotion in the past. With proper motivation, a joyous crowd of participants would be only too eager to dig and dig. It wouldn't take too much because so many wanted to enjoy surfing and with flinging beach lovers over the hill taking a good chunk of their kilowatt reserve. The tunnel would be the greatest. During construction they could produce a lot of kilowatts All of the tunnels were designed to have a slight slope from the middle to the exits, the load of dirt and rock being removed would give the peddler attached to a trailer a 100 percent generation guarantee. On phase off it was perfect.

The worker who were stationed at the front had the most difficult occupation. There was some vibration from the electric augers gouging into the face, forging ahead to meet the same operations from the opposite direction. There was some dust to contend with but a slight spray of water settled most of it. A conveyor scooped the bits and pieces and an operator controlled the amount that was loaded into each trailer for a peddler to take to the opening area and dumped. The operation was simple and tedious and like ants, constant effort got results. Downhill grade and a heavy load made easy generation.

83-Voting

Construction of eight tube tunnel cost is 3.7 mega watts. Recovery was expected in 7 orbits. Engineering and material for completion was local. Dumping area contained, no runoff. Completion date five orbits.

This was a major project. But as in the past, eager hearts participated with vigor. There were many volunteers for other projects. Their kilowatt reserve was more than the average person ever needed. One had seen 92 orbits and never made a claim to his reserve except for his pellets and every new moon tube fee. Voting was done on everyone's monitor. Unrolling it brought up the this rotations ballot plus issues for the next 5 rotation's subjects.

The next rotation's vote was to extend the tubes through the marshes by the bay. It was a local one but it brought a lot of ire from everywhere. If it was out of their voting area, they would buzz every acquaintance in the voting area and express their opinion. Every vote was taken seriously by everyone. There were no one that would not express their opinion. Every subject was on the ballot. Every person voted every rotation. Not expressing yourself would cost 2 kilowatts. The incapacitated would have their person in charge relieve them of their obligated duty. Incarcerated in the quiet place were also obligated to vote. Whole body Rejuvenation Retreat: no ballots issued. When Almaaz was in quarantine, she voted.

84-Who votes

"Scorpio, have you been interested in what is being voted on today?" asked Aires?

"Not really," he answered, giving a glance into his general area.

"I would like you to bring up today's decision to be voted on, please."

"Can I just finish my bird study project?" he pleaded.

"By all means, I'll wait," he returned. Reading his monitor for the decisions that were decided the past phase and was into the next three phases, Scorpio brought up the voting ballot on his monitor, then asked to be excused to visit the private place. Returning after placing his waste container into the pickup box in front of their dwelling, Aires had his long spiel down fairly well and did not want to bore his offspring with a lengthy lecture on rhyme and reason and facts and consequences. "First is a brief history of why we do,"

Aires proudly commented. "Second is that I want you to know why I find it extremely important for me to cast my ballot. Voting over the many orbits have made conditions what they are this rotation. It was thought that the most learned or the most aggressive one would lead everyone to a better place here on earth. Physically or mentally handicapped people have the ability to cast their ballots. It is understandable that they're are ones who cannot comprehend where their next pellets are coming from, let alone foresee what their vote is going to accomplish. Anyone who can pedal can vote. Anyone who can consume pellets can vote. Exceptions were made, but the main force behind who can cast a ballot was, is and always will be, society cares for everyone and voting is their response to that love. Ballot issues would be long forgotten but the words that are written have become part of our every rotation life. What we vote on this rotation will become words for the way."

85-Marsh vote

Aires rambled on and he could notice that Scorpio was getting a little restless. "The second part is on your monitor now. Do you know what to be voted on?" he asked.

"Sure do. The last bounce ball game it was in one of the opposing players made a comment on it. He said it was something about scaring all of the marsh birds away just to make it easier to get to the research building. The only ones that would benefit from were the Grade 3ers who need a little more exercise and wattage generation," the very young expert opinioned.

"WOW, can thoughts and desires ever get twisted! Probably his donor gave him those words. It could not be further from the truth. I am totally familiar with the area and know for a fact that the only disturbance to the birds will be the initial phase of construction when the pylons are sunk for the pillars. One fine two tube route across 50 hectares is not going to destroy anything. Construction will begin and end before the next in migration of the foul. The birds will not even know anyone is pedaling in the tubes. My," he said, "how could anyone ever think like that?"

"What say you and I buzz the misinformed? That would be something I could add to my bird project," Scorpio suggested?

"Duty calls first, but I have to make this an exception. Dysfunctional ignoramus. Idiot," were rare words out of Aires mouth.

86-Marsh discussion

Aires buzzed the many not too-friendly worded donor and the offspring answered monitor. Looking at the split viewing he recognized Scorpio but not his donor. "I can't play tomorrow. Have a long trip down river," were his first words before Scorpio could get to even say hello. Scorpio cut in and told his friend what his reason for calling and could he get his donor in the discussion. "Quiet time. Available in 15 minutes" came across the screen. Aires said, "Great, we need ours and it will give me time to repossess my thoughts." Fifteen minutes later another try was made and now some swaying of feelings about the marshes was about to take place.

Aires introduced himself, brought up the marsh matter and now Scorpio, his friend Struve and his donor were in open debate. Aires had the beginning words and it didn't take long for Struve's donor to make a comment, "Grade 3 would be the only ones using the tube."

87-Marsh discussion

"On that point I will have to agree with you. I never even thought about it that way. What if a side rail was set for parking in the tubes to observe the birds?" Aires brought up."

"Hey, that would be great," both of the young males seemed to come out simultaneously. "That's not on the ballot for today. I would go for that, but not the way it stands now," Struve's donor said firmly. "That means the issue should be brought up with all of the details in it. I was dead set for it, but now that the side observing rail came up." Aires said "I'm going to vote against it too as it is now. Why don't we both send the same thought to engineering for reissue of the ballot. I'll be buzzing others and share my views. Spare time is something that I have very little of. I'll let my fingers do the walking and send a blanket to all of my acquaintances. It was nice talking to you and I feel honored to have Struve in our circle." Finished, all four wished each other a goodbye.

It was so important to have communications and never let them die due to ignorance or anger. "Thank you our creator, for delivering to me an offspring such as Scorpio," Aires said to himself. "My choosing his incubator 17 orbits ago sure was one of the greatest gifts I could have. Research paid off. The physical attraction fling only lasts for a short time. The wisdom our past voters had made all of this happen. Who would ever have thought that something like having all the ringed males make such a difference. It caused a lot agony for all males. Many used to have multiple partners, so how could it ever get such a overwhelming majority of votes on the first ballot?

88-Tau delivering

Harmony in any department was the primary goal of the leader. Choices had to be made with wisdom. There were times when anyone could be wounded by a decision. Wounded was the word usually used. The word wound had a connotation of something visible . Something that could be treated with medication or by cleaning the damaged area. Aires was to get his test.

The excitement of Code 6 brought about extreme levels of adrenaline in everyone involved. Procedures for delivery were robot like in most cases. The health care unit dwelling that Mintaka brought Tau was the fourth of the rotation. Aires was in his place in an adjacent dwelling monitoring all of the supply reserves. Each article was censored so that it took just a matter of seconds to physically show that it was in its proper place.

Tau was huge. She had waited until 30 orbits before joining the mating area. It took another three before she was chosen. It was not uncommon. Tau was confident that all would go well. Her past gene pool deliveries had never had any complications. Never was now to be changed.

Safety precautions are routine with every one schooled in its priority. Kooky things happen though at the kookiest times. How could such a stupid incident about to cause so much grief to Tau?

89-Baby is born

Ninety eight percent of all births were natural. Locals, oral medications or any other pain controls were rarely used. Tau had none. The only joy of her existence was monitored and was in perfect position to come into the world. Sensors attached to her showed that all little one inside of her was in perfect harmony. She was naked with all of the birthing technicians and Mintaka kneeling at her side. She had all of the prenatal exercises down pat. Squatting naked while the team watched her every movement did not bother her at all. The pain of delivery was eased by her thinking about what she was going to hold in just a few moments. "New life is coming. The top of the head is here," was said loud and clear from Mintaka, nearly in the prone position. One of the technicians was getting ready to use her stethoscope on the neck of Tau and it somehow snagged onto her suit and the ear piece swung like a slingshot and hit Tau in her left eye. With the pain she was in she barely felt it. She let out a scream and those standing thought it was from her eye injury and others thought it was the normal sounds coming from a delivering incubator.

"It's here. It's a female," calmly said the technician. Everyone heard its cry and saw that it was covered with Meconium plug. The usual procedure of having the umbilical cord that was clamped then have Mintaka cut it was over-ridden by eye damage that was done to Tau. She could have walked to the clean up area but instead was immediately placed on a gurney. "I want my offspring now," screamed Tau. The lead technician thought the covering of the new born could infect the open wound on Tau. Mintaka shouted at the technician holding the baby in its special newborn wrap, "You had better do as Tau wishes. Do you hear me? NOW!" The technician hesitated for just a fraction of a second and that was too long. Mintaka's anger overwhelmed him, with his arms about to pull the newborn infant from the technician's arms when the infant was placed on Tau's chest.

90-Baby is perfect

The other technicians were hovering over the newborn trying to clean the mess that was swallowed inside its mother. Mintaka was in charge. The newborn was the priority. Dilemma unsolved. There was no greater force than procreators love for their offspring. Decisions had to be made. Ingesting too much of the babies waste could have life long complications. Code 6 after the original Code 6 had Aires running to the newborn dwelling. Nearly out of air, he arrived just in time to see the gurney being rolled outside in the direction of the eye dwelling. He was told in a few words. Meconium and infant ingesting it. Everyone knew that the newborn was of primary concern. Two huge security personal were commanded by Aires to tranquilize Mintaka and return the gurney to the newborn dwelling, remove all of the possible damaging Meconium from the breathing and digestive tract. The process was started in a matter of seconds. The pain in Tau's eye was causing the technician from the eye dwelling some concern. The damage was one thing but the pain was another. He was cleaning one area of Tau and the delivery room personnel were cleaning the other. Mintaka was in another world on the gurney next to Tau's. The newborn was cleaned and still crying but was returned to its incubator in less than 15 minutes. Tears in the undamaged eye left Tau with no sight at all. She could feel her baby. Her eye damage was of little concern to her now. The joy of touching it filled her with a warmth only an incubator could know. The beauty of new life is what it is all about. The future is now secure with creation of a new human so perfect. The rings are delivering the promise of the best of new humanity. When first voted, the dreamers knew the greatness of procreation and the weakness of the procreators.

91-Tau's eye not lost

Aires had all involved in the delivery of another perfect human but causing severe eye damage to its incubator. All were standing with no one really knowing where to start. "Thank you all for another perfect human. Our future is now secure. The beauty of new life is paramount to any other of our being greater than we ourselves. Love is now showing its light onto what the originator of our species intended. Each and every one that is procreated is why our training is so important for it to not have any problems in its life from our mistakes. This is our first in which the incubator was injured by all of us, not just you Betelgeuse. Our greatest concern is for how the little one can be affected by the damage to her incubator's eye. It is too early for the eye technicians to determine what can be salvaged and not have a total loss of sight for her left eye. He finished with. "Let us all now have a quiet time" Mintaka had his and then some. His companions, the security guards, escorted him to the eye dwelling and each gave him a bear hug congratulating him on having such a perfect offspring. He was now himself but the Record Keeper had the incident for posterity.

Tau was holding her offspring while a large cone shaped device was focused onto the her swollen left eye. Her right eye was covered and the prospect of being blind forever entered her mind. Cuddling the little one to her chest destroyed her panic. She was constantly touching the only exposed skin on its face. This caused its mouth to pucker up, wanting to suck. The training plus instinct for the little ones urge to suck was a wonderful feeling. "Oh, how beautiful the bonding," Tau felt deep within herself when her offspring began to suck. The feeling caused tears to flow from her damaged eye to flow. A good sign that that part was not injured.

92-Tau's eye repaired

Tau was typical of every other incubator. Her only reason for accepting a seed was for this loving creation. Years she had waited to have become of age. The research that she did in selecting a mate. The acquaintance time she had. She did not accept two prospective mates she brought to her dwelling. Her third selection refused to further their relationship. The fourth time in mate selection was the magic number. Mintaka was worth waiting for. He was overjoyed by his selection too. It was the first time he was in the mate selection arena. It wasn't until three orbits and two phases that she conceived.

It was their choice because Tau was on a research project nearing completion like most of the gifted intelligent were doing. The following phase after her group developed one more detection process of the decline of the small intestine nutrient absorption in the elderly. She was to be part of the implementation of their study into the automated waste testing but declined and was granted permission to become an incubator.

The ophthalmologist, optician, and surgeon were hovering over Tau like hen's with their chick. Nothing that was shown on the enlarging monitor or her vitals escaped them. She was unknown to them, but her medical history was all open for viewing. It was all there for her delivery so there was no transmission delay of any minutes. The cone scanner took the image of Tau's damaged eye area and transposed it into a hologram large enough for anyone to walk into. The lead ophthalmologist pulled the edges of the scratched eyeball together, his assistant guiding the thin string from the inside of the huge holo and placed the needle into the correct distance from the other side of the break.

93-Adjusting to Alnitak

Micro surgery like this has been done for many generations. The technicians felt it best that her other eye be immobilized to speed up the healing process.

Alnitak was held most of the time by her procreators but the pediatrician advised them to give the young some time on its own. Mintaka wanted to keep the little one in his back pack or his baby front pack carrier every moment he was awake. Over-zealous procreators sometimes could cause the offspring to develop within itself constant motion and require it for the rest of their lives. Newborn Alnitak was to become her own person. Guidance from her procreators, her neighbors, instructors were all geared to have that happen. No one was to intentionally guide her to any selection of any field. To do so would cause a lot of frustration after she realized that it was not what her inner feelings were in the first place. She could change anytime she wished but that decision would be entirely her own.

Tau could walk around her dwelling and do everything she had normally done guided by Mintaka. Seated or lying most of the time caused no anxiety in her because Alnitak was there for her to touch and nurse. Mintaka bathed and changed Alnitak. Her diaper and wand water waste were all placed for daily pickup in front of their dwelling. If there were any discrepancies or even the slightest deviation from the normal, someone from the pediatrician's staff would give them a call.

94-Identification chip imbedded

The eighth rotation after delivery identification was to be done. It was to be with her for the rest of her orbits. The process would cause her no pain or any other discomfort. A staff of twelve was required for this to happen to every newborn that survived to the eighth rotation. That was the official time when a new life would be processed with

The Record Keeper. It was questioned over the many generations as to why so many. Traditions were frowned upon. Changes would rarely be made by vote. Why twelve? Only one person performed the procedure. What were the other eleven needed and why did they all have to be qualified for such a simple task?

Identification was forever. No mistakes in the slightest would be allowed to happen. While the one made a tiny incision in the top of Alnitak's head, the others entered eleven different avenues of electronic inspection on the validity of the chip that was made for her the day she was delivered. Each had a sensor that detected that it was Alnitak. Some wandered out of the dwelling and as far as fifty meters which was the maximum range of detection. That was much further than the third generation when it was first implemented. Each of then took turns for the next five rotations and constantly had Alnitak in their view. Never was she ever to be let out of their sight. When the tiny incision was completely healed and her vitals monitored if there was no detectable tampering, which could not happen, Alnitak was now officially entered into The Record Keeper. Every one of her actions from her first tooth, step, word, verse repeated, song sung and more would be recorded for posterity to monitor. When she last needed a diaper, temper tantrum, attention span, non-obedience to her procreators or instructors would also be in The Record Keeper. In the mating arena it was vital for the research for the perfect offspring.

95-Tau's head gear

When half way through the second phase, the eye guard was to turn translucent to allow Tau's eyes to become adjusted to light. She panicked when she could only observe it on her right eye. The staff from the optical group were familiar with what caused her anxiety and immediately instructed her not to try to move her direction of vision to cause the eyeball to move. Those nerves were still under sedation and would take another rotation or so to return to their normal state. The technician in charge soothed her anxieties by informing her that was normal. "The right eye had no sedation so it could relay light through the stem to the brain. The left eye could not, but it was functioning perfectly," the technician told her. Tau was over-anxious in seeing her procreation. Her life long dream. What she was created for. New life from her and the donor she selected.

"Now Tau," the technician informed her, "you are going to have to wear the head guard much longer than normal. I say longer than normal because your offspring accepts, even at this early age, your first image. To totally remove it when you are not in need of it, would cause Alnitak not to recognize you. Her thoughts are primary. Any changes in the process of removing your head guard will be ever so gradual and with her view of each. We demand that you sing while holding her or even nursing while your donor, as we will instruct him, removes the multilayered head gear. Over the generations it was noted that newborns retained some of the pain of the birthing process.

96-Tau hums to Alnitak

Stress related to the length of time in the birth canal, rough handling by delivery personnel, room temperature or other environmental changes from what existed in the womb did cause unrest to what looks like fear in the new arrival. Some cried a little more and took longer to react to nurse its colostrums. With that behind us, please relax and your free flow of milk will not be retarded. Just hum or sing just as you did when you were incubating," she said softly. Tau sat with infant Alnitak in her arms seated comfortably in a cart that was hooked up to Mintaka's bicycle They all were glad that the added pain was now gone. All of the monitoring and testing that was being done to his incubator and offspring did not allow him to be completely rested. The stress of the ordeal did have its toll. Mintaka was keeping his speed at a minimum and still could not raise his generation level as high as he thought he could. The muscle power was not there. He was exhausted. The cleaning crew sanitized their dwelling shortly before their arrival. This would be done every rotation until Alnitak was four phases into this environment. The young ones attain immunity to most infections by its mother's milk plus its own newborn defenses and cleanliness of the dwelling. The latter would slowly be cut back.

97-Eye inquiry

Aires had to make a full inquiry to the eye injury. All of the personnel that were present when it happened plus what had transpired in The Record Keeper. Everyone was glued to the monitor keeping a close eye on Betelgeuse. The activity was placed in slow motion. He watched the stethoscope around her neck and her tugging on it. It was stuck on something out of view of the camera. Betelgeuse had the same uniform she had when the accident happened. "Please place the identical stethoscope we see in the monitor and repeat your actions similar to the one we are viewing now," Aires told her.

She complied, crouched herself over and tried to duplicate her actions and took a hold of the sensor part of the stethoscope and pulled it over her shoulder. "That is not the same one used before," one of the other technicians noticed. "Start over again using the same hand, please," Aires demanded. This she did and was upright. Another correction was needed. Trying to duplicate the same actions was getting too stressful for Betelgeuse. She started to cry uncontrollably. Aires held her in his arms trying to soothe her misery. "Quirks occur and they will never happen again if certain hazards are eliminated. All around us they lurk waiting for the perfect opportunity to maim. Take your time and your composure will return. I know you very well. Please relax and follow through as it is on the monitor," Aires pleaded then added, "Let's take a quiet time now."

It took more than five minutes for her to be able to speak and another two or three before she could look at the monitor and watch herself and assume the same position that she had when the accident occurred. "Please Betelgeuse, quiet time, please," Aires said with a very soothing voice.

98-Inquiry complete

This time everything was duplicated even to the speed in which she tried to remove the stethoscope from around her neck. Relaxed from their rest they proceeded from where they left off. Aires was standing on the blind side of the camera and noticed that the tubes were just slipping over the uniform flap on her shoulder. Viewing the other shoulder strap on her left shoulder was normal. How could the tubes ever come around her neck and spring right into the pregnant woman's face doing such a catastrophic damage to her left eye? The technician was noted in different positions before the accident and it was obvious that on her right shoulder strap was pulled over one of the tubes. In the process of trying to remove it, the stethoscope had to separate the strap from her shoulder causing all of the tension on the tubes. A fluke accident. It never happened before. It was now Aires responsibility to see that it never happened again. The uniforms that everyone wore were of the same design. A flaw in them all? Aires had a major project to pursue. It was his phase off time and he wished he could release all of his responsibilities from his mind. The leader this phase had to start and Aires would follow his lead. Arriving to his dwelling he found no one there. His schedule was very irregular. Three phases sometimes left Almaaz feel like she was in a lonely place. Scorpio was constantly in his preferred studies, bounce which he loved and his weird musical instrument he found in the archives of antiquities. Her dwelling was constantly being monitored and when she noticed that her mate was there she took off from the beach and notified him that she would be there as quick as she could. They had one phase off together. What a treat. Her medallion had no color. Scorpio called and asked for permission to participate in a bounce tournament the next few days and was graciously granted his wish.

99-Bounce tournament

Bounce tournaments were quite well attended. Aires and Almaaz could see his every move. There were hundreds of cameras focused where ever someone wished to focus. The priority to view was given to any of the participants procreators. When they beamed their camera onto Scorpio it would follow him thorough his ID. Scorpio wasn't the fastest but he played a smart game. He could judge very well at what height he would bounce in front of an opposing player and knowing their weight from the pre-game stats, so that it would just be high enough above their middle to get them out of the way and land on his feet and follow through, attacking another player. The game was violent in comparison to other sports. When two opposing players running at full speed and met with their center of gravity equal, they would bounce back two or more meters. This usually brought a roar from the crowd. Aires could transmit some of his cheers, too, but at a much lower decibel. It was rare for him to miss seeing Scorpio in his favorite game.

Academic challenge took a lot of Scorpio's time. The young man who was going to become seventeen orbits did very well especially in world geography and insects. Centipedes just fascinated him to no end. Why that particular one his procreators could not understand. He said many times that when he could sufficiently move as an adult, he was going to pedal through the tubes then sail to do his research jungle. His studies at this early age were focused on just that. Aires never had wanderlust like his offspring. How could someone so young pick such an unusual insect in some distant bug infested tropical forest?

100-Scorpio away

When he decided to leave, they may never see each other again. Routes over water could shorten the time but they do not generate any kilowatts. Pedaling was used to propel the boat. Research into any field was the primary concern of everyone participating in the tubes. So if Scorpio had his dreams, they would not be dashed because his procreator's fear of his safety.

It was just a matter of time and weaning was in the process just like now with the bounce tournament. Aires and Almaaz could observe him while he was in any viewing area. He knew that too. His time was so scheduled that there was very little time for unfavorable thoughts or ugly actions. His pellets and water were delivered to him where ever he might be. His waste was picked up every rotation. His suit refreshing was done as usual in the dwelling he was occupying with his other teammates. There were times when Scorpio would not be physically present with his procreators for a phase or so. They each knew each others whereabouts. Scorpio could just about leave for his dream "buggy" place anytime. Responsible adults were everywhere the tubes were.

The range of most was usually no more than a rotations pedal. Any new comer into their area would be like a new story book unfolding. All could be had on their rolled out monitor but the conversations with a visitor from far away was a special treat. Everyone knew the history of everyone else so that was not the attraction, it was the affection to any visitor. Another person to console. A new life to oversee. A being who might be the perfect one to guide them in the next day's voting. Any new arrivals were something to celebrate.

101-Scorpio's other dreams

Almaaz and Aires had their phase off. They voted every rotation. The time it took to cast a ballot with only thirty three words took only a few minutes. Scorpio was also notified by them about getting into a good voting habit. The results were not reported until twenty four hours after the deadline for the last time zone vote was past. They were totally refreshed for another three phases of duty.

Almaaz's experiments in different electrical charges on the bacteria she selected was a challenge. It was easy to follow one at a time but to view it for many orbits and note if there was any personality change in them. How could anyone observe a personality in bacteria? What human could have the patience for such an absurd project? Even if it could be done, would it have any merit? How many kilowatts were needed for this project? A zillion questions could be asked and they probably would never be answered with facts. Research into anything was always encouraged. Some started out with a tiny battery and magnets and ended up with a repelling beam that sent objects into space.

Space flight was common with the propulsion sled and the repelling beam. It took many rotations to perfect and now was considered as simple as pedaling a bicycle. The sled took the longest to construct. There were a few 25,000 meter inclines that would have sufficed but to get a anything through the sound and heat was a challenge. When Scorpio was ten, he had dreams of being a space engineer. At eleven, the bottom of the ocean fascinated him. Thirteen was when the caterpillars kicked in.

102-Alcor

Sleds used for space projects were similar to that Health Team or Security Personnel, only on a much larger scale. The maximum on that one was 2,000 Kilograms. Any new projects of this kind were defeated on numerous ballots because the energy needed for each space flight did not return its valued to the peddlers.

Alcor, the chief space engineer, would have like to send everything into space. It was like he was addicted to observe the ease in which loads were moved. There was a group that wanted his removal from that position. His designs were the primary factor in the latest accomplishments. He was oblivious of the ballot process on progress- and against him. His whole force was in having life's work in constant motion. He abandoned his mate and had his mat wherever he felt he could better his dream. There was never a phase off. The one thing that he was faithful was his quiet time. He revered that, Once he confided to another engineer that it was there that most of his ideas were given birth. On one of them the Health Team had to tranquilize him. He arose from a deep sleep screaming, "That's it! That's it!" He ran from one dwelling into the another for fifteen minutes screaming at the top of his voice. He was in a state of total elation. Arising from his induced sleep, he groggily said with slurring words, "That's it. That's it," and laid down again in another deep snooze.

103-Airless tube

The commotion that Alcor caused drew a crowd. One was Mizor, his co-worker on many projects. When he saw Alcor in such a pitiful sate, He nearly lost his gentle ways. His first look at Alcor in the fetal position on the cold ground was very upsetting. How could someone ever allow this to happen? Cornering the obvious initiators of the sedation he questioned, "Is that any way to subdue the great joy of victory in research? Was there any danger or was any physical harm done to anyone? Antidote this sleeping genius and let him express his feelings to the maximum! Now!" The now could he heard for a few hundred meters. They obliged. In a few minutes the groggy Alcor asked why they were standing around him. Mizor obliged and it was now he who needed the tranquilizer. "What was on my mind? What were my thoughts? What was it? Oh, how could you put me to sleep? Look at me! Take a good look! Please, anyone, please do you have any inkling of what it was about? Please! Please! Did I add any other words/"

Aires saw the commotion from his dwelling and rushed to see Alcor arise from his sleep and return to it. Now totally coherent and listening to Alcor, "I was told that the only words you said were that's it and mumbled air tube." Jumping up and yelling again, louder than before he was put to sleep, Alcor bellowed, "THE AIRLESS TUBE.

HOW COULD WE ALL BE SO BLIND!" Lying onto his mat, it was quiet time again.

104-Alcor explains

The usual method for quiet time was for everyone to repeat the same word or words over and over again. Alcor's were, "Beam repulsion, beam dispersion. Beam repulsion, beam dispersion." Mizor's repetitions were irrelevant to his duties. "Be at my dwelling before sundown." Others were mumbling their own thing with some having totally incoherent gibberish. What quiet time was doing for one was totally different for another. To each their own. All that mattered was, being refreshed when arising from their pad.

Alcor nudged Mizor, who was soundly asleep and startled him. Sitting up on his pad, Mizor he gazed around him and yelled, "Where are my pellets?" Alcor gently grabbed him by one ear and whispered into it and said, "I need you now." Mizor shook his head like he was trying to fling water from it a dive. His gaze slowly came into focus and he stood like nothing happened.

"Mizor, the repulsion beam that sends objects into space is always at the earth's side. It is doing the same on its return. Particles causing heat resistance has been a nagging problem and we have always accepted it as, there and normal. The G-force build up at 94 kilometers, depending on the angle of descent. Humans could tolerate much greater ones but heat was the major problem. If those particles were removed, no heat would be generated and its speed be calculated to what G-force of its cargo. Do you follow me, my dear accomplice in our joy of research?" asked Alcor.

105-Alcor's habits

Alcor was exhilarated by research. He successfully instilled others with his attitude. While he was doing calculating which was transferred onto walls of any dwelling he was in, he would hum his favorite tunes. The words to them eluded him and even the titles. The notes were perfectly in tune. He loved string instruments, especially the mandolin. He found that strings let out a vibration that would emotionally transfer into others and have an effect on them without their slightest awareness of why they acted in a certain manner. He wanted to follow that line but he knew that its lead came from others and if he would stumble into some segments of its possible reality, he would forward it lovingly to the Strings Theory Research. His mind was focused on the beam tunnel and he did not want other matters to interrupt.

Alcor asked the director of dwelling to have a new dwelling close to the beam pro-repulsion one. This new projects would require the top students from the next graduating class. Other research projects clamored for top students. Who would get them? They were so many things going on within him that there were times he would walk into a dwelling and awaken a stranger. One occasion, totally exhausted, he entered a dwelling he thought was his, rolled out his mat and was asleep in no time. The occupants were roused by snoring that sounded like a card on bicycle spokes with whistling and grunting awakened him. He rolled up his mat and left with out a word.

106-Alcor not physical

Alcor never had what you rally called a mate. Attractions to females was never a priority. He was not ringed until after his 14th orbit. Bedwetting was part of his way of life shortly before then. His clumsy ways awarded him with many bumps and bruises. He never had a broken bone or similar injuries because he never generated enough speed to cause anything violent to occur. He fuddled aimlessly and was considered a loon. For anyone to question him as to why he had no drive was not proper. The medical team had his history and was daily monitored as was everyone else. He accidentally wandered into a mate finding area and was physically grabbed by a female. She was given her chip and cried for love ever since. He had to force himself to pedal to create watts for his reserve even though he knew he was a grade 3. His niche was daydreaming. He would ponder in silence with or without his eyes open, not moving a muscle. He called it extended quiet time. The only thing that drove him into motion was the notice that appeared frequently on his monitor: ACCESS TO SERVICES DENIED: NO WATTS GENERATED. He knew that notice was coming and procrastinated. Why?

His procreators were puzzled and the attitude group from the health team visited Alcor. The last time was 3 orbits ago. He would get excited with experimenting and let out loud yelps but generating watts was just a so-so. He knew what watts did for all society. He knew everything around him was delivered by cooperative watt generation. He had no physical impairments and was just a slightly stooped middle aged male.

107-No watts-no monitor

"We have it that you have been denied access to services," the leader stated. "Are you never going to learn the consequences or you lack of kilowatt reserve? We are here to be advisors, administrators and will help you create within yourself the ideal attitude to have your priority be the generation of watt, watts and more watts. Our first question to you is, "Are you a member of the Tube Society?'" You know well that I am. I was created for it. My procreators chose each other to have one of the greatest peddlers. My first bike was the smallest made and I still remember my first kilowatt reserve and that was well before others beyond my orbit. Three orbits have gone by and I explained to you then and I will do the same now. I was totally engrossed into my research and my reserve was not even given the slightest attention. Do you know what I just gave the Tubers? Do you know how many mega-mega watts will be saved by my team? Can you fathom the depth of my concentration into the unknown? Why on this beautiful earth are you harassing me on such a trivial matter about not having any wattage reserve?" Alcor said with a tear running down his right cheek. "You are a grade three. Have you looked at yourself lately? Your brilliance is to be commended. The joy of your team is the greatest. There is a long list of applicants wishing to be part of your research. All those plusses are noting to the standard that has been set to your physical health. You are being totally engrossed into your way of living is going to have to change. We are denying your new research dwelling. We know that you are physically capable of generation. You will be expected to have a reasonable amount of watts in reserve before you wish will be granted.

108-Must exercise

"You are advised to not pedal more than fifteen minutes of every hour because of your body condition for the next three rotations. You will add five minutes to that every rotation until it reaches an hour. Break for an hour then repeat this four times a rotation. Keep your generation level low for the first five rotations. If you try to over-extend your ability to pedal, you could damage or strain your frame and your internal organs. We all know your body carries a great brain so if you want that wonderful and exciting brain of your to participate in the research in a new dwelling you anticipate to "play" in, you must get with the program, please," she very gently informed Alcor. "Plus you must have every off phase away from your research dwelling."

Quiet time was the first thing that entered his mind when he exited the dwelling. He tried to say pedal, projection tube would creep in. "Pedal, pedal, pedal, ray, pedal, ray repulsion, wave length, pedal, projection tunnel, GET YOUR ACT TOGETHER AND YOU BETTER DO IT QUICK! "He yelled at himself. Somehow he did doze off. Awakening, he didn't remember where he left his regular bike but knew that more were available. It was very difficult for him to pedal up the slight grade into the tube. His dream of a new research dwelling was what drove him to work. The first five minutes caused him discomfort over his whole body. His back ached, his left leg was about to give out and he had to leave at the first exit. He asked himself, "How could I ever sacrifice my body for research? How stupid can I be?" He tried to shame himself and that made things worse. "Shame on you Alcor, you dummy." That really aggravated him.

109-Alcor is pushed

He was out of breath. His left leg had a cramp. His heart was racing at 124 bpm. Frustration, Exhaustion. Depression. The list of horrible things could go on and on, He unrolled his mat, took another quiet time crying. This did not help his situation, Frustration led to anger. He got so angry at himself that he wanted to whack his head against the handle bars of the bicycle. His shaking was ever so obvious that everyone walking or pedaling did not get near him.

Betelgeuse had just exited the tube and saw this strange man acting in a weird way. The delivery room had no scheduled berthing. Cautiously she pedaled close to Alcor and gently asked him, "Male, can I be of assistance to you?" "Yes. Make a 50,000 kilowatt donation to my reserve!" he blurted out. "Male, you know that is impossible. I can push you through the tube if you are incapable of reaching your destination," was her response. "That will be fine. Anything is better than me cowering here like an idiot," he said. Rolled up his mat, unrolled his monitor and saw that he had generated 10 wats.

Betelgeuse followed him into the tube for the return. Alcor pedaled as hard as he could and his rate was ten. Six orbit children's setting. Betelgeuse began pushing Alcor with her rate at 60. When their speed increased he was asked to raise his to 90. Accidentally it was made 100 and both were working at maximum effort. When he exited, his reserve now was 300 watts.

110-Alcor is obedient

He thanked the female as she pedaled back into the tube. A huge smile came across Alcor's face and he just loved the beautiful moment of someone caring for him. Depression entered again. "Why did I shame myself? Ignorance is something I could have used but I knew perfectly well I needed my exercise. Stupidity could have been another reason of which I'm not part of. Alcor, give some of you joy to the bicycles. Alcor, you must love what the tube society has voted on as the proper way of existence. Alcor, please be quiet now and roll out your mat. This is your dwelling. Alcor lie down and relax……….." and he was asleep.

It was ten hours later when he awakened, bathed, put on his cleaned suit, jumped onto his bicycle and off he went. He felt like he could have gone 24 hours without stopping but he knew that he was being monitored by the health team. The little bit of exercise relaxed him for the long sleep and gave a terrific boost to his moral. It was his phase off and in the past orbit he has never left his station for even one phase.

Alcor strictly followed the health team's advice. If they had to call on him again it would be a deduction of watts which he wanted no part of. What was he going to do with so much time. If he only knew what was waiting for him. He felt good about the woman pushing him and that gave him a real high spirit. Then a flash back hit him hard about the tears by the exit; down the valley of despair. He had to fight off more tears.

111-Alcor meets Betelgeuse

Changing a way of doing things over the orbits was going to be more difficult than Alcor imagined. Habits and patterns were done by rote. His nibbling on pellets every rotation was another habit. Lucky for him there was no need to change that. The tube generation was great for his nervous system. He had a whole phase to do nothing but generate. The third rotation was the toughest to handle. His body ached. He even felt like his ears were in pain. He no one to console with. His love, research, had abandoned him. The beam tunnel was on the other side of the earth. A thought came to his mind that he could research through the system and do it from wherever his monitor could pick up a signal. He entered the tube and exited where he had his last emotional moments hoping to maybe meet the female who was his new spark of being.

There was a lot of traffic trying to get access onto the system and keep an eye out for the female. His whole mind was totally occupied. That was until a blip appeared on his monitor: ACCESS DENIED UNTIL FOURTH PHASE-Health Team. This was difficult for him to take. He started to fume, then shouted to himself, "quiet time." His mat was already unrolled so he put himself prone and kept repeating, "I must met her. I must meet her," then dozed off. The hustle bustle around him didn't bother his sleep. Sitting on his mat he heart started to race when he said aloud, "It's the female. It's the female" Most everyone looked in his direction and he was unaware of their stares. Betelgeuse was preparing for her quiet time, acknowledged him with a nod and laid down.

112-Alcor finding himself

His ups and downs were in sharp contrast with each other. Down-thoughts about leg pains. Up-kilowatt generation. Down-health team visit. Up-the female. Down-no new research dwelling. Up-the female and he was back to sleep.

He never had any feelings for any person. Female or male. All of his existence was for what entered his mind of earthly research. That was it. Nothing more. Nothing less. Research, research and more research. It was the love of his life. His only love. He was never lonely or depressed for any reason. Why did all of these new kinds of ways enter into his life? All of the different moods were entirely new to him. The health team visit three orbits ago had no after effect like this one. He was forced to pedal the tubes. He was again forced to be away from his lab on his off phase. Was this taking away from his independence? If all of the forcing was being done, why was he so enthusiastic about seeking the female? The off phase was now needed for personal off duty use. Why were all these new changes so welcoming? It was like a new spark that entered his life. The downs tried to lower him into the depth of depression, but the happy feeling that he had within himself by far overruled even to the point of him cheering for himself in front of everyone who happened to be near.

113-Alcor startles Betelgeuse

Alcor moves his mat next Betelgeuse's and just sat there and gazed at something emotionally moved him more than any other human. The only feeling he had in the past were for his totally engrossing research. Was the chance meeting directly related to his health team directives? He felt so comfortable with himself. Was the meeting from one of the other eleven dimensions? He was curious but not possessed by them. He could hear her repeat something but it was inaudible. It seemed like it was an eternity for her to find the end of quiet time. She did not stop her mumbling when she shifted from her back to her right side. He thought it was now that they could converse but the matter of two minutes, she was asleep. He moved so he could look at her face. The female had him in a trance and he loved it.

Finally awakening she saw Alcor's most radiant smile right in front of her. She recognized him and thought to herself, "How could anyone get our of therapy so quick?" All she had to do was squeeze her monitor and any of the dozen of services would protect her from whoever he thought he was. The smile on his face looked sincere but his mouth was not symmetrical. It could have passed for a snarl in the twilight. "Thank you," was all he said. "How long have you been watching me?" she asked. ""I dared not interrupt your quiet time. When you napped I moved my mat so I could thank you for giving me a new grasp of being," he answered. "All I did was help you generate," Betelgeuse responded. Alcor told her his health team dilemma and her eyes began to lighten up. She was dead wrong in her quick judgment of this brilliant scientist. She noticed that his body shape was not one that had a lot of kilowatts in reserve.

114-Alcor in love

Rolling up her mat and securing in on her back, she picked up her bike and was ready to pedal off. Alcor was totally out of sync of conversing with anyone except if they were beam talking. All that could come out of his mouth was, "Please."
"Yes!"
"I want like to talk to you for a moment more."
"About what?"
"Anything that might please you."
"Do you have a mate?"
"Yes and no. All of my life research has been my mate." He knew that she did not have a mate because she was not sporting a fertility medallion.
"What dwelling are you straining you gray matter in?"
"Please scan my ID and you will have all the information you need. May I scan yours?"
She obliged and he responded. Looking at each others credentials an explosion of feelings reached between each other.
"Do you wish to come to my dwelling?" she asked.
Alcor was in a tizzy. He felt tongue tied and flat-footed and felt a fog surrounding his head. Never had he experienced such a close encounter with a female. His whole body quivered and he was totally lost in his thoughts.

115-Dwelling offer deferred

"If you don't get yourself back to normal quickly, I'm leaving," she said.

'Oh, please excuse me for acting like I am. You are the first female that had ever asked me like you did. I was lost and did not know how to react. I do accept your offer. You will have to be patient with me. Please, again I beg of you to be patient with me" he pleaded.

"My nursing career has trained me to deal with all kinds of personalities and yours is a rare one. I think it's best that we defer my offer until a later date. I do hope that you can get the system to assist you in practicing your female approach with the hologram. I would like to know you better and you can have permission to use my form to be your holo female. Is that OK with you? She asked. "That is more than I expected. I'm still in shock. Thank you. Thank you. Which of the 11 dimensions was responsible?" Alcor stuttered. "I don't really know which one but I do know that I now feel vibrations from some distant place and I like it. As soon as you complete the male-female meeting hologram program, please buzz me. I have responsibilities the next three phases so take your time and I will also take that same program again. I t has been many orbits since I last completed it and maybe some of my services on the health team might have distorted my proper actions," she said smiling.

116-Bounce rules

Returning from a whole phase of Bounce, Scorpio returned to his dwelling exhausted. He just about to collapsed onto his mat, but first he had to place his suit into the sanitizer, bathed before getting into his nap suit, It was such a fun filled phase. He had the highest percentage of wins of anyone. He would have liked to be able to choose who would be on his team. The rules were made so that with eight positions on a team, all of the participants would be drafted into teams of eight, No substitutes. Of the eight positions, each one again would be drafted into position. Sometimes the fastest runners would be drafted to play one of the five lineman and the slowest drafted to the three backfield positions. The first left lineman would organize the first offensive play, the one to the right of him the second and so on until all of the eight would have their turn then back to the front left lineman. The general play book, which all teams had access to, had hundreds of offensive and defensive plays. The middle backfield could make slight modifications if he so desired. When the center lineman threw the ball to any of the three backfield players, it was the start of some real bouncing.

Defense was the most fun. They would be aligned as the alternating leaders desired. Being the flyer was what Scorpio liked the most. Usually he would be at least ten meters from the ball, and when he saw it move, he would run full speed at the player who had the ball, which was behind his offensive line. Then Scorpio would jump as high as he could, striking the opposing player above his chest. Scorpio's speed was the major factor in having one or sometimes two opponents topple over with Scorpio on the backfield person and the ball at his finger tips.

117-Bounce

Halting that player from advancing to the end of the 100 meter field was the goal. Each player on offense would then get a point. There were no lines on the field. Infrared beams marked the sides and ends. A beam from the side would be focused on the middle of the ball. To start the game the ball was placed in the exact middle of the field. Opposing players would gather at opposite ends of the field. When a whistle was sounded a mad rush was made for the ball. The first player to place the ball in their carrying pouch would have the first play of the game. All plays were ended when the ball was stationary for five seconds or touched the ground. If out of bounds a whistle would sound and siren blared when the ball crossed the end line. There were no referees. Anything goes.

Tournaments were usually held at the last day of each phase of the moon. The bounce uniform was designed to cushion the whole body and still allow mobility. Who would have ever thought that the most popular game would develop from a covering for small children who were strapped into their bicycle carts.

Each field had a dwelling for uniform storage. That uniform was worn over the player's suit. When the game was over the bounce uniform was placed in the sanitizer, them put in appropriate weight size rack. The Physical Activity Team (PAT) maintained them.

118-Scorpio loses monitor

The nap did Scorpio wonders. He awoke refreshed like it was an all night sleep. The rare caterpillars in his jungle paradise possessed him. His monitor had, "ACCESS TO THE SYSTEM DENIED--LACK OF KILOWATTS". "That cannot be. No Way," he grumbled. His total engrossment into his favorite activity for the past three rotations and not pedaling slowly eroded his reserve. His pellets and other services were on constant withdrawals. The dwelling next to his he most likely could locate a construction site where he could replenish his reserve a lot faster than pedaling the tubes. He knocked on the entrance, then knocked again and was just ready to leave when a very old man in a wheel chair slowly opened it, much to Scorpio's surprise; he saw a bunch of children, much younger than himself running around. He thought to himself, "Why was someone so frail in that dwelling with so many children?"

"May I help you in any way?" he said in such a low voice that it was like a whisper. "You sure can. I have no reserve and I need access to the closest construction site. I know that there is one three kilometers from her," Scorpio said. "Young man, I have to generate using my arms as you can see that my legs are useless. Do you want to use my kilowatts from my puny reserve? I strongly advise you to hop onto your pedaling thing and jump over to wherever you want to and generate while doing it," the man whispered. "I'm sorry I bothered you. I thought all of those children were part of a nursery. Why do you have them here?" Scorpio asked. "I'm cleared as a Social Adult Personnel (SAP) and I need a donation of kilowatts," He answered.

119-Kidnapping

"May I buzz my incubator, please," Scorpio said.

"For that, yes by all means," he assured.

"Incu, can you check for me if that construction site at exit 2045 is in operation now? I'm out of Kilowatts and you know what came up on my monitor," Scorpio explained.

"Are you using the old man's monitor now?" Incu demanded.

"Yes, as you can see," responded Scorpio.

"Young man, if you want your dreams about your caterpillars to come true, you just pedal yourself to that place. It would be nice if you would more than double the watts you used from the old man for this buzz. Ask him if he needs any favors. Bye now," Incu said.

"My incubator suggested that I ask you if there is anything I can do to return the watts that I used in making this call. I want to leave now and will be back tomorrow if that is OK with you," Scorpio asked. "Yes there is. The Kooky Klowns are performing in the nearby park and I want one of my wards to return now. She was gone longer than I permitted. Please take this sending unit and she will respond. The range from here should have been adequate, but it seems not," whispered the barely audible old man.

The park came on his monitor. Turning the camera to view the entire area, "There she is. She is the one with the zebra stripe suit. What is that woman doing holding her hand? What is that weird cap on the little one? Hurry over there now! Hurry!" This time the old man's voice was very understandable. He notified the Security Online Services and reported the incident. He did not take his eyes off the youngster while wheeling himself through the entrance.

120-Scorpio tranquilized

He looked in the general direction of the area where the clown were performing and a hundred meters or so at least twenty SOS personnel gliding in. There was no way his ward would be abducted.

Pedaling as fast as he could, Scorpio saw the little tike, moved much faster than their casual walk. He stopped his bike in their path and immediately the woman hugged the little girl and shouted, "You are not going to take my little girl from me!" Scorpio laid down his bike and told the woman that she belonged to the old man and would like to have her returned immediately. "I can't let my little girl go anywhere but to my dwelling with me," she sobbed. Scorpio, in his youthful impatience, reached to grab the girl when the SOS group surrounded the three. Scorpio and the woman were covered with the "sleep" blanket with some of it covering the little girl. They were all tranquilized.

Scorpio and the abductor were taken to the nearby lonesome place and given neck monitors. The old man saw all that happen and notified the SOS that the young man was not part of the kidnapping. Scorpio was asleep. His monitor was dead. SOS could not understand the excited old gentleman. What an experience a 15 orbit male was getting.

Aires returned for the rotation to his dwelling to be confronted by the old man who could hardly breathe and tried to shout with only air coming out. "Is that the kook that I see next door with the little kids?" he said to himself. Four tiny children ran out of the dwelling with the old man gasping, "Get the kids!"

121-Aires tranquilized

He took off and corralled them, holding one, and guiding the other two to the old man's dwelling. The little male was just a little too frisky for Aires and tried to take off again. Aires grabbed his arm and he let out a loud scream. All this happened when the SOS were returning the drowsy little girl in the zebra suit. Two of the SOS ran up to the four and one asked Aires if he knew the children. All it took for another blanket treatment was when Aires said, "No." Off he goes to the lonesome place.

The old man was wheeling with excitement, and tried to explain to the SOS but was out of breath. So the SOS did their operations just as they were trained. They scanned the three infants and The Record Keeper showed that they were to be at the dwelling in the charge of Sirus. If any harm were to come to any child, their safety was paramount. "Are you Sirus?" the old man was asked. He could only nod. "You will have to answer me with a yes or no!" they demanded. He took as deep breath as his old body could take and wheezed out a, "Yes."

The three were brought to the old man, and as soon as the SOS let them loose, they took off again and the SOS after them. The lead SOS female said, "We can't leave these 4 with someone in such a handicapped condition. Get someone from Child Protective Services!"

Sirus asked one of the SOS to push him to his dwelling and they obliged.

122-Scorpio in a Lonesome Place

Scorpio was awake but completely confused as to where he was. That bib-like thing around his neck was very puzzling. He tried to shout to the SOS walking away and his first try was supposed to be his last. A sharp piercing pain entered the top of his head. It was so sever it seemed like his eyeballs ere going to burst. He unrolled his monitor and entered his donor and on the screen came "NO ACCESS TO SERVICES. LACK OF KILOWATTS." Trying to access any source to the outside, he noticed that the SOS brought a very relaxed male into the next Lonesome Place, "That's my do……."

and poor Scorpio gets another lesson in shouting. The pain went away and with all of the education in how the collar worked, he did not try to shout again. Scorpio attracts the attention of a SOS male and asks for the report of his donor who is now his neighbor. It did show that "Attempted kidnapping" was the charge. "Please bring up the surveillance of that incident." begged Scorpio. "The dwelling with the old male is next to ours. See the Caducei over our entrance. My donor was probably trying to return the little ones. The wheelchair male can only control them when they are inside his dwelling. I was with him when we saw a female taking his ward from the recreation area.

123-Aires and Scorpio released

Awakening, Aires saw his Scorpio waving his arms. "How could that be? He is so you…." and falls back to sleep. A few minutes later he is aroused by a SOS standing over him. "You can return to your dwelling now. We are sorry for the slight discomfort we have cause you and I know you will understand why this happened. You can bring up our report. Your actions justified our actions."
"You know what happened" said Scorpio and excitedly he says to the SOS male. "Look at the beautiful words on your monitor, 'All charges dropped. Free to leave' and mine should be the same. Verbally, the one in charge said a series of numbers then across his monitor came, "All charges dropped. Free to leave." Scorpio felt a buzz in his neck and was told to be stationary for a moment. His bib separated by the SOS, he was now a free person. He was going to shout for joy but the painful experience he just had caused him to whisper, then talk, then a little louder then he shouted at the top of his voice, "DONOR, I AM COMING TO THE RESCUE!"
Aires heard the yell but was ever so distress to see a woman lying on the ground in the Lonesome Place next to his. He saw her go into a full run the collapse in pain from the securing device. How could the system be so cruel to the helpless. This was a priority of his-to have the mentally impaired tubers have a more compassionate confinement.

Turning around he saw his offspring running toward him, yelling again, "DONOR, I AM COMING TO THE RESCUE!"

124-Reckless bicycling

After giving Scorpio a real loving donor hug, Aires pedals to his place of duty. Scorpio is overly eager to generate watts and get to his dwelling gets caught by SOS. The path he took was quite busy with walkers and zigzagged his way through. He could see the old man's dwelling and gave the urge for more speed. "SOS! Oh no. Not again!" he all but shouts to himself. Stopping on command to an upheld hand, he was then told the obvious.

He was stopped two moons ago. He tried to explain his anxiety but to no avail. SOS female said, "This is your second offense. You have a choice. The Lonesome Place for three rotations or pedal the penalty fee before you retire. "I'll take the second one. I have to notify my incubator," Scorpio asks then adds, "if I may. "I'll go with you the SOS responds.

125-Watts for the fine

Incu had just cast her vote for that rotation and asked if Scorpio did the same and what was the SOS person at door for? It was total confusion for the young male. "I was in the Lonesome Place and so was Donor. It was all a mistake and we are both free. The SOS is here to see that if I have your approval to generate my reckless bicycling I received after I was released."

"Scorpio. Scorpio. Do you have any idea how long it will take you to generate enough for the fee? I doubt if you can, but your procrastination in generating brought this about and all I can say for you now is, go for it. I will always wish you the best. Can I have a hug before you go? I will loan you a kilowatt for you to be able to communicate with me."

SOS and Almaaz waved him goodbye. Scorpio's first destination was the construction site and his luck had now changed for the better. The line waiting to hook up onto a trailer was a little long and it would be a good time for him to take his quiet time. Caterpillar. Leg coordination he said over and over. He was soon sound asleep.

When he awoke, there were three less in line than when he first arrived. With the anxiety of getting involved in another new venture, he didn't notice the cool temperature. Unrolling his monitor, he brought up the ballot and voted while waiting in line.

126-Generating watts

He was next in line to hook onto a trailer. He had never done this before so he closely observed the female on how she did it. It did not seem to complicated but now that it was his turn, he was all thumbs. It was taking him too long and the next female in line saw that he was having difficulties so she generously assisted him in his real life education. Once inside the tunnel, it was kind of spooky. The air he was breathing was nowhere as easy to inhale as the outside one was. The trailer had some weight and his generation for the upgrade was struggling with was only at 15.

Five was the marker on the finished side-walls. His gap between the one in front of him was widening but he could not get enough extra strength to catch up even with his rate set to zero. Peddlers in the other two lanes were passing him by. Passing the Six Kilometer marker, he could see he was getting closer to his destination. Stopping to load his trailer was a relief. In less than a minute, he was on the decline return with 200 Kilograms of rock. His load was much heavier than he, the bike, and the trailer. All he had to do was get started which took all of his muscle. Ever so slowly it seemed for the young male, but it was now moving faster than the other bikers in the other lane. "Slow down, young buck. If you dump that monster on your back, it is going to take you a lot of trips to cover the cost to clean up the mess you are going to make," yelled the white haired male in the next lane. Increasing his generation rate and bring about the other's speed, he could not believe the number. 172. Adrenaline was now pouring into his system.

127-Double rate

Scorpio's procreation rotation was approaching ever so slowly for him. He wanted another orbit in the worst way. He developed average for a male of 15 orbits. His donor said that he was just a little older than he was when he was ringed. Never was he going to procrastinate again. Unrolling his monitor and securing it to his handlebars, he contacted Incu. As they conversed she could see what his operations were like. He told her his generation rate and she shouted praise for him and told him now would be a good time for him to get into the history channel because he was going to be tested for the orbits between 100 and 200 BOT. Beginning of Tubes. His incubator also said that she would load more kilowatts so he could bring up that channel.

The return trip was ever so easy, and his generation so high, Scorpio was in his glory. The screen flashed an announcement-ALL RETURN TRIPS FROM THE FACE WILL BE REWARDED DOUBLE THE GENERATION RATE. How much luckier could a young male of 15 be. The next trip up the incline seemed to be so much easier. He now felt like an adult. The third trip was going to be his last. He was exhausted and his wisdom about his ability to perform in this exercise superseded his desire to load up his reserve. Checking it, he found that he was ten kWh past his fine fee. That in itself was a great pleasure. Now he was ready for the long bike ride to his dwelling and much needed rest.

128-Scorpio exhausted

Aires and Almaaz were waiting for him. Their completely exhausted offspring was going to fall onto his mat but was told that he would have to bathe after placing his suit into the sanitizer. He obliged, and ever so slowly without saying a word, flopped onto his mat.

Aires told Almaaz that he had an incident similar to Scorpio's when he was a few orbits older. It seemed that Kilowatts were always there. Not checking on the reserve constantly, a youth's kWs could vanish and being denied the joy of the system hurt. "Have you looked at your reserve lately?" asks his mate. "Let us both inquire now," she returned. Unrolling their monitors and asking for Kilowatt reserve it listed the ones used and the balance. "I've got 3,429 kWh," bragged Aires. "Mine is 978, but you have a rate of 2.5 rate and I only have a 1.75," in a voice that sounded like a complaint. "If you want to spend a phase on the beach, you are going to do some serious pedaling. While we are there we cannot do any generation. Any problem with spending more time in the tubes than at the holo exhibit of little bacteria?" He pleads

"My research is so dear to me. The Health Team has not contacted me as to my 5 Kilo weight gain, so until they do, my cute little things are my babies," said Almaaz. "Does the Health Team have to threaten you? Why can't you do it on your own? You know that there are fees for their visit and they don't come cheap. Aires, stop it now," Aires says to himself." then adds, "The incubator of my offspring knows what to do without any aggravated coaching,"

129-Muscles ache

At 1300 hours, Scorpio rolled over on his mat and let out a groan. He had to visit the private place in a hurry and all of his muscles were so sore he could hardly move. The urge to go was more painful than his aches. Relieving himself the putting on his suit fresh out of the sanitizer, he was buzzed. "We are short one bouncer and we need you," pleaded a bounce player. "I cannot," answered Scorpio. "What's the matter? Is your turn to clean your dwelling? Or maybe you have a headache?" asked the caller. "You know better than to tease me. If you did what I did last night, you'd be in a medical dwelling," Scorpio nearly yelled back . "Did you get bit by one of your caterpillars or some other bug?" teased his bounce buddy. "The new tunnel for three trips and now I'm so sore I can hardly walk," groaned Scorpio. "You've got to be stupid to do something like that,. Will you ever learn that greed will do you in?" was another tease. "I'll get back with you when I heal these aching muscles. I'm sure that there is someone else that you can find," Scorpio said rolling up his monitor.

He tried to loosen up by walking around his dwelling and saw that some of the plants needed watering. He filled the containers to less than half full. He was surprised that even though he was sore, they did not feel as heavy as he thought they would feel. That chore done, he used his wand and emptied it into the proper container and placed it with the daily waste to be tested. Every bite of body loss was inspected. The automated system could handle much more than it does now. The only problem was the malfunction of he mechanical devices. It seemed to everyone that the more any testing mechanisms were programmed to perform, the greater was its risk of shutting down.

130-Hologram teacher

Knowing that his body was not frozen at its joints, he could relax and bring up 100 to 300 BOT. It was now 317 BOT. The voting files were his greatest asset. Each ballot had only 33 words. Starting at 100 BOT, he just read the highlights of each and their percentage of the win or loss. Surprisingly to him was that on the second moon, third phase the percentage of votes needed to have won was changed from 66.66% to 75%. He know that it still is the same now. Reading the ballot in detail he found that there were too m any losers at the lower number, Originally it was 50% plus one. The next issued for the next rotation was that any intentions on an issue being on a ballot must not be related to anything that was in the past orbit. It won.

A 15 orbit's retention of all that was not related to bugs was going to be tested as soon as his incubator and holo teacher would try him. Holo teacher's lessons were finely tuned by a group of instructors after many orbits of research and testing for the highest retention rate for the next rotation, phase, moon, orbit and five orbits. The hologram teachers were used everywhere. The only drawback was that its central system could only engage 262,144 at one time for any one subject. Overload has happened only on rare occasions, Eleventh power systems are now being perfected. One is being tested by the Medical Team, which gets everything first, gives off smells, grunts and a hologram within a hologram all projected from a monitor. Research brought many marvels to be enjoyed. If a human was not in research, they were in services. There were research teams generating all their power needs. If more was needed it was placed on the ballot.

131-BOT history

The tunnel that his Donor, Incubator, and he pedaled through was on a ballot in 203 BOT with an estimated cost of 323,570,000 kWh. Curious as to what the final cost was, Scorpio entered engineering and found it was 412,230,907kWh. With a rough estimate of 88 difference, he figured that the engineers were off by nearly 30%. He probably thought to himself that they probably gave peddlers generous bonus'. He was happy that he made a few extra kW last rotation and will find the completion cost in three orbits.

Scorpio's goal was to speedily read every ballot for 20 orbits every rotation. Within 5 rotations he would have to digest 28,000 ballots. The third new moon and the next 3 phases after the start of another orbit was quiet time for everyone and no voting. With 3 orbits read and 17 more to go, he felt he could do it.

In walks his procreators. They held hands and smiled. "What have you been up to, my ever growing offspring?" asks Donor. "History, history and more history," responded Scorpio. Right back Donor responded, "Great. I always wanted to know if the lesson that I took was still in the system. I want to see progress in action." He got the history channel on his monitor, and was shocked at the amount of hair that most of the males had.

132-Scorpio wants to study

"I used to have some difficulty getting my face shield on, but with the bush I see, it could never happen. Freedom to be odd sure has its drawbacks. What's with the ballot you are reading now? Is that the one we still ridicule to this day? Free tranquilizers for the over-passionate females. I see it failed. They claimed that males were ringed and thy had nothing to ease their anxieties. Sorry females, if you had the many pains of the rings, it would be a different story. That was a long time ago. Scorpio, did you know that?" "Please Donor, I have a lot of ballots to go through before the next phase and I will be tested by Incu and the holo," pleads Scorpio. "Wow, I'm ever so pleased that you are getting aggressive with you studies, but what happened to the little male we used to have?" kidded Aires. "The jungle intrigues me too to no end. I hope to be there in a few orbits. Have you been following the weather there? It is so----," Scorpio catches himself talking then repeats 3 times, "I have to study!" Aires asks Almaaz, "chess?"

The set they were using was a lot larger and heavier than the one from their last dwelling. The note in the game box stated that the marble used in the pieces was from the mountain just to the west of here and was chiseled by Sirus. "That is the old man that lives next to us.. His misshapen hands now can barely hold a liter of water, let alone create masterpieces like these. Just feel how smooth the finish is. They are beautiful. Next rotation I have to compliment him. Are you going to try to beat the champ, my loving incubator?" asked Aires. "Do you know what time it is now?" she asks. Aires looked at his monitor and without saying a word, laid down on his mat and all three of them had a quiet time.

133-Voting history

Scorpio repeated over and over again: Leg coordination. Caterpillar. Leg coordination. Caterpillar. A nap was out of the question. His anxiety about the tests overwhelmed him. Leg Coordination. Caterpillar. Caterpillar. Leg coordination. When he awoke from his quiet time, the chess set was put away and his procreators were fast asleep.

BOT had a few goodies on the ballot. UNLIMITED WORDS PERMITTED ON ANY BALLOT. REASONS: BETTER UNDERSTANDING OF THE ISSUES. Lost by 93 to 7 percent. Three phases later: SIXTY SIX WORDS PERMITTED ON ANY BALLOT. Same reason. Lost 92 to 8 percent. Three phases later: 51 WORDS PERMITTED ON ANY BALLOT. Same reason. Lost 89 to 11 percent. They were all counted electronically and stored until all had voted and it was then and only then so that the voters would not be swayed by the earlier ones cast.

BOT had: ADD THREE CENTIMETERS OF CUSHION ON ALL BOUNCE COVERING. REASON: BRUISED THIGH IN GAME 302, 6TH MOOM 3RD PHASE. Won 51 to 49. Scorpio said to himself that 49 percent of the tubers were upset. He can see why it was changed to the present 75% approval.

BOT. MATE SELECTION FOR TWO PHASES. REASON: LONGER DISCUSSIONS WITH OTHER POSSILE MATES, Lost 84 to 16

134-Past votes

Quiet time seemed to come much sooner than usual. Scorpio was totally engrossed by the voting that was done. He could see why things are as they are this rotation. Everyone that cast a vote must have one thing, and only one thing, in their minds: What is best for all tubers? Caterpillars. Leg coordination. Leg coordination zzzzzzzzzzzzz.

He awakened by thunder that was really a blast. He was also in a little pain from the rings. He hobbled to the private place, relived himself and then back to his duties. 241 BOT: INCREASE DWELLINGS BY TEN PERCENT--Reason: SERVICE PERSONNEL INCREASE TO EVERY OTHER PHASE OFF DUTY. Lost 87% to 13%. "Donor this last one here puzzles me. Why would such a nice thing lose so badly?" "When you get to the first 100 orbits of your history of the tubers it will come clearly why. The tubers have always voted for the maximum efficiency of our system. Figures are thrown at us every rotation. Researchers donate heavily in time toward their pleasures of life. The repetitious manner of service personnel can become boring if the individual wishes that to happen. You just went through a bout of not being able to enter the system. You had other interests and forgot that you are part of the tubers and are responsible for everything that you do. Humans as well as everything in the universe always follow the least line of resistance. A narrow window of zeal for tubers must be maintained for us to function proficiently. The system must have a large majority of voters with good will contributing their joy at being part of the whole tube picture. What was the percentage?" asked Aires. "13 percent," answered Scorpio. "It would be nice at 1 percent," returned Aires.

135-Studies distractions

Scorpio entered his jungle to find there was a research party there now. There six and they were all involved with plants. None were of the "buggy" kind. One there was in the process of having her application approved. Curios of why it was such a large group, Scorpio buzzes them all at one time and he got an eye opener. Each were on his split screen and they were all females over 50 orbits. They all used tact informing him that they were together for many orbits and that a young male would not enjoy their habits. One of the most forceful reasons was his age, he would have too much energy for them and it would be best for him to try another group more to his speed. He told Aires of his inquiry and Aires asked if he see the list of names. When donor browses over it, up popped a big red flag which he recognized very quickly. "It's best you were rejected and please don't feel so bad about it. That group has done more to pellet additive development than any other group. None of them have entered the mate choosing events" Aires dropped it at that and did not want to dwell on why. "Your incubator would like for you to be with for two more orbits. With the your last few incidents, we desire that you have a fully developed frontal lobe. You know that the tubes are sparse where you plan to be. Medical facilities are in most cases, distant. Your healthful youth is the only thing meeting the demands of your dreams. You are going to be so distant that we may never touch each other again. The monitor is great. Holos are close to being there but to touch you there is no equal. Now that we have my feelings thrown into your "future basket", I have to buzz my hobby buddy, and what about your history studies? asks his donor.

136-Alcor very happy

Alcor returned to his research dwelling in full vigor and smiled, much to the surprise of his fellow scientists. "Is it a female? I'm puzzled, but it sure is a pleasure to see such a lively change in you. You have had some exciting innovations in your development of sending projectiles into space but somehow this one seems to be different. Hurry up and give us the details. Please do it now. Is it a secret or something like that. What is taking you so long to let us know? his assistant asked. "I would if you would be quiet for a moment. You know that I was refused access to the system because a lack of kilowatts. That was the best thing that ever happened to me. There I was totally exhausted and had to leave the tube and rest, and this wonderful female livens up the whole reason of my existence. Never have I experienced such a wonderful emotion. Wonderful. Wonderful and a hundred more of them. She is a technician at the birthing center," said Alcor in one breath. "Does she have a small scar on the right side of her forehead?

asks Alioth. "Yes, she does, and another under her chin. Do you know this female? Alcor wanted to know.

"Betelgeuse has the same incubator as I" Alioth calmly answered. "That cannot be. Can it? Alcor asks again. Where have you been since you were ringed? Everyone know that any unattached female who attracts a male can incubate another offspring. It so happens that my donor was being catapulted on a rescue service when his soft landing device failed. I do not want to go into details because it is still painful for me after all of these many orbits. I saw some male enter her dwelling at the beginning of the last phase and that was you, you young buck," Alioth said with a huge grin,

137-Fear gene

"We spent a lot of time talking and she knew where I had my science dwelling and she never mentioned you at all. Why? demanded Alcor. "It's a long story and old incubator tales sometimes are best left alone. Don't you think we should proceed with the developments of the ray tunnel? pleads Alioth. "It will be a phase before we meet again and how do you expect me to concentrate on anything but that wonderful female? I have to know all about the one that brought a great light into my life. I dislike making a command, but please, please tell me," Alcor begged.

"Your love's genes have brought along some fears. It seems that it is the only defect in her past. My incubator knew that more 5 generations ago a male refused to pedal the suspended tube over a wide river. There was a lot of traffic on the two tubes and with freight carts occupying the one, he caused a huge traffic jam behind him. SOS rescue personnel were catapulted and the cover solar panels were removed over him. He was in such a panic mode that his hands clung onto the bicycle. It was impossible for them to be separated from the bike until after he was blanketed. My incubator thought that was because the number of orbits that it would not have any effect on his offspring. Her donor was after mine so I had a rare opportunity to be her dominant teacher. It is rare for any dwelling to have two offspring. Her donor and our incubator were so occupied in their research it gave me the responsibility of teaching her how to pedal. Need I say more on how she received those scars? It took years of therapy for her to get near a bicycle. I carted her all over the place, as did her procreators. There were so many times that I could have increased my Kilowatts if it were not having to lug her around.

138-Alcor in love

"We don't hate each other, but there is little reference that we have the same incubator. How she retained the fear from such a young orbit, I'll never know, as did her therapists. Now you know the story. Trust me, she seems perfect in every other detail. Now can we get on with our new thrusts in to the future?" gently asks Alioth. "Thank you," said Alcor with one of his snarl smiles.
It took Alcor most of the rotation to follow the research into the project that got him blanketed. The adrenaline was starting to hit its peak and he was reverting back into the same old Alcor. He could not hide any of his innermost feelings. He was an open book. Once, his mind was so totally engrossed into his thoughts, he eliminated into his packet while at his desk. He was conscious enough to deposit it into the disposal container, much to the delight to everyone nearby. Alioth thought to himself, "Those two sure make a duzy pair."
Sending a beam of light all the way to the moon and beyond was a common thing. What was needed was a beam to do something to the atoms that were causing friction and heat buildup of any object passing at higher speeds. Muscle by the heat shields were common, but any imperfection would scatter what was behind it. Why not lovingly remove the particles to allow a speedy passage, then return them to their original place. Most of the battles would be won but a loss would be great. He was forcing himself onto Betelgeuse. In the middle of his atom studies the new-found female dominated his thoughts. Was his mind split?

139-Repulse beam

Alcor thinking to himself as to how atoms can be moved without touching each one individually? If they will not move then the design of the heat shield must be proportional to the amount of heat generated. That happens when the velocity to sent an object into space. There must be another force to recon with. The repulse beam! He calls Mizor to his research place and quietly asked him about the repulse beam. Mizor is puzzled by the question., slowly refreshed Alcor on to what he came up with originally. "Oh, yes. That's great. Thank you Alioth." I'm Mizor" said Mizor. "Oh yes, you certainly are. Please help me. Something is wrong somewhere. Some quiet time. I am in desperate need of it.," requests Alcor, and Mizor obliges.

Mizor was the first to arise and was fully refreshed. He checked the fine details of the beam generator and found that the whole generator was not in true North position. He questioned a veteran engineer as to why it was so when he had his phase off. "Is it right for the chief engineer of propulsion to know all of the intricate operations to have a bird that can fly. Is this corner of your responsibility? asks Mizor. "I don't think so. Where in the operations manual is it shown as my area? asks Megrez. They both unroll their monitors and bring up the operations manual and sure enough it was Megrez's responsibility.

140-Repulse beam

Alcor asks, "Why has that simple procedure ever been programmed into the check list?" Mizor returns with, "You changed it because the constant deviation of true north. "Then rewrite it so that it gives a reminder to do so," Alcor suggested, but it sounded more like a command.

According to my theory, we have two choices of moving aside the atmosphere atoms in the path of a moving object. One is to repulse them away from the beam or have a series of beams which have the same exterior pattern of the object and attract the atoms to them. The engineering team will be given this challenge on the fabrication of my theory. Megrez, please bring up the list of them and their locations, Megrez, are you awake? Megrez," Alcor shouted. "It will not work," was his response. "It was determined five orbits ago that the amount of energy to send the beams and the atom removal from the flight path was much greater than having a free fall and letting the heat shield do its thing.

"That was before the attract and repulse beams, Alcor said.

Megrez replied, "The only way it would be energy wise is if the beam projectors were on the bird."

"That would be impossible," Mizor retorted. "Just the weight of the beam projector and its volume would make it energy prohibitive.

Alcor tried to reach Alioth at his dwelling and on his monitor came, "PHASE OFF".

141-Alcor gets blanket

"Isn't this system ever going to allow progress with its personnel available at all times?

How are ever going to get this thing to become a reality when I get PO and QT over and over again? What we are discussing now was a specialty." Usually he was slow to anger, but this time in his frustration he shouted, "QUIET TIME". He rolled out his mat and started to repeat some tranquilizing words, "Betelgeuse. Betelgeuse." This helped a little to relax but complete rest eluded him. "Space beam. Space beam" only made it worse. In fact, he was getting irritated. It was recommended to him by the health team if his anxiety was too great for any quiet time it would be best for him to generate watts. The others were resting, so quietly he snuck off to the nearest tube. Setting his generation rate as high as he could, he pedaled to the next and returned to lie on his mat for a few minutes before quiet time was over.

They all arose from their third QT of he day, and brought every mathematical tool at their disposal. Scientist Mizor suggested that they use the new computer designed for hologram transmission. Alcor enters the request and gets: ACCESS TO SYSTEM DENIED; NO BALLOTS CAST IN TWO SUCCESSIVE ROTATIONS. This frustrated to no end. He lets out a scream like a wild man. Megrez and Mizor get the tranquilizing blanket, threw it over him and called the health team.

142-Betelgeuse sings

When he awoke, paradise looked him in the eye. Betelgeuse smiled and rubbed his cheeks with both hands. "I didn't know this side of you. Your dedication is robbing you of your true value in the tubes. Relax. Relax. Close your eyes and just think of the time we spent together when I first met you. Relax. Relax." She massaged his temples and sung at the same time. Relax, my sweet Alcor. Relax. Relax, my sweet Alcor." She did this until his blood pressure dropped to a safe level and his brain waves were not hitting the limits of the sensing device.

When Betelgeuse stopped her singing and rubbing, Alcor sat up and gave a huge smile like he never could do before. "Please confide in me as to what caused this to occur? "PO and voting. That was it," and starts to get red around his neck. "Please lie down again," She repeats the same procedure which was successful just a few moments before. When all his stresses relaxed again, and with him still lying down, she asked him the same question. "I don't know if I can. For me to tell anyone about my feelings when I have never done it before is only going to cause me getting blanketed again. Not now. Please. Especially to you," he pleaded. "How could you ever expect us to share the same dwelling if you don' allow complete confidence in sharing your most intimate feelings with anyone? Especially me. The Record Keeper knows you have your rings and I have no mating chip and it know all of your wonderful past." she says in the most soothing voice.

143-Scorpio studies

Scorpio was so intent on going to his jungle that it became an obsession with him. His studies on the area were as good or even better than any of the locals. It seemed that being a researcher was in his genes. His 16th orbit was not too distant and it was then he could be tested for his rite of passage. Examiners were not a gentle bunch. The general term for them was "brutal". He knew that he could easily perform the physical and the educational tasks, but it was the emotional part that gave him the most anxieties. He could not leave his procreators if he was not functional in society. He was called again for a bounce game but always refused. He was away from the game longer than he had ever been before. He had to study history and caterpillars. To him that took priority over all of his other pleasures. Who could he ask about preparing for what emotional demands are ever tested? Where and who should be first?"

His dream dwelling was brought in on the hologram and the camera's view was nowhere as exciting as being there. The leaves, fallen trees and moveable rocks could not be touched. What he saw was OK, but the real thing was to be there. He brought the last camera on the end of the tube to view the mountain range and that just made him eager to leave this very moment. That was not possible. Rite of Passage was first.

144-Scorpio dreaming

To have dreams like he did was common and ever so many times offspring would leave for their distant research dreams and never physically have contact with their procreators ever again. The holo was just like being there. Aires' procreators were some distance from his last responsibility and the last move increased that. He would buzz them occasionally and question their health status. He could have checked with The Record Keeper but his emotional ties were part of nature's bonding.

Aires returned to smell the jungle mold in the dwelling. "Scorpio, you surely have got yourself hooked onto a good one. Do you think that you could find a better spot? One that would have wild orchids growing or maybe the smell of the mist from a waterfall? I'll only be here for a few minutes before I leave for the sing-a-long in the park by the bay. How are you going to put that huge python hanging in the tree into a sack? His eyes are huge. Please hold you camera view on the python's head for a few moments. Just a little closer. That's it. Now put on your sniffer. His breath would take the hide off a horse. He doesn't stink but his breath is horrible. Are you sure you want that for a neighbor?"

"Before I exit for this scouting, I must tell you when I go, you and Incu will be dearly missed," said Scorpio. "What's with the dearly part? Questions his donor. "You have never used that word in a very long time. Is it from your etiquette supervisor or are you hormones starting to really kick in? What ever it is, you are the star of the earth."

145-Donor's procreators

"How many orbits were you when your procreators left on their vocation"? asked Scorpio.

"Nineteen."

"Donor, you have not seen them since?" he questioned.

'Nope."

"Do you miss them?"

"I have my own life and am completely content. The holo is there for our disposal. We are both charged for its use, so I try to not use their reserve. Our conversations are at a minimum. Strange as it seems, the more orbits I become, the more I think about my donor. It seems that the male that I am. I devote to my incubator. The male

I want to be, I, feel that I owe that drive to my donor. Don't ask me why," said Aires.

"Do you think that you will see them again?" asked Scorpio.

"I'll let you answer that question. You have been toying around with that stinking jungle and seem to l love it. Is your frontal lobe developed enough to foresee the distance that is from here? I will tell you now that I will never, even with prodding from your incubator, never pedal across the vast distance of water." said Aires then added. "The propulsion sled could get me there in a matter of minutes, but at what KWh expense?"

'I take that if I leave we may never touch each other again," says Scorpio with a very sad look on his face.

"That is why we have anxieties about you leaving before you have matured enough to make a sound decision. There are some of many orbits who still cannot make a sound choice that stand the pressure of time."

146-Aires' youth

"What was growing up like at my age for you?" asks Scorpio.

"Not too much different. Pedal, pedal and more pedaling. Choices were about the same. Technology has made generation of electricity so much easier. A lot of children do not have the physical problems that were loved out of existence. My procreators were into frozen embryos. A group wanted them to participate in a new breakthrough. I was 19. When they left, we embraced and wished each other the best. That was the last time I touched them. I have kept myself occupied with my education and had enough other social activities that I never had any idle moments. I didn't like bounce. Have you ever checked my past in The Record Keeper? It will tell you everything except how content I was." said Aires. "Please do it now and it will give me a chance to reminisce." he added.

Scorpio unrolled his monitor and said,' Let's compare, OK? Birth weight 47 grams heavier. Length 3 centimeters longer. First tooth 3 moons earlier. I'm winning so far," said Scorpio. "Nocturnal bladder control you were 2 orbits and 3 moons. Mine, 3 orbits and 10 moons." "Is that a tie of are you still ahead?" jokingly Aires said. "Donor, you know that had nothing to do with any kind of emotions on my part. Do you think that I inherited it from Incu?" Scorpio asked. "Do you want to bring up Incu's too? Asked Aires. "This is a male thing, so we'll just get into that stuff. You did not like bounce so what was your favorite activity?" asked Scorpio. "Chess, cribbage, Monopoly and music were about it." said Aires.

147-Aires' grades

"What's Monopoly? I never heard of it." Scorpio said puzzled.
"It's a game that is played with the intentions of owning everything."
"Who would ever want to do that kind of thing?" demanded Scorpio.
"It took a few generations for that kind of attitude to be tranquilized. If you notice that in voting there are some that get quite perturbed about an issue. Coaxing others to vote their way is one thing, but demanding is another. Can you picture that kind of person who would own everything? The game is still available for historians. said Aires. "None of them are very aerobic," Scorpio noted. "With generating, it's enough." Aires replied.
Look at the 89.5 on the language final! Is that yours? What happened?" asked Scorpio.
"Let me try to remember. All of my other ones were much higher, Look at he others about the same date and show my picture," Aires requested. "Wow! Look at those pimples! That can't be you! That's you?" excited Scorpio shouted. "I believe that was when I was so self conscious of my looks that I remember shying away from everyone. It was a very low time of my hormonal change. Look at some of the numbers an orbit before and after.

"They are 93.8 or higher. I know how you must have felt. A tiny zit and I just about panic. I fell sorry for you. Why did that happen?" Scorpio questioned. "Dieticians tried everything and the dermatologists were my constant attendants. There was similar case 4 generations previous where the male was affected by the same problem. The solution was to allow it to proceed with its pattern. No great harm will be done as you can see," responded Aires then said, "Quiet time."

148-Hypertension

The next rotation Aires flopped off his bicycle and just about made it into his duty dwelling. It was a long work period. His dedication to the health of everyone in his area was very important to him. Automatic tests were the simple part. It seemed that the list of names that needed personal attention was just a little longer than usual. He grouped them into categories and found that hypertension in one area must have some stress causing it. Those living there had not changed dramatically so he had to find out why.

Three assistants were assigned to electronically monitor the area for the next phase, plus five more to physically pedal and walk it, There was usually a reason for many to be affected with the same malady. It didn't take long to find the answer, thanks to the wind blowing in the right direction. The odor coming from the lagoon wasn't nauseating, but was noticeable with the right combinations of factors. Not one complaint was forwarded to the health team. It seemed that everyone thought it was normal and was accepted. It took sets of new nostrils in the neighborhood to notice something different, The olfactory sensing devices, as sensitive as they were, did not give off an alarm.

Scorpio was questioning Aires about his upcoming Rite of Passage when was buzzed by his assistant. If it were not for his quiet times through the rotation he would never have had enough energy left to answer the buzz nor spend time with his offspring. "Algol, thank you for doing such great detective work," said Aires, then adds, "I believe when we had the same problem before. Dwellings were built in the area 20 or so orbits ago. The Old Era had raw sewage dumped into many wells. Check with The Record Keeper on the

149-Sewer gas

Clean up method used on the one they found. Be careful and use radiation detectors because in the Old Era there were visitors that tried to set camp for causing mischief for their neighbors to the north. I'm surprised that the amount of time that has elapsed that the organic matter has not totally decomposed and the methane absorbed by the surrounding strata. If there are any difficulties in procuring services from the hazardous waste recovery department, please inform me. I shouldn't have said that because that group has the highest accumulated KWh of any other and they have the least number of researchers. Thanks for your diligent assistance. I'll be here when you return," said Aires.

"Now where were we? asked Aires. "Oh yes, your total independence. For you, it will not be too difficult. Scorpio, have you taken notice on your absence from our dwelling this past orbit? Your scholastic ability has been superb and then some. The short period of not having any KWh gave you an eye opener as to your responsibility to the system. Have you looked at your reserve lately?" "I have pedaled 40K. I'm having some anxieties about the emotional responses that I have to give. There really is no holo or procreator's assistance on what might be questioned," Scorpio said with a frown. "What can I probably expect?" "You had two speed violations and those most likely be in our Rite of Passage arena. Another will be your knowledge of your past few generations. You might be forced into a closed chamber when you least expect it. Simulated catapult is going to be a tough one. Plus more simulations, especially in the research area." said Aires.

150-Is Scorpio a clone

"They will come when you are most fatigued; totally exhausted from. This is why you must keep yourself fit at all times. It will be some time before you are called, so be prepared. Love life and enjoy all that you do. Have a high spirit and all will fall into order for an exciting ritual. Never, and I must emphasize the never, allow fear to guide your judgments. Love everything around you. And that is about it. Don't get anxious about your test. You will not know the day or time which will be any time in the next seven moons. I must get some sleep now. When Incu returns you must say that I need as much rest as I can get so no chess tonight. Now I say quiet time." Aires said then visited the private place, took his container to its proper place, rolled out his mat in the corner and in a matter of minutes was sound asleep.

Scorpio unrolled his monitor and projected holograms into the middle of the dwelling. He visited the last ten donors, set the sequence of 15 seconds each, then the same for incubators. He glanced in the full length mirror an tried to compare their facial features and body forms to his. The only one that had any semblance to him was a donor seven generations back. He was brought into the holo again. All that Scorpio could do was stare at a donor as his and there he was 175 orbits ago. How could all the mixtures of mates produce something so similar and not be a clone? This was a shock to him. Was he a clone? Generally clones were forbidden because life was meant for procreation as humans were created, even in the Old Era.

151-Clone

He had to be one; there was no other way they could be so identical. He loved his incubator and donor, but now he had some doubts as to their motives for not telling him. Cloning was available for one generation in animals but never in humans. Exiting the holo he brought up cloning in the Old Era, and found that the practice was just a passing fad that ceased when offspring had peculiar ambitions. A few governments that wanted to control the world had started growing many thousands of clones but found that they were destroyed by their own folly. Scorpio brought back the holo to view clones in this generation and found that a female had some odd characteristics with a DNA check, and the synapses speed detector, Scorpio found that two generations back a walk-in who came into the tube area was the culprit. A few clones survived and still might be in the lineage of our time. Some of their quirks were evident, and when told of it the cloning every one of them refused to enter the mating ritual because did not want to disrupt the joy of being a tuber. Their offspring might amplify their "not normal" activities. They were awarded lifetime Kilowatts and no duties to perform. Everyone chose to follow their routines for two reasons. They did not want to be focused on and disliked doing nothing.

"Am I going to be one of them? Everything was going so right, and now this! Why? Why? And a thousand times WHY??? Why me?" Scorpio said to himself. He looked down at Aires lying with his back to him and had nothing but contempt in his heart. He was growing furious. There was no way someone 175 orbits ago could look just like him.

152-Scorpio a clone?

His frustrations were so great he had to have the answer now! There was his donor. He knew that Aires might know the answer, but it was his incubator that was the one who would positively know. He debated about waking his very tired donor or waiting until Incu returned from her rotation of research. He could not wait. He brought up the hologram and what he firmly believed was his origin and started again with tears in his eyes. "How could they do this to me? These damn rings have caused me much pain so far, and I don't want to go through life as a clone." He walked through the hologram and was about to wake his donor, when in walked Incu.

She greeted Scorpio, reached out to hug her offspring, but he backed off and doubled his uncontrollable bawl. That awaked Aires and both of his procreators puzzled at his terrible discomfort. There standing by them was Scorpio in the hologram. "Incu, how did he get into the holo? There he is a fetal position crying, but who is that?" Aires said with alarm. He checked the date of the holo and it was 175 orbits ago. Now, alarmed, he said, "Almaaz, is there anything you did not tell me." Her face turned red and the veins on her neck protruded more than ever before. "It is Scorpio and yet it cannot be! Impossible! Your were the donor! You were my mate! No other sperm has ever entered my body except yours! He thinks that he is a clone! May the one in the other dimensions please help explain this to all of us! Please! Please," she pleaded. They both huddled next to Scorpio on the floor and tried to comfort him as they did many times before when he would hurt himself in one of his playful activities.

153-Soothing Scorpio

Almaaz laid on the floor and tried to get her face next to his. Scorpio clasped his hands over the top of his head and pulled himself firmly into a fetal position crying much louder. Incu patiently stroked the back of his hands and started to hum his favorite tune. It seemed like eternity, but the volume of his wails subsided. He then gasped for air, similar to a hiccup. Still humming, Incu waited patiently. Time was all it took. To force the issue would only have exacerbated an ugly situation. Donor had to get the anxiety out of his system and wanted to generate Kilowatts, but did not want to leave his side. There were also some answers to be had, right now.

It took nearly 10 minutes before the humming took effect, and Scorpio got into a seated position with Incu's arm around him. He used the sleeve of his suit to wipe away the tears and the fluid leaking from his nose. Aires brought the wash wand for him to use, but he refused it. "Youth has a propensity to make rash judgments. We both see "you" standing in the holo. But I assure you that nature has a way of bringing about what you might call a clone. Is that what this is all about? Incu asks. Scorpio barely whispered, "yes" then started to bawl again. Incu started another hum. This time Scorpio took the wand from his donor and gently touched one side of his nose to give a good blow to clear that passage, then did the same with the other side. He washed his face, and now seemed to have control of his emotions.

154-DNA test

"Youth can make rational judgments, but sometimes they can be tainted by panic. Your frontal lobe has not been fully developed, and what you thought to be looked so real. I'm sure if I were in a similar situation that I would probably have reacted just as you are right now," Incu said, holding tightly onto Scorpio. She continued, "Science has brought us marvels as to what and how truth can be factually proven. Isn't that right?" "Yes. But that holo is me. All me and no one else," Scorpio responded with disgust. "The ancestor is so identical to you it is unbelievable. Now that you have brought yourself into such a dilemma, you must get yourself out of it by following simple guidelines that have been established. Do you know what to do?" she asked. "Yes," responded Scorpio. "Do it now," was her very stern command.

Scorpio asked to use Donor's monitor. Aires unrolled and handed it to Scorpio who brought up the DNA procurement procedures.. The instructions were for the donor to place either palm on the upper right of the monitor and the incubator to do the same on the upper left and the offspring to place both palms on the bottom middle. Their hands tingled like a thousand needles were piercing them and it lasted for at least 10 seconds; then an automated voice asked that they remove their hands. There were thousands of red lines drawn from the youth's palms to the other two and they seemed to be so close together that they looked like they were the background.

155-Scorpio no clone

It just took a matter of minutes when The Record Keeper gave a detailed family tree for the past three generations. I could have gone further back, if requested, to the time of its origin. "What do you read from the results?" Aires asked. "It does positively show that you two are my procreators," Scorpio responded. "What would you have done if the Rite of Passage team had called you while you were in the middle of your wrongly judged clone panic?" asked Aires. "Would you have come close to passing any of the three parts? Do you believe that your frontal lobe has matured to where you can function on your own? Your ordeal was a little too much stress on your physical emotions. Please don't answer any of my questions. Just relax and let's all of us take a quiet time" Donor said.

Almaaz was the first one to arise and voted on extension of the tubes nearby and read the next 7 rotation's issues. They were usually that far in advance so most everyone could discuss them and evaluate their positions. Outside their dwelling plants needed watering, so Almaaz added exercise that she would get from carrying containers of water. She poured the water into another trough with tubes going down each row of maize and dripping a drop at a time near the base of each plant. She checked most of the plants for insect destruction. She found a section with borers. Unrolling her monitor, she presented the problem and a solution was returned. The plant maintenance dwelling had everything from planting to harvesting. There were three syringes and enough mineral oil for the three of them. Returning to her dwelling to recruit two assistance, Almaaz found them just starting another game of chess.

156-Plant watering

They told her they would be there as soon as they finished the game they had just started. "Why don't I take the place of either of you and the other fill the drip troughs?" she suggested. Aires and Scorpio looked at each other, made a simultaneous move to the exit and took off in a full run to the irrigation bladder. The first one who got there would pick the troughs that were the closest. Aires was forty and was in nearly perfect physical condition, but was no match for the Bounce player Scorpio. Scorpio filled his container and told donor who just arrived, "Fill yours and I'll help as soon as my area is completed." "I think we should have been doing this a few rotations ago," Aires said with regret. I hate to see plants curl their leaves because of my negligence. I pedal to the tubes past this area and it seems like the other dimensions are communicating with us. You will notice in just a short time after they receive their living fluid, they will say 'thank you'. There are many varieties of maize and they all are wishing quietly that they will be chosen next to bring human and other animal's some comfort in this three dimensional world. Almaaz carried the liter of mineral oil in a pouch tied to her waist. She refilled the syringe after putting a drop on the silk of the maize. She noticed a female adult borer landing on the silk and squished it between her fingers. She said to herself,"there goes many unlaid eggs." As she was applying the drops, she would to the same for more egg layers. She unrolled her monitor and buzzed maize pest control and reported it. She would continue doing the same to the other stalks. When her mate and offspring had completed their task, they came to assist her.

157-Bug catchers

Aires liked to sing when he did any of his chores. The beat he took was in sync with each drop of oil. Scorpio following the same tunes and he would have sung had he known the words. Whey they reached the opening at the end of the field there was a long string of bicyclers, some of them were pulling someone in a cart. A loud shrill whistle caused all of them to stop and lay down their bikes. There was a leader of each three mentally handicapped workers. They were all given tiny nets. As they unrolled their monitors, they were shown that they were to catch in their nets and what to do when they did. They all seemed regimented so that none would get too far ahead of the others. It seemed that they were looking to the left and right and keeping in line more than they were looking for bugs. Aires followed one of the leaders and reflected on his attitude toward the mentally less fortunate. The health field had many avenues to a healthy society. Aires knew that it was much better for these to be participating in whatever they could possibly do, rather than sit in some dwelling and lapse into nothingness.

One of the younger ones was lagging behind and needed a little prodding, so the one that was responsible for her took out his net and did some twirls in front of her humming a repetitious tune. This amused her and she started to do the same and tried to net non-existing insects. Her speed got herself in line with all of the others, and she kept doing the same over and over again. This was good because any borers in her row would fly to the next one and be caught by someone who was just a little more talented.

158-Brain damage

Aires' observation of the leaders was a new attraction for him. How could anyone get so many people with such a variety of abilities to be organized in their assigned tasks and seem to be enjoying themselves? Beautiful, he thought to himself. It took every bit of an hour for them to reach the end of the field and return in another row. At 1357 hours a whistle blew. the leaders unrolled their mats and laid down for a quiet time with all of the workers doing the same. Aires could hardly believe what he saw. Again, beautiful came to his mind.

How could so many have such a disability? He checked The Record Keeper for their history, ancestry, the extent of their disability and probable cause. None were genetic. Their bodies looked great for pedaling. At least most of them did, As he quickly browsed the list, Aires was surprised that insect bite was the probable cause. Encephalitis. Further down in this report was that they had not used their faces shields. He was wearing his now because of the infestation of mosquitoes, plus the likelihood of a long leaf cutting a stripe across his face. Three had serious injuries from falling from a vehicle. He thought there would have more than that. He had had some nasty falls in his life time. His suit had a cushion built in as did all of the others. The bug pickers were scattered all over the place. Some laid down between the rows of maize. Aires took his quiet time too.

Almaaz and Scorpio finished their task and napped, then took a walk to collect their pellets. The four day supply for Almaaz was about half the weight of her offspring's. There was a sticker on Scorpio's container: Report to the nearest medical center.

159-Melons

Scorpio asked, "Why the sticker?"

"Not an emergency. If it were, you would have been buzzed," answered Incu, then added, "were you in the melon field lately?"

"Yes," he said.

"How any melons did you eat?" she asked.

"I don't know. Two or three. They were delicious," he said with a big grin.

"That is probably why. Any change in diet will show up in your "package" to them. I would no be too alarmed. You will get a lecture on dental care, plus one on gluttony," she calmly informed him.

Scorpio pedaled to the medical dwelling and found no one there. A monitor note was hanging on the inside of the entrance which he had overlooked on the way in. It said, "WILL BE BACK IN 10 MINUTES. GENERATING IN THE TUBES." No sooner had he read the note, in walked the health team member puffing from his vigorous pedaling. He unrolled his monitor and asked Scorpio if he had any intestinal cramps or pressure yesterday. He said that he did, but they were gone now. "We also had your friend here just a while ago, and melons were his problem. I'll bet they were delicious. Weren't they?" he asked. "They sure were. I would have gone there this rotation if I had more time," he answered. "This is he first time that you have ever had a note from us. We do hope that it is the last. The pellet food has been especially designed for you is sufficient and perfectly balanced for you and you only. Your friend's and family's may be similar looking, but again I must say yours are formulated for only you."

160-Dental checkup

Your teeth look perfect but they will not be that way if you place "other" foods into your system. An apple taste could be in some pellets if you so desired. Let's see. Here your palate's requests. Hmmm, chocolate, strawberry, mustard/garlic combination, yuck. Where did you acquire a taste for poppy seed and honey? The worker asked. "I don't know. Most likely from the holo smell thing that you guys gave us to sample. It sure is neat the way I can get these combinations. Place a hand on each of the two that I want, rub my hands together and there it is. How does that work? When I remove my hands from the holo, the smells are gone," Scorpio asked. "How it gets from the olfactory producer in The Record Keeper for anyone to have access to is beyond me. They have been in there for many generations. Now and then we have a lot of requests for combinations of smells; we place that on the common list. I believe it is quiet time now," the worker says. They unroll their mats and both were asleep in just a few minutes.

The health worker awoke and started to vacuum the floor and walls, and that awoke Scorpio. He sat up and stared into nothingness. His sleep was so deep that he did not where he was. Taking out his wand, he washed his face and hands, and was still a little groggy. When he finally came back to himself, he asked if he could leave. "I'll be right with you just as soon as I finish this wall," the worker answered. Done with that chore, he asked Scorpio to spell "Too much to much." "Too much too much," Scorpio spelled each letter. "Nope," the worker stated. "It's spelled this way, TOO MUCH TO MUCH. The first "too" is just like when you had he melons. The second "to" is what we all desire. We have a tendency to go to excesses." That is gluttony.

161-Teeth OK

"You had some minor problems with eating too many melons and if you have a chance you will go back to the field and do the same thing again," he said. "I doubt it," Scorpio responded. "That's great. Now have a seat in this chair because I want examine your teeth. I see that you are due for your two moon exam in a few rotations, so let's do it now." When Scorpio opened his mouth, the health worker a decay detector wand from its sanitized container, and in a slow motion started on Scorpio's right molar from the inside, across all of his teeth to the other molar. He did the same to Scorpio's lower jaw teeth, from the outside top and bottom. No cavities or other dental problems were detected.
"I see that you have a tooth that is not aligning itself with the two adjacent ones so I'm going to make you a device that you place over your teeth when you eat your pellets. That will force it back in line. When you finished munching on our pellets, rinse you mouth with your wand. Are there any questions you have for me?" he asked. "Yes," said Scorpio. "Why do I have to return every two moons?" "Your age and goodbye for now and I will see you here in two moons," returned the health worker. He then went back to vacuuming before Scorpio left the dwelling.

162-Other Side

Scorpio pedaled to his dwelling and was ready for a quiet time when he saw his neighbor lying in front of his dwelling on a mat next to his wheel chair in a very unusual position. Curiosity got the best of him. Putting down his bicycle he walked cautiously over to the old man. He gave a little twitch, then a groaned "Ahhhhhhhh." Startled, he looked up at Scorpio and said, "Hi."

Scorpio asked, "Are you having any problems?"

"I did have a minor one. Can't you smell it?" he says with a smile.

"I'm up wind and I'm glad of it," he returned with a bigger smile.

"Young offspring, I have been observing you since you moved here and I see in The Record Keeper you are a fine student. Have you any future interests that seem to dominate your thoughts?" he asked.

"I sure do. Caterpillars fascinate me. Every quiet time, 'leg coordination and caterpillar' get me to relax," Scorpio said with confidence.

"That's nice. Most your orbits still want to play. Great for you. I've had 108 of them and have changed my dreams many times. Each time I changed the past ones were like a crutch to the next. Have you ever thought of exploring into the other dimensions?" he asked.

"My donor started into that field but found it too complex to enjoy his experiments. He mentions many times that the seed from the "OTHER SIDE" was incubated by an earthly female, and the male offspring tried to gently persuade humans on the benefits following his instructions. That male was treated very badly and killed by their standards, but he was returned to the "OTHER SIDE" alive. Part of my home education was to read all of his teachings written by others. I could not ever understand how he had such wisdom and never wrote one word," Scorpio answered.

163-Other Side

"I'm impressed that you are aware of so much. Thanks to your donor and probably your incubator too. Do you have a few minutes? I have some to add to that, if you don't mind," the old person pleaded.

"Please do, but first I would like to know your orbit number," Scorpio said.

Castor then asks Scorpio to take a guess.

"I could easily find it in The Record Keeper but I would say in the vicinity of 108," Scorpio said with a smile.

"That's right. How did you know?" he asked.

With a bigger smile Scorpio said, "You just told me."

"You sure are attentive. Well, I would not be in this wheel chair if it weren't for getting dizzy on our exit ramp and falling off my bicycle. That's enough about me. The Other Side is what is important, you know. Do you ever have the feeling that you are being followed by something that is all around you? If you have a problem, do you feel you can talk to The Other Side? Humans have been researching for generations all the way back to the old era and even reports that they conversed with someone. The elusive Other Side. I'm positively sure that there is someone alive now that is going to cross the abyss and show us the beautiful harmony we can enjoy. The beginning of the tubes was the greatest evolution of humans in some time. Humans have no choice but to wait on this side and dream. Free thinkers say that there are a total of eleven dimensions. We just work with three. It would be someone like you, through scientific research, could have us all feel the fourth, then the others.

164-Castor

Scorpio entered his dwelling, unrolled his monitor and brought up Castor, the old man he was just talking to. He had a very long list of accomplishments. His procreators were recently honored for enhancing the ability of oat plant to absorb more moisture from the air than from the soil in which it was planted. They were a team, inseparable long before they were mated. Scorpio thought to himself that they were fortunate that their genes blended for a beautiful procreation. He never entered the mating pool. Why would any person not enter the mating pool? His choice. His scholastic marks were not the greatest in his teens, twenties and thirties but they took off when he reached 40. Seventy four years in research on the Other Side. That is a lot of time for not having any success in his search of nothingness. He had a bout with lack of Kilowatts when he was 85 orbits. Reason: Depression. Scorpio thought to himself that he would have had that problem after only a few years with no success in what he was looking for. From 98 to the present he delivered water and picking up "packages." The names of the four children in Castro's care were there, too. The reason why he was chosen for the task was that the child care center was closed for lack of interest. He also noticed that his donor had an incident of being sent to the lonesome place. There were scrolls on Castor. The Record Keeper has no secrets.

165-Bounce game

Scorpio was buzzed and it was Struve. "Hey, old buddy. We have a real game going on here. One of the guys has to leave in fifteen minutes and we need you. Please come."
Scorpio jumped on his bike and took off at breakneck speed. There was no one in the park and he did not let up on the pedals. This was the first time that happened. Usually there was a crowd and the lesson he learned made him cautious even if no one was in sight. After parking his bike and running to the uniform storage, #7 arrived. He took off his bounce uniform and gave it to Scorpio. "How many points did you score today?" he asked. Nearly out of breath he said, "Only six. We would have had a lot more but for that one fast female. I put her into my address book." "I'll bet it is the same one that I have there, too. What is her number this rotation," Scorpio asks? "Number 4. She is all over the field. She has an uncanny ability to hit just right and knock two of us off the field with the same hit. She is a lefty, so if you have a chance, hit her from that side. That is, if you can." He left and Scorpio put on the bounce uniform over his suit, raring to go. When he got to the field the other team scored because there were only seven on the field. The scoreboard showed that the team he was going to play for was down 6 points.
The ball was set down on the forty meter line with sixty meters to reach the goal line.

Scorpio got into the huddle as the leader this play and gave instructions on what the next play was going to be. "Numbers 1 and 5 are to make an X and cross in front of their #4. He is going to fake a handoff to #6 with #8 running in front of him. We all move on the fifth audible."

166-Bounce game

They lined up and Scorpio watched where number 4. She was about four meters behind the line where the ball sat. Calmly, Scorpio said in his speaker to the ear phones of all the players, which both teams had, "Pass, run, stop, go, stop." His team followed his instructions. In the fake handoff, it brought number 4 to follow two players thinking that one of them had the ball. She flung herself high, and pulled her knees as much as she could. The two running without the ball make a barrel roll onto the ground and she skipped off the second one and was totally out of the play. Scorpio throws the ball to number 8 who had only one defensive player near him. The ball is a little high so number 8 had to leap with one out stretched hand. The ball clinging to Velcro on his mitt and he easily ran for 6 points. Tie game.

The ball was placed on the forty meter line and now it was up to Scorpio's team to stop them from scoring. Number 4 kept herself a meter or so from the line so that she would have a running start to build up momentum for a good block. The other players on Scorpio's team said that all of the plays they had to stop were running. They had not thrown one pass. "That's great," he said. "Everybody back up from the line at least four meters. See #4, never hit her on her right side. She has a habit of flying sideways when she wants to clear a path. Do a quick barrel roll and she will fly over you. Their player with the ball will be right there for you to bring down and hold in place."

167-Bounce game

They all heard King, Queen, Pawn and they all moved in unison toward Scorpio's right. He was more intent of giving #4 a good hit than he is looking for the ball. He told himself that was intimidation at its greatest. Scorpio's #8 barrel rolled in front of the lead runner. Their #5 is knocked to the right with #4 in front of the ball carrier. Her path was for Scorpio's #5, and she did not see him fast approaching. He gave her a flying leap, she barrel rolled and Scorpio bounced off the turf well beyond her path. Luckily for him, the ball carrier was held down on his forty three meter line. The sensors on the sides of the field would mark exactly the farthest forward spot.

Who was intimidating who? He had to do something because he felt that he was more athletic than she was. The very next play was a repeat and Scorpio had another chance. This time he made a fake to fly high but tried an ankle hit, only to have her make a little jump and he passed under her. The opponents made 23 meters on that play. They had two more plays to make it to the goal line before they would have to go on defense from their farthest forward spot.

The next play was the same except to the left. Advantage Scorpio. He was at least five meters back of the line which gave him a running start. At full speed, he leapt as high as he could into the air, rolled off the tops of all the other Bouncers and landed smack into the ball carrier. Scorpio knocked him to the ground but, kept rolling. His team mates came to the rescue and held him there with a loss of meters. The next play they also had a loss which gave the ball to Scorpio's team.

168-Bounce game

Each game was one hour long with no time-outs. With three minutes left, the game was tied. Scorpio had to win. The other team felt the same. The last point maker worked and Scorpio would try the same. Twenty seven meters. Same play again eighteen meters. Thirty to the goal line. This time #6 took the handoff, with #8 running interference, and that made 20 meters. They had one more play and ten meters to go for a win. Scorpio was all fired up and #4 was still on his mind but the win was greater. Initially he wanted the same play they used all the time, but instead he decided to carry the ball himself. Number 4 suspected something and did not get suckered into a running play or the pass. Scorpio's Numbers 2, 3 and 4 charged forward making a wedge with him behind them. Seeing the play she charged all four, as did another of her defensive team mates. She did her usual flying cross body at the shoulders of #3 knocking him into #2. That leaves his #4 and one defensive player between Scorpio and the goal line. He tried the same as his female #4 but was not very successful. He hit at an angle, giving Scorpio six points. Now there were thirty seconds to go and one more play from the forty meter line.

Scorpio said "I know they are going to pass." He told his two fastest runners to stay back. Sure enough, their leader was behind #4 and was getting ready to throw when Scorpio and his team mate #3 flung themselves at #4 who was stationery. What an advantage they had. She was never jolted so much on one hit! The leader threw the ball and it was deflected into the air, landing right into Scorpio's hands. Scorpio got up and starts to run to the goal line, his #3 between their #7 preventing him from grabbing Scorpio. Number 4 recovers from the hit and took off after the ball. Scorpio turned his head just enough to see through the edge of his visor lightening ready to strike.

169-Rite of Passage

"It can't be now! Why now? He buzzed his donor to make a report and was notified that ACCESS DENIED. NO CONTACT WITH ANYONE BUT RITE OF PASSAGE COMMITTEE. He wanted to clean up a little before he left but when he tried to use his wand and the suit cleaner, neither would work. "They got me," he said to himself. He got on his bicycle and into the tube and had about ten kilometers to get there. No sooner then getting on, he was buzzed. Scorpio unrolled the monitor comes up with: "SETTING TO 75% NOW". He never set it that high but he has to comply, while thinking that 72% would suffice. After 30 seconds he was buzzed again 3% MORE NOW. The MORE NOW was in red. He complied. He arrived totally exhausted and hardly able to catch his breath. Eleven males with full beards said in unison, "REMOVE YOUR SUIT NOW". He obliged and got naked. An 5 centimeter diameter rope was dropped from the high ceiling and Scorpio was told to climb the ten meters to the top. He was too tired even to try, but this is what his donor warned him: He would tried when he least expected it. Slowly he climbed about 3 meters hand over hand, then had to use his legs to hold the rope when taking the next higher grip. The rope shook violently at the top which impeded his climb to nearly a halt and the lights were turned off. He kept climbing, even though it seemed he was stuck there. It seemed forever when he touched the beam that held the rope and the second tester yelled up to him, "LET GO OF THE ROPE." He knew that he could not do that. He was too high and would seriously injure himself if he did. Again and louder, "LET GO OF THE ROPE!" He knew that no one was ever injured in these tests but he was positive he was going to be. Then the testers shouted, "FOR THE LAST TIME, LET GO OF THE ROPE! NOW!"

170-Rite of Passage

He let go and tried to prepare himself so that his feet would land on the floor and winced when he was going to make contact. In the fraction of a second that when the rope was being vibrated it was moved over a pool of water. It was ice cold and when his head came above his whole body spasms into one solid block of ice. He was going to go under. The lights were turned on. Where the energy came from to move to the ladder at the side of the pool he did not know. "PICK UP THE BALL AT THE BOTTOM OF THE POOL AND PLACE IT INTO THE RED BASKET." These are not humans! They are something else. This is not right! Donor, how could you ever do such a thing to me! "PICK UP THE BALL AT THE BOTTOM OF THE POOL! NOW!"

Taking a deep breath, Scorpio dove to the bottom of the pool which was about three meters, grabbed the ball. It was too heavy for him to swim up with it, so he carries it to the ladder at the side of the pool and made it to the top place where he was told.

How will this make me into a man? Most of the work that he will do will never be as physical as this. This is not right he said to himself again, ready to curse his donor. "STAND ON THE BLUE PAD AND ADD THE TEN FIVE DIGIT NUMBERS!" Scorpio did the first column then the second and then noticed that the bottom of his feet were warm. It sure beat the cold that he had to endure so far. Halfway through the third column his soles got hotter. He finished that one, started on the fourth, and his feet were hot. While on the fifth, Scorpio danced then finished in pain and hopped off the pad. He looked for blisters on his soles but there were none. They felt like they were cooked.

171-Rite of Passage

"WRITE A FOUR LINE SONNET ABOUT YOUR DONOR."
What is a sonnet?
"MARK AS WHOLE NOTES THE FOLLOWING SOUNDS."
A piano key was pressed and Scorpio made an elliptical mark between the bottom line and the next one up. The same key was struck on the piano, and when Scorpio placed the stylus onto his monitor to make the same mark in the same place he heard a loud bang from two huge cymbals that were probably done electronically. There was some ringing in his ears.
"ONE MORE TIME," the tester insisted.
The piano key was struck for the third time and Scorpio knew exactly what it was because his donor gave him many music lessons. He made the whole note mark and definitely knew that the note was an F and then again B A N G went the cymbals and Scorpio thought his ear drums had burst.

The ringing in his ears was becoming painful and he could barely hear a guitar string being plucked. Aires had done this many, many times and he knew that it was an F. He was not sure which octave it was because of the ringing, but he made a mark on the top line.

172-Rite of Passage

He heard the noise of a thunderous water fall and again a piano key was struck. Scorpio marks a C. The next distracting sound was in a nursery, where, at least, it took ten hungry, crying babies made very disturbing noises. A violin played the next note and he marked an A. He was sure that he made the right marks and was now thanking his donor for all of the time that he had spent with him.

"HOW WIDE ARE THE HANDLEBAR SLIDES INSIDE THE TUBES?"

"One meter," he answers quickly but is barely audible because he is ready to collapse.

"LOUDER."

"ONE METRE" he yells as loud as he could.

"WHY DO YOU HAVE TO WEAR YOUR RINGS?"

Trying to buy some time so he can get back some of his energy Scorpio asks, "Do you want them in any special order?"

"WHY DO YOU HAVE TO WEAR YOUR RINGS?"

Shivering naked in the very cool room he knew the answers but his mind was in a state of confusion. He was never placed in such disturbing circumstances. How much more of this could he endure? He looked down at his genitals. They were retracted because of the freezing conditions he was in and the rings seem to dominate the area. His pubic hair was very thin and just starting to grow.

"DO YOU WANT IT TO BE COLDER IN HERE? PLEASE ANSWER QUICKLY."

Scorpio's teeth were chattering, his lips were very dry, and his whole body quivered from the cold. This time he couldn't wait to analyze himself, question his donor or allow his mind to be disturbed by the pressure put on him. His answers now had to be spontaneous.

173-Quiet time

Page missed intentionally for you to take your quiet time.

174-Rite of Passage

"LOWER THE TEMPERATURE FIVE DEGREES."
Scorpio pleaded, "Please don't."
"REQUEST DENIED."
Scorpio's lips were blue from the cold as he gave the answer that he was told many times by his donor: social responsibility holo, Sirus, his elderly neighbor and a few other males who casually mentioned it over the past few years said, "Male's instincts are too strong to be responsible for the well being of the world."
"ADD TO THAT."
"The primary design of a male's body is to implant seed into a female for procreation. The pleasure of the act is minuscule to the incubation of a superior offspring," Scorpio shouted. He felt like the air passing past him was a little warmer.
"ADD TO THAT."
"It was voted by 89 percent of males the last three orbits. Social acceptance of it was overwhelming because of dedication to the offspring was primary. Females were content after bonding and knowing that the interaction chip which was imbedded in her would allow only coition with the male she had chosen.
"WERE YOU INFORMED ABOUT SEXUALLY TRANSMITTED DISEASES?"
"No. What are they," he asks and feels the air getting much, much colder."
"AFTER LEAVING HERE BRING THOSE DISEASES UP FROM THE FIRST GENERATION. ONE MOMENT PLEASE."

The air grew so cold that when Scorpio exhaled it seemed to be visible for nearly a meter. How much more of this must he be able to withstand? He crouched into a ball with his back to the breeze, leaving very little exterior skin exposed.

175-Rite of Passage denied

"YOUR RITE OF PASSAGE HAS BEEN DENIED."
Quickly Scorpio rose to his feet and faced the blank wall where the voices were coming from. Shocked, but calmly he shivering said, "I have tried my best. You are in control and I must accept your decision. Please, may I leave this most uncomfortable frigid environment now that you have made your decision."
"ARE YOU NOT GOING TO CONTEST NOW?"
"No. I have tried my best. The Rite of Passage is not for me to judge. Only you can judge my ability to perform the responsibilities of a male in the Tube Society." Scorpio's voice was somewhat distorted by the extreme cold that passed by him now. Standing made it so much colder.
"WHAT DO YOU THINK THAT MADE YOU FAIL?"
"Write that something you wanted me to do, is all that I can think of," he said and started to walk toward an exit.
"STOP. WHY ARE YOU NOT EMOTIONAL IN ANY WAY ABOUT OUR DECISION?"
"I least expected to have this done to me this rotation. My youth is still with me and the next time you call, I'm sure that I will do much better," he answered then collapsed to the floor.
How long he lay there he did not know. Slowly he became aware that he was lying on his mat in his own dwelling. Lying on a mat next to his was his donor. Aires was smiling more vigorously than Scorpio had ever seen before. It took a few minutes before he was coherent, then he lapsed to some brain fog. He felt like he was half asleep and was starting to get upset about Aires smiling and that brought about some of his normal alertness.

176-Scorpio passes

"Donor, why are you so happy?" Scorpio growled and that was never his manner of speaking. "You are now a male that can participate in any of the leadership roles that we have in our society. I am so proud of you!" Aires said in a very jubilant state. "My Rite of Passage was denied, but you are acting with more zest than if I had just scored all the points in a game of bounce. Is there something that I do not know?" he asked. "You had the most severe judges and they were brutal. I was buzzed and told that you have completed the Rite of Passage. I did not even know that you were there. Finding you on the floor completely sedated, I dressed you, placed you on a cart and brought you here. The next time you look at your rings you will notice that they are now a different color. You can now compete in any of the mature male activities," Aires still smiled.

"I was told that my Rite of Passage was denied. I was freezing, but coherent enough to hear that I failed," Scorpio sternly said in what was nearly a shout. "The same is done to nearly all of the candidates to frustrate them to find out if they are emotionally stable enough to accept a fate decided by others," Aires answered. He brings up on his monitor the results of Scorpio's latest ordeal.

Rope climb 93. Drop 80. "What happened for such a low score?" his donor asks?

"When I started to climb, the floor was firm and from the height that I was at the top, I would have injured myself as would anyone else. I let go because I was commanded to. I was expecting the worst, but the water cushion was a complete surprise. How was I to know that I was to put my whole faith in the examiners? Was that water ever cold!" Scorpio shivered from the thought of it.

177-Praise from Donor

"You don't know what a sonnet is?" asked Aires, and continues with "There are different ways of writing poetry and this is one of them. I'm not too sure of the exactness of it myself. Bring it up on your monitor when you have time." "Why did you not ever tell me what to expect in the test?" Scorpio asking with a very stern facial expression? "Now I'm going to tell you something that you will have to remember for a long time," Aires looking directly into Scorpio's eyes. "Every Rite of Passage is different. If I would have coached you on what I had to do, you would have failed miserably. Never tell your offspring what you have just done. Every male is unique unto himself. Someday I will have to perform the same duties the males tested you on. The program you had was chosen by twelve of the most senior males in our community. They are the ones that have been tested by time as to what is most desired in our future. What got you the highest score was your answers after you were told that you had failed. Remember when I once told you about emotions? They are acquired by your association with your family and peers, and mostly they are passed on to you from the past generations. You did great! I'm so proud of you. In my decision to choose your incubator, that was one of the factors. Her third generation in the Tubes had a recorded incident. After reading the report and seeing his struggles in the bag, I think he did not have enough air to breath and was just following nature's first instinct, self preservation. Now that you have passed, quietly proceed with whatever you would have done, as though nothing has happened. You are the greatest!"

178-Adult responsibilities

Awakening the next day, Scorpio felt like a different person. For years he had on his mind the Rite of Passage. He envisioned that it would last for days and he would have to hike and bike in the primitive parts of Tubes and perform all kinds of survival projects. What surprised him also was that none of his friends that went through it ever talked about it. It was mentioned a few times that some of the males had to go through it more than once. He unrolled his monitor and brought up all of the duties of ringed males that have gone through his last uncivilized ordeal. The first on the list was that they all must be prepared to comprehend the responsibilities that are required for seeking offspring. The second on the list was the incubator. Why was he "required" to know that when it would be orbits before he was eligible to enter the mating area? Out of his monitor come the holo instructor that will accept any questions that he might have. He could not tell if it were male or female because a robe covered "its" face. "Why are you dressed as you are," Scorpio asks? The voice that answered was also indeterminate in gender. "No reason except in this area of instruction, it is best that the student does not have any predisposed opinions to the gender of the teacher."

"You are doing a great job," complimented the youth and added, "Why is such a high priority placed on the offspring?" "Humans have been procreating since the beginning of their existence and the amount of physical and mental defects have multiplied exponentially to where the main efforts of society have been to care for the maimed. Even in these rotations, certain diets and exercises have been strongly requested for some that have inherited a defect of the slightest degree. Look at yourself. You are a perfect example of choices that your donor and incubator have made," Holo answered.

179-Gene knowledge

"There is a female that I have grown fond of and I have the feeling that she also thinks of me a lot. I checked her gene pool and it was recommended that I refrain from emotional involvement. I know that it will be at least 10 orbits before I can approach any female and with her approval begin the procreation process. Why was I told that?" He asked?

"The Record Keeper has that you have passed the Rite of Passage and now are qualified to know the details. There are a few blood types that complicate the procreation of a healthy offspring. Do you have the name of the female in question?" asked the holo.

"Yes I do," he said firmly. "You can do it on your own. All you have to do is enter your name and the female's and The Record Keeper will show you a list of reasons for denying union. It will also show pictures of offspring from previous unions. It will show you the problems that the offspring had during their life time. Once you see how their life was, please compare theirs to yours. This is why it is extremely important that you always select the female that is most compatible to your genes for offspring before you allow yourself to become emotionally involved. Have I answered your inquiry sufficiently?" asked the robed encyclopedia.

"If I should have any reproductive defects does that mean that I will never be able to have a female companion?" Scorpio asks with a very stern voice. The holo answered, "The sex drive of both male and female is very strong, and all that The Tubes asks is that any sexual contact between the two be delayed until they have emotionally matured. A female can choose you with the understanding that there will be no offspring." Scorpio asked, "The age now for first mating is determined by whom?"

180-Voting is heartbeat

"The age is determined by voters and the need to control the maximum amount of humans that can inhabit The Tubes without destroying all of the other occupants of it. Look around you and think what would happen if the lagoons and all living things that exist in them were destroyed by human intrusion. The Tubes built into areas were minimal, and the only time humans were there was during the installation. You have pedaled, and if traffic is not congested, you can observe all of the wild life because they are oblivious of you being there. The solar panels on the tubes were designed so they seem transparent. As time goes by, you will notice that you have freedom of movement in any place in The Tubes. Vegetation has been restored to nearly its original state before the Old Era changed it dramatically, and all of the wild animals are controlling their numbers by nature's edict. If there any changes, the voters will determine it. Are there any other questions?"

"I've seen my procreators vote many times but I find it difficult to understand why it is required and only one vote can be missed occasionally," says Scorpio. "The voter is like a heartbeat. The Tubes are a living thing and must constantly be given positive thoughts of the desires of 75% of the inhabitants. A change is very difficult. Now and then there comes a human with the wisdom to see the need for change and that person chooses a well organized approach. Whatever the 75% decide, it is final. Are there any more questions?" the robed holo asked. "Enough for this rotation," said Scorpio. He unrolled his mat and the holo disappeared so the young male could enjoy his quiet time. It seemed like an hour passed but still exhausted young male wished he could have rested much longer. Almaaz had tossed a pellet into the air and it fell into her open mouth. This was a tough one, so she worked much harder to break it apart with her teeth.

181-Mating pool age

"I now have two great males in my dwelling," Almaaz said with a grin. "What is going to be the first thing that you want to do now that you are one of us?" She put a lot of emphasis on 'us.'

"I haven't put to much thought into the voting patterns, and I do hope that you would give me your past marks. You have mentioned many times how you felt, but it seemed that I was not too concerned about anything but bounce or chess or what the holo had for me. Your biology, astronomy and physical fitness instructions penetrated, but somehow the voting went over my head. Donor and his other dimensions I had always had some difficulty comprehending. Micro electronics was great the way the holo did it. Excuse me for wandering from the voting thing," Scorpio said with interest. Incu requested, "Let's roll out our monitors so we can see what is in for us this rotation. Notice that there ten lines with a three word topic. You have to bring each of them in to have the 33 words or less explanation of the topic. The large one on the top is the issue to be decided today. The ones below are numbered and will work their way to the top of the list in sequence. It's best that you read them all so you can have the next ten revolutions to decide after conversing with others or do some research on your own in The Record Keeper or the library." Almaaz popped a pellet and chewed it with vigor. "This one has been here many times. CHANGE THE ELIGIBLE ORBITS TO ENTER THE MATING POOL FROM 24.7 TO 23.2 STARTING ON THE FIRST ROTATION OF THE NEXT ORBIT. It seems that the newly ringed and those waiting in the mating pool have some inner desires that they want satisfied. The dwelling occupancy is at 96.5%."

182-Mating age vote

There might be a need in a few different locations, but the dwelling service crews can shift them with the greatest of ease. The highest mating pool age was 27.9. The lowest was 18.4 and that was after the tsunami of BOT-147. The flow of the system is going along very well now. Pellet products have not used fertilizer of any kind because of the plant rotation of crops. The soil has a four rotation fallow and one for crops. Look at yourself. Is there anything that you would like to change on the mating age? If not cast a NO vote." Scorpio now voted for the first time as a Rite of Passage male. He voted NO.

They looked at the next issued. It was about eligibility of the elderly to care for children. The rule now is that they must be under 87 orbits. CHANGE THE AGE OF THE ELDERLY FROM 87 TO ANY AGE IF PHYSICALLY AND MENTALLY CAPABLE. The reminder of the 33 words were the wattage donation increased from 300 to 750 per hour. That was one that Scorpio knew a little about. Castor had some children with him before Scorpio was taken to the Lonesome Place. Scorpio told Incu about Castor's inability to control the energetic youngsters and felt that he was going to vote YES the next rotation. He did see many that were pedaling and wondered how they ever stayed on their bicycles.

Incu told Scorpio to read all of the issues that would be coming up and to question Donor or herself. Incu tossed another pellet high into the air, nearly hitting the top of the dwelling and caught it with her mouth easily. Her grazing of food did help her by not overburdening her digestive system by consuming one rotation's rations at one sitting.

183-Incu's eye

While Scorpio was reading the future ballot issues, Almaaz took out her art supplies and started to sketch the landscape view from the front entrance of their dwelling. It was damp windless evening with the sun half way on the horizon. She was surprised that the beautiful colors that are usually present. She had been having some weird sensations in the back of her left eye, but never paid much attention to it because it only lasted for a few moments. She set up her tripod with a 200X300 cm pad, took out her colored pencils and drew a straight line for the horizon and half round disc for the sun. "When will the hues arrive?" she asked herself." She occasionally glanced at the sun every minute or so, but now the other objects also were turning a brown color. This was the first time that anything like this ever happened. She grabbed all of her art supplies and returned them inside the dwelling and walked over to Scorpio who was watching an area where an engineering proposal for a tube tunnel to be dug.
"Scorpio, please look into both of my eyes and see if you see anything unusual," she said.
"They look the same to me," he answered.
"I cannot see any colors!" she says with somewhat of an alarm. "Please come with me to the eye dwelling." It took them less than 15 minutes. The service person asked Almaaz to unroll her monitor and answer all of the 32 questions. Using her stylus she hurriedly answered all of them then looked up only to see the service person ready to walk out of the front entrance. In a loud voice she asked, "I hope you are not leaving!"

184-Color blind

"I'm just going to look out the front entrance for the one that should have been here two hours ago. The bird watching group was to leave from my area's center and pedal 30 km the to bay. I did not want to start with you if she was in sight." He peeks out the door but saws no one. "Sorry about the delay," he apologized "You are more important than my off duty pleasure." "I have lost color in my vision," Almaaz said in distress, but projected a very calm appearance.
"Please relax. Could you please start to hum one of your favorite tunes?" the technician asked. Almaaz started with the one that she used to put Scorpio to sleep. What she was humming was monitored and was now being played softly by a violinist in a very soothing way over what seemed to be speakers everywhere in the dwelling. The technician told Almaaz that he was going to place a few drops of a clear liquid onto each of her eyes. He held her eye lid open and Almaaz's self preservation instincts dominated her attempt to keep them open. When the drop hit her eye and automatically blinked. The music played soothing and finally some drops landed in here eyes. The technician told her, to take her quiet time now. Scorpio rolled out his mat and rested too, as well as the technician.
Betelgeuse walks into eye dwelling and finds all three asleep. Seeing someone on the litter, she opened the current file and discovered Almaaz had a major problem. Betelgeuse entered The Record Keeper and brought out all of the related histories of other patients. This was an easy one to compare because there were only eight. She got a holo on one where the whole eyeball was one meter round and in full color.

185-Eye exam

Betelgeuse walks into it because she wanted to get a closer look at the cones at the rear of the eye. She went further and observed the optical nerve and its color. She could also hear a heart beat. This is a perfectly healthy eye, and any slight deviation to it is going to be a problem for the patient. She prepared herself to compare this image to the one of Almaaz. She marveled at how researchers had developed technology so that a technician could do some of the most complex diagnosis just by comparisons like this one. Of the three sleepers, the technician, sat up first. "You were late!" he baked.

"When you come back with some loose feathers sticking out from your face mask, I'll give you the reason. Go see nature at its best. Sorry," said Betelgeuse calmly as she watches him race to his bicycle and speed off on it to the nearby ramp.

She turned off the music, and the sudden silence awakened the two stretched out visitors. "You have 8 minutes before your eyes can be scanned. In the mean time I want you to have a full physical," Betelgeuse said. She wheeled the gurney over to the examiner and instructed her to roll over onto it, lie face down and place her face into the opening of the table. Betelgeuse verbally instructed the automatic optical examiner to start. As soon as the beam gets to where she has her monitor, FOREIGN OBJECT. PLEASE RESTART. "Please remove your pad with whatever is in it and the monitor," Said Betelgeuse.

Almaaz got herself into a sitting position and removed both then returned to the face down position. The start command is given again, and the blue line across her body moved ever so slowly. No sooner had it started, when Almaaz let off with a ground shaking sneeze. EXCESS MOVEMENT. PLEASE RESTART.

186-Eye exam

The blue line moved from head to toe. Then Almaaz rolled over onto her back. The blue light line moved from toe to head and made and announcement: COMPLETE.

Betelgeuse told her patient that in a few moments the results would be announced. PLEASE QUOTE PATIENTS PROBLEM. Betelgeuse speaks slowly one word at a time, "Loss of color detection in both eyes." Again they have to wait. Almaaz is now, for the first time in her life, starting to sweat because of the stress of her ailment and the test results. REPEAT SCAN OF PATIENTS OPTIC NERVE TO BRAIN came the next directive. Betelgeuse pulled the blue line mechanism so it crossed just over her eyebrows and said, "Start." It moved now at one fourth the speed of its last test. As it moved and the image appeared along side of the hollowed image a little anxiety the nurse displayed. Scorpio is compared the two images and grew alarmed at the odd thing showing in Almaaz's. He was going to say something but Betelgeuse held her index finger over her lips for him to be quiet. The blue line was over the bottom of her eye and Almaaz had to sneeze again. This time she pushed up on her nose and it worked just long enough for the scanner to complete its mission. COMPLETE and with that Almaaz let loose another wall-busting sneeze.

Almaaz sat on the examining table until helped off by Scorpio. "What do they call this machine?" he asked. "Molecular interloper," Betelgeuse immediately said "It gets between, over and around everything."

187-Eye exam

"Let us just walk through and find any differences to why you are having the color problem. Position yourself between the healthy one and yours and see if you can find any differences," Betelgeuse directed

Almaaz backed herself across the room to get a full view of both, then walked slowly toward them. "Nothing so far," Almaaz said as she walks into the healthy one then to the cones at the rear of the eyeball. She suspected that it was there where color separated. She looked over it very carefully, then went to her own and noticed that the tips of the cones of hers were slightly rounded. Scorpio noticed the same and told her about it, and that they appear a little darker especially on the edges. "I've seen something similar to this," the technician said "Have you been around any active bacteria lately?" she asked.

"That is what my research is in now. We have it so isolated though that none could have escaped its confinement area," Almaaz said with authority.

All the other holo examples are brought into view and examined by the three. This was something very exciting for Scorpio. His total interest was because it concerns his incubator. In his excitement Scorpio rushed from one holo to the next looking only at the cones and their color and shapes. The most distant one in the eye dwelling seemed to have a similarity. He shouted, "It's this one!" Almaaz rushed over but Betelgeuse, knowing that all must be closely observed, looked at each holo in sequence before staring at the one Scorpio picked and tells him that he had a good eye. "I'm sending your hologram to the Retina Research Center and they will have to give final confirmations as to your color blindness," Betelgeuse stated.

188-Eye exam

"How long will that take?" she asks.

Betelgeuse responded, "Let's find out." She gave the verbal command to her monitor, "Send patient's and number 18 to the Eye Research Center." The holos disappeared. "We still have a copy here and one is in The Record Keeper forever. Are you in any kind of pain now?" "None whatsoever. I can see some colors at a distance but it is the close objects that have none. It's totally weird. Have you seen anything like this before?" Almaaz asked

"I'm new here. I was in obstetrics and was transferred here by a vote of that team," the nurse said in a very somber voice. "Are you the one that caused the female that was delivering to nearly lose an eye?" Scorpio asks.

"Yes. That was me. I was overjoyed that she was able to retain 20/30 vision from that eye," Betelgeuse said. "I like my service here much better. I have to retrain, but with the holograms it will not be too difficult. Oh, here is our response." HAVE PATIENT SEATED FOR A RETINA OBSERVATION. Betelgeuse directed Almaaz to the seat and moved the two cone shaped devices, adjusting them to focus on each eye. Her blinking didn't help matters, so Betelgeuse quickly used lid retainers so the viewing would continue uninterrupted. It took about 30 seconds. EXAMINATION COMPLETED.

Almaaz wiped the tears that were flowing after the lid mechanism was removed, and she felt a buzz on her monitor. Unrolling her monitor she saw EXCESSIVE TIME IN MAGNETIC FIELD. "Her first and only words were, "OH NO!!!!

189-Healing time

"Those bacterium had their revenge. Why was I not informed about this if it has happened before? I've got to find out." She unrolled her monitor again and contacted the health director. "Please bring up my problem with the eye dwelling," she requested. "Done," he said. "Your research project was never entered into The Record Keeper. There was no way for you to be prohibited from continuing. Why did you not follow new project warnings?" he asked. "It had been a long time. It totally slipped my mind." Then it dawns on Almaaz that the research dwelling director should have informed her, and told the health director so. "Stop what you are doing now. Call me in three phases. Your color loss should be returned by then," He said in a very tranquil voice. Relieved, Almaaz lets out a huge sigh of relief, packed her stuff and pedaled off for their dwelling.

"Incu," Scorpio asked, "Is there any chance that I can enter the gliding competition that is going to be held the next Full Moon?" "You get a 95 or better on your Physics and Geography exam, and if your Donor agrees, the record distance is yours to try," she answered with a great big smile. "I thought I was going to have to do some coaxing or begging. Thank you Incu. Thank you, again and again. What do you think Donor will say," he asked with a blank expression.

Incu had three phases off from her research. She had kilowatts in reserve. More is always better. How best to get some. Carting packets.

190-Glider

Arriving at their dwelling they did not see Aires' vehicle and wondered where he might be, Almaaz unrolled her monitor and paged. A minute later he responded, "Yes?" with a lot of music in the background. "I see by the locator that you are not too distant and with the beautiful sounds, do you mind if I come to listen? she very softly pleaded. "Great, I know that you will see me at my best with this group. Please hurry," was his response. Scorpio had other things on his mind, so he plugged the bike discharge cord into his dwelling and went inside and took a few pellets.

The holo simulator was close to the real thing, but pretend took away most of the feelings. Scorpio placed himself on his mat with the holo surrounding him. The launch part of the glide was the same for every participant. They had no control over it. The ten kilo weight differences were very strict. If anyone was a milligram over on the weigh-in, he or she would have weight added to qualify to the next higher weight class. The projectile, which he was going to become, was triangulated so that the start of the glide was nearly at the same point for everyone. He would be given a buzz by the automated system when it was ready. He had talked to his donor some time ago and a lot of the finer parts of it were gone over thoroughly. Aires never won an event but did come in the top ten every time. The winner would be reimbursed his launch kilowatt hours and the other nine would be given their place's amount, with the tenth getting back ten percent.

191-Glider and music

Scorpio felt the buzz, pulled the latch cord, and the simulator holo took over. He felt his "wings" move up on one side and tried to correct the movement to give himself the greatest lift. The glide could last for at least ten minutes. He did his launch and glide seven times, and finally had to stop because his watt reserve was getting on the low side.

He heard some singing when his donor and incubator entered holding hands. "I wish you would have come with me to see one of the best musicians, "Incu said. "The beautiful sounds were better than I have ever heard before! I wonder how so many talented ones could congregate in such a small area. I just loved it. You have to spend some more time in music and become part of 'The closest thing to the other dimensions'."

"I do like music very much but it seems that I have so many other things that are drawing me away," Scorpio said. Incu replied, "Could you just do five minutes a rotation please? You can use the holo keyboard or the ones that are in the recreation dwelling. Please do it every rotation for just a short time. Please."

Scorpio stretched his monitor to display the 88 keys and started to satisfy his incubator. Generally he was doing very well but hit between the keys a few times and in less than five minutes he stooped and asked, "Donor, may I have your permission to participate in the gliding competition that is occurring in the next phase.?" "I would be honored if you would. Do you have enough in your reserve? he asked.

192-kWh and beads

"I'm sure I do," Scorpio said unrolling his monitor. "Kilowatt reserve," he requested and it showed that he had 437 kWh. "How did you accumulate so many? That's great." his donor said with surprise. "Every time I go to play a bounce game, I hook up onto a freight cart and it automatically give me the same it would have used from the tube system," smiled Scorpio. "What is the launch fee this orbit," asks Aires. "It used to be 187 kWh but it was changed to 142 because more powerful magnets were used and using just as much power. Then there was the standard launch vehicle fee and that from what

I researched has not changed in the past five generations. I would like if you would also be a contestant too. Wouldn't it be nice to see where I come in first and you just a few meters behind me?" Aires said smiling from ear to ear. "No. I had my fling. Now the only exercise that I need is when I bike to generate some electricity. It's fun and I don't want to ruin your day by taking it away from you," Aires smiled and gave Scorpio another hug. "I do hope the wind is at your back and may the love of our other dimensions lengthen your flight."

"Donor, can I go with you to your health dwelling the next few rotation?" asked Scorpio. "What's this I hear? You have never had any interest in the health field. It has always been caterpillars and bugs. Now and then you talk in your sleep and it's always the same, 'coordinated leg movement,' so is there a change or do you feel it should add to your bugs?" asks Aires. Scorpio returned with a very serious face, "Since we have moved here, there seems to be a different of so many. Have you noticed how much neater all of the dwellings are? Quiet time is groups and some alone mumbling with some kind of beads. I have never seen anything like it before coming here. Do you know why?"

193-Beads

"What does that have to do with the health field?" asked Aires. "I just can't walk up to these people with their beads and ask about what they are doing to satisfy my curiosity, can I?" Scorpio evades a question with a question? "Offspring, you are going to have to learn that if you put true loving curiosity into anything, people will respond likewise. So go for it. It's easy to offend someone when you approach with an attitude of degrading humor to ignorant demands. Just relax and thoroughly observe many times before you want answers," calmly Aires answered. Scorpio replied quickly, "Please give me some kind of hint about what those beads do and why they are so prevalent here. Why don't you and Incu use them?"

"Scorpio, I have been in the research field and so has your incubator, and in all of the time that we can remember, a fact must be substantiated and proven by many. I am in the administrative end of the medical field but it took many orbits for me to obtain that position. I was voted in by 75% of my peers. Earthly science is not taken lightly. Superstitions can devastate the health of a community. In the Past Era there were many different groups that flourished rampantly with each one seeking power and control over the other. Outside the tube area, they still decimate themselves. To be part of the tubes, love, which was given to us from someone that was from another dimension and returned is primary in any actions by anyone of us. They believe that man had an earthly incubator, who by the way was the only human to be touched by the other dimension. That female was the only human that was taken away from the earth to return with visions through the eyes of many children and one adult male.

194-Beads

Those beads are man-made pleas to try to get her attention," Aires paused.
Scorpio excitedly asked, "Why here and not at any of the other dwellings we
had?" Aires, somewhat anxious about furthering the conversation said, "OK that is your last question now. I did want to come to this medical facility, and a bonus was that this was the only community with a spirit of togetherness in the system. It is because of those little beads. Are the beads part of another dimension?" Aires replies, "They all know that we cannot get to the other dimensions. They say that the other dimensions must come to us." "Please can I ask you just one more yes or no question," pleads Scorpio.
"Last one for sure," Aires says smiling. "Does Incu know about you and the beads," was Scorpio's last question. With a kind of somber answer he said, "She knows of them but not my desires," then

added, "I have a music concert in the park in a few minutes, so bye for now."

Scorpio unrolled his monitor and asked for a keyboard. In holo, all 88 keys appeared. Some buttons he pushed gave the piano the same sound that a roll player would sound like. He asked for the notes of a nursery rhyme he sang to many times as a child, and then played with the volume up higher than his procreators would allow. Singing along with his playing drew Scorpio's attention to and elderly female who just happened to be pedaling by. Scorpio made the offbeat noise.

195-Beads

Scorpio walked to the door and peeked out, but did not see anyone. He was surprised to hear a voice from around the corner, "Hello good neighbor. I have not heard that one you are playing since I was a child." The female said then added, "Where did you come up with that tune?"

"From my incubator," Scorpio answered.

"May I ask her name please?" says the female.

"Almaaz," Scorpio answered.

"It has to be her! She has a scar on the underside of her left arm and she has the most beautiful voice. Where is she now because I must see her?" asks the gentle one.

Scorpio spoke to his monitor, "Almaaz please," and there she appeared smiling.

"What is it," she asks?

"Someone to see you," he said and moved his monitor to focus on the female.

"I thought I'd never see you again.! What a pleasant surprise. My number one bead lady," Almaaz excitedly said. "Alphard, please stay where you are. I'll be at the dwelling in a few minutes. Please, can you wait? I must see you."

The visiting female pressed the location button on Scorpio's monitor and then says to Almaaz, "Stay where you are because I have some unfinished business in the dwelling next to where you are now. Is that OK with you?"

"By all means," she said and the keyboard reappeared for Scorpio.

"Now I know where your tune came from, offspring. You have been truly rewarded," She spoke like it was part of a song.

196-Beads

Scorpio watched as she sped away and he estimated that her speed was well above the speed limit. Her anxiety to meet her long gone friend was too much to observe the limit.

She blazed by the crowded park, is where it is closely monitored, and sure enough the enforcement regulator stopped her. Scorpio immediately buzzes Incu and tells her of her friends speed problem. Almaaz leaves her post and pedaled to the park to see her being led to the lonesome place. She is very discreet in getting the attention of Alphard, because if there are gestures of any kind, she might be a neighbor for one rotation. Now that the females knew that they both are in the same area, Almaaz returned to her research station. What a treat, she told herself, but with deep reservations about the activities of Alphard. Alphard was brilliant and was voted by 98% of her peers to become the director of the amniotic fluid research center some distance away. She refused the offer because she was so devoted to her research in the other dimension. She never had a mate and if it were not for the quiet times, the moon phase rotations off or the annual four moon phase off, she would be constantly meditating or experimenting with finding where "she" went. Almaaz knew Alphard and her friends and had a different outlook on that dimension but just the overflowing joy of her personality attracted most everyone to her. Almaaz was hooked.

"I wonder which dwelling she was going to visit. The only ones I can see other than my workplace are the butterfly, toad and the archeological files," she said to herself.

197-Alphard speeding

"I should have asked Alphard what she was going to do here and now it has aroused my interest in what she was going to do. Maybe I should browse around all three of them….. It would be futile, so it's best that I return to my dwelling," she said to herself and pedaled with her generation drag as high as she could. The downhill was nice especially this time of the rotation.

"You are going to run out of watts doing all of that practice with the gliding holo," she said to Scorpio as she walked into the dwelling. "I have lots to spare. Practice makes perfect. I do hope to do as well as Donor and maybe just a little better. I know that you will not be able to attend the launching. I will let you know my launch time as soon as I register. Is there any advice you can give?" he asked" None that would be of any mechanical value. I was never interested and heights bother me a little. The only thing that I can say is that if you ever want to be good in anything you have to do a lot of research and absorb all of it. Talk to some of the elderly who have participated. If you feel there is a little more you should know about any part of the contest, seek and you shall find yourself to be among the best. So that is my best advice my flying bird," she said smiling and gave him a big hug.

"I'm sorry to see your friend was given a lonesome for one rotation. I know how she feels. No big deal but, I'm sure she probably has something to do to keep her from being too stressed," said Scorpio.

"You know," said Incu with a very curious look on her face, "She will make more out of it that you think. In the past, she did spend much more quiet time than anyone that I have ever known. The Lonesome Place will give her undivided attention to what she is doing research in. Being upset is not part of her being. I'm still wondering which dwelling she was going to visit: Toad, butterfly or archeology?"

198-Mental problem female

Alphard was deep in thought and had her eyes closed most of the time. A bird happened to land on the tree next to her Lonesome Place dwelling and chirped a few times and drew her attention just enough for her to see a female in the next "Place" was flailing her arms and walking in a big circle. "So that is where Antares is?" she said to herself then waved to attract her attention. She looked at Alphard and fell to her knees. Alphard pressed the "need" button and a voice came through her monitor. She unrolled it and asked the voice, "Why is my neighbor not getting any medical attention?" "The female was visited by a technician one hour ago and the patient was found comfortable," was the response.
"I would like very much to comfort her now if I may. Please," was her request.
"Your request will be forwarded to the health services." came back the answer.
Alphard saw her neighbor still on her knees and knelt too. The other woman stood and started to walk toward Alphard then suddenly stopped. She took a few steps backward then falls to her knees again. She knew enough to feel her circle of containment. Alphard placed her palms together and the woman docs likewise.
The monitor buzzed: You will be observed making contact with the uncontrollable one. You can walk to her, but be aware you are doing so at your own risk. You will only be a minute away from help from an attendant who will activate her collar if your safety is in danger. Alphard stood and slowly walked toward the troubled female still kneeling with her palms together. When Alphard was about two meters away, Antares stands, turned and ran to her dwelling.

199-My little female

Alphard cautiously walked toward the dwelling entrance and saw the frightened female cowering on the floor in a fetal position and crying. At the entrance, Alphard started to sing. The crying stopped and humming of the tune comes from the inside. Alphard took out her beads and started to sing, as she has done thousands of times. Slowly, Antares crawled toward the opening, still humming, stood then starts to hum the same tune. The singing and humming kept up for five minutes. Then all of a sudden, Antares grabs the beads from Alphard's hands and ran back into the dwelling. Startled, Alphard kneels and continued to sing with both of her palms up, pleading for the sick female to return her most prized possession. Alphard was shocked to see the crying one inside suddenly throw the beads at her, then sing words that neither rhymed or had a tune of any kinds with "my little female" repeated over and over again.

"Music is working," Alphard said to herself. She finished one circle on the beads, arose turns and slowly walked toward her dwelling for the rotation. No sooner than she crossed the first parameter, Antares started to hum and holds her palms up and, "Please give me the beads." They are yours to keep only if I can give you a hug," said Alphard. "NO!" was the loud answer. "Please, can you just hold your palm against mine?"

Cautiously, Antares walked up to her humming neighbor, slowly took the beads then reached for a hug. The two females embraced each other with tears flowing down Alphard' face.

200-Alphard tried

They walked back to their own dwellings, and that was the last time that rotation that the sick one was outside hers.

When her speeding penalty time was over, Alphard pressed her "need" button and asked if she could remain a few more rotations and might be of some assistance to her very ill neighbor. The voice from her monitor answered: "Your request will be forwarded to the health department." Alphard took a quiet time and started to mumble her bead thing. Using her fingers to keep count, she found herself totally relaxed while waiting for an answer. She completed one circle and was half-way through the next when she was buzzed. "Your medical expertise not sufficient."

This disturbed her but she had no choice. She pedaled to the butterfly dwelling and would have enjoyed the companionship of her long lost friend but, her obsession with the other dimensions, she was completely possessed by thoughts that all around in open sight the other dimensions were hiding. She could have done all of this research on her monitor from wherever she might be, but the open drawers of thousands of butterflies are the real thing. She walked into the large room filled with local butterflies fluttering everywhere and some landed on her. She viewed different stages from a plain caterpillar to colorful work of beauty. We humans must find that our procreation is only to seek the other dimensions. Science has done wonders to make every rotation full of excitement-learning and living without fear of hunger, most diseases and being dominated by foreign aggressors. But with all the learning, the other elusive dimensions remain elusive.

201-Fling

Scorpio unrolled his monitor, brought up the fling rules, and was totally engrossed by them. He had done it many times before and knew that because of the danger, he MUST achieve a 100 percent to participate. With him not having any previous flings, he could only participate during daylight. He chose the best time. Aires said that the evening is better when the air is more humid. He checked the weather report for wind direction and their approximate speed. He knew that he would given kilos to make the weight class. The weight strip would be attached, from his shoulders to his knees and have the same density its entire length.

Everything needed was entered and with the anxiety of this "first time" move, he felt a strange buzz come over him. Inside of him were little feelings that said, "Check one more time" and another saying, "PRESS ENTER." The last time he had that feeling was when he walked onto the bounce field for the first time with a uniform on and that to him was ever so long ago.

The louder of the two prevailed and he was now officially a contestant. Viewing his application he noted that he had been preapproved by his procreators. His kilowatts were deducted. That part included the banana outfit, fling sled and all of the personnel at the launch site. Sixteen orbits and allowed to make these decisions was normal. Bounce at the earliest was also tested by the youngest of participants. They had to fill in all of the blanks on the registration form, enter and be deducted the kilowatts from their reserve.

202-Fling

He checked the names and ages of the other entrants and who does he see, but the female who gave higher g-force hits than anyone else. Why was she to become part of his game again? Strange he thought to himself. There were 26 in all in his weight class. One was a female who was 63 orbits and had 6 wins. He wished that there was a juvenile class which would have made it easier for a championship. He turned on the cameras to the launch site and adjacent preparation dwellings, the landing area, a close up on the ramp itself, and the infamous "banana." That was one thing he paid most attention to. The site was 12 kilometers away and for him it was a must to get fitted. He told Incu about his plans. "There is no need to do that," she said. "There is the utility dwelling with all kinds of equipment. Donor is very familiar with you desires," she continued and opened her monitor and buzzes him. She could only get part of him with the camera shot. His response was, "I'll be right with you." She noticed that he was pushing himself off the floor. "Were you on quiet time? I'm sorry if I disturbed you, but Scorpio needs to be fitted with a fling banana at the utility dwelling." "The earliest that I can be there is 0345. Is that OK with him?" Scorpio said it was fine. "Remember when I told you about asking someone who was a flinger. Is there a person other than donor who could forward some expertise?" "I have a female who has won 6 times, but I doubt if she would share," Scorpio said with a downhearted look. "The world is full of beautiful people," Incu said then added, "Why don't you give her a buzz?"

203-63 orbit champion

"You have time before your fitting with donor. How did you get her name?" asks Incu.

" It was on the list of my competitors," answered Scorpio. He unrolled his monitor, scrolled to her name and address and gave her a buzz. "Yes, may I help you?" the female voice said. "My name is Scorpio," "I know. Is that your Incubator with you?" "Yes it is. May I spend some time with you to get some pointers on the upcoming competition?" "I'd love to. It's quiet time for me now. But by the time you travel from you dwelling to mine it will be over. Almaaz would you like to come too/" the fine toned woman asked. "I have made previous arrangements so that would be impossible. Is there some time we could swap previous orbit tales?" asked Almaaz? "I'm leaving now, if that is OK with you," said Scorpio. "You sure are an eager one! Almaaz, you set the time," she said.

Scorpio timed himself to give the female at least 15 minutes of quiet time. Her dwelling was surrounded by flowers. The large rose bush with the tiny pink flowers was ringed with a different variety of lower plants with white petals. It was like a beacon for her dwelling. When he racked his bike, she exited her dwelling. "Scorpio, you are so much taller than you look on my monitor." "May I call you Hydra? asked Scorpio" "That's my name, young male. That is all that I know that I am," then she added, "with all of that formality over, let's get on with why you are here."

"The first thing that you must know is how to be fitted with launch gear. I just happen to have some here. As you know they are all the same for our weight class," she said.

"I have buzz my donor for him not to meet me at the utility dwelling for a fitting there at 0345," Scorpio cut in.

204-Hydra's bird

As Scorpio spoke to his donor on his monitor, Hydra beckoned for him to enter her dwelling. He nearly tripped over a bucket of water while walking with his open monitor in front of him, recovered quite gingerly and rolled it up. Inside her dwelling were all kind of plants. "WOW! What do you have here? I have never seen anything like this before!" Scorpio said with nearly a shout. "WOW!"

"All of this is a labor of love. Everyone has priorities and the plants are one of mine. I utilize every minute of my time, every rotation. What you see here only takes a few moments to nurture. The oxygen that they add to the inside here may not be readily noticed, but it's there. Now this is the outfit or one like that you will be wearing," she said smiling. " I have it on the floor, just lower yourself onto it face down."

Scorpio laid down and Hydra locked on the waist strap, then told the young male to extend his arms to the top of the wing vanes. She binds his arms with the three evenly spaced straps. The nose cone was clear so he would have full vision. It is hinged to the base, the largest of the four vanes. The top vane slid under the nose, as did the two wing ones. The device was aerodynamically designed to act like a disc when spread. The older female slid on the foot rest and told Scorpio she was going to force it very tightly against the soles of his feet. "Now I want you to bring your arms back. With your palms hold onto the bar, twist them so that they will be perpendicular to the floor. Have you ever done this before?" she asked. 'No," he answered. "You are doing everything so smoothly. I'll bet you did it with the holo," she said with full confidence. "Yup," was his answer.

205-Hydra teaching Scorpio

"How does that feel so far?" she asked.
"Great."

"Young flinger, you will have to push your wings out from the tucked in position. The force of air is going to be great. It will be impossible to do so before you reach your apogee. You will notice the simulator screen just under your nose cone. I had it made specially for myself," She said

"Nothing is moving!" shouts Scorpio!

"Not yet, young chick. Be patient. You and the holo did the chute thing probably many times. This is going to be about as close as you can get to the real thing-all except the vibrations. What is the maximum speed of the fling?"

Scorpio said, "290 kilometers per hour."

"Excellent. The air rushing past you is going to be great. It will rapidly decrease until the peak of your fling. What will your speed be then?"

"Zero," said Scorpio

"Determining when it is zero is critical," Hydra stated. "Notice the spring loaded ball inside the tube. That is the decider. When you see it touch the end of the tube, there is no thrust. For simulation sake, a magnet will slowly lose its power and allow the ball to touch the end. It is then that it is zero. I will adjust the magnetism manually. See. That is when you spread your wings. Got it?"

"I'm ready," Scorpio answered nervously.

206-Hydra teaching Scorpio

"Oh, another thing. It's best if you close your eyes while being on the thruster. There is nothing to look at. Ready or not, here goes. Ready? Three. Two. One. Go!" Hydra's shrill voice gave Scorpio added excitement. "You will be on the thruster sled for nine seconds. When you feel the vibrations stop, open your eyes immediately. It is that moment that you will get the thrill of your life. The first launch is the greatest." The simulator's vibration stopped and the huge monitor under his nose cone made the dwelling get smaller and smaller at a terrific rate. He could see the horizon, the beach, previously launched flingers, a lonesome place, and birds all around him. He issued a loud "WOW!"

He was amazed at how real the simulator screen was. He was brought back to reality by "that voice" again, "Where is the ball in the tube?" "It's against the end of the tube," he responded. "When did it get there?" Hydra asked. "I'm not sure. I was marveling my new surroundings," he said.

"You failed that launch, young chick. Two more launches and I have to go."

"Ready? Three. Two. One. GO!" Scorpio tried this time to count the 10 seconds before opening his eyes. He was surprised at his speed on the ramp. Then, ZOOM, saw the open sky and the same scenery he had the last time. Watching his ball touch the end in the tube, he pushed his arms out maneuvering the wings to be parallel to the ground. His left wing was out long before the right one was. She told him about it and asked him to retract the wings and try again. He did and the same thing happened again. Once more, the wings were not coming out evenly.

207-Hydra's generosity

"One more time! Bring your wings back into the launch position. Good. Ready? Three. Two. One. GO," Hydra screeched. This time Scorpio could watch the scenery and the ball in the tube. He extended his wings and still his left was out before his right one was. He knew he had to work on that. He felt a tug on his binders and in a matter of seconds he was able to get up. "Thank you ever so much for spending your valuable time with me. How can I thank you? Can I come here again? That was great. Thanks again!" Scorpio chattered. "No problem. If you wish to use my winning device you are welcome to. I will not be around for the next few days, so if either of your procreators assist you in using it, do so," Hydra said with a very comforting smile. "Why are you doing this for me?" asked Scorpio? "You were the only one who asked," she replied. "Young flying chick, in life nearly everyone is very kind and generous. There is no greater joy than in sharing knowledge, especially with the young. If you have a desire to learn anything, look around you and seek the person or persons that have participated in whatever you desire, ask kindly and your wish will be granted nearly every time. Ask and you will receive. Do you know anyone that was a flinger?" she asked. "My donor was for many years," replied Scorpio. "My only request is that you are not using this equipment alone. I'm late, so let yourself out." She waved goodbye and pedaled away. Scorpio unrolled his monitor and buzzed his donor. "What is your request this time my champion?" asked Aires.

"Donor, I have a simulator to use but I must have you assist me. Would you have time to come here?" "Can you wait a half hour or so my favorite offspring?" "Awake me when you get here," said Scorpio.

208-Donor at Hydras

Scorpio unrolled his mat for quiet time and was asleep in a matter of minutes. He didn't need to repeat over and over again, Leg coordination. It was nearly an hour before Aires arrived, much to the benefit of Scorpio.

"So this is you new hangout?" Aires asks the groggy youth after gently shaking him.

"My first time here and it was great!"

"How did you make the acquaintance with the young woman?"

"Donor she is old. I mean real old. Her name was on the list of competitors. Incu told me to network with a winner. That picture you are looking at is not my mentor. Who that is I do not know. Hydra has won six times. I will only be able to compete against her this one orbit. I do hope I make the weight class and not have to go to the next higher one this launch. What is that you are looking at?" asks Scorpio. Donor asked, "Did you ever see this?" Irritated Scorpio said, "Donor, I never saw anything like that before. Snooping around in someone's dwelling is not proper. Let's get to the simulator."

Aires set down the tiny beaded rope nearly exactly as he found it. "Scorpio, aren't you the least bit curious?" "No," said Scorpio, "My only interest here is to use this simulator."

"Hey. This is neat. Only an engineer would possess this. Did she say tell you her vocation? She can't be real old if she is still Flinging. What's her name again?" Donor asked. "Hydra," Scorpio said. "Hydra." Aires unrolled his monitor and brings up the name, then Flinger with it. "Sure enough she was the one who beat him on my first Fling. It seemed to me that she was old 25 orbits ago when I had my first launch," said Donor.

209-Donor teaching Scorpio

"Scorpio, she is good. We've got our work cut out for us. This is why she wins. She practices with a simple device like the zero propulsion tube. I do hope that you can observe now that males do not have a superior guide to inventions. I will have to say now that I am going to confront her as to why she never made it public before. That little tube is great. OK, now let's get you into this device again." "Let me adjust the hand hold bars. Your arms are just a little longer than Hydra's. Now, how's that?" "It is a lot better than the "ghost" bars on the hologram. Do you want me to stretch my arms or just be relaxed?" asked Scorpio. Donor answered, "Feel comfortable. Just lie there, close your eyes, inhale three times and slowly exhale the last time."

Scorpio exhaled slowly with his eyes closed. He felt his donor move his right bar, a few centimeters and lock the bar into the wing. Then he did the other. "I had to move the right one four centimeters and the left one nine. When you did some practice with Hydra were the wing extensions coming out evenly?" "No. The left one was out slightly before the right. My face is very close to the nose cone. Could you put in some of the torso pads to raise me up just a few centimeters?" "No problem." Scorpio twisted his body and pulled vigorously on the hand holds. The three straps on each arm were releasing their hold on him, and he pushed himself so that he was on his hands and knees. "That's it," he said and twisted the bars to have the straps clamp themselves onto his arms. He started to move the wings into the launch position when Aires was buzzed.

210-Ballot presentation

"Your presence is requested immediately in the Ballot Presentation dwelling."

"I've got to go," said Aires. "Loosen yourself and buzz me as soon as you get to our dwelling." He was undecided to pedal or fling the five kilometers. The "immediately" term puzzled him. Ballot presentations are not an utmost urgency, so he decided to pedal. His new responsibility required this, and though he had viewed them many times on the "open circuit," the adrenaline was flowing within him at an unbelievable rate. He wasn't even aware of the speed that he was pedaling. Scorpio buzzed and asked him about something on his competition against Hydra and was told that it would have to wait until he returned.

When Aires parked his bicycle, he counted fifteen others. He walked into the entrance and an attendant of the dwelling motioned for him to be seated in the first row. He got a printed sheet of the upcoming decision that had to be made, and he settled himself for some rest after the exhausting ride. He noticed two empty seats, so there must be others coming. He could rest and browse over the sheet he was given. It read:

Old Era area requesting to become peddlers.

Area of their authority is ninety kilometers east of our development.

Land mass of approximately 39,500 square kilometers. Previous drought and recent hurricane caused very serious food and health problems.

They have accepted our scouts: devastation confirmed.

Decision on ballot to be our terms of acceptance.

211-Old Era request

From the start of the tubes all of the additions have been contiguous. This would be the first time that one would be far away. There was Old Era hostile land that had to be considered. The materials to convert to our standards would be immense. To what extent did they know about our personal restrictions? How many orbits would it take? All of this had to be taken into consideration and still have only thirty three words on the ballot. A very interesting challenge for Aires.

One more entered into the dwelling completely out of breath and was directed to the third and last row. Why this kind of seating arrangement? It was then that the attendant announced, "The last ballot preparer will not be here because of health reasons. We must wait another four hours before his assistant can arrive.

Aires rolled his mat to the corner of the dwelling and proceeded to take his quiet time. It didn't take long for him to sleep. It was not long before he heard a quiet snore from the nearby mat's female.

Refreshed from his nap, he had a lot of time to search for expertise on each one of the lines in the ballot proposal. He knew, in their misery, they would not have much time living in their horrible conditions. Why did they not make this request before the twin disasters? He was very comfortable living with the Tubes. Why would anyone want to live otherwise. He knew that there were a few Tubers who demanded to be released to the Old Era and were granted their wish. Most males returned, begging to be ringed again. He buzzed Almaaz to find that she and Scorpio were at the beach. He displayed the ballot proposal and wanted her opinion.

212-Aires consulting Almaaz

I wish you could be here instead of sweating it out with a bunch of experts trying to make something out of nothing. Just kidding. When the drought was going on, I suggested sending them pellets from our two orbit reserve, but the suggestion was lost in channels, or was refused by the ones with lots of sand. There is not much I can add other than each male is made well aware of the rings and females accepting wearing the ovulation indicator forever. You can place anything on our ballot, but it is the sand people that must know that they have to vote with the electronic monitors we will supply them. It must be 95 percent for our requirements or nothing else. If you do place their addition, it must be under the conditions that we monitor their vote first. I'm going to leave now because I cannot see Scorpio," excitedly said Almaaz and vanished from Aires' monitor.

Aires scanned the beach and saw a group of teen. Almaaz approached them. Focusing the sounding device, Aires heard, "Hey, you got sand over my face cover. I can't move! That's enough," a giggling female shouted. "You didn't stop when I said so last phase, so here comes some more." Incu recognized the male's voice and kept on walking knowing that to defend him now would most likely embarrass him. She is buzzed by Aires, "Was that our joy in the huddle of young ones?" She returned with, "Here I am worried, and he is having the time of his life." "Hey, you've an urgent demand on you. Is there anything else you need?" "Nope." He said, "Bye."

213-Old Era Request

"Thank you. I have one more question. When the last Old Era were assimilated with us, how did the females fare?" he asked. "Surprisingly well, like I said with a drastic change in ways of living, we will always have some on the extreme fringe of what is acceptable. There were a few who could only tolerate the lonesome place until they met their natural demise. They refused to return to some other Old Era lands and were belligerent to the Tube's way. Uncontrolled hormones can be devastating. They tolerated the time limit of medications, but once off, were back to their "old" ways and back to the lonesome place. They were miserable. We tried to comfort them but they were lost forever. It took two orbits before anyone could participate in the mating pool, and now there is some dour humor into itself. If the sand people vote 100 percent to be one with us, they are ignorant of the agony that they will have to endure. Are there any other questions?" "With your emotional knowledge my wish now is that you should be here instead of myself. Thank you very much and good bye. Can I buzz you again on this subject?" Aires asked.. "Are not we all here to make this an earthly paradise?" she responds then adds the, "Our curiosities in the mystery of our other dimensions." Thirty three words. The Sands people request to become Tube people. Then equally peopled sections to be phased in at one phase of the moon at a time starting from the westerly beach section and ending in contiguous sections. Word count did show three too many.

214-Old Era request

Tubers should have been aware of Sands people dire needs and the past shipments of pellets to them via sea craft. The land route was not possible because of graft and high fees.

Aires entered his ballot words. The attendant then returned to him all of the others that were completed. Thirty three ballot proposals would be submitted. He found a few that were very interesting. Everyone in the dwelling had the general feeling that if the whole world had organized living conditions as the Tubers, turmoil would be at a minimum. They also knew the male Tubers knew their boundaries, but surprisingly it was the unhampered females who were in distress more than the males. Aires' mind started to drift from his task at hand, so he rolled out his mat just outside the dwelling and was asleep in a matter of minutes.

A bell awoke him and the attendant buzzed all of the ones attending. "PROPOSALS WILL BE DISCUSSED AT 2100 HOURS. VOTING BEGINS AT 2200 HOURS."

He knew that the Sand People were in total distress. They also knew what the living conditions were like with the Tube People. This ballot proposal had to contain two things. A timetable for the Sand People to adapt comfortably and how best to help them transition.

The voting done by the Tubers must have 75% acceptance or more, the ballot must be made favorable, if that be the goal of the ones submitting proposals.

Aires had seen satellite close up views of the whole area. The automated total physical testing devices were pouring in results of The Sand People's unhealthy way of living. One area on the southeast corner had some green plants visible. He thought to himself, "We A are taking on a burden that we do not need!" They were approached every 10 orbits for the last 10 generations and each time they refused. Why did that society have to wait until it was on its death pad before requesting admittance?

215-Sands ballot

The gene pool could use some additions. The combination of a family gene with another was 12 generations apart now. No human should exist under the horrible conditions that they were in now. Their population was 300,000 just 15 orbits ago and is now decreasing every rotation. Aires had to make the ballot favorably suggest their addition. The ballot he proposed was being digested by the others and he had just a half hour to finish the last nine entries. There were proposals that had the ten section approach yet. One he thought that merit, suggested that the Sand People choose a leader for each group of hundred. Another proposed that groups of one thousand be transported here and after orientation be IDed and ringed then returned with starter supplies and instructors for tubing construction. One had 37 words and was not even looked at. By the time he read all of the other 32, he was unsure of what was in the first one. Quickly he started browsing them on his monitor and found only two more worth mentioning. He reread them all again. The attendant rang the bell and asked for a vote. It was now 2100 hours.

All of the attendees saw a proposal with eight votes. Four had five votes. "This is the first time this has happened," the attendant said. "So that means we will have to limit ourselves in the amount of time we each have the floor." Two minutes was decided upon. Twenty eight was huge for discussions. This is the price we have to pay for a tranquil "family" Aires said to himself, then asked the attendant for a ten minute quiet time that was granted.

216-Sands ballot

Aires rolled out his pad and tried to meditate. He repeated the number "one" over and again and again but could not get himself to be totally relaxed. His mind wandered aimlessly to thoughts of things past. How was he going to concentrate on preparing a ballot for voting while being preoccupied with thoughts that had nothing to do with anything, Random thoughts of a lot to do about nothing. "Sir. The ten minutes plus are up," the attendant said, shaking Aires shoulder. "The bell for us to resume our duties went to the limit and your snoring prevented all of the others from utilizing their quiet time to the maximum. Aires was groggy and somewhat incoherent being awakened from a deep, deep sleep. He wobbled to the private place, then deposited his "packet" by the entrance, and emerged from his stupor.

Everyone had out their monitor to view what the programming device entered from all of the entered ballot proposals. It read: TWELVE PERSONS FROM THE TEN AREAS OF THE SANDS PEOPLE TO BE TRANSPORTED TO OUR COAST TRAINING FACILITY. ONE MOON BEFORE EACH ARE RETURNED WITH ONE-HUNDRED RINGED MALES AND ALL THE BEGINNINGS TUBE MATERIAL.

That had everything that Aires wanted and touched "approval" and it was not more than two minutes later that all of those present did the same. It would not be the daily voting item for one phase. It would have to take that many rotations for every one of the Tubers to view what was what they were going to vote on.

Rested from his pre-voting snooze, Aires was eager to get back to his dwelling. He was walking to the exit when he heard his name called. Turning he saw a very old female. "Yes. May I help you?" he asked.

217-Old woman

"How well do you know Alphard? She asked.

"My mate knows her," he responded.

"How well do you personally know Alphard? She asked again.

"I know nothing about her. Why do you ask?" Aires said with curiosity.

"Have her visit your medical facility and question her on her ability to relax. Then try to integrate her into a common Tuber. Please," she pleaded.

"As you noticed my snoring at quiet time, I do not have any relaxation problems. Can you give me your thoughts as to why I should respond to your request? He asked with a firm voice.

"I'll say nothing more for now. Goodbye and may the wind always be at your back," she said as she walked out the exit.

Aires watched her ride the bike to the nearby tube entrance. I'm more than burdened with responsibilities and it is the medical personnel who delve into those areas. He was administrative.

"Scorpio, I'm on my way back. What were you going to ask me?" said Aires.

"Does she have the same body shape as when you were in competition with her?" Scorpio questioned.

"I have not seen her in years, so I do not know. Let me see her body stats from her last visit to the medical facility." Aires brought up her past medical history and found that she was 2.018 K lighter than when he "let" her win. "Scorpio, with the added years plus the muscle loss, she has to be a super human to even come close to winning. Since she has so much interest in you, and with your personality, she will pour out to you the finer movements of gliding."

218-Scorpio disciplined

"Donor, there are 87 other entrants in my weight class. One flinger every 60 seconds will leave the sky full of birds. Last orbit, five meters were awarded to a flinger for avoiding contact with another. Can you come with me for a practice fling? I will schedule one in two rotations if that is OK with you. I have to leave for my bounce game now and will see you as soon as I can." Scorpio was ready to say more but was cut short by his donor.

"Hold on. Do you think that life is just one game after another? Your last results on mechanical design were nowhere near your potential. That class takes a lot of drawings. Are they all completed? This better be your last bounce until all of your assignments are completed. Do not even think of bounce or fling until those are done. Did you hear me?" Aires said with authority.

"Donor, these are the bounce finals. Fling championships are just one moon away. I have to prepare myself if I am going to invest so many kilowatts. I'll get my classes up to par." Again he wanted to ramble, but was cut short. "Scorpio, I know that you do not have a hearing problem. I'm positive you have a reasoning one. Your frontal lobe still has a lot to be entered, so until that time, play your bounce today but that's it until there are positive class results. That is final and there will be no more pleading. Understood?" demanded Aires. He rolled up his monitor and raised his generation level to 9. He knew that it would relieve him from the minor anxiety he had just encountered.

219-Alphard

Aires arrived exhausted. A wand cleaning in the private place while his suit had all foreign objects removed refreshed him. As soon as he it was done his monitor buzzed: LOWER THE AGE MALES CAN ENTER THE MATING POOL FROM 24.3 TO 22.7. REASON: SANDS PEOPLE PROBABLY MAKE A REQUEST TO BECOME TUBERS.

"No" his first response since he conversed with Scorpio. Every frustrated female will vote yes he knew from reading hospital reports, admittance and outpatients' records. Doctors that treated females with anxieties and no pattern or diagnosable disease always wrote:

Exceedingly strong desires. No medication was prescribed. They had a choice; Extreme kilowatt generation, counseling or The Lonesome Place. Scorpio cast his vote: "NO".

Aires buzzed Almaaz and found that she was with Alphard. Ironic how that female would come into their lives. "What time do you think you will return here?" he asked.

"I'm about to leave in a few minutes. Is there anything you need me for? I'll be there within 15 minutes." She was walking out of Alphard's dwelling when Aires interrupted, "I would like to visit with your friend if she will allow."

Alphard asked Aires, "Did you speak to my elderly friend?"

"Yes, I did for just a moment. She aroused my curiosity more than you can imagine. I'm leaving my dwelling now." he said..

220-Alphard

"Almaaz, do you ever give any thought to superstition?"

"Very seldom. In fact, rare. I have been reared and structured to only follow the facts of reality. All of my reasoning has to be based on this real world. Alphard, I did not want to come to this area because we had wonderful recreation facilities.. I've heard of some movements overran these beautiful places with firmly structured Tubers to disseminate thoughts of *bead superstition*. It was one of the reasons that Aires was granted by the Supreme Board of Directors permission to migrate here. Aires is a no-nonsense Tuber. I have been granted the female's "dream" mate. His love for organization is special. His desire is to have all under his jurisdiction maintained a loving attitude toward their duties. He understands that the human brain is a magnificent gift to humans and is to be used to its maximum potential. Aires has mentioned a few times to me that there is something above our known facts about life. It has been puzzling him. He is working with his staff to spend their time on the pattern he discovered. Non- conformists seem to dominate the workplace. He had difficulties in comprehending their ways. He viewed their dwellings and found floral arrangements with artistic designs so beautiful in comparison to the obligated patterns found in other areas." Almaaz was interrupted by a noise at the entrance then said, "My mate is here."

Alphard rushed to the entrance to give Aires a warm and firm hug. He wondered why he received such a reception from an unmated female. He embraced her with a little less enthusiasm and looked over her shoulder into the staring eyes of Almaaz.

221-Alphard

"Do you greet all of your visitors this way?" "I believe you are really the first, Aires."

"Something tells me that an air of mystery is present"

"Aires, now what would give you of such a thought?"

"The elderly female mentioning you this rotation and now my mate visiting and my presence here tell me something is happening," Aires says.

"Can I ask you the same question that I just asked Almaaz about superstition?" Alphard responded.

"What about it?"

"Have you ever given any thought to superstitions?" she asked.

"Yes, many times," he answered. "The Old Era was plagued with fears founded on irrational beliefs. Statues made of gold, bones of animals, hallucinogenic drugs and many other earthly devices were pursued in frenzies, trying to gain favor with some kind of mystical super power for them or against whomever they disliked. Why do you ask? And what does that have to do with the elderly female I met earlier?"

"The elderly one is my incubator. She has done a lot of research into the fourth dimension. I'm sure you have read some of her works. Does the name Norma mean anything to you?" Alphard asked.

"Everyone knows the name. I thought she was no longer alive. How could she be your incubator with such an orbit difference?" Aires asked then unrolled his monitor and entered *Norma*. Before he got her response he shouted out, "Wow! Unbelievable! I saw at 226A her pedal away with vigor; A female of 132 orbits." He then entered Alphard and saw 98 orbits and a long list of accomplishments. The brilliant female with endless energy standing next to him was more than twice his orbits.

222-Alphard

Why do you look at me so strangely, Aires? She asked. "I'm having difficulty comprehending your genes. Your donor is still pedaling. Why did your incubator join the mating pool late in her fertile years?" Aires had a long list of questions to ask her but was cut short by Almaaz. "Aires, we do have to go because Scorpio's bounce just finished and I want to be in our dwelling before he returns. If you wish to converse with Alphard in detail, I know it will take a lot of time to absorb what she has accumulated, so meet with her in your next phase off. I'm sure she will share her beliefs," said Almaaz heading for the exit. "Can I give you a hug, Alphard? You are a person that I am going to spend a lot of time with, I do hope that you will enlighten me on your thoughts about your donor's and your own research projects, I hate to leave now, but my offspring needs some family attitudes reinforced by our presence when he returns," said Aires. Alphard gave him a hug nearly as firm as the one he received upon arrival.

Almaaz and Aires pedaled to the tube entrance and did not converse for the first five minutes. "That female is not of the ordinary kind. Almaaz, did you suspect that she was that many orbits/" With your research into the low magnetic pull field, do you feel that may intertwine with her thoughts on superstition on the fourth dimension" "I just became aware of her serious thoughts shortly before you arrived. I'll have to have some discussions with you and maybe we could delve into the unknown. Interesting, but most of those beliefs end up on the tube to nowhere." Almaaz said, puffing from the generation number she had set.

223-Scorpio Bounce game

From the tube exit to the short pedal to their dwelling, the conversation was nothing but Alphard. Scorpio should have returned by now but had not. Aires unrolled his monitor to view the bounce game and saw the score tied for the third time overtime. They awakened from their quiet time by Scorpio's loud shouts, "Look at this!" He unrolled his monitor and replayed his bounce game. Sitting up groggily on their mats they saw what Scorpio programmed. "That was you? Wow! How on earth did you manage to get by the defensive back? With a move like that, you will be chosen for the area team!" said Almaaz, now wide awake.

"With a play like that you should have added incentive to complete some quality work for your industrial drawings. That was a great move," Aires said moving toward Scorpio. "And that deserves one of the greatest hugs you have ever gotten from me. I was never that good."

"To win was great but out maneuvering that #8 took a lot of replays. She is the greatest player ever," Scorpio said with a very excited voice.

"Who do you mean She?" asked his donor,

"That female and I were always on opposing teams. That gave me a lot of time to study her offense and defensive moves. You are going to hear a lot about Cepella. She is 3 orbits before mine and is fearless. I was attracted to her in our first game 2 orbits ago. I doubt if we will ever compete again because we're at the borderline of that weight class. The 4 teams in our division will have only 10 chosen for the area competition." No sooner he said that when he was buzzed.

224-Bounce and school

A list of then players was shown and Scorpio became more excited about Cepella's name than he did his own. "This is it! I made it! I had the feeling that I would! I made it! Thank you, judges! Thank you, teammates! Thank you my most loving donor and incubator! It is from you that I did so well! Thank you! Thank you!"

Almaaz and Aires embraced him with tears of joy pouring from his donor. Slowly Aires had to bring his offspring back to earth and face the realities of what his priorities must be. Aires unrolled his monitor and brings brought up Scorpio's Industrial Drawing class and he grudgingly showed the quality and percentage of completions to Almaaz. "Those are so very close to what I would have as being acceptable. He has 8 rotations before the 3 rotations pedal to the area competition games. I'm sure they will be done. I will go even further than that," Almaaz emphasized, "they will be done. Right, my Bouncer?"

"Incu, for you anything," he said with a huge smile. Scorpio unrolled his monitor. He asked it to show a few drawings that were completed and ready to be handed in. The beam that he chose for the ravine anchor for a tube was not accepted because it was the wrong size. He chose one that was one size too small. He felt that to be on the economic side, it would be OK if the stress was only .004K and over. He had 6 more drawings and the complexity of them would take some time to complete. He was more than sure that they would be graded in about 3 rotations, giving him ample time to correct any errors he might make.

225-Myths

"Scorpio, I have no doubts that you will have your duties completed in ample time. I really do not want to distract you but I want to get your feelings on something that your donor and I were just confronted with. Your orbits plus new technology being introduced, have you ever heard anything about superstition? Asked Almaaz.

"That is one word that we thoroughly discussed on our group holo. Am I right in saying that it is a belief founded on irrational feelings especially based on fear? I've seen what was done in the Old Era with dolls with pins, or breathing in smoke from ground bones of reptiles being burnt. The one I found that was most ridiculous was people gazing into a glass ball and predicting some body's future.

The Sand People we are monitoring now use blood from chickens. There were so many other false beliefs it was humorous. I could go on and on about them, but," he said with a huge smile, "I have work to do." "I'll have to admit. Scorpio, your frontal reasoning lobe has developed sooner than mine had at your stage in life. One more thing, please; How much thought have you given to the other dimensions?" asked Aires.

"Some. We have been given seeds of curiosity of our past. Science has developed so many theories about what happened orbits and orbits ago. The last one was molecular arrangements of fossils. That one was debated last phase. It's a little too far advanced for me to comprehend, so that thought will have to wait," said Scorpio. "Why are you bringing that subject up with me? I'm still curious to why our move here was your idea and was not discussed with Incu. Your visit with the bead lady sure brought some spark into our dwelling," said Scorpio

226-Beads

Almaaz queried her mate, "What was the secret of yours? This is the first time that something like this has happened. Were you afraid of exposing your mystical feelings about the beads? I was perfectly content at our last location. I had thoughts of them too; but to make a move of this magnitude is surprising to me. Are there more secrets hidden in your cranial closet? Now that the beads one is exposed and we are relocated, bring all of what you expect to explore out in the open. I have no intentions of discouraging your path to how they came into being. In fact, after knowing Alphard, I would probably be more aggressive in that pursuit than you. I'm a little perturbed for you not confiding in me. That's all. I'll get over it. Scorpio, your innocence is to be commended. Donor and I will keep you posted of our findings. You better get yourself organized on your learning project."

Incu was all wound up and could have talked for hours. She had feelings of not being one with Aires. One second she knew that he would do nothing to harm her. The next second she would say to herself, "Why didn't he tell me?" He does show all kinds of affection. Then why such a secret? It's not a secret and he probably forgot to mention it. He knew that the area we left was comfortable and so is this one. The more she debated within herself, the more doubt entered her mind. Aires saw her discomfort and the only thing that would ease the situation was, "Quiet time". All three unrolled their mats and were "out" in a matter of minutes. Incu was the first one up. She unrolled her monitor and entered beads. It did show an example of one. It also showed a string of them as an ornament around an Old Era person's neck. They were made of different materials such 231A as glass, pearls, diamonds or even kernels of corn. What could be so special about beads?

227-Beads

What was so special about a string of beads? Why Alphard was so mystical attracted to them? Why did Incu bring up the subject of superstition? Were Alphard and her incubator alone in the mystery or were there others? Almaaz was mesmerized and drawn into the whirlpool and seemed to be in a trance of another dimension when. "My next three phases on duty will give you ample time to explore our new attraction," said Aires.

"The low magnetic experiment dwelling here does not have the same equipment as I used to "toying" with, but they will suffice. If the staff has the same drive as the ones we left behind, I will have less time for Alphard than you will," Almaaz said.

Scorpio awakened in pain then rushed to the private place. Exiting from it he seems so relieved like a great burden was removed from him. He returned to his mat and on his monitor was a list of drawings to complete. Wind sway of 30 KPH on a tube suspended between two anchor piers one hundred meters apart. Forty KPH. Fifty KPH. The list asked for drawings of the same section with wind increments of 10 KPH to the point where the tube would be torn from its mooring to the pillars. The correct answers were easily available on charts; but the mathematical formulas and his calculations had to be shown. He ate a few pellets. Then with a stylus, he started his chore on his monitor. On the left upper quadrant were formulas to choose from. The bottom left had the specs on the material used on the tubes.

228-Beads

She heard of rumors of the Old Era peoples using beads for meditation. Any use of meditation these rotations were considered superstition. Facts were the only reason to follow. Facts. Reality of numbers. Holos were programmed to give exciting effects to a myriad of situations knowingly faked: Walking on the moon in a bounce suit, chasing reptiles on Mars in a tropical forest. Many other Holos were available to enhance the imagination. Almaaz entered sweat beads, liquid beads on a solid surface and again she entered necklace beads only to get the same results as the one she previously entered. She tried to bring up Old Era mystical beliefs, but got no results. She thought to herself, "WHY?" There was no forbidden literature or history that she knew of. Tubers were given complete access to all and everything; or were they?

"You sure are engrossed in your monitor," said Aires as he rolled over on his mat. "I've been watching you for the past few minutes. Can I have a glimpse of what's up?"

"Sure, I have no secrets. Now that the reason why we are here is out in the open, let's go full force into the unknown. Beads are slightly mentioned as an ornament hanging around the neck with no other special reason," said Almaaz.

Scorpio, now awakened by their conversation mentioned, "If it's not found, bring up ballot issues on beads. Almaaz tried with no results. "Try ballot meditations," added Aires.

"Nothing. Do you think that there is another name used for the ballot issue?" Incu asked. "If there is one, I'm sure Alphard or her Incubator would know."

229-Micro magnetism

"My duties are calling me. It will be three phases until I have the opportunity to follow up on what is totally foreign to us." Aires rolled up his mat, tucked in his monitor and pedaled to the tube entrance.

"Incu, I have been fascinated by caterpillars ever since I can remember. They have been pushed aside for now, but I still want a few moments for some studies on them. The complete metamorphosis of two completely different forms is all tied into one. How can that be? It brings up the same feelings about the fourth dimension. Can we be something different in another time? There must be something there," said Scorpio.

"How is it that at your youthful orbits you have such deep thoughts? Elderly scholars usually delve into them, especially the ones that have difficulty pedaling," said Incu.

"I really don't know. You are my incubator and know our genetic history better than I. Were there any others that had something similar to my abilities at my orbits?" he asked.

"It is difficult to compare. In fact I would not even venture into that path of thought just to prove your status. Pride might sneak in the back entrance and cause you to gloat and seek added compensations. Let's just be thankful that you have the ability to reason as much as you do," joyfully answered his incubator. "Next phase, a new magnetic detector is being freighted here that can detect one-hundred thousandths of a Tesla. It's going to be exciting for me to have full use of it. It was brought about by an accident by an interstellar technician then developed fully by an engineer from our last area. You might be interested in it." Then she tried to add a little humor, "The legs of your little bugs are coordinated by micro-magnetism."

230-Sands ballot

Incu and Scorpio got buzzed at the same time. Each unrolled their monitor to find: TWELVE PERSONS FROM THE TEN AREAS

OF THE SANDS PEOPLE TO BE TRANSPORTED TO OUR COAST TRAINING FACILITY. ONE MOON BEFORE EACH IS RETURNED WITH ONE-HUNDRED RINGED MALES AND ALL BEGINNING TUBE MATERIAL.

They read it and Scorpio said, "I'm qualified to go. How do I get my name on the list? It would be exciting." Incu replies, "This is the first time in my generation that anything like this has happened. I doubt if you would meet the criteria for a start up of the tubes. With your energy you might be involved with pellet distribution. I truthfully would not like to see you be part of it because of the unruliness of the Sand People. They have been monitored for some time on what they practiced and most likely still are. You would not be able to cope. Bring current observation cameras on the most devastated area. That one on the north exit of the river to the ocean. Do you have it? Focus in on the smoke coming from the dwelling, if you want to call it that." "Are those flies on the little children's faces? They should have their suits on. Where are all the other incubators for that many young ones? Look up the hill a 100 meters or so. What are dogs eating? Is that what I think it is?" Scorpio said with disgust. Incu focused in on the remains of an adult male nearly dismembered by the hungry animals. How could a society allow itself to degenerate into such conditions? Tears rolled down her face, and then she focused back on the hut. Eight young surrounded a prone female. They all were huddled together facing outward. "Do you want to enter into another world with these conditions?" asked Incu.

231-Sand ballot

"This has not been voted on yet," Incu said while wiping her tears. Scorpio excitingly said, "I'm going to give my yes and I wish I could give more votes if I could." "Give the whole situation some thought before you wildly give your consent for this huge undertaking. Do you know how many mega watts are going to be needed before the first voyage is made with materials?. Everyone who votes yes will have to donate kilowatts to the gigantic project. It's nice to feel compassion for the humans that are existing on nothing but bare dirt." Incu added, "Bring up a list of materials that The Record Keeper has on the last acceptance to the tubes."

Scorpio did so, and then had some second thoughts about his vote. The list of materials needed was over 100 lines. He noticed that there were items that are not being used in construction these rotations. Iron beams were long made obsolete. Copper cables had disappeared. His mechanical drawings had lists of currently used of items available. "Incu, how does anyone predict what is needed?"

"The Record Keeper is the only source. All of the entries of human habitation were entered with their physical conditions. The remainder was done by IT. We could do it line by line now, but it would take nearly an orbit to do so. How do you feel with only this much research done?" asked Incu.

"There's more? Isn't it all done? The Record Keeper did it all," said Scorpio.

"The greatest yet to come is the attitude of the Tubers after a vote. I know the vote will determine if we help or not, but if you think it is best that we do have 75% or more, how will the others accept defeat?" she asked.

232-Sand ballot

"Incu, if something like this has not occurred in your generation, how would anyone know how to vote? I know that they could do some research into it and most likely they would all come to the same conclusion wouldn't they?" asked Scorpio

"Not necessarily. Some might vote yes out of compassion, some for new Tube places to go; more area for Tube security. The no's don't have the extra energy to contribute, or they are comfortable as it is, or fear contracting new diseases. The world is made of many parts and how you vote on this issue will bring changes, definitely for the better for the Sand People. It just might make it better for us in the long run. Voting allows us to make decisions and whatever is decided, we will have to accept the results," said Incu in a mournful voice. "Buzz anyone you know. If your mind is made up now, vote copy everyone you know. You might even send it to those who will be selected to join the first 1,000 to voyage to the Sands."

Scorpio had some tough decisions to make. He had the bounce tournaments, his fling competition and mechanical drawings that were due and regular studies. Then there was music which he had participated in a moon, friends to visit and he knew that he could hardly accomplish all of his requirements, and then add the Sands project on top of it all. He did have some time to jot down his thoughts about it, though. How does someone start this kind of request and have all of the people he knows respond? His thoughts were settled very quickly by Incu saying, "Quiet time."

233-Record Keeper list

Aires got buzzed with the following:

Record Keeper

Directors of the following facilities are to list personnel to be available if the Sand People are going to be admitted to our society.

Communication--Class 1-2-3

Water Purification--Class1-2-3

Medical Administrators--Class 1

Medical--Class 1-2-3

Dietitians--Class 2-3

Dwelling erectors--Class1-2-3

Tube installers--Class 1-2-3

Bicycle Administrators--Class 1-2-3

Transportation--(land) Class 1-2-3

Transportation--(sea) Class 1-2-3

Archeology--Class 1

Identification: Sands that have been found to be free of communicable diseases and/or have a survival possibility of one moon.
List to be available one rotation after the results of the vote are known.

234-Sand ballot

Scorpio took a 15 minute power nap. He didn't even have to repeat the caterpillar thing over and over. As soon as he awoke he unrolled his monitor and started to write: The vote that will be taken in five rotations will make the people of the Sand have something that will be greatly appreciated. Each day hundreds are dying from animal predators, lack of food and sanitation. Last orbit the number of Tubers incapacitated by disease were from a bacteria that originated with the Sands. Please focus on their land and view the misery that is a breeding ground for new and perhaps more deadly virus or bacteria strains.

PLEASE VOTE YES

Incu was keeping herself busy contacting Alphard. She should have answered Almaaz's buzz. She tries one more time and gave up for the moment. "I see you are writing the Sand vote notice. May I see it before you send it?" "Please. I wish you would. This is a first for me. I knew about the Sand People for some time, but this vote is something I had given an opportunity to concentrate on. I'll send it to only your monitor," Scorpio said.

After reading it twice, Incu said "I marvel at your ability. You have even not reached your 16th orbit! Your donor and I have mixed a superior offspring. The only thing that I would add is the number of our incapacitated and dead. The middle of the epidemic, 3,027 were ill and died. The bacteria detector was a little late in accurately naming the virus which did so much damage. "One more thing you should add is that mating age will be lowered to repopulate the Sand area."

235-Sand ballot

Scorpio wanted to change one more thing. We appreciate that they voted 95%. They clearly had their self-preservation instinct intact. The 5 rotations was a known fact too. How could he make it appealing for a yes vote? The vote that will be taken in five 5 rotations will be greatly appreciated by the people of the Sand. Each day hundreds are dying from animal predators, lack of food and sanitation. Last orbit, Tubers were incapacitated by a rare disease that originated with the Sands. Please focus on their land and view the misery that is a breeding ground for new and, perhaps more deadly virus or bacteria strains.

PLEASE VOTE YES

He felt that the focus on their land should be first, their misery the second, their disease affect on us third and last, the mating age.

PLEASE VOTE YES ON THE SANDS BALLOT.

The yes was lost in the notice and he wanted more emphasis on it.

YES

PLEASE VOTE YES ON THE SANDS BALLOT

Please focus on their land

Misery at its worst. Each day hundreds are dying from lack of love.

Our 3,027 ill and one death last orbit was from a disease originating from the Sands.

Mating age will be lowered to repopulate the Sands area.

236-Sand ballot

Scorpio entered his list of personal contacts, and then entered recently ringed males from every section of the Tubes. One female, Cepella, was the one whose he most wanted to know. SEND. His ballot efforts were completed.

The next rotation a list of contributors to the YES vote was much longer than to the NO. In brackets were the orbits of the contributors,

In the 15 orbit group there was only one. Zero in the 16 and five in the 17. The numbers increased with 37 orbits having the highest, 54,327. There were only four more rotations before the vote was to be cast.

This was the first time that Scorpio had any interest in a ballot. He viewed the Sand People's misery often. He tried to hurry his drawings, and when submitted, they were rejected. Again he corrected and submitted and again had another failure. Quiet time was a must. Leg coordination. Leg coordination. Over and over again, but it did not seem to work. Why was he getting himself so excited about an issue that he had no control over? Leg Coordination. Caterpillar. Leg Coordination. Caterpillar. Leg Coordination.

Sitting up groggy on his mat, Scorpio did not realize that he had slept so long. "I must have needed the rest." He opened his monitor and was going to check if there were any responses to his ballot opinion then decided quickly that his drawing were of greater importance. Checking all of the data that he entered, he noted that a simple formula from one of his first classes was missing from the stress entry. Simple error. Lack of concentration on the task at hand. Thank you.

237-The perfect drawing

His next drawing was Laying Bicycle Runners on Beach Sand. The only givens were the grade of the sand and the distance from the water to the nearest vegetation. This one had the least amount of references, but he noted, "Only <u>one</u> attempt for the perfect drawing will be accepted." He had to concentrate on this one. Reading all of the needed references once was not enough to satisfy him. One chance was all he would have.

Incu entered and saw her offspring totally engrossed in his duty. That was nice to see. Quietly she tip toed toward the private place then heard, "That was an easy one." "What is an easy one?" she asked. "Oh, I didn't even know you were in the dwelling," he answered, "It's about my second drawing. Would you like to check it out?"

"It will have to wait for a few minutes," she replied and rushed off. In a matter of less than five minutes, she returned with three packets, body waste, body cleaning wand and suit cleaning residue. She placed them in the Pick Up container near their front entrance.

"This was your first. Now that you know how it is done, it will be a stepping stone for all of the others similar to this one. Why did you submit it so many times?" she asked.

"In a hurry. Did not have a stress formula. Simple mistake. Quiet time did its thing. How is my second one?" he asked.

"Just glancing at what you have down so far, something's wrong," Incu noticed.

"It sure is. In the reference it states that a slight bow must be made to allow for the expansion and contraction. The runner ends, because of no anchors, have to be solidly connected. Thank you, Incu," he said with excitement. "So that's why we don't have a straight away on the beach exit."

238-School work

"You will have to do the last one yourself. I shouldn't have assisted you at all. Incubators can't resist their loving instinct. I took my quiet time while visiting Alphard so now it's clean up time." She grabbed the long handled wand and started with the ceiling which was curved to the side walls. She moved the wand back and forth, following the lined texture of the design. The floor was done in the same way. Removing the soiled tissue from the wand, Almaaz placed it into a deposit bag at the entrance with the others she had deposited just moments before. The pick-up cycle steered it toward the his next packages then stopped. "Remember me?" the peddler asks Almaaz? "Sure do. For a three, you sure picked a non-demanding generation. Watts are watts no matter where they come from. You know, your timing could not have been more perfect. My offspring has a drawing to make of the space propulsion ramp. Could you just peek at how he doing? Now don't do it all for him," she smiled. "What brings you here?"

"Long story. Get to that later. I will, if you will finish this route for me. The watts will be credited to my account." he emphasized. "If you have never done this before, just follow the planned route on the bicycle's monitor. It will tell you all you need to know."

Almaaz could not believe that she had the designer of the space project here.

"Incu, this one is going to take a little longer than I thought. I just scrolled through 200 lines and there are more than that to go. I might have it finished before the Sand ballot. I think I'm going to need another quiet time," said Scorpio.

239-Alcor waste pickup

"That is a very good idea," said Alcor unrolling his mat.

"Who are you?" asked Scorpio.

"After quiet time. Your incubator is pedaling my waste pick-up route while I meddle with your next project. Quiet time," repeated Alcor.

"Leg coordination. Caterpillar." Scorpio mumbled a few times and before he could go to sleep, snoring was vibrating the dwelling. Scorpio turned up the volume of the relaxing music to overcome the noise, but it seemed that he could feel it through his suit. After a brief nap Scorpio walked up to the now quiet stranger, still sleeping. He scanned the male to find that he was the author of the drawings. What luck! He feels that his last drawing will be perfect. Browsing through the remainder of the lines, Scorpio started again. How on this earth did anyone ever come up with this design? Or invent and coordinate this massive project to get not only to other Tube areas on our planet but to other planets too? His presence here is like a star from the heavens shining on Scorpio. His guest rolled over and suddenly the whole inside of the dwelling just smelled rotten. Scorpio gagged, rushing to the private place and used his watts to place the exhaust fan to its highest setting. He held his breath to the exit and sat outside waiting for the sleeping bear to come out of hibernation. He wondered where Incu was until she buzzed him explaining why she is riding the waste pick-up route. "You're so lucky," he replied without giving any details."

Sitting up, Alcor mumbled, "I'm used to living alone, so if what I think happened here is done again, just leave or grin and bear it. OK, I will go through the whole project verbally once, and then I leave. Is that clear?"

240-Alcor drawings

"I might over-extend what is needed for you for your drawing. What I will say probably will help you understand why this design was perfected. First, the ramp that you are looking at was not our latest. The many launches would have been able to carry three percent more cargo if the axis to the earth were only one degree of parallel to the equator. We lose one way and gain another, so let's not get into that when it does not apply to your task. I get carried away you know. I'm a little excited that I can refresh some of my first designs. To help you get the overall picture, first you must ask yourself, 'Why is this ramp necessary?" He rambled on about his first drawing, other scientists, their names and accomplishments, places he had been to, his heaviest payload, near-miss of a deer on a ramp, and his donor's encounter with a panther when Scorpio cut in, "It sure is nice to be given most all of that, but I had that three orbits ago in "Space Purpose" and it does not help me with the drawings."

"Sorry about that. I just love my work so much the peripheral tidbits come out with vigor. OK. Let's get to the text. The first section is about the purpose of the project. The second, design of the ramp. Material and energy for propulsion follow. Your knowledge so far from what I see in your last two drawings will be enough. Your drawings for the ramp could nearly be copied from the text. Bring up the ramp on your monitor. Show a launch. Great. Now how much more do you need? It's so simple. Here comes your Incubator, so I have to leave. It was ever so nice to meet you." He gave Almaaz a nod as he exited toward the tube, and have the packet trailer delivered to the automatic testing site.

241-Alcor's brilliance

"Was the visit worthwhile for you, my budding world traveler?"
"By all means. He told me more than any of the texts could have. So many times the trivial things add to the subject. He sure had enough time. Look at this! Mastered the Boolean theorem at 17 orbits. I'm still working on string vibrations and trigonometry. Why is it that such a brilliant mind never procreated? His offspring at half the genius would have surpassed most everyone. I wish I could have more contact with him."
"My little flower of the future. there is more to life than procreating. The most important thing for Tubers is that any new life be loved and given emotional security by physical contact. The most harm any of us can do to the young is not to love them. His interests were so dominating he had no time to participate in wanding a stinky and messy newborn's anus. His physical desires," Incu redirected the conversation, "You will have orbits of education into your responsibilities if your wish is to procreate. You have a task at hand to concentrate on, so allow yourself one look at the orbit schedule for males and you will find that this very subject will be addressed."
Scorpio projected his drawing onto the dwelling wall and matched it to the one that Alcor had made. He made them identical, and then added a little something. He put in a deer at the lower altitudes where they might wander. He felt proud of himself then got a rude awakening when his monitor buzzed announcing low wattage reserve. He had so many things to do and using his monitor had top priority.

242-Low watts

"Incu, I am going to pedal some freight in the tubes now. There is a bounce game at exit 2520. I'll push a load to that exit, play some bounce and I should return home in about three hours. Donor checked to see if my drawings were done. Is there anything that you might want before I leave?" he asked. "Just a hug." Incu answered. Scorpio entered the tube and saw no carts, but decided to park until one does come by. He could create watts without one, but so many more would be added to his reserve if he towed or pushed a cart. He heard some squeaking noises coming from the bottleneck-causing cart. He hooked onto it and had a difficult time pedaling to the nearby exit and delivered it to the wheel repair dwelling. The attendant gave Scorpio 500 additional watts for his volunteering. If he had not volunteered, service personnel would have to be dispatched to remove the errant cart. He reentered the tube with one of the long line of freight carts to be hooked onto. Unhooking before exiting the tube, was only too eager to get into a vigorous game of bounce.

There were no bounce uniforms available, two other players waiting before him. This was not a championship, so continuous play was in effect. When exhaustion caused the player to exit the game, he removed his outfit for the first in line. When Scorpio saw how sluggish some of the ones on the field were, he knew that his wait would not be too long. He unrolled his monitor to see how many responses he had from his vote yes notice. There were many. Only one stated, "No way." Reading what came after that puzzled Scorpio. "At 108 orbits, I have no need for any new adventures," signed, Sirus..

243-Sirus's vote

"No wonder he had to care for the youngsters. Having no friends to enlighten his life pushed him into a corner that was nearly like a Lonesome Place. Scorpio buzzed him with a note: Quiet time. Scorpio checked what time that was entered. It was long over a normal quiet time and buzzed Sirus again. "Oh, it's you again," he grumbled. "It's nice to see you," cheerfully replied Scorpio. "What's with this yes vote? There has not been an addition to our sphere in my lifetime. All things are going fine. Why add new stresses and even a cut in our watt generation to give overactive groins and greed our ways. I doubt if we can convert them to the disciplined ways we have. They are next to animals. I looked at the river you wanted and all that I see is bodies floating to the sea. They cannot have any respect at all if they just dump the dead into the water. Do you know how many generations it will take, if we do accept them by 75% vote, to have some semblance of sanity? After the tubes are installed, all that you will have from them is Grade 1 peddlers. My mind is made up and I have contacted everyone I know to do the same." Sirus was firm.

Did you fall from your bike because your dizziness was that caused by bacteria we contracted from them? I have to agree with most of what you said but I cannot see anyone living under the conditions they are in now. Is there anything I can do for you to vote yes the next rotation?" begged Scorpio.

"Get me my vigor that I had before I contracted those horrible bacteria," he demanded.

"You know I can't do that." Then Scorpio countered with, "If their ways are not changed by us giving them a place in our society, a worse virus or bacteria might do all of us in."

244-Sirus upset

"Young male, where are you getting your philosophy from? Most your age would be bouncing, flinging or doing some other non-productive activities. I have been pedaling my entire life and always have had enough in reserve. My incubator nurtured me to do the best I could do in whatever I did," rambled the old male until Scorpio cut in, "So do just enough and draw a line to your "best," and do no more?"

"This is the first conversation that I have had like this and it is making me nervous. I need a quiet time," said Sirus with what was now a high pitched voice. Scorpio's monitor shows in very big letters, "QUIET TIME!"

The next rotation the vote occurred. Voting buzzed Scorpio and the usual once a moon request to lower the mating age. He voted yes, because of the need for society, and anticipation for the hopeful upcoming admission of the Sands People. Being a ringed male had this responsibility added to his other juvenile activities.

The name Struve appeared on Scorpio's list of personal contacts and he buzzes him. When Scorpio looked at him on his monitor, he did not look much older than when they last played bounce over an orbit ago. "What's with the buzz?" was Struve's first words.

"I'm letting everyone I know about the next rotation's vote on The Sand People. I hope you have some thoughts on that," Scorpio said.

"I wouldn't vote to admit them if I could," Struve blurted out.

"What do you mean?" questioned Scorpio.

245-Struve

"In the first place, I have not been ringed. And the second, the feeling in our dwelling is that if they are allowed to follow their non-planned existence, they will all die and their neighbors are lurking by their boundaries to just walk in and take over. How is your bounce doing? I just had my first fling two phases ago and did great. All of my wattage is going toward flinging. It's super great. I felt like a leaf floating for kilometers. I love the sensation that just the tiniest arm or hip movement can maneuver. I did not make a landing. I was about 50 meters above the ground and the angle of my descent was too great and the automatic helium safety balloon went BAM and I floated down softly. All I have been doing lately is hauling freight, freight and more freight. It's so much fun! The holo practice is OK, but the real thing is so great! My donor took the championship four times. If you need the best for instructions I know he will only be too glad to help. I haven't bounced in two moons. I have enough exercise pedaling. Flinging is so great," rambled Struve.

Scorpio had the vote only on his mind and had a few buzzes to make so he congratulated him on his first flight. "Are any of your procreators available now? I would like to speak to one, please.

"Sure, both are here. Which one do you want first to change your mind? Donor, this is Scorpio. Remember him? They were the ones with the prettiest flowers around their dwelling," says Struve focusing his monitor to past the fling champion, his donor.

"I just found from Struve that your dwelling is against the admission of the Sands People to our society and I wish I could convince you otherwise," pleaded Scorpio.

246-Struve

"Let me tell you something first. I was a scout and have some scars to show my past close call. A couple of threes in the Veterinary lab needed a cat. Not just an ordinary feline which we had enough of. They wanted a special one from the Sands. We were told that it was going to be extinct. To the Sands, it was food. We were mini-subbed and had rope ends hidden in the sandy beach. We cornered one, only for it to climb up a leafless tree; the only tree around in broad daylight. Out of a cave, which we were not aware of, comes the dirtiest person I have ever seen. He returns to the cave and comes out shooting the cat. We took off for the ropes, yelled to the mini-sub to GO and it was then I felt a severe pain in my right arm." He pulled his suit aside and Scorpio saw the obvious scar. "The place smelled horrible. Our daily testing dwelling smells better. You don't want any of them anywhere near us or have anything to do with them. They're filthy! It would take ten generations for them just to learn how to pedal." "I'm sure you have seen our start in the tubes. We've come a long way. Please view our first generation scenes and give it another thought. I would like you to vote yes," pleaded Scorpio. Struve's incubator came into focus." Thank you for buzzing. Have your rings been uncomfortable? Do you have flowers around your new dwelling?

How is your incubator? Has your donor made any improvements on his new assignment?"

Scorpio felt that something was amiss by all of her questions. She could have obtained all of the ones she asked except the first. Sounds like she was being dominated by the male. "The answer to the rings question is that pain contributes to respect. No flowers, just "no water" plants. Incu is doing fine. Why don't you give her a buzz. Donor has his hands full with the addition of his curiosity about the beads."

247-Struve

"What's this about beads? Struve's donor said. The cruddy killer had some around his neck. Let me show you what I viewed at the time of his crazy attack," He brought up on his monitor to show Scorpio. "I could not figure out what the small pieces were made from. Here let me get you a closer look. See? They all look like tiny vertebra from something. To me, they look like bragging rights to something that he killed. Every time I look at them all I can think of is the stink!" He shouted like a crisis existed right now.

"That sure was a close call. Did anyone ever get one of those cats?" After Scorpio asks the question, he knew immediately that was the wrong question to ask.

For another five minutes, he rambled on while Scorpio forced himself to seem interested. Had this male frozen himself in time to that one incident? Had he lost the capacity to show some emotions to the real purpose of our existence? Scorpio thought, "I'm glad he is not my donor." Feeling within himself he could not convince this tuber. Scorpio tried unsuccessfully to quit the call. Another few minutes of the same, he asked if he to talk to Struve again and was granted his wish. "Struve, I have to make a few more buzzes. Give your incubator a hug and remember what I am trying to do for the next rotation's vote. Thank you and goodbye," said Scorpio. "What an environment to mature in." Poor Struve he said to himself.

How large is this earth he is walking on? It's immense! Huge! Scorpio felt content and had more than enough to occupy himself. Why was he burdened with this new activity? Now he doubted his involvement on the next rotation's vote. Scorpio gave himself a quiet time and was sound asleep after the third leg coordination. Caterpillar..leg…

248-Cepella

Cepella had her best game of bounce in some time. Her energy level had not lost its touch. The bounce game did not have male and female leagues. The weight of the player determined which league one would play in.. Every 10 Kilogram had its own weight class. Cepella was 3 orbits older than Scorpio. When she took off her playing suit she noticed that she was buzzed by Scorpio. "Yes?" she responded to his return buzz.

"Why are you all sweated? Just finish a game of bounce?" he asked?

"Had a great one," then she turned her head and tried to mask a cough.

"What's with the cough?" he questions.

"Nothing much. I think it's an allergy," she stifled another small one.

"I do hope that is it. I'm out for yes votes on the next rotations Sand vote. Have you given it very much attention?" He asked

"Hasn't everyone? It's been many orbits since another land joined us. It seems that everyone in our dwelling area is for it." Then she coughed.

"We have so many things in common except the 'you know what'," he said. "When was the last time you entered the physical testing machine? If you haven't, please do so quickly. You are the only person that I really enjoy smashing on the field."

"My semi-orbit one is due in a moon but I'll give it a visit this next phase. Do you think that I could talk to your donor about something?" she asked.

"Just buzz the administrator in 7520 area. He knows a lot about your bounce ability. He is quite busy with anticipation of a yes vote next rotation." Scorpio thanked her for her affirmative vote.

249-Cepella

Scorpio immediately buzzed Donor and mentioned his friend's problem. Donor assured him he would expedite her health problems to the appropriate channel. He brought up Cepella's health records and reviewed them carefully. He took them to the Master Physician in the next dwelling and found her on her monitor. He waited for a few moments, and then saw her face turn red. "Wow that must have been some communication. Is something wrong? Is there anything that I can do to help?" he eagerly asked.

"It was from the far east province. Seems that there is an outbreak of those rare bacteria again. We had it controlled and the rascal mutated slightly so all of the vaccines that were given are useless. Prepare yourselves for an onslaught. I have to put these health dwellings in a lock down. The Master physician buzzed her assistant and commanded that the 22 unoccupied dwellings be sterilized immediately. Her next call was to Supply and had them put in full production body suits. When she was questioned as to how many? The reply was, "Don't stop until told to do so!"

Aires was buzzed and saw the young female that Scorpio talked a lot about. Before she could say one word he said with a firm voice, "I see you are at the bounce field and you must stay exactly where you are right now. Do not allow anyone near you. If you can, take the bounce suit with you. If anyone should approach you yell out CONTAGIOUS. A medical staff person will be with you shortly with a body suit. It will be placed on you. Do not move! Do you understand?"

Her monitor showed the sky, so Aires transferred to the field monitor and focuses on the bounce suit rack and saw her lying prone. He could do nothing for her. It was just a matter of minutes later and the medical team "suited her" and flagged the area where she lay.

250-Epidemic

It was a three day pedal to the province that was struck with the bacteria. Was there someone that brought it with them here? Aires told the Tube Director to stop all traffic going west of the far east province immediately. There was no questioning the Health Administrator. The peddlers exited at the first ramp and the freight just parked on the runners. Everyone in the Tube Lands was buzzed and told about the epidemic that they have just been struck with. No one could move anywhere. The only personnel that could be mobile were the food, water and packet pickup with their trailers. They were in body suits with a filter as a back pack. The food was pellets were generic. They would suffice until a decision could be made when it was thought that the bacterium was under control. Many took quiet time. A music group that was heading for a competition on the far east started to play some oldies. No one seemed to be in panic mode except the grade three administrators.

Chess boards were brought out. One champion had ten set up for all comers at once. Jugglers came out of the "wood work," an old saying which had no meaning to anyone. Some juveniles started a bounce game without suits and were quickly stopped by the enforcement regulators. There were enough health problems awaiting them now. They could pass and run, but there would absolutely no contact. Aires put emphasis on absolutely. It was just like the third moon quiet time.

A juggler, who was going east and forced to exit, unrolled his monitor and summoned medical help. In a matter of minutes, he was suited and carted off to the medical facility. The same was done to all of the pregnant females-even those without any symptoms. They had to stay in their enclosed suits and no one was allowed near their dwellings except other suited medical personnel. They were given priority over all others.

251-Cepella dies

The 22 dwellings had only a few patients with the epidemic symptoms. Aires was hoping that it was just a scare and not the real thing. All Scorpio could do now was to use this time to get more yes votes for next rotation's vote. He buzzed Sirus, "Yes I know. So what? It's panic by the threes. The far east province had 37. That's not much."

"This is the first rotation. Just do me a favor, please. If when you awake the next rotation and there are more guaranteed, buzz the same ones you did and tell them to vote yes. Is that asking too much?" Scorpio pleaded. "Young male, you are something else. I have to admire your persistence. If I wanted a friend it would be you. I'm a late sleeper so before I hit the mat for the night, and there are some dramatic changes for the worse, I'll do them then. Even if I do vote yes, it is against my feelings toward them. The yes vote is only for self preservation," Sirus said.

Scorpio traced to where Cepella was taken only to find that she had died. Tears flowed down his cheeks. How could the bacteria be so deadly? She was so energetic and healthy. It had to be something else. An autopsy would be taken as soon as the morgue could perform it. He buzzed his donor for that request only to find that he had already had an emergency one ordered.

Scorpio watched her body removed from the body bag after it was scanned for any other possible cause. It was no delight to see her dead body. The scanner found a huge clot of blood just above her stomach. It was an aorta that burst. She had no pain when she fell. It was quick. This was the first person that Scorpio had any personal involvement with who had died. It was a shock. He could not believe it. It was not real.

252-Cepella dies

How could someone so full of life just fall over? Why was it not detected before? He had donor bring up her last physical and concentrate on the aorta area. He showed Scorpio there was aortal wall weakness. More would have to be researched as to why is happened. "Medical research is a must for me," he told Donor. "I admire your devotion to your friend. Give yourself some time before you make a statement like that. There will be researchers looking into why that happened. Look at the statistics on burst aortas. The chart will show you all that you want to know." He tied Scorpio's monitor to his. There was another female younger than Cepella who died. It does seem that females are more prone to it at the younger part of the chart and males totally dominate in the aged. "Scorpio, two of the most dramatic happenings will be facing you the next rotations. It's time to get yourself some rest. You are going to need it." Scorpio felt that he didn't sleep at all. The first thing he did was cast a yes vote. He wanted to be there when Cepella was placed in the ground, but the quarantine was in effect and he could only watch on his monitor. He had seen burials before, but this one was a friend. It would be an hour before it would be done. There were calls to be made on the ballot but he could not concentrate on anything else but the burial. She was such a perfect person and had so many things in common, even though she was nearly four orbits older. He lay down on his mat and stripped everything from his mind except the violent contact he had on the bounce field. She was good. The best. He kept telling himself, "It can't be true. It is not his bounce buddy. It had to be someone else." He knew that The Record Keeper did not make mistakes. The scanner identified the burst aorta with Cepella.

253-Cepella buried

Scorpio's only thought was the morgue. He wanted to follow all that was going to happen to his friend's body. The workers, wearing body suits because of the epidemic scare, cut two meters from a huge roll of white cotton cloth that was more than 3 meters wide. The cut piece was placed on a rectangular table, and then the body of Cepella was placed on it. One side of the material was pulled over her and tucked under the opposite side. The top was pulled over her face and the bottom over her feet. The other side was pulled over her and tucked under her side. She was completely wrapped. Straps were brought over to secure her to the table. The table was lifted by the workers onto a cart and bicycled to the Land of Memories.

The Land of Memories was maintained better than any other place. The memory of everyone placed here was revered. It was they who made the Tubes have such a wonderful and relaxed place to live. It was they who lived and thought how to love all that around them. His eyes were focused on the cart the whole time her body was being moved. "It can't be her" kept popping up in his mind again and again.

The cart was pedaled to a long trench that was more than two meters wide. Her body was removed from the table and placed onto the bottom of the trench that was one meter deep. The two workers who brought her there proceeded to shovel dirt over her body. A plastic plate was set on its edge one meter from the previous one buried. The first plate was being removed slowly as the hole was being filled and used for the next burial. The previously removed grass sod was placed over it all and this is her final resting place. When this bacteria epidemic is over, he wants to visit the place and pretend he will be holding her hand.

254-People dying

Where did everyone go? No one was in sight. Scorpio looked out of his dwelling and was told to remain inside by Incu. "Scorpio, there are very few more aware of the deadly bacteria than I am. I've seen how they multiply under the microscope. If it is the same one I saw last orbit, it divided five times at once. It seemed to explode when coming in contact with humans. Our dwelling filter will take a lot of health problems away but the one that I am most fearful of is just about too small to be removed. Just relax and find something to do." "I have a feeling that the Sands vote will be yes," said Scorpio unrolling his monitor to brings up a full view of all of the Sands land. The terrain has a lot of ocean beach with a rise to nearly six hundred meters. There is hardly any vegetation. Zooming in, he saw pockets of people with what seemed to be children in the middle. If this is what is going to be inherited by a yes vote, Sirus was right. How could any society degenerate to such a state? He asks for a human count and it gave 22,874. It was over 30,000 just last moon. Another moon at the pace and population will be less than 10,000. He had difficulty comprehending the situation. Boat loads of pellets were shipped. Where did the food go? He focused onto the crowd around concrete bunkers. They were holding guns. Some of them being fired at the few people trying to get close to the buildings. If the food was in them, there was no sharing being done. How was a vote under those conditions ever held? There was sure no love in this community. How was this insanity going to be converted with guns and violence? He zoomed in onto the hillside and noticed that a small fire was burning with some kind of rodent being barbecued. Zooming to the far end of the land, he saw a fairly large number of people whose conditions did not resemble what he had just seen.

255-Sands misery

Sticks that resembled a fence surrounded a village. The fence was something that was never used by the tubers. He had read in the Old Era that they kept animals from their growing crops or their huts. To him they were there to keep out the "human" animals that were hungry. How could anyone ever allow conditions to deteriorate to such a miserable level? Allow was something Scorpio could not comprehend. Allow what to happen. Allow. Everything in the tube areas were voted on and all accepted it as part of their own nature. The peace and tranquility they are now enjoying took many centuries to obtain. Sirus was right and so were Struve's procreators. What ugliness that is there now could contaminate the tubes not with invisible microbes but with immovable attitudes. "Oh Scorpio, where are you going with the 'yes' vote?" he asked himself.

Scanning the area he noticed a small structure with a board pointing up and a smaller one stuck sideways on it. He never saw that before. Next to the building were rows of formed stones. He tried to bring up on his monitor things from the Old Era, but none of that was available. Back to the Sands he saw emaciated humans. He could see some of the plants and most were brown. Lack of water was destroying the vegetation first. "I have to be on the first wave to the Sands," Scorpio thought, "I must be." Not having reached his 16th orbit though, he would have to do some serious convincing. His procreators made it well known to him many times; your frontal lobe has not been fully developed. If it were not, why am I having emotional feeling for those destitute foreigners? He wondered. His drawings were completed and the fling competition was in three rotations. His main task how after trying to get yes votes, was to visit Hydra and use her fling. Checking the responses to his request, 20 said they were going to vote yes and only one said no. He felt he could now pursue his desire to be on the first wave to the stink, drought, dead and dying and all of the other miseries of the Sands.

256-Hydra

He buzzed Hydra who responded, "Hi, my flinger buddy."
"Do you have time for another lesson?" Scorpio begged.
"Sure do. I need you to watch me on the flinger too," she returned
The fifteen minute pedal set at 27 was a speedy run for Scorpio. He buzzed Incu and told her his whereabouts and Incu said, "Now remember what I told you before, 'never be afraid to ask'. You will now have a lifelong friend and a loving one too. Enjoy and give Hydra a hug from me." Hydra had just watered all of her plants and was reading, Hints on Flinging. Scorpio walked in and seeing it on her monitor asked, "Why would a champion like yourself need such triviality?" "Ninety-nine percent of what is here I have known and some of it is not beneficial for me. It is that lonely one percent that I seek. I found one I used in the past, and it escaped my practice,

and now I ask myself how could I be so forgetful? Every fling, all of my movements are automatic. Now look at this one," she said to Scorpio.

It showed the wind direction and the slight shift of the legs to just allow the flinger to move a minute amount to the direction of the shift. "That is one that we will have to practice today," he said, "I have to give you a hug from Incu first."

"I am going to get into this unfolded banana thing first. I was using it yesterday and felt very comfortable. I will talk on each movement using the slow motion so listen without commenting," she said, then drew back her arms to fold back the wings. The energized holo engulfed the mechanism and off she went.

257-Hydra's flinger

The catapult ramp at half speed zoomed in on 18 seconds and she became a bird floating like a disc. "This is the most crucial part of the fling. Watch my arms move out in unison. You cannot see it from where you are standing, but the marble was at the end of my propulsion when I shifted the wings. From the underside all of the birds look like a saucer so you can see how having yourself exactly flat to the prevailing breeze is so crucial. You have to feel within yourself the slightest movement of the air going past you. Windsocks on the ground are everywhere, and a glance at them is very useful. It could be different at 1,000, 500, 300 meters. I want you to holo in full time and the wind directions slightly so I can show you my arm, body and leg movements."

On the holo, Scorpio watched her body moving constantly to every one of his changes. She made a sudden dip, picked up speed and was asked why. "Have you ever noticed a leaf float to the ground? It has no control. You must maintain some forward movement. If this bird was to have no forward thrust, I could have the rear of this thing lead the way to the ground." She said, "Watch this!" The front shifted down a 45 degree angle and zoom; her speed caused the built-in vibration to give her a thrill ride. Shifting her weight to the rear, she leveled then curved upward. She told Scorpio to watch her right hand push down, and banked that way. Now the left; now the right; right; left. She got herself into the landing pattern and showed the glide angle. The moment before touchdown, quick body movements allowed for a gentle landing. "Now it's your turn," she said, unstrapping herself and beckoning Scorpio to a new thrill.

258-Hydra's flinger

Scorpio had a little difficulty with the arm straps and asked Hydra to adjust the hand bars and place a mat under his chest. Strapped in and wings folded back, he was ready for propulsion. Hydra said that she would set the wind speed at 5 KPH and keep it blowing from the same direction. He then heard Ready, 3-2-1-Go! Off he went. It seemed like the real thing, vibrations and all. Watching the marble touch the tube end, he pushed out his wings with the right one still coming out a little faster to give him a tilt to the left.

"Let's back up to that part again. Notice that the ball is nearly touching the tube end. Now, coordinate your arms. Push harder with your left; Still too much right. One more time and we observe you through the rest of your flight. Now, that is much better but it need some polishing. I'll let do your own thing now all the way to the landing and comment after that so off you go, Scorpio!"

It was a dream comes true. What would he have done without the coaching of Hydra? His home holo was nothing like this one. Shifting and moving with the holo computers were amazing. The gliding gave an exhilarating feeling shifts back and forth, the down glide to pick-up speed, the upward movements, shift left, shift right then back again gave. Landing was near and he had to prepare for that. All of a sudden, he heard a POOF. "What was that?" he asked Hydra. "That sound was the helium safety balloon exploding because your angle of descent was too steep at less than 50 meters. Let's try that part again" she said. The holo was brought back to

300 meters and Scorpio was gliding again. He had to learn more patience. Slowly he came in. He was just about 5 meters from the ground and another POOF.

259-Hydra's flinger

"Tomorrow I cannot be here and your donor will be on duty. That means that you have one more day here before your first real flight. I'll be waiting for you at 900 hours on the 269th.

Scorpio unstrapped himself and asked if Hydra would like some wattage for the time she gave to him and the use of her holo and fling. "Young man, if you were 6 orbits older and I was 40 younger, I would have an eye on you. You are a pleasure to have around. The holo used less than 300 watts. If you see someone in need, give it to them, OK? Good-bye for now and give Almaaz this hug in return for the one I got from her."

Entering the tube, Scorpio heard a screech as another cart with a bad wheel barely moved along. By instinct he pushed his bike back to it, hooked up and put his generation at zero to work harder than he ever had before. This was a bad, bad one. He moved about 2 KPH when three maintenance crew workers backed up to grab onto Scorpio's bike. The four of them took it down the ramp to where two of the crew replaced the defective wheel.

"The last time I did that, 500 watts was added to my account," Scorpio told one of the crew members.

"I'll notify my supervisor and see what we can do this time, OK," he responded. "Check your reserve in a few rotations. I'm sure you will see it in there. Thanks for your concern for the bad wheel."

260-Bacteria

Scorpio arrived at his dwelling to find that this was the first time in a very long while that he had no demands on his time. He thought of buzzing a list of voting young persons to get a yes vote on admitting the Sands to the Tubes. Holo bounce would nice too. His second thought won over and he told himself just a few minutes and then do the buzzing.

"How did you do against the bounce programmer?" asked Incu.

'Not very well. Oh my goodness. I don't believe that I was talking my way through the game this long. I'm going to buzz for some votes," said Scorpio

"Quiet time," said Incu.

"I have to do a lot of buzzing," Scorpio excitedly returned.

"Quiet time. Leg coordination. caterpillars. Relax. Please." Incu rolled out her mat, and dozed off in a very short time. She is buzzed and unrolling her monitor she saw in huge bold red letters, NOW. REPORT TO LOW MAGNETIC DWELLING. Without disturbing the sleeping Scorpio, she left pedaling her fastest with the lowest setting.

Not again; Total isolation probably. I do hope it is not as long as the last time. Is it something that the birds brought from the Sands? Did, whatever it is, come with the wind? Her thoughts were rambling at 60 KPH. Arriving at her station she removed all of her clothing, completely covered herself in a containment suit, attached the apparatus and read her schedule of duties. She is ready for whatever would be asked of her.

BACTERIA STRAIN UNKNOWN. SIX REPORTED DEATHS.

261-Bacteria

Almaaz viewed it as having some resemblance to what she had seen before. The bacteria shapes were compared and they seemed identical. This one was covered with follicles. How could such a germ cause such havoc? There were many bacteria to work with. She applied the tiniest of magnetic field surrounding it and its follicles seemed to tilt towards the slightly stronger fields. Removed the field completely, then applied fields incrementally stronger, observing its reaction. Sometimes from one direction then another, then from all sides. She noticed that when she applied a strong shock, it pulled its follicles into itself and did not move at all. When she removing the field, it came back to life.

A cadaver was delivered to her lab dwelling in a sealed bag. Inserting an evacuation tube into the cadaver using sterilized opening, she withdrew some feces then inserted another withdrew tissue from one of its many sores. The laboratory was crowded with the other teams. It was their phase off, but because the bacteria were killing the Sands People, their own lives were at stake.

262-Bacteria

Almaaz placed a tiny part of her sample into a vacuum chamber. She closely observed it through her electron microscope. She noticed that when she had 3 kilo inside the chamber, they started to explode. What kind of shielding they have? They were like popcorn. Was the covering that they had on themselves that made them so immune to any kind of medication?

She tried the same test with samples from the sores that and did not get the same results. Why? She lowered the pressure again and the bacteria just expanded a little with no bursting of any of them. She lowered it at a steady pace to a near vacuum, and nothing unusual happened. Why?

The bacteria looked identical in every way. Why was the one that went through the blood stream and the one that just went through the digestive system so differently? Her observer, who was just a technician but had many orbits in the lab, said, "A live tissue would be interesting."

"Thank you." Almaaz buzzed the supervisor of the lab and requested live tissue. She was told that one should be available within the hour. "Please take your quiet time now." Removing and getting back into all of her sanitation gear would be too time consuming especially when the dying human would arrive. So they rested in their special engineered recliners that fit their backpack and other safety equipment on their outfits.

263-Bacteria

Scorpio buzzed his incubator and got a "quiet time" so left a message. "Incu, Donor and I are going to my first fling tomorrow and I would like for you to be there too. We are practicing at Hydra's dwelling." An alarm awakened the sleepers in the lab announcing arrival of the dying human. Almaaz saw her name 5th on the wall monitor list. She and her assistant were ready with all of the equipment needed for the withdrawals and were in line nervously waiting. Number one withdrew tissue as soon as the brain waves ceased. Number 2, 3 and 4 were told that their withdrawal tubes were exposed and to return with sterile ones after being scolded for their inept practice.

Almaaz withdrew sore tissue and feces and a sample from a tear on the face and one from the back of the throat of the strapped-down female. "This microscopic monster is sure leaving its mark on our Tubes," Almaaz said to herself. Taking the samples to her station, she placed three of them into the "live condition" chamber. The tear was placed into the automated testing device and in less than 60 seconds 37 results were given. They ranged from acidity to lube percentage to zymosis. Viewing the tear under the microscope, Almaaz saw the multiplication going in full force. She saw a cell split into three cells. There was not enough human fluid to multiply again. Almaaz increased the magnetic field from atmosphere to its maximum and observed its reaction to various powers. What kind of element does it have within itself to react to such a field?

She removed the Petri dish and the slides from the testing equipment and placed them into the destruction chamber. She would have liked to preserve them, but her observer said that there were too many others wanting to do the same.

264-Bacteria

The saliva from the back of the victim's throat did not have one bacterium. Why? Could they have all been eliminated from digestive juices in the mouth? She asked her assistant see if there were others getting samples from the patient. "You know that I cannot leave your side for anything," was his reply.

"Then place my name on the list for more withdrawals," she commanded.

He did then kept a close eye on the removal and procedure of placing the other specimens for examination. Almaaz relayed the information from the saliva test to her supervisor who enters it into The Record Keeper. The stool test bacteria "popped" and the sore bacteria did not. Why? In a magnetic field they reacted the same. The supervisor was told of the same and they found that the phenomenon was never recorded in The Record Keeper. Was it because of the new testing equipment that had just arrived two moons ago? "How would it in any way determine how to combat its deadly effectiveness? Wondered Almaaz. Almaaz was told that she could withdraw more samples from the expired female. There were no intrusive devices to extend her life. Almaaz placed a tube down her throat, withdrew. The next time she went further down, and the third time into her stomach. The first sample had none. The second very few. But the sample from the stomach held a blob of bacteria. It must be the saliva that is destroying the bacteria. Almaaz made her report to the supervisor and informed her that she was leaving unless there was a present need for her services. She was exhausted and did not realize that she had just spent 14 hours inside the research dwelling. Her feeding tube, plus the waste bag let Almaaz have her sterile suit the whole time.

265-Almaaz's donor

She and her observer individually cleared the decontamination chamber, checked their monitors, said goodbye to each other and pedaled away.

Almaaz had five quiet times and was not ready for a good night's sleep. She buzzed Aires who was just leaving Hydra's and pedaling to their dwelling. It would only be a matter of minutes before they all would be together again.

Almaaz arrived first to find that someone had their mat in the middle of their dwelling and was snoring; sound asleep. She did not recognize the male and let him do his thing. The private place was a must for her immediately. She put the fan on high speed; and used her wand for a thorough clean up while her clothing was electronically cleaned. She dressed and placed her packets outside for pick up and saw the two "men" in her life pedaling up the hill. The three embraced each other and Almaaz asked each of them how long they had their face covers off. "Just from the bottom of the hill to here," Aires answers. "Seal your body now," she demanded, then told them of the sleeping male inside. They entered and speaking louder than usual trying to arouse him but nothing happened. Aires touched him on his arm and he stirred a little. The male has a burning fever, Aires noted. Almaaz buzzed the Enforcement Regulators and in a matter of minutes six glided to the front of their dwelling with all of the equipment needed to enclose him into a sterile bag. Scorpio, knowing that they will be needing a trailer, secured one from the nearby tube entrance. His identification was that of Almaaz's donor. She had not seen him in many orbits, and their communications had been on the lax side. The beard, which she had never seen, was a full bushy growth.

266-Almaaz's donor

Why did he come to visit at this time without informing her? Communications was ever so simple. The surprise visit left her in a very uncomfortable situation. She wanted to be rested for Scorpio's maiden flight, but now being with her donor in his distress was a must too. "Incu, why did you sound so distressed about our face cover when we first arrived?" asked Scorpio.

"In the testing lab I noticed that the deadly bacteria enter the body, I think, through the eyes and multiply like a thunderstorm in full force. It has not been confirmed yet but seeing what I did, I am not going to wait for commands from the health department. Now that our dwelling might be contaminated and I was in there, we have to find somewhere to stay while being extremely attentive to any ailments" she answered. She buzzed the dwelling scheduler telling her the dilemma. A dwelling was available two kilometers away and they were told they would have to be put through the portable contamination chamber before they could enter it.

Almaaz knew where the dwelling was and told them that she would be with them as soon as she learned what kind of medical attention her donor would receive. "Almaaz, you know that you will not be able to be near your donor, so why pedal there? You can get all the information about him and even view him on your monitor," said Aires.

"I have not seen him in such a long time and I want to be close by in case he has a few alert moments," she replied.

267-Almaaz's donor

"You know someone in research talking like you do, surprises me," said Aires.

"I must be talking out of the tubes. Sorry. Thanks for bringing me back to my senses. Ready to ride. Let's go." They all followed Almaaz.

Upon arriving they could not enter since there was no sanitizer there yet. They walked around the dwelling that seemed like it was not occupied for some time. The condensation drip containers were overflowing. Ten 20 Kilo containers had to be emptied into the plant bladder at least 300 meters down the hill. Lucky for them that it was in that direction. Scorpio and Incu carried one while Donor took two with ease. Scorpio could have taken two but did not want to strain himself for tomorrow's fling competition. Puffing from the exertion on the last walk back to the dwelling Scorpio said," Why couldn't a tube be used and let gravity do all of the work?"

"That will be your next project," smiled Donor. "It sure is taking the decontamination team a long time to get here. I guess their work load is horrendous with all of that is going on," he added.

Scorpio unrolled his monitor for another holo fling.

Donor heard a concert at the tube entrance. Wanted to go, but since contact with Incu's donor he decided to bring it up on his monitor. Incu buzzed her donor and got a response from the technician. "May I help you?"

"Shauia was brought to your dwelling. Can you give me any information on his health status?" Incu asked.

268-Scorpio's fling

The technician answered, "He is now being heavily medicated for the infectious "pop" bacteria. He is not able to walk but is communicating. He will be in quarantine for a moon. I will inform him of your buzz and he should be able to talk to you in a rotation or so. Thank you for calling." Incu's monitor went blank.

"If it were not for the nocturnal flesh-eating felines, I would unroll my mat here in the open and have a night of star gazing," said Incu.

"I doubt if we will be bothered by anything wild. The netting will discourage most everything so let's use it." Donor started to unroll it when the four man decontamination team arrived towing the decontamination trailer.

Donor got into the unfolded trailer, undressed completely, placed his suit into a small chamber and had cool air blowing past his nude body. If there was any bacterium outside his body they would be destroyed. It also eliminated all of the bacteria in his nostrils. Keeping his eyes closed was a must for the short time he was in the chamber. He dressed himself. Now it was Incu's turn, then Scorpio. Having the decontamination done, they all entered the dwelling and were ready for a good night's sleep. With all of the confusion, Scorpio had only the fling on his mind. Would he get a good rest? Unrolling his mat he was sound asleep in a few minutes. Arising he looked at the weather report and everything was perfect. The slight breeze would make things better. He was all excited and wanted to leave as soon as the sun came over the horizon. "It is best for a morning run so let's go for it," said Aires. It was a good hour to the fling ramp and Scorpio was winded from the pedaling. He hoped that he has enough strength for the flight. At his age, his recouping energy was not too difficult. There were 12 in line awaiting their turn and he was the 13th with a group of flingers walking to register. He looked for Hydra but she was not in sight.

269-Almaaz's donor

Almaaz buzzed her donor and asked why he was visiting without informing her of his arrival. He said that he wanted to get the yes vote for the Sands People and just got carried away by giving personal visits to many who befriended him over the past orbits. He was only 40 kilometers away so a surprise was in order. It would have worked if it were not for the bug from across the water. "Now that I'm here and feel like I will make a full recovery, is there anything that I might say that might interest you?" "There are a few blank spots before I entered the mating pool but they can wait until you have a full recovery. It has been so long ago and one moon will not make that much of a difference." Her donor cut in, "What is this about one moon," he demanded.

"I was informed by the technician that you will be in quarantine for a moon?" she said.

"The medication has worked wonders and I feel like I can leave now. I have a lot of campaigning to do. I am going to talk to the technician now," He took one step off his mat and fell to the floor. Almaaz had nothing but the ceiling of the dwelling and buzzed the technician. He informed her that her donor was now being restrained because of the delirium he was in. Almaaz knowing how the female that she took the tissue from acted, and hoped that her donor's disease was not to that stage yet. Her screen went blank. She buzzed the dwelling monitor and saw three medical attendants with full body covers and a breathing back pack surrounding her donor. One step away, and now she saw that the restraint straps kept him from injuring himself. He was the only patient in the dwelling. The other two technicians moved away from him for her to see that he was totally relaxed or anesthetized.

270-Scorpio's fling

She wanted to watch her donor and it was now time that Scorpio was strapping himself into the flinger. Donor was hovering nearby, but the rules stated that the entrant must not have any assistance of any kind, not even verbal. Donor was pleased to see his offspring do so well in strapping himself in and watched the flight crew place the safety helium container on Scorpio's back. He then folded in his wings and the "banana" was ready. He relayed that he was ready then heard, "Ready-1-2-3-go and off he flew. There was no noise of any kind. The undercarriage did make a sliding noise and that was it. The anxiety of having their Scorpio on his first fling was emotional for the both of them. He was just a speck in the sky and getting smaller. Donor pointed his monitor lens, and there, with a full screen, was his dream comes true. He had no idea how fast Scorpio was going but he did know that he was still climbing and would be at the apogee in a moment or so. "Incu, you keep your monitor on your donor and mine will be on Scorpio. There," he shouts, "he is opening his wings. He looks great. Wow. He had a slight drift to the left but not much. Look at that bird. His balance is great. Thank you, Hydra. Thank you, holo. For a first time, he is wonderful!" Incu had her eyes on Scorpio and tears of joy ran down her face, with a face cover in place she could not wipe them and in fact was somewhat proud to show them. They were hardly visible under the tinted cover. They got on their bikes towing trailers and pedaled to the direction Scorpio was gliding. He looked like a flying saucer. There must be a hundred in the sky with a few more to be flung; A sky full of birds. Some of them below 300 meters had their balloon pop. Their angle of descent was too great and if the safety devices were not in place they would crash into the ground. It had been 15 minutes since flight was given to Scorpio.

271-Scorpio's fling

The distant birds were getting fewer and fewer and the colorful safety balloons were all over the place. Pedaling, they lost Scorpio in with all of the others. Stopping, they focused on the birds, and then quickly found him gliding ever so smoothly. Off again. Now it was easier to spot him amongst the others. "He is gliding so great. Oh, what a joy to watch. He is great. Lean right. Lean right. Lean right! Scorpio, lean right!" He shouted knowing that Scorpio cannot hear him. Scorpio made an adjustment, losing some height and leveled again. The sky now had much fewer "birds." Donor and Incu pedaled past some of them that had landed in the open fields. Trees were also a problem. If a bird was going to crash into one, the helium balloon would ease the hit or take the flinger out of harm's way. Scorpio was now less than 300 meters and doing very well, floating down to earth like a leaf. Beautiful, beautiful was all that was going thorough donor's mind. It seemed that he was going to float forever. They pedaled closer to where they felt he is going to land, and waited, watching him like a hawk. He glided to the ground with a rolling belly flop for a perfect landing. His position was automatically relayed to the control at the launch site.

Scorpio loosened all of his binding. He was in another world, totally elated at his accomplishment. Standing next to his bird were two proud procreators. "I think you did very well in the competition. I watched you most of the way down and saw only a slight drift and that was it. Great! Were you ever frightened or had a stomach full of butterflies? You seem cool and collected now. You were great. How do you feel?" asked Donor.

272-Scorpio's fling

"I'm still hurting from the squeezing of the launch suit. It seemed to be all over me. Incu, you love me a lot and have given me some of the most soft hugs, but what I got from the suit was really a life saving work of love. The view when I reached the top was so beautiful. A view from the tower on hill 76-21 was nothing compared to this indescribable panoramic view. I glided through a cloud of insects of some kind and that was weird. My caterpillar studies never mentioned anything like that. The eagle eye magnifier did great but when looking at the ground details, I lost the inner feelings of my gliding," Scorpio rambled on in what seemed to be a non-breathing description of his flight. "Did you see Hydra?" he added.

"I should have looked at the roster, but we were totally focused on you," said Aires. He unrolled his monitor and viewed the name list of the flingers. "She was 6th to launch. The results showed that she had the longest flight this rotation. Here is yours: 27. "That is great for the first time. My first flight ended with a bam. Thanks to the balloon I am here today. I was 30 meters off the ground and tilted too much to miss a tree and would have slid hard to the ground. What about you Incu? How was your first flight?"

"It was my first and last. I was all over the place. Sliding sideways with no control, then over-reacting and going the other way I had a back slip and did all kinds of things, then got to 100 meters and had the "bam" balloon give some sanity to the flight. The heights and the physical compression suit took all of the joy out of it and now you know," Incu said, and then let out a gasp.

273-Sand ballot

"Incu please let me pedal you back to the launch site. Better yet, I'll take back the lighter banana so I can set my rate a little higher and you bring back Incu. Sound good?" pleaded Scorpio. "My, are you a thinker. Sure. Let's load your fling onto your trailer. You could do it yourself, but it will give us a little work coordination task," said Donor.

The pedal time took 10 minutes and was 4.5 kilometers. They checked the fling into a slot and Scorpio was scanned and buzzed, "Condition of fling?"

"No damage. Some grass from the landing," he responded to a speaker hidden somewhere.

"Thank you," the automated voice sounded.

"There is a sing-a-long two exits from ours. What say we go there? I'm in a mood to exercise my vocals. Scorpio, I have not heard you in a long time. Let's go, please" begged Donor.

"Sounds great," Scorpio answered. "I have a lot to sing about. The only song that should not be sung is 'Back to Earth With a Bang.' There will probably be some flingers there." No sooner he finished saying that than all three of them were buzzed and like an automated piece of equipment, they all unrolled their monitors.

TWELVE PERSONS FROM EACH OF THE TEN AREAS OF SANDS PEOPLE BE TRANSPORTED TO OUR COAST TRAINING FACILITY FOR ONE MOON. EACH RETURNED WITH 100 RINGED MALES AND ALL BEGINNINGS OF TUBE MATERIAL.
YES   NO

274-Scorpio votes

"Scorpio, this is your vote. You have a choice. Do you want it to be a secret one or one that you want everyone to know your feelings about this issue?" asks Donor. "Because of my position, I would rather not have anyone know how I vote, ever. I have voted that way for a long time. You know that you made a few buzzes and so most everyone knows how your feeling are. May I suggest that even though you are going to vote yes, press the 'SECRET' and not The Record Keeper," said Donor. "You are young. If this is approved with 75%

of us voters and the project meets with disaster by some fluke, you will agonize within yourself and not be heckled by the losers. It has happened before and the losers screamed over and over again, 'SEE, I TOLD YOU SO.' Be aware that once you cast your first vote, you will obligated to do so 6 rotations every phase with the third moon off every orbit with no voting. Do you want to start voting now?"

"I sure do and I want everyone to know how I feel about The Sand People. For me, it partly out of compassion for the misery that they are enduring and the health of our Tubers . I am going to enter into the selection pool to be in the first wave to float there. I will make a difference," Scorpio boasted.

"What talents do you have to offer?" asks Incu.

"My energy and I have done everything from installing the tubes, erecting a dwelling, preparing soil and seeding, bicycle repair and a few more. I have done all of these things on the holo," says Scorpio. Incu cut in, "Do you know that you will be required to wear full cover for the entire time that you are there?"

275-Free time

"I do here most of the time and that will not be a problem. What concerns me is that a lack of sufficient enforcement regulators will leave any installers of all of the facilities open targets for the unruly. Viewing them on the holo and smelling their stench make the jungle caterpillars roses. I know that I can handle it. Trust me," said Scorpio.

Incu said she doubted that he would be chosen for the first wave floating to the Sands. She knew that there would be enough qualified and eager adults. Almaaz realized this was a downer for Scorpio and it was obvious by the look on his face.

Aires announced, "We're here. What a crowd! I'll enter my name on the soloist list and wait my turn. The program director will buzz me when and if I am chosen. How about a nice quiet time for now," said Donor unrolling his mat. The three plus a dozen or so were asleep in the shade of a huge tree.

The weather was beautiful with a 2 or 3 KPH breeze. Huge white clouds kept the sun from baking the crowd. Out of the shade of the tree, it was noticeable that their suits were in the cool mode. While still being covered and not allowing insects to leave their mark, it felt as though a person was naked. The rack of 3 meter poles were near the ramp exit With its sharp pin for insertion into the ground. The eye/ear from the monitor could be placed on the top of it for viewing whoever might be performing. All that was needed was for the spectator to focus it in the direction of what they want to view or hear.

276-Tube song

"Scorpio, I would like very much if you would accompany me," pleaded Donor.
"You are so nice to hear and I would ruin it for you," he answered.
"Please, your voice is changing and that might make it something special. Unroll your monitor and bring up 'The Future'." "I know that one from my preteen orbits. If I do, will you let me go to the Sands?" Scorpio begged. "You sure are a determined one. Incu, what do you say to that?" he asked. "I'm not for it, but let's make a deal. Try for the 3ʳᵈ or 4ᵗʰ wave please," she answered somewhat mournfully. "Deal. Thank you both," smiles Scorpio, "Now that our name is on the list, do you want to practice?" "Not too loud now. If you listen to the words it will give our place so much more meaning when you get to the Sands," responded Aires. Then they both sang softly so as not to disturb the act going on.

WHERE ARE WE GOING AND WHAT DO WE DO
NOWHERE SPECIAL, JUST BLUNDERING AWAY
IS THERE A SPECIAL DIRECTION TO GO
EVERYWHERE YOUR FEELINGS TELL YOU THE WAY

JUST GO WITH THE FLOW AND FIND YOURSELF THE
WAY
KEEP A KIND HEART IN THE WORDS THAT YOU SAY
THEY WILL MARVEL YOURSELF TO WHERE THEY
CAME
IT IS WITHIN YOU THAT THE TUBES CAN STAY

277-Fee time

From the start and Incu noticed an old male lip syncing with them
then. She placed her index finger across her lips, and then pointed
to the performer. He blew her back a "thank you" kiss.
The performing group was playing a beautiful tune from the Old
Era. Couples were dancing between the lounging spectators. Donor
asked Incu if she would like to move with the next one and with the
smile she gave him it said yes..
Incu waved her palm in front of Scorpio's face and he did not even
blink. "Where are you, my young dreamer?" she asked. "Somewhere
between being a Sands Commander and learning their language," he
responded. Donor cut in, "Beautiful dreams, but when reality kicks
in, a pick and shovel will most likely be your thing."
The music stopped and the director of this rotation's activities
announced the last event would be the Future Song. Donor and
Scorpio stood and all of the eye/ear rods were turned in their direction.
The transmitting camera operator did the same. The musicians did
the first two lines, then back to the first with Donor and Scorpio
singing with full vigor. Before the first verse was sung, others started
in. Standing, they drowned out the two starters. When the two
verses were done the director said, "One more time".

278-Food supply

Everyone was singing at the top of their voices while walking to their
bicycles to return home. What a way to end an event.

The next rotation, Scorpio awakened and checked his monitor for Incu's instructions. Empty the condensation containers into the bathing bladder first, then into the plant drip on the uphill side. He wished they had a new dwelling where the condensation was designed to drain directly into them. Four dumps and it was done. The exit chute for the generic encapsulated food pellets that were used for insulation in everyone's dwelling was right there and out of impulse, Scorpio released a few. He devoured his morning portion, and for some reason was never this hungry before. He was unaware of the chute lever's silent alarm to the Dwelling Erectors. No sooner did he crack one chute open and eat a few, a flinger comes gliding next to him. He was surprised by the visit and the delivery vehicle bringing his next three day supply.

"What's going with you, young bucks? This is the second fling I had this morning. Has no one told you about NO TAMPERING with the two year food supply? I see this is your first," the Dwelling Director added, "You have a choice, trailer me and my bird back, or 30KW!"

279-Pellet insulation

"You get the ride, but first I must gobble some of the good stuff. Generic are barely edible," Scorpio said while loading his backpack with handfuls of the newly delivered pellets. He hooked onto the two trailers while the Dwelling Erector sealed the chute and tagged it.

"Why wasn't the chute tagged before? Is it because we have an older dwelling?" Scorpio asks. "You're right. No big deal. It's not of major concern. They are scattered all over the place. Hey!!!! Can you set your generator up a bit? Your speed down this hill is making me a little nervous!" shouted his passenger. Scorpio obliged. "Did you start the song last rotation?"

"My donor and I," answered Scorpio. "How was my voice?"

"I really couldn't tell. Before the second line, my mate was straining her vocals to the max. I could never understand why that song gets so much attention. Its tune is not the greatest," he said.

"Have you read each word and dwelled on them?" asked Scorpio

"Not really," he replied.

Scorpio asked the worker, "Who do you see in the Land of Memories to move some dirt?" "The caretaker can usually be seen pedaling somewhere in the vicinity," answered the worker.

280-Bartering

Scorpio delivers the flinger and while unloading his bird he asks Scorpio if he could have some of the power he generated.

"Would half be OK," asks Scorpio?

"More than that. How about ¾" he asked.

"You know, when we were at my dwelling you said just a ride back. What's with this extra stuff," Scorpio scornfully replied!

Well, you're young and I tire easily, so every little bit helps," he pleaded.

"I'll make a deal with you. I'll give you 90 percent or nothing depending if you have less in the reserve than I do," Scorpio said.

"50 percent will be fine," he said. Scorpio voiced his donation into his monitor.

"Thank you young male. I like your bartering over kWs," the worker said then got onto his bike and pedaled away with tags fluttering out of his backpack.

Scorpio pedaled three kilometers to the Land of Memories where Cepella was buried. Since she was brought here, quite a few more added to the line. He notices a couple crying near a newly planted tree. He took his monitor and held it over the row he thought she was and noticed that nearly all were over 100 orbits. One was 142. Electrocuted: adjusting a flinger.

281-Cepella's procreators

Glancing up Scorpio said, "Oh, I'm sorry! I'm looking for Cepella." "She is here," the male answered. "She is our offspring. We came to see if there were any discrepancies in her history. We could have done it from our dwelling 300 kilometers north. This visit is soothing our loneliness. Who might you be?"

"Scorpio, the offspring of Aires and Almaaz. Cepella was one of the greatest bouncers I have ever played. You sure were fortunate to have someone so talented. How many orbits when she started?"

"She was in uniform as soon as she could walk. Her energy was so great that she was always injuring herself by running into things," said the male. "The bounce suit saved her from destroying herself. My donor was a record sprinter and I guess that is where her genes came from. I missed it somehow."

"After our first game I put her into my address book as someone who I would want for a mate, but our DNA's were incompatible. She was better than any male and I'm so glad that a tree was planted next to her. You can be comforted that I will visit this spot many times." Scorpio then added, "The Tubes have lost a great member. Thank you for procreating such a great female."

Scorpio left and when he got to a knoll overlooking the Land lf Memories, he laid down his bike, and unrolled his mat for a quiet time. He glanced in the direction of Cepella and saw her procreators doing the same. They had a long way to return and he wished that there would always be a breeze at their backs.

282-Digger

Awakened and sitting, he noticed a group digging. Pedaling with his generation set to its highest level he panted heavily when he arrived. Watching the work in progress, he noted 10 rectangles in a line. A very crude male used a pick, burying it to the handle each swing. He was powerful. He shoveled the loose dirt onto a platform.

Scorpio questioned the male in charge, "Why are his ankles chained together? "Why don't you ask him yourself?" "I'd rather not," said Scorpio with a frightened look on his face. "Well, if you must know, he is a mean one from the Lonesome Place. Digging is the only relief from anxieties that plague him. Without this strenuous work to where he exhausts himself, he would growl like a dog and drool a river. I have to be near him with a blanket. He refuses quiet time. While shoveling, he is quiet as a lamb. At sunset he is chained to a tree, given 3 liters of beer, has a good night's rest and is ready for his chores the next sunrise. He has been doing this for the last three orbits since I arrived here without a rotation off. If you want to see something exciting, be here when he has to be dragged on a blanket back to his paradise. Would you like to dig next to him?" he asks Scorpio.

"No thank you," he answered. "I want to go to the Sands and my donor said this is the kind of work I most likely will be doing. An accident would dampen my dreams. Do you have another section where I could work myself?"

"Sorry. This digging machine is well ahead of the need as you can see from the empty holes. There is another Field of Memories10 kilometers west of here. Try there," he said..

283-Vote 87%

Scorpio entered the tube, discharged all of his built up current, and checked his reserve: 647KwH. That is the most he had ever had. In 3 moons, 16 orbits will be his. He raised his generation rate to make him nearly exhausts himself as he exited. A short pedal away for a dwelling discharge. The sky was full of stars and he found his namesake.

Aires and Almaaz returned to find Scorpio getting a full view on the holo of the Sands. He didn't understand why they didn't bury the bodies instead of just throwing them into the river. "Donor, look at the flow of corpses. Look at the river. That is not a river but a moving Field of Memories. How can society degenerate to such depths? I am having doubts of even going there. Why? Why? Why?" cried the young male.

"Voting result was 87 percent for occupying the Sands," said Aires then added, "They were dying at an alarming rate. We have had tragedies in the past and our way has made us what we are today. Humble yourself and try not to understand a very vexing situation. Be patient and think of only good things to replace the bad. Make your quiet time a time for rest and deep thought. Will a vaccine that is still in research be developed in time? Full body cover is the only salvation for the tube people. Did you learn anything special at the Field of Memories?"

284-Cepella's gene pool

"The Field of Memories was something special," said Scorpio. I wanted to dig but was scared by a male who was the closest thing to an animal. He was digging with leg irons and would not stop for anything, even quiet time. While there, Cepella's procreators told me their memories of her. She was energetic from birth. They put her in a bounce uniform to keep her from injuring herself. Oh, by the way, I noticed her incubator was not wearing a necklace like the one you wear all the time."

"Most females wear them forever out of habit," said Incu. "She probably found it a nuisance. When a female does not produce eggs because of age or some other reason, it is not bright red anymore." She then unrolled her monitor and entered: Cepella. It took a few seconds and a complete history came up. Her incubator was 37 orbits before she entered the mating pool. One orbit later she delivered Cepella. "Look at the sprinters in her gene pool. Two generations back the donor still holds the record for the 100 meter dash and third in the 5K run. Speed and stamina," read Incu then added. "And our bunch has never been near the top ten."

285-Beads

"I'm ready for a quiet time," said donor. He unrolled his mat and was snoring in a matter of a minute or so. Incu tried to get some rest but couldn't because of the misery that was thrashing The Sand People. Scorpio lay on his mat saying over and over again, caterpillar/ butterfly but it did not work. He glanced at Incu. She was mumbling something ever so quietly, but he could not make out the words. He noticed her holding onto some kind of chain. He had never seen it before. It was quiet time and he would have to wait to find out.

Scorpio finally napped and when he awoke, Donor and Incu were gone. Checking his monitor, he noted that they would be gone for a few rotations and would be at their work stations. He buzzed Incu and the first question was to ask her about the chain. Before he said a word, she remarked, "Follow this bacteria closely! This is the monster that is going to cause misery to a lot of people."

"What color is it," he asked.

"Yellow. Isn't your monitor picking it up? Now watch the splitting. This one is just in half. Watch when I add human tissue. Watch closely," she cautioned.

"Wow!" Shouted Scorpio. "Unbelievable! We are in for a slaughter."

"Buzz Donor and ask if your services can be used for shipments from our shore." Then she added, "Make sure you have a good fit on your clothing." Upon contact donor instructed Scorpio to come to his work station immediately. Donor said, "A report from the eastern medical facility has the area in quarantine. No one is allowed to pedal to the west." Scorpio pedaled to his Donor's facility with no generation.

286-Scorpio with Donor

Donor motioned his offspring to come over to him, and then instructs him to bring his bike into the dwelling. The in-swinging door was slammed shut by the higher air pressure inside. No dust, bacteria or any other foreign object penetrated the tiniest of openings. Donor helped Scorpio get into a lab uniform. Bounce suits were similar except that this one was clear. The vibration Scorpio was now feeling was from a tiny air compressor. This outfit was a double safety feature.

Donor informed everyone that the first wave of Sands would arrive the next rotation and he was in charge of their program. "One hundred is no great number, but it will take a lot of personnel to cart them to special dwellings."

"Scorpio, while you are waiting, I want you to read all of the sanitary procedures, patterns of dispersion of the bacteria and other safety regulations," Donor firmly instructed him, and then announced, "It is quiet time."

Scorpio found it very awkward being enclosed naked in a suit. An elderly scientist told him that the suit was clear so any skin blotches would be noticed.

Butterflies/caterpillars/butterflies/caterpillar/butterflies.

287-Safety uniform

His outfit was not conducive to relaxation. The first line on his monitor instructed: DO NOT PANIC--- TRAIN YOURSELF TO DO THINGS AUTOMATICALLY---IF YOU MUST DEVIATE FROM THE PRESCRIBED PROCEDUDRES, REASON IT THOROUGHLY OR QUESTION OTHERS, IF TIME PERMITS.

It showed pictures of many different body surface eruptions. He never realized that there were so different ones that could harm humans. No human could remember all of them and many were similar. The automated visual observer was a must. He viewed the Sands bacteria and asked for a holo. "Larger please." It was magnified to his body size. He saw tiny blond hair covering it. No openings or irregular surfaces. The hairs must be its survival tool he told himself. Suddenly a crack appeared, then another and another. There were four fragments and each rounded itself and grew slowly into the same size as the original. Human tissue was a magnet for this tiny monster. Its growth rate was unbelievable. What Scorpio was viewing was available to everyone. A message scrolled across his monitor: TISSUE-DEAD-HUMAN-----GROWTH THREE TIMES WITH LIVE HUMAN TISSUE.

The holo bacteria vanished and another scrolled message came with another bacteria: LIVE TISSUE FROM A SCIENTIST BEING ATTACKED . Wow! Scorpio said to himself. He now felt that he wanted to be in his clear plastic uniform forever.

288-Safety regulations

He read the pattern of dispersion transmitted by humans. Touching a Sands was forbidden. The arriving 100 would most likely have some bacteria on their bodies.

Reading the safety regulations could be done by scrolling long lines or short ones. Scroll speed, letter size, font, color of print was available to the reader. Absorption of the text was different for everyone. Scorpio chose ½ line length with two lines visible. He tried scrolling the next two but found that just flashing two lines at a time did best. He had some questions for donor but he was in conference with six scientists.

One hour of this concentration was enough. Bringing up The Sand's north flowing river with all of the bloated bodies sickened him. A look at the eastern border revealed some greenery. Further east there was more human activity. A flash came on the monitor: ***ASSISTANCE NEEDED IN BRINGING MATERIALS TO SHORE SIDE FOR THE SANDS PROJECT PRIORITY***

Scorpio knew this one was cleared through The Record Keeper. He buzzed donor and got a busy signal. He knew he was behind that door. He wanted to knock but didn't knowing Donor's stress during the situation made Scorpio go back to his reading. He wanted to leave but the contamination in that dwelling would prohibit it. He was less than one fourth into the manual but needed another quiet time.

289-Sands dying

Almaaz was expecting the notice. She could not leave but was keep abreast of the ugly situation. Data entered into The Record Keeper was digested, and at the alarm it was to regurgitated. There was no break in the efforts of her department.

Was some factor overlooked which could bring this monster under control? The latest count of Sands was less than 23,000. In another moon it would be less than ½ of that. Bodies lay where they died. Survivors, exhausted, wandered aimlessly.

The east area of the Sands had vegetation and some activity. Satellite views showed children. Scorpio saw mechanical equipment moving, but speculated that there was a lack of fuel or operators. It would be a matter of time before their misery would be relieved. The Tubes neighbor to the east was slightly aware of the plague and would probably end with the same calamity.

Aires came out of his conference and buzzed Almaaz. "I wonder how long we will be apart?" were his first words. "This is more than a toy to be played with. I miss you and Scorpio very much." He sounded like tears were near. "Just be patient," he replied, "Your offspring is in quiet time. Have you ever found why the remaining ones there survived? Do we have to bring a few more here? We have examined one hundred that just landed. A few are not going to survive."

290-Epilepsy

Every one of the arriving Sands was placed into clear bags. They all accepted it. Some were sickly. When they left the Sands, all were in good health. The Tubers were like someone visiting a zoo or an aquarium. They were like tiny fish being transported in a plastic bag. None were threatening. A computer translator gave directions to them. The Tubers heard their responses, but it was comical because their words and their lips were not in sync. Someone blew a whistle and all activity stopped. Mats were scattered everywhere. From a bag they heard, "Hey, don't you have work to do?" From each translator came, "Please enjoy a nap or meditate now, please."

One of the bagged female Sands tugged on the closing flap, and with much effort made a tiny opening that set off an alarm. Many sleeping giants rushed her into over-bags. "How did you know that?" she yelled. Pointing to the tear, a Tuber told her to never do that again. Frightened at the demand, she started shaking, went limp and from her mouth came foam. She was rolled on her side to keep from gagging. Slowly her body relaxed and went into a deep sleep. A camera focused on her actions prompted The Record Keeper to respond: EPILEPSY. Later when she received a thorough physical, medication would be supplied to relieve her from this ever happening again.

291-Epilepsy

Epilepsy was diagnosed but she seemed to have another problem. Being naked inside the clear body cover made probes easier to enter all of her body orifices. A sedative would not be needed for the comatose state she was in. Every move was observed. Data slowly emerges from The Record Keeper. Bacteria had destroyed the nerve cells at the base of her brain. She had no chance of recovery. Almaaz was desperate to solve the mystery. The key to the bacteria's multiplication speed was, she thought, in the cilia that covered it. After each division the hairs would burrow into the flesh. She entered her thoughts in with the others that were scrolling on her monitor. She magnified the hairs and found each end had a bur, just like a cocklebur.

She buzzed Scorpio and he was overjoyed to get away from the boring manual. After asking how he was and he telling her she said, "There is all kinds of excitement here. Right now I'm trying to find how the yellow hairs can absorb nutrients so quickly from live human tissue." "Incu, I saw a holo of it and was thinking. Maybe they are like when you stroke a comb across fabric and hold it next to your hair, the hair stands up," offered Scorpio. "Hey, that's great.

I never thought of it that way. I have been with low voltage with other things but now I have a real project. I have to run, my fellow scientist." She disconnected.

292-Sirus sick

Aires buzzed Alcor, the space engineer, and saw his department in quiet time; he left a message and took his own quiet time.

Scorpio, following the bacteria activity, magnifies a frozen one to his size. Its hair ends were sharp and hinged. He was as concerned with finding how to control it as were his incubator and other scientists. "Caterpillars have hairs, but do not have the clinging ability," Scorpio mused. "This hairy monster does not pupate either."

His flashed on Sirus, his elderly neighbor of an orbit ago; he gave him a buzz. "Scorpio, I noticed recently that your reserve is doing very well. I don't think you want to take this ride. Three transporters are taking me on my last trip." "A trip to where?" asked Scorpio. "Research needs live tissue, so I'm it," he said smiling. "What do you mean?" Questioned Scorpio. The elderly male coughed, swallowed hard and said, "I am going to let scientists mate me with a cute blond neighbor." Scorpio gasped, "Aren't you a little too old for that?" "Young buck, never underestimate the ability of anyone. The blond I have my eye on is from the Sands." "Your humor is crude," is all that Scorpio could say.

"Scorpio, do you remember the time you used my monitor, well, if you would donate that time, my balance would just about be zero." "Your wish granted," said Scorpio. "What about the butterfly carvings? I marveled at how thin you made the wings. Did you attach the wings or was it all one piece of wood?"

293-Guinea Pig Sirus

Sirus lets loose a rib-breaking cough and could not regain his breath to give him an answer. Scorpio watched as three medical aids placed him onto a cart. He did not get his answer. Scorpio had a feeling within himself about the aged male. He never was much to socialize. His responses were with the least amount of words. This was the longest conversation he had ever had with his neighbor of an orbit ago. He buzzed Incu and informed her about Sirus' donation. "Incu, could you follow up what is going to be done with him? All of the Tubers are to focus on the blond bacteria, so he must be part of it. You will know the finer details. I am completing my studies on the digestive system of the caterpillar and the butterfly, Quiet time." "Scorpio, I miss you," were her only words.

It was a real puzzle to him how the same, if you call it that, the same insect had so many opposite habits. He had so many other interests, his first love was nearly lost. Caterpillar-butterfly, cater-pill--ar------ ---butt----er-------f------l----------y.

The first hundred Sands tests were complete, with 62 were placed in isolation. The others were placed, four or five in dwellings. No males were ringed and were separated from females. Ivan, the hairiest of the remaining 37, was complaining about his feelings of being naked. All complaints that were not medical were directed to Aires.

"Ivan, will you please unroll the plastic on the floor so we can talk to each other?" pleaded Aires.

294-Ivan plus 3

"How did you know my name?" he responded.

"Ivan, when you were being given your medical tests, photographs were taken. I see Manuel, Filipe and Francois are with you," Aires said. "Please unroll the monitor so we can see each other. It is yours to keep forever."

He was like a cat calculating if the rodent he wants is something he could win the battle with for his next meal. Slowly the Sands male dropped to his knees and touched the monitor with one finger. Aires said, "Just pic------------" and did not get to finish. Ivan frightened, picked up a chair to strike the monitor. Aires, speaking through the rolled monitor said, "Ivan, look at the ceiling near the entrance. Do you see the dome? I can see you. I'm very sorry I frightened you. Please unroll the monitor. I want you to see me and my people. I will not speak until you unroll the monitor."

Francois, the fearless one, picked it up, unrolled it and handed it to Ivan. He got a thank you from Aires, who then said, "Francois, pick up any of the other ones. Filipe and Manuel, please do the same." They all, except Ivan, had huge smiles on their faces. It was the first time they had seen a piece of plastic talking to them. I have many things to tell you. The first is how to get rid of your body waste. On the shelf near the entrance are collection pads," instructed Aires.

295-Diaper for Sands

"What is that?" asks Francois?

"You would probably call it a diaper," Aires continued. "If you have to urinate, the pad will absorb it two or three times. If you have to eliminate___" "You mean, take a shit," Francois cutting in. "Yes, that is right. Remove the diaper, lay it on the floor and dump onto it. Take the wand by the handle and squeeze it to clean your bottom," and again Francois cut in, "You mean, wash your ass," "Yes, you're right again. Take the rolled up collection pad and the plastic bag from the wand and put them in the chute by the entrance. You will not be allowed to leave this dwelling for a moon" Francois cuts in again, "What's a moon?" "It is 28 rotations or what you call days." Francois asked, "Why don't you just say a month?" "We count on a slightly different calendar," said Aires.

Each took a collection pad with only Francois putting it on right. They look at each other and started laughing. It was hilarious for Aires to see them in that state of amusement. He said, "A technician will be entering to remove all of your body hair. You all have lice. You will then have a scanning wand moved over your whole body to record any scars, skin blemishes, warts or any other skin problems." Francois asked, "Why the yellow line by the entrance?"

"Do not cross it," Aires warned, "You will get an electrical shock. The closer you get to the entrance the more powerful it will be. A dietician will visit and question you as to what flavor you would like your pellets. A uniform technician will fit you for clothing, and if you have any emotional needs that technician will make a visit. Good bye."

296-Manuel's wife dies

"We are powerless to control the situation in your homeland. Use the monitor for anything you wish. If there is writing, just place your finger on the word you do not understand and it will be voiced to you. Again I have to say to you, the monitor is yours forever. It will be one of the best friends you will ever have. It will tell you everything that is expected of you and will obey your every command.

Manuel unrolled his "plastic" and it said, "Your name is Manuel Galente. Once you speak to me I will know it is you. If anyone tries to talk to me, I will be mute."

"My name is Manuel Galente and I have a wife. Her name is Maria. She lives in Duvalle in The Sands. Can you tell me how she is doing?

"Do you have a street address?

"297 Dupree Street." The area was shown but not in detail as Manuel would like.

'My house is near where Dupree crosses Plantain Street. Can I get a closer look?" One is shown, and he yelled, "Closer. Closer" He then a shrieked! She is dead! My Maria is dead! Oh my God, my Maria is dead. My dog is by her. I must get back to bury her!" Wearing only his waste collector, he ran to the door grabbed the handle, and was thrown to the ground. He was wriggling while he was being dragged across the yellow line. Manuel felt the full effect of the shocking device. He lay there for three or more minutes, and then opened his eyes, and stares at the ceiling, "She is gone. My Maria is in heaven. May her soul rest in peace."

297-Rings explained

"How soon can I get to be with her?" groggily he pleaded to his monitor.

"You will be in this dwelling for one moon. You will not leave this dwelling until you have been ringed and your training complete," it responded.

"Years ago I have heard of the rings for men and they can never have sex. Never for me! I want to go back to the Sands like I am now!" he cried out.

A female appeared on his monitor in a very colorful suit and calmly said, "Please relax. Males here have accepted it and find it very beneficial to our society. Males can have sex only with the mate they have chosen."

"I must get back to the Sands! I will not be ringed!" he shouted at the monitor.

"The Sands voted to become one with us. You have no choice. You can go to the land to the north and they will slaughter anyone who enters their territory," said the female.

"Do the rings hurt when applied?" he queried"

"No pain. You will feel them at first but in time they will become part of you." She added, "You will then be able to have sex with the mate you choose. There is a technician approaching your dwelling. You were told about your hair removal. They look at their monitor and see a huge male park his bike, climb into an enormous clear plastic bag and seal himself into it. The entrance opened and he squeezed in and said, "Hello."

298-Haircut

"We cannot understand that word," said Manuel.

"Oh. I'm sorry. It means greetings," the technician points to their monitor and they obliged. "Who wants to be first?" Filipe walks forward. "Just stand where you are and in a minute I will have you as hairless as a fish."

The awkwardness of the bacteria proof bag did not seem to hamper any of his activities. The hair cutting device vacuumed what it removed into a clear plastic bag. As soon as he touched Philippe, he jerks away then relaxes and his hair was patiently removed. "These scars on your back are huge. How did you get them?"

"The mayor's wife was very fond of me," was all he said.

Ivan added quickly, "He got away easy."

"That can never happen here," the technician said while still cutting hair. "The rings will guarantee pain that brings tears. You will have only one sex partner. In a moon or so you will be able to control yourselves. Have you been enjoying the food pellets? I see that all of you need some meat on your bones." Francois tried to cut in but the technician just kept on talking. "I'm sure the dietician will make things right for you. We have some real nice females but; no rings-no females "Now I have one fish, so let me start on you, hairy boy."

299-How to bathe

Shaving Ivan took three times as long. The technician thought to himself, "When this guy enters the mating pool, I wonder which female is going to want to mate with a gorilla?" He had to use two bags for him. He shaved the other two and scanned their bodies with the recorder wand. "You were given a physical, so there is no more for you to do than follow the directions on your monitor."

"What about clothes?" asks Manuel.

"The uniform technician will be here shortly. Have you been shown your sanitation procedures?" he asked and they all nodded. "Well, let me show it to you again. This door leads to the private place and it has a fan to take away the stink. That stack has the, what you call, diapers. The other stack is for your washing wand. Ivan, let me give you a bath to show how to properly use it. Take off your collection pad." He attaches a hose onto a liter of room temperature water, and then holds it near Ivan's chest showing how far from his skin to hold it. He wands his chest and one arm, then lets him finish his whole body. The liter was empty and the technician attaches another. More than half of that was used too. "Less than a liter is what you will use when you get good at taking a bath," said the technician.

Philippe was next and complained that the water was too cold. "If you want it warmer, hold the bottle under your armpit for a while or let it sit in the sun," advised the technician.

300-Uniform

After he washed it seemed that his skin was two shades lighter. He was dirty! The technician took the second wand and handed it to Manuel. He cleaned himself and was told that he did not do a very good job around his butt. He did that part again and was surprised how little water he used. They were told to observe the color of the wastewater and if it was a blood color, report it to health department immediately.

"Now for the bags: The identification for them is made from the necklace that you are wearing. Everyone's is different. Do not mix; Very important. If you do, the examiners will identify an error and you will be charged. He was explaining again how to drop their solid waste into the collection pad when another technician entered.

"You guys look like a bunch of newborns. I brought four suits with me. Who wants to be first?" he asked.

Philippe, as usual, stepped forward first. "Let me explain how to put it on. The two leg sections are the same. The waist section middle flap is on the back side. The top section with the hood, sleeves and gloves is easy to understand. The breathing face mask is used when biting bugs are around. Mosquitoes cause malaria, so when they and a few other troublemakers are in season, wearing it is a must. Snakes can bite through it."

Philippe put his leg into one piece and he said it felt like there was a lubricant inside of it. His toes were in place in no time. He did the other then wrapped the waist section around himself. Reaching between his legs, he pulled the flap and stuck it to the front. He put on the jacket with a seal down the front, and then put on the hood. The face mask felt like it was not there at all. That was a surprise to him.

301-Uniform

"I must leave you now. My clean air container is nearly exhausted. Get yourselves into you new outfits and the dietician will be with you shortly." He said good bye, and left.

Manuel grieving over the death of his wife was reluctant to do anything. He was crying in a chair when the dietician entered. She was a petite female, one fourth the size of the monster that just left. Manuel glanced up at her and tried to cover his bottom with the waist band in a roll. "Shame is unknown here. Ringed males cannot express themselves." Philippe's traditions kicked in and he approached her rapidly, even knowing that she is in her bubble. She held up a clear plastic rod and said, "This thing is a foreign educator." Totally oblivious of what she just said, a slight touch on Philips's wrist made him scream in pain. "No touch, no pain," she said then asked Manuel to get dressed. She doubted if he could retain very much in the misery he was in. After he had his outfit in place correctly, she noticed Philippe head cover allowing some skin to show on his back.

"Philippe, your headpiece is not in place correctly. May I help you?" she asked.

"Madam, you can touch me wherever you want," he answered.

"In time you will have no problems," she said as she made a minor adjustment.

302-Pellets

"The slot on the side of the entrance will be for your pellets," the dietician said very slowly. "Pellets are all that you will ever get. If you want to know how they are made and what from, please ask your monitor. Now, if you have any kind of rash or trouble breathing, tell you monitor immediately. Manuel, the physical you had showed that you are a diabetic. The pellets marked for you are only for you and no one else. You are not to have any of the others, ever. Manuel, I must stress gain, do not touch anyone's pellets. None of you eat Manuel's. We want to get your bodies ready for the return trip to the Sands. Philippe, if your urge to play with females is overwhelming, tell your monitor. Are there any questions or problems you want to talk about before I leave?"

Manuel asked if he could get a view of his house, to see what happened to his wife. "Did you forget? Just ask your monitor," she calmly instructed him.

"I can see my house and my wife was not lying in front of it. My dog is not there either. Can I get someone to look inside?

Did you ask your monitor?" she said.

Without any hesitation he asked, "Monitor, I want to see inside my house," and his wish was granted. He saw her sitting at their table eating and then throwing some food to the dog.

Before the dietician is about to exit she asked again, "Are there any more requests or questions?" They, not paying any attention, are concentrating on Manuel's monitor.

303-Call to Sands

"Can I talk to her?" he asked the monitor?

"Nearest communication, 1 kilometer. Message relay doubtful," it answered.

"Mister Monitor, let me talk to anyone nearest to my home," he pleaded.

A phone rang many times but no one answered.

'Mr. Monitor is there another one you can get for me?" he asked.

A phone rings eight times and he heard, "What?"

All excited to talk with someone from the Sands, Manuel tried to act as calm as possible, "Can you deliver a message to my wife in Duvall?"

"I cannot leave. Everyone is either too sick or have the same problem I have; if I leave, all of my belongings will be stolen," he answered, "Where are you calling from?"

"I'm on a 28 day detention with the Tube people," he answered.

"What did you do wrong?" he asked.

"I should have said that the ones that survived are in quarantine," he responded.

"You mean some of our healthiest have died?"

304-Thieves

"Yes. Scientists have found the bacteria that are killing us and hope to have some medicine that will help us. I do hope it is very soon. How many are still living around your home?" he asked.

"Six from my house I have shallow-buried. Four houses on one side are empty and the next one has one out of ten. Three out of four the other ways, then many are empty. I just leave long enough to get food or water from the empty houses. I do not know why I am still here. I have begged the Lord to please take me. I have to leave now, I hear thieves coming! I have to hide! They never seem to get sick." They all heard a loud bang and the phone drop. Quiet for a minute then, "Pardon me. May I help you? I am with Federal Security. Can I be of any assistance to you?" the educated voice asked.

"Oh, yes please! I want to let my wife know that I am fine and hope that she is the same," Manuel pleaded

"Could you give me her address and I will gladly do you the service?" he said with the gentlest of voices.

"I would like to have your service number so I can have future contact with you?" Manual requested.

"239045," he readily gave his number.

305-Breakthrough

"I will call you right back. I am having a problem with my ill friend." Manuel answered and knowing that the man was not with the Federal Security. He knows that there were never any zeros in any of their numbers. He waited about ten minutes, saw the dietician leave, then asked for the same number. The line was dead. He asked his monitor to view the address of that phone number and saw a male lying in front of his house. How cruel can life be? Why is it that the miserable have to endure more misery? How can this resolved as soon as possible? Philippe, François and Ivan are sound asleep on their mats. Manuel was exhausted too. He unrolled his mat, tried to sleep but it eluded him. He was just getting cozy when his monitors flashed. Aires noticed they were on quiet time and does not buzz. Manuel saw Aires looking directly at him and said, "I'm awake."

"Manuel," excitingly Aires said, "We have a break through with the Blond Bacteria and have to rush your schedule up considerably. Please eat to your heart's content. Make sure you drink enough water to digest your pellets. You will be placed in a static chamber for three rotations then you will be ringed. After that you will be able to mingle with us tubers. Would you like that?"

He let out a loud cheer, waking up the three, and then told them the good news. They all started to sing:

306-Sands singing

My many children are my wealth
My many wives are best in good health
When I get tired, old and gray
My many children are with me to pray
Now children remember, the day is long
Nothing is better than a joyous song
Making love is part of our way
The more of us to grace our stay
We sing the best for last
Our bed is for more than rest
To have each other is our greatest desire
The beauty of love and now to retire

They sang it over and over and being in such joyous mood they asked their monitor for some alcoholic beverages. The female asked, "What is your preference?"

"Anything you've got and please make it quick," shouted Francois. This is the most vocal he had been since arriving at The Tubes.

307-More alcohol

The fourth repeat was interrupted by a huge male in his bag entering their dwelling with four tiny containers of liquid. The all rushed him with Francois getting there first. Francois grabbed one and the others took one handed to them. Francois, struggling to open his, noticed Ivan gulping his down.

"How did you do that? Open mine," he demanded.

Ivan pulled on the cap firmly and pulled it off. He was about to put that bottle next to his lips when Francois grabbed it, took one gulp and it was empty.

Loudly, Francois shouted into his monitor, "That was nothing! Bring ten more!"

"That is all you will get," responded the monitor "Do not act like children."

"What's with this children crap? I want another drink! I'm a real good boy, so what do you say? I'll even say please! Please and a hundred pleases!" begged Francois.

The tiny dietician came in view and told them they are in the middle of a medical testing program and alcohol will distort the results. Her saying that infuriated Francois.

"Look, either I get my drink or I'll rip up my suit. Is that clear?" he screamed .

"You will get no more." The screen went blank.

308-Broken neck

Ivan tried to sooth Francois as he grabbed anything to throw. He picked up his mat and threw it in Ivan's direction. It unrolled and fell harmlessly to the floor. He was about to throw his monitor when Ivan got him into a headlock, then shouted, "You damn fool; we are trying to help our Sands and you act like a child. One squeeze and I'll break your neck if you don't calm down!" then he tightened up his grasp.

Francois went limp and Ivan let him fall to the floor. Unknown to them, the dwelling camera recorded the event.

"What in the hell am I going to do? I can't run and hide. I'm stuck here." They removed his face cover and splashed water onto his face. It did nothing. Manuel checked his heartbeat and found none. Philippi tried the same and felt that he is getting a little cooler. Ivan yelled out, "I'm in deep doo-doo. How can an idiot like Francois bring me so much agony? This is more than I can handle!" His monitor buzzed and it was Aires. He noticed from the ceiling camera and asked, "Who is on quiet time without a mat?"

"I think the bug killed him!" said Ivan looking at the floor.

"He had no symptoms of any kind. Are you sure?" questioned Aires.

"I did it. I broke his neck. He was going nuts and I tried to calm him. I didn't mean to. It just happened!" Ivan cries out.

309-Demagnetizer

Aires had two flingers at their door in a matter of minutes but they could not enter because of the quarantine. Bubbles would be available from a medical center 2 ½ kilometers away. While Aires waited he reviewed the incident filed from the ceiling camera. He then told the three to drag Francois to the entrance and go to the private place. He was going to have the two flingers use tongs and place the body of Francois into the body bag but decided that the Blond Bacteria showed no mercy.

It took three minutes for the bags to be delivered. The peddler helped the two into the bags and left. Entering the dwelling, they heard the three from the private place and were leery of what they were going to do. One of the flingers felt for a pulse. There was none. He placed a tubeless stethoscope onto the male's chest; there were no sounds. Placing him into a bag and sealing it, they loaded him onto a cart and delivered him to the morgue.

Aires had been so busy the past few rotations he had no contact with Almaaz or Scorpio. His mate was on quiet time. Buzzing Scorpio, he found that he was digging in the Field of Memories. "Scorpio, did you ever mention anything about hair and static electricity to anyone?"

"I casually said something to Incu. Why?"

The life of the Blondie is short. The life cycle is a little more than one rotation. A prolific multiplier. I just read a report stating that by just placing an infected person into a demagnetizing chamber for two rotations destroys all of the hairy monsters," said Aires.

310-Ivan sorry

Francois' body was delivered to the morgue. They had just finished their 14th body this rotation. It was a busy one. They were all exhausted and their leader said, "Let's check if he has any beats; if not? quiet time." They had just voted and were told that he was informed by Aires to vote NO and the reason. There was no life left in Francois. They all unrolled their mats and in a matter of minutes they all looked like the one they were about to dissect.

Ivan was terrified by what he thought was going to happen to him. He did not mean to hurt François. He just wanted to calm him down. Francois was delirious. Manuel and Philippe said they would tell whoever they must talk to it was an accident. Ivan said, "I broke his neck. I didn't hear a snap, but I did have a good grip on him. Why did he get so mad over a drink of alcohol? Oh Francois, I'm sorry. If I could bring you back to life I would. I'm so sorry!"

Manuel placed his hand on Ivan's cleanly shaven head and tried to console him. He started to sing the same song they had just sung earlier. It had some effect but his tears did not stop.

Quiet times bring tranquility to you inner self. Take one now. Please.

311-Ivan cleared

About an hour later, Aires buzzed the three Sands people with a report of the cause of Francois' death. "He had a blood clot in his heart. It is not rare that hyper personalities cause their hearts to beat at such a fast rate that no blood is pumped at all. The scuffle you had with him was justified. He was dead when you first felt his limp body. We will take care of his burial here. I want the three of you to bathe by 9 AM. Each of you will be placed into a chamber to destroy any Blondies you might have in your bodies. After that, the Ringing Team is going to pay you a visit. Trust me. You will hardly feel them being applied. I wish I could spend more time with you to show all of the benefits we have. They are mostly because of the rings. The female medallion is part of it too. So, be patient and use your monitor to explore our homeland. I'm sure you will cooperate with us in making yours the same. Oh, Ivan. I just received a report that you were exonerated in the death of your countryman. Please console yourself. His emotional problem would have done him in sooner or later. Is there anything I can do for you now?"

"Your alcohol person says I am limited for the good stuff. How about some nice juicy pork chops, mashed potatoes with gravy and a huge salad?" he said drooling.

"Sorry. We only have some fresh fruit to infuse pellet with the flavor of your choice. Oh, by the way, three stationary bicycles will be delivered. Get your body used to using pedaling. You will be using a bike lot. Take your break times to rejuvenate your whole person. Good bye and may the wind be always at your back," said Aires.

312-Scorpio chosen

Scorpio was buzzed by the medical department and told he was chosen to be on the first wave to be delivered to the Sands. He had a choice of assembling static chambers, moving dirt or preparing their first organized lonesome place. "I definitely want to be working with the chambers," he quickly responded.

"Report to the erection plant 14 kilometers north at exit 127," said the male with a very low voice. "The plant manager will be expecting you in the next rotation. Inform your procreators of your schedule. You will not be returning for an orbit or so."

Scorpio was excited to no end. He buzzed Incu, quiet time. The same for donor. He left a message for Incu about his new assignment and wanted to visit her. It was his quiet time too.

Almaaz buzzed Aires as soon as she read her message. "He is too young to be on such a dangerous mission! He is unaware of the problems they have! He would not know how to handle a monster in an unruly crowd! He would never-" Aires cut in, "He is going to be a male of prominence. He does not have any growth of facial hair, but he does have the wisdom of many twice his age. I have one item to complete here and will be with you with in the half hour. Relax and make him feel like a hero."

Scorpio buzzed her work dwelling. Signs and flashing lights were at every entrance. Almaaz decontaminated herself and was outside much faster than she had ever been before.

313-Last hugs

Incu waited for Scorpio and got very impatient. She looked at the exit ramp of the tube, to see the pride of her life. The one that she dreamed from her youth. The special procreation that would make the Tubes better than it ever was before. Someone who would be kind, intelligent, energetic enough to generate many kilowatts, the most desired male in the mating pool. Then gets a tap on her shoulder. "Scorpio."

Her eyes filled with tears. Scorpio hugged his incubator with fervor. "I have to be at exit 127 the next rotation to enter the assembly dwelling for static chamber construction. When enough are completed, I will be on my way to the Sands. Isn't that great?" he said without taking one breath.

"Scorpio! Scorpio! Do you know what you are getting yourself into? Not only will you have the plague of the bacteria, but also the unruliness of the unethical Sands people!" As her sobbing got louder, she squeezed him tighter.

Scorpio, startled at her emotions, did not understand her misery. He wants to look at her and explain how happy he was but her grip did not release. Donor arrived and was unaware of what Incu said. He joined the two with more hugs.

"I'm sorry. I could not contain myself. Please don't be upset with me. The one that I suckled, nurtured and embraced to my chest so many times is now going to be placed in surroundings that are inhuman," she cried.

314-Parting tears

"I will be fine," Scorpio said trying to calm his incubator. There will be many of the Tubers there. You always wanted our place to be better than it was in the past. Others in this world are in need of the same!"

"Sure. Sure. We want everyone in the world to have the joys we have. Their minds are not the same as ours. It took many generations to bring the conditions we have now." Donor interrupted, "The Sands people's backs are up against a wall and theirs have nowhere to go. Why did it take such a catastrophe for us to come to their aid? They voted for us to assist them. We voted to bring them our ways," Incu shouted, "I know it is for the better, but do you think that they will just roll over and become one of us? They are animals. Their misery is inbred!" Donor calmly said, "Breed in, breed out."

"Do you know how many generations that will take? I don't want my Scorpio breeding into that flock. They have no history of their genes.

I doubt if they have any inkling of who their second generation back was. They are animals. Lower than animals. Low----" Donor cut in sharply, "Please control yourself! All you are doing is making a bad situation worse. Scorpio, you will have over 8 or 9 orbits to join the mating pool. With the Sands situation, it may be a lot sooner. Whichever it is, you must be always aware that the only reason for procreation is for your offspring to be a child of two loving procreators. We have had perfect couples who made their offspring miserable.

315-Scorpio leaving

When you get to the Sands you will have enough to keep yourself busy without even thinking about mating. Your rings will be your salvation. The responsibilities will occupy most of your time. You have also your holo teachers. They are still in my schedule too. Do not be excited about what is going to be happening. The environment will be new but in time you will adapt to any conditions that are forced on you." Sobbing Incu blurted "Scorpio, I'm sorry. So sorry I over-reacted. I want nothing but the best for you. Donor, please forgive me. I am going to miss my sweet Scorpio ever so much." She released her grip on him and took a step back and admired his whole body through eyes that were full of tears.

"I never dreamed that I would be getting this kind of send-off. I thought it would be similar to me going to a championship bounce game. Incu, I will be extremely cautious in my dealings with the Sands. I promise not to venture away from the probable security that will surround the testing chambers. My curiosity into butterflies will still be there and maybe in time bounce will be one of their most loved sports. Please don't worry about me. I will be fine," he said with a huge smile of confidence.

"Offspring," calmly Donor said, "You be a kind and loving person and most things will come your way. Your intelligence will make all around you better for everyone. Relax and remember us by knowing that we will love you always."

Jack B. Sudar

316-Scorpio leaves

"I am going to leave now. Everything is happening so quickly. Can I give you a hug before I leave? I have to be there the next rotation. I am all excited about what I am going to be doing." He gave Donor a real tight hug and he said to Scorpio, "Be careful, be patient, and be yourself. Remember, the Tubes are our way of life and the strangers will need some time to adapt. Be very patient with them. I'm so proud of you."

He turned to Incu who cried and could not say a word. She hugged him and did not want to let go. Scorpio did nothing to discourage it. He knew without any doubts, she gave him an inner joy of life only an incubator could instill.

When Incu let go of her grip on Scorpio, she noticed a tear in his eye. He got on his bicycle and pedaled to the tube entrance. They wave to him as he went up the ramp. He turned back for a last look, and raised his right hand to say goodbye.

A JAGGED SEASON
FALL IN BONNET, TEXAS

GEORGE WILLIAM

iUniverse, Inc.
New York   Bloomington

iUniverse books may be ordered through booksellers or by contacting:

iUniverse
1663 Liberty Drive
Bloomington, IN 47403
www.iuniverse.com
1-800-Authors (1-800-288-4677)

Because of the dynamic nature of the Internet, any Web addresses or links
contained in this book may have changed since publication and may no longer be
valid. The views expressed in this work are solely those of the author and do not
necessarily reflect the views of the publisher, and the publisher hereby disclaims
any responsibility for them.

ISBN: 978-1-4401-2593-5 (sc)
ISBN: 978-1-4401-2591-1 (dj)
ISBN: 978-1-4401-2592-8 (ebook)

Library of Congress Control Number: 2009923280

Printed in the United States of America

iUniverse rev. date: 03/04/2009

For
Christopher, Catherine, Stephanie, Jennifer and Anthony

A JAGGED SEASON

CHAPTER ONE

Heroes don't often come to Bonnet, so we leech onto those we get. We don't want them to leave. We don't want them to change. We don't care if they die as long as they remain icons frozen in image. We preserve them like canned fruits and vegetables—peaches, apples, beans, running backs—then store them so we can reach up and take them from their aging places on our shelves—getting our fixes from their past moments of glory and never considering that those moments might be theirs. They belong to us. What they do, they do for us; we can do with them as we please. We meant for my nephew Cobus to be our next hero.

Our little town rests, as it has for 150 years, on a cedar-covered limestone plateau in the Hill Country of Texas. Caliche dust and heat are our constant companions. We are farmers where we can get water and rangeland ranchers where it's harder to find. We raise cattle and ride horses; we hunt deer, hogs, and dove. It's thirty minutes by pickup to Llano, the rope-throwing capital of the world. We're real cowboys, but the truth is the town gets its personality from the way the football season goes. Ten weeks in the fall tell whether we'll have to bite our tongues when the bastards from Bee Tree drop by to rub our faces in it, or whether

1

we get to be the cocky sons-a-bitches who drive to their place
once a week to remind them how we're going to kick their asses
all over the field again next November.

Half the town turns out for the games. They start coming
as infants in car seats and keep coming until they are no longer
able. Mathilda Hannah—Tildy—hasn't missed a game in thirty
years, and she always sits in the same seat. She sat there when
Doug and I were in high school and played for Bonnet. She
sat there with Macey, Amanda, and Inez on the last evening in
August, twenty years later, watching Doug's son play for Bonnet
against Solvado.

It was Cobus's senior year. By half, Bonnet led twenty-four to
nothing, and we were standing and buzzin' about the way they'd
played and about how Cobus had run—breaking tackles and
knocking Solvado boys over. We were already thinking about the
state championship, and some of us were crazy enough to talk
about it with nine and a half games still remaining.

Doug wasn't that crazy. At least he didn't show it. He took it
all in. Ten or twelve of his friends—I always called them friends;
he did sometimes—gave him a hard time about how much better
Cobus was playing than Doug ever had.

"Goddammit, that boy can run," said fat Alex Trombetta,
blowing cigar smoke in our faces. "You know, these kids are a lot
bigger and stronger than they were when you and I played, aren't
they, Douggy?"

Doug hated to be called Douggy, so I knew he was cringing.
Al Trombetta had been in school a full ten years before Doug and
me. To look at him now did not give one the slightest impression
that he had ever accomplished anything on a football field other
than to take up a lot of space. Even if he was right about the kids
being stronger, I couldn't imagine anyone being bigger than he
was.

"This is not the same game you played, is it, Doug?" offered
Bud Granger.

How did he know? He'd moved here ten years after Doug graduated.

I tried to smooth over the barbs by smirking at Doug in a way I hoped would let him know that laughing at himself—at ourselves—was really okay. I should have known better.

"And you thought you were good," I said, stupidly.

There was no thinking about it. Doug had a gift—smooth—always choosing to finesse a defender out of a few yards with a glide step or a quick shift of the hips. Sometimes, Cobus left me wincing with insecure images of unnecessary force. Doug never had. Doug had been grace and agility—pure athletic beauty. He was tall and slender and ran with long strides. Changes of speed and direction were so subtle that the average rigidly muscled high school defender had no chance. Once Doug was in the open field he was never stopped. He didn't run; he danced effortlessly—like Fred Astaire in a uniform. *Fred.* He'd liked it when we called him that, until he couldn't play any more. I called him that once, later, and he threw a glass across the room and then walked out as it shattered against the wall with me scurrying to avoid the shards.

Doug had a scholarship to the University of Texas. He blew out his knee in the first week of practice and never played football again.

So Doug knew full well what was happening with Cobus. He had lived it. Maybe that's why he didn't say much; he understood the fragility of it all and knew that none of them would ever understand. I was the only one in the crowd who even had a clue that he really was proud of his son and afraid for him at the same time. I knew because Doug lived with me then and had for seven years since the summer Sally divorced him. Sally is my sister. Doug was my roommate. I am his ex-wife's brother and Cobus's uncle. So I was proud of Cobus too, only I didn't hide it. I was loud and crazy like the rest of them, slapping Doug on the back, trying to get him loosen up a bit—a grin, a twitch in the corner of his lip—anything. When Doug moved in with me, I inherited the job of making him happy. It was a job with plenty of security because it was never finished.

He didn't break a smile until just before half-time ended. He had recognized something, or someone, and he lit up some. I thought the boys must have come back onto the field, and he smiled because he saw Cobus—but that wasn't it. I turned to look at the field, and, except for six junior high boys playing a quick game of touch, it was empty.

Tildy was ascending the seats with septuagenarians in tow, calling out to Doug. All of us knew Tildy, but that was nothing more than an occasional hello at the post office. This picture of her, a five-foot-one, ponytailed, seventy-four-year-old woman attacking the bleachers and brandishing her purse to fend off any helping hand that was offered, made him smile. I should have known he wasn't smiling at Cobus.

"Douglas. Douglas Meadhran," she called as she stretched her leg up onto the next seat.

Her voice was sharp with plenty of volume to be heard over our noise. The clamor around us stopped as all eyes fixed on her for a moment with the same bemused stare I had seen on Doug's face. We held that gaze until the boys came back onto the field, which, fortunately, they did just as Tildy and her entourage made it to the halfway mark of their ascent—bleacher row number seven. The cheer that rose for the team and the anticipation of the beginning of the second half stole the attention of the crowd back from the old gals.

Tildy kept coming. It would have been much easier for her to use the steps in the aisle, but her personality dictated the direct approach—a bee-line right up the seats. She made it up to our level without elevating her breathing by as much as a pant—a feat which young Cobus himself may not have been able to accomplish in a like amount of time. Amanda and Inez were a bit more winded but followed closely, nevertheless. It was a humid Texas night and Macey, who was overweight, was panting heavily and perspiring through her cotton dress by the time she made it to us, half a minute behind the others.

She said, "I would have been here sooner, but I stopped to breathe. My, my, it's hot."

The people in our section of the bleachers moved aside to make way for the four women. Tildy sat at the left side of Doug with her hand on his shoulder; Macey, Amanda, and Inez sat so they could hear everything that was being said between Tildy and Doug—each one of them leaning forward a bit more than the one in front of her—each one with the same intensely eager look on her face.

It wasn't that any of them lacked a mind of her own, but Tildy was their leader, and they were perfectly content to follow.

I was on the right of Doug and leaned in to hear Tildy like her group leaned from the left. Doug was polite. If he was at all nonplused by the presence of the visitors, he didn't show it. He sat when they did. He kept a submissive grin on his face while he listened to Tildy speak—never acting for a minute like he was the least bit annoyed at having the game interrupted. Tildy began by talking about football; I assumed that was the entire purpose of her climb up the bleachers.

"Your boy's not nearly as good as you were," she said.

Doug's earlier simper changed to a broad toothy smile when she said that. I hadn't been able to perk him up in weeks, and she did it in ten seconds.

"I know," he said. "There's not many around here who remember that though."

He was referring to the prodding he had endured a few minutes before. It had been delivered with good intention, but apparently he had not taken it entirely that way. How were we to know what he was feeling? I made a mental note not to compare him to Cobus again. I filed it away alongside the Fred Astaire reference.

"Well, I remember, Douglas," said Tildy, without a hint of a grin. To her, football was sacrosanct. "You were the best that's ever come out of this county. Your boy's good. He can knock a few people down, but he doesn't stop my heart like you did. No one else has since."

It was as though she had known that the entire town was making a fuss about Cobus—making fools of ourselves, trying to get on Doug's good side by reminding him of what must have been a painful memory. Maybe even watching football was painful for him—even his own son. How could we have known that? Maybe Tildy knew and had come up to rescue him. That thought didn't cross my mind then—I was too perplexed by her presence—but it has since.

Doug simply said, "Thank you." I could feel him relaxing. Something about Tildy warmed him; I knew he trusted her and was glad she was sitting beside him. I had never been sure he trusted anyone, and I knew he didn't always care to be with most of the men who usually surrounded him.

"Golf," said Tildy.

"Golf?" asked Doug, mystified.

"Golf, Mr. Meadhran," said Macey, wiping the perspiration from the folds beneath her chin with a handkerchief.

After the knee surgery, Doug moved back to Bonnet for his rehabilitation. He worked hard at first with Sally visiting him every day, helping him with his exercises. I don't remember that Mom and Dad were even that upset when Sally became pregnant with Cobus. I'm sure they were; I just don't remember it. It probably doesn't happen any more often in small towns than it does in other places. It's more visible, though; it's accepted more. Kids marry younger out here than they do in the city, anyway, and everyone figured that Doug and Sally would probably have been married sooner or later. Cobus just made it sooner. He was born the year after Sally graduated from high school. That's when Doug started feeling like everything he did turned out wrong. He didn't talk about it then like he came to talk to me about it later but, looking back, I'm sure he felt that way. There was a chance he could have gone back to the University—or even a smaller school—to try football again, but when he found out about the baby, he quit his rehabilitation and took a job.

Peach Pit, Texas has a golf course—eighteen miles south of Bonnet. Doug, like a lot of us, had worked there in the summers on the grounds crew. It was steady work and we liked the hours because it was a lot cooler at four in the morning watering greens than it was at four in the afternoon in the grain elevator at my daddy's feed mill.

Squinty Spencer was the pro in Peach Pit; he ran the whole show. He owned the pro shop, taught lessons, acted as the greenskeeper and slipped behind the grill to fry hamburgers when the need arose. He'd lost his left eye playing mumblety-peg as a kid, donned a patch and forever the name of Squinty. He won a lot of tournaments around Texas. In 1958 he made it all the way to the U.S. Open where they paired him with Sam Snead. Squinty shot forty-seven on the front side and then packed his bags. Depth perception was a problem for him; he couldn't play on big, undulating greens because he couldn't gauge distance with only one eye. He realized then that the only way he was going to make much money from golf was by teaching it. He never played another tournament; he became one of the best teachers in an area of the country that has produced the finest in the game.

The day after Sally told Doug she was pregnant, he asked Squinty for a job. He said it had to pay more than it had before, though, because of the baby. Squinty found as much for Doug to do as he could. He kept him busy inside when the weather was bad, cleaning the clubhouse, working behind the cash register, or in the snack bar—outside when spring came, repairing the equipment, picking the range, or preparing the greens and fairways. Squinty did something else for Doug, too. Any time things were slow around the pro shop, he would talk to Doug about golf. We had all played without knowing much about the game, and most of us got to where we could shoot around ninety by cheating four or five strokes a round. Doug usually found a way to beat us when we played, but we didn't pay any attention to the way he swung the club. We didn't know a bad swing from a good one.

Doug began hitting balls with Squinty watching. Squinty saw right away what the rest of us learned later. Doug had one of the finest pairs of hands that have ever held a club. Squinty told anyone who would listen to him that Doug had been born for one thing and it wasn't football. Squinty said that Doug had been born to swing a golf club.

"Doug," said Tildy, "we've come to ask you for instruction in the game of golf."

"That's right, Mr. Meadhran—Doug," said Amanda.

Amanda was the smallest of the four—almost frail. Where Tildy was often without hat or sunglasses, Amanda was never seen with any of her skin exposed. Her skin was white—the same white eggshell color—all year round. Not Tildy. She had kindly tanned lines outlining her smile and surrounding her bright blue eyes with a permanent, mischievous squint. She wore granny glasses, which on her, ironically, didn't make her look granny at all—especially with the ponytail. She looked like she'd attended Woodstock and traded handmade jewelry for the golden wire rims.

"Miss Hannah," said Doug, tightening his grin, "I'm not a professional."

"That's in name only. And, considering the amount of time we will be spending together for the next ten weeks, I expect you to address me as Tildy. You know the others—Macey, Inez, and Amanda. That's what they wish to be called. We shall call you Doug."

His full smile returned.

"I'd love to call you Tildy," he said, shaking his head in mild disbelief at the prospect of teaching the ladies to play. "But, if you really want to take some lessons, you should drive on down to Peach Pit to see Squinty. He's the best there is, you know."

Perhaps he was thinking they would appreciate someone more their own age. I know I was.

"I've known Beaufort Spencer since nineteen fifty-five," she said. "I'm sure he's a fine professional. But I don't have the time or inclination to drive to Peach Pit every day. Besides, he never played the game like you."

Squinty was in his late sixties that fall—six or seven years younger than Tildy.

"Beaufort?" I chuckled, immediately wishing I'd not acted so amused.

"A mother does not name a newborn *Squinty*," said Tildy. "He was named for his grandfather who was killed at San Juan when he followed Teddy Roosevelt up the hill."

"Every day?" asked Inez. "You didn't say we would have to play golf every day, Tildy."

Tildy didn't turn her head to respond to Inez. She kept her hypnotic attention pinned on Doug's bewildered face. He was totally at her mercy.

"I'm sure Douglas will agree with me; if we are to win a golfing tournament at the last of October, then it will be necessary to practice every day."

"The last of October?" said Doug, his smile disappearing entirely, giving way to a pained grimace.

"We are ready to start practice on Sunday," she continued. "We wish to practice for one hour, under your tutelage, beginning at six-fifteen every morning. After our supper each evening we will practice for an additional hour on our own."

The time of day certainly didn't bother Doug—neither did the every day part. He was at his pasture most mornings by that time. I'm sure Tildy was aware of that fact. I could tell he was figuring how impossible it would be to get anyone to the point of even making it around nine holes of golf in ten weeks—let alone ready for a competition.

Everyone around us stood as Cobus took a pitch-out from Tommy. The defensive end fell down when Cobus shifted gears and turned the corner. He was gone. Nobody came close to touching him.

Macey stood, yelling with the rest of us.

"Oh, my," she screamed. "Oh, my, my." That's what Macey always screamed.

Inez said, "Did he make a touchdown, Macey?"

Inez's vision had never been good; she was extremely nearsighted. The way she looked right past you, never really focusing, made you think that she wasn't perceptive in other ways, but that wasn't true. She was as sharp as Tildy, only her handicap made her more cautious. She always stood, sat, yelled, or groaned with the rest of the crowd and then let a companion fill in the details later.

"Oh, my."

"Macey. Did he score a touchdown?" She tugged at Macey's dress like a kid pulling at her big sis for attention.

"Oh, my," said Macey again, alternately waving her hankie and using it to wipe her chins. "Didn't you see it?"

"Of course she didn't see it, Macey," said Amanda, deliberately answering for Inez—knowing Inez would never deliver the sting deserved. "How could she with you jumping up and down on that bleacher seat, blocking her vision with that…that handkerchief of yours?"

"Inez," said Tildy, with staccato delivery, "Tommy took one step back and underhanded a straight pitch to Cobus. He shuffle-stepped, waiting for Jerry Grune to throw a block, turned up inside the end who fell down on the right side, and then he ran a straight line to the end zone—forty-three yards."

I don't know how she saw it because she and Doug never stood up. When I turned around to hear her play-by-play she was still sitting—as if there wasn't a game there—as if she hadn't seen a thing—riveting Doug as well as any snake charmer with her golf tournament talk.

"What tournament?" he said.

"We will be playing against four ladies from the Bee Tree Women's Golf League. They're much younger than we—probably as young as your friend Beaufort Spencer—but that won't matter.

We will play them in Peach Pit rather than on their home field. Am I using the right terms? I think it only proper that we play at a neutral site."

The concept of neutral site was interesting since the four had never played at any site before, as Bonnet didn't have a golf course anyway.

"Home course," murmured Doug.

"Yes. Of course. Home course."

Doug was beaten all right. As I watched him squirming to form one last feeble objection, it occurred to me that not only had he given in, he was looking forward to it. He was already planning how he was going to go about it. He was in a trance like he was playing again. When he'd played, I could walk up to him during a round and speak to him; he'd look right through me—like I wasn't there. He looked like that now.

"I'm not a pro, you know," he said.

"If I'm not mistaken," said Tildy, "that only means you can't take money from us. Is that correct?"

"Yes."

"We hadn't planned on paying."

"That's fine," he mumbled. I doubt if he even heard her. Just like he didn't notice a few seconds later when Cobus recovered a fumble in Solvado's end zone.

"Oh, my," gasped Macey.

He didn't see the last twenty-one points the boys scored. His mind was all tied up by Tildy and her tournament. It had taken her less than ten minutes and then she went back to watching the game. She didn't miss a down—hadn't in over thirty years.

The final score was fifty-two to three, with Cobus scoring four times, and Doug didn't see much of it.

CHAPTER TWO

A L TROMBETTA'S CAFÉ-BAR, THE only eatery in Bonnet, doesn't have a name. *Café* is stenciled proudly on one window and *Bar* on the other. We crowd around the rustic oak table after games—home and away—to spout opinions on the coach, players, weather, and anything else we think deserves our attention. Bud Granger is the most vocal. Doug's the quietest. Families dine in homemade, vinyl-covered booths lining the wall, and eight stools front the bar where some sit to drink. Our gathering table clogs the middle of the room, between bar and booths, so we eat and drink.

It was the first game, so we'd forgotten the unwritten rules about how much we could or could not expect Doug to join in our bull. We couldn't slap him on the back, we couldn't compare him to his son, and we couldn't talk about a state championship with nine games left. We should have remembered those rules by halftime—he'd sent us enough signals—but either the lopsided win or Tildy made us a little slower than we should have been.

Big Al, holding a tray of empty beer bottles, leaned over and rested his arm on Doug's shoulder so he could talk in his ear. He'd done that to me before; he breathes so loud that it's hard to hear his words over the air. "Goddammit, Doug," he exhaled, mixing stale cigar breath with the aroma of beer, "when in tarnation are you going to loosen up? We're going to win the goddamned state championship, and you'll be sitting here with that same sour look on your puss."

"Pass me the fries," said Doug to me.

Bud said, "Come on, Doug, you've got to admit he's the best high school player you've ever seen."

Doug said, "Al, get me some ketchup, will you?"

Al inhaled as he stood. "Well, you can ignore it if you want,"—breathed out again—"but you ain't foolin' me for a second. You want it just as bad as the rest of us."

Doug finally smiled at that one—a mock smile. He closed his eyes, incredulously shaking his head, disbelieving that he had to listen to the same crap again this year as last. The boys were supposed to have won the championship then, but they hadn't. They never had. Bonnet had always fallen short with a fumble, a missed extra point, a dropped pass; it was different every year, only the same. Now we sounded like we'd forgotten how it felt to lose by a point and a touchdown called back at the end of the game—forgotten how it felt to read it in the paper the next day—how it should have gone our way.

The year Bee Tree beat us in the district final, they dropped by the next week after they'd rolled over their regional opponent, before they lost a close one to that year's champions, and told us how lucky they'd been to beat us. It really should have been us, they said. That year we were a lot better than they were, they said. Now, sitting around Al's table at the start of a new season, we'd forgotten how it felt to hear that. I'd forgotten. Doug hadn't.

Bud, seeing Doug's sarcastic grin and apparently thinking it genuine, said, "See, I knew you were thinking the same way as the rest of us. You crazy son of a gun. By God, Doug," he said, "don't you really think Cobus is the best you've ever seen?"

Doug's eyes narrowed. He lifted his head, looking directly at Bud, so there would be no chance Bud could misunderstand.

"You know, Bud," Doug spoke lowly with a gravelly rumble in his voice, "you could take everything you know about football…"

Suddenly, seeing three auras of invincibility beam through the café door, I clamped my hand on Doug's shoulder and said, "Hey, here's Cobus. Hey, Cobus, come over here."

I think, thank God, Bud was already drunk enough that he didn't fully get how angry Doug was. Doug stared a hole through the back of Bud's head after Bud turned around to see the boys come in. Doug twitched his shoulder to throw my hand off.

"There they are," said Al. "Best in state."

"Hey," said Bud, "you think you guys poured it on enough? Jesus. It's a little embarrassing, you know."

The boys came for this backhanded praise. It was one of their spoils.

Tommy said, smirking, "Sorry, Mr. Granger, we'll try to keep it close next time."

"God, Tommy, you threw a great pass in the third quarter," I said.

"Thanks, Mr. McCheyne," he replied, becoming animated, choreographing a mini drop-back while he talked. "I was supposed to throw it to Cobus on that one, but I saw Michael had the corner-back turned around, so I let it fly to him instead. I knew he'd run under it."

"No, not *that* pass," I said. "The one you threw to Cobus when he got his feet tied up and fell all over that Solvado cheerleader."

Michael said, "Shit… Mr. McCheyne. I mean, thanks, sir." He grinned a broad, schoolboy toothy grin while I shook my head with feigned disapproval of his irreverence. I was the boys' science teacher; in the classroom they kept their Texas bearing intact, drawling *yes sir* and *no sir* when spoken to. After a game, in the café, they became good ol' boys too easily—and too young.

"Hell, Uncle Robbie," said Cobus, to me, "I called for that play in the huddle. I told Michael to see how close…" He lowered his voice, glancing around to make sure there were no women paying any attention, and then said, "…to see how close he could come to her… her sweater." He cupped his hands over the inappropriate area of his chest.

"You cocky punk," I said, in a way that sounded too much like I was proud of the macho bonding thing that he was attempting, "somebody ought to kick your ass."

Michael Martinez rested his arm on Tommy's shoulders and said, angelically, "Please, sir, may we?"

Cobus knew to duck on that, but he wasn't fast enough; Michael cuffed him behind his right ear. Tommy lunged for Cobus to fend off whatever retaliation he might try. They knocked over a chair, and one of the boys yelled *shit* again. Al didn't care; he thought the whole thing was great—that it was what a café-bar was for.

Doug didn't like it though. Using the fire left over in his voice from his earlier disgust with Bud, he barked, "That's enough, boys!"

They stopped right away, surprised because Doug never raised his voice to anyone. If he was angry, he usually did nothing more than bite his lip.

"Sorry, Dad," said Cobus.

"Sorry, Mr. Meadhran," said Michael, picking himself up, grinning, using the lull in the action to deliver one last shot to Cobus's ribs.

"Come over here a minute, son," said Doug, finally more relaxed. The sound of his own voice when he'd snapped at the boys had shocked his emotions back in check. I rarely heard him speak harshly to Cobus. He had his way of keeping the boy guessing about what he was feeling, like he kept us all guessing. He pulled out the empty chair beside him so Cobus would sit. Doug put his arm around the boy and leaned in and spoke quietly so, even if we could hear, we would know it was none of our business. "Don't juke so much. You pulled yourself off balance on that run when you faked too hard before you turned outside. That's why you fell. You already had him beat with your speed."

"Yessir," said Cobus seriously—listening to his dad—listening to the legend.

And that's all Doug ever said about the game. Not, *good game, son*; not, *that forty-three yard run from scrimmage was great, son*; not even, *next week's game will be a lot tougher*—which might have been in character. He wasn't one of those hard-driving fathers who pushed his boy to the point of breaking. If Cobus wanted to play, it was his business, but Doug expected him to play the game right. He was a purist and not just with football. All the boys appreciated that. A week later, each of them, privately so the others wouldn't know, asked Doug if he'd noticed his more subtle faking.

"Al, get these boys a cheeseburger," said Doug. "You boys pull up a chair. Cuthbert, move over and let these boys sit down."

Cuthbert and Galey, the Alden brothers, slid their chairs apart, making room at the table. Two minutes before, Doug had been ready to jump down Bud's throat and then the boys'; now he was fine, wanting to buy a round of cheeseburgers. Who could figure him?

"Comin' up," said Al. "Ah, hell… They're on me. Martinez, come on back here in the cooler and get whatever y'all want to drink."

"Whatever we want, Al?"

"Sure, in the red cooler—get whatever y'all want…" Al let go with that high-pitched, squeaky one-note laugh of his. The red cooler was soft drinks; the silver one held beer. Not once had any Bonnet schoolboy talked Al out of a bottle of beer.

As the front door of the café banged shut, Al said, "Here's the man of the hour," with his voice still high-pitched from laughing.

It was Samuel "Hutch" Hutcheson. He'd been the head coach in Bonnet for two years. We liked him. He was eternally upbeat—always sure something big was going to happen to him or the team, tomorrow, next week, or next year. He'd been an assistant at the University in the nineties and done well there. They said he was on his way to a head job of his own at a small college—maybe at one of the private schools around Dallas. His last year there, the University had a dismal season. The coach was fired and Hutch became a casualty of war.

Hutch told us the story, admitting he had been young and headstrong. He said he let his pride get in the way of the facts and he left football. He didn't watch a game for three years. He helped his dad with his hardware store in a farm town sixty miles southwest of Bonnet. After his father passed away, he ran it himself for two more years. Then, on impulse, he sold it to a young couple. An old friend, said Hutch, just happened to mention to him about the job in Bonnet. He joked with Hutch about coaches never getting it out of their blood—told him he hadn't fooled a soul with his, *I don't really even like the game much,* act. The very next customers through the door, according to Hutch, were a couple who had dreamed of owning a hardware store. Hutch claimed the coincidence was too much to ignore—providence. That same afternoon he called Vernon, our principal, and was offered the job on the phone. He hung up from Vernon, reached the folks who wanted his store, and made them an offer they couldn't refuse—a wonderful deal for them. One of those, *run the store the best you can, pay when it goes well, and worry about details later,* arrangements. Things can still be that way in south central Texas. I'm not sure how prudent it is; but many, like Hutch, do business in that manner.

Hutch spoke often of returning to the college ranks and made no secret of the fact he would be in Bonnet only temporarily. He'd made a commitment to Vernon to stay for two years. He believed coaching college football represented the pinnacle of his profession; until he was there he wouldn't consider himself a success. His attitude wasn't affected, though. He gave the town and the boys a hundred percent and treated them with the same respect he expected from them. More than that, the boys genuinely liked the man—wanted to please him—considered him their leader.

Hutch, confident and shining, ready to slap high-fives with everyone in the café, walked to the bar stool nearest our table and positioned himself, back to the bar, so he could join in on our conversation. Al sat a beer beside Hutch before he had a chance to lay his clipboard down.

"This one's on me," said Big Al. Al didn't make much money after the games.

Doug stood and shook Hutch's hand.

"Good job, Coach," he said quietly—sincerely.

"Why, thanks, Doug. Cobus played well."

"They all did," said Doug.

"Great way to start," I said, raising my bottle of beer in a salute. "Now what? How you gonna top that?"

"The great thing about this game," said Hutch, "is that it never lets you rest. You never dare think you've got it figured out."

One after another, around the table, we congratulated him. He, like the boys, had come for this—the camaraderie after the win. I suppose it was a far cry from sitting with a half-dozen big-time coaches after a University game, but we loved to talk football as well as anyone. And, even though he had the credentials, he was never the kind who would make us think we weren't on his level. He treated us as equals. He didn't worry, like some coaches do, about keeping distance from fans or his players. Hutch came around to spend time with us more often than even his assistants, most of whom had lived in the Bonnet community longer than he had. They had families and Hutch was single—lived alone— but he always gave the impression he'd rather be wherever he was than any place else.

Bud Granger said, "Who else looks good, Hutch? I mean, who do you think we might face in the playoffs?"

That was it. Doug could take it no longer. Fortunately, he'd already let go of some of the steam he'd built up over Bud's apparent ignorance of the transience of success. At least, he was able to say what he needed without exploding clean across the table.

"Good God, Bud," he said forcefully—not as angrily this time, but commandingly. "The boys have nine games left to play. Do you mind if we enjoy this one before we hang the trophy over the bar?"

"Dad!" said Cobus, surprised at this intensity he'd seldom seen.

Doug continued, "You boys listen, too. Hutch, jump in here any time you want, if you think I'm out of line." Even though he was speaking with passion, I sensed he was in control, that he'd thought about what he was saying.

"Why do you think every coach who's been asked that question, responds with, 'We're not looking that far ahead, we're taking one game at a time'?"

He didn't wait for an answer. "Because it's true, that's why. It's the oldest cliché there is, but it's the way you play the game. You block, you tackle, you execute play by play. On Saturday, after every Friday night, you start all over again. Football is played one game, one down, one week at a time. Why in hell must we be too damned stupid to watch it the same way?"

I didn't know whether to apologize for Doug or applaud. Applause would have broken a deafening silence. Cobus was too shocked to be embarrassed. He looked at me and then at his coach to see what his reaction should be—as if we would know.

Amazingly, it was Bud who did the right thing. He laughed at Doug. It was the first time in memory that Doug had stated an opinion so vehemently. He usually left it to us to interpret the meaning of his curled lip, tight jaw, or snorts, but Bud rolled right on along like Doug was always shooting his mouth off about one thing or another—like the rest of us.

Bud took another sip of beer and said, through bloodshot eyes, "Tell us then, Doug, how do you think we'll do in the state playoffs?"

Doug looked around, saw how much of the attention of the room was focused on him, saw how we waited for what he would say next, paused for a second as it sunk in that Bud was trying to make a joke, and he finally let go with a country Texas gut laugh. We all did then—especially Hutch. He was the one who slapped Doug on the back.

"Aw, shit," said Doug.

Only Cobus and the boys weren't laughing; they didn't know if they'd been chastised, challenged, or praised—although they looked like they knew it wasn't praise. They weren't even sure if Doug had been talking to them. Tommy looked down at the floor shuffling his foot back and forth; Michael Martinez's eyes were wide; Cobus pursed his lips, eerily resembling looks I'd seen too many times on his dad.

Big Al bailed them out of their uneasiness. He wound down his machine-gun string of soprano cackles, saying, "You boys want these burgers to go?"

Cobus jumped on that. "Yessir," he said, nodding decidedly.

Hutch laughed again, "You boys better get out of here. All this Texas philosophy might get too deep for you."

"Yessir," said Cobus, grinning, finally.

Tommy couldn't let that slip by; "I'll do my best to explain it to Cobus, Coach, but Martinez will never understand—since you really can't call him a Texan."

"Pardon me, Coach," said Michael Martinez, professorial finger raised, serious look on his face, "I need to explain something to your *former* starting quarterback."

Michael turned away from us so we wouldn't hear, although I did make out the words *home boy*. He could capture your attention—always ready to take center stage. In the classroom it could be disruptive; on the football field they called it leadership; in the bar he was entertaining.

He turned back to us with angelic look again, "I must apologize for my friend's lack of maturity."

"See what I mean?" said Tommy, backing as he spoke, heading for the door. "He's always doing that Mexican macho thing of his. I wish he could prove his manhood the normal way."

Michael Martinez smiled an understanding smile, nodded patronizingly, saying to Cobus, "Amigo, will you bring the refreshments when you come? I will be in the street tending to our injured friend."

He turned and followed his bolting teammate, slamming the door behind them.

Schoolboy humor washed right past me; it all sounded the same. The others at the table ignored it as well. Big Al was the boys' only audience. They hadn't cared if they had one. While he packed cheeseburgers in paper bags, his laughter resembled shrill bursts from a poorly played flute.

Cobus was uninterested, too, for only the moment, in his teammates' inconsequential capers; he turned to Doug, changing the direction of the conversation, and he said, "Dad, what are you doing tomorrow?"

After thinking about it, Doug said, "Pretty busy. Why? What do you have in mind?"

"You want to drive up to Austin to the game?"

"I don't know, Cobus," he answered, sounding as if the prospect of fighting traffic and crowds would be as unpleasant as the Saturday morning chores he had scheduled. "Any scalped seats will be sixty rows up. I need to clean out that back storeroom. On the other hand, if I could talk you into doing that for me…"

"God, Dad. If it wasn't football season, I would—and you know I would—but you wouldn't want me to risk injury, would you?" Cobus smirked, thinking he was funny. He was as good at any teenager I'd seen when it came to getting out of work.

"Oh, hell no," I said. "We wouldn't want to risk that."

Doug owned the grocery store in town. His father had started it at the age of thirty-six. He'd been a butcher. The store was his life's work, and he ran it until he died the summer Doug was twenty-seven.

Doug's story was similar to Hutch's. Doug helped his father and then stayed on after he died. Neither Doug nor Hutch wanted to be stuck in a store for the rest of his life; they were athletes and needed to be outside. They loved competition and the challenge of pushing themselves to the limit. There was a difference, though. After a couple of years of giving it his best try, tackling every day in the hardware store with the same intensity he'd coached his sport, Hutch threw in the towel. He got on with doing what he should have been doing all along.

Doug, resigned to the fact that he would never be able to leave, thought he would die behind the counter the way his father had died. He went to work every day with the memory and the expectation of the inevitable.

He spoke about the differences between his father and him—how the store had been everything to his dad—how his father had a dream—chased it, found it, lived it. Doug could say his father had been one of those fortunate men who had accomplished exactly what he'd wanted in life. Doug could say that, he just couldn't believe it. For Doug, the store was so suffocating that he had a recording in the back of his mind telling him his dad must have hated it too. Doug stayed because of guilt—punishing himself for hating it—sacrificing himself because he believed that his father must have given up the better part of himself for him—afraid that he might be wrong about who he thought he was—who Squinty told him he was.

On one hand, I'd been kidding with Cobus, laughing at the way he squirmed his way out of helping his dad in the back of the store; on the other, I was low-grade pissed at him when he didn't do what had to be done—like I was frustrated with Doug for always doing what had to be done—never taking time for himself.

"I'd be glad to watch the store for you," I said.

Doug had good help in the store. Norma and Cassie had been there so long they thought the store was theirs with Doug working for them. Still, he appreciated it when I made myself available. He welcomed the slave labor.

"I don't think so," he said.

"Do you mind if I go with the guys then?" asked Cobus.

I bit my tongue.

"I don't care," said his father. "Do you need any money?"

Well, that made sense. If he wasn't going to help around the store, then at least hand him money to make him think he was earning his keep.

"Sure," he said, acting surprised. Although I don't know why—Doug had never turned him down.

Doug reached into his pocket for Cobus's cash injection as Al handed over two bags of cheeseburgers.

"Thanks, Al," Cobus said. "Thanks, Dad. I'll be home around seven or eight tomorrow evening."

"Tell your mother where you're going," said Doug.

He was responsible for his son from Saturday through Monday; Sally had him the rest of the week. Doug and she communicated well enough and supported each other when it came to Cobus, even if one of them didn't agree with the other about what might be going on with the boy. If there was an important decision to be made, Doug checked with Sally first. If Sally had to make a judgment concerning Cobus, she made sure she informed Doug just as soon as she'd made it.

Cobus was just about out the door when Hutch said, "Cobus. Wait there just a minute."

Cobus paused, puzzled look on his face, as Hutch turned his back to his star halfback in order to speak to Doug privately. "Doug," he said, "I've got two tickets to the State game in San Marcos. I'd like him to meet Coach Hollingsworth."

Hollingsworth was the head coach at the State University in San Marcos.

Doug said, "Sure. That's fine with me. You'd better ask him though."

"Wait up, Cobus," said Hutch, "I'm leaving with you."

I turned to Doug after the door shut, and asked, "Do you think he'd ever consider any school other than the University of Texas?"

"I don't know," said Doug. "How can anybody tell from one minute 'til the next how a teenager thinks?"

He stopped for a slow draw from his beer, banged it down hard on the table, and then, looking right at Bud, said, "If we can beat Bee Tree—'cause you sure as hell know they're going to be there at the end— we might have a shot at winning the whole thing."

CHAPTER THREE

O N SATURDAY, TILDY WOKE me up banging on the door at precisely 6:15 AM. Doug was up. I heard him say "Why, hello Tildy. Today? It wasn't today, was it? I thought we were going to start tomorrow."

"We are. We are," she said, "But I want you to look at these clubs—tell me if they're good for me."

"Where did you get these?" said Doug with surprise in his voice. "I've never seen a set of these. They're brand new."

I listened from my bedroom, wanting to wrap tighter in the sheet—as if it would do any good against the morning sunlight and rapidly elevating heat of the first day of September. I decided instead to roll on out to see what had him excited.

"They belonged to my father," she said with pride. "He was a fine golfer. My father won many amateur tournaments in the South and abroad after the Great War."

"World War One?"

"Yes. He was an army officer—like his father and grandfather had been, but Dr. Allister would never speak of the war," said Tildy.

"Allister? Was that your father's name?"

"Yes. Mine, too, for the first eighteen years of my life."

"I'm learning all sorts of things about you, Tildy," said Doug.

I'd heard the stories that Tildy had married young and moved to a cattle ranch south of Bonnet with her husband in the fifties. I'd heard he was killed on an oil rig, but not many had known either of them then, so not many remembered.

I stumbled in barefooted, in jeans and T-shirt, after passing a comb through my hair. Doug was standing, hand on the bag of clubs, listening to Tildy. I greeted them by offering to make coffee.

"Good morning, Robbie," said Tildy nodding in my direction. "Yes, coffee will be fine. I take one teaspoon of sugar and a jigger of two percent milk."

"I'll take a cup, too," said Doug, using my interruption as an opportunity to examine the clubs.

"Where did you grow up, Tildy?"

"Atlanta, Georgia."

"I knew you had more bearing than could have been learned in Bonnet," I quipped.

"Quite," she said, with a mock English, high-brow accent.

"What tournaments did he play?" asked Doug, cradling a putter like it was made of crystal.

"He played them all. For nine summers in a row, he and Mother drove their Cadillac across Dixie to play with the finest golfers of the time. He crossed the Mason Dixon line only once—when the United States Amateur Championship was held at Merion, Pennsylvania in 1930."

"The year of Bobby Jones' grand slam."

"Oh yes. That was the reason he went. My father went north only two times in his life. The other time was to board a ship from the New York harbor to Europe at the expense of the government."

"Pennsylvania is not that far north, Tildy," I said.

"It was for my father. He was a professor at the University of Atlanta—regarded as one of the foremost Civil War historians of his day. His grandfather—my great-grandfather—was a general of the Confederate Army. Dr. Allister left no doubt as to where his allegiance would have lain had *that* war been fought again."

"Did your father actually play in that Amateur?" he asked.

"Oh yes, he would have played in more if they would have been in the South. He was out of the competition by the last day—had been beaten in the quarter-finals. Of course he stayed for Mr. Jones' final triumph." A broad smile crossed her face. "Mr. Jones and my father were friends from the time Mr. Jones was a boy. They both grew up on the East Lake course in Atlanta."

"Tildy," said Doug, now seating himself across from her—staring at her, captivated, "you *knew* Bobby Jones?"

I placed their cups of coffee in front of them and pulled a chair of my own. Doug was agog. After he stopped playing, never losing his love for the game, he had become an insatiable reader of its history. The game was still his passion. The shelves in his room contained the golf books of a hundred and fifty years. He covered his walls with pictures of the great ones, from Vardon and Taylor through Hogan, Palmer, and Nicklaus. The latest addition to his shrine was a bobble-head doll of Tiger.

Watching Tildy and Doug, I could tell it was rapidly becoming one of those rare moments when a lifetime connection is formed. It happened to Doug as we sat drinking our morning coffee.

"Knew him? Doug, I was in love with him. No woman who ever saw him wasn't. Mr. Bobby Jones was one the most glamorous men of the twentieth century—still was in the early forties when my earliest memories came into focus. Of course, he just called me Little Twig."

"Little Twig?" I said.

"Because I was so small."

"You were with him enough for him to give you a nickname?" asked Doug, star-struck.

"Oh my, yes. He and Dr. Allister were together all the time. After Mr. Jones won the Amateur, my father threw a party for him—they said it was the biggest Atlanta had seen since antebellum."

"Your father must have been an excellent golfer."

"He was wonderful, Doug," said Tildy, playful eyes flashing, bouncing parcels of light around the room. "He and Mr. Jones had the same teacher."

"Stewart Maiden," said Doug.

"Yes. Stewart Maiden," said Tildy, startled that he knew that. I wasn't. "Why, both of them would go for months without touching a club. But when they did, to watch them play was artistry you will never be able to imagine."

"I promise you, Tildy, tonight I will fall asleep trying."

She took a long sip from her coffee, holding it gently with both hands. I noticed how young and strong her hands looked. Sculptured. Athletic and nimble.

He was in a trance.

"Now, tell me," she said. "What do you think about the clubs?"

"Tildy, they're beautiful."

"Oh good. Then I don't have to worry about clubs."

"Not exactly," he said with a cringe.

"Uh-oh," said Tildy, "what's wrong with them?"

"There's not a thing wrong with them. Tommy Armours, 1952—a complete set. You even have the putter, Tildy. The woods don't have a scratch on them—oil-hardened persimmon Eye-O-Matics. This is the most beautiful set of golf clubs I've ever seen."

"They've never been played, you know."

"I can see that." He was like a kid on Christmas morning. "There can't be two or three sets of these in the world in this condition."

"So that's why I shouldn't play them? Because they're in such good shape?" she asked.

"No, of course not," said Doug. "Golf clubs are meant to be played. They're all new sometime. In fact, until only a few years ago there were many pros who continued to play these as their clubs of choice. My own set, thirty years old, is a third-generation version of these. This type of club is not as much in demand any longer, so they don't make them."

I knew he didn't think much of the current trend toward a high-tech solution to the game of golf. Every time he read about squabbles between the USGA and manufacturers who wanted to put everything on a golf club but heat-seeking missile technology, he would say the same thing—that every golf club made since 1975 prevents people from learning how to play the game the way it was meant to be played. Once I tried to point out that the newer equipment made the game available to a lot more people—made it easier for them to play—he said, "The sport of horseshoes has fallen off in recent years. Let 'em try horseshoes. Maybe they could move the stakes closer together."

Examining a five-iron, I said, "Tildy, the reason these won't work for you is they're men's clubs—too long, too heavy, and too stiff for you."

"Oh." She mulled it over for less than two seconds, and added, "Well, then I will drive to Austin and get new ones. Do you think the salesmen there will know what's best for me?"

Then, while Doug was forming his answer, trying to think of the best place to send her for what she needed, Tildy exclaimed, "Doug, since these are worthless to me, take them for yourself. You play them. They're yours."

Doug's eyes grew wide, his face crimson. "Tildy, you can't be serious," he said, not exactly trying to talk her out of it. "These clubs are worth a lot to collectors. Why would you want me to have them?"

"If they are as fine a set of clubs as you say, then shouldn't they be in the hands of someone who could use them properly?" asked Tildy.

He could only smile. It was as if he'd known from the minute he laid eyes on the clubs they were meant to be his. He picked them up gently as a father carrying a newborn—pulling the head covers off each wood in turn—running his fingers over the polished steel of the irons. Doug placed a seven-iron on the floor and folded his hands around the leather grip. He waggled the club twice, flexing the muscles in his jaws like I'd seen him do a thousand times in preparation for a shot. Neither Tildy nor I said a word while he checked the swing weight of each club with the tactile brilliance in his fingertips. Doug's hands on a club weren't those of an athlete gripping his weapon, they were the hands of a surgeon guiding a scalpel to the heart or of a jeweler sculpting the diamond of a lifetime. I could appreciate the genius I was watching, even though my touch with a club had frequently been likened to that of Lizzie Borden's.

"Tildy," said Doug, "I hope you don't have anything else planned for the rest of the day; you and I are going to drive to Austin where I'm going to buy you the best set of clubs we can find and then I will treat you to the most elegant lunch in the city."

"Doug Meadhran, you're the first man to ask me on a date in more than forty years," said Tildy, doing her best to act coquettish. "I wouldn't miss this for the world. I'll be ready in an hour. You're not paying though; I need *something* to do with my money," she said decisively.

"We'll discuss payment later," said Doug, sure of himself.

Then Tildy, deliberately avoiding the subject, asked, "Where are you taking me—to one of those romantic discount golf stores or a real pro shop?"

"We'll try both—many. We'll stop by Ben Crenshaw's course on the way."

"Oh, good," she said, "I haven't seen Ben in years."

"Tildy, how do you know Ben Crenshaw?" he asked—then halted. "No, on second thought don't answer that. Don't say another word. I don't need any more shocks before six-thirty in the morning. We'll have hours together in the car. I have feeling we'll need them."

"Oh, yes," she said, "I have lots of stories I can tell you." She stood to go, sighing deeply—content that the morning was going exactly as she had planned.

As she reached for the kitchen door, I said, "Tildy, you never did tell us where you got the golf clubs."

"I thought I said they were my father's."

"He bought them?" I said. "He never used them."

"Oh, no. He didn't buy them. Whose name is on the clubs?"

"Tommy Armour. They're MacGregor Tommy Armours," said Doug.

"That's right. That's who gave them to Dr. Allister—Tommy Armour," said Tildy walking out, letting the screen door slam behind her.

"Tildy!" said Doug.

She didn't respond. He watched her walk sprightly away from the house, and then, speaking with his back to me, asked, "Is that offer to watch over the store still good?"

"Sure, it is."

"You don't have to stay all day, just drop by a couple of times to check on Norma and Cassie. See if they need you to lift anything."

"Thanks a lot," I said. "I knew you didn't need me for my brain."

"You're right," said Doug, turning back to his new clubs as Tildy walked out of our sight, leaving me to guess whether he was kidding or not. "They shouldn't need anything lifted or moved. They can take care of the store. Go ahead with whatever you had planned. Go to Sally's."

"I'll stop in to see the ladies. Don't worry about it."

"I wasn't," he said. "I was thinking about what just happened. That store was the last thing on my mind."

"Will you have the heart to hit these?" I said, picking up the five-iron again.

"Watch me," said Doug.

"I plan to."

CHAPTER FOUR

Cobus went with Hutch to San Marcos. I helped Norma and Cassie open the store at eight o'clock and then stood around for an hour trying to act useful, wondering how long I'd have to do that before I became as bored with the place as Doug was.

I politely asked the ladies if there was anything else I could do for them, and their answer was, "Oh, are you still here?"

I told them to be sure to call me if they needed anything— that I'd be at Sally's. Cassie responded with, "Thank you ever so much, Mrs. Quandt. That will be forty-three dollars and ninety-two cents."

"Would you like paper or plastic?" added Norma, smiling politely to Mrs. Quandt, who had a basket full of party favors for Mr. Quandt's fifty-third birthday.

It occurred to me that the most insignificant rejection, even if imagined, is effective. I straightened a table of six watermelons, the heaviest thing I could find, and then backed out, holding the door in the process for Mrs. Quandt. I threw a wave in the direction of the two would-be grocery moguls; they waved vigorously in return—to Mrs. Quandt. As I closed the door, I heard Cassie say, "Norma, I'm going to throw those watermelons away, they're getting too soft. I'm putting tissue on special. I'll put a display on the table. Doug bought too much toilet paper from that salesman. I don't know what he was thinking."

"Do you need any help?" asked Norma.

"Oh, no. Of course not."

Sally is more fun than anyone I've ever known. She's good at everything she tries, so she tries everything. She's smart. She's pretty. She can talk anybody out of anything she wants. Her only problem is finishing what she starts. Sally tends to get distracted. I asked her once if there might be a deep-seated reason for her abandonment of projects before they were finished—fear of success or something. She giggled at that, saying, "Oh, no. I'll finish it all one day—unless something better comes along."

She took up scuba diving when Cobus was a freshman. The dive shop nearest to Bonnet is over sixty miles away, and she drove to class there one night a week for eight weeks. She loved it. The gear alone cost her a thousand dollars. The kid teaching the class told her not to buy all that stuff, that the fee for the class included equipment rental. Sally wanted the best, though, so she bought the place out. She subscribed to two magazines and joined a diver's club. She stuck a red-and-white-striped sign on the back of her car that said, *Divers are deep people.*

The night Sally got home with the equipment, she called me and told me to get over to her house as quickly as I could. She sounded like she was calling from inside of the refrigerator. Her voice was tinny and faint, with an echo. I could barely understand her, and she repeated, "Come as quickly as you can." I panicked, of course, believing I was hearing the death rattle. I knew she'd been to her first scuba class; I thought she had the bends. I rushed over to find her in the front room in wetsuit, weight belt, tank, and mask. Sally was breathing compressed air through the regulator.

"Whaddya think?" she said. What was there to say? I watched television while she flapped around the living room in fins, sucked air through tubes, and practiced stiff-kneed kicking.

"I'm going to Cancun," she gurgle-shouted through the mouthpiece between hollow-sounding drags of compressed air.

I said, "You're growing a cocoon?"

"Cancun. Cancun. I'm going to Cancun," said Sally. I understood, then, why whales hum and whistle their songs instead of singing the words out loud.

"If you plan to molt, I hope you're wearing clothes," I said, flipping through the channels with the clicker. I'd lost interest when she didn't have the bends. Wearing a wetsuit in the house just wasn't surprising—not for Sally.

She spat the mouthpiece from her lips, saying succinctly, "I'm going to Cancun, Mexico for my final exam."

"Oh," I said.

She went to Cancun—passed with flying colors—and came back with rock-climbing gear—ropes, karabiners, black-soled canvas shoes, leather shorts, and an international orange safety helmet. She wore it all off the plane—including the helmet. Sally claimed she had to because she was over weight limit and couldn't check any more luggage. On her suitcase was a bumper sticker proclaiming, *Climbers live on the edge.* The scuba magazine subscription ran out; the scuba equipment went in the closet, and she hasn't touched it since. The rock-climbing gear went into the closet four months later, after the trip to Yosemite.

Her overflowing closet drove Mother crazy when we were growing up. Now we—including Mother—expected Sally to find adventure for the rest of us—the rest of us who would have loved to do what she did, but lacked the money, time, or guts.

The fall Cobus was a senior, Sally discovered commodities. She withdrew five thousand dollars from her savings and opened an account to trade futures. She bought forty thousand pounds of pork bellies on margin and then sat back to watch the charts. When I arrived at nine o'clock on Saturday morning, she had them spread out on the floor, pencil between her teeth, calculator in hand, figuring how much money she was going to make.

"Hey, Robbie," she said, pressing the equal key, "if I can guess right on twenty-six contracts in a row, I'll make three and a half million dollars."

"What are the odds of that?" I asked, trying hard not to sound skeptical.

"Let's see—if it's just a guess, which it's not, 'cause I'm better than that, it's the same as flipping a coin and coming up heads twenty-six times straight." She punched the keys on the calculator again. "That's the reciprocal of one-half to the twenty-sixth power, which is…one in sixty-seven million. Oh."

"Better than *Reader's Digest* sweepstakes then."

"Yes, but… I don't want to think about it," she said, rolling up the charts and stuffing them in the corner, disturbingly near the closet. "Let's talk."

Sally never *just talked* unless it was serious. She tossed gems of wisdom your way while doing something else—like deciphering charts or practice climbing the banister. Now, she plopped herself on the couch, crossed her legs, folded her arms across her chest, smiled up at me wide-eyed and said, "What should we talk about?"

"I hadn't thought about it. I just came by to see what you were doing."

"Nothing. Tell me about school."

"School?"

"How are your classes this year?"

I'd been teaching in Bonnet for fourteen years and I couldn't recall that she'd asked me once how my classes were. She knew how they were. She knew everyone in town—knew all the kids—which ones were good students and which were rowdy. I decided the question meant she was beginning a new project, that she'd probably read a self-help book on *Enlightenment by Embracing Your Family.*

"My classes?"

"Yeah. How are your classes?"

"You know," I said, sitting back in the La-Z-Boy. "Same as always."

"Oh. Do you like that? I mean, does that get old? Same thing every year?"

"No. The kids make it fun."

I had no idea where the line of small talk was headed. Sally didn't do small talk.

"Is Cobus doing okay?"

"Sure. He'll get his customary B." That, too, was the same as always. He was good at doing what it took to get by—like most boys. The girls, as a rule, took it more seriously. In a small town, you don't break those rules; individuality doesn't surface until you emerge from your teens, if ever.

"How about the faculty? Do you get along with all of them?"

"I don't do things socially with some of them, but we all get along."

"How's the new math teacher?"

That's what she was driving at. She'd heard I'd been seen with Kjirsten. They weren't even dates; it was only coffee after school at Al's, which is not exactly the world's most romantic bistro.

"Now I know what you're leading up to. You're trying to pair me up with Kjirsten. I have two cups of coffee with a new colleague, and right away you want to play matchmaker."

"I do?" said Sally, feigning surprise. "I see…a colleague."

"I suppose you and Mom already have me married off. Who else has been talking about us? Who said something?"

"About what?"

"About Kjirsten and me dating."

"Are you dating? What's her name? Kjirsten?"

"Well, no, not exactly."

"Not exactly."

"You've heard something, haven't you?"

"About you and the math teacher?"

"Yes. She is attractive, isn't she?" I asked, trying not to act too excited to be talking about her.

Sally responded, "I've only seen her once, —jogging. She was red-faced and sweat-covered in her tights and head-band, but she looked like she might be cute under all that."

"Cute. She's great. She's tall, athletic, younger."

"How much?"

"About five-ten."

"Very funny," said Sally. "I mean, how much younger is she?"

"I'm not really sure. Five or six years."

"Five or six years? She looks eighteen," she said, with a smirk on her face that I interpreted to mean *you dirty old man.*

"Okay, she's thirty."

"Aren't you thirty-eight?"

"Yes."

"I see, *older brother.*"

"What? What is wrong with it?"

"Nothing. Nothing at all. Especially since you're not even dating."

"Oh," I said, disappointed at hearing I really wasn't. "Yeah, I guess that's right."

"Robbie?"

"What?"

"I think she's lovely. I can't think of anything nicer than for it to work out for you."

"Thanks, sis," I said. "She is nice, isn't she?"

"I'd be able to answer that if you'd bring her by."

"How about this week?" I asked.

Suddenly, Sally paused for a second, studying my face, like she was trying to guess how I'd react to unexpected news. She took a deep breath and held it, gathering the courage to say, "I have a better idea."

"This is going to be good, isn't it?" I asked, suspiciously.

"I hope so. Why don't you two come by Tuesday evening at five-thirty, and the four of us will drive to Peach Pit and have a steak at the Elks Club."

"The four of us? Cobus? I don't want to spend an evening with Cobus. After teaching all day, I want to be with grownups." I could say that since I was his uncle.

"Hutch."

"Hutch?"

"Hutch Hutcheson."

"Coach Hutcheson?" I said. "Cobus's coach? You want to have dinner with Coach? Do you want to talk about football?"

Hutch was a football coach; I had not considered that he had a life outside of that. As for Sally, she was sister, mother, daughter, ex, provider of adventure—and that was all she was supposed to be.

"We can talk football, if you wish," said Sally, "but I doubt if you'll want to."

"I mean, what reason do I give for wanting to have dinner with him?"

"Why would you naturally assume that *you* have to tell him anything? That is so *big brother* of you," she snapped. "It never crossed your mind, did it, that Hutch and I could have reasons for going out to dinner other than football or Cobus or you?"

"Are we discussing a sensitive subject which I know nothing about?" I asked, now thoroughly confused. "Hutch and you?"

"What do you think?" Cheery again. Instant mood swing.

"What do I think about what? Are we in the same discussion?"

"You're being dense, Robbie."

"You and Hutch?" She was deliberately leading me on. I knew she was. It had to be a new game of hers where no one else could know the rules.

"I like him a lot."

"You don't even know him, do you?"

"I think I know him well enough."

"I like him too," I said. "He's okay; I don't think he's dating anyone. Maybe he'd like to go along with us." I still wasn't seeing the whole picture. "Do you want me to ask him or not?"

"No. No. No, I don't want you to ask him, big brother. He is, too, dating someone. Very seriously, I'd say. I'll ask him myself when he comes over tonight, after he drops Cobus at Doug's."

"Oh. He's coming over tonight?"

"I rather imagine. We've been together every night that Cobus hasn't been here, since July."

Click. A light came on with that one. *Every night* said there was something more going on than an occasional happenstance meeting at the IGA. I wasn't quite as dense as I'd been ten seconds ago.

"Hutch Hutcheson? You and Hutch Hutcheson? Every night? What do you mean every night? Are you two…?"

"Yes."

"My God, little sister. What do you two do together all that time? Scratch that. I mean, that's great."

"I think so, too."

And I thought she'd been giving me a hard time about Kjirsten. She was building a line of defense, stalling for time, keeping me off-guard as long as she could before dropping it on me. It was what she'd been trying to say all morning. Her roundabout way of telling me was Sally's surprise. As I sat there watching the light in her face make her look like a teenager again, it gradually sunk in how important this was to her. Sally was talking about permanence with Hutch; I hadn't even been aware they knew each other. Nobody can keep secrets like that in a small town. Somebody, sometime, will guess lucky; lies will no longer hide the truth and then everybody will know. But they had done it. I didn't know if I should be proud of her for pulling this one over on the rest of us or hurt that she hadn't told me sooner. Although I can't honestly say I would have been any better at keeping it a secret than anyone else.

"How long have you two been seeing each other?" I was up now, pacing—prancing—around the front room; feelings were trying to exit through nerve endings and dancing on the surface of my skin. If I'd been a sister of Sally's, instead of brother, the appropriate action would have been to squeal. I fought it back.

"Well," she said, "if you'll sit down I'll tell you. Since December, a year ago. We ran into each other in Austin doing last-minute frantic Christmas shopping—totally by accident. I didn't know him at all then, other than as the cute guy who spent a lot of time with my son on a football field." Sally was on a roll; she'd hidden this for nine months, and now it was burbling out.

"I helped him pick gifts for seven or eight of his female relatives; he helped me with a stereo for Cobus and then he bought me an early dinner. After we ate, we bought more presents. There's something about four hours of Christmas shopping that reveals a lot about a person and his family."

"You just ran into him, and he asked you to help with all of that?" I asked, arching an eyebrow.

"Of course not, silly. He asked me what I thought about perfume for a twelve-year-old niece, and I sort of took over from there."

"This I believe."

"He kept apologizing. That's how I got the free dinner."

"And you've been seeing each other since?"

"He called me a day or two later," said Sally, "to tell me thanks and how much fun he'd had. I told him I'd love see him again. 'How about Saturday?' I asked. 'My treat.' And the rest, big brother, is history—current and future."

"You always were shy," I smirked.

She'd done it again. I thought I knew her so well, and she'd pulled out the stops and surprised me one more time than I thought possible. It was way better than Cancun. I hadn't gone to Cancun; I had the feeling I would be riding along on this one all the way to the end of the roller coaster.

"You're not already married, are you?"

"Of course not. Don't be silly. Do you think I'd get married without you there?"

I wasn't sure about that—after all, I hadn't been asked to Cancun. "I'll be there. I'll be there," I said. "Unless, of course, you do something crazy, like saying your vows while parachuting off the face of El Capitan."

"Doesn't that sound like fun?"

Change the subject now, Robbie, I thought. Don't give her any ideas.

I felt like a kid carrying a lone flower home to Mom only to find her admiring the bouquet sister had gathered. As inspiring as Sally was, she had a way of keeping us from doing things for ourselves; she overwhelmed. I caught myself resenting Hutch for only a moment. I'd worked hard to collect the courage to care about my feelings for Kjirsten. Now I fought to keep them relevant alongside Sally's surprise.

I said, "Cobus has not even hinted at this. He is really keeping it quiet. He must not be too upset at the idea."

"He doesn't know," said Sally, cringing.

"Oops."

"I know. I know. Today's the day we tell everyone who matters to us. Mom, you, Cobus—even Doug. Doug has to hear it today, too."

"You haven't told Mom yet?"

"She's coming over at noon, and we're going to lunch. I wanted to use you to practice on."

"That fits in with the rest of my morning," I mumbled.

"What?"

"Nothing," I sighed, smiling. "She'll be excited, won't she?"

"She'd better be. Of course she will. I'm her daughter. It's Doug I'm worried about."

"Uh-oh."

He'd had two good days. A seventy-something woman with a remarkable history was responsible for that. As recently as Thursday, though, he'd sat in the same kitchen as he did with

Tildy and the golf clubs and told me how much he still missed Sally. I'd lost count of how many times he'd said that in seven years. Moving pictures in his mind played on an endless slow-motion loop. They wouldn't leave him alone. They wouldn't leave me alone, either, because he would pin me down and make me watch them again with him. After a couple of beers, or a tiring day of work, the movie would start over.

When Sally first told him she was leaving, he thought if he could rewind it enough times for her, then she wouldn't go. "Sally, don't you remember when we drove to the coast and camped on the beach while I played in the Houston Open?" he'd said, playing back every detail, as if she'd forgotten it—as if the memory would make her say, *Oh, Doug, I'd forgotten; how could I have forgotten that? I'll never leave you now.* It only made it worse and he couldn't see it. Not once did it make her think about staying with him; it made her feel more wretched about leaving.

After she was gone, he kept the film loop rolling for me—like I could bring her back if I heard the sound track enough times. At first it was, "I know she misses me. I know she remembers how good things really were." He kept old pictures and mementos; once he handed me a scrapbook from the Texas Amateur—the one he won. "This was one of the best times of my life," he said. "I thought about calling her to see if she remembers it. What do you think? You remember that, don't you, Robbie?" I remembered; he'd won on the final nine, rolling in forty-footers like they were tap-ins.

Now, seven years after she left him, the show had become more subtle, but still it played on. Thursday, sitting in the kitchen, third beer of the hour in hand, he'd said, "Do you remember, Robbie, the time I played in the tournament in Little Rock and Sally and I went up alone in the motor home?"

It was Dad and Mom's Winnebago. The old kind—the shoebox on wheels.

"You kept Cobus, remember?"

Of course I did; it was the weekend the boy had diarrhea and a temperature of a hundred and three for fifty hours straight. Mom and I spent Saturday night in the hospital with the baby.

"It was quite a weekend, Robbie," he'd said. "I wonder if she feels the same as I do when she thinks of that?" he'd asked.

Probably not. Her memories were of being on the phone while he played golf, wanting to be with her son; of trying desperately to act normal so Doug wouldn't suspect his boy was as sick as he was—so Doug could have a good tournament. It never dawned on him that all the good memories happened in the first four years of his marriage. I never said it, but it all ended the day he quit playing. No movies existed for any time after he'd won in Little Rock by twelve strokes.

"What do you mean, *uh-oh*?" said Sally now, echoing well the tone of apprehension in my voice.

"I'm just agreeing with you. I'm worried about Doug, too."

"I'll tell him today. I'm going to call him to see if we can talk."

"That will be tough."

"Why. What's wrong?"

"He's out of town until late this afternoon. He went to Austin with Tildy Hannah."

"Tildy Hannah?"

"It's a long, crazy story."

"What time do you think he'll be back? I really want to tell him before he hears it from someone else." She was disappointed. She had worked up the mettle and the means to get it over with in one day. It would tarnish the excitement if it didn't go exactly as she had planned.

"I don't know. This trip is a strange one. He might be back this afternoon, but who knows? It'll be all right, though. I'd just be sure I told Doug before Cobus."

"Why? Cobus will be okay; he likes Hutch." She really hadn't considered the possibility that her son might not take it well.

"Sally, I teach kids Cobus's age all day long, and the only thing you can be sure of is their volatility. They can always be trusted to overreact."

She gritted her teeth for a second and, after exhaling a tensioned sigh, said, "I hope this day ends as well as it started."

"Let me ask you something," I said.

"What? I wish you'd quit drizzling on my parade."

"No, just a question. If you had no fears about Cobus, then why did you keep this a secret for so long? Why not just date in the open?"

"Doug. I was worried about Doug's reaction."

"What about Hutch? What did he say?"

"The same thing as you. He was polite about Doug. He was concerned about Cobus." Sally frowned as all the possibilities she'd never considered stared her in the face. "Cobus has to be okay," she said. "Hutch is telling him today on the way to the game."

"Boy, you are shooting from the hip. I guess that rules out telling Doug first."

"Hutch wanted to tell Cobus. He said he spends more time with him in intense situations than I do."

"That's true," I said. Then, jumping in with both feet, I said, "I'll tell Doug for you."

"Robbie, I don't want you to have to do that."

"I spend more time in intense situations with him than you do," I said, resigned to my role. "Besides, I think it's important he isn't surprised by Cobus with it. And what's he going to say when you tell him? *Gee, Sally, that's great?* No. You and I both know what he's going to say. I've heard it a few times over the last seven years. Let him tell it to me. It's my job, isn't it? He'll probably feel better about that. He considers me a neutral party."

"Are you sure?"

"Yes, I'll tell him," I said, thinking it probably didn't matter a whole hell of a lot who told who. I knew it was going to be a lot more interesting fall than it had been when all we had to think about was the Bee Tree football team and the Bee Tree Women's Golf League. I longed for the time, an hour before, when all that was on my mind was a beautiful blue-eyed math teacher named Kjirsten.

CHAPTER FIVE

I CLEANED THE HOUSE waiting for Doug and Cobus, or Cobus and Doug—whoever came first. It was Doug and Tildy— each of them clutching new clubs to their respective bodies like four-year-olds with stuffed bears. Doug had the shining Tommy Armours arranged tightly in a burnt orange carry bag slung over his shoulder and across his back. Tildy held her bag—strikingly bright, a metallic sapphire-blue design that could be seen at midnight from six fairways away—tightly to her breast with both arms in front of her.

"I can't believe it, Tildy," I said, suspiciously eyeing her space-age irons—the kind Doug hated. "Mr. Tradition let you buy these?"

"Oh, he wanted me to buy *classic* clubs. For half an hour, Ben Crenshaw and Douglas discussed the pros and cons of casting with a fat perimeter versus forging. I had no acquaintance with that of which they were speaking."

"That's perimeter weighting," said Doug.

"That's what I said," continued Tildy, never missing a beat in the rhythm of her reenactment of what must have been a rather tedious technical digression, "Fat perimeters. Ben kept saying fat perimeters forgive missed hits."

"That's *miss hits*, Tildy," Doug said. "Nothing forgives *missed hits*."

"That's what I said. Doug wanted me to buy something that would match the *fundamental* swing he will teach me. My swing. The one that doesn't exist. He's worried about esthetic appeal, and I haven't attempted to swing at a ball since choices for clubs included hickory shafts."

"Looks like you won the argument," I said.

"I ignored them both," said Tildy. "I made him take me to *Golf-Smart*, or whatever it's called. I bought this bag and then clubs to match it."

Doug stood by, trying his best to act golfier-than-thou.

"Come on, Tildy," I said, "they don't make blue golf clubs."

"Oh?" said Doug, pulling a furry white head-cover off her driver. "Look at these."

They were blue sapphire, all right—the same blindingly bright color of her bag.

"Aren't they beautiful?" said Tildy, sitting the bag on the kitchen floor and then running her hand over the enamel like Doug had done when first touching his Tommy Armours.

"They will attract attention," I said.

Tildy said, "I heard my father say a dozen times that when he was playing well, he could swing a broomstick and hit the ball. These broomsticks just happen to match my bag."

"Humph," said Doug, leaving me wondering if he was clearing his throat or holding back a disgustingly graphic comment on pastel clubs, pastel golf bags, clubs being likened to brooms, or all three. Truth is, he wasn't doing a good job of acting. He made sure we saw through his thin veil of mock disapproval right into the bond that had fused him and the woman we had both come to know only that morning.

"They're lovely, Tildy," I said. "Don't pay any attention to him."

"I'm sure I haven't," said Tildy, decidedly allowing her Southern air to punctuate.

Tildy left and Doug beamed. If Cobus or I would have tried to buy clubs that didn't meet his personal standard, he would have been critical. More, he would have made us feel so self-conscious about it that we would have bought the ones he chose or no clubs at all. She made him laugh. She got her way. By the time she was done with him, not only did Tildy have him agreeing to her choice, she had him liking it. They were her clubs. They were part of her aura and, now, so was he. Since morning, for Doug, there had become two kinds of people in the world—Tildy and everybody else.

"Blue golf clubs," Doug said to me. "Blue. There's another reason she wanted those particular clubs, you know." She even had him liking the color. Mr. Black and White liked the blue color of her clubs.

"Another reason?"

"Yes. She bought those clubs because they had four sets of them."

"Four sets?"

"Oh, yes, Robbie old boy," he said, taking on—to the best of his ability—the same tone of Georgia aristocracy that Tildy had used on him. "The Bonnet Lady Mustang Golf League now has a perfectly matched collection of four blue golf bags, four sets of blue metal woods, and four sets of perimeter-fatted irons. She bought the four most expensive pull carts in the shop. Naturally she bought eight blue golf gloves—one for each of the eight hands on her team."

"Let me guess about the golf balls," I said. "I bet they weren't white."

"Sixteen dozen. She bought sixteen dozen fluorescent blue golf balls. Says she wants to practice with the same balls they're going to play."

"This had to cost a fortune," I said, uneasy, as always, with the concept of using money for anything more than basic survival.

"I'm not done," continued Doug. "For each of her friends, she bought three outfits complete with shoes." Doug rattled off the list of blouses, sweaters, skirts—all matching—right down to socks with little fuzzy balls on the heels—describing color, style, even fabric like he was a buyer for a women's sports wear boutique. The day had been an awakening for him and he had memorized every microscopic detail. "She bought them uniforms. Golf team uniforms."

"How much?"

"Three thousand two hundred and forty seven dollars. Wrote a check. The clerk took it and stuck it in the cash register without blinking an eye."

"I take it you didn't offer to pay."

"She let me buy lunch."

It was, by then, four in the afternoon. Every day, at the same time, for as long as he had lived with me, Doug slept for thirty minutes. He would sneak out of the store, leaving it in the good hands of Cassie and Norma, and then come home for his nap. He'd return after five. The ladies went home then and he closed at six. On Saturdays he closed at five.

"Today is day sixty-three," said Doug, flipping back the pages of the Meadhran Grocery calendar on the kitchen wall.

"What?" I said. "What is day sixty-three?"

"Today is. It's sixty-three days until the Bonnet Lady Mustang Golf League has their tournament in Peach Pit. Sixty-three days to teach them to play."

"Look out, Bee Tree," I mumbled.

"Hey," said Doug, "they'd better."

I couldn't believe it; he was intense. He had already slipped into his tournament trance and he wasn't even playing.

"Well, one thing for sure," I said.

"What's that?"

"They'll look the best."

"If they think I'm wearing blue plaid pants, they've got another think coming," said Doug.

I was thinking that it would be entirely Tildy's decision.

He picked up the phone and called Cassie at the store, telling her that he was back in town but would not be in to close. She must have said something like, *Who is this?*, because when he hung up he said, "I'm not real sure of my function there any more."

"Just be glad you can lift the heavy stuff," I said.

He grabbed his clubs from where he'd laid them on the kitchen table.

"One thing for sure," said Doug, "I can lift these." His voice had a new ring of confidence; words came quickly. His movements were snappier, too. He pivoted, letting the clubs swing sharply around his back, and said, "I'm going to the pasture. Wanna come along?"

"No nap?"

"I'll be there if you want to hit some balls," he said. "I'll be there if you don't."

I finished drying the dishes, grabbed my own clubs, and jumped in my truck to drive to his pasture. On the way, I drove by Sally's. She wasn't home so it was my job to tell him of her surprise.

The pasture was his space. Doug bought the land for the sole purpose of hitting golf balls after his father died. It was at the western edge of town, jigsawed between the last street of houses and a bean field on the Alden brothers' ranch. The pasture had belonged to them, but when the price of beef dropped and raising cattle on purchased grain was losing more money than they could make, they plowed it under for beans and cotton. They plowed it all except for the strip they sold Doug.

He cut the hearty buffalo grass every Sunday if it needed it or not. He was at home on his strip of pasture whether he was hitting golf balls or merely sitting on his mower making the place into an imaginary little golf course. I sat in the truck watching

him. I was working up a way to tell him. I had to; he had to
know before Cobus got home. I wasn't a neutral party. I needed
to protect all of them.

I watched the rhythmic motions of his flawless swing as he
struck shot after shot. He started with the small pendulum arc
of a lofted club, letting the clubface drop on the ball from waist
height—lobbing the balls with such softness that they rolled
quietly to rest, side by side. He methodically lengthened the arc
with his new clubs so the golf balls began to stretch out in a line
from him toward the end of the field, like pearls on an invisible
rope. He switched to one of the middle irons—a six or seven.
The club swung itself; Doug merely had to slide gently to the
side to let it pass without inhibition—like a matador you know
has moved by only the ripple of his cape. The iron exploded into
the grass, and the ball climbed like a rocket, to its peak, and
then, flame extinguished, fell quietly to its target a hundred and
seventy yards away. He'd said many times that he could tell he
was hitting the ball well when the distances were consistent. I
watched. He had placed a bag as a target and each shot fell beside
it—one a foot or two to the left, the next a foot or two to the
right. I believed even that variation was by design.

This was a daily regimen for him—as necessary as breathing.
All the trepidation I'd had as I drove up was gone. Watching
Doug swing was like attending a symphony. I was as overcome
by the artistry of his gift as I would have been by the crescendo
of a hundred strings.

I stood beside him and said, "I need to tell you something
before Cobus gets home."

He never changed his rhythm—grass erupting, holding
textbook finish, standing, exhaling methodically. They say the
best shooters of guns pull their triggers between heartbeats. Doug
swings that way—body under command of mind—reaching for a
new ball, flipping it onto a tuft of grass with the head of his club,
feet rolling into place, fingers rolling onto the leather, inhaling,
pausing, club at the top once more without you knowing it's

moved—and then at last, and suddenly, the slap of the club on the ball again.

"Uh-oh," he said, watching the flight of his shot, "what's the boy done now?"

"It's not him," I said, "It's Sally." He had no response this time, only another shot. "I spoke with her this morning. She's with Mom. I thought she'd be home by now." I watched the ball roll a foot and a half to the left of the shag bag, downrange. "She's been seeing someone. She called me over to tell me about it, so I guess it's pretty serious." He placed a new ball on a small mound of turf. "It's Hutch. They've been seeing each other almost a year. Even Cobus doesn't know."

"I knew," he said, and pulled the trigger again.

"How? She didn't think you did," I said.

Silently we stood for a moment as the ball bounced once and landed in the open canvas bag.

"It doesn't matter. I just know," said Doug, never interrupting his flow—never changing expression.

I'd come thinking I'd have to direct the conversation—worried how he'd react. I had a whole list of things ready to say, like *you knew this was going to happen sooner or later*, or *don't walk away angry, just stay and practice a while longer*, or *she isn't doing it to hurt you*. But he knew already. He didn't do or say one thing I'd predicted he would.

The tempo of his swing never changed. He said, "I knew this was coming. A girl like Sally. I'm surprised she's stayed alone this long."

His next shot bounced off the side of the bag a hundred-seventy yards out. As always, he was the director; I was the spectator. For three minutes I stood beside him, quietly, hearing only the crack when he hit the ball. I saw seven successive shots hit the bag—two of them dropping in. Even for Doug, this display challenged believability.

"I've never seen you hit the ball like this," I said. "I've never seen anyone do this before."

"Neither have I," he replied, allowing a hint of a smile.

"Why didn't you say something?"

"I don't like to brag," said Doug, now grinning fully. "Who'd believe it?"

"No, not about this," I said. "About Hutch and Sally."

He said, "Hell, I figured everyone else was trying to keep it a secret from me. I thought I was the last to know."

Doug hit a five-iron 195 yards—towering, with the height of an eight.

"Looks like you were the first," I said, watching the ball land on the same line as the rest.

Never breaking rhythm, never pausing, never looking up, he said, "Dad didn't want me to play golf."

Crack. Straight as an arrow.

"What?"

"He never got angry when I told him Sally was pregnant. He just said, 'You'd better come work in the store. You'll need a job.' I'd already taken the job with Squinty. Dad said, 'There's no permanence in that; you'd better come work in the store.' I didn't answer him. I went to work in Peach Pit."

"Your dad was proud of the way you played," I said.

For the first time, Doug paused his practice—looked at me—like a look was response enough to what I'd said. As if saying, *you have no idea what went on.*

He began again. "A week before Cobus was born he took me for a long drive to tell me that my wife and child would be my only concerns from then on. He said I had to give up playing games. He said he needed help in the store and it was time to stay home."

I'd never seen Doug's father raise as much as an eyebrow, let alone his voice to anyone. "What came of it? How did it end?" I asked.

"You know what happened," Doug said, opening his stance, facing a few degrees left of his target as he addressed the ball again. He edged his grip an eighth-inch left so the club faced slightly to the right when he sat it behind the ball. With the same swing, club taking less turf, barely clipping the grass, the ball started left, rose even higher, and then fell like a feather moving on the wind from left to right, dropping on the line—the same long white line he was painting with pearls. "I kept playing golf," he said.

"Did Squinty talk you into it?" I asked.

"Nope. He said I should work things out with my dad. He couldn't—wouldn't—come between us. I told him it was my decision and I wanted him to help me become as good as I could."

"How'd he answer?"

"He loaded me in his car and we went to see Harvey Pennick. Harvey was the only man I ever knew Squinty to look up to when it came to teaching golf. Harvey was very old then, but I saw him many times; you know that. A year later, I spent a week at the country club without Harvey saying much other than his favorite platitude—*If a doctor gives you a bottle of medicine, don't drink it all at once.* I was there a week and that's all he said. Best lesson I ever had. I had a message waiting for me when I got home; they offered me a golf scholarship to the University. Sally said she'd work. We lived in married student housing, found college girls to help take care of Cobus, and I graduated four years later. We never had a dime but those were great years. Maybe the best of my life."

"But your dad," I said, "what about your dad? I don't believe he didn't want you to play."

"How many tournaments did he attend?" asked Doug, smashing a five-iron like a jackhammer.

The ball screamed along the line, lower than the rest as if boring into a wind, and then hit the ground hard, running away from us, still on the rope.

"He was working hard in those days," I said, trying to recall if his dad had gone to any tournaments.

"Yeah. By the second year, I was winning just about everything I entered. My father never said a word."

He hit another screaming five-iron—not climbing above thirty feet—a bullet. He pitched the club on the ground without holding his finish like he usually did, and then he grabbed a three.

"I'm sure he was proud of you," I said, standing again, nervous, not knowing the right thing to say.

Smash! The three-iron resounded like a shotgun.

"You remember that summer, don't you Robbie? The summer they said that getting my tour card would be a cakewalk. The summer I won in Dallas, and Houston, and then later in Little Rock, one week before qualifying school?"

"Sure, I do," I said.

But Doug never played in that qualifying school or any other. Out of the blue, he'd said he'd done all he wanted in golf so he was through with tournament play. We were horrified. I'd said something to him when he announced he was quitting and he gave me a look I'll never forget. It was vicious. It must have been the same look he gave anybody who asked him, because no one ever mentioned it again—until now.

He hit another shotgun blast.

He talked with no pause between words or shots, "I got back from Little Rock, and he took me for another ride. I guess he figured I couldn't walk away from him at sixty miles an hour in the Buick. I thought he wanted to tell me he'd sponsor me on the tour. That was somewhat naïve of me. He had me in the car to tell me I'd almost killed my son by leaving town when he was sick. He told me how Cobus almost died from the flu and he asked me when I was going to grow up and stop fucking up everything I touched. He wanted to know when I was going to earn my keep. I told him I didn't want to work in his godforsaken store. I told him I hated the goddamned place. He told me I was nothing without the store—how he'd given money to Sally every week so she could pay the bills and we could eat while I was in school—*while I was playing games*, he said. I didn't believe him."

Doug struck another three-iron—this one softer, climbing high then feathering to the ground like the ones he'd been hitting when I told him about Sally.

"I'm sure it wasn't much," I said. "Sally never mentioned it."

"I made him take me home and yelled something eloquent, like *fuck you*, when I got out of the car."

He stopped to clean the club and then he said, "I started to work in the store the next morning after Sally confirmed it all. He'd given us a lot of money. I had no idea. I was stupid. They'd all been lying to me, like he said, just so I could play a game. I never took another unearned penny from him. I worked side by side with him for the next two years and we didn't talk about anything but the business until the day I found him dead behind the butcher counter."

All he was telling me was news—as much as Sally's surprise had been that morning. Everybody said Doug's dad was the nicest guy they ever knew. He was a hard worker, they said. In Bonnet, naming someone a hard worker is the highest compliment. Maybe there was a blueprint that dictated that Doug's dad would have had a problem with whatever Doug had done. Maybe Doug had been right all along and his dad had hated the store—resenting Doug for being able to get away from it. Perhaps he'd loved the store like we all thought and was panicked at the idea that the store wouldn't carry on after he was gone.

Like I could fix it if I could only say the right thing, I tried, "I'm sure it was something else, Doug. I know he didn't mean it."

"If he didn't mean it, he wasted a lot of energy beating it into me," said Doug.

He'd never spoken to me about anything this personal. I doubt he'd ever said any of it to anyone. It was as if telling him about Sally had unlocked it—had given him permission to pass it on to me. "What else did he say?" I asked.

"He didn't *say* much of anything else at all," said Doug. "I said he beat it into me. I left out part of the drive in the Buick. When we got to the country, he stopped the car, walked around to my door, belt in hand, pulled me out on the side of the road, and beat the shit out of me."

"Come on," I said. "I can't believe this, Doug. Not your dad."

Doug never blinked or wavered; he just stood holding my eyes with his, giving me time for it to sink in. I'd admired his dad. I would drop by the store just to see him when I was a kid. He'd give us boys pop or a candy bar if we'd straighten a shelf or two. He was important; a store was important. I liked being around him. Now, thinking back, I remember how many of those times I was around him without Doug being there—even when we were young—before high school.

"Hell, Doug," I said, "my old man hit me once. I came home drunk and puked all over the kitchen counter. I mouthed off to him the next morning when he climbed all over my case about it and he hit me. I had it coming."

I was trying to laugh it off so Doug would know I thought what had happened was okay. Bonnet boys are tough. We play football. We drink. Every now and then we get into a fight with our dads. It goes on. An hour later you make up, you shake hands, he gives you a pat on the back, and maybe you even hug. It happens. Some might say they're proud of it. I wouldn't go that far. I'm still embarrassed about the time Dad hit me—because I was a jerk. I had it coming.

"Once or twice would have been okay," said Doug, standing stoically before me.

While I stood on Doug's own corner of freedom, his pasture, trying to keep myself from repeating anything stupid, like *I know he didn't mean it*, Cobus walked up to us. He carried his own clubs—something I hadn't seen in three years. I could tell by the look on his face that Hutch had told Cobus about Sally and him. I could see that Cobus was scared and had come to be with his dad, so I left. I reached out to put my hand on Doug's shoulder but stopped—not because he gave me any message that my hand wasn't welcome—but because I wasn't sure it was the right thing to do—for Doug, I mean.

CHAPTER SIX

HALF AN HOUR LATER, Sally and Mother arrived at Sally's. I'd called every five minutes since I left the golf pasture. I said, "Good, you're home. I'm coming over," and hung up. I didn't want to be in my house when Cobus and Doug came in. They needed to be alone.

"You took long enough," I said, entering Sally's kitchen more forcefully than I'd intended, pushing the screen door so hard that it banged against the wall. "Oops. Sorry."

"Oh, I know we're late," said Sally. "Mom and I drove to Austin."

"Austin?" I'd rushed over, and then bounded from the car up the steps to the kitchen; I must have been speaking loudly—out of breath. It occurred to me that I wasn't the one who should be panicking. I wasn't getting married or trying to win a football championship or playing in a golf tournament in a few weeks. My mother wasn't about to ruin my entire senior year by marrying my coach.

"Why, what's wrong?" she asked, startled at my addled entry.

"Nothing. I wondered how your day went, that's all, and I wanted to invite myself for dinner."

"I thought you might decide to join us," Sally said with a knowing smirk. "You haven't had dinner with me for almost a week.

"We were going to Peach Pit," she said, "but we were talking and we kept right on driving past the turnoff."

"Okay, let's have it," I said. "What was Mom's reaction?"

"Why don't you ask her?" she said with her head in the cupboard. "She's in the front room."

"Hi, Mom," I shouted. "What do you think of our girl?" Then, without waiting for a reply, still foraging for leftovers, "Hey, Sal, what did you have in mind for supper? Mom, are you staying?"

"Hello, Robbie," said my mother. "Of course I'm staying. I want to meet Hutch. I've spent an entire afternoon listening to how wonderful he is. That's earned me a place at the table."

I sneaked a look at Sally. She looked happy; she listened— smiled—while tucking away the few groceries she and Mother had bought.

"I suppose to earn my place I have to cook," I said.

"I hope you've already earned your place," said Sally. "And yes, you have to cook." She pulled four packages of sirloin from the bottom of the sack she was emptying, saying, "What do you think of these?" And then in a whisper, "You did tell him, didn't you?"

"Oh, those are gorgeous," I said, suddenly realizing how hungry I was. I nodded a reply to her question while mouthing the word *yes.*

Mother knew what we were talking about and could probably hear us, but we whispered anyway. Besides, with Mother you could shout and she would hear exactly what she chose to hear. She was skilled at either ignoring completely that which was unpleasant or tucking it away until she was in the proper frame of mind to deal with it—usually long after the rest of us had dealt with it. When asked about that trait, she liked to reply that most problems solved themselves if she ignored them long enough. Of course they did. The rest of us did all the work while she hummed merrily along.

"He talked about his dad," I said, still feigning to keep the conversation between Sally and me. "He didn't talk about you like I thought he would. He talked about his father."

"What did he say about Cobus?" asked Sally quietly as she placed four potatoes in the microwave.

"Not a thing. He talked about his dad. I can't believe what he told me." I unwrapped the steaks and placed them on a platter alongside all the charcoal grilling paraphernalia I could find. "He told me he used to get into fights with his dad."

"Do you want me to make a salad?" shouted Mom from the living room.

"No, Mom," answered Sally. "I don't expect Hutch for half an hour. Why don't you rest for a while?"

"I'll just rest then. Is that okay?" I heard the footrest snap into place as she leaned back.

"Yes, Mother," said Sally.

"I'm going to rest my eyes. Wake me up in twenty minutes. I don't want to sleep longer than twenty minutes."

"Don't worry, Mom," I said. "The smell of the sirloins will wake you up."

"I don't want to miss those sirloins," she said. "Be sure to wake me up for those sirloins."

"I wouldn't call them fights," said Sally, frowning. "A fight implies a two-way exchange. They were mostly one-sided affairs."

"You knew about it then?"

"Robbie, I was married to Doug for twelve years."

"It went on then? After you were married?"

"No. Most of it was before—long before. Doug and his dad didn't communicate at all while we were married."

Sally grew anxious. She was uncomfortable with the subject. She wasn't as good as Mother at dispensing with painful topics, but she was trying. "I don't want to talk about this now, Robbie," she said, washing a head of lettuce. "Is that okay?" She scrubbed the lettuce with hurried, nervous movements.

Of course she didn't want to talk about it. This was her day—the day when everyone would be happy for her. She wanted to talk about Hutch and how he made her feel. She'd wanted me to say Doug would be fine. I regretted having said things that caused her to think of anything but bliss.

"Did you see Cobus?" she said after a minute of affected lettuce-chopping.

I was supposed to say he was going to be all right, too. "He came out to the pasture as I was talking to Doug. He had his clubs with him, but he seemed fine." I lied. The look on his face had been one I'd seen on his dad a hundred times. He was panicked. I knew it and I knew she didn't want to hear it. "He didn't say anything though. I don't even know if he's heard yet. He was okay."

"No, he wasn't," said Sally. "Listen to what you said. He had his clubs with him. Cobus doesn't even like golf. He's out there hitting golf balls for the same reason his dad does—to forget."

Great. Everything out of my mouth had upset her.

"I have an idea," she said.

"What?"

"There. The salad is ready." She slid it into the refrigerator. "See if I have any mince in that cabinet."

"What idea? Mince?"

"Mince. For a mince pie. Yes, that's my idea," she said, as if I should understand why mince pie would be regarded as a revelation. "I'm going to make a mince pie."

She had done it, just like Mother. Zip. In the closet it went. She wasn't going to think about it any more. She was going to make a pie.

"Mince pie is Cobus's favorite," said Sally, pulling a frozen crust from the freezer. "He calls it mincemeat only there's no meat in it. I'll make him his *mincemeat* pie and then call him to come over after dinner. If he's feeling bad, it will cheer him up. It always does."

It struck me that Cobus considered what he'd learned this afternoon a bit more serious than his usual problems—a failed test or not enough gas money for Saturday night. I didn't say it, but I thought it—this time it might take more than mincemeat pie.

"It's my favorite, too," I said. "Maybe it'll cheer me up." I punctuated with a sigh.

"What could you possibly need to be cheered up about, big brother?" said Sally, opening the can of mince pie filling.

"It has been a long day for me, too, you know." I'd planned to loll around all day Saturday and think about Kjirsten—or call her up—or take her out. Instead, I'd been stock boy, psychologist, and now cook. I'd wanted to ask Sally's advice about dating the beautiful golden-haired girl but now it dawned on me that I would be the only one Cobus could turn to who didn't have a real stake in this, so I had to remain sane.

"Poor baby," Sally said, patting my head as she sashayed by with two frozen piecrusts. "Why don't you go rest your eyes, too?"

"No, no. Far be it from me to be weary."

Hutch rolled his red pickup to a stop in front of Sally's house and walked slowly up the walk. I could tell by the way he moved that he was down—not like I'd seen him Friday night in the café with head high and bounding strides. He looked tired.

Sally saw him, jumped up, and beat him to the front door. "Mom," she said as she scurried by, "wake up. It's Hutch. He's here early."

Mom said, "Oh," and stood to meet her presumed future son-in-law—doing her best to straighten her hair and press the wrinkles from her slacks with her hands.

Sally offered Hutch a hug and a kiss. His response was guarded—embarrassed—but he smiled and kissed her back quickly.

"Hi, Robbie," he said, offering his hand and widening his grin.

"Well, Coach. Hello," I said, eagerly returning the handshake. It was easy to picture him as part of the family.

Hutch said, "Hello, Mrs. McCheyne." He was shy like any Texas boy would be meeting his best girl's mom for the first time.

"Why, hello, Mr. Hutcheson," said Mother, still smoothing her slacks. "It's good to finally meet you."

"Hutch," he insisted.

"Oh," said Mother. "Hutch."

She placed her hand in his and they shared their nervous handshake. I stood and watched the man who would marry my sister. I realized how much I liked him. His smile was genuine; his movements and words were easy. I wondered if Mother was doing the same thing that I was—comparing him to Doug. Doug was graceful and athletic, too. Almost always, his words were quiet like Hutch's were now; but with Doug you always felt he was holding something back—that there was something hiding behind his eyes. Hutch's eyes said, *come on in, what you see is what you get.* I liked them both.

Sally jumped in to rescue them from the awkwardness of their first meeting. She threw her arms around both of them at once and squeezed hard. For a moment, an image of her in cheerleading skirt and sweater flashed—a scene from the past. She was that happy—as excited as a pompom girl.

"What do you think, Mom?" said Sally with arm now around Hutch alone—presenting him to us.

"I think this is all wonderful," said Mother.

"I'm not so sure," I offered, trying to raise one eyebrow. "Is this going to cancel my open invitation for a free dinner?"

Sally said, "As long as you cook, you're welcome any time you like."

"Well, then," I said, "I think this is great," and returned to the kitchen.

Mother said, "Now I want to hear the story about the two of you. How did you meet?"

I know she'd heard every detail from Sally but Hutch was glad to tell it his way. While he spoke, with Sally interjecting corrections and additions, I finished supper. Mother and Sally set the table while he sipped a bottle of beer. Hutch and Little Sister had a gentle way of talking—bouncing words and phrases off each other—laughing for no apparent reason or getting laughter out of Mother and me—for no apparent reason. What they had together was contagious; it was easy.

Then, as I was serving the main course to Hutch, she said, "Well—tell me how it went with Cobus."

He didn't say anything. He took a sip from his beer and stared out into the street.

"Uh-oh," said Sally. "You did tell him didn't you?"

Hutch peered through the window as if trying to view the future. He murmured, "Yeah, I told him," with no expression.

"Oh, he'll be okay," said Mother. "What did he say? I'm sure he'll be fine. I know for sure he likes you a lot, Hutch. Robbie, please pass the Worcestershire. He's always talking about you, Hutch. What could he have said today?"

"Nothing," said Hutch, allowing his lips to tighten into a sad frown—still looking into the distance.

Sally sat with a startled look on her face. Either she had never seen Hutch like he was at that moment, or had, and was afraid of the foreboding. She had worked so hard for the day to be perfect; now, it was as if she knew it was about to fall apart.

Mother said, "Hutch, will you pass the salt and pepper, please? I know I'm not supposed to eat so much salt. But I love it. How can you cook without salt?"

"What did he say?" said Sally with a frightened, fawn look in her brown eyes.

"Not one thing," said Hutch, his frown appearing more perplexed than sad. "I told him on the way down. We'd been getting on fine; he started out talking about the University of

Texas with me saying little or nothing at all. Before we had gone thirty miles he changed his train of thought and spoke about San Marcos. He talked a mile a minute. I listened."

Hutch cut a bite of steak and Mother said, "See, I knew he'd be okay. Sounds to me like he was fine."

"Mother," I said, "Hutch hadn't told him yet."

"Well, I'll bet he'll be just fine," she said. "Would you pass me the ketchup?"

Sally handed the ketchup across the table and said to Hutch, "Go on, sweetheart."

While Mother mixed a ketchup and Worcestershire paste, Hutch continued with his description of the afternoon. "Cobus finally said, 'You know, I'll bet I'd get to play a lot more in San Marcos than I would at U. T.' I said, 'Your Mom and I would surely love to see you play in San Marcos.' Of course, we'd love to see him play in Austin, too, but it was a way of broaching what I wanted to say."

"Did he get what you were saying?" asked Sally.

"Not at first. It was so far removed from anything he'd ever considered that I had to say it nine or ten different ways. He denied it every time."

"Like how?" she asked.

"Cobus said, 'Mom will probably come with Uncle Robbie.' I replied, 'Robbie can come, too, but I'll be with your mom. I'll be going a lot of places with her.' 'What do you mean?' he said. 'I mean, I like your mom a lot,' I said. 'So?' said Cobus. 'So, I mean your mom and I have been seeing each other for some months now and we're fond of each other. We've become very close.'"

"Robbie, will you pour me another glass of water?" asked Mother.

"Cobus said nothing after that until I said we'd be getting married."

"And…" said Sally.

"And, he said *shit*."

Hutch paused for a minute, finished his beer with one long draw, cast his blank gaze out of the window again and then added, "He didn't say another word all day. Not one. I could tell by his breathing and body movements on the way home that he was becoming angrier with each mile. I stopped in front of his dad's and tried to talk to him again. I didn't get two words out. He slammed the door and ran into the house. I sat there for a while hoping he'd return. When he didn't, I drove out into the country for half an hour or so and then I came here."

I looked up and Cobus was standing in the front room. How long he had been there, I don't know. I don't know how much he heard—if anything. It didn't matter. Nothing he could have heard would have changed how he felt. I watched the look on his face morph from confusion to fury. The reality of seeing Hutch and his mother together began to sink in. I could see he was going to fight this with every tool he had available to him. The first tool he grabbed was anger.

When Sally saw him, she quickly said, "Hi, hon, would you like something to eat?"

"I don't want anything," said Cobus, looking daggers at his mother.

If I could have attached words to his glare they might have been *what in the hell do you think you are doing, Mother?* Instead, what came from his mouth was, "Hi, Grandmother. Hi, Uncle Robbie."

He continued to stare angrily at Sally.

Mother said, "Honey, come and give your grandmother a hug."

He did. Then he said, staring at no one in particular, "I've come to get my clothes. I'm going to stay at Dad's for a while."

Sally was handling it much better than I was. Calmly, she said, "Can't that wait, Cobus? I've made you a mincemeat pie."

"I'm not hungry. I'm moving out."

He started for his room and Mother said, "Cobus, you just wait right there. I'm going to fix you a piece of pie."

"No thanks, Grandmother," he said, and left the room.

Cobus's room was the first one down the hallway from the dining room. He shut the door with a bang.

Mother said, "I'm going to cut him a piece of mince pie and take it to him," and she left for the kitchen.

From the bedroom we heard Cobus say, "Where are my basketball shoes?"

Sally didn't say anything. Hutch didn't say anything; I knew he had a rule against the boys playing basketball during football season. Cobus said it to hurt them—it worked. I heard him tearing through his closet, throwing shoes, books, and balls against the wall.

He said, as loudly as he could, "Where the hell are my basketball shoes?"

"I'm going in there," said Sally.

"This is difficult for him," said Hutch. "Don't say anything to him."

I was thinking that was what the boy intended—to say or do whatever he felt without consequence. Often, he got away with shirking responsibilities or he got money from Sally or Doug without earning it. Perhaps those transgressions were practice for what was happening now—and for what was to come.

The day and the news that had earlier been so exciting had become painful. For a second, I caught myself feeling the same way Hutch did—sorry for Cobus and for what he was going through. Then I caught myself again. Here were two of the most important people in Cobus's life—wanting to share one of the happiest times of their lives with him—and Cobus was thinking of Cobus. His perfect view of the world—the one which placed him at its center—was being restaged to include a second spotlight focused elsewhere.

I said, "Let me talk to him."

I must have sounded angry—I was—because Sally and Hutch's heads snapped to look at me.

Mother said, "There. That's a nice big piece of pie. It's still warm. I wonder if he'll want milk with it." Raising her voice only slightly, she said, "Cobus would you like milk with your pie?" Then, to herself, "I'll pour him a big glass of milk."

"No," Sally said to me. "You can't go. It has to be me."

She stood to go to Cobus in his room. I wondered if she intended to lock him in his closet where he could still be heard rummaging through eighteen years of accumulated boyhood junk.

Sally said, "Robbie, don't look at me like that. I can handle him."

I was embarrassed that I must have looked like I disapproved when I really wanted her to know I was on her side.

I said, "I wasn't looking like anything."

"Do you want me to go with you?" said Hutch.

"No," she said. "Just me."

"I will, you know".

"No."

Mother said, "I'll cut pie for everyone."

Hutch and I enjoyed one of those awkward moments when it's obvious that everything you say is said merely to have something to say.

"I hadn't expected this," said Hutch. "I was concerned how the other boys on the team might ride him, but I never expected this explosive reaction."

I said, "I thought I knew him fairly well. I'm really disappointed in him."

From the bedroom, I heard Cobus say, "No, Mom; this sucks. This is the worst thing you have ever done to me."

"I didn't know I was doing it to you," she replied, with real anger in her own voice. "I thought I was doing it for me."

"I guess you are, then," said Cobus, with a cruel ring. "You are thinking *only* of yourself. That's called selfish. Have you stopped at all to think about anyone else—me, for instance?"

"Yes, I have."

"Right. What about Dad? Do you know what this will do to him? This will kill him. This is the most embarrassing thing you could ever do."

"Come on, Cobus. We've been divorced for seven years. Do you expect me to be alone for the rest of my life?"

"You are not alone. You have me, Grandmother, Uncle Robbie, and a hundred friends. You even still have Dad, if you'd give him a chance."

Sally didn't respond. What could she say? Cobus had to know there was no chance for the two of them. Could he have possibly been holding out hope that they would get back together one day? Maybe he had grown comfortable with life as it was. Maybe he felt that the separate lives on opposite sides of our little town were his family. They were certainly his world. This must have been like divorce all over again.

"There's plenty of people who don't rush out and get married just to keep from being alone," he continued. "Uncle Robbie isn't married and he is perfectly happy with only the rest of us as his family. You don't have to go out and bring in someone else."

Surely he wouldn't have said that if he knew I could hear him—which I could, clearly. The walls were paper-thin and their conversation bounced off the hardwood floor of his room, under the crack in the door and down the hallway to us. I felt like we should turn on TV or talk loudly or do the dishes but Hutch had an important stake in how it would turn out so we sat poking at what remained of supper without really eating—saying little. Even Mother remained silent. Could it be that she was eavesdropping, too? I didn't think she ever allowed anything unpleasant to enter her head.

"Why don't you wait a few days before you move all this stuff to your father's house?" Sally said. "You'll feel better in a day or two."

"No. I'm moving out."

"Please don't, Cobus."

"Not only that. If you marry *my* coach, I'll not be there at the wedding and I'll never come to visit you."

"Then that will be your choice," said Sally. "It will not be mine."

Cobus threw the door open as wildly as he had shut it and strode angrily into the dining room. As if on cue, Hutch and I stood and gathered the nearly empty plates from the table. The boy stood watching us. Sally came from behind him and began clearing dishes along with us.

Mother said, "Cobus, honey, I cut mincemeat pie for you and poured a glass of milk. Please eat your pie while it is warm."

Hutch and I turned to see what he would do. The spotlight was on him, just like he liked it. He looked at us, made eye contact with each of us in turn, and then said, "Thanks, Grandmother." Cobus took the pie, jammed himself into the La-Z-Boy, and flipped on MTV.

While he ate, we washed dishes—all four of us—banging into each other in the crowded kitchen. Then, after barely enough time had passed for an eighteen-year-old angry football player to wolf down all but one bite of pie and a swallow of milk, Mother said, "Your mother made that pie just for you Cobus. Isn't it wonderful?"

"God," he said. "Dad's waiting dinner on me." He bolted back to his bedroom, grabbed as much as he could carry in one load—including his basketball shoes placed pointedly on top of the pile for all to see—and hurried to the front door, saying, "Thanks, Grandma. I'll see you tomorrow. I love you," as the screen door slammed behind him. The last bite of pie, left alone to enjoy the beat of the deafening MTV, sat untouched on the arm of the chair.

I did my best to make Sally and Hutch feel like things would be all right. I hoped I was more convincing than how I felt. They tried to be positive, too—switching quickly from guesses about how soon Cobus would come around to talk about their own plans for the future. It all sounded lovely—only not as imminent as it had seemed earlier in the day.

When they lapsed into their dreams, Mother and I took our cue to leave. I drove her home and endured her proclamations of how wonderful Hutch was and how nice it was that he and Cobus were already so close. Hadn't she been in the same universe as the rest of us that evening? How could she possibly think things would ever be normal again—let alone warm and toasty?

When I got home, Doug was asleep in his chair and the boy was not around. I don't think he'd been home at all.

CHAPTER SEVEN

I DIDN'T HEAR COBUS come in Saturday night, but his truck was in front of the house so I figured he was okay.

Doug and his newly acquired students beat me to the tee. It was six forty-five on Sunday morning. The ladies were in a line along the back of the pasture-turned-golf-range, each with her own pile of blue golf balls stacked beside her. Doug stood in front of them with the strangest collection of implements I had ever seen in a golfing arena. The beach ball stood out because of its colors. The ax, an old stump, weed cutter, yardsticks, and oak logs blended into the Texas rural landscape more naturally than the beach ball, but they, too, looked miscast as tools for golf.

I walked to the group and asked if I could watch their practice. I think Doug was uneasy about having an audience—even if it was me. Tildy jumped in and insisted that I stay and the other ladies echoed their welcome, although Inez wasn't sure who I was until I walked closer to the group.

Doug wanted them to chop wood. He had purchased a new ax from the farm supply store—a light one for the women to handle.

He said to them, "If you can chop wood, you can play golf."

He placed an oak log on the stump and split it with one quick blow. He did it twice more—once with each of the halves made by his first swing. He created four equal-sized pieces of wood. He hadn't quartered the piece of oak to display the athletic ease with which he could chop wood—although he'd accomplished that—he made four smaller pieces of wood for his protégés.

The ladies lived in the Texas Hill Country. Except for Tildy, who had been raised in Atlanta, they had been reared on Texas farms or in the town of Bonnet. They could easily remember a time when their houses had few modern appliances. They had all—even Tildy—cooked on wood-burning stoves. Chopping wood was an ingrained memory.

Each of the ladies, in turn, split her log cleanly and quickly. Naturally, they lacked the power that Doug had displayed, although Macey came close. Nevertheless, they were able to accurately deliver crisp blows to their logs until they were halved.

Doug said, "I knew this would be easy."

Then he picked up the idiot stick—that's what we'd always called the L-shaped weed cutter. It was like a hockey stick with a serrated edge.

Doug said, "If you can cut dandelions, you can play golf."

He went to a rogue patch of yellow-headed foliage where he cut a swatch of weeds with the sickle and then handed it to Tildy. She wielded the tool with the same confidence as she had the ax.

I said, "Tildy, you surely didn't cut weeds when you were growing up." I assumed Tildy had been raised in a more genteel fashion.

"Why, Robbie," said Tildy, "I didn't know how to do anything until I moved to Texas. The weeds of Atlanta are just now beginning to return; Sherman burned them all, you know." She swiped at a daisy and scattered its petals to the breeze.

Doug took the beach ball—small as beach balls go, the size of a basketball. He picked up the ax again and then wedged the ball between his elbows. He had placed another log on the block and he split the log as he had the first—only this time he kept the beach ball between his arms.

"This is easy, too," he explained, and handed the odd props to Macey.

Amanda grumbled, "I don't really see the purpose of this."

"Look at it this way," he pointed out with a smile, "if you ever need to build a fire on the beach, you'll be prepared."

The ladies were much too serious to laugh at themselves. Inez wanted to and Macey started until an icy stare from Amanda froze them both. Tildy ignored all and was riveted with fascination on Doug's manner of teaching.

Macey had difficulty placing the beach ball comfortably between her arms. Her breasts were large and her arms sagged heavily. I didn't think there would be enough room for the beach ball but with Doug and the others standing by patiently, Macey leaned forward from the waist—allowing the backside of her anatomy to act as an anchor to prevent her from toppling forward—allowing her arms to hang from the shoulders—there was plenty of room for her to hold the beach ball and ax with good vision of the log.

I would have been quick to say, *Macey, try it this way, or that way*—or quick to say, *Macey, you don't have to do this with a beach ball,* but Doug didn't say a word. Amanda started to. Perhaps she was anticipating an embarrassing moment that never happened, but Tildy gently placed her hand on Amanda's arm and muffled whatever was about to be uttered.

I became immediately aware that Macey, bent from the waist with back straight, knees slightly flexed, beach ball resting comfortably between her arms and on her chest with ax in hand, was in a perfect golfing posture. She stopped her panting which had grown steadily while she explored the refinements of beach ball chopping. She raised the ax high over her head and then returned it crashing to the wood, splitting it with one blow, as had her teacher.

Inez clapped and yelled, "Yeah, Macey."

Amanda growled, "Harrumph."

Macey gasped, "Oh, my."

Tildy smiled.

Doug said, "Now get ready to do it again, but don't chop 'til I tell you."

She squinted at him, panting again, as a few beads of sweat formed across her upper lip. She said, "Oh, Doug, let one of the others do it next. Tildy, you come and try it."

Amanda questioned, "Are you sure this is the best way to learn golf? I mean, with beach balls and axes?"

Doug started to respond, but Tildy did, resolutely. "We will not question Doug's instruction again. Macey, do it once more."

Macey, not quite sure if she or Amanda, or both, had committed a transgression, said, "I was only trying to be fair, Tildy."

Doug said, "Macey, I want *you* to swing the ax again because you are doing something so beautifully well that I need to point it out to everyone."

"Oh, my," she exclaimed, blushing.

"Oh, my," echoed Amanda somewhat less enthusiastically.

Macey took her position again and then a deep breath—breasts, arms, and beach ball rising as one in anticipation of the destruction she was about to deliver—and Doug commanded, "Now, stop."

Walking down the street or up the stadium stairs, Macey would give you the impression that putting one foot in front of the other required more energy than she could sustain for more than a few painful seconds. Now, with a beach ball squeezed into the triangle formed between arms and cleavage, she looked surprisingly athletic—strong—capable of swinging the ax with ease.

"Hold that position as long as you can." Doug spoke enthusiastically now—apparently excited that his method was working better than he had anticipated. He pointed to the salient parts of her posture. "This is perfect. Her back is straight, her head held high, knees flexed for power, and weight evenly distributed—front to back—across her feet. This is what we want to copy when we hold a golf club."

I said, "That's called the address position."

"It doesn't matter what you call it," responded Doug quickly and sharply enough to make me vow that I would never interject again.

"This is how you stand up to a golf ball with club in hand," he continued, turning decisively away from me. "Be like Macey and the ax. Go ahead and swing now, Macey."

She explosively expelled a burst of air which she had held, purple faced, since Doug had ordered her to freeze in mid-chop and she cut the oak as emphatically as she had done before.

When it was Amanda's turn she whimpered, "I don't know how you expect me to do this; I won't be able to see the wood through the beach ball." Her whine said to me that she could do it if we would make the same fuss over her that had been made over Macey.

Doug said it didn't matter if she couldn't see the log—all she had to do was lift the ax and then, if she could keep her body from getting in the way, the tool would find its own path back to the wood.

Her first two chops were awkward attempts that missed entirely. She grunted and strained to force the ax toward the target with a stranglehold on the handle that popped the veins out on her forearms turning her knuckles white and face red.

Doug stepped in, gently placing his hand on Amanda's— quietly, with voice soft and low, saying, "Your hands are way too tight, Amanda. Let's relax them." I could see the tension begin to leave her arms, and he said, "Even more. I want you to be able to feel the ax handle in your fingertips; hold it lightly."

Her face returned to a natural hue. When Doug felt what he wanted, he loosed his grip; his voice dropped to a whisper. "Now, slowly raise the head of the ax. Let it climb with your arms following—never pushing, never straining—only following. When the head coasts to a stop, let your arms fall; do nothing; let them fall."

Amanda's ax rose, mirror finish catching a glint from the sun, and the razor edge fell, splitting clean the air and then the oak into a pair of splinterless staves.

"See," he said, "if you let it, it will swing itself."

As Tildy had been in control of Doug the night she asked him to teach them, he now held them in the palms of his hands. Tildy was wide-eyed; Amanda beamed. The gentle give and take of influence between the friends would continue throughout the following weeks.

Inez did not have the trouble Amanda had when she split her log with the beach ball and ax. Her vision was so poor that she was used to doing things by feel.

When Tildy swung, her athleticism became evident. Her touch was quick, light, and sure with never a doubt as to its accuracy.

After an hour of chopping and cutting followed by a fencing tournament with hands wrapped around yardsticks-turned-scimitars in a manner remarkably resembling the proper way to hold a golf club, Doug allowed each of them to make one swing with her own seven-iron. Each swing was smooth; each ball well struck. There was none of the earlier embarrassment or giggling—they were too tired and too in his grasp for that by then. They were each successful.

Doug took the clubs and balls away from the women and placed all in the back of his truck. He shouted through the open window as he started the engine to drive away, "Cut some weeds or wood for a while. I'll see you in the morning."

I saw a wry upturn on the corner of his lips as he drove away with tires spitting gravel. I turned to see what must have been a reflection of the confused amazement on my own face in the eyes of Amanda, Macey, and Inez. Tildy stood alone, clearly silhouetted against the rising sun, tilting at imaginary samurai warriors with her yardstick, unaware of the fog enveloping rest of us.

Monday evening, when Cobus came from practice, Doug and I saw the first preview of the rest of the football season. Cobus had moved in permanently—at least for the time being. At Sally's he was accustomed to dinner being served when he walked through the door. Doug had never been much for cooking so I knew if the boy was to have anything more substantial than four or five bowls of Cap'n Crunch washed down with a quart of Coke, I had to fix it.

I grilled four Texas-sized cheeseburgers—two for the boy, the others for his dad and me. I thought it would be a perfect meal for a teenage boy, but he picked at it; he ate a few bites of one burger and some chips and that was all. He made it hard for me to enjoy my own meal.

"What's wrong, Cobus?" I asked finally, after silently waiting on a dinner conversation to begin—after five minutes of waiting for him to break the quiet—five minutes of chewing our potato chips rhythmically like a three-beat country song. When Doug began chewing out of time, ruining the beat, I decided I had to be the one to talk or it was not going to happen. When Cobus didn't answer, I added, "Aren't the cheeseburgers good?"

"What?" he murmured, irritatingly.

He hadn't heard me or the potato chip percussion.

"The cheeseburgers. Is there something wrong?"

"I'm not hungry," he said, as if a starvation diet was his normal fare—his voice challenging my right to interrupt his mood.

"You must be hungry," I responded with my tone matching his more than I'd intended. "You've just come from a two-hour football practice. You must be starving."

"Football practice sucked," he said matter-of-factly.

"I'll fix you something else, then," I said, trying my best to sound hurt, knowing full well there must have been something wrong with the cheeseburgers.

Doug had a book about Bobby Jones propped against a milk carton in front of him. If he had noticed the building tension at the table, he hadn't shown it. I didn't think he'd heard a thing, but when Cobus mentioned practice he looked up from his reading.

"What sucked?" he asked quietly.

"Nothing," mumbled the boy, making eye contact with neither of us.

"Good," responded Doug, returning to Bobby Jones, apparently intuitive enough not to push his son or afraid of what he might hear if he did.

"The whole thing sucked," exclaimed Cobus suddenly, after a pause of a few markedly silent seconds, as if a revelation had landed upon him. "His practices have nothing to do with anything. I'm surprised we ever win at all."

Doug stabbed his finger into his book, marking his place in a way that let us know he was not exactly thrilled with the direction the conversation had taken and that he resented his reading being interrupted. He'd been a supporter of Hutch since the coach moved to Bonnet. I knew he had little use for the type of football second-guessing that often went on around town. I imagined he had even less use for it when it came from a high school player who had just come from practice—even if it was his own son.

He looked up with fire in his eyes; I thought he would cauterize Bonnet's star running back, but he backed down before he said anything and then asked politely, pointedly, "Cobus, do you think you might give me just one example?"

"No, sir."

Visibly biting his lip, Doug eyed the boy for a second and then continued reading at the point of his finger bookmark without responding. I was still searching for some food to serve

Cobus—something better than what had been the best possible of all meals half an hour earlier.

"I mean," said Cobus, with volume and tempo increasing, "Tommy threw eight incomplete passes the other night and all we did today was tackle, tackle, tackle. I'm not the only one, either. Everybody thinks it's stupid."

If I remembered my high school football correctly, no boy ever liked *stupid* fundamentals like blocking and tackling. Throwing and catching are much easier on the bones than banging and falling. Doug didn't bother to raise an eyebrow over Cobus's comment—it wasn't worth it. Instead, he closed his eyes, trying to restrain his billowing anger. Cobus's criticism of the day's practice crescendoed to a sermon. He bit off a healthy bite of burger to punctuate the primeval wisdom he was imparting. At least he was eating. I shut the refrigerator door and began cleaning the table.

Chomping and spewing, Cobus said, "I spoke to Derek Richards's dad and he told me that I have to carry the ball at least thirty times a game if we expect to keep winning. He's talking about winning the big games. The one's we've never been able to win because… because of…"

Cobus stopped just short of saying because of *the coach.* This time Doug left his eyes open and shut the book. "Thirty times a game," he said, nodding as if to thank the boy for the enlightenment.

"That's what Mr. Richards said. You know he played four years at the University of Texas, Dad. He knows what he's talking about. He played on some really good teams there. He said I need to touch the ball thirty times a game. But all we do is practice tackling and blocking and punting and kicking. Tonight we practiced punting and punt receiving for about an hour. I think I had the ball once. Then all the coach could do was tell me what I was doing wrong. He said I can't cut to the left."

If I knew Hutch, and I was getting to know him better with each passing day, he'd probably said something like, *Cobus you're a good runner but you cut to the right better than you cut to the left,* which is natural for right-handers. *Use your practice time to practice the hard stuff until it becomes natural.* He would never have said the boy wasn't good at anything. I'm sure Cobus looked at him, threw the football down in anger and walked over to a group of boys who were practicing blocking and tackling. Hutch would have been too embarrassed to stop him.

I knew Baron Richards, too. He'd been on the scout squad at the university for four years in the late seventies. He was a practice holder for place kickers and a fifth-string, sometimes defensive back. Baron was a good enough guy—I guessed. He meant well—I supposed. He probably got carried away and wanted to make Cobus feel good. He'd probably said it in the heat of excitement after the game.

Doug closed his eyes again, held them that way for a few seconds, and then opened them wide and said, "When did he say that?"

"Friday night—after the game."

"How long are your games, son?"

I couldn't believe Doug. His boy had just said hurtful things and the man was calmly changing the subject—carrying on most of his end of the conversation with eye gestures. If any of the rest of us ever said anything to remind him that he hadn't been able to play at the University, he made it as painful for us as it was for him.

"Forty-eight minutes," said Cobus curtly, as if he resented being asked a question when the answer was obvious.

"That means your team owns the ball for about twenty-four minutes a night. You think you personally should carry the ball thirty times?"

"You don't understand."

"Then make me understand. You think you should carry it thirty times in twenty-four minutes?"

Cobus stopped eating again, turned red, and yelled, "You don't understand!"

I knew teenagers enough to know that *you don't understand* is a battle cry shouted when whomever they're arguing with begins to make sense.

"Listen to me, boy." Doug spoke directly to his son, looking at him hard, riveting his eyes on Cobus's eyes, trying to hold the boy with a stare.

"You listen," screamed Cobus, jumping away from the glare and the table, knocking his cheeseburger to the floor. "He's a stupid coach. He doesn't know what he's doing and I don't even know if I want to play football anymore. I hate him."

That sucked the anger out of Doug and any control of the situation he'd begun to wrench from his son. Cobus wasn't angry at football or at Hutch because of football. It didn't make it hurt any less, but it was clear that there was a lot more going on than football.

"Sit down, son," said Doug, shaken. He'd spent a lifetime hiding any emotion that dared creep up on him and he looked scared. He was scared for his son and for himself. He was vulnerable—not strong like he always was or wanted to be. The only way he could see to handle the situation was to be submissive and that scared him because he had no idea how to do that.

Cobus didn't sit down, but he did stop before he made it out of the kitchen. He stood in the doorway to the rest of the house with his back turned to us.

Doug kept talking, "Look, Cobus, I know this is hard for you, but don't hurt yourself because of something else going on. Your whole life is football. That's all you ever wanted to do or be. Now you've got it better than you dreamed. Don't throw that away. You'll regret it the rest of your life."

"What do you know about it?" Cobus asked quietly, back still turned.

He didn't know that his dad had seen every dream he'd ever dreamt die with a whimper.

"I guess I don't know what you're feeling," said his dad—saying anything to agree with his son—lying to him because he knew more than the boy how it felt to be betrayed—lying because he knew how it felt to kill what he loved most because he wouldn't fight who he loved most.

"I'm not feeling anything," said Cobus, with no feeling. "I hate football. And you're right; it's been my whole life and that's not good. I don't have another life. Maybe it's time I started thinking about that. I'll need to take over the store someday and I don't even know the first thing about it. It's time I learned about the store."

Doug wouldn't respond and he didn't want me to see his face so he looked at the floor.

I said, "Cobus, you won't feel this way in the morning. We can talk about it tomorrow. Do your homework, get a good night's sleep, and you'll see things differently when you wake up. Okay?"

He stood there, like he was waiting for his dad to say something else, but Doug couldn't, so the boy went to his room like I'd suggested. Immediately, I wished he hadn't done what I'd suggested.

But for the sounds of me cleaning dishes, the house had been still. I hadn't noticed when Doug left for a walk. He returned as I scoured the sink.

"Hey," I said, sponge and cleanser in hand. "I didn't even know you were gone. Where've you been?"

"Walking."

"Walking? Where walking?"

"Walking. Thinking and walking."

"What did you think about?"

"I'm going to play golf."

"What?"

"Golf. I'm going to play golf."

"Tonight?"

"No, not tonight. I mean I'm going to *play* golf. I'm going to pick up where I left off fifteen years ago. Whaddya think?"

"Sure," I said, "I think."

CHAPTER EIGHT

DOUG HAD DECIDED TO play tournament golf again. I knew he could hit the ball as well as anyone when he stood in the privacy of his own personal driving range, but playing tournament golf was a different story. He wasn't thinking of playing in local best ball events—he wanted to play professionally, on the tour. He hadn't played in fifteen years. He hadn't putted; he hadn't hit sand shots, chip shots, or any shots requiring other than a full swing. He was thirty-eight years old and I thought it a bit late to begin competition at the only level that could ever satisfy him. I was supportive, though, while afraid of the consequences if he were to fail.

On Tuesday morning, I wanted to talk to Doug about Cobus; instead, I found myself listening to his own personal plans for the next twenty years. He'd decided less than twelve hours before to play competitive golf again and he already knew the route he would take to return to top form. He had every detail choreographed—down to practice schedules and budgets. When first I'd heard Sally's surprise, I'd braced myself for the tough job of holding him together. Then, when Cobus fell apart, I figured Doug was a goner, too. Instead, he was fine, making plans for the future and I was the confused and sullen one. I was concerned he was moving too fast—setting himself up for serious disappointment—like someone marrying on the rebound.

"What about Cobus?" I asked when I could wedge a word into his planning frenzy.

"What about him?" said Doug, sounding wholly ignorant of the boy's battles.

"You're planning to be gone a lot in the next year."

"I hope it lasts longer than a year."

I wasn't sure it would, but I played along. "Okay, a lot of years. What about Cobus?"

"He'll be in college, playing football, chasing women, and drinking beer. He won't need me."

I said, "You heard him last night. He isn't even planning to finish this football season, let alone play in any others."

"Tour qualifying is in November."

He hadn't heard a thing.

"The PGA Tour? This November?" I asked. "You're talking about playing against professional golfers?"

"Yep. Whaddya think?"

"I think you've lost your mind."

"Hell, I probably won't qualify anyway. I'll play one round, zip it up, and come home."

Now that sounded like the old Doug. I didn't disagree with him.

I said, "You still haven't said anything about Cobus. I think you should move a little slower, maybe wait until after he graduates and then start playing again. Really, don't you think he's going to need you this year?"

In a flash, I knew he was unhappy with me; if not angry, sadly disillusioned.

He said, "For as long as I can remember, you have prodded and pleaded for me to take care of myself. You have reminded me a dozen times a week that I was too tied to the past, Sally, Cobus, my father, or you."

I didn't know he'd been listening.

"Now," he continued, "you want to keep me from going where you've pushed me for so long. Were you lying to me then or now?"

He was right. I had switched roles without realizing it—without knowing why. He had turned a corner, was going a better way now, and I wanted to reel him back. It occurred to me, with sickening clarity, that of all the people in my life, I might be the one who was scared the most. Sally was changing; Cobus wanted change; Doug was changing; and all I could think of was clinging to the past. I wanted things to be as they had always been, like Friday night, when the boys hit hard and Bonnet ran up the score. I wanted things to be as they were before Tildy Hannah climbed the bleachers and before Saturday and Sally's surprise.

"I'm not lying," I murmured. "I only want... I want things to be okay."

He said, "Last night, Cobus said hurtful things. Did you hear them? Did he do it intentionally? I don't know. Teenagers think pain, happiness, and everything in between come cheaper than they do. Can you believe what he said about Baron Richards playing football at the University? Is Cobus so stupid he doesn't know how that might make me feel? Jesus Christ, I'm not the one who's marrying his coach. Maybe pain is necessary to sever the ties between boyhood and manhood—between dependence and independence. Cobus saying he was going to work in the store hurt more than his cracks about football. He knows I hate that place. He hates it. In one sentence, he brought my whole life into focus. I saw me in him and my father in me. I wanted to hit him."

I almost said I'd wanted to hit the boy, too, but I didn't. I said, "I know."

"Then I knew," said Doug, "I knew why my father hit me. He wasn't hitting me; he was beating himself up and he couldn't stop because every time he did it, he hated himself more, so he hit harder, until he hated himself so much he died. The ultimate

beating: —he died and left me in the store. But I didn't hit the boy
last night. I'll never hit him. It's his life; the only way he'll work it
out is on his own without the rest of us shoring him up."

He was talking about me, too.

I didn't want to stand in front of Cobus's class that morning and
teach. I was afraid that I might see too much of myself mirrored
in a spoiled, confused adolescent. I went to football practice at
the end of the school day to see if things would be any better than
they'd been the day before. I sat alone in the bleachers.

Cobus came late, dragging himself slowly onto the field.
Other boys worked intensely in groups with their coaches.
Quarterbacks threw short patterns to the ends. Michael
Martinez cut hard to the sidelines after five yards and Tommy
Jarvis, practicing quick three-step drop-backs, fired him bullets.
He liked to throw hard. Jason Roberts and three boys kicked
field goals without a coach, working well on their own, gradually
making their way back from the five-yard line to the extent of their
range. Tackles and guards did what they do best—hit. Across the
field they banged a two-man sled, throwing the front end high
into the air with a coach standing on the back. The sounds of
football came from that group—the short shrill blasts from the
coach's whistle rhythmically prodding the boys to blast the sled
again—the loud grunts, explosive bursts of air from their lungs,
and the *pop, pop, pop* of shoulder pads. In the middle of the field,
running backs worked on blocking, too. They ran at freshmen
and small sophomores holding inflatable dummies. Younger
players were allowed to carry the ball for a few collisions, but
they were knocked on their butts by starters using the dummies
as battering rams.

Cobus shuffled on to the end of the field where Jason Roberts
kicked with three other boys; he took his place in line like he was
going to kick. This was the first football practice I'd seen in a

dozen years, but even I knew that Cobus was not supposed to be kicking. The four boys looked at him as if to say, *what are you doing here?*, but Cobus was a leader and no one challenged him. He led them in a wrong direction.

He kicked one and then it was his turn to hold the ball for the next kicker. Instead of holding it, he pulled the ball away from Jason and jumped up, motioning for the others to go out for a pass. Jason didn't; he was irritated; the others scattered across the end of the field so Cobus could loft one to them. He threw it high as he could and they ran under it to the end zone. They banged into each other jumping for the ball and fell in a heap—presumably laughing at the fun. One of the boys grabbed the ball and was in motion to throw it back when Hutch saw them. He blew his whistle while gesturing for the team to move to their next drills.

He gave instructions to one of his assistants and then walked toward Cobus who was moving slowly—generally in the right direction. Hutch met him halfway there and attempted to put a kind hand on Cobus's shoulder, which the boy shrugged off vigorously. Cobus wanted no part of Hutch; he walked and then rudely trotted away. I heard Hutch call out, "Give me one minute, Cobus."

Cobus kept jogging—into the backfield of an offensive set, pushing aside a freshman who had lined up to take the hand-off, and then he ran the play himself. He took the ball from the quarterback and needlessly ran at a defender, knocking the unsuspecting boy to the ground long after the assistant had blown the play dead. Hutch walked to the scene. As head coach he was the one to deliver the reprimand needed. He did nothing.

I thought how interesting that body language was as loud as it was. From my place in the bleachers, I could feel the chaos being provoked by one person. He had injected anarchy into a finely disciplined organization. The other players were bewildered; the assistant coaches were furious; Hutch was humiliated, but continued to do nothing. Judging from the speed with which disorder flourished, I gathered that similar things must have happened the afternoon before. The reaction looked to be, *oh no, here we go again.*

To my dismay, I watched them run play after play in which Cobus ran the wrong direction, forgot to run, dropped the ball, or tripped over his feet and fell. This was the heralded high school running back from Bonnet, Texas who was being recruited by thirty schools from a five-state region. Each time he screwed up he yelled *fuck* as loudly as he could and then either slammed his fist into the ground, threw the ball to the ground, or shoved a teammate in the general direction of the ground.

Finally, after watching the confusion for as long as he could stand it, Hutch's number one assistant coach, Scotty Campbell, took Cobus by the side of the helmet and dragged him from the scene. Cobus had no quarrel with Scotty, of course, and he went along half willingly, half dragging his feet. I was glad Scotty did it because I was seriously considering walking onto the field and dragging the boy off myself.

If it would have been me, I would have been torn between saying, *you'd better get you shit together, boy, or I will personally kick your butt all over this field*, and sympathizing by offering to listen. Scotty was plenty big enough for the former; I was glad he was man enough to try the latter. I'd mellowed in twenty-four hours. If I'd been at practice on Monday, I would have been cheering for the butt-kicking.

Scotty returned to practice leaving Cobus brooding with head down, away from the rest of the team. They executed better with him on the sidelines, if not with the spark you'd expect from a championship-bound team. The boys were disciplined enough or perhaps polite enough not to stare at Cobus and they continued their practice. When he finally returned to the workout, he went through the motions without enthusiasm and, thankfully, without his earlier lack of control.

I left the stands, started the half-mile walk home, and saw a familiar figure coming my way. I made out only color at first—a yellow splash bounding over the gravel. It cheered me up before I knew what I was looking at. Bouncing along with ponytail flipping up behind like the tail of a fawn, making me feel good for the first time since Saturday morning, was Kjirsten. Kjirsten... Oh my God, I was supposed to invite Kjirsten to dinner with Hutch and Sally. I'd forgotten. It was Tuesday.

Kjirsten ran toward me in the sexiest yellow jogging suit I had ever seen, waving, calling my name with a smile that made it hard breathe, let alone think. I felt myself returning the smile and the wave as she stopped in front of me. I felt her grab my hand, saying, "Where have you been?" Although I could tell she hadn't been jogging long, her face was blush pink. She was beautiful.

"Kjirsten. I'm really glad to see you."

"Robbie, do you know you don't have to leave our meetings to chance? You can see me any time. I sat by the phone all weekend pining, waiting, hoping in vain for the ring that never came."

I was reasonably sure she was toying with me. Her mocking doe-eyed expression said as much, but in my state of mind I trusted no assumption to my besieged imagination.

"What? Really?"

"Of course not. You think I don't have any thing better to do than wait around on you?" she said, flicking her ponytail so it fell long down her back.

"I'm sorry," I said, as if I wasn't confused enough—but how was she to know that? "I really had planned on calling." I really had.

"Sorry for what? Oh, so you didn't call? I wasn't home, you know. I went to Houston to visit my sister. She's playing matchmaker again. She set me up with an oil guy. How shallow does little sister Heidi think I am? I can't believe she would be influenced by all that money. I suppose she was blinded by his rugged good looks. Besides, I don't look good in diamonds so I gave them back. So, tell me, why are you glad to see me?"

She squeezed my hand, tossing her mane again.

"I was supposed to ask you out—for tonight—but I forgot."

"Oh, Robbie," she said, batting eyelids at me as if my deepening mortification wasn't enough, "You make me feel so, so wanted."

I tried to look sheepish, rolling my eyes, wanting to show her that I knew I was being a jerk.

"Let's try again," I said. "I know it's short notice, but I want to take you to dinner—tonight—to the Elks Club in Peach Pit. Whaddya say?"

"Ooh. Sounds wonderful. The Elks club. Too bad."

"Too bad. Too bad. What do you mean too bad?"

"I mean, I already have plans for tonight. I mean, it's usually okay to ask me out two minutes before it's time to go, but this time I have plans."

At that moment I was reasonably certain I was having the last casual conversation with Kjirsten I would ever have. I also figured that by the time she finished sharing the story with everyone in Bonnet who knew me, I would have to drive to Dallas for a social life.

"I'm sorry." I hate apologies.

"Sorry again? You were sorry a minute ago." She took her hand from mine, tweaked my cheek, and then said, "Oh, okay, if you promise to quit pouting, you can come along."

Honest to God, she pinched my cheek, and I was not pouting. Come along? What did she mean come along?

"I surrender, Kjirsten. You win. I have no idea what you're talking about. I'd love to go anywhere with you. I'd like that very much. I'll go tonight, tomorrow night, any time you say; just tell me what you mean before my brain turns to grits."

"We'll pick you up at five-thirty. Wear your new boots and something western. I like that green shirt of yours with the pearl buttons. I've got to go."

She kissed me right on the lips then flailed me in the face with her ponytail as she turned to jog back in the direction from which she'd come.

"Kjirsten," I yelled after her. "Where are we going? Who are we going with?"

She waved back at me without turning around.

I forgot every problem I'd ever had. I wasn't thinking about Cobus or Doug or anyone but Kjirsten. I stopped by the store on the way home to tell Doug I wouldn't be there to fix supper. I called Sally to tell her I wouldn't be going to the Elks Club. I thought it funny that she didn't argue with me or say anything about not giving her more notice. She giggled like she'd expected it, which irritated me because I was the one person in the family who was always reliable. After all, she was the one who hadn't called since Saturday to confirm our night out.

I had one hour to get ready. After a ten minute panic-stricken search, I found the mother-of-pearl, button-down western shirt under a pile of dirty clothes in Cobus's room. How he'd stacked clothing that high and that filthy in less than three days was a mystery to me. I wished I had time to get angry with him for borrowing a brand new favorite shirt without asking. I'd only worn it myself once. How did Kjirsten know about it anyway? I rinsed it, threw it in the dryer with the best pair of clean jeans I could find, hoping like hell they'd both iron up easily. By the time I finished showering, I had thirty minutes.

Out of the shower, shirt not quite dry, I polished boots in my underwear while the iron heated. I drenched shirt, jeans, and floor with spray starch—pressing with hot steam 'til the cotton was crisp as a paper-thin pane of glass. It's the only way I know to wear western clothes. As I shut the iron off, a car slid to a stop on the gravel in front of the house, driver laying on the horn.

I toyed with making her—them—whoever it was—wait until I could make myself look good. I chose the splash-cologne, slick-down-wet-hair, button-shirt-while-running-for-the-car method of dressing instead. I was glad I did because Kjirsten and Sally, with horn still blaring, were sharing hysterics at my expense.

No wonder Sally had been so forgiving when I'd thought I was breaking a date with her. Sometime between Saturday and then, Sally and *pinch me on the cheek, you can come along if you don't pout* Kjirsten had become best friends and had plotted my torment with every waking moment.

"Hey, cowboy," said the long-legged blond girl.

"Hey, good-lookin'," said Little Sister, leaning on the horn one more time. "Let's party."

Damned if I'd let them know they put one over on me.

"I knew what you were up to," I said, trying to be casual—hiding excitement behind cowboy cool—excitement over two mostly crazy women who cared enough to go to all this trouble on my account—excitement when it hit me just how much I had come to care for the one in the ponytail.

"Don't even think you fooled me," I said when they stopped hooting enough to hear me—and that started them hooting again.

"Get your cowboy jeans in the car," said the ponytail. "Don't talk. Men in the back."

I had to dive into the back because Sally hit the gas the minute I opened the door. I was pretty sure that this was not the role model Bonnet expected from its teachers.

"We're going to the Elks Club, aren't we?" I said, righting myself enough to speak.

"The Elks Club it is," said Kjirsten. "Peach Pit, Texas here we come."

"Well, don't forget Hutch," I said, feeling unfairly outnumbered.

"Who?" laughed Sally, honking this time at a bright blue half-ton Chevy pickup with roll bar and top-mount lights flying by as we rounded the corner toward the school and Hutch. Sally stuck her hand high out the window and waved at Cobus as he raced by. She stopped laughing. In the rearview mirror, I imagined a twinge of sadness in her eyes when he drove on without a wave or answer from his horn. Maybe he hadn't seen us in time.

I looked again and she was smiling once more at the new man in her life standing alongside the road, waving at us as we skidded to a stop beside him.

CHAPTER NINE

"HUTCH HAS SOME NEWS," said Sally.

"More news?"

We sat in the Peach Pit Elks Club while local members played bingo in the back room. The restaurant was empty. Being so, the *maitre d'* had secured us a table under the collection of polished longhorn cattle horns hanging on the wall as far away from the sounds of bingo as we could get. That was *maitre d'* and Vietnam War veteran Buggy Strait who'd stuck his head out from the bingo room to say, "Y'all set yourself. I'll git there soon's this card's over."

"Please, no more news," I said again.

"Okay," Hutch said. "No more news. So let's eat."

"Oh, tell us Hutch," said Kjirsten. "Don't listen to him. Tell us everything."

Sally said, "Hutch got a call from the athletic director at El Paso A&M. The coach is retiring this year; they want Hutch to apply."

"Hutch, that's wonderful," said Kjirsten.

"It's a long way away," he said.

"No kidding," I said, remembering clearly the last conversation I'd had with Doug. Suddenly, people in my life were thinking of moving away from me. It meant Sally would be leaving, too. "That's five hundred miles."

"I don't mean it's a long way away in miles," Hutch said. "I mean, a lot of things have to happen before I can move to El Paso."

I said, "El Paso. Do I have to remind you how hot it is in El Paso?" just as Buggy Strait showed up with a pitcher of ice water, ready to take our order.

"Hell," drawled Buggy, voice deep and rumbly like a distant roll of thunder. "Don't you know El Paso gets dry heat? Everybody knows dry heat ain't hot. They git so much dry heat in El Paso they bundle up all summer long."

"That's right," said Kjirsten. "Just like people in Montana go naked in the winter 'cause it's a dry cold." I loved the way she fit in anywhere.

"Robbie," said Sally, "I hope you're not going to be a stick-in-the-mud about this. This is Hutch's lifelong dream."

"Oh, I know," I said, when it dawned on me I was throwing the same bucket of water on Hutch's parade that I'd splashed on Doug's that morning. "It does sound great. I'll say they couldn't be getting a better man. I hate to see you move away, that's all."

"Touching," rumbled Buggy. "If y'all wanna eat, you'd best tell me now. They're gittin' ready to start the next game. I'll *be* there for the next game."

"Garçon," said Kjirsten, with her best high-brow accent, "would you be so kind as to enumerate the day's specials?"

"We got specials. Thawed out too many chicken-fried steaks for bingo. You want chicken-fried steaks, you git 'em half price. Tonight only."

"What's that come with?"

"Potato, beans, with thousand island, ranch, or blue cheese on your salad."

"Baked?"

"You were expectin' *au gratin*?"

"Sounds like we all want chicken-fried steak," said Hutch.

"I thought so," rasped Buggy. "I'll bring coffee."

When Buggy left, Hutch said, "Look, you guys, I don't want this going any further. I don't have a job offer. The coach hasn't even officially retired yet. I got a call from an old friend discussing possibilities, that's all."

"Yeah," I said. "Let's not rent a U-Haul yet."

"Right," he said. "There's plenty enough going on now to occupy us without worrying about what may or may not happen six or eight months from now. Besides, they said they'd move me. We won't need a U-Haul."

For the next hour, we knew when Buggy would return to our table; his appearances followed thirty seconds after the shriek of *Bingo!* from a back-room patron. Then, for two minutes we would have his undivided attention—two minutes only, for as soon as the next card was called, Buggy would growl, "They're playin' my song," and then leave us.

There are few places I've dined—of course, I'm not as well traveled as, say, Tildy and her friends—that can match the flavor of chicken-fried steak cooked Hill Country, Texas-style. It's not the flank leather they try to pass off as steak in the so-called popular cafés in Austin. It's the best locally grown sirloin that can be butchered. Buggy, or whoever is cooking, smothers it with enough Southern-style sausage gravy to push it off the end of the fat charts. It's not politically correct, it's not nutritionally correct; it's wonderful. It leaves you spent—gluttonously speaking.

Sally ate a full plate, as, of course, did Hutch and I. Kjirsten did a good job of making it look like she was eating as much as any of the rest of us while still managing to take most of hers home. At least one of us would enjoy full circulation without the aid of surgery. I saw Hutch lean back in his chair, rolling his eyes inward, and I thought we were going to lose him to a cholesterol overdose. He was saved by the breakup of the bingo and the emergence of Bonnet's four oldest football fans. Of course, I wasn't surprised to see Tildy and her friends—I'd seen them so regularly since Friday that I would have been surprised if they hadn't been there.

Tildy made a bee-line for our table when she spied Hutch. He and I stood to greet her and she graciously offered her hand to him. "I must tell you, Coach," said Tildy with enthusiasm, "Friday's game was so much fun." She spoke directly to him, not wholly ignoring the rest of us, but capturing his attention entirely. "We must do it again this week."

Tildy would talk football any time, night or day, as long as she was sure the other participants in the conversation were as knowledgeable about the game as she. Coach qualified. The rest of us probably did not.

He stood, wiping his hands on a napkin, before shaking Tildy's. "We will do the best we can."

Tildy said, "This team reminds me of the 1970 Bonnet team."

I assumed she had a technical comparison, player by player, of the two teams. There was certainly no one at the table who remembered the 1970 team. I was a toddler and Sally and Kjirsten were younger than I.

"I'm not given much to nostalgia," Tildy continued, "but that team stood out because they were blessed with wonderful talent. Bradford Keegan played quarterback then. Do you know Bradford? He lives in Two Rivers now—has seven kids."

Bradford ran the Two Rivers tire store. The only knowledge I had of him was that his huge hands were permanently black from the tires.

Tildy went on. "Brad didn't throw a very pretty pass but he found a way to get the job done. For a quarterback, he loved to hit people, too—played corner on defense. That team also had Jackson Prothro. He was the best kicker this county has known. He kicked beautiful high spirals that hung on the air forever. He kicked field goals as well. Look on the record board above the trophy case in the main hall of the high school; you'll see he still owns the record for Bonnet's longest field goal."

I didn't recall the name but I remembered the record was fifty-two yards.

"Jackson lives down near your hometown," said Tildy to Hutch.

"Sure, I know Jackson," Hutch said. "He played four years for Nebraska, then one season for New Orleans. He's a lawyer now."

Tildy nodded.

"But it was Linus Everly who was the best of them all. Young Cobus reminds me so of Linus Everly," said Tildy, looking at Sally. "He was a ferocious runner and a punishing linebacker. If ever an opposing player jumped offside when Linus was on defense, he would make him pay. The offending player, upon realizing his transgression, would go limp and Linus would use the opportunity to bury shoulder pads and helmet into the poor boy's ribcage. More than once Linus injured a player with that tactic."

Sally winced, either from the image of unnecessary violence Tildy had painted, or from the comparison she had drawn to Cobus.

Tildy smiled, softening the impact of the story. "Of course, in those days, coaches encouraged that type of play more than they do now. In fact, any time a player was injured it was considered to be his fault because he had allowed himself to be hit instead of hitting, so Linus was encouraged.

"It was Linus's team. Old Coach Cecil made no bones about it. The season rested on one boy's shoulders. There was talent at every position—but we all understood that Linus would take us over the top. Mind you, I'm not saying Cecil was right or wrong to place the responsibility for the success of the team squarely on the back of one player—it's the way Bonnet football was in 1970."

Macey, realizing Tildy's story might continue for longer than she would find it comfortable to stand, pulled a chair from the table next to ours and sat. With a menu she unconsciously fanned herself while her friend held our attention. I sat, too. Hutch remained standing since it was he to whom Tildy was directing her conversation. Behind Tildy, Amanda and Inez let their focus wander. Inez, standing, rocked back and forth as if keeping time to a melody heard only by her. Amanda's lips moved silently, perhaps mouthing the lyrics to the song of Inez.

Tildy placed her forefinger to her lips, pausing to reflect on the point she was about to make. "That was the first time we were picked in all the polls to win the championship—then didn't."

I hoped she wasn't making a prediction. I hoped Hutch didn't think she was making a prediction.

"Bonnet rolled over each of the first five teams they faced in the fall of 1970 by an average margin of forty-three points," she said.

"Wow," said Hutch. "Why haven't we heard of this team? Forty-three points a game. That must be a record."

I'd grown up in Bonnet and began playing and loving football four years after Tildy's wonder team had played. I'd never heard anything about them.

"Everyone knew we were going to win it all," said Tildy, with a shrug of her shoulders to emphasize the inevitability of victory. "We read about it in all Central Texas papers. Many made reservations in Dallas for the championship game. They did that because Coach Cecil promised us we would win."

Macey still fanned herself while Amanda and Inez rocked and sang silently. Kjirsten rested her head on her hands, which were folded in front of her with elbows on the table. She was captivated by Tildy—by the energy Tildy bounced off us as she spoke. Kjirsten admired Tildy. I understood that. They were alike in many ways. I admired them both.

Sally looked as if she was trying to understand how Tildy could make comparisons of Cobus's team, which had played only one game, to a group of boys who had played more than thirty years ago. She was either thinking that or I thought she was thinking that because I was thinking that.

"A strange thing happened on the way to Dallas. We never got there," said Tildy, pulling a chair and sitting beside Macey. Hutch sat, too.

Amanda and Inez wandered around the room looking at the pictures of past Elks Club presidents and board members. There were pictures of Willie Nelson and John Wayne, too, but Amanda and Inez looked at portraits of the Elks. They had known and outlived most of them.

"In the fifth game, Linus Everly was magnificent. Thirty-two points on offense and two on defense. Thirty-four points. Five touchdowns. Ran for a two-point conversion. Scored a safety by knocking down the enemy halfback just as he took the handoff from the beleaguered quarterback. Nearly took the handoff himself. He ran for 248 yards and had nine tackles. The best single game performance I've seen by a Texas high school player."

"It would be the best I've ever heard of," said Hutch. "Only I've never heard of it."

Tildy paused, and then spoke more quietly.

"In the sixth game, Linus did not appear. No one knew why. No one knew where he was. He didn't come to the game."

Sally was bothered by this. "What happened to him?" she asked.

"It's a sad story," said Tildy. "Not the saddest story I know, but a sad one."

Macey said, "This is the saddest story I know." I looked at Macey and knew she was telling the truth.

"The night of the sixth game, Coach Cecil paced the sidelines. Of course, all coaches pace sidelines. He didn't watch the action on the field, though. He watched the gate to the football field. He was expecting—hoping—to see Linus drive up in that old pickup. The sixth game was one they should have won with ease—without Linus. But Cecil's mind wasn't there and, because of that, neither were the minds of his players. Four or five times during the game he sent one of his coaches to call the boy's home or to drive around Bonnet to find him. They did not find Linus and they lost that night by two touchdowns."

"Now *I* think it's a sad story," said Hutch. "That was really the end of their season, wasn't it? A good football team is as much smoke, mirrors, and magical spell as it is talent and strategy. When you break the spell, it's over. I've seen it a hundred times."

"What happened to Linus?" asked Sally. "Was he okay?"

Hutch added, "I bet they lost most of the rest of their games."

It was no wonder I'd never heard of them. In Bonnet, we choose to remember the winners.

Buggy came by and refreshed our coffee. Macey asked for water.

Kjirsten asked, "Where was he? Why didn't he come that night?"

"From the sounds of things, I don't think he ever came again," I said.

"He was never seen again," said Tildy, after sipping from Macey's water.

I said, "He was dead, wasn't he?"

"Oh, no, he wasn't dead," chirped Amanda as she strolled by the table on her fifth orbit of the room—still gazing at the pictures with humming Inez.

Tildy continued telling her story mainly to Hutch as if we weren't there. "After the game, Cecil didn't even wait to shake the hand of the other team's coach and players. He ran to his car and sped straight away to the place Linus lived—where he lived with his daddy—a hired hand's shack out by Spurling's south place. It was empty—bare of furniture or any other any sign it had been occupied. Of course, they had lived there. Some of the boys on the team had been there only two days before. Nothing was wrong then. Linus wasn't embarrassed about the house or way he lived. He liked his friends to come by. Linus's daddy had been fine, too. The boys liked him. He'd talk football or arm-wrestle them. He could beat them all, too."

Spurling's south place, she'd said. That brought a flicker of recollection. There was a crumbling old foundation in an overgrown windbreak—a place Daddy and I'd find quail in November. There was no shack; only a few broken boards of weathering wood. I remembered Daddy said the place had been knocked down with a bulldozer. Daddy said folks had lived there and then disappeared. He said they were strange and no one knew what became of them. I knew who owned the land near Spurling's.

"I know this place, Tildy," I blurted. "There's nothing there but broken cement. I remember rumors. I don't remember the football or a boy named Linus, but I remember folks saying no one ever knew what happened to the folks who lived in that place."

Tildy, this time addressing me, giving credence to my memories, said, "As far as I know, there are but two people in this town who know what happened to Linus."

Macey stopped fanning. She was surprised by this. It had been apparent until then that she'd heard much of—or remembered much of—what Tildy was telling. "You mean you know what happened to Linus, Tildy?" she asked dramatically, as always.

Inez and Amanda stopped their strolling and humming.

"Of course I do," said Tildy. "Linus's daddy worked for me. It was my shack they lived in.

"Linus's daddy'd had a problem with alcohol. When he came to me in the summer of '69 and asked for a job, he'd been out of the Louisiana State Prison for only a month. I don't believe he ever planned to stay in this town longer than the time it took to fill up his tank, but I'd hung a sign in the window of the Texaco station sayin' I was in need of a hired man. The job came with a place to live. He told me up front he'd been in prison and why. Driving drunk, he'd killed his own wife and a family of four, and served two years for manslaughter. When he told me that, I knew I didn't have to ask him if he'd stopped drinking. I took him on and he worked for me for nearly eighteen months.

"Linus came to live with his daddy in early September. Some said he'd been with his grandmother. He was a good football player that first year, but the second year he was magnificent. He found a home here."

When Tildy stopped for another sip of water, Sally said, "His daddy started drinking again and did something to the boy, didn't he, Tildy?"

"No," said Tildy. "I do not believe he had one drink while he lived in Bonnet. That Friday afternoon, Linus had been in class. *Ready for the game*, his friends all said. He went home to rest. When he arrived there, I was with his daddy, begging him to stay, but his truck was already packed with what things belonged to them and I could not stop it. He looked at the boy and said, 'The sheriff was by this morning. Boy, we have to go.' If Linus was surprised, he didn't show it. He handed me the keys to the old truck that I'd lent him—given him—politely saying, 'Thank you, ma'am. Will you please tell my friends good-bye for me and wish them luck?' His daddy shook my hand and they drove away. That was the last I ever saw them. By the time the game began, they were a hundred miles away.

"The sheriff, Murton Banks, from Bee Tree, had rousted him—told him to leave the county by the day's end or go back to prison. He didn't have a reason—didn't have to. Didn't like Louisiana trash, he said. That's all. That's the whole story. I didn't say anything to Coach Cecil—perhaps I should have. I have regretted it for years."

"To what end?" asked Hutch of no one. "There was nothing you could have changed."

"Tildy," I said timidly—afraid of the answer, "Why does this team—Hutch's team—remind you of that one?"

"Oh, my goodness," she said with a startled laugh. "That was my opening statement wasn't it? How did I ever get on to telling you about all of that? Please forgive me. The similarity of which I was speaking was merely with regard to the outstanding talent of the two teams. That was a very good team and so is this one.

That is what I wanted to say. How did I digress so far? I love your team, Hutch."

Hutch and Kjirsten laughed. I smiled. Sally didn't.

"Sally, I was trying to say what a wonderful football player your son has become. He is such a leader on the field and I marvel at how the other boys follow him. How proud you must be."

I wondered if Hutch and Sally were cringing as much as I at the memories of the young leader's performance on Saturday evening in Sally's home.

Hutch said the correct thing for a coach. "This is, on the whole, a mature group of boys. There are quite a few individuals who will assume a leadership role when I ask it of them."

"I can see that," said Tildy.

"It's the same way in school," I added. "There are many leaders."

Tildy stood to leave and ended her conversation by saying, "Hutch, don't change a thing. I can't wait until Friday night to see what happens next." Then, as an afterthought, "Sally, don't you change a thing either."

When she left, Hutch said, "They *are* a mature group of boys—a good team. Don't you think so, Robbie?"

CHAPTER TEN

TEXAS HIGH SCHOOL FOOTBALL boys are rowdy. They get pumped up, loud, and in the face of their opponents. They are vulgar. Football players like to hit things. They slash and bruise with their hands and arms and butt with their heads. They'll turn their entire armor-clad bodies into weapons of punishment whenever they can. If they can't find a player from another team to hit, they'll beat on each other. It doesn't matter if there's a game or not. When two boys pass each other in the hallway in the school, they beat on each other. If they pass each other on the street, they shove with a grunt and an inciting sneer. Merely standing together in a line or waiting for a hamburger in the café is an invitation to slap each other around. It's the code of conduct for the boys, like a secret handshake that's not so secret. If you don't do it, you can't be in the club and, frankly, you'll never be a very good football player.

I'd seen Cobus or Tommy Jarvis or Michael knock a player flat on the field and then stand over him with their own particular versions of in-your-face taunts. I'd seen them with arms flexed and chest thrown out after a sack as if to say, *I'm king in this jungle,* thumping their chests like an alpha male ape—strutting, crowing, and waving fists and towels to fire up the crowd.

Some hate it when they see pros or college players act that way. They hate it whether it comes from their hometown boys or from the other teams'. Some say they don't understand the bravado when tackling or scoring touchdowns is brag enough. They're right; they don't understand. It's not mean; it's not personal. There is no malicious thought or intent; there's no thought at all. It's what they do these days and it may be different in form from some other time, but it's different in form only. I suspect strutting and crowing have been around since the dawn of games when it was a challenge to capture another tribe's winter cache. Of course, strutting then would have included the head of an unsuccessful invader skewered on a stick.

Cobus was mean on Friday night. Friday night, in the second game of the season when we played against the hapless Peach Pit Broncos, he had malicious thought; he made it personal. I saw it right away. On the first series of downs when Peach Pit had the ball, I saw him kick at the Bronco quarterback after throwing him to the ground. The overmatched quarterback had already handed the ball off and was no longer part of the play. Cobus did it on purpose. Doug saw it, too. Cobus flung the boy down and stepped on him. The referee missed it, but he didn't miss it two plays later when Cobus chased a receiver out of bounds and slammed him into the Bonnet bench. The ref threw a flag.

Hutch grabbed Cobus and held him long enough to say three words to him before my nephew reared his shoulder and flipped the coach's reining attempt madly aside. The fifteen-yard penalty and whatever Hutch said to the boy worked for most of the rest of the first half. Cobus held his rage at bay and didn't intentionally maim anyone, but the chemistry had changed.

Confidence is an elusive gift. The boys received theirs from Cobus. They used a look in his eye, firmness of his lip, or the spring in his step to fire their own passions for the game. On the best nights, Cobus sprinted to and from the huddle with his right hand clenched in a victory fist, urging his teammates on, and their fires raged. In those games, we were treated to great

Texas high school football. It could have been Tommy or Jason who provided the spark, but early in their lives they had learned how easy it was to get it from Cobus.

In the stands, we warmed ourselves on Cobus's fire, too, only in our case it was thievery because we never gave anything back. We consumed it. That night against Peach Pit, after Cobus's passion for the game flamed out, he violently tried to recreate the burn but ignition failed him.

Bonnet was leading the game twenty-one to three when the third quarter began. Peach Pit had scored a field goal when Cobus fumbled the ball on his own twenty-yard line late in the first half. Cobus gave Tommy a shove on the sidelines after that. He blamed it on Tommy, but it wasn't Tommy's fault.

We led twenty-one to three and were winning easily—without his passion. The boys hadn't learned yet how to fuel their own and in the stands we had frittered away all we'd been allotted. We sat quietly, clapping politely or trying to raise the level of our cheers loud enough to be heard above the murmurs of those who had grown disinterested. The boys walked to the huddle and then back to the line. Hutch was a good coach so they ran plays with precision—surgically, but boringly, excising a win from Peach Pit.

With four minutes gone in the third quarter, Cobus tore his helmet from his head and threw it at a Peach Pit player who had tackled him cleanly in the open field. On a normal night, the boy wouldn't have been able to bring Cobus down—shouldn't have laid a hand on him—so Cobus threw his helmet, hitting his opponent squarely in the middle of the back as he walked away.

The boys had seen too many brawls on television to have the restraint to stay on their own sidelines. It's an event that high school football players dream will happen at least once in their lives. Both benches emptied and the melee was on. The hit kid went after Cobus, casting his own helmet aside in the process. The Peach Pit boy blew past the referee who feebly tried to get between them. Cobus went low and cut the kid's legs from under him. In a flash, Cobus was sitting on top of the boy, pummeling his head.

Before he could inflict any real damage, the stampede bowled into Cobus, burying him under an old-fashioned dog pile. By the time the coaches and referees amassed enough strength in numbers to peel away the brawlers and send them back to their own sidelines, the two who started the mess had been at the bottom of the heap for so long that they were putty.

Hutch ran straight away to the head referee and spoke rapidly. We all knew the ref was going to throw Cobus out of the game—perhaps the boy from Peach Pit as well. The Peach Pit coach had his back to Hutch's powwow while he tried to calm his team down. I know he thought both boys would be ejected. When he turned around, Hutch was walking toward Bonnet's team's bench with his arm around the referee—like they were best of buddies. They probably were.

What could Hutch possibly have said that would excuse Cobus's actions? How could the referee not have tossed Cobus? The zebra pointed and shook his finger at Hutch on the sideline while speaking with enough animation to make it appear that he was still in control. Each time he pointed and shook, Hutch nodded with understanding; each time Hutch nodded it became more apparent he'd found the right words to convince the ref to allow Cobus to play out the game. That Hutch even had the brass to ask for mercy for the punk was embarrassing—shocking. After all, he was Sally and Doug's son, not mine.

The Peach Pit coach ran onto the field, honoring the unwritten coaching rule that says a coach must never allow an opposing coach to have the exclusive ear of an official. He was way too late. It was the referee's turn to put an arm around the animated one. The ref nodded with understanding while the livid-faced coach from Peach Pit gestured toward my nephew. The coach was angry enough that he might have been tossed out himself on another night. Thank God the ref had the presence of mind to refrain from booting the coach. If he'd have done that,

I *would* have been embarrassed—at least for Doug and Sally's sake.

Afraid to look, I turned to see how Doug was taking the scene. He was gone. He'd sat beside me for the duration of every game in which Cobus had played since seventh grade—through rainstorms, hailstorms, windstorms, and blue northers—now with one little fracas, he'd bolted. I watched the sideline thinking perhaps he would appear there to talk to his son or maybe pull Cobus from the game himself. He didn't.

The rest of the game was a fog, with robot-players trance-walking their routines—with no bounce, no spring, little life. Four and out. Four and out. Touchdown by proxy. Final score—twenty-eight to three.

Out of habit, I went to the café—without Doug. Bud had beaten everyone there, as usual, with half a beer gone before the rest of us walked through the door.

Bonnet, Texas is a small town—small enough to walk every place you go. There are those, though, like the elderly or ill and Bud Granger, who find it necessary to drive the few blocks from their homes to the field. Tildy doesn't count in the elderly group—she out-walks us all.

There is room for a few cars to park near the north end of the field. At one time they parked right behind the end zone. They stopped that when a kid from Beaucoup went too deep on a post pattern and kissed the front grill of a '69 Chevelle. Bud parks as close as they'll let him and prides himself on being the first one to leave the field at the end of the game… or he prides himself on being the first one to the café. Either way, he's the first to down one beer and start on his second.

I arrived with Galey and Cuthbert Alden, who said, "Hey, Big Al."

"Hey, boys," wheezed Al. "Bud beat you guys here." He punctuated with his, "Hee, hee, hee" staccato cackle without looking up from the tap. He gulped another throat full of air, not stopping talking for breathing, and said, "Hey, Doug."

"Doug's not here," I started, quickly groping for excuses for him—hoping I wouldn't have to recall all the details of the game—hoping I wouldn't have to explain to them what Doug was feeling before I'd figured it out myself.

"Sure, I am," said Doug, striding through the door behind me, catching it before it slammed like any other Friday night.

Trying not to act too confused, I began to ask, "Where—"

"Where, what?" he asked, brushing past me with no glance or pause for an answer.

"Hey there, Al," he said, "how's about a beer?"

With beer foam slopping over the rim, big Al set a mug on the bar.

"Hee, hee," tittered Al at me, "where the hell did you think he was?"

"I thought—"

"Too much," quipped Doug with a smirk. "You think too much."

"Hee, hee."

Bud Granger, already red-faced from the beer he'd guzzled, turned and began his melodrama before my roommate had even a chance to pull his chair.

"Wow. What spunk that boy has," he said with an emphatic gesture of his fist.

Before he could burble another word, I said, "Hey, Bud, mind if we join you?" which was a ridiculous question since we always sat in the same place.

"Why, sure," he sputtered.

For the moment, I'd kept him from pissing Doug off.

Baron Richards sat back in the corner of his booth, alone, trying to act like he wasn't eavesdropping on our every word—not that it was hard to do, as loud as we were, and not that we were that interesting. Did he think he needed an invitation to sit with us? It was understandable since I wouldn't have sat with him if I'd been invited—which I wasn't.

Doug rebuffed me the first time I attempted to ask him where he'd spent the last half of the game. Probing him wasn't usually unbearably painful until the third rejection. I could even recall a time when persistence had provided me with an answer, so I tried again. "Doug, where were—"

Red-faced Bud crudely stepped all over my question with, "Tell me, Douggy..."

A minute before, I had tried to save his butt by interrupting his "what spunk" line. When he interrupted back with *tell me, Douggy,* he was on his own.

He continued to spew, oblivious of the thin ice on which he skated. "Have you ever seen as much spunk as that boy of yours showed tonight? Have ya, Douggy?"

Oh, how he hated to be called Douggy. A week before there would have been nothing I could have done to stop Doug from saying what he might regret for some time.

Bud Granger was really quite harmless. He was drunk and slobbery, loud and obnoxious. I prepared to jump in one more time to bail him out when Doug—full of surprises—did it himself.

He gently leaned in closer to Bud, kindly sliding his arm around the sot's ubiquitous trunk, and with his barely audible, gravely whisper, said, "Spunk, Bud? So you call it spunk? I don't call it spunk. I'm his own old man and I wish he hadn't done it. He didn't need to do it. I'd rather call it a cheap shot. But if you say we should call it spunk, we'll call it spunk. How about punk spunk?"

"Hah! Punk spunk. I like that," said Bud smugly—smugly, because for the first time in memory, someone—Doug—was actually paying attention to him and giving rare credence to his babblings. It was either credence or cleverly disguised mockery.

Marvin Duncan entered the café. I liked it when he showed up. Marvin Duncan, proprietor of the Duncan Fertilizer Company, didn't join us after every game, but when he did, he was usually able to offer a measure of sanity to our tortured musings. Doug figured Marv was able to sift through our rhetoric better than most because he was an expert with what we were spreading.

Doug caught Marvin's reflection in the mirror and turned from his touching embrace of Bud Granger to offer Marv a seat. "Marv, come on over here," said Doug. "Join us, will you? I want to talk to you."

Bud continued rambling. "Yessir, Douggy, that boy of yours sure knows how to get them players fired up," he said, taking another long draw from his beer.

Far too sarcastically, I added, "Oh, yeah. He showed enough spunk tonight to fire up both teams, the refs, coaches, and most of us folks in the stands."

Unfortunately, I'd not been able to hide my displeasure at Cobus's earlier antics—nor was I able to disguise my disapproval of his father's apparent indifference to them. I regretted my lack of self-control at once, wincing, but not quickly enough to avoid Doug's daggers. So much for indifference. Sure, he could go out of his way to placate old Bud. I was left to dangle—still wondering where he'd gone during the game and wondering how he was planning to deal with his son now.

"Hey, Doug," said Marvin, with a wink and then a gesture directed toward Al indicating he wanted the big guy to pour him a beer. Big Al complied, lifting his large belly from its resting place on the bar and throwing a towel over his shoulder as he pulled the tap.

Marvin sat beside me, saying, "Hi, Robbie," with a friendly pat on my shoulder. He proceeded 'round the table with greetings to Bud, Galey, and Cuthbert.

Poor Galey and Cuthbert. They hadn't had a chance for an edgewise word with Bud and Doug carrying on like they had. They may have been content to sit back and watch the show but I was searching for a voice on my side. I asked Cuthbert if he'd ever seen a brawl like the one we'd seen—hoping he might confirm it was out of the ordinary—out of line.

"I wuz in one," he said. "Baseball."

It wasn't exactly the answer I'd hoped for.

Cuthbert was a nervous talker. His head bobbed. He sat up and moved around in his seat. He brushed his hair with his hand. He always talked that way and brother Galey always jumped in to complete his thoughts for him.

"Damnedest thing you never saw," said brother Galey. Cuthbert sat back in his seat to restrain his fidgeting. "Cuthbert slid home, caught his spike in the grass, an' flipped up into the catcher an' knocked him over in a cloud a dust. He wuz tryin' to avoid the sumbitch all together an' didn't do nothin' but cause a ruckus."

"Yup. Big mess," said Cuthbert sitting up again—brushing back his hair with his other hand. "Jest like tonight."

Galey said, "Loads of fun. It wuz a high point of our baseball-playin' days."

Now they both sat back in their chairs and folded their arms across their chests. No more fidgeting and done talking—for the moment.

Marvin shook his head, saying with a click of his tongue—a *tsk*. "How soon we forget, Robbie."

"What?" I asked, wondering if I really wanted to know. "Forget what?"

"Your youth."

Marvin was ten years older than Doug and I, so it was entirely possible he was remembering something I couldn't.

"Aromas," said Marvin, and a fuzzy image formed in my head. "Your freshman year, I believe. Up in Aromas. District freshman basketball semis. Any recollection?"

Now the old memory was clear. It wasn't fuzzy after all. How'd he remember that? Okay, so we'd emptied our bench too, for our own little riot in the middle of the Aromas gym floor.

"That was different," I said. "Wasn't it, Doug? It was a lot different."

"Don't ask me," Doug said. "You're the one who hit that big Dutchman."

"Yeah. Well, it was a lot different. He had it coming. That oaf was all elbows."

"Heh, heh," chuckled Al—shrill as a banshee. "You'd better have another beer, Robbie old boy."

I hadn't even noticed that mine was gone. It was. I took another.

Doug finally turned his attention entirely away from Bud and toward Marvin. "Hey, Marvin," he began, "I need help growing grass."

"Not in Bonnet, Texas," chortle-gasped Big Al.

Doug ignored that and continued, "Putting green grass. I want to put a putting green in on my practice range. A good one. Golf-course quality. You know anything about putting greens?"

"Sure, I do," said Marvin with a confident nod. "We helped with all the greens in Peach Pit when they rebuilt. That was two years ago and they're doing great."

"I thought so. It doesn't have to be that big. I want some ridges and valleys, though."

"Like Augusta, I suppose," I said sincerely.

"Exactly."

Cuthbert began twitching, sitting higher in his chair so I knew he was going to speak. With total departure from the conversation the rest of us shared, he said, "I remember where I wuz, Doug, the day I learnt yer knee'd been blowed out."

Brother Galey hadn't been prepared for Cuthbert to talk so he didn't interrupt yet. He sat up and nodded in agreement. Cuthbert would have to speak his second full sentence alone so he wrung his hands and then ran first one then the other through his hair. He adjusted his glasses, sniffed and continued, "We wuz cuttin' beans. It wuz a bad day all around."

Apparently that was enough information for Galey to pick up the story, which was a good thing because I was afraid Cuthbert would fidget himself out of his chair. Galey said, "We turnt the International over with a whole load of beans."

Cuthbert shifted from one cheek to the other and sat back while brother Galey continued.

"Gary Spurling come by to help us load it all back wit' his Allis front loader and he said you'd blowed out yer knee real bad. We figured you'd make a comeback. We'd got our season tickets to the University and wuz plannin' on seein' ever' one of your games."

Fidgety Cuthbert twitched and asked, "Did you ever wonder if'n you coulda made a comeback?"

"Nope," said Doug without hesitation. "Wasn't in the cards. Good thing I found golf, huh?"

"Well, that weren't the same," allowed Galey. "We couldn't watch that."

Bud Granger jumped in with, "I'll have to agree with that one, Douggy. Golf just ain't the same as football. Besides you never amounted to much with golf anyhow."

Doug didn't flinch. He continued with his patience, or he continued with his patronizing, whichever version is preferable.

"Now, Bud," said Doug, kindly. "Never is such a long time."

He turned back to Marvin, "I want two or three hills. Let's make my green thirty by fifty feet. I'll need a long flat area along with hills. How much sand will that take?"

Marvin thought for a second, and said, "Tell you what. Let's get together in the morning and we'll figure out what you'll need. Too late for Bermuda grass now—we'll plug that in the spring. We'll seed rye for the winter. I'll mix you a special batch of the same putting green brew they use in Peach Pit. You can use my truck and front loader for the weekend; take whatever you think you'll need. Mix sand, fertilizer, and your soil. Take my tiller, too. We'll settle up next week some time."

"I'll be there at seven AM."

"Well, I won't, but I will by eight."

Doug was as excited as a kid waiting for a new toy. Sounded like fun to me, too. I could picture myself putting away a few hundred hours on his green in the evenings. I'd even mow the grass if he'd let me, which he wouldn't.

"Didn't you ever think about coachin' or somethin'?" asked Galey, still not in touch with the idea that Doug hadn't done a thing with football for nearly twenty years.

"Nah. Coaching's not for me. Anyway, I can still play golf and playin's better than coaching."

"Well, I hain't never seen you play golf. Don't s'pose I never will, neither. But I'd bet a full-growed heifer that your golfin' wuz never as purdy as yer running of the football."

Galey said that and then he and Cuthbert crossed their arms and sat back, resolved that they were right and there wasn't nuttin' else to say.

"Oh, yes, it wuz," I said with absolute conviction that his golf swing was as purdy—pretty—as anyone who ever ran any football—including himself.

"Iz," corrected Doug.

"Iz."

Marvin, always well grounded in the present, asked Doug, "What's all this renewed interest in your golf game lately? I see you out there at six in the morning and you're still there as the sun sets."

"I'm going to play again."

"I'm assuming you don't mean with the boys on Saturday morning down at the Peach Pit Country Club and Grill."

Bud, showing fully his lack of understanding for the topic, slobbered, "You don't expect him to drive all the way to Austin every Saturday just to play golf, do you?"

Cuthbert, uncrossing his arms, folding them again, uncrossing them again, offered, "You wasn't thinkin' of building no golf course in Bonnet, wuz you?"

Brother Galey, not bothering to uncross his arms, said, "I don't know where you'd put it, no how."

The train of thought to get from *I'm going to play golf again* to *there's no place to put a golf course in Bonnet*, was mind boggling at best—more like frightening.

"I want to play on the tour. The pro tour," said Doug speaking strictly to Marvin now—and me, I hoped.

"I don't see why not," said Marvin, with a nod of understanding. "You can start on that junior tour—who sponsors it? Nike?"

"Used to be Nike. They change sponsors every couple years. Now it's an insurance company."

"Now, Doug, just who do you think is going to run your store?" gurgled Bud.

"I know the answer to that," I said. "Norma and Cassie. They run the whole place now. They'd just as soon Doug not show up anyhow."

"Harumph," grunted Bud Granger right through another gulp of beer.

Al pulled a chair to join us. There weren't as many customers in Al's café as usual, so he had the time to sit a while. Maybe the boys' brawl had zapped enough energy from folks that they chose home instead.

Cuthbert cleared his throat and sat way up high in his chair, leaning right up against the table. He placed his arms down flat on the table without fidgeting, so I knew he was about to utter something profound.

"Well, I wisht you'd a been able to play football, jest so me an' Galey coulda come and watched."

Galey fidgeted for Cuthbert. "We don't know about no golf. We only know 'bout football. We wisht you'd stayed a football player. We picked up all them beans we spilt and we never lost one penny on account o' that, but yer knee stayed blowed out and we never got to the University to see you play."

"Harumph," spat Bud again.

That may have been as close to the philosophy of the meaning of life as Galey and Cuthbert would ever come.

Marvin smiled, chuckled, and then said, "You boys ever think about going to those games without Doug havin' to be there?"

"We did one time," said Galey, looking pathetically nostalgic. "It weren't the same at all. There weren't no one there could run as good as Doug. We didn't know none of them other players. There wuz too many people. We left at the halftime and come on home. We give our tickets to Tildy Hannah and she went with a different person ever' week."

"Harumph."

That night, when Doug and I were home alone—while he was reading and I washed the dishes the nephew left for me—I asked him one more time where he'd gone during the game.

"Under the bleachers."

"So you saw the end of the game at least."

"Yeah. If you can call it a game. Pretty ugly, huh?"

"It was okay. Not the best ever, but okay." I tried hard not to sound negative. I'd done that earlier and it didn't make me feel any better. Maybe he wanted me to say what had happened was okay. Maybe it was okay—like the old boys in the café had said.

"It was shit. It's hard to wake up and realize your own kid's a jerk."

"He's not really, you know."

"Yeah, well, he's doing his best to prove otherwise."

"He'll get through this. You wait and see."

"Well if he doesn't hurry, he's going to fuck everything up."

I almost asked, *fuck what up, the team, the golf, Sally, Hutch—what?* But I didn't. I didn't want to know what he thought the answer was. I didn't say anything.

Doug said, "Hey, pard, wanna help me build that green tomorrow? Then Sunday, I'll treat you to a round of golf. I'll see if I can get us on Crenshaw's course west of Austin. Whaddya say?"

Hot, physical labor sounded good.

"Sure," I said.

"Maybe Cobus'll help, too," said Doug.

"Sure."

CHAPTER ELEVEN

I WAS IN BED when Cobus came home

I heard Doug say, "I'm doing some work on the practice range in the morning. I'll get you up early. Plan to spend the whole day working with me."

Cobus tried to resist, but he was tired. "I was going to go—"

"Cancel whatever you had planned. I need you to spend the whole day with me."

A brief pause, then, "Whatever."

That was as close to, *sure, Dad, I'd love to*, as Doug would ever get. At that, it wasn't a bad substitute.

Cobus didn't say a word when Doug woke him up at six on Saturday morning. He threw on jean shorts and old sneakers and, after wolfing half a box of cereal, rode with me to the practice tee.

Doug beat us there by ten minutes. It had taken him less than half that time to mark an area on the grass with yellow twine where he wanted to build his green. He'd built it in his head a dozen times already.

The task before us was simple enough. It required some brawn and little brain. Between Cobus and me, we could supply both.

We shackled ourselves to Doug's old walk-behind rototiller. Marvin promised a riding tiller for later in the morning; until then, Cobus and I took turns being dragged by the noisy steel-toothed beast. Thank God it was September and the Texas sun didn't reach full bake 'til ten. Cobus ran the machine and I walked beside, breaking clods of grass and dirt with a shovel or my boot. Every twenty minutes we stopped to down a pint of ice water. Doug had it easy. Tildy and the gals came for their morning session and he gave golf lessons while the boy and I busted sod.

Doug relaxed at a table with umbrella and chairs at the back of the practice tee. Every time I looked up from clod clomping, he was sitting in the shade, sipping Macey's lemonade and munching oatmeal cookies.

The women held hands in pairs and dry-swung each other through the movements of their swings. Since, except for Tildy, they had acquired nothing remotely resembling muscle memory, Doug used this method daily to remind their sinews and tendons of the proper golf movements and to help them stretch out the pains of the previous day. He made them chip balls directly at each other, still in pairs, from less than twenty feet apart. He believed that would teach them the touch they needed faster than chipping to a basket or an imaginary hole. If they hit it too hard, they could maim each other. Short or erratic shots, causing a partner to walk to retrieve the ball, elicited complaints of increasing volume—in Macey's case, greatly increasing volume— until the ball striker got it right.

After my third glass of water, I watched the women blast shot after shot from a pile or sand. Sand flew into the breeze; the breeze blew it back into their faces while Doug sipped away.

They never complained. Complaining at your partner's wild chipping was orchestrated; complaining about sand in the face was not allowed.

He allowed them to hit thirty-six full-swing shots each day—never more than five with any one club and never more than two of those in a row. He believed the more closely they could approximate a real round of golf, the better they would play on an actual golf course.

By the time they were finished with the last of their swings, Cobus and I had tilled the designated area. It was only eight-fifteen in the morning; it felt like we'd been digging for hours. When Marvin Duncan arrived with garden tractor tiller in tow, Tildy and friends were pouring lemonade while Doug stretched and yawned away the stiffness of nearly two hours in his chair.

I didn't entirely mind that Cobus and I tilled while Doug sat in the shade. I needed the exercise and Cobus needed time to brood, but I wasn't entirely clear on the reason for the walk-behind tiller when a garden tractor was on its way. I believe I was trapped in the middle of a point being made for Cobus's sake.

I felt fulfilled when Marvin said, "You've got the hard part done."

"Good," I said. "This ground is fighting back."

"Use my baby John Deere to work in a few tons of sand and fertilizer and you'll be ready to plant. Work it first one way and then the other. Work it back and forth until the entire mixture of soil and sand is as fine as the sand itself. Build the hills as you go—you'll need to do that with a shovel. You'll be ready to plant by four o'clock."

I felt so much better.

We finished earlier than four o'clock. After Tildy and her band of septuagenarian golfing neophytes departed the scene, Doug worked as hard as Cobus and I the rest of the day. He made runs to the fertilizer yard with Marvin's dump truck while Cobus and I worked with baby John Deere. The clods were gone by the third circle through the ever-softening patch of dirt.

At ten o'clock, Cobus remembered that Jason Roberts's daddy had a tractor with a blade on the front he used to move feed and manure. Cobus left and returned with the Godsend in twenty minutes, and from then on we used our shovels for leaning only. Cobus ran the blade and I drove the John Deere tiller. Doug raked it all out by hand until it was as fine as sand like Marvin told us. We built three of the prettiest putting mounds into the green, and sloped them all so the water would run easily off to the sides instead of collecting in low areas. I told Doug it was just like Augusta.

At noon, Doug bought burgers from Al. Cobus ate by himself, sitting against the manure blade while Doug and I sat at the table with the umbrella. Two hours later, though, Cobus was eager to talk about the work we'd done and how he thought his dad should have built a putting green much sooner. He was proud of his work. You would not have known it was the same boy who, the night before, had been angry enough to throw a blanket of depression over an entire town.

Doug planned for the day to work on the boy like it did. It worked so well that I caught myself believing things were okay with Cobus—that his demons had been exorcised. For a few minutes, he was laughing again—the way you should laugh when you're eighteen with no cares in the world.

He said he wanted Doug to help him with his golf swing. He said he was looking forward to playing golf when he got to college—wherever that was to be. The last fifteen minutes before Doug gave him fifty bucks and sent him off with the Roberts's tractor, they stood on the tee and hit trick shots while I sat under the umbrella and watched—amazed as always at their athleticism. Doug offered me fifty bucks, too. I told him to stick it in Cobus's college fund. I'd done it for the exercise.

Doug stayed behind to spread seed on his creation and to start the water. He wanted to stand alone and admire his new baby all the way 'til sunset.

I opted for a shower and a nap. A golf tournament, whose name and sponsor changed yearly, was on television, and that and nine hours of work in the sun made it easy to fall asleep. When I awoke at six, I was too sunburned and too tired to cook. Besides, Doug wasn't home and who knew where Cobus had gone. With fifty dollars in his pocket, it might have been the moon.

It had been two days since I'd dined with Little Sister. I didn't want her to become accustomed to eating without me. Sally stood where I knew she'd be—at the counter in her kitchen with vegetables lined up and ready for chopping. It was Chinese night, Sally style, which meant she chopped vegetables in chunks as big as would fit in the wok. On Mexican night, Sally chopped vegetables in chunks as big as would fit in a store-bought tortilla. On soup nights, she was restricted to chopping chunks only as small as would fit in an adult's mouth. One Christmas, Cobus and I bought her the best food processor we could afford, which meant I paid for it. She accepted graciously and used it twice. When I hinted she should get it out, she said it was too hard to clean—besides, she had only a few vegetables to chop. She never understood the point we were trying to make about the size of her potatoes.

Sally had finished with lettuce shredding and was butchering carrots. She hadn't yet chopped onion when I found her crying, so I knew she was crying not for the vegetables' sake. She cried for Cobus's sake or she cried for her own sake because of Cobus.

Sally laughed at herself when she cried. She chopped, laughed, and then cried and chopped again. As she sobbed, she shook all over with a twelve-inch chef's knife in her hand. Sally saw me and rushed to throw her arms around me with knife clutched in her quivering fingers. I ducked as she flung her weapon past my left cheek and I held very still while she held me tightly with blade pressed against my ear.

When she quit convulsing, sobbing, and laughing with cold, cleaving steel and pulled away from me at last, I instinctively reached for my severed lobe. I breathed again only when I knew for sure that all of my body parts remained intact.

Sally waved the knife at a heap of nephew's dirty clothes, which flowed from the front room. A mud and dirt wardrobe of t-shirts and denim draped the arms of the chair. Crumpled briefs were strewn on the floor. Once-white socks were especially crusty. At practice, the boys stretched in socks until the coaches arrived. For wind sprints, they kicked off their cleats and ran again in socks in the cool grass of the field. From the size of the pile, I calculated how long the mess had been crammed into the bottom of a locker that should have been condemned. I had no desire to approach the burgeoning life form, although I considering collecting specimens for the sake of science.

Sally shook the knife at the accretion, laugh-sobbing, "He—*sob*—dumped them there—*laugh*—and said 'Wash these.' *Sob*. He didn't say, 'Wash these, Mom.' *Sob*. He didn't say 'Wash these, please.' *Laugh*. He took the beer. *Sniff*."

"What beer?" I asked, desperately trying to decide on which of her emotions to hang mine.

"A six-pack of beer. *Sniff*. He knows that's a rule. He can't take beer out of the house. *Sob*. I said, 'Don't take the beer, please, Cobus'. *Sob*."

"What'd he say?" I said.

"*Laugh*. He said, 'Wash those.' *Laugh*."

Some might consider it normal for a teenage boy to have no compunction at leaving his mother a filthy stack of laundry, but Sally was a good parent. She'd taught him to wash his own dirty clothes while he was in junior high. Doug and I didn't do it for him. We barely found time for our own.

"Well," I said.

"Well, what? *Laugh*."

That was three laughs without a sob. Sally was bouncing back.

"Well, are you going to do the wash?"

"No! *Laugh.* First, I was going to take them to your place and dump them in his room. Then I was going to call the Salvation Army to come get them. Now—*sinister laugh*—I'm going to flip the flipping pile of... shtuff out on the lawn to see how long he'll let it lie."

That's as close as she ever came to swearing. At that she blushed. She must have had terribly nasty words floating around in her head to turn as pink as she did.

"When he left," said Sally, wiping remnants of tears from her face with her knife hand, causing me to massage my ear lobe again, "he took beer with him and then spun his tires. He threw gravel everywhere. It's all over the porch."

I recalled how he'd spoken to his father a few nights before and how cruel he'd been with little effort and no remorse. Sally had gotten off easy. She would bounce back. She could swim, climb, or chop her way through the thrashed fields of life's chaff better than the rest of could muddle through ours. She would put this twisted gift of love from her son into one corner of her closet and his next salvo in another. Some went on the shelf; some fell on the floor; but always, the door would close. How easy it was, I thought, to sweep a little gravel from the porch and into the dirt, never having to deal with it again.

Doug dealt with his gifts of love chaff by beating them into the golf balls on his perfect patch of grass—always picking them up and then bringing them back to beat them again, tearing up the grass, and sometimes the rest of us, in the process. I had come to count on him to maul enough turf for both of us. There were times when Sally's castoffs landed squarely on me without her knowing it. Like water, my own feelings flowed to the lowest point of those that surrounded me. When they puddled, I did my best to hide it, but Doug was too good at lapping up any depression that spilled, so he'd drag it to the range and I'd tag along to shag. I could even count on him to invent despair for no apparent reason; then he could beat balls with me shagging along to earn credits for yet unnamed miseries. Now, I was no longer sure I could depend on him to morph enough of his own worry into ball-flogging to drain me of mine. He hit balls more than ever, but he did it for golf's sake—certainly not for me. It was tough to dispense with my gloom when he drank lemonade like nothing was wrong at all. For as long as I had lived with him, Doug had wrapped himself in clouds; now a few beams escaped where once a storm had challenged the sun.

In the old days—the old days, two weeks before—when Cobus would bring his friends around to party with country music blaring and the girls begging the boys to dance, the house was bright in spite of Doug. He'd shut the door to his room with enough force to make us wonder why he was angry. I'd stay long enough to apologize for him once more and then leave the house to the kids. Doug should have cleared out, too, instead of being the mystery behind door number one. They didn't want me around and they sure didn't want him around, but often he'd stay. They rose above it. I would throw them out at midnight when I returned to music so loud it shook the windows of my truck a block away. I was glad we lived way on the edge of town so I didn't have to grovel to more than one or two neighbors on Sunday morning.

Since the day Cobus learned about Sally and Hutch, the house had rung with the silence of friends no longer there. He didn't bring them around and I missed them. Sally's surprise had ignited his anguish but the longer it burned the more I knew it was fueled by a deeper festering agony. Maybe he had worked hard for a long time to hide it. Sally was good at it; why shouldn't he be? Maybe Doug's years of moping had taught his boy to keep it boxed. On Friday night, the box broke with contents spewing across the football field. On Saturday morning, he'd tried to pick up the pieces with a shovel and tiller, but when he was alone again, the box dumped its dirty laundry all over a chair in his mother's front room.

I was sad when Sally and Doug broke up. Cobus had hidden his sorrow most of his life. I'd been guilty of channeling all of my grief through my best friend; maybe Cobus used his father that way, too. I'd fallen into the trap of believing the boy was always okay. His tough exterior was no more than a veneer. Now that Doug was no longer willing to be our surrogate, we had to find ways of our own to lash out. As scary as it was, Cobus was finding his. Mine would have to wait.

"There," Sally said, putting down the knife at last. "The vegetables are ready to wok."

Some were too small; some were too big; a few were just right.

"Okay," I said. "I'm hungry."

Then without thinking it through—though it wouldn't have made any difference—I added, "I'll tell you what. You wok while I sort clothes."

"What clothes?"

"Cobus's clothes, of course. I know, and you know, you will do them sooner or later."

"Oh, no, I won't."

"Sure, you will," I said smugly while walking toward the offensive heap. "You'd have probably done it late at night when you're too tired to keep from crying yourself into a blue funk."

"I don't think so," she said too resolutely to convince me that she really meant it.

"Ha!"

"I won't stop you though. Wash away big brother—to your heart's content."

"Just think how this lets you off the hook," I said over my shoulder, while gingerly poking a pair of Jockey briefs with only the tips of my fingers. "You can say quite truthfully, without any reservation, that you had nothing to do with his clothes."

"I know," said Sally, giddy at the realization that she had one-upped her impudent offspring. "Wash away. Wash away."

I stayed until I'd washed and folded all four loads. Every time Sally tried instinctively to grab a pair of socks to fold them, I slapped her hand.

I got home before the boy and put his clothes away for him. I had enough time to straighten the rest of his room, too, and make up his bed like Sally would have done—if she'd a mind to. I wasn't about to tell him it was me, though. Sally would need all the ammunition she could gather in the next few weeks and this was good for a couple of rounds. I was awake when he rolled in at midnight. He wasn't drunk. I listened as intently as I could, without actually following him, when he closed the door to his room. He opened one drawer and then another, quietly, so I had to stop breathing to hear his reaction. *Wow! Look at this*, would have been nice, or even a heart felt, *hmmm*. I know if you could hear smiles, I would have heard him smile. You can't, so I didn't. Finally he said, "Good night, Uncle Robbie," so I could start breathing again.

On Wednesday, I watched practice and the energy that was gone the week before was still gone. It stayed away for the next game when we drove to Wynet to play the Roadrunners. It rained on and off. The boys fumbled on and off. They dropped some passes and caught one or two. They missed one field goal, kicked another, and eked out a touchdown. Bonnet won ten to nothing. The boys walked slowly to the bus and slowly we followed them home.

Sitting at Big Al's round table, Bud said, "Weren't they somethin'? Them conditions were awful and Bonnet rose up above it and whupped the boys from Wynet. Woo-hee, what a team."

It was a little rain, that's all it was; we should have won by forty.

CHAPTER TWELVE

KJIRSTEN LOOKED AT THE putt from every angle. Ten feet from the hole there was a sharp break left, so she allowed for that. The pace would quicken once it rolled over the break. It was all touch. The green was very fast. It had rained earlier that afternoon but the green drained well and was as fast as if the short grass had baked in the sun for days.

"Take your time," I said. "You can't hit this hard or your next putt will be as long as this one."

"Hmmm," she said, down on one knee directly behind the ball, taking a last look before she stroked it.

Kjirsten was wonderfully athletic, and though she hadn't played much golf, her balance and posture looked natural as she stood over the putt. She had long, beautiful fingers that folded softly around the grip, caressing it as if it were an inborn extension of her own graceful arms. Her stroke was smooth. First the ball was still and then it was rolling peacefully across the grass, quietly with no bounce or waver, seeking a new place to rest.

"That looks good," I said, leaning and then walking to the left so I could get a good look at the angle as it took the break.

The ball clanked off of the plastic clown's big red tongue much harder than she had hoped and it caromed left down the hill. Fortunately, she hit the brick in the middle of the carpet with enough force to bounce the purple ball back into the Ferris wheel at the right moment. The wheel's bright yellow paddle spanked the ball as it came around, shooting it straight to the cup, which was cut into a hillock of fake grass-covered concrete. The ball hit the mound, hopped up and plopped straight into the bottom of the first hole—the circus hole at the Brown Family's Dog and Suds and Miniature Golf Park in Peach Pit, Texas. It was a Tuesday night and we were alone together for the first time in two weeks.

"Wow. What a shot," I said incredulously. "You are the luckiest person I know."

"I'd better be, because I have no idea what I'm doing."

I missed my shot, of course. The red ball got caught in the Ferris wheel and was spat out the other side. It took me three more to get down from there.

On the way to Peach Pit, I had begun to tell Kjirsten a story. We were interrupted by two calves that had broken out of their pasture and were wandering on the open road. We stopped to help the farmer herd them back through the hole in the fence.

Bits and pieces of the story had floated around the school, and probably the town, for most of the day. I knew all of what had happened because Hutch told me himself. I hadn't really cared if I got the chance to finish the story or not. It was much more fun to play miniature golf. She begged me to continue. Looking back, I wonder if she was trying to distract me so she could beat me at putt-putt. If she'd had any idea how much of a distraction she was to me without doing anything at all, she might not have bothered.

The second hole didn't have moving parts. I stood over my putt trying to decide whether it was better to bounce it off the back rail or to try to make it straight away. Kjirsten wasn't aware of the pitfalls of putting to a plateau. Naively, she rolled her ball to the edge of the hole and easily made two. More dumb luck, I rationalized.

When I was ready to take my backswing, she said, "So, go on with your story. Did Cobus just walk into Hutch's office out of the blue?"

"Nope," I said, stroking the ball smoothly as I could. "Hutch called him in. He grabbed him before school and asked him to talk."

I stroked it too well. It was on line, but came to a stop shy of the crest of the plateau and rolled back to the rubber mat where I stood. I hit it again, this time disregarding smoothness, sending it over the plateau to the back rail.

"Hutch wanted to make peace with Cobus. He wanted the old Cobus back again. There has been no energy in the practices and the games have been boring at best."

Kjirsten asked, "Is that all Cobus's fault?"

I sank the next one from the back side of the plateau.

"No question. He's the team captain. He's a senior and the best player. If he wanted, he could use his leadership to lead the rest of them over a cliff. They might not like it, but they would dive over the edge."

"Nice shot," said Kjirsten sincerely.

"Thanks."

Hole three was a water hole.

"Hutch started by saying, 'Cobus, I know you're angry about your mother and me.' Cobus didn't say a word. He didn't blink. Hutch said, 'I'd like to talk this out. If you can tell me what's in your head, I can help you work through it.' As much as Hutch wants to win, he wants more for Cobus to stop hurting. He certainly wants Cobus to stop hurting Sally."

"This is a lot harder on her than she ever dreamed it would be," observed Kjirsten as she putted past the fishpond, stopping the ball in front of the bridge.

"It's harder on all of us than we could have imagined. Do you want to finish?"

"No, no. I'll wait on you."

Mine stopped near hers.

"Cobus still didn't respond, so Hutch asked him, 'Would you have preferred we tried to keep this a secret for a while longer?'

"Hutch told me that Cobus stared at him, eyes cold as ice, and said, 'I want this fucking soap opera to never have happened at all.' Hutch said, 'That's not fair, Cobus. We've been discreet. We've done nothing to embarrass you. We never would.'"

I putted first because she would have had to stand on my ball to putt hers. It worked. It went up and over the little Japanese bridge directly into the center of the hole.

"Ooh," said Kjirsten gleefully, and then with concentration as she attempted to match my mastery. "What did Cobus say to that?"

She lipped out. I gained one; I was three down after three.

"He said…" I paused because I was about to repeat something more graphic and personal than Kjirsten and I had ever breathed before.

"He said…"

"Come on, spit it out," said Kjirsten slipping her arm around me and pulling me close as we walked to the loopity-loop hole. She gave me confidence to say what I had to say.

"Cobus said, 'How the fuck do you know what is fucking embarrassing to me? And just what does discreet mean anyway?' Hutch told me he took a deep breath and tried to answer like it was a real question instead of shark bait. He said, 'Discreet means we will never do anything embarrassing in public—to you, ourselves, or—' Cobus interrupted him and said, 'I know what the fuck discreet means. It means you'll make sure you sneak off to some motel in Peach Pit instead of…instead of here in your office where all my friends can listen in.'"

Kjirsten was quiet. She gently placed her ball on the mat and hit it too softly to make it through the loopity-loop and it rolled back to her.

"Oops," she said quietly.

She was so quiet for a moment that I was afraid I'd offended her. She hit the ball hard enough this time and resolutely said, "There."

She stood up, smiling, put both arms around me and kissed me quickly—her eyes telling me everything was fine and was going to be fine. She said, "Make sure you hit it hard enough."

After her kiss, that was not a problem.

As I lined up, she spoke comfortably. "I feel so bad for Hutch. I feel bad for you. I'm trying to feel bad for Cobus, but it's a bit more difficult."

"Don't worry about me. You are finding ways to make me forget the last words I spoke, let alone what I heard eight hours ago. As for Cobus, I don't know how Hutch kept from doing substantial bodily harm to the boy."

I hit my ball too hard and it banged into the loopity-loop and dropped with a thud at its base.

"Damn."

"Well," said Kjirsten, with way more understanding than I had shown, "Hutch must have realized, even at that moment, how much Cobus must be hurting. Pain was speaking, not Cobus."

"Hutch told me he felt like he'd been shot. He did his best to calm Cobus down, saying 'I know you don't mean that Cobus. I will ignore it this time, but you must realize that I think a great deal of your mother and I won't let you talk like that.'"

I moved my ball back to the drop area in front of the loopity-loop and hit it again. The ball swirled up and around and then through the shoot and I sunk it.

"Wow," exclaimed Kjirsten.

"Sometimes I get lucky, too."

She made her easy one, but I'd gained another.

"Did Cobus back down at all, or apologize?"

The gauntlet was next—a conveyer belt with masked warriors painted and running toward us. We had to putt against the rolling charge—like trying to run up a down escalator.

"He sure didn't apologize, but he did change the subject away from Sally. I can only hope that somewhere inside he hid a morsel of guilt."

"You know he did."

The warriors rolled at us two by two.

"Whoa," she said. "Scary."

"Yeah."

She made me putt first and I stupidly tried to gauge a speed that would stop the ball on the other side of the conveyer. I putted too slowly and the belt shot the ball back past us into a patch of sand. I jumped aside to keep the ball from shattering my ankle. Kjirsten laughed and I got the giggles and whiffed the next one completely. The third time, I sent the pill scurrying across the moving mat, past the hole and down the other side. Kjirsten, still laughing, sent hers to be with mine with a good whack. She made three and I a four. I was back to three down and ready for the sixth hole—the maze.

"What did he change the subject to?" asked Kjirsten. She placed her ball in front of one of the six entrances to the maze. There were a number of ways through. The shortest routes had very small entrances. Kjirsten chose a larger tunnel—a longer path, but an easy three-putt.

"Cobus said, 'You're supposed to be the football coach. Why don't you just talk to me about that?' Hutch said, 'Sure, Cobus, we need to talk about football. I know you and I are having our problems, but can we keep it off the field?'"

I tried one of the smaller openings to the maze. The ball bounced off the front and over to the side in front of the chute Kjirsten had taken.

"Oh, good," she said perkily, "you're coming the same way I did."

"I meant to do that."

"What did Cobus say?"

"He said, 'You're the coach. It's not my fault that practices are totally worthless.' Hutch replied, 'Cobus, come on, you have to admit that you've been somewhat distracting.'

I hit mine beside Kjirsten's and continued.

"Then Cobus said, 'If practices weren't so stupid I might be more interested. Everyone is talking about it. Our offense sucks. Everyone says I should be carrying the ball thirty times a game.' Hutch interrupted him and asked, 'Who is everyone?' Cobus said, 'Mr. Richards—Derek's dad. He thinks you don't know what you're doing. Coach Ashworth thinks that way, too.'"

Kjirsten said, "Bret Ashworth never had a coherent thought of his own in his life."

"Kjirsten!" I said, trying to sound shocked. "I've never heard you utter a negative word about anyone. I don't know whether to be sad that you're not perfect or relieved that you're as mortal as the rest of us."

"Oops. Ignore that while I climb back up on my pedestal."

"Hutch took the comment about Ashworth with a grain of salt, too. Ashworth's as malleable as lead and about as quick-witted. Hutch is concerned about Baron Richards, however. He knows that one sour voice in a town can cause a great deal of discord."

"He's right," agreed Kjirsten, as we skulked to the dungeon hole with its chains, rack, and blade on a pendulum.

"I want to change my luck," I said. "I'm going first."

"Like you did at the gauntlet."

"I was thinking more of the loopity-loop."

"The hole where you got lucky."

"Yeah." It was too easy. I didn't touch it. I didn't look up. I placed my golf ball on the mat, timed the pendulum perfectly, and lipped out.

As I tapped in, she said, "Way to go, lucky."

I looked up then, quickly, but Kjirsten was already crouched over her putt with long blonde hair hanging across her shoulders and down her arms, covering her face. I couldn't see her face, her smile, or her eyes, but I knew they were full of mischief. She putted it past the pendulum and it stopped short of the hole.

"So did Cobus say anything else?" she asked as she finished it off, doing an excellent job of keeping me grounded.

"Oh, yeah. He ripped Hutch for fifteen minutes or more. He poked to find a soft spot where he could inflict the most pain."

Number nine was the pinball hole with flippers, bells, and colored lights. Flippers wagged back and forth into the putting line.

"Go ahead, lucky," she said.

I avoided the flippers but banged if off the bell and it ricocheted behind a plastic bumper. Kjirsten hit a flipper and we both made three.

"The scariest thing Cobus said was that he doesn't enjoy football anymore. It's killing Hutch to think he's destroyed the boy's love of the game."

Kjirsten made me feel better when she observed, "There's nothing Hutch can do to take that away from Cobus. Either he loves it or he doesn't. Just because he's so good at it, doesn't mean he has to love it. Cobus may find the pressure of choosing a college and being number one to be more stressful than he'd bargained for."

I said, "So you think Hutch and Sally are unfortunate outlets for anxiety that was already there."

"Could be," said Kjirsten, slipping her arm around me again as we strolled past the snack bar. "Would you like a Coke?"

"I'm fine. You?"

"No, thanks," she said. "It may be that he really isn't enjoying the game right now, but it's not Hutch's fault."

"The problem," I said, "is that he's so worked up, it may be hard to get to the truth."

She said, "Especially if his head is being crammed full of gibberish by Baron Richards and Bret Ashworth."

I wanted to agree by calling them jerks or assholes, but I behaved and said only, "Yeah."

"They're jerks," she said.

"Yeah."

"Sounds to me like he needs an understanding uncle to talk some sense into him," said Kjirsten, pulling me closer as we walked.

"I wish Doug would sit him down and have a long talk with him, but he won't."

"He will when he figures out the right thing to say."

"He's trying. Golf-green tilling worked for a while. You're right; I need to help if I can. I'll say something to Doug; maybe between us we can get through to the troubled child."

We stood in front of the windmill and she kissed me again.

"I know he'll be okay soon," she said, still holding me tight. "He has the perfect uncle to see him through this."

In the end I lost by three strokes. I handled it well, whining for no more than a minute—okay, two minutes.

In Bonnet, I went in with her to her house and we sat on the couch and talked, and kissed, and talked, and then kissed and kissed again— right up 'til midnight. Never in my life had it been so easy to be with someone or so hard to get up and leave.

CHAPTER THIRTEEN

O N WEDNESDAY, THE THRILL of the evening before stayed with me until football practice. I walked in the clouds, hoping I wouldn't get caught smiling for no reason at all by one of the kids. It was all I could do to keep from throwing my arms around Kjirsten in the hallway when I saw her. She blushed too and did her best to avoid my eyes; if our eyes would have met, we could not have hidden what we were feeling inside. Any student seeing us would have known, and soon—within thirty seconds or so—it would have been all over the school. The teasing would have been merciless. If things happened with Kjirsten as I dreamed they would, kidding would come sooner or later—and it would be fun when it did. It was in our best interests, though, to keep the urchins at bay as long as we could.

I went to the boys' practice after school, fully intending to gather ammunition for a long talk with Doug and Cobus later in the evening. Kjirsten had given me the courage for that. Practice was worse, and stranger, than I had anticipated.

Baron Richards was there. He'd parked near the field like Bud Granger did for the games. Richards leaned against his truck and took notes on Hutch's practice. One of his cronies was there with him—Jacob Swindel's father, Amos.

Neither Derek Richards nor Jacob Swindel would ever amount to much as football players. In Jacob's case, there was little chance he would get off the river bottom his father called a farm. Derek might attend junior college but he certainly would not play football there. Where he would go after college was anybody's guess. He rarely uttered a word that had not first been spoken by his father, so it was hard to imagine him conquering the world on his own.

Baron Richards believed his boy was being shortchanged. He thought Derek should be involved in more big plays. As it was, he played a good deal. He started on defense and muddled through a number of offensive downs as tight end. I'd overheard Richards say they should throw more to the ends.

Derek may have been an okay utility defensive player or dependable blocker on a better-than-average high school team, but a pass receiver he was not. He had hands like hatchets. Even in practice with nobody on him, he dropped two out of three. More often than not, he tangled his feet and fell when he tried to keep his eye on the spiral and run at the same time.

I watched Baron Richards on Wednesday night. He jotted a note every time Cobus or Derek was involved in a play. His buddy Amos pointed out details to him and he scribbled furiously on his yellow pad like he understood what they were watching.

During water breaks, Cobus, Derek, and Jacob walked over to Richards for a blatant in-your-face rendezvous. After the second water break, I got hot. When the three boys returned to the field, they created chaos. The other boys weren't stupid. They knew what was going on and, to their credit, wanted nothing to do with the rebels. So unless a coach forced him, Tommy Jarvis stopped throwing the ball to them. On handoffs, too, Tommy did his best to give the ball to anybody but Cobus. The one time Jacob touched the football he was gang-tackled and they made sure it took plenty of time to unpile. They were too smart to try that with Cobus. Jacob was a dupe; Cobus was a time bomb.

The boys stood around between drills in two distinct groups. Cobus and his merry band stood haughtily, arms folded, daring all to challenge them. Tommy Jarvis and the rest who had their heads on straight turned their backs on the renegades. Before my eyes, friendships that Cobus had known since he was old enough to distinguish one face from another were disintegrating.

The third time the brat pack walked off the field, Cobus dragged assistant coach Bret Ashworth with him. Ashworth was clueless. He had no idea he was a pawn in a plot to upstage Hutch. Richards put his arm around Ashworth like they were the best of friends. He flipped through the pages of the legal pad, pausing to draw plays in the air or point to imaginary images on the field. Ashworth, the dolt, nodded wide-eyed like he was hearing an epiphany.

I was boiling. I couldn't decide with whom I was most angry—Richards for having the gall to trespass on Hutch's turf, Bret Ashworth for being born stupid, Cobus for being so cruelly mutinous, or Hutch for letting it happen.

Hutch knew what was going on. He was trying to protect Cobus and thereby Sally; in doing so he was allowing the fabric of his domain to unravel. I prayed he would be good enough to catch himself and the rest of them in time to prevent complete dissolution.

Ashworth walked back to the field and straightaway to Hutch. The head coach listened attentively to his assistant, patted him on the back as if to thank him for his input, and then walked briskly to the sideline where Baron Richards was holding court. Hutch was more controlled than I could have been. I would have started with Richards's throat and pleaded to the judge for leniency later.

Hutch shook hands with the meddler and showed no signs of the rage that must have churned inside. The meeting was short as was the remainder of practice. Richards stayed until the end but there was little else for him to observe. Hutch lined the boys up and ran their butts off for twenty minutes. He rode them hard, with their helmets fully strapped, until two puked. He talked to them all while they lay on the grass gasping or chugging water. It was not a fire 'em up, rah-rah speech or an X's and O's talk. He spoke to them of character, commitment, and pride. His words were lost on some; they turned away. For those who nodded affirmably as he spoke, his talk was not needed in the first place. He was able to speak sense into a few of the boys, especially the younger ones who were confused.

Still, at the end of practice, the team was divided. Many more were on the good side of the line than were on the bad, but there was division. If I hadn't been so close to it all, I would have found it interesting to reflect on how little it had taken to split what had been a cohesive and smoothly running team. One scared teenager with too many untamed demons and one self-righteous, meddling parent had driven a serrated wedge that would be painful to extract.

I stayed after practice to give moral support to Hutch. He said to me that he had reached an agreement with Baron Richards. He'd told Richards that he was welcome at practice any time, and that his comments would be appreciated whenever he wanted to share them. But, Hutch said, he wanted none of the boys or coaches spoken to during practice. Hutch requested that Richards direct his comments to him rather than assistants or players. Hutch called it an agreement, but he also said that Richards hadn't said anything in response. That didn't sound much like an agreement to me—more like wishful thinking on Hutch's part. I feared his entreaty had fallen on deaf ears.

Kjirsten had invited me for dinner and I was high with the anticipation of two evenings in a row with her. Within a minute of walking through her front door and into a world quickly becoming ours alone, I'd forgotten the pain I'd seen at the football field. Maybe if I would have stayed later at Kjirsten's home or we'd been at a place where I could have spent the night, I would have forgotten it forever. We both had papers to correct so I left early and happy. Happy for the entire length of time it took me to drive from Kjirsten's house to mine—about a minute and a half.

At home, in my house, the afternoon was still alive and well, rearing its ugly head. Baron Richards's Ford pickup was parked in my spot in my driveway, and he was standing in my living room pointing his finger and preaching to my best friend, Doug. I'd had enough of Richards for one day and here he was—his space tromping all over mine.

I knew in a quick, angry minute what was up. Doug didn't know what I knew yet, but he was about to find out; I had no trouble fantasizing what Richards was going to look like when Doug and I were through heaving the son of a bitch's carcass through the screen door. I fantasized all the way to the weekend when I was going to have to waste my entire Saturday morning installing a new door because of his fat ass.

Richards looked at me like I wasn't there and went on blowing his garbage. "That coach has got just two things on his mind and neither one of them is any good for our boys," he spouted.

If he was waiting for Doug to ask what the two things were, he would wait a long time. I knew Doug's curled lip look—I hadn't seen it in a few weeks, but I knew it well.

"He doesn't care about our boys," continued Richards haughtily. "He's thinking only about getting out of here and coaching in some college somewhere. Why, I heard he's been calling all over Texas trying to get a job."

Baron Richards and the truth were distant strangers.

"I don't believe that's been happening at all," I said.

Doug rolled his eyes at me as if to say, *don't bother responding to this asshole.*

"Well, you haven't been talking to the people I have," Richards said smugly. "Why, I spoke to a man who knew him when he coached at the University. That's what he did there:

called all over to athletic directors. That's his mode of operation, you know."

He was talking about a time ten years before. Calling around sounded to me like a good strategy for finding a job.

"What does that have to do with now?" I asked, trying to imitate Doug's frown. Doug remained motionless. I imagined—hoped—he was a bobcat, waiting to pounce.

"You just know he's doing the same thing now," said Richards. He was like a preacher now—arms folded and head held high with indignant, self-aggrandizing virtue.

I tried, but I couldn't stay out of it.

"So you don't really know that he's been doing that now, do you?" I asked, staring straight into his eyes, trying to see if I could detect any signs of intelligent life.

"I don't mean to offend, Mr. McCheyne," he said, leering down his bulbous snob-nose at me.

Mr. McCheyne? Where did that come from? When did Bonnet, Texas become so goddamned formal? What a jerk. Did he have any idea how far past offense he'd gone by breathing the same air I needed?

"I don't mean to offend," continued Richards, oblivious to the telepathy I was ray-gunning his direction. "But, after all, you are the perhaps too close to the other distraction that has befallen our good coach. I can't expect you to be objective. My comments are really directed at Doug, here. He would certainly understand our distaste for the goings-on behind our backs and behind closed doors."

Finally Doug spoke, moving slowly toward Baron Richards like a bear, stalking.

"Just what the hell do you mean by that?" he growled. His fists were clenched—like mine. Doug stood tall—looming—filling the room with his fury—with wolf-eyes—slits homing on the jugular.

"Yoo-hoo, Doug," sang Tildy, her happy voice ringing through the screen door, bouncing all about the room, dousing, for the moment, our madness.

She banged loudly on the door with the head of her seven-iron. "Yoo-hoo."

Doug snapped back from the hot place he'd been seconds before, confused, for a moment, at the discordance of Tildy's cheer and our seething ire. He went straight away to the door to show her into the room. How quickly he changed into a cheerful person when he saw her. I, too, was glad she was there—relieved.

Richards was too clueless to be relieved or annoyed at Tildy's welcome intrusion. He wasn't aware of how close he'd been to a good country thrashing.

"Tildy, hello. Please come in," said Doug warmly, taking her hand.

"Oh, my, I'm sorry," she exclaimed in her best voice of surprise. "I didn't know you had company. Perhaps I should wait until tomorrow. It's not that important."

"Nonsense," I replied, turning my back on the befuddled Richards and striding across the room to offer our good friend my hand, too.

"Well, it is just golf, you know. I can come back."

"No, no," begged Doug.

Richards cleared his throat. "Ahem. I can wait a minute. I've got one or two more things to say here, so you go ahead, Mrs. Hannah. If you say it won't take long."

"Take as long as you like," whispered Doug.

"Well, if you're sure," Tildy said hesitantly. "I don't know. But, perhaps…just look at this. I didn't hit the ball so well today. I practice on my own, you know."

"Yes, I know," said Doug with a prideful smile.

"Just watch my swing—just once," she said taking her club and her stance into the dining room. It had high ceilings and plenty of room to swing a club. The Spartan furniture arrangement was intentional. Doug had long since worn a patch on the carpet in front of the dining room mirror where Tildy now stood. She assumed her normally graceful stance but jerked the club back uncharacteristically and took a quick swing that was awkward by her standards.

"Aha," proclaimed Doug. "You're laying off your takeaway."

"Ooh," she said. "Just show me what you mean—just once—then leave me alone while you go back to your important meeting."

"It's not that important," I said.

"It's not that important," said Doug taking one of his favorite teaching postures along side of Tildy's left arm. He gently placed his tanned sculptured hands on her small ones and pushed her club back twice.

The first time he said, "You are here."

The second time he said, "You should be here."

"That's it!" exclaimed Tildy with joy. "Now get out and let me watch myself in the mirror."

He said, "Ha," and walked with me back to find the self-ordained preacher still standing cross-armed in the front room. Since Tildy was swinging away just a few feet away around the corner we spoke in hushed tones, although they began as grimly as they had been when interrupted. Doug took charge right away, not wanting Richards to build a head of steam.

"Look here *Mister* Richards," said my roommate standing closely enough to Baron Richards's red face to fog his spectacles. I was hoping Doug had eaten a plate full of his favorite garlic pork sausage he liked to grind up at the store.

Doug curled his lip like a frothing Doberman and continued, "I don't have a clue what your confused mind has cooked up about my good friend Hutch, but I know enough about your kind to know that the sewers you crawl around in are full of nothing but bullshit."

Richards sagged his confrontational posture and began stammering, "I didn't…I don't…we don't need that sort of talk here…I only mean…I'm concerned about his coaching."

He tried to step back from Doug's advance but Doug came on like Joe Frazier. No rope-a-dope would help this pseudo-preacher's pompous ass.

"His coaching? His coaching? What the hell do you know about coaching? Nothing. Not one goddamned thing at all. What the hell do you know about football? Not one goddamned thing at all. I saw you play football when you were a punk. You don't have the athletic savvy of a meal worm."

I knew Doug had that in him and what a perfect time to let it out. What a perfect maggot to pour it on.

"Well, Doug," said the now whimpering Baron Richards, "I see no need to make this personal."

"And you think Hutch won't take it personally?" I asked, letting him know I was just as ready to take him on as was Doug.

"Just how far are you planning to take this half-baked vendetta?" questioned Doug.

"Well, I'm only trying to make people aware that there are things going on which deserve scrutiny. We certainly don't plan to cause any disruption. We wish to help out."

"I bet," I snarled.

"Let me be as clear about this as I possibly can," said Doug, moving ever closer, lowering his voice another notch. "You'll get no help from this house. Every place you turn, I'll be standing in your way."

You would have thought that would have been enough to put him on the mat for good, but Richards rose up and fired one last combination of cheap shots—below the belt.

"You should know, Doug," said Richards, coating *Doug* with syrup, "that your son Cobus is the one who has apprised me of these goings-on. I'm sure he felt that he wasn't close enough to you to say anything, but aren't you glad he felt he could approach me?"

The snake staggered my best friend with that strike. Doug backed off—his eyes widened in pain, his lip unfurled and flagged. I reeled, too. How I wish I'd been quick enough to jump before the venom was injected into our hearts.

"I'm sorry I'm the one who must bring these things to your attention," hissed the serpent. "You must know—I hate to tell you this—you know your wife has been—shall we say—indiscreet with our good coach. It's a shame when two people put their own needs above those of others who depend on them."

There was no foundation to any of what he said, of course. Sally hadn't been Doug's wife for seven years. She and Hutch had been nothing but discreet—even when there was no need for caution. They had worked so hard to protect the rest of us from this sort of vile slander. His lies were painful because we knew they would not stop with us.

Had he mentioned Sally and Hutch first, Doug and I would have thrown him out before he said another word. But what he said about Cobus was close enough to fears Doug held—that many fathers secretly harbor about their sons—to stop us in our tracks while he spread the rest of his poison.

Doug and I were raised in Bonnet—a small town in the Hill Country of Texas. We grew up with real cowboys. Some busted broncos. Some rode bulls. Some of us stayed in town to play hard-nosed football. We all know how to fight and most of us have done it more times than good sense would allow. Doug and I, at times, had had no trouble with the concept of a good fight. We were younger then and almost always drunk. We didn't need beer or youth for Baron Richards. He was reason enough. Doug grabbed him by his synthetic turquoise bolo tie to hold his head still so he could punch him, and the sound of Tildy breaking a lamp in the front room shattered the air.

"Ooh, goodness. Ooh, goodness," Tildy cried while Doug and I dropped all attention from the viper Richards and went running to her aid.

Tildy stood holding her seven-iron in one hand with her other clamped firmly across her mouth with a look of surprise. The lamp lay in pieces all around her feet with its cord still attached to the wall and its light flickering one last time before dying in a final instant of brilliance.

It took only a second for Doug and me to see that she was not harmed. There was no damage other than the Sears and Roebuck terra-cotta lamp, which wasn't worth much more than the bulb. As soon as he knew she was okay, Doug laughed.

"Tildy," he said with a wide toothy grin, "I'm glad you did that. Now that lamp matches its mate. There were two until I smashed the first with a wedge. Now there are none."

"I'm so-o sorry," she said in her best woeful voice.

She moved, finally, and reached in her pocket and pulled out a fifty-dollar bill. She tried to hand it to Doug and that made him laugh harder.

"Fifty dollars! Tildy, the pair of lamps didn't cost me ten. Put your money away. I won't hear another word of it."

He clasped her hands with kindness and sincerity so effectively that she put up very little fight.

"Are you sure?" she asked timidly.

"I'll tell you what," said my friend Doug. "I'll get the broom. You hold the dustpan and we'll call it even."

He wasn't going to let go of her hands until she agreed, so she said, "It's a deal."

My heart had stopped pounding from the shock of the glass breaking and from the rush of the fight that never was. The fight. Baron Richards. Where was he anyway? My head snapped around to look back into the front room where he'd neared disfigurement. He had slithered away during the commotion and was pulling out of the drive.

"Oh," said Tildy. "I hope I didn't interrupt your meeting. Were you finished?"

"We were finished," said Doug, with grin turning sheepish while he swept away the shards.

"Finished," I agreed, rolling my eyes, in mock contempt of ourselves.

When she and Doug were content that the well-struck lamp proved she was no longer laying the club off, Tildy left. I couldn't decide if she'd saved Baron Richards's hide with her new backswing, or Doug's and mine, or all three.

I asked Doug if he thought we'd pushed Richards too far with our tough guy act.

"Nah," said Doug. "It wouldn't have mattered what we would have done to the son of a bitch—unless, I suppose, we'd killed him outright. He's going to keep doing what he's doing until he's knocked on every door in town."

"Whaddya think? Is there anything we should do to stop him?" I asked.

Doug answered, "The problem with trying to catch vermin is that you have to be willing to crawl in the same gutters they do. I won't do one thing to give credence to anything that guy does."

Then after a moment's reflection he added, "Except to let Hutch know we're on his side."

"Yeah," I said, nodding agreement.

Cobus came out of his room and walked past us like we weren't there. He rummaged in the refrigerator and grabbed a half-gallon of milk. He found a box of Oreos in the cupboard and grabbed a couple thousand calories' worth. Cobus went back into his room with his bedtime snack without looking at us and without breathing a word.

Doug and I were a bit wide eyed. I was red faced.

"I didn't know he was home," I whispered.

"Hmm," sounded Doug with a pleased glint in his eye. "I didn't either. I never heard a sound. I figured he was at Tommy's."

I was going to tell him about the afternoon's practice and how I knew that there was probably little chance the boy had any friends left at all. I didn't. Perhaps in the morning, I thought. Instead, I asked, "How much do you think he heard?"

"Ha," blurted Doug loudly enough to be heard through a bedroom door. "I hope he heard the whole goddamned thing."

I motioned for Doug to follow me into the kitchen where I knew Cobus wouldn't hear. I tried to apologize for the crap Richards had said to Doug, but Doug knew the truth.

"He's a coward," he said, speaking of Richards. "They crow loudest. They puff up biggest. Then, in the end, they turn their yellow backs and run the fastest...like he did."

I put my arm around him and for once he didn't cringe or pull away. I whispered, "Would you have really hit him?"

"Nah," said Doug. "That's kid stuff. I wouldn't even know how any more."

"Yeah," I said, relieved to hear he felt that way, too.

Then, with a cocky smirk, the golfer added, "He didn't know that, though."

"Yeah."

CHAPTER FOURTEEN

D RY FORK, TEXAS SITS up on a sometimes-tributary of the
Guadalupe River. Water trickles through the branch for
most of the spring. Legend says they built the town there not for
the wayward creek, but because the table on which the town now
sits could be counted on to remain high and dry throughout the
rainy season. It was a favorite stop on the cattle drives for that
reason—water in the draw, ample grass on the high ground, and
whiskey and whores in the Dry Fork saloon.

The Bonnet caravan meandered to Dry Fork on Friday night
to play the Dry Fork Rattlers. Over the years, the Rattlers had
the reputation of being a tough, hard-hitting football team. They
were not usually big enough or deep enough to win it all, but
they'd been giant-killers many times. They knew how to block
and gang-tackle better than many teams with more talent. If you
weren't ready to play them, they could beat you.

Bonnet won the toss and marched down the field like we'd
seen them do before—like we'd come to expect. Hutch knew
the Rattlers were not as fast as Bonnet, so he had Tommy come
out throwing. Tommy was sharp. His drop back and footwork
were as quick as anyone's. Michael Martinez was a flash that the
Rattlers couldn't catch. He caught the first three bullets Tommy

threw—one from the left side, one from the right, and one down the middle. Twelve yards—first down. Fifteen yards—first down. Eighteen yards—first down.

Fifty-eight seconds were gone from the clock and the Mustangs had the ball on the Rattlers' thirty-five-yard line. Cobus went in motion to the left. Tommy rolled right while Martinez flew down the right sideline. Michael was by everyone in a heartbeat. The foot race was no contest. As soon as Michael got one step past the line of scrimmage, five Rattlers took off after him and fell further into his wake with each step. Cobus crossed the middle of the field unnoticed and watched with the rest of us while Tommy planted and let fly with a beautiful high spiral toward the end zone flag. All Michael had to do was run under it. He did, but caught it one step out of bounds so they brought it back to try all over again.

The Rattler coach sent a new play in with a defensive back. He'd seen Cobus standing alone and figured, like I did, that it might be a good time to throw the ball to him—since most everyone else in the Dry Fork grandstands was expecting the ball to go to Michael again.

Hutch sent in the play with Derek Richards. Derek lined up at tight end on the right side with Michael in the slot behind like the play before. Tommy play-faked to Cobus and he burst through the middle of the line. Tommy sprinted right with the ball hidden well on his right hip. Derek lumbered on down the sideline where Michael had gone before, attracting only a mild interest from the Rattler defenders—they'd scouted him well enough. Michael sped across the middle to the opposite flag and Cobus curled back in toward the center seven yards off the line of scrimmage. Tommy hit Cobus with a strike to the numbers; Cobus planted a foot and then pivoted—ready to streak toward the end zone but the Rattler defensive back was ready. He hit Cobus like a battering ram and the ball popped out. Cobus did his best to jump on it but he was beaten to the punch by three of the enemy. The Dry Fork boys were well disciplined; they bounced up and made the change to offense with no dancing or strutting—like they'd expected this to happen all along. Cobus walked to the Bonnet bench and threw his helmet into the water cooler.

The Rattlers ran a trick play on the first snap from scrimmage. The ball was on the right hash mark and the boys in orange and white with the coiled rattlers on their helmets huddled far to the left, up on the line. It looked like they didn't know what they were doing. The Bonnet Mustangs in their deep blue and black away uniforms stood opposite the ball mulling around, preparing their vaunted defense. The Dry Fork center broke from his huddle early, as centers often do, and trotted to the ball to take his stance—alone. He looked strangely naked crouched over the ball, ready to snap with no quarterback there to accept it.

Suddenly, on a silent signal, the Rattlers whirled around where they stood—still a full fifteen yards left of their center—and dropped in unison to their three point stances. They were in perfect formation, only they looked stupid with no ball and no defense opposite them.

Hutch started yelling and jumping up and down, waving his arms frantically, trying to get the attention of our boys. He knew what was up but he hadn't caught on quickly enough because he was trying to talk to Cobus, who was pouting on the end of the bench. As soon as I saw Hutch going crazy I figured it out, too. Even Doug started yelling. It was an old junior high trick you see for the first and, hopefully, the last time in the seventh grade.

The center snapped a long spiral sideways across the field to the Rattler running back and all eleven Dry Fork Rattlers were off to the races—chased by the fooled Bonnet boys. They looked like the Keystone Cops chasing a band of thieves down the field. We had fast defensive backs, but not that fast. The kid from Dry Fork made it to the Bonnet goal line and stepped across just as our Roy Calbo caught up with him—too late of course. A seventy-five-yard run from scrimmage on their first play of the game and the Rattlers led seven to nothing.

Hutch's assistant, Bret Ashworth, ran out onto the field, red-faced, yelling at the referees. Then he left, red-faced, when they explained that the play was perfectly legal.

The boys were bewildered, but Hutch got them fired right back up—all except Cobus, of course, who still sulked. After all they'd been moving down the field with ease before the fumble. Besides, you can't count a trick play. Bonnet was still the superior team—clearly.

So, we were ready and on offense again. Cobus took the kickoff and ran it to the thirty-five. Already, the Dry Fork coaching staff had adjusted to Michael Martinez and double-teamed him from the time he stepped up to the line. That left a hole in the field that Cobus and Tommy should have had no trouble finding.

Sure enough, on the first play, Cobus caught a beauty for an eight-yard gain. For a naïve instant I let myself believe that Cobus was going to be the old Cobus—now that he was in a game—now that he was running and catching and hitting. I had that familiar feeling—for a flash of time—that Bonnet was as good as ever. The cheerleaders chanted, *Here we go, Mustangs,* and I rocked to the beat.

Cobus ran a down and out, only he forgot the out. Tommy threw the ball perfectly to where Cobus was supposed to be—right to where he wasn't—into the hands of the Dry Fork linebacker. The Rattler had a clear lane to the end zone and made it fourteen to zip with Bonnet holding zip. As before, the boys from Dry Fork took their good fortune in stride—no vulgar displays of bravado—not even a high-five.

This time, Cobus left his helmet on and bent over with elbows on knees and head between his legs like he would be sick. He had reason enough to be sick. I was sick.

Okay. It was still early. We were still Bonnet. *Here we go, Mustangs!* I wish those cheerleaders would pay more attention to the game. Cobus sat out the kickoff but Hutch sent him back in with a pat on the butt for the next series.

Tommy called three plays. He gave the ball to Cobus twice and Cobus covered the ball like he was carrying a newborn—afraid to hit or be hit—afraid to run and cut. He gained one and lost two. The third play Tommy looked for Michael running deep but he was blanketed and Tommy threw it over his head and into the stands.

I could hear the Dry Fork cheerleaders chanting, *Here we go, Rattlers!* Their cheerleaders were paying attention.

Football coaches say a football game can get out of control faster than any other sport. It's odd that it happens when there's so much time between plays—time to think about what you're going to do next—time to plan for what they're going to pull next.

The Rattlers took their positions in the center of the twenty yard line and ran a sweep right. No gain. Great tackle by Jason Roberts. Fourteen points was nothing. Bonnet could make that up in a jiffy.

Now the Rattlers were on the right hash mark and... and they huddled up fifteen yards to the left again. How stupid did they think our boys were? Ha! We weren't going to fall for that chicanery twice in one game. The Mustang defense quickly repositioned themselves in front of the misplaced huddle. Our center stayed put over the ball, across from theirs. Their center broke early like before. It wasn't the same kid, I noticed, but he did the same thing. Hutch started yelling again as the boy snapped the ball across the field. The Mustangs came rushing across the line, and this time the quarterback threw the ball back to the center, who, being much smaller and faster than the slug we had attempting to stop him, was already fifteen yards down field when he caught it. He never looked back, of course. It was twenty-one to nothing and our air-headed cheerleaders sang, *Here we go, Mustangs, here we go!*

Cobus threw his helmet into the water cooler and he hadn't even been in the game. It was good to see he still cared.

Hutch saw it happen and cornered my nephew. Later, Hutch told me he told Cobus to sit down for the rest of the half. He said he hadn't been angry or confrontational. He said, "Cobus, you'd better sit out the rest of the half and cool down. Be ready to play for the second half."

Our eyes were focused on the field for the kickoff and the next few plays, so I didn't see him leave. I looked down to where he'd been sitting and his jersey was folded on the bench with his number draping to the ground, plainly visible below the helmet resting on top.

The game was lost, then. It was certainly lost for me. It was lost for Doug. And when it was finally over, it was lost on the scoreboard—twenty one to three. Then the Dry Fork Rattlers allowed themselves their high-fives. Their cheerleaders shouted, *Way to go, Rattlers, way to go!* They had it right.

Cobus had quit the team.

On the way home the old tight-jawed Doug came back. I rode with him in the front. Cobus sat in the back, looking oddly out of place in his football pants and bare chest with his shoulder pads beside him. None of us spoke and we didn't go to the café.

On Saturday morning, I went to Sally's for breakfast. Hutch was there, sitting quietly at the table reading *The Austin American Statesman.* Sally was breaking eggs.

"Hey, Robbie," Hutch said, looking genuinely happy to see me. "It says here we got beat last night by the Dry Fork Rattlers."

"Damn media," I said, leaning over the stove to kiss Sally on the cheek. "They obviously don't know that Dry Fork can't beat us."

Sally said, "Neither did Dry Fork."

"Well, at least we're talking about it," I observed.

"Oh, yeah," said Hutch. "Football coaches aren't allowed to cry. It's in our contract."

"I can't say much for the way they beat us." It was the best condolence I could conger.

"Hey," said Hutch without hesitation. "We're the top dog. If I was them, I'd have done the same thing. Witchcraft, lyin', cheatin', stealin'—anything goes when you're trying to knock the king off the hill. My hat's off to those guys. Thanks for the sentiment, though."

"Yeah," I said. I knew he was right.

Sally broke two more eggs into the mix for me.

She took a deep breath and asked me, "What did Cobus say?"

I said, "Not a thing."

I was glad of that, because I was sure that if he had, it would not have been pleasant.

"Nothing?" asked Sally. "He didn't say a word?"

"Okay, one word. He said 'Yes.' The car was quiet as a tomb on the way home. Then, when we walked into the house, Doug growled, 'I suppose you think you're quitting the team.' Cobus said, 'Yes,' and went to his room."

Sally asked, "Would you two like me to chop up some onion and ham to mix in with the eggs?"

We both answered, "No, thanks," at precisely the same time.

"It's for the best," said Hutch, putting the paper aside and grasping his coffee cup firmly with both hands.

"Who's best?" I asked.

"Everyone's," he said wryly.

Sally said, "You don't really mean that, do you?"

"Sure, I do," said Hutch with surety. "He needs a break. He's having a hard time right now. A break will do him good. A break will do us all good."

"What about the team?" I asked, trying to calculate our chances of making it all the way to the state championship now.

"The team will be…" he paused for a moment, smiling at Sally who was scrambling eggs in a black iron skillet., "the team will be what they are—a fine group of young men who do the best they can every week."

Doug phoned for me as Sally was serving breakfast. He'd finagled a tee time for two at The Falls course west of Austin and wanted to know if I'd join him. I hesitated long enough for him to say the pro would pick up our greens fees, and then I said yes. I had to promise I wouldn't embarrass him off the first tee, though. He said I could hit it any place I wanted once we were out of sight of the pro shop, but on the first tee, please, I was to attempt to hit it straight.

I wolfed the eggs and bacon and then grabbed two pieces of toast, my cup of coffee, and bolted for the door. We had an hour and a half for a one-hour drive and I had to change clothes and get my clubs. I mumbled a mouthful thanks to Hutch and Sally and left. After the screen door slammed behind me, I heard Sally say, "Hutch, what did you mean by a break will do us all good?"

I started my truck and left, wondering what his answer would be and glad that I didn't hear it.

Standing on the first tee at The Falls, I whispered to Doug, "What have you gotten me into?"

"Isn't this great?" asserted Doug.

He was fired up. This was the perfect tonic after the previous evening's debacle. Perfect for both of us.

"Just look at these guys," I said quietly while a young blonde Adonis addressed the ball.

"They're kids," he said full of confidence.

I turned my back so the young men couldn't see the terror on my face, and sputtered, "It's the University of Texas golf team."

The blonde one hit an absolute rocket two hundred and ninety yards down the sprinkler line in the middle of the first fairway.

This was the foursome ahead of us. We were paired with two more perfect golfing bodies to make up the second group.

"It's only six of them," said Doug. "This is the second group—the B-Team. The first squad is playing in a tournament at their own course."

"The B-Team," I echoed, as a mere boy with the arms and hands of a lumberjack airmailed a Titleist past his teammate.

"My God, Doug," I exclaimed, holding back a shriek, "he hit it three hundred and twenty yards."

"Yeah, pretty cool, huh?"

"Humiliating," I muttered as the next kid in the group hit his beside the ball of the blonde one.

By the time the last of the foursome was ready to launch his mortar, a crowd of Saturday morning regulars had gathered to watch the show. A rippling of applause started the four men off down the fairway after their tee shots.

"A gallery," I said to Doug. "I have to tee off in front of a gallery."

"These old boys aren't a gallery," he snorted. "They're Saturday morning golf cronies. That's barely a recognizable life form."

A crusty cowboy golfer standing nearby heard Doug's remark, grinned a toothy grin, and then spat a stream of tobacco into the high grass behind the tee box to emphasize my partner's point. That made me feel more at home until I took a good look at the two we were paired with.

One had a ponytail, earring, and gold necklace. The other had perfect hair, piled high, swept back like a not-yet-fallen TV preacher and held in place with half a can of hair spray.

"Howdy boys," drawled Doug. "I'm Doug and this is my sidekick, Robbie."

"Hi," said the ponytail to Doug, shaking his hand. "Call me Gizmo."

Then he said, to me, "Hey, dude," and grabbed—slapped—my hand.

Okay, I could play with this guy. I didn't care how good he was, if he called himself Gizmo and me "dude," he couldn't possibly take the game as seriously as, say, Bill Murray.

The second golfer's handshake was much more controlled than Gizmo's.

"Hello, sir," he said, politely—deferentially. "My name is Randall. It's an honor to play with you."

"Ha," I laughed. "It's no honor to play with me. You must mean Doug. Although I can assure you he's not always that honorable either."

"Hello, Randall," said Doug. "Ignore my partner, please. If you want to think of this as an honor, go right ahead."

"C'mon, dude," prodded Gizmo. "Hit that pill."

"I'd rather have Mr. … uh … Doug tee off first," offered Randall reservedly.

"No way, dude, frosh first. Flog it."

I felt better knowing the kid was as nervous as I was. He stepped up to the tee and hit a nice drive—not as far as the other boys', but it was good enough—stopping in the right rough—out about two-eighty.

"Good one, dude."

Gizmo teed it up with no hint of a practice swing or waggle. His swing wasn't textbook like the other boys' but he was fluid—naturally athletic-looking, like another I had come to know over the years. He hit a big draw, and it rolled it behind the lone tree on the left of the fairway.

"Duuuude. That's not the way to start."

I said, "I'm next."

I did not want to be the last one to tee off, leaving the crowd with the final image of my excuse for a golf swing emblazoned on their retinas. I hit it okay, though, even if the hack was too fast for stop-action film. The ball flew higher than I'd wanted but still managed a flight of two-thirty.

"Way to go, dude," said Gizmo, offering a high, closed-fist five. I took it. Who knew? It might be my only chance.

Doug wasted no time. He waggled twice, like I'd seen him do ten thousand times, and then he put the Doug swing on the ball. It wasn't as high as the boys' but it had eyes for the right side of the fairway—two-seventy, and we were off. The cronies held their applause this time—thank God.

After Randall and I had hit our approaches, mine to the bunker, his to the fringe, and Gizmo had concocted a curving, miracle shot under the tree, Doug's placement of tee shot became apparent. He had a level lie with an uncontested shot to the flag. Anything left of the middle of the fairway and the second shot would have had to clear the deep bunkers guarding the left front of the green. He dropped a perfect six-iron shot to just below the pin.

Doug lipped out his ten-foot attempt at a birdie, Randall and Gizmo each got up and down for their pars, and I was happy to walk off the first hole with a bogey. Most of my apprehension from the first tee box had disappeared as soon as we left our gallery behind.

As we waited on the second tee for the green to clear, with Randall off to the side checking and then rechecking his backswing, Gizmo leaning back on the bench catching an apparent nap, Doug, out of the blue said, "I'm going to miss watching Cobus play football."

I knew at that moment he had asked me to join him for golf so he could talk about it. He hadn't said a word the evening before or on the drive to the course. It dawned on me then that we were in the one place Doug could always feel safe. He could cleanse his soul on the green grass of the fairways. Nothing could touch him there. Nothing could hurt him.

"It's hard when you build a dream for someone else," he continued, not sadly, but reflectively. "You begin to believe that it's really their dream, too, and finally you forget it was all yours in the first place. It's a trap, you know. It's not real."

"Aw, Doug, don't you know he really loves the game?" I asked him, hoping his answer was yes—hoping the truth was yes.

"Oh, sure, he does. He doesn't know it yet, but he does. Right now he's scared that he has no identity. He's afraid he's nobody without football and he wants to find out—he has to find out."

"Then why didn't he talk to someone—you, me, Hutch—anyone?"

It was time to tee off on the second, and Doug said, "Because there's a war raging inside of him and he's got no clue which side he's fighting for... let alone how to fight it."

The four of us hit acceptable shots to the par three. We each had our own standards, of course; acceptable for me was entirely different from acceptable for Doug or either of the two University of Texas players. At least I avoided the cottonmouth-infested creek. Still, Gizmo's standards remained loosely defined. When he hit a low runner that never rose above ten feet before dribbling to a stop on the fringe, he smiled with a sparkle in his eye and said, "Check that out. It's my wind ball." The air was beautifully calm on that autumn Hill Country day. Wind was not an issue.

Doug took a shine to Gizmo right away. It would have been hard not to like him. He made us laugh. Randall, the freshman, was still new enough and young enough that he would politely wait on each of us to laugh first, but then he would, too.

Doug and I stopped by my ball, which was a good forty yards from the pin. Gizmo and Randall walked ahead with Gizmo explaining to Randall how to hit a wind ball and Randall listening intently.

I said to Doug, "It sounds as if you are speaking as one who knows more about how your son feels than you'd like to let on."

"I don't mind letting on at all," said my friend Doug. "I know exactly what he's going through."

"You never quit the game, though."

"Sure, I did," he said.

I took my stance.

"You were injured," I said. "It was career-ending."

I thinned a pitch shot that skidded past the pin into the trap.

"Shucks," I grumbled.

The two players from the University each putted their approach while Doug and I watched. Doug lagged his beautifully, leaving himself a two-footer for an easy par. Gizmo and Randall were impressed with the fifty-foot roll.

"Great shot, dude," said Gizmo, with a congratulatory fist raised for Doug.

After that, Doug and I didn't have a chance to speak again for over an hour. By then I was six over, Doug was one under and the boys were somewhere in between.

On the eighth hole, a long par five that meanders alongside Flintlock Creek, Gizmo snapped it into the trees on the left. Randall, who was now experimenting with Gizmo's surefire method of hitting a controlled fade, also hit a long pulled draw to the rough that left him stymied. Doug hit it high and soft to the right side where the hole opened up for him. My slice put me on the same general line as my friend, albeit twenty-five yards behind.

The Texas players took off together with Gizmo saying, "Catch you later," while Doug and I headed for the opposite side of the fairway.

"I could have made a comeback in football," said Doug as soon as we were out of earshot.

"I don't know, Doug," I responded, trying my best to remember the details of his injury, "an ACL tear is a tough one to bounce back from."

"It wasn't as bad as they thought. When they got in there it was still eighty percent intact. There was less surgery than they had feared. It was relatively simple—even for those days."

I still wanted to give him an excuse, so I offered, "Yeah, but the rehabilitation was brutal. I remember that."

"What you remember," he said, with chagrin, "is me *complaining* about how brutal it was."

"I think it's been so long you've forgotten how bad it was."

I was okay with the thought of my hero being felled by a crippling injury. I wasn't sure how I felt about him deciding on his own to quit football. I stopped myself short of whining, *but yer knee stayed blowed out and I never got to go to the University to see you play*, like Cuthbert Alden had done in the café. Then I remembered the thrill of watching Doug hit a golf ball.

"Maybe, partner. Maybe," he said with a knowing wink, "but, if I'd decided to make a football comeback, we might not be standing here right now."

We had reached the location of my sliced tee shot, which was nestled in a deep divot and I wished I was standing six inches to the left, but he was right; I didn't want to trade a thing.

"Hit a good hard five-iron out of there," Doug drawled, "and that puppy will run like a scared rabbit."

He was right again.

We walked to his ball and he laced a gem to the right front of the green.

We heard the familiar whack of a ball being struck with the echo of the sound in the trees and Gizmo let out a whoop. I heard the *tick, tick, tick* of branches and looked up to see Gizmo's ball squirt out and run to the throat of the green. Randall was still trying to hit a Gizmo fade, so he hooked it into the trees again and went on to bogey the hole.

By the time we finished the nine, Doug was one over. Gizmo, although he'd seen places on the course that few others had before, was somehow even par. He sank putts from everywhere. Randall wasn't playing as well as he would have liked. He shot forty. And me—well, I hit a few good shots and was having a great time.

Doug and I grabbed a hot dog at the turn and sat on the bench enjoying our lunch while Gizmo hit the can. Randall was still trying to decide what he wanted at the snack bar when Doug matter-of-factly said, "The interesting thing is, not only do I understand what my son is going through, now I know how my father felt."

He tore a big bite out of his Polish dog while I asked, "Do you think your father felt the same way you feel now?"

"Sure, he did. He expressed it differently, that's all. He was frustrated as hell because he knew I'd walked away from a dream he'd had for me since the first time he saw me play. He didn't want me to have to work a day in that goddamned store. He saw football as my way out."

Doug spoke without emotion—like he was an observer looking from the outside in on himself. He'd thought it through and was at peace with it.

I mumbled with a mouth full of wiener, "I thought you said he told you—demanded—that you come to work in the store."

Doug gulped Coke and explained, "Yeah. Well, that was only anger talkin'. Desperation. I can see that as plain as day, now. *I* was his dream. When I walked out on it, he gave up. He grabbed at anything he could to keep from drowning; it happened to be me. His dream didn't allow for golf. He didn't understand golf. He only knew football. If there was no football for me, there was nothin'."

I thought about Doug stuck in that store all those years— hating it like he believed his father had, and how a little lady by the name of Tildy had rescued him. I was still worried about Cobus, but seeing Doug like he was that day at The Falls and listening to Doug coming to grips with the irreversible switchbacks of his life, gave me a glimmer of hope for my confused nephew. He would be okay. I had no idea when, but he was Doug's boy and he was Sally's boy. He would work it out.

Doug went on to shoot even par that day. He played the back nine of a championship course he'd never seen before in one under. Gizmo's adventures finally caught up with him and he tripled seventeen to end up five over. He beat Randall by one. I broke ninety and was delighted.

As we walked off eighteen, Randall stammered, "Doug— and Robbie—thank you—thank you, sirs. I hope we can play again."

Gizmo, with his hand extended and his cap bill flipped skyward as if he was catching the sun, said to Doug, "Dude, it was an honor."

For Gizmo, that was the ultimate act of veneration.

CHAPTER FIFTEEN

I ENTERED SALLY'S CANDLELIT sanctum where the suffocating aroma of rose overwhelmed what little pure air remained. The image of an Egyptian goddess lay on her rug with perfumed shrouds draped over her still body 'til only a slit remained through which her eyes might follow whatever figures were invading her shrine. Fifty candles in little jars sat on pedestals around the room, their flickering lights entwining with the last minutes of sunlight dying from the windows.

After a few shaky paces into the maze, terrified at the thought of knocking over a flame and igniting the house, I dropped to all fours and crept toward the mound of sheets, my head swirling from the essence of rose. I peeked into the slit and whispered—afraid of the answer to my question, "Sally, is that you?"

The barely audible word escaped her lips, "Water."

"What?" I asked with my ear to her mask.

"Water. Bring me water."

"I'll be right back," I aspirated, now gagging from the rose perfume.

She remained motionless while I crawled to the kitchen. I did manage to stand upright to pour the water and then shuffle my way back to the bundle of sheets without tripping and spilling.

I knelt beside my sister, the mummy, as she imitated life and sat up.

Her hand snaked its way from beneath their covers to limply grasp the tumbler I held for her. As she arose, the cloths fell from her face to reveal the wilting smile and glazed eyes of an out-of-body experience that had not quite yet returned home.

Her limp eyelids sagged and then closed as she sipped and sighed, "Ooh, yes," revealing more of the ecstasy in her soul than I had really ever wanted to witness.

"You're scaring me, Sally," I said, sitting now alongside, gingerly moving her rose rags away from my butt, afraid of becoming the smell that was liquidating my brain cells by the billions.

"Isn't the attar wonderful?" she asked, caressing herself with an invisible aura.

"I suppose it is," I slurred, genuinely fearful of passing out, "if you're a honey bee or a hummingbird looking for the succulent sex organ of a flowering plant."

"Oh, no, this is the spirit of rose."

"Isn't that what I just said?"

"It gives me strength. It fills me with confidence."

I wanted to say it filled me with nausea, but I held my tongue. Her eyes still were closed. She finished her water and then dropped the glass and turned her palms skyward like a rose bud uncovering for the first time to the gift of light.

"Sally, where did you get this stuff? There must be fifty candles."

"Fifty," she mumbled—eyelids opening slowly—finally. She dropped her heavenly pose and, with her fingers, pinned the last drooping sheet to her shoulder.

"Yes, fifty. Fifty roses. Confidence, strength, hope."

"Are you naked under there?" I exclaimed in mock shock.

"All pores must be opened to the oils for purification to be whole," she said with a turn of her nose upward in an air of virtuosity.

"You're naked. For God's sake, hold on to the sheet."

"A wrap. It's a wrap."

"Then for God's sake, stay wrapped."

"Ooh, yes."

Again commenced the flagging eyelids and ecstatic sigh.

"And stop it with the 'Ooh, yes.' It's me—your brother, Robbie."

That caused her body to fully reattach itself, at last.

"Oh," she said matter-of-factly with a flip of her hair, "yes."

"Where did you get fifty candles and... and the rose oil?"

"My closet," she said, as if I should have known.

I should have known.

"I know you remember Alice Beckworth," said Sally with a twinkle that told me she knew more about Alice Beckworth and me than I might have hoped.

"Alice Beckworth. Alice..." I was trying to act like recollections of Alice were foggy when in fact the mention of her name vividly resurrected twenty-year-old memories. Alice and I had... we'd been... we were very young then, but the remembrance made me feel like I was betraying Kjirsten and I blushed. I snapped back to the present and realized the memory was about two people who no longer existed.

"Well, whether you remember or not, I attended her wedding while you were off getting your degree," said Sally, ignoring my simulated amnesia.

I *had* forgotten that Sally went to the wedding—if I ever knew. Alice married some guy she'd met in school from Santa Something, California. They left Texas and I hadn't heard anyone mention her name until now.

"So what does that have to do with the candles and the oils and the nakedness?" I smirked. I quite deliberately did not connect any of my Alice memories to what appeared before me now.

"Well, she had a hippie wedding with peasant dresses and sandals and rings of flowers in her hair and a tofu wedding cake and sitar music and self-written vows that promised to love just as long as they loved and, of course, lots of—"

"Candles," I said, raising my finger as the light went on.

The light really did snap on as our mother entered the room. I had not heard her drive up.

"Oh, look at you, Sally," said Mom with no moment of startled hesitation, "you've found Alice's candles. Doesn't it smell wonderful in here? It lifts my spirits just to walk into this room. Roses, roses, roses. And look, you've found the oil, too. How beautiful it all is... What's wrong, dear?"

Not only had our mother remembered the candles, she had apparently known, in a flash, they were a signal that more was amiss with Little Sister than fleeting whimsy.

"Nothing's wrong," said Sally, looking away quickly from both of us. She arose from the floor clutching her wraps and began to extinguish the candles one by one with little puffs of air. She looked like a sad ghost now as she floated from light to light leaving only wisps of fading smoke where once the flames had danced.

Mother spoke while folding the sheets that remained on the floor, "Oh, good, I'm glad nothing's wrong. I was just recalling that the last time these candles were lit—you remember, don't you?—must have been seven years ago—you and I wrapped each other up and lay here on this very floor talking and crying for hours."

"I remember," whispered Sally.

"What?" I asked, with all the sensitivity of a blue norther. "What do you remember? Why were you crying?"

Sally chose to leave the room instead of answering me. When I put two and two together and realized that seven years ago she and Doug had divorced, I was sorry I'd asked. Mother was worried that Sally was burning candles to help her work through more sadness. Then I remembered the last thing I'd heard Sally ask Hutch that morning was, "What do you mean, *a break will do us all good?*" and I felt an empty feeling in the pit of my stomach.

Mother said, "Robbie, why don't you find something to fix for supper while I talk to Sally?"

Good idea.

A few minutes later, Mother and Little Sister—sister still wrapped, only now in sweats with a towel around her wet hair—walked into the kitchen as I finished setting her entire collection of leftovers on the table. While Mother and I dove into our potpourri of Tupperware delights, Sally picked at her food, absorbing barely enough blood sugar to sustain conversation.

Hutch was concerned about Cobus; Sally believed he was saying they should slow their relationship. I knew how he felt about her and I knew that wasn't the case. Nevertheless, all she'd heard was that he wanted to pull back. Hoping that I could offer a man's interpretation, I asked her to repeat his exact words.

"He said that we probably should have had the good sense to keep things a secret until after Cobus's senior year," said Sally with resignation.

"There," I said. "He isn't saying anything should change. He's merely musing how things might have been easier if Cobus had not been in the middle of his senior year when you two fell in love."

"See," she sighed, with shoulders slumping, "you think we shouldn't be together, too."

So much for a man's interpretation.

"Fiddlesticks," said Mother.

"Well," lamented Sally. Any relaxation she had absorbed from the rose wrap had now deserted her as lines of worry crept over her face. "Maybe they're right. Maybe now isn't the right time for Hutch and me."

"Fiddlesticks," said Mother again, flippantly sure that hers was the only opinion that mattered. "Up until a few hours ago, you were the happiest you've been in seven years."

"Well, maybe I should have waited eight."

"Fiddlesticks," I chimed, unable to resist hearing what the word would sound like coming from my own lips.

"One more year would not have made that boy of yours behave any better," Mother said, tapping her finger on the table to emphasize her point.

"It might have," said Sally, wide-eyed at Mother's strength of conviction.

"It wouldn't have. And think how sad you would have been if he was away at college acting out like he is now."

I was wondering how my mother knew so much about teenage bad boy behavior, and I asked, "So you think Cobus is merely acting out?" I was also wondering why I suddenly felt uneasy.

"Oh, sure, honey," Mom said to me. "Next year he'll be away at college and he won't have us to clean up after his tantrums."

"Maybe he won't have any reasons to throw tantrums," said Sally.

"Oh, sure he will, honey," said Mom. "You have no idea how youngsters will act when they're on their own for the first time. Bad grades and weeks without hearing from your son are worrisome, but a phone call from police saying they're holding him overnight for drinking is devastating. Yes, you can feel grateful that your son has you nearby so you can help him."

"Aw, Mom," I said, suddenly feeling like a guilt-ridden teenager again, "it was just the campus police. Besides, my grades were only bad my freshman year, and I know I never went weeks without calling."

"Oh, I know, sweetie. I was trying to make a point. You called all the time and we always sent the money you needed right away."

"Now, Mom—"

I'd forgotten the conversation was not about me at all. Sally hadn't; she interrupted and said, "I don't know what good it does to be here for him when the closest he'll get is to drop a pile of laundry on the living room rug."

"Oh, honey, he'll come when he needs you." Mom sounded so sure of herself. I wasn't so sure and I longed for her insight.

Where Mother had been able to stealthily enter the front room when Sally was wrapped in rose rags, Cobus came through the front door with a resounding bang. Belligerent entrances and obnoxious exits were all too quickly becoming his trademark. He must have noticed us at the table, but I did not detect a hint of a glance our way before he blew into his room.

Sally's instinct was to rise and go to him, but Mother stopped her. She held Sally's hand, then turned to me and said, "Robbie, why don't you two take a walk around the block and let Grandma have a talk with Grandson?"

"Oh, Mom," protested Sally, "I don't even have my shoes on."

"That is such a silly comment coming from one who could barely be forced to wear shoes for the first sixteen years of her life."

"Oh, Mom." Sally sighed and I took her hand from Mother to lead her outside. She stopped on the porch to pull on her sandals, which were always there.

Sally and I walked arm in arm using the intermittent light from street lamps as our guide. It was still early October and the summer critters had not yet abandoned their territories to winter ones, so the night sounds were summer sounds. The peepers and crickets sang to us while we strolled quietly. When we returned, Cobus was gone. Mother was still there.

"Well, Sally," said our Mother smugly beaming, "I think you are going to find that everything will be better in the morning."

That did not reflect my understanding of reality.

"Mother, what did you say to him?" asked Sally skeptically.

"Well, I told him he should be having the time of his life right now and that he should play his football with everything he's got. That's what I said, 'Give it everything you've got.' I told him that all of us love his football and the best thing he could do for you was to play the very best he knows how. I told him he would never have this chance again and how grateful he should be that he has a coach like Hutch who cares about him as much as your Hutch does."

"And what did Cobus say to that, Mom," I asked, thinking *Sure, Mom, I bet that really got through to him.*

"Oh, he didn't say much. That's how I know I was getting through to him."

Sally smiled and said sweetly, "Thanks, Mom."

Sally knew Cobus loved his grandmother dearly, but loving her dearly and heeding her advice were two entirely different things. Sally also knew, as I did, that nothing would be different in the morning.

I stopped by Kjirsten's to talk her into having a cup of coffee with me at Al's café. It didn't take much talking. I needed to be cheered up and she did that by opening her door and saying to me, "I was thinking and wishing that somebody—anybody—would drop by and take me out for coffee. You'll do. Let's ride, cowboy."

We quickly found that I wasn't the only one who needed cheer. Hutch sat alone in a pinewood booth reading a week-old *El Paso Herald*. Uninvited, we plopped ourselves across the table from him and stared until our silly grins forced him to stop ignoring us and fold his paper away.

"God, you two look like trouble," he said.

We said nothing and kept up our childish glaring until he finally said, "I suppose you want me to buy you coffee."

"Works every time," whispered Kjirsten, with a nonchalant flip of her ponytail.

Big Al read our minds, clanged down two cups, and then poured in his manner that allowed most of the coffee to make it into the mug.

"I've got two big pieces of pecan pie left," said Big Al.

Kjirsten playfully asked, "How about tiramisu?"

Big Al's face curled with bewilderment, "Terra-me-what?"

Kjirsten said, "Oh, Al, you must get out more. Coffee will be fine tonight, but some day soon I must teach you to make *terra-me-what*."

Big Al snickered, "Heh, heh, heh." Then he leaned over to me and whispered so everyone could hear, "Next thing you know, she'll want lattes and steamed milk."

He walked away with his *heh, heh, heh,* and I turned back to Hutch and, pointing to his El Paso newspaper, asked, "You're not picking out houses already, are you?"

"Nah. Just reading the want ads. I figure one more game like last night and I'll need to hire on someplace as far away from Bonnet as I can get."

Kjirsten said, "The number for truck drivin' school is 1-800-OPENROAD."

"That's it," he said, sounding like his fate was sealed. "I'll git me a big ol' Kenworth, an' head out to see Amurica."

With thumbs and forefingers, I framed an imaginary motion picture of Hutch in a big rig and said, "I can see you and Little Sister now, drivin' on down to Albuquerque with a load of pigs. You got your arms all tattooed and she's got no teeth. She's tough as nails and throws them sows 'round just like they're so many sacks o' cotton."

Big Al looked at me like I'd lost my senses.

Hutch quit playing the game and said, "Right now, I'm not sure Sally would go with me."

Kjirsten looked him straight in the eye and said, without a moment's hesitation, "Hutch, if there's only one thing I know, it's that Sally would follow you to the ends of the earth. I don't care how things feel or look right now, but I promise you she'd ride in a Kenworth or on an old gray mare if that's what it took to be with you."

She squeezed my hand under the table as she said it, and it felt like she was talking to me alone. Then I remembered that Hutch and Sally were the problem of the moment and he reminded me by saying, sadly, "You should have heard her this morning, Kjirsten. She is so sad about Cobus and she has no idea how to handle him."

"I know, Hutch," I said, still holding tightly to Kjirsten's hand, "I just came from Sally's. Sure, she's distraught. She's mixed up. But she's not mixed up about you. If you two weren't such a mess right now it'd be funny—her thinking you're having second thoughts and you thinking she would let you go anywhere without her. I feel like a high school messenger boy delivering notes back and forth. One thing makes it easy—the message is loud and clear: you two love birds are head over heels for each other."

Kjirsten squeezed my hand again.

Looking like he'd been stabbed, Hutch said, "Sally thinks I'm having second thoughts?"

I guess he missed the part where I said she was head over heels for him.

"Not any more she doesn't. Mom and I set her straight. Mom said if she could raise me, then Sally and her son would come through this crisis smelling like roses." I didn't tell them she already smelled like roses.

"I need to go over there right now," said Hutch, standing to leave. "I want to let her know that I've not had one other thought but her for the past year."

"Now listen, pard'," I said with my best tough-guy Texas drawl, "don't get too mushy on me. Let Little Sister rest tonight. She's gonna be fine. Mom was puttin' her to bed when I left. Let them do their girl-talk thang."

"You're right, I suppose," Hutch murmured, and sat back down.

"Of course I am. Have another cup of coffee and sit here with Kjirsten and me. Al, please bring us another pot."

Big Al obliged and spill-poured another round.

We hadn't done a good enough job yet of lightening Hutch's dark cloud, and he said, "The hard thing now is, for the first time in a long time, I don't have a real good concept of who I am."

Kjirsten never allowed me to take ownership of my own blue moods for more than half a minute and she wasn't going to let Hutch spiral into one now.

"Who do you want to be?" she said, casting a line in his direction.

"I thought I wanted to be a football coach."

"And you know what?" posed Kjirsten, with her *my view of your world is so obvious that I can't believe you don't get it* air.

Hutch took her bait and responded, "What?"

"You *are* a football coach," she said.

"Yeah. I know. It's just that—"

"It's just what?" she said setting the hook. "You're not just any old football coach, you're our football coach. Are you the coach of a great group of boys? Yes. Do you win lots of games? Yes. Does anyone and everyone in this town who matters as much as a cockroach admire you and respect you and want to be you? Yes."

She was reeling him in and I flowed along in the wake. In my mind, she had just placed Baron Richards a notch lower on the evolutionary scale than a cockroach. I felt closer to her than ever.

Big Al, who had the ears of a bat and was eavesdropping like always, said, "Please don't say cockroach around a restaurant owner, darlin'; it makes him nervous."

"Oops, sorry, Al," she said, smiling, without looking away from Hutch. "I should have said rat."

"Thanks, sweetie," Al said. "Rats make Big Al feel so much better."

Kjirsten gave Hutch no time to argue with her offerings; she kept on pumping. "Who do you want to be?" she asked again.

Hutch finally felt good enough about where she was taking him, and he replied, "I want to be married to Sally."

"And Sally wants to be married to you. Sally's mom wants Sally to be married to you. Sally's brother wants Sally to be married to you. I even have it on good authority that Sally's ex-husband wants Sally to be married to you."

With that, Kjirsten had pulled him all the way up from his depths, and he broke a wide relaxed grin for the first time—like he'd forgotten he had any troubles at all.

Then she reminded him.

"So it sounds to me like you have a perfectly wonderful concept of who you are. Problem is, a confused young man is interfering with your concept because he doesn't yet own one of his own."

I probably would have let him float in the clouds a while longer, but since she'd reined him back to reality, I went along and offered my own brand of cowboy psychology.

I said, "Yeah, buddy. It doesn't sound to me like there's much you can do but be yourself and let the chips fall where they may."

I was talking about letting my own troubled nephew dangle 'til he worked through it. I was worried sick about the kid, but Kjirsten had made it clear that Cobus's problem was his alone, and there was not much Hutch or I could do to help.

Hutch kneaded his hands on the table and said to us, "There have been moments in the past couple of weeks when I've wanted this football season to be over with so I could sneak out of Bonnet and take a job in El Paso or Albuquerque or Saskatchewan or anywhere they'd have me. Then I think, God, how miserable I'd be without Sally. Then I think, Sally can't go 'til she's sorted it out with Cobus and I'm right back where I started—thinkin' round in circles."

While we sat in the silence of Hutch's last thought, Big Al did something I'd never known him to do before or since. He got serious. Gone for the moment were his staccato laugh and carefree smile. He walked his large frame over to our table and squeezed himself in beside Hutch. Hutch moved over as far as he could against the wall of the booth. A picture of him being crushed by the big guy flashed, but Al stopped sliding before that happened. He left a good portion of himself hanging out past the end of the bench.

Big Al, breathing loudly with each word coming laboriously, wheezed, "I'm sure sorry, Coach. You gotta excuse me for overhearin' y'all, but I cain't help that lest I turn on the dishwasher to drown y'all out. And y'all don't want me to do that 'cause then y'all couldn't hear yourselves neither, so I just overhear and I cain't help it."

Well, we knew that. If you ate in Al's place very much, which we all did, you knew you were sharing your life with him. We were used to him laughing at us when he thought what we said was funny, which was most of what we said, but we sure weren't used to the serious side of him.

He took long, hard breaths through his nose like he was letting out steam from all the work it took to form his thoughts. "I been here a long time in Bonnet, Texas. Hell, I been here in this café most the hours of my whole life. So there's some things I jest know 'bout and what I know 'bout most is people. You're a real man to them boys, Coach."

I wasn't sure what kind of man that made me, but I knew what Al meant. In Bonnet, Texas, there is no higher praise than to call a man a man.

Al looked at Kjirsten and sheepishly said, "Miss Kjirsten, I don't mean to offend. But these boys have gotta become men; I don't know how else to say it—you bein' a woman and all."

Kjirsten reached out and touched his arm from across the table and said the perfect thing. "Al, you're talking to one Texas girl who's damn proud to be sittin' in the company of three real men. Real is the only way I like 'em."

Al blushed at that, rubbed his whisker-shadowed chin, shyly looked down at the floor, and said one more thing to Hutch. "Some of them boys got hard times comin', Coach, and some's surely got hard times now, but they're gonna' know how to stand up in the face of what's dealt them 'cause they're learnin' how by watchin' you. They'll be real men because of you."

And I'd called myself the cowboy psychologist.

CHAPTER SIXTEEN

BARON RICHARDS DIDN'T HAVE the guts to throw me out, but he sure wasn't happy I was there. Bret Ashworth the dupe, so naïve, believing the crap Richards spewed about being interested in only the good of the team, was stupid enough to invite me. If Richards would have had the good sense to hold his get-together at his own home, I wouldn't have had the nerve to crash the party. Instead, he convened his band of renegade wannabes in the Bonnet First—and only—Southern Baptist Church, and that made it more or less public. I suppose Richards thought meeting at the church added an air of sanctimony that blessed his perversions. Since I'd been saved three times that I remembered, at least once by Baptists, I figured the church wouldn't burst into flames on account of my presence, so in I went.

I'd asked Doug to go with me. He found that too humorous an invitation for a reply. I went mostly to see who came. Amos Swindel was there, and Ashworth, along with three dads of boys on the team who'd been hanging out with my nephew Cobus too much for their own good. There wasn't a flyspeck's worth of leadership in the group—to say nothing of courage.

It restored my faith in Bonnet's townsfolk to see that they'd stayed away in droves, although, that didn't faze Baron

Richards much. He was so inspirational with his Sunday-school chalkboard that it was all I could do to keep from grabbing a couple of hymnals and shakin' them like pompoms to lead the sheep in a cheer for good ol' Bonnet High. The sheep sat there wide-eyed while he drew his plays, most of which were designed to get the ball to his own son. Every third or fourth one involved one of the others' boys, but mostly the ball was to go to flat-footed, slow-legged Derek Richards.

Daddy Richards's twisted logic went, "Amos, if they would just fake the ball to Cobus Meadhran, they could throw a swing pass to your boy Jacob. Next down, you just know that end-around play would work with my Derek. Ever'body knows the ball's going to Cobus, so I figure we don't give it to him. Use him to decoy. Spread that ball around. Keep 'em off balance. We can't become so interpretable as to give the ball to the same boy all the time."

The first thing wrong with that idea was that Cobus got the ball because Cobus got the yards even when everyone knew he was getting the ball. The second was—and it was not clear to me how Richards had missed the importance of this simple fact—Cobus was no longer on the team!

Amos Swindel, with the skin on his forehead scrunched up from thinking too hard, interrupted Richards saying, "Baron, I'm pretty sure I heard Cobus was off the team for good. I even heard he turnt in his uniform."

"Oh, that doesn't mean a thing, Amos. I talked to that boy and he allowed as how he'll come back as soon as changes are made. I'll make that happen. I'll be dropping by to see Coach Hutcheson tomorrow to let him know how it has to be if he plans on winning many more games. Don't you agree, Coach Ashworth, that something's gotta be done?"

Bret Ashworth scratched his ear and spoke hesitantly. "Well, we have them plays you're drawin' in the book, alright. But Coach Hutch told the boys that it weren't the play-callin' that beat us the other night. He said it was execution."

Good, I thought, Ashworth is going to stand up to the ass.

Richards crossed his arms atop his chest indignantly and postured. "Ain't it always so? When things go south, a man will look to the east, the west, and north 'fore he'll look to himself."

Ashworth stammered, "I know what you're sayin'... I guess there's things we could do...but don't ya think the defense let down, too?"

Hang in there, Ashworth, don't start waffling.

So damned cocksure of himself, Richards said, "That's what they all like to throw in your face when they cain't figure out a way to score."

Ashworth looked pained at the dilemma his conscience was offering him. He whined, "We didn't get as many points as we thought we might the other night. Perhaps you could talk to Coach Hutch. It cain't hurt to have another idea."

So much for standing up to the ass. When you can't be with the one you suck up to, then suck up to the one you're with.

I wasn't much better. I leaned against the wall in the back and kept my mouth shut. Not that it would have done any good. Fighting with Richards would have been pointless. Besides, it wasn't clear that he was building much of an army. Sheep don't follow well when led by wolves in wolves' clothing.

I was glad he'd stuck to football. If he'd tried to surface any of his claptrap about Sally and Hutch, I would have had to say something. As long as he stayed with football, he was impotent.

Still, he'd wedged his foot in the shut doors that were their minds. The best way to keep him locked out was for Hutch and the boys to keep winning. Surely that would happen because this was the year we were going all the way.

We won on Friday night. The Whitworth, Texas Stars weren't much of a challenge. The towns get smaller with each westward passing mile. They love their football out there, but it's hard for those little towns to get enough boys in school to field a healthy team—let alone attract experienced coaches to teach them the game. The Whitworth boys rode two hours on a noisy bus to get beaten by the Mustangs and then they turned around and rode two hours home.

The score was lopsided enough for the old boys at the round table in Al's Café to resume their fantasies of winning the state championship. They conjured up more paths to the finals than were mathematically possible and sounded like they believed every one of them would happen.

"Laurel Mountain is unbeaten," Bud said, "but there ain't no possible way in hell they stay that way."

"Yup," echoed Cuthbert. "Ain't no way."

Then Bud said "Now take Bee Tree. It doesn't matter if they get beat or they don't. They gotta come through us and we'll kick their butts."

Galey repeated, "You are right about that, and there ain't no way Laurel Mountain ain't gonna git beat."

We didn't play Laurel Mountain during the regular season, but they were in our division. Since they were unbeaten after five games, they held their fate in their own hands; we were already behind the eight ball. Doug wasn't there, of course. Good thing; I wouldn't have wanted to apologize for his comebacks to anything the old boys might have said about Cobus. As it was, Cobus's name didn't come up. Most likely it was on account of me. The codgers did not speak unkindly about the recently departed in front of his family—not in that first week after his demise, anyway.

I don't recall uttering a word. I drank beer. I sipped and stared straight ahead until Bud Granger looked up from another bottle emptying gulp and slurred, "Robb-O, I do believe you're beginning to act just like your friend Doug."

How I hated to be called Robb-O.

"Hell," said fidgety Cuthbert, "you even look like Doug with your mouth all tight like that."

They thought they were funny.

Brother Galey quipped, "I thought you *was* Doug."

Didn't they know we'd beaten Whitworth only because they were grossly overmatched? No good football was played Friday night. We'd won the game without spirit. Whitworth was bad enough that our boys could play sloppy and still win and that's what they did. I took it as long as I could, then gulped the last of my beer and excused myself. They didn't much notice. As I walked away, I heard Bud say, "Lookin' at our schedule, I can't see as how there's anyone left that can beat us."

I wondered if folks in the towns of teams that won championships talked that way. I wondered if the attitudes of men who sat in cafés jawing and predicting could affect the outcome of the games. Then I thought that the likes of Bud Granger couldn't affect the outcome of anything. It was a Doug sort of thought; I wondered if I really had become him.

On my way out, I passed Baron Richards and Amos Swindel sitting at what had become Richards's regular table in the corner by the door. Ironically, that night, Tommy had thrown a bullet of a pass to Richards's son Derek, hitting him in the worst place possible—his hands. The ball bounced harmlessly away as the klutz swatted at it with the grace of a jackhammer. Still, his old man continued to draw plays on his yellow pad, pathetically believing that if coaches would only teach it right, the true talents of his son would shine through.

On Saturday morning, Doug woke me up with obnoxious cheeriness. Whistling Hank Williams' songs is a good thing for any Texas boy to do—but not at 6:00 AM on a Saturday.

Doug clanged the pots and pans looking for a skillet and then began frying eggs and bacon to the tune of "Kaw-Liga". If he wasn't going to let me sleep in, then I might as well join him.

"What the hell are you so happy about?" I mumbled, staggering into the kitchen.

I was still in my boxers and a t-shirt that read, "Don't Mess With Texas." I threw a pot on the stove, added a pint of water, and then sat a box of grits on the counter.

"I knew you wouldn't let me cook alone," said the super-athlete, trying his best to act hurt.

"You can't have eggs and bacon without grits," I growled through sleep still pooled in the bottom of my throat. I tossed a cup on the counter and splashed it full of coffee. "Besides," I continued between slurps, "I'm not good at lying or sitting around while someone else chars perfectly good eggs and bacon."

"I wasn't going to burn 'em." He pouted, doing such a good job of acting that he almost convinced me.

"And why should this time be any different?"

With that, he sat down with his own cup of coffee and opened the Saturday morning *Austin American Statesman*, leaving me at the stove with the skillet and the pot. I'd Tom Sawyered myself into doing all the cooking while he read the paper. It was just as well; I hadn't recharged the fire extinguisher since the last time he cooked. As I poured dry grits into the pot, Doug, never looking up from his paper, said, "Why don't you come to the range with me and help me teach the ladies about the rules and etiquette of golf?"

I wouldn't have missed that for all the blackened bacon in Bonnet.

Doug had tried to get Tildy and the girls to throw their clubs and carts into the back of his truck, but they wouldn't have any of that. At least three of them wouldn't. Macey whined when Tildy, Inez, and Amanda started down the range pulling their carts behind them.

Macey said, "Tildy, I want to ride in the back. I haven't ridden in the back of a truck in such along time. Can't we ride in the back of the truck?"

Amanda shot back, "Macey, it would seem to me that if Tildy could go to the all the expense of buying these wonderful new golf carts for us, the least you could do is show some appreciation by being thrilled to pull them."

Macey was ten steps behind the others, scurrying to catch up.

Tildy said, "Now, Amanda, I know Macey is grateful. She's every bit as grateful as you. She only wants to ride in the truck."

Macey, already beginning to huff because she was walking faster than she normally walked, wheezed, "I only wanted to ride in the truck."

Doug and I stood without speaking as the four of them strolled down the range pulling their equipment behind them. The range was four hundred yards in length and we watched their single file procession until they neared the end. Tildy looked like a mama duck with three ducklings in tow—their two wheeled carts wobbling back and forth like tail feathers on a waddle. He shook his head at the sight; I shrugged, and then we hopped in the pickup and sped to join them. At the end of the range, he jumped out to start the day's lesson.

"The first thing I want y'all to do," said my friend, now the teacher, "is leave your golf carts where they are and come stand by me."

He stood squarely in the middle of a closely trimmed patch of grass that was longer than it was wide.

"This freshly mowed grass is called the tee or tee box." As he spoke, he traced the expanse of the area with his hands.

"Then I'll always call it the tee box," Inez stated. "I have already memorized that the little green wooden pegs are called tees. They shall be tees and this shall be the box into which I stick my tees."

"Inez," questioned Amanda sharply, "you do know that not all tees are green, don't you? I happen to know that most are white."

"All of mine are green, certainly. Tildy gave me a sack of a thousand green tees. So, for as long as I live, my tees will be green."

Being legally blind, seeing only vague colors and shapes, Inez found comfort in similar things being the same. If all tees were green when she held them an inch away from her coke-bottle lenses, she could be sure it was tees she was sticking into tee boxes and not pencils. Her pencils were red.

Doug kept smiling and said, "The first point of golf etiquette we'll learn today is that carts are not to be brought onto the tee box."

Two of the ladies' carts were clearly on the makeshift tee box and Amanda was ruffled at her apparent transgression.

"Well, how was I to know that?" exclaimed Amanda, and she marched promptly to remove her cart. Macey followed and moved hers, too.

"You weren't," said Tildy to the point. "Doug was merely using this opportunity to teach us proper golf procedure—the etiquette of the game."

Amanda, still so concerned about making any semblance of a mistake, moaned, "He did tell us to leave our carts where they were."

"At most courses," continued Doug, oblivious to the cacophony, "every tee box will have three or more sets of markers—blue markers, white markers, red markers."

Doug pointed to three pairs of bricks he'd painted and placed on the ground like you'd find on a real golf course.

"Notice, the red markers are in the front—closer to the green. Most courses use red to mark the ladies' tee box. Folks just call 'em the ladies tees."

This was the third use of the word *tee* to describe a different place or thing. I had visions of Macey trying to hit the ball off of a brick or of Inez painting one green and putting it in her bag.

Doug took a deep breath and caught each of their eyes to make sure his latest bit of lexicon had sunk in before continuing. He explained to them about honors and teeing the ball within two club lengths behind the markers. He showed them where to stand when it was another's turn to play. He covered the concept of placing the ball in play and how scoring the hole had not really begun until that happened. Amanda had trouble with the idea that Inez could knock the ball off the tee as many times as she wanted and it wouldn't count against her unless she'd made an honest attempt at the ball.

With an all-too-transparent reference to her nearsighted friend, Amanda snipped, "If the ball has been knocked off of one's little green tee, then how are we to know if it was due to one's actual attempts to hit the ball or an involuntary spasm?"

While it was a fact that Inez's swing was quicker than some, and she often bumped the ball off her green tee while addressing it because she couldn't see it well, it wasn't fair to call her swing a spasm. A high-speed lurch, perhaps, but not a spasm.

Doug said, "It's a game of honor. You accept your opponent's word."

"Harumph," snorted Amanda. "I hope honor doesn't take all day."

Tildy strode over and stood in front of Amanda with hands on her hips and mock on her face. "Now, Amanda, would you please explain to me just what in hell you have to do with your day?"

Amanda, Inez, and Macey's eyes grew big as the golf balls in their hands. It appeared they hadn't heard Tildy say *hell* much.

When Amanda collected herself she meekly offered, "I do like to go for my walks."

Without turning around, Tildy asked, "Doug, how long is a golf course?"

"Nine holes is a couple miles, I suppose," said my roommate.

"How far do you walk, Amanda?"

"Now, Tildy, you know I walk two miles every day."

Tildy took her friend's hands. "Yes, you do, dear; so when we golf, we will walk two laughter-filled miles while swinging at silly little golf balls. Some swings we'll miss and some we'll hit. We'll be too old to count them, but we'll walk on. We'll smell the flowers. We will feel the breeze on our skin and the green grass beneath our toes. Now, don't you really hope it takes all day?"

I looked at Macey and she was leaning against Doug and removing her shoes and socks. Quietly, with a falsetto tremor in her voice, she said, "Oh, Tildy. I want to feel the grass on my toes now."

I was shocked when the other three ladies began snickering. Then I saw Doug was holding in a laugh and I was angry with him for making fun of poor Macey. She had obviously slipped into a distant world of her own. Was I the only one who could see it? Then she tilted her head revealing a deviously wry smile and winked at me. She stood and tossed her shoes on the grass and then snapped to a drill sergeants' pose, barking, "Now, if all of you are through sniveling and waxing melodramatic, can we please git on with golfin'? I'm feeling a strong need to whack at something." She looked at me and added, "You need to loosen up too, sonny."

Okay, so she wasn't losing it. She was sharp as a tack and she'd been toying with me and I was the only one who hadn't seen it. Now, Doug had to walk away to keep from laughing at me. The others felt no need to hold back and tittered away.

Doug had strung bright yellow rope for a good distance along one side of the range and he'd made a giant circle with red rope directly in front of the tee box. On the right hand side, there was white rope running for a few hundred feet. He explained to the ladies that the ropes represented hazards and out-of-bounds markers. That was all well and good until they hit their golf balls into the forbidden areas and couldn't understand why they couldn't place it back into play with no penalty. Out of bounds was the worst. I agreed with them that it was unfair, which didn't make things any easier for Doug. The one-stroke penalty and loss of distance was too harsh and Amanda fought it all the way—especially when she'd hit a good shot that rolled no more than an inch across the rope and my roommate made her walk all the way back to hit another. It served the purpose of illustrating the prudence of hitting a provisional ball before walking to find the original. I wouldn't have taken bets either way on what the decision would have been if the United States Golf Association had been given the choice of listening to her squawk or changing the out-of-bounds rule forever.

It took over an hour to finish the first hole with Doug stopping every stroke or two to emphasize the rules. Macey observed that it would take until after dark to finish nine holes, but Doug stuck to his plan. After a glass of lemonade, he hopped up and said, "Let's do it again."

Tildy clapped her hands together excitedly and exclaimed, "Super! Let's all ride in the back of the truck."

I held my breath, expecting whines from them at the prospect of another hour to play one hole, but not a word was said. Macey was proud of her ride in the bed of the pickup and sat up on the rail looking as regal as Queen Victoria. The others didn't look nearly as tired as I felt. On the contrary, they had begun to exhibit the first looks of determination on their faces. They had practiced for weeks, hitting balls, chipping, and putting—all for only the fine art of hitting balls, chipping, and putting. Now, for the first time, they had a bigger purpose.

If Tildy really believed, as she'd sensitively promised Amanda, that their rounds of golf would be peaceful strolls across the fairways with time taken to smell the roses along the way, she was shy of the truth. If she was actually afraid, as she had humbly surmised, that they would miss as many shots as they hit, she'd underestimated their resolve.

By the time we reached the end of the fairway again, with the four who'd earlier been nervous chatterers—unsure whether or not they had stepped onto the right pasture—there wasn't a quibble to be heard. Doug and I lifted first the women and then their bright blue golf carts from the back of the truck and they went straight about the business of the game. Their change of demeanor was dramatic. They'd been four seventy-something women who were dabbling in a silly game of golf until then. Suddenly, after one glass of lemonade, they were golfers. They spoke in the hushed determined tones of seasoned combatants. They selected their clubs like duelers choosing pistols for forty paces and then strode to the tee—each in their turn. They waggled, pulled their triggers, and put their balls in play.

CHAPTER SEVENTEEN

To show support for Hutch, I went to football practice every afternoon of week six. On two days, Kjirsten went with me and we sat alone in the bleachers. She graded papers while I stretched my legs to the bench in front and leaned back to bask in the October afternoon sun like a terrapin on a log.

The boys on the field acted like programmed androids. They did everything right. On Thursday afternoon, Kjirsten looked up and asked me how practice was going and I said they hadn't made a mistake all week. She smiled and said that was super, but she didn't get what I meant. They didn't miss tackles, they didn't drop passes, and their faces were masks of no expression. I found myself longing for the days when Cobus was throwing helmets.

Aromas is another Hill Country town like Whitworth where the boys have a hard time matching up to teams from towns the size of Bonnet. Not that Bonnet is a sprawling metropolis, but we do lay claim to a population of round about a thousand while most of the little towns west of the Guadalupe have a hard time finding five or six hundred souls for a census. Most of those they do scrape up are on Social Security.

In our town, we dream only of championships. We sneer at ourselves for less than perfection, so we sneer a lot. In the Aromas and Whitworths of Texas, they're more content to wait patiently upon the times they beat the one team they can't. It's not that no small school ever wins a championship—a small school wins one every year in the divisions 1A and 2A. There are so many more schools in those divisions, though, that for any one of them, winning it all doesn't cross their minds until the trophy is theirs. In Bonnet, the big prize always taunts like a dangling carrot just beyond our reach.

So every year most of the little schools play up—out of their division—once or twice with the hopes of slaying Goliath. Every year Goliath gets slain more than once or twice. Aromas was our David that fall; we were their Goliath.

Our Mustangs played like they'd practiced—methodically, rigidly, heartlessly; and that's how they got beat—one heartless play at a time. If my own heart hadn't begun fading away that night, too, along with our boys', it would have been fun to cheer on the little school from out west—high-fiving after every play. It had been so long since that first game of ours when we were the ones slapping each other on the back and saying the magic forbidden words—*we're number one.* Now we sat jacketed against the October evening chill, hearing their muffled din from across the field—scarcely aware of the blurred images of their streamers in the air and pom-pom girls cartwheeling their cute little skirts into the night and their fans standing—never sitting—like us.

Now we were beaten twice and the talk around the table could no longer be about winning a championship—only about how we had lost it and where to place the blame. I know it was sadness the men felt and not the rancor they spewed. We don't teach boys and men to speak to sadness in Texas so what they're feeling can come out plain mean.

Galey and Cuthbert, the brothers Alden, whined at me like I could do something to prevent what had already taken place because I was guilty of being related to my nephew Cobus. In their minds, they were sure we wouldn't have lost if he hadn't quit. The Aldens didn't know their musings struck painful chords.

Trouble was, I couldn't disagree with Cuthbert when he said, "I sure don't git why that boy run off like he done. You jest know things woulda been different if'n he'd stuck around."

I mumbled something about it being the same as losing a star player to injury, but inside I knew it was different. A good player gets hurt and the rest of the squad rallies 'round the one who gave it up for the team, and they're better for it. When Cobus walked away, he took their spirit. Tildy had been right that night at the Peach Pit Elks Club when she told us Cobus was their leader. They were still following him.

Bud Granger's bleary-eyed incoherence was more to the point. He leaned in toward the center of the table as if to lower his voice, and then spoke too loudly anyway. He slurred, "I heard that boy quit 'cause he don't want Coach Hutch dating his mama." He turned his head my way and squinted like he was trying to look into my thoughts and asked what he assumed was a question in perfectly good taste. "Whaddya think, Robbie? You think something funny's going on with them two?"

Something funny? Why couldn't these old boys just stick to football? At least there was a pretense, then, that they knew something about what they were regurgitating. No, there was nothing funny going on. Whether or not Cobus's feelings and antics were justified didn't matter; because of him there was little laughter coming from Sally or Hutch.

No laughter came from my lips either. I looked at Bud Granger. I looked over at Galey and Cuthbert and suddenly I was scared to death I might end up like them. I forgot for the moment that my life had any purpose. I forgot the energy I got from the kids in the school and all the reasons I'd come back to Bonnet. I forgot how Kjirsten made me feel.

All I could see was the vile stagnation in the lives of these men that I'd been willing to call my friends only a few minutes before. They'd never been goin' places together friends, or callin' up to chat friends or even sharin' your feelings with friends. I had those. I had Doug. I had Kjirsten. These goats were just drinking-in-the-bar-after-the-game kinds of friends, and that had been good enough. Now, I realized how pathetic their lives must have been if their only concern was how a prize had been taken from them by a man and a woman who'd dared to fall in love, and by a boy who'd dared to act his age. They wanted to point fingers and call names because they felt like they'd lost what had never been or even been promised. The prize—the championship—would not have been theirs had it been won, but they clung tightly to their self-given right to throw stones at those who stole it from them. Calling them my friends wasn't good enough any more.

I stood up from the table without speaking or even so much as a glance in anger. As I walked away, I heard Bud Granger say, "I tell you. He's turning into Doug."

Then Galey said, "I think that boy Cobus turnt into Doug, too. He's quit playing just like his old man done. It's like they got no dedication to their own hometown."

I grabbed the door so it wouldn't slam behind me. I wanted to leave them with a whimper. I figured that was the last football Friday night I'd spend in Big Al's. Baron Richards passed me on his way in and I knew he had a big, round table of fresh converts waiting.

I didn't want to be alone and I didn't want to be with anyone. I wanted to see Sally. I wanted to see Hutch. I needed Kjirsten. And where the hell was Doug, anyway? I wish I'd had the good sense to go home and get up close and personal with Jack Daniel's.

I chose to go to Sally's.

That was the night Hutch and Sally agreed to stop seeing each other and there was nothing I could do to stop it. It was decided by the time I walked in the door.

Hutch paced back and forth in Sally's front room with breaths coming in short chops like he was drowning two feet from shore and couldn't wade out of the undertow. Sally cried because she loved them both, and she knew one was in pain and the other was fading from her as fleetingly as the tears falling from her cheeks into the torrent.

Hutch was crying, too, not with tears, but on the inside; the tremble in his words gave him away. He said, "I'm no good for the boys this way, Sal. When those kids walk out on the field, football should be the only world they know. It's gotta be a safe haven for them—a place they want to be. Right now, I can't keep the rest of the world at bay. It follows them into practice and into the games, nipping at their heels like yapping little curs. They can't get on with what they ought to be about because they're looking over their shoulders."

Sally stopped crying because she was angry at what she thought he'd said. Sharply, she snapped, "So this is just about football. You lose a game and you think we should stop seeing each other."

What was left of my heart was breaking for them but I felt like an outsider. I offered, "I should go, you guys. You don't need me around while you work this out."

Together, without taking their eyes from each other, they said, "Stay!"

I sat on the couch and shut my mouth—for the moment.

"Aw, hon," said Hutch, sadly exasperated at being unable to express himself, "it's not about the game. It's not about any game. It's about those boys and it's about you and Cobus. I'm only sayin' we ought to take a few weeks to let things work themselves out. You need some time with your boy and I'll take some time with the other boys to help straighten them out." He added emphatically, "And I don't mean straighten them out for football's sake. I mean straighten them out for their own sake."

Sally, crying again, "Cobus won't even talk to me. He won't come around."

"Aw, sure, he will, hon," said the rugged football coach, stammering now, like a kid scratching up excuses. "Sure, he will.

He'll come 'round if he knows I'm not here and you can talk it out."

I wasn't sure he would come—right away, at least—there were more forces tugging at the boy than Sally and Hutch.

Then Sally wrapped her arms around him, burying her face in his shoulder, and sobbed, "I love him so, and I don't know what I've done to make him hate me."

In unison, Hutch and I said, "Oh, sweetie, he loves you."

Sally chuckle-sobbed at the two tough Texans calling her sweetie.

I didn't know what to feel. I was angry with the boy for what he'd done; the other side of the story was that he was hurting, too. Having a chance to make it up with his ma might be just what he needed. I was bitterly angry at the contemptibly petty Baron Richards-types in the town, and there was no other side to that story.

Sally said, "Maybe I can take him out of school and get away for a while. Just Cobus and me. He likes to fish. Maybe he can teach me to fish."

I knew that wouldn't work. Besides, there was no room in Sally's closet for fishing rods. Hutch still held her tightly and stroked her back. They stood together in the middle of the room while I offered the first thing that came to my mind. "Sally, I think he's got to come around on his own. Even if you could get him to go away with you, he might feel like he was forced into it."

"See," said Hutch, "Robbie thinks this is for the best, too."

Damn. The last thing I wanted to do is take one side or the other—especially if it had anything to do with keeping the two of them apart for even a minute.

"I don't know what's best at all," I said, wishing there was a way I could say the right thing when I knew there wasn't a right thing. "I only meant that Cobus will be okay. It might not be tomorrow or the next day, but he's gonna be okay. I was trying to say that it has to be up to him—on his own terms—when he was ready."

"I know," she said.

Hutch said, "Sal, I want you to be here for him when he comes to you, that's all."

"I will. I will be here. I've always been here."

He said, "But, don't you see, I can't be here when he comes to work it out. Like those boys on the field need their safe haven, he needs his, too, and it's with his ma. Me being here makes it seem unsafe for him."

She didn't say anything back this time. She sniffed quietly with her face still in his chest—rocking gently as they embraced.

"It's only for a few weeks," he said. "After the season, everything will be different. You'll see. We'll take it a little slower and he'll get used to it."

Then I said, "Sure. By then the folks in town will stop feeding him full of crap. Football will be over and he'll feel good about himself again."

Sally pushed away from Hutch enough to see my face and asked pointedly, "What folks in town? What kind of crap?"

Beautiful. She hadn't known about Richards and his vitriolic vendetta or any of the other mindless scuttlebutt. I had to open my big mouth and add to her misery. God, how I wished I'd chosen Jack Daniel's for a friend that night.

Hutch looked like I'd shot him. He knew some of what the bad guys had been spreadin', but not all. Sally knew none of it. Treading water fast, I said, "I mean mostly the boys in school pullin' at him to come back to the team."

Sally knew I was backpedaling. She wanted to protect Hutch from a truth that she didn't even know. "Oh," she said, reading my lying eyes. "That makes sense. That has to be tough on him."

Hutch crinkled his brow and stated haltingly, "Well, that doesn't sound too much like crap. Sounds pretty normal to me. We all want him back."

Seizing the opportunity to change the subject away from the foot that was in my mouth, Sally looked into the coach's face and asked, "You'd take him back?"

Coach said, "In a minute, I would. He has to come to me, though. If—when—he has the courage to do that, he'll be ready to play. He'll have fought the battles he needs to fight. I don't know if he can fight them all between now and the last game, let alone win them, but I'll be there with open arms if he does. If he doesn't, I have the sad feeling he'll regret not finishing his senior season for a long time to come. That's one reason I want him to have you without me around—but only one. Even if he doesn't come back to play one last time—he needs to make up with you."

She realized how sincere he was about Cobus—the other boys, too—and tears began again.

This time I wouldn't let them talk me out of leaving. I could foresee the outcome anyway. I wanted to come up with an alternative to Hutch's reasoning; I couldn't and neither could Sally. He was making too much sense. The thought flashed to me that Cobus could go on pouting all year and Hutch would stay away and Sally would still be alone at the end of it all. I didn't want that to burble out of my mouth and add to the agony of the moment; I gave them the closest thing to a hug I could muster and walked away.

The boys in the café left me thinking I couldn't feel much lower; at Sally's, I discovered how foolish I'd been to think that. I thought it would be safe to go home and crawl between the covers. I was foolish to think that, too.

When I pulled into the drive, Cobus was leaning on the cab of Derek Richards's truck, talking to Derek and Jacob Swindel. I realized how much I missed Cobus's old friends coming around. Tommy and Michael used to brighten the place up with their antics and noise and, as I liked to remember it, they came by every night. Now Cobus was hanging around with two boys who had dark clouds hanging over their heads. Swindel's cloud came from an acute occlusion of reason and Derek Richards's was formed by the evil spawned from his own father.

I saw the boys stash their beer under the seat when they saw me. Cobus waved them off and they pulled away gunning gravel from their tires while he walked fast into the house to avoid me.

After the uplifting evening I'd already had, seeing him with the two future pillars of society was the last straw. I was able to move quickly enough to cut him off before he locked himself in his room—again. The only sound I'd heard from him for two weeks was the click of the lock in his door. All I wanted was to convince him to drop by to see his mom. It went uglier than I'd planned.

"Cobus."

"Hi, Uncle Robbie," he mumbled, and kept walking.

"Cobus. Stop a minute. Stop and talk to me."

He stopped, but kept his head lowered so I wouldn't see his chew, but he was too late for that.

He said, "I have to pee."

"Well, then, pee; then come out and talk to me."

"I have homework."

Cobus hadn't uttered those words in four years of high school and I did not believe he was going to do schoolwork at eleven o'clock on Friday night. I knew from the few glimpses I'd caught of him lately—groggy and disheveled—that he'd been doing little else but sleep. I imagined his grades were taking a beating.

"Just five minutes," I said. "Just talk with me for five minutes. I'll fix you something to eat."

"I'll listen, but I don't have anything to say and I'm not hungry. I ate at Derek's."

When he returned to the kitchen I set a package of Oreos in front of him at the table with a glass of milk. He ate them, staring straight ahead while we talked.

"How's Tommy?" I asked, knowing they hadn't seen each other.

"Don't know."

"I miss him coming around."

His reply was a gulp of milk.

I wasn't there to talk about Tommy, so I took a deep breath and went where I knew I'd find trouble.

"Your ma misses you," I said.

I looked into his vacant gaze.

I tried gain. "Do you know she misses you and wants to see you?"

"She doesn't need me."

"Come on, Cobus. You don't believe that. You're her whole life."

"Yeah, right. Are you forgetting Mr. Football?"

He jammed two of the chocolate cookies into his mouth at once.

"If it comes to a choice between you and him—between you and anyone else—she chooses you."

He smacked his response between swallows. "She already chose."

He still hadn't looked at anything but the night coming through the window on the wall across the room.

"You're right about that," I said sharply. I'd used up all of my allotment of patience for the evening. "She chose you. Because of you, she's stopped seeing him. She's putting her whole life on hold waiting for you."

"Oh, I'm so sorry. Did the lovebirds have a little spat?" he sneered.

"No, there was no spat. And if you'd stop acting the spoiled brat for more than thirty seconds you'd see just how many people care—really care about you."

He stopped chomping and flexed his jaw looking more like Doug than Doug had looked in recent weeks and I knew I had my old job back. I'd sat at that table a thousand times trying to unclench the jaw, only it hadn't been Cobus's jaw, it had been his old man's. I'd never once in seven years succeeded in prying it apart—Tildy's magic had done that in a heartbeat—but, like always, I was fool enough to try again. I hoped for the boy's sake it wouldn't take seven years and the good witch from the north, because there was no guarantee that there'd be a spell strong enough to cast away the demons that had come to dwell in his head.

"So, she dumped him," said the boy, chewing deliberately loudly.

"No, she didn't dump him. Can't you get it through your head that she'd give up everything else she ever loved to make you happy?"

He sat motionless again, this time without the clench— only the lip of derision. When he spoke, he spoke quietly— resolutely—like he was seeing a different version of reality for the first time. "Like she gave up Dad for me? I suppose she thinks giving up Dad made me happy, too."

Then I, too, saw his different version of reality for the first time. I was the one struck motionless with the stare into the night.

At last I said in a whisper, "Is that what this is all about? Is it about your mom and your dad?"

Where could I start? What could I tell him about his father's life that would help him now? The child was only eighteen but it had taken twenty years to get him to this place. When he didn't answer me, I tried once more. "It wasn't your fault they got a divorce, you know."

A dispassionate smile grayed his lips and he closed his eyes softly, shaking his head gently. "You said she did it all for me."

How could I explain that Sally had divorced his father so the boy wouldn't drown in the same darkness that was suffocating her life? She'd done it for herself so she could breathe again. She did it for Doug so he could learn to breathe on his own for the first time. If I said to Cobus that she'd done it for him, I knew he'd hate himself more than he already did.

"Cobus, you don't remember how it was. She did it—they—both of them did it for all of you. Doug is better off now and your mom is better off—you are, too."

"How do you know if I'm better off? Things were fine the way they were. Six more months and I'd have been out of here—gone to college—and Dad would have had a chance with Mom again. Then I'd have been better off."

Doug's old movie was playing again. The lines were, *if only I'd done this—maybe if I do that—when things are better—then she'll take me back*; only now the words were coming from Doug's son, Cobus. Cobus played his father's part perfectly, but for the first time I refused to stick to the script. I did not sit quietly in the audience while the show ran to the end of the reel. The pent-up years of standing by while the grownups in Cobus's world avoided telling the boy what he needed to hear bubbled to the surface in me as Cobus munched Oreos. They wanted to protect against losing him and it was happening anyway. They'd tiptoed around him most of his life while he raised himself. In Bonnet, you could get away with that because the town was good enough for a boy to turn out okay by raising himself—as long as real life stayed out of the way.

I stood, frustrated, and paced the room. My voice was louder than I expected when I heard it; it surprised both of us. "Cobus," I said, "they were never going to get back together."

"You don't know that, Uncle Robbie. You don't know what might have happened and I don't have a clue what might have happened. I don't even know what's going to happen five minutes from now with this fucking nightmare."

Cobus shoved the table away with enough force to topple his glass and spill what was left of his milk across the table. I grabbed the glass with one hand to stop it before it crashed to the floor and then spun and reached for Cobus with the other. I caught only a piece of his shirt, but he turned and pulled away from me hard.

"Aw, Cobus, come on. Sit back down."

It was too late for that, of course. I didn't care that I'd have to clean up the milk—although it had begun to seep into the crack between the leaves of the table. I wanted him to stay longer.

He sputtered, "I'm going to bed," and bounced off the wall a couple of times as he stumbled down the hall toward his bedroom. He was more frustrated than he was angry. I was the same way.

"Okay, go to bed," I shouted after him as I grabbed a kitchen towel to mop up the mess. "But I'm fixing a huge breakfast in the morning."

"I'm not hungry," were his last words as he shut his door.

I let him go. Even I, who could never let go of anything until I had beaten it unrecognizable, knew enough to let it go until breakfast.

In four hours, we'd lost a game to a team our JV squad could have handled on most nights; I'd lost four of my old friends to chronic idiocy; my sister and once and maybe future brother-in-law lost each other; and Cobus lost his cool and his milk and cookies.

Kjirsten became the only reason the day wasn't a total loss. I was so keyed up that not even cleaning the kitchen could calm me down enough to think about sleep. I walked across town to her house not believing she'd still be awake at midnight, but hoping she was.

I saw the soft, gray-blue light of a television filling the window of her front room. The glow was an invitation to knock as far as I was concerned. I didn't have to say anything. She could tell by the sheepish roll of my eyes that my evening had gone straight to hell since I'd kissed her goodnight after the game.

"Aw, baby," she said simply, quietly, lovingly.

She was in her pajamas and we stood on the porch and she held me and then kissed me and said to come in. I spent the night in her arms and that was what I needed.

CHAPTER EIGHTEEN

W E WERE LUCKY TO have Vernon Wieselmeyer as our high
school principal. He'd retired once and moved to lakefront
serenity on Lake Johnson with his own dock thirty minutes from
Bonnet. His fishing-boat community was on its second generation
of fixed income thumb-twiddlers. The World War II veterans had
been passing away in earnest for some years and the new crop was
made up of teachers and state employees who'd accepted early
retirement to make room for the hoards of baby-boomers' babies
the state schools were graduating.

Wesley Pilgrim had been our principal for two years and
never liked it. His was a classic case of a good basketball coach
being promoted into administration and then suffocating under
stacks of paperwork, school board politics, and parents who
knew how to do his job better than he did. Sometime in October
of Wesley's third year, he ran into Vernon at a ball game and their
conspiring commenced. Wesley talked the board into a leave of
absence while Vernon was to fill in for him for only one year.
After five years, Wesley was back to coaching and Vernon was
still filling in.

Our 223 student population was a step down in size from the
Dallas suburb magnet school that Vernon built from scratch and

grew to three thousand in the fifteen years he was principal. He was famous. At least he was famous in high school administration circles. And now he loved to keep the day-to-day machinery oiled in the halls of Bonnet High.

Vernon made it look so easy—fielding the unreasonable insanity that besieged him daily. Wesley had never learned to handle it well, but Vernon had done it for so long that it was second nature to him. He'd seen it all and dealt with it. On Monday morning when I checked in at the mailboxes in the faculty lounge, Baron Richards had Vernon sitting captive at the table next to the coffee machine. Richards had invaded the sanctity of my teachers' lounge! He had the same stern wrinkles etched into his forehead as always while Vernon smiled patiently with frequent understanding nods.

"Please understand, Principal Wieselmeyer, that my—our— concerns are not about football, *per se*. I know that a man in your position has to be principally concerned about academics— reading and math and the like." Richards spoke under his breath, afraid that even the most innocent of conversations might somehow be overheard.

What was he afraid of? I guessed the more paranoid practitioners of the faith needed to be ever vigilant. There may by transgressors lurking around every corner—like me.

"You might be surprised," said Vernon kindly. "Football, basketball, or the junior class play, —you name it, are very important to these kids."

A less confident principal might have insisted that they move to his office so closed doors could guard his words. I'm sure Richards would have liked that; it might have added an artificial air of importance to his pleadings, but Vernon sat comfortably sipping coffee and nodding greetings to the string of sleepy-eyed Monday morning teachers as they shuffled in and out of the lounge. I loitered at the mailboxes, the coffee machine, the copy machine, and then finally sat down at the computer to feign an actual teacher task. I was going to hear every word regardless of how low Baron Richards lowered his voice.

"Yes, yes," Richards said solemnly, "and I would think character development must be top priority in every discipline."

Vernon continued his train of speech which was aligned enough with Richards's to make it seem as if they were in the same conversation when, if you listened carefully, they weren't.

"To say nothing of the community. These activities that the kids do after the bell rings are memories that linger long after the grades on the card are forgotten." Often when Vernon made such declarations, he looked as if he'd surprised himself with his own revelation. He hadn't, of course; after years of practice, his coy facial language was a disarming technique that had become instinctively integral to his bag of diplomatic tricks.

Richards curled his brow furrows deeper as if trying to signal the self-proclaimed importance of his proclamations. "All of our children's role models should be above reproach—giving not even a hint of impropriety." Richards never looked surprised at anything that emanated from his own mouth. He believed he channeled a higher wisdom and therefore assumed that all he spoke was anointed with a certain brilliance.

Covering all the bases, Vernon said, "Of course, the push is always for better test scores. But football—Texas schoolboy football—what could build character better than that?"

"Ah," said Richards, perhaps sensing a move toward common ground, "but if the mentor exhibits less than good character, the boys may be led in wrong directions."

Vernon raised a thoughtful finger to his cheek and added, "I'll venture to say there are more senators and congressmen, lawyers and doctors, and leaders of the community who have come through the ranks of Texas football than there are those who solely buried their noses in their books for four years."

"But their mentors… What about their mentors?" When Richards's voice grew louder, it raised in pitch as well.

"The girls, too, you know," Vernon added, passing on Richards's question, "you'll find the women who rise to the pinnacles have most often excelled at sports in school."

"No doubt, Principal Wieselmeyer," Richards said tensely— face flushing, "girls' sports have given them more things to do. I'm sure they need their outlets. But I'd like to talk about Coach Hutcheson."

"Good man," said Vernon resolutely, at last looking Richards squarely in the eye. "Lucky to have him. Good coach. Good man. What about him?"

"His character," whisper-hissed Baron Richards through clenched teeth. "We are concerned about his character."

By this time, when Doug and I had been in a similarly ireful conversation with Richards, we had been close to manslaughter and Tildy had rescued us with a seven-iron and a lamp. Vernon's pulse did not appear to have elevated a beat.

"Well, I don't know who *we* are," he said in his best grandfatherly voice, "but if I were you I wouldn't be too worried. Coach and the boys will win a few more games before the year is out. I'm always impressed at how a coach's character improves with the winning of a few games—just as I'm amazed at how his character becomes blurred when the score runs against him."

Richards tried to speak affirmably. "I never meant to hint that I was caring only about the win-loss record. I care about appearances, propriety, and—well—Christianity. I care about those boys."

"As do we all, Mr. Richards," responded Vernon, agreeing completely for the first and only time, "as do we all." The principal rose, offering his hand to Richards, who took it weakly and obligingly as Vernon brought the talk to a close. "I need to get the school day going now, but I'll visit with the coach and suggest that he telephone you to discuss your issues. Are you parked in front? Come, I'll walk you out."

I managed a look up from the computer as they left the room with the principal's hand on Richards's shoulder—guiding—

almost pushing him out the door. I'd swear that Vernon glanced my way and winked. He'd deny it, but I'd swear to it.

I'd gone to Hutch's practices the week before to show support and I wasn't about to stop. Those practices had been robotically boring—methodical to a fault. After the loss to Aromas, Monday and Tuesday practices degenerated into chaos. Everything Hutch tried backfired.

Tommy and Michael were late—for valid reasons, I'm sure—so Derek Richards and his cohort Jacob Swindel filled in for them to lead the stretching. It was not what the team needed after the previous Friday's embarrassment. There are few things as pathetic as a pretender stealing the mantle of leadership when no one is willing to follow.

Freshman harassment, by tradition, is rough in the first couple of weeks of practice in August, but that winds down quickly as the squads are broken into their season's groupings. By October, stretching at the beginning of practice and windsprints at the end remain the only activities that the freshman, JV, and varsity squads perform as one large group. Even a school the size of Bonnet High suits enough boys to man three squads. Some of the JV boys dress with the varsity for the games but rarely does a freshman. After two-a-day practices are finished, the frosh are invisible to the upper classmen and glad of it.

Every new leader needs to make a statement. As self-appointed team leader for the day, Baron Richards's boy Derek made his statement by picking on the freshmen for no apparent reason. They certainly had nothing to do with the loss on Friday.

"It's high time this team started putting out," shouted Derek. "Helmets on today. Helmets on!"

"Mushman. Put your helmet on!" Derek Richards was more than loud; he was angry loud. "You hear me Mush Man?!!"

Maschmann was the boy's name, not Mushman or Mush Man. He was a good kid—a second-string freshman, short on talent, but long on heart and pretty tough, considering his lack of physical gifts.

"Yes, sir!" Maschmann answered sharply, if not spitefully.

The others, including more than a few upperclassmen who were stretching with helmets off, grudgingly pulled them on—most after rolling their eyes or casting sidelong glances at each other as if to say, *gimme a break.*

Derek Richards was just getting started. He opened calisthenics with windsprints. Windsprints were for the end of practice—at least they were for every team I'd ever played on. The coaches were huddled at the other end of the field going over the day's schedule and Derek was trying to run windsprints. He began bellowing those unintelligible jungle-like sounds that football players regurgitate periodically to get themselves psyched up for the mayhem they are about to inflict. Derek's problem was that no one bellowed back. Some echoed with whimpers—but not bellows.

"Are we going to get better?" Derek screamed with spittle spraying from his mouth like the spray nozzle of a hose spewing more stale air than water.

"Yeah!" Some answered loudly enough to be heard. Most merely mouthed their response. The freshmen were thoroughly pissed off at him and said nothing.

"I can't hear you!" he screamed, as he started another sprint across the field. If he weren't so pitiable, I would have been laughing out loud. He was quite a picture trying to lead sprints with his duck-toed size thirteen shoes flapping on the grass. The rest of the boys let him lead, which meant that the sprints weren't fast enough for most of them to break into a pant—let alone a sweat.

"Yeah!" His cronies—all two of them—responded more loudly than they had the first time, but the rest barely mumbled. The frosh remained pissed and mute.

"Mushman, I can't hear you or any of your frosh pukes."

That was all Maschmann could take. "Hey, fuck you," he shouted, not using much sense considering that the total weight advantage the seniors held over the freshmen was measured in thousands of pounds. Then he added the spark that incited the chase. "At least we won our game last week."

Derek and six seniors began running after the freshmen, who exhibited enough good sense to run in the direction of the coaches. The coaches sprinted toward the mob from the other end of the field. Jacob Swindel caught up with Maschmann at the same time Hutch met the freshman head on. Hutch grabbed the poor kid around the waist and swung him out of Swindel's reach.

Swindel shouted, "I'll get you, fuckin' punk," apparently oblivious to the fact that Hutch would find that objectionable.

"Hey!" shouted Hutch, holding the freshman boy like a sack of flour with one hand while he attempted to hold back Swindel with the other. "What's going on?!!"

The rest of the pack skidded to a halt when they realized the coaches had stepped between the factions.

"Nothing, Coach. Sorry," said Jacob Swindel through clenched teeth, still glaring at the freshman.

"Sorry is right," said Hutch.

Hutch knew better than to react spontaneously, so, for the time being, he was content to break up the mess and put the boys to work. He loudly commanded the entire group—all three teams. "Freshmen, you get down here with your coaches and the rest of you back to the other end of the field with me." A couple of the boys hesitated, and Hutch added, "Now!" as forcefully as he ever addressed the team.

Most of them sprinted to their places but Coach stopped Swindel and Richards in their tracks. "You two stay here," he growled.

Up to that point everything had been loud enough for me to hear from my front row seat in the bleachers, but I couldn't make out what Hutch said to those two. Later he told me he tried to pump them up by telling them how important they were to the team. I would have been kicking their butts, but he tried to use it as an opportunity for team building. He also promised them that if he heard of them even looking cross-eyed at any of the freshmen—especially Maschmann—they would sit out the next game, but mostly he said he pumped them up.

Hutch's best efforts aside, all that adrenaline rushing through the boys ruined the rest of practice. Nothing went right. Backs ran the wrong way, guards and tackles blocked the wrong defenders, and there were five or six offsides violations. The only time any passes were caught was when a defender tripped over a painted yardage line and fell down. The worse it went, the louder and more incoherent the assistant coaches became. Bret Ashworth, who was working with the varsity defensive backs, gave up entirely. He took a play out of Derek Richards's book and started his group running sprints in the middle of practice. He didn't ask Hutch; he took his group of eight boys, marched them to the sideline and started them running. With that, Hutch's practice schedule was jumbled beyond recognition.

Hutch stood with hands on his hips and watched while his assistant went off on his tangent. Hutch improvised well because his character would never have allowed him to show up a subordinate in front of the boys. He made it look like it was all planned—moving smoothly into the next set of drills that didn't require the presence of defensive backs—but I knew he was frustrated. Hell, they all were—we all were.

Our mistake had been living out the future before reality rewrote the dream. Now it had crumbled and the hopes of a championship seemed dashed, so we took it out on ourselves. I fought to remind myself that there were more important things transpiring than the football season. I worked hard to stay angry at the rest of the town, stubbornly refusing to let their irrationality invade mine. I did that so I wouldn't think about what might have been if Hutch and Sally had only waited.

Watching a football practice in shambles did not make it easy
not to think that.

The next day was no better. The first northern front of the fall
blew through Monday night and it rained cold all day Tuesday.
Later in the fall after a few more rains and gray windy days, the
boys would get used to it—even look forward to working hard
in the crisp air as long as it was dry—but Tuesday was the first
cold rain. The boys moved slow and klutzy in the mud. Derek
Richards didn't look so out of place when they all slopped in the
water, fumbling and falling down.

To make matters worse, if that was possible, Derek's old man
picked Tuesday to make one of his hovering visits to the practice
field with his minions. I sat huddled in my rain suit with bucket
hat pulled down low, hoping the rain would run off the brim
and down my back instead of down my neck. It sorta worked
some of the time. I was as wet and miserable as the team and
coaches.

Baron Richards and two other men stood stoically in long,
retro rain slickers—the kind Old West lawmen wore when they
marched down the street three abreast to roust the stranger in
town. They wore Stetsons and stood in the mist at the end of the
field—apparitions in the rain, looking immune to the cold—
condensation from their breaths swirling around their heads.

Finally Hutch put an end to the charade that passed for
practice and he sent the boys to the showers half an hour early.
The three ghosts of the James Gang climbed into their pickups
and drove away as the team filed lethargically from the swampy
field toward the lockers. Thank God that was over. I was shivering
so hard that water sprayed off my rain jacket like a wet dog shake-
drying his coat after a swim in the Pedernales.

Hutch watched the boys and his assistants leave the field; he
stood alone for a moment staring blankly after the last of them.
After a frozen eternity, he suddenly appeared to find an infusion
of strength. He stood straighter than he had all afternoon. It
wasn't that I'd noticed him slouching or thought that he was

lacking energy, but all at once he was walking toward me with a purpose in his step that I realized I hadn't seen in weeks.

I stiffly rose from bleachers to greet the coach. I figured Hutch was going to ask me to his place for a beer. I was hoping he wouldn't ask me to Al's place; I wasn't ready to go back yet. He did neither. He splashed his way up to me then stopped in a puddle in front of where I was extricating myself from my crouch and said, "That's it." Then he strode briskly away with a wake following him in the rising waters on the field.

"That's it?" What the hell did he mean by, "That's it"? I didn't get a chance to ask. By the time I could draw a breath, Hutch was already out of sight. That was all I would find out on Tuesday. I couldn't go to Kjirsten's and I couldn't go to Sally's. Kjirsten had taken Sally to Austin for the evening. Doug had left Sunday for Oklahoma to golf with old friends. I was left alone to toss and turn all night wondering what *it* was.

I wondered until practice the next day. I arrived as stretching was supposed to be happening, but wasn't. The boys sat on the field in small groups—not organized. One or two of the freshmen made a pretense of stretching but, even with all that had occurred, the younger boys still took their cues from the older ones—who were doing nothing. They only gear they had with them was their helmets—no pads. It wasn't as cold as it had been on Tuesday and it was dry; they wore sweatshirts.

There were no coaches in sight and by then it was ten minutes later than time to start practice. I stood from the bleachers and walked onto the field.

I overheard Jacob Swindel laughingly say, "Maybe he's going to tell us he's quitting."

Derek and his two pals sat with their back to me; they didn't notice me strolling through their disorderly midst; they couldn't hear me and didn't know I could hear them.

"You think?" asked Derek's normally silent sidekick, Mason Brett. Brett played on defense and was a good enough kid— average in school but he excelled at following. It was too bad he hadn't started following a more positive image when he was younger. Now he had absorbed too much of the mindset of Derek and Jacob to exhibit a mind of his own.

"Wouldn't you like to see that?" snickered Derek.

I knelt quietly beside Derek and asked, "See what?"

Without missing a beat or even so much as feigning surprise, he said, "Oh. Hi, Mr. McCheyne. We were wondering what Coach is going to say to us."

"Say?"

"Yeah," he said, making no eye contact with me. "The coach told us to come out without pads and he said he wanted to talk to us."

"Did he say what he wanted to talk about?"

I was worried and hoped it wasn't noticeable. I had a sick feeling that Jacob's comment was close to the mark.

"No, sir," said Jacob. "He said he'd be out after he spoke with the other coaches."

My sick feeling approached nausea. I stood without saying anything more and started toward the gym where I was going to prevent my friend Hutch making the second biggest mistake of his life. Before I reached the fifty-yard line, all six coaches, led by Hutch, walked out the door.

I met them on the twenty and stood in front of the entire entourage doing my best to posture a stature that said *stop before you do anything stupid.*

What I actually said was, "I was just coming to get you guys. The natives are getting restless." It wasn't the bold confrontation that I'd hoped would come out of my mouth, but it did slow their confident stroll toward the team.

Hutch said, "Hey, Robbie, I'm glad you're here. I want you to hear what I have to say to the team."

He had a wry smile on his face. I had expected extreme sobriety from a man who was about to walk away from his first love—second love counting Sally, but I wasn't counting.

His assistants kept walking and I stood in front of Hutch so he'd have to stop or knock me down. I waited until I was sure they were out of earshot and I whispered to Hutch, "What are you up to?"

He put his arm on my shoulder and his grin widened, "This is it, Robbie."

"Okay, I was up all night wondering what *it* is. What are you up to?"

"I'm taking back control."

I could feel my own brow wrinkling, and I said, "What do you mean by that?"

"Follow me. You won't be disappointed."

With a snap of his head, the smile on his lips reformed into the pursed look of unshakeable determination. He brushed past me with his eyes focused on what he was about to do and I fell in tow like a kid after the Pied Piper.

Hutch walked briskly to the front of his audience. He was tall with the posture of a battlefield general. Even when not at his best, he commanded a presence; Wednesday he was in top form.

"Gentlemen," he began, "things are going to change."

Here it came. I held my breath waiting for the hammer to drop.

"You are going to change, all of the coaches you see here are going to change, and I am going to change."

I knew it. He was going to change himself out for one of his assistants.

"What does that mean, Coach?" asked Tommy Jarvis. They, too, believed he was about to resign.

"I mean things—in this case, a team—our team—cannot stay the same. They never can. They either get worse or they get better, but they cannot stay the same." He paused and looked them over to make sure he was connecting.

And he went on, "It doesn't take much smarts, boys, to understand that since the very first game we played, things have gotten worse every week."

"I wonder why that is?" grumbled Derek under his breath. I barely heard him, but he was audible and Hutch heard, too.

"I will tell you why, Mr. Richards," barked Hutch with the viciousness of an angry drill sergeant and a white-hot stare. "Because every single one of us gave up on what we set out to accomplish on the first hot day of practice last August. The first time something went just a little bit wrong—was different than we had envisioned—you—me—we invented ways to self-destruct. We did it to ourselves. I contributed to the destruction; the coaches standing here contributed, and each and every one of you have contributed. The saddest part is the entire town, even your parents, gave up on you. And we allowed it to happen."

At the mention of parents the last of the boys who were staring at the ground looked up.

"I'm not blaming your parents," he said. "It's not their team. It's not their family."

"Family?" asked Michael.

"That's right, Michael, we're a family. Like all families, we see the best and the worst of each other. Sometimes we cause the best and the worst in each other, but through it all we stay loyal. That's what good families do. And today the bickering is going to stop. We're done feeling sorry for ourselves and we're going to lock the door and solve our own problems. Your girlfriend can't help. Your grandmother can't make it better. Nobody's gonna fix what's broken here but us—not your teachers, not Mr. McCheyne standing there, not even your parents." Then after a moment of reflection he added, "Especially not your parents."

Hutch paced silently, phrasing first in his mind what he wanted to say before continuing aloud.

"I want each and every one of you to think about why you play football," he said, finally, with the ring of an evangelist beckoning his flock to answer the call. "First, I'm going to tell you why I do this—what this game means to me—then I'm going to put you on the spot. I'm going to ask some of you to stand up and tell us all why you're here. If you can't do that, then maybe you're here for the wrong reasons and maybe you should look for another after-school activity."

He paced while he spoke. "I began playing Pop Warner football when I was seven years old. I was on the field every spring and then August through November for the next twenty years. One day, all the reasons I played the game got jumbled up in my head along with my stubborn pride and I walked away. I stuck football in a closet of my mind and closed a door. When I finally opened it again, I remembered everything I loved about the game and I have not forgotten it since.

"I love the smells of football—the fresh, wet grass for April practices—the medicines in the locker room—alcohol, tape, balm. I even love the smell of your lockers when you leave your jocks there over the weekend." Then he smiled and added, "Although I don't love that as much as the fresh-cut grass in the spring."

I saw grins on the faces of the boys for the first time.

"I love the sounds—the jibes and bad dirty jokes when we hand out uniforms in August. All summer long I can hardly wait to hear those wonderful explosive cracks and pops the first day you put on pads. I love the silence we hear at the end of those hot, hot, two-a-day practices when we're all so tired that all we can do is pant like beat-down old hound dogs."

As he spoke I sensed the energy flowing from Hutch to the boys. Wonderment was beginning to light their faces the way it should have been all season long.

"Tommy," he said suddenly pointing a finger at the quarterback, "what sounds do you like?"

"Me, Coach?" he said, wide-eyed.

"Sure, what are your favorite sounds of football?"

Tommy's old look of impishness returned, and he said, "I like the sound of the cheerleaders shaking their pom-poms."

Now they were laughing.

Then Martinez leaned in and said into Tommy's ear, loudly enough for all of us to hear, "What do pom-poms *smell* like, amigo?"

Over their catcalls and jeers Hutch tried his best to act serious and said, "All right, all right. Let's keep it clean."

I turned away in case there was a smirk on my face they shouldn't see.

"Derek," said Hutch, looking at the one boy who was trying his best not to enjoy the moment, "what's your favorite sound?"

That stopped the laughter. Then the only sound, for what seemed forever, was dead quiet. Derek had been spouting negative rhetoric for a long time and Coach was asking him to be a leader in the most positive moment the boys had enjoyed for weeks. Derek said nothing for a full minute and Coach let the seconds tick away. I was afraid all of the good that had just taken place was about to be lost.

Then Derek said very quietly but with full-on eye contact with his coach, "I like the sound of the yellin' and the screamin'."

Coach returned the stare and allowed another ten seconds of breathless silence to pass before, with chest puffed out and hands on hips, he shouted at Derek like a drill sergeant again, "I can't heeear you!"

Then he beamed a broad toothy grin.

The laughter returned spontaneously and Derek jumped to his feet and shouted as loudly as he could, "I love the yellin' and the screamin'. I like to say oooohrah and… and… oooohrah."

More laughing.

"Hey," shouted Scotty Campbell, Hutch's assistant, "I like that too. Oooohrah." He shouted it with a wave of his fist and all the boys echoed, "Oooohrah."

Hutch chuckled because now he was hearing the sounds he'd been longing to hear for weeks. They shouted two more times before Hutch motioned for them to quiet down.

"Ahhh…that is music to my ears," he said. "There are so many things I like about this game and I could go on forever, but more than anything else I love the camaraderie. That's why I put up with the physical pain of practice when I played and that's why I can handle the bad days I have as your coach."

He looked around to ask another boy to speak up and strangely enough none lowered their eyes the way they would in class if a teacher was looking for an involuntary volunteer.

"Jason," he said, singling out the kicker, "what's camaraderie?"

Jason scrunched up his face and made a valiant guess. "Friendship?"

"That's a big part of it, but not all. Soldiers talk about camaraderie after they've been through boot camp or even a battle. Camaraderie is the bond that occurs when a group of men endure a trauma together, and no one else can ever really know what they've gone through.

"We haven't been to war, but a football season might be compared to a battle. It's stressful and painful. It's also exhilarating and more fun than most other things you'll ever do, and no one else can ever really know what it was like to be part of it."

He'd talked for longer than most high school boys would normally endure, but he hadn't lost any of them.

"Just one more thing, gentlemen, and then we'll commence with some more of Derek's yellin' and screamin'. Did you notice that I never once brought up winning and losing? I do not want anyone to go away from here thinking I don't care about winning. I hate to lose." He paused. "I *really* hate to lose, but the one thing I want you to take away from this practice tonight, is that we play football for many other reasons as well. They are sounds and smells and friendships and even pains that will be a part of you the rest of your lives.

"Which brings us back to family. These memories belong to us. All those great folks who come to watch us play have their memories, too, and that's fine, but the memories we make together on this field are ours alone and no one can steal them from us. Let's make them great ones. I'm proud to be your coach and I'm proud to have you as my team."

He turned to his assistants. Hutch, the battlefield general again, commanded his men, "Coaches, put these players through their paces. We have a game to play on Friday, and we are going to look good. Oooohrah!"

We all, even I, shouted *oooohrah*, and then I jogged off the field to resume my rightful place lounging in the bleachers, because, after all, it was not my camaraderie.

CHAPTER NINETEEN

There is no better time or place to watch football than on a chilly October night in south central Texas. On Friday, Michael Martinez was voted homecoming king and Jeannie Gail, our cheerleading captain, was his queen. At halftime, the Junior Class pep squad rolled out a long red carpet that stretched from the end zone to the fifty-yard line. They dragged out the same dilapidated wooden stage every year. White enamel paint held it together. In the crisp air, the sparkle of the lights bouncing off the white platform and the cheesy crown on Michael's head made the coronation look as grand as Charles and Diana's wedding. Kjirsten told me that as she squeezed my hand hard when the royal couple was presented to their court. We're still that corny in Texas.

The Bonnet boys won their homecoming game. They made it look so easy. The Scottville Highlanders were a pretty good team. Certainly they were better than Aromas. How does that happen so often in sports? One week the boys play so poorly that folks in town can't speak to each other without lowering their eyes. The strain of losing is so unbearable that lovers fall out of love and the air itself turns cold at the offense of ugly football. The next Friday night the same boys piece together a mosaic of power and grace that reawakens the intoxicating mania of your unrealistic dreams.

I know I said I was through going to the Al's café after the games—or any time else, for that matter—but this was different. Kjirsten was with me and I wouldn't be obliged to sit at the round table with the old boys. Had she not been with me, I might have gone anyway considering how the easy win made me forget my grudges. The entire cast was there, of course. A casual patron entering Al's café but once every ten years would believe he had stepped through a hole in time to the identical scene of beer guzzling codgers reciting the same Friday night script of a decade before.

"Hey, Robbie," called out Bud Granger with a raised long-neck, "we saved you a place." Then he saw Kjirsten, and added, "Well, lookie here. We saved a place for your little lady, too." He slid over to make enough room to squeeze another chair between Cuthbert and him. He wasn't slurring his words yet, but he wasn't exactly focused either.

Kjirsten clinched my arm with a fingernail squeeze that I knew to mean, *God, please don't make me sit there.* There was no need for the tactile message because I had no intention of exposing her to their particular brand of malt-enhanced chivalry.

"Thanks, Bud," I said as sheepishly as a schoolboy on a first date. Then, "If y'all don't mind—no offense—if it's all the same, I believe we'll take a table by the jukebox," which was a stupid thing to say because the jukebox hadn't worked since "Achy Breaky Heart" was a hit.

"Well, seein' as who yer escortin', I can't hardly say as I blame you."

It didn't really matter where we sat in Al's because no table was entirely out of earshot of another, but if they were counting on me jumping into their conversations, I would disappoint them.

It was the first chance I'd had to talk to Kjirsten about the team's transformation—from Monday and Tuesday's storm and angst, to Wednesday's calm and, finally, Friday's homecoming victory. I scooted into the booth beside her so I could speak quietly with my head turned away from the prattle behind me.

Big Al hollered, "I'll be right there, you two."

After the roller coaster week, it felt good to sit close to Kjirsten and unwind. She leaned forward to see around me and yelled over the din, "Hey, Al, you have any decaf?"

"I'll put it on," he answered as he headed into the kitchen to the brewing machine.

"So, to get them playing better he talked about the sounds and smells of football?" Kjirsten asked quietly with a sprinkle of wonder in her voice.

"Yeah," I said. "At first I thought he'd flipped out, but the boys loved it. It even worked on the assistants. He was able to get them all to remember the good things about the game."

Bud Granger couldn't hear us; he'd been drinking steadily since the end of the game and was either intentionally speaking loudly enough for us to hear him or he was loud on account of the beer.

"I heard he laid into them boys in practice," pronounced Bud haughtily.

"Well it's about time," said Cuthbert. "I'd ha' kicked their butts a whole lot sooner."

Brother Galey eloquently added, "I'd ha' sit thar buts on the bench and played the freshmen; that's whut I'd a done."

My eyes must have been as big as half dollars because Kjirsten saw the look on my face and had to turn away to keep from laughing at what we'd heard. I shook my head with incredulity and said to Kjirsten, "On Monday, Hutch had every reason to lose his cool and make examples out of a couple of jackasses who deserved it, and he didn't. Maybe he held his tongue because he felt like some of the trouble was of his own making, but he did not *lay into them*."

The door banged and I looked up to see Doug enter the café for the first Friday night since Cobus left the team. He slowed his stride long enough to scan the room to find the most neutral place to sit.

Cuthbert saw Doug when I did, and he slid the same chair back they'd offered to me. I quickly called out, "Hey, Doug, over here," to lure him away.

"Hey, Doug, you drinkin' beer or coffee?" shouted Bud, even more loudly than I had done.

"Huh?" Doug was perplexed that Bud would consider anything but beer.

"Beer or coffee? They're drinking coffee at that table. Don't seem right, does it? Coffee, on a Friday night." As if on cue, Big Al came out of the kitchen with two cups and the pot of decaf.

Doug said, "That looks good, Al. Bring me a cup will you?" And he made a beeline to our table with no more of an acknowledgment to Bud and the Alden brothers than a cowboy nod.

We were both glad to see him. He'd been in Oklahoma earlier in the week and our paths hadn't crossed since he'd returned. Kjirsten didn't know Doug well and she'd asked me a number of times to set up something so we could all get together. She said she had friends in Austin she wanted him to meet. Each time she'd mentioned that, a tug at my heart told me I wasn't as used to the idea of him being with someone else as my head was. I know it wasn't logical to be excited for Sally and Hutch while, at the same time, feeling a mystery twinge of sadness at the thought of Doug moving on with his life. I harbored more of the same irrationality that was tearing Cobus apart than I wanted to admit.

"Howdy, roommate," I said, standing and offering my hand. He shook it strongly, like always, but his smile was aimed at Kjirsten.

"Kjirsten," he asked, "would you mind if a weary bag of bones joined you for a cup of coffee?"

"I'd be honored," she replied kindly.

He looked worn out.

I asked, "How come you're so tired?"

He grinned and said, "Well, I walked thirty-six today and then raced back here in time to see the game."

He was still wearing his wind shirt and Texas Longhorns ball cap.

"Oh, good, you saw the game then," I said. He had not sat in the bleachers with me for three games.

"Yeah. It was good to see the boys having fun again."

Kjirsten asked, "Did you get anything to eat?"

Big Al was attempting to pour our three cups of coffee without spilling a fourth on the table. He asked, "You want me to fix you a steak?"

"Nah, I ate hot dogs—three snack bar hot dogs at the game."

"Mmmmm," Kjirsten said.

"Humph," snorted Al. "I guess I cain't be too hurt, seein' as how you ain't 'et in here fer a month of Sundays." He snickered the high-pitched Al laugh and patted Doug on the back to let him know he was glad to see him. Al made his way back to the round table to collect the empties in preparation for their next round.

"How was the golf?" I asked.

"Shit."

"Shit? What do you mean, shit?"

Kjirsten said, "Tsk, tsk, boys. Such talk."

"Oops. Sorry, Miss Kjirsten," said Doug sincerely. "I meant to say it was a long day on the golf course."

I said, "What'd you do? Shoot even par instead of sixty-eight?"

"Eighty."

"Yeah, right."

"Yup. Seventy-five this morning and an even eighty blows after lunch."

"What'd you do, play left handed?" I still thought he was pullin' my leg.

"I might as well have. I couldn't putt worth a damn."

"Oh well, that'll pass. You're a great putter."

"I had four three-putts and a four-putt in the afternoon round. That's not so great."

I said, "Ouch."

Kjirsten said, "Shit."

Doug and I said, "Kjirsten!" at the same time.

"Oops," she said with that same playful sparkle in her eyes that made me fall in love with her in the first place.

"I don't know what was wrong," sighed Doug, trying to rub the fatigue from his brow. "I'm tired, I guess. I played five days straight in the wet and cold. I hadn't seen those guys in a while and we felt obligated to get all we could out of the occasion. You can't shoot good scores in those conditions—nobody can. I got too used to playing bad golf but the beer and old friends made it all worthwhile."

It was good to see him uncovering a semblance of life outside of Bonnet. His rendezvous in the rain had been with three teammates from his all too brief stint at the University. I was surprised they'd kept in touch all that time. I hadn't known. That was the pull he had on people. Even through his blue years, when he'd said mostly nothing to all of us, we still coveted his companionship. His aura of greatness found a way to shine through no matter what he did to dim it. We liked to be near him.

Kjirsten reached across the table and sympathetically took Doug's hands from where he was warming them on his cup and she said, "Sleep in tomorrow, lounge around in the morning, and you'll be back in top form before lunch."

"Sleep in?" he snickered. "That'll be the day. I've missed five days of practice with Tildy. I'm sure she's fit to be tied. We'll be at the range before eight."

"Well, then, after you're done with Tildy and the gals, it wouldn't hurt you to take the rest of the day off. In fact, I think you should take the whole weekend off and read a good book."

"You know, Kjirsten," said my best friend with an air of resignation, "that's the best idea I've heard all week."

That made her feel good and she sat back smugly folding her hands around her own coffee cup—content that she'd solved all his troubles. I knew he'd never take the weekend off from golf. His date with the rest of his life—the qualifying tournament for the tour—loomed ever closer and I knew he was feeling the time slip away from him. He was pressing too hard. The weary lines on his face told me that but he was not going to take the weekend off.

I was aware of hovering. I looked up to see Bud Granger standing over us—swaying slightly—staring at Doug as if working up the courage to say something he knew he shouldn't. If Bud was weighing the prudence of uttering his usual claptrap, then it was a good bet he should keep his mouth shut. He turned around and I thought he was leaving without a word; instead, he reached for a chair. He pulled it to the end of our table, turning it backwards so he could straddle it and lean on the back.

I rolled my eyes; Kjirsten was gracious and Doug laughed. "Well, hello, Bud. Have a seat, why don't you?"

Bud had the closest thing to a serious look on his face he could muster. He looked like a cross between W. C. Fields and Emmett Kelly. He said, "Doug, you know I hain't give up on the boys making the playoffs."

"Oh, you haven't, have you?" Doug winked at Kjirsten and sipped his coffee.

Bud continued with his vision. "I know there ain't many who think that, seein' as how we've lost two, Beaucoup's lost one and Bee Tree not none."

"To say nothing of the fact that we have both of them left to play plus Tickle Creek," I said with a skeptical squint. Kjirsten pinched my arm to get me to shut up. She was having too much fun.

"I know all that," Bud said. Then he lowered his voice and leaned in a little. "But if Cobus comes back now, we can whip both them teams. Beaucoup could beat Bee Tree, and Tickle Creek ain't nothin'."

It made a semblance of mathematical sense. In Bud Granger's scenario, Bee Tree, Beaucoup, and Bonnet would each have two losses. If we'd beat them both, it would be us who would face Laurel Mountain in regionals. In the real world, it had become too far-fetched for any rational-thinking Bonnet fan to think that way. They may have played okay that night, but a week before, the boys had been the sorriest-looking team you'd ever want to see. And what the hell did he mean, *if Cobus comes back now.*

Doug put his coffee cup down real slow. He was the one who lowered his voice now and turned his eyes to pierce Bud's glassy gaze. "Has my boy told you he's aimin' to play any football?"

Kjirsten squeezed the blood out of my arm. She was no longer having fun.

"Nn…not exactly," stammered Bud. "I figured—"

"You figured what?" growled Doug.

Surely even Bud had enough sense to stop before he ruined a perfectly fine evening.

"Doug, I mean… I figured he'd come back out since that coach stopped runnin' around with yer ex."

Okay, so he didn't have any sense.

Doug didn't say a word. His look brought our conversation to a screeching halt. He'd been ready to snap back when he thought our tipsy friend was spreading foolish rumors about Cobus, but now he had no response. He slumped. He looked so tired that I wanted to cry for him. He turned to Kjirsten, smiled meekly and said, "You know, Miss Kjirsten, if you don't mind, I'm going to call it a day."

Kjirsten replied so warmly to Doug that, had I not already suffered an emotional meltdown, I might have been jealous. "I think we should take you home and tuck you in," she whispered.

Doug had barely enough energy for a resigned chuckle as he stood. "Now there's an offer I haven't had lately, but I'd best take this walk alone."

A specter of an image that I knew all too well hung on his face. I had hoped I'd never see that sadness again and now I hoped it was only the temporary flag of exhaustion. He left the café to a chorus of, "Take 'er easy, Doug," from the boys at the round table. He tossed a barely perceptible gesture of good-bye and left.

Bud, still sitting at our table caressing his now empty bottle, was deliriously oblivious to the fact that he'd had anything to do with the diminished numbers in our booth. He scrunched up his face in bewilderment and asked, "Did Doug look tired to you?"

I was through being pissed at these guys. I retreated to the comfort of sarcasm. It was for my comfort only because it was surely lost on Bud. "Naw, Bud," I said with clenched jaw. "I think you perked him up. I bet he's all excited about Cobus playin' again."

Kjirsten was the rudder that kept me from sailing too far off the deep end. "Oh, Bud, don't pay any attention to him," she said, cocking a patronizing thumb toward me. "He's too close to the boy. Who knows what a teenager's going to do next? One thing's for sure, if he catches wind that we want him to come back and play, he'll run the other way."

"Ya' think so?" asked Bud, helpless against her. Feminine charm flowing Bud's direction was rare enough that he was overwhelmed.

"Oh sure," she said, donning her schoolteacher persona. "You know how kids are, so you better stop spreadin' rumors that might stir things up."

Bud sat back and, for once, laughed at himself. He said, "Well, Miss Kjirsten, I wouldn't worry too much about my ramblin'. Don't you know that no one listens to ol' Bud?"

With that, he showed more clarity than I thought possible. I was so shocked that I offered my own self-deprecation. "You know, Bud, I guess we're all smitten by the sound of our own voices."

Kjirsten rescued us from our pointless digressions. "Okay, you two, as brilliant as all this talk is, Doug had the best idea of all."

"What's that?" I asked, not recalling that Doug had shared a positive thought.

"It's time to go home."

Relieved, I sighed and said, "Oh, that idea. Finally, one of us makes good sense."

Bud decided he needed another beer and he graciously bade us goodnight and then returned to Galey and brother Cuthbert who were both fidgeting at being left alone with Big Al. Al was machine-gunning them with one-liners and jokes they didn't get. He was enjoying himself, though, and laughed enough for the three of them. Still, they were glad to have Bud back. They weren't comfortable sitting at the round table without him. It upset the delicate balance of their universe.

Kjirsten planned to leave early on Saturday to drive to Houston to visit her parents for the weekend. I dropped her off with a quick kiss goodnight and the promise of a real date the following weekend.

Doug left only ten minutes before we did. Nevertheless, I was surprised to find him awake when I got home. He was sitting in the front room reading under the new lamp.

I said, "Hey, pard. I thought you were tired."

"I am. I thought reading Stephen King would calm my nerves. It's no good. My eyes are so sore that the pages are a blur."

"Your nerves? What's wrong with your nerves?"

"I'm too goddamned old."

"After the week you've had, you probably feel like you're sixty."

Doug closed the book without ever turning a page and spoke with his eyes closed. "Eighty," he said. "I feel like I'm eighty."

"A good night's sleep will knock off forty years."

"Yeah, well, I'll still be twenty years too old."

"All right, old man. What are you blabbering about?"

"Charlie Wyvern's son played with us last weekend. He's a year younger than Cobus."

"I remember Charlie. He was a hell of a golfer."

"He still is. He played on the tour a couple years. Now he's head pro at a club."

"What'd he do? Beat you?"

"No. Not Charlie. Charlie junior. Charlie's seventeen-year-old boy."

"Uh-oh."

Doug opened one eye, squinting a feeble grin at me while he spoke.

"That skinny, flat-bellied kid hit it thirty yards past me and he hasn't even grown into his strength yet."

There was no reasoning with him. All the speeches I could have made—the same ones I'd heard him recite so many times—would have fallen on deaf ears. He loved to preach about the importance of the short game. For hours, he could stand under the two-hundred-year-old oak on his range and hit thousands of shots that were under a hundred yards—high, low, soft, driving—with every club in his bag. He knew how much more important that was than launching three-hundred-yard drives. Yet here he was feeling sorry for himself because a spindly-armed, freewheeling kid could hit it further than he could.

I said, "Aw, pard, I know you had a rough week. So what if he hit it further than you a few times?"

"Did I mention he putted like a magician?"

I was groping for anything to clear the fog of hopelessness that now obscured him.

"Doug, I keep telling you that you'll feel much better about this in the morning. It was the kid's home course. It was cold and rainy and you had an off couple of days. That's all. I remember a guy a while back who said that with two days' practice he could putt with anybody in the world."

"That was a long while back and a different guy."

"Bullshit. You're the same guy. Same stroke. Same hands."

"I appreciate what you're trying to do for me, buddy, but I gotta tell you it feels like pork chops hanging at the end of my arms instead of hands."

I still had my keys in my hand; without any forethought, I flung them hard at Doug's head. It was a game we played when we were in high school. We'd throw things at each other under the pretense of honing our reflexes. We'd keep it up until one of us missed and got a split lip—usually me. I hadn't tried that stunt in nearly twenty years and now I'd done it instinctively. The instant the key ring left my hand I was shocked at my own impulsiveness, but it wasn't a problem. Doug's hand flicked from the book he was holding as quickly as a frog's tongue, and he snatched the keys out of the air before they had a chance to jingle.

"Aha!" I said. "I never saw a pork chop do that."

Doug took my keys and shoved them in his pocket without so much as a grin. "Well, that just proves my point," he said, as dejectedly as before.

"Huh?"

"Fast twitch."

"Huh?"

"Fast twitch muscles. Us guys with fast twitch muscles can't control them when we get old. They go off like they did just now and I putt like an epileptic. Hogan had fast twitch muscles everywhere from his toes to his teeth and he couldn't putt worth a damn when he got older. Ben Crenshaw's stroke is long, slow, and syrupy. He'll be putting like God when he's ninety."

All I could do was shake my head and snort. "Okay, you have lost it. If you don't git yourself into bed right now, I'll put you there myself."

"That's just like you to think you could take on fast twitch muscles." He slowly peeled himself out of the chair, and added with a groan, "I'd better turn in before you get hurt."

"Smartest thing you've said all night."

As he walked by, he slapped me on the back to appease me. He said, "Don't worry about me. I'm tired. Like you said, I'll feel better in the morning."

"Are you sure?"

"Yeah, I'm sure. You've been telling me to go to bed for an hour. You promised me that sleep would fix everything and I choose to believe you."

I was no longer sure who was trying to convince whom.

"That's right. Everything."

"Good. See ya in the morning."

When he reached his bedroom door he paused and turned back toward me.

"Did Sally and Hutch break up?" he asked.

"It's nothing," I said.

"They still in love?"

"Really, Doug. They're going to be fine." I felt funny talking to him about his ex-wife's new love.

"You didn't answer my question."

"Yes, they love each other. That's not the problem."

"What's that mean?"

I sighed. "That means they're confused about the best way to handle Cobus."

He stood thinking and scratching his cheek. Finally, he said, "I'd better talk to the boy." Then he turned and entered his room closing the door behind him.

My first thought was, *it's about time.* Then I remembered that I'd already tried to talk to Cobus and only made things worse.

What I actually said was, "Hey! What about my keys?"

Silence. Nothing but silence.

CHAPTER TWENTY

T HE TEMPERATURE WAS STILL in the fifties at eight on Saturday morning, but Doug and the gals were already at the range. Inez was bundled in a knitted sweater, scarf and matching beret. I guessed she'd knitted them all herself. Amanda and Tildy wore sweat suit outfits and sneakers but Macey was in the same-style, loose-fitting cotton blouse she always wore. She enjoyed the cool of autumn.

I was the coffee runner. I thawed out a dozen Round Rock donuts while the coffee was brewing and then delivered the treats to them. I hadn't seen them practice in a couple of weeks. I marveled at the progress they'd made since the beginning of their quest. They'd been so ragtag—emotional, argumentative, uncoordinated—now they moved and talked like they belonged on a golf course.

I could tell Doug was pleased. The night before he'd been so down; it was good to see him smiling and relaxed. He moved quietly from protégé to protégé making small adjustments only. Their swings were what they were going to be. He helped Amanda with the way she practiced. She was such a perfectionist that she wanted to keep hitting the same shot until she hit it just right. Doug finally convinced her that golf is about managing mistakes.

It's human nature to want to quit on a good one. Doug made her quit after bad ones. Then he'd let her switch to a different club and try again.

He helped Inez as much as he could with her distances. It was rough for her since she couldn't see a thing. Doug chose the distances and Inez picked clubs.

He said, "Fifty yards," and Inez lowered her head down close to the numbers on the clubs in her bag and fumbled through them until she found the right one.

"Five-iron," whispered Inez.

She swung slowly and deliberately, making a sweet crisp click when she hit the ball. Inez didn't take any turf. She always hit it thin but it would get up in the air enough to go the distance they practiced.

"Exactly," said Doug, as the ball rolled to a stop by the white flag in the middle of the field.

Macey loved to swing hard at the ball whether she hit it well or not. Every fifth attempt or so, she'd hit her three-wood over two hundred yards somewhere onto the makeshift fairway. A good bit of the distance was covered on a roll over the baked range, but she hit it two hundred yards nevertheless. She hit others two hundred yards, too, but they were outside the bounds of what one could reasonably call the fairway.

Tildy made one graceful swing after another. By now we all knew that she had played before—not that she was trying to keep secrets from anyone. Doug didn't say much to her. He didn't have to. She practiced rhythmically and smartly, humming quietly while she worked. She'd stop every now and then to toss Doug a softball question to which she already knew the answer. It was her way of making sure Doug stuck to her vision of the curriculum.

After an hour, we sat at the picnic table drinking coffee. Macey finished the last three donuts thinking no one would notice.

Doug put his cup down, clapped his hands together in front of him, and then with a broad grin, said, "Ladies, we are ready for our first round of golf."

With a quick inhale, Macey exclaimed, "Oh, my. Surely we can't be ready for that."

"Of course, you are," he said. "Did you think we would stay on this pasture forever? I'd have to start charging you greens fees."

With a snort Tildy added, "It's about time. You do remember, ladies, don't you, that we are to play in a tournament in two weeks' time?"

Addled, Inez cried, "A tournament! Mathilda, I can't believe we are going through with this. Those gals at Bee Tree have been playing for years. I thought... I thought..."

Amanda blurted, "Humph! You thought? Surely, you didn't. Surely, if you had thought you would have remembered that not once in thirty years have any of us ever seen Mathilda Hannah back down, change her mind, turn around, or give up, even when it was clearly prudent to do so."

I was instantly curious to learn about their imprudent adventures, but figured I most likely never would—not from Tildy, anyway. Any unplanned outcome, no matter how dire, would undoubtedly be a resounding triumph by her retelling.

Tildy, ignoring them all, never taking her eyes from Doug, excitedly said, "When? Today?"

Macey mumbled, "I can't possibly go today. I have too much to do today—too, too much. Today isn't good."

Seizing the opportunity, Doug said, "Great. That settles it then. Tomorrow it is. Sunday afternoon—Peach Pit, Texas, in the fall. What could be better than that? I will call Squinty and set it up."

"No need," said Tildy, her gaze still affixed on Bonnet's greatest athlete like a schoolgirl with an unquenchable crush.

Three of us at once said, "What?"

"No need," said Tildy, matter-of-factly. "Beaufort, or Squinty, as you call him, knows we're coming. Three o'clock. We will meet you there, Doug."

She had already made arrangements as if she knew in advance that Sunday would be the day. Of course, she did.

Doug laughed out loud. Macey whispered, "Oh, my." Inez sighed, and Amanda grabbed a club and began hitting balls again.

While I cleaned the cups and donut box from the table, I facetiously quipped, "Tomorrow just doesn't work for me. I suppose I could cancel my date, but you might have asked me if tomorrow would be good."

Doug raised an eyebrow and asked me, "Who are you, again?"

The women acted like I wasn't there.

I didn't go along on Sunday afternoon for their first round on a real course. Not because I wasn't invited, that wouldn't have kept me away, but because I spent the day with Kjirsten—canning tomatoes.

So, when Doug strolled in that evening, whistling "Kaw-Liga," sniffing the remaining wafts of boiled juice to find me on hands and knees scrubbing red goo from the floor, stove, and table legs, he said, "Tomatoes?"

"No," I said, without interrupting the rhythm of my flying rag, "I'm cleaning evidence from the scene of a stabbing."

He ignored me—naturally.

"The gals were great," he said. "Couldn't have been better."

That made me smile, but he didn't see it because I didn't look up. There's something about sweating furiously on hands and knees with onlookers bantering casually that makes you redouble your efforts.

Pretending to pant, I asked, "What'd they shoot?"

"Don't know. Didn't keep score. They need to work on their putting. That's our mission this week. It was a lot of fun though. You and Kjirsten will need to come with us next Sunday."

"Maybe—if I get this kitchen cleaned before then. I suppose you want supper."

"Nope. Tildy bought steaks for all of us at Buggy's place."

"Oh?"

With that he said, "See ya' later, pard," and left again for parts unknown.

I remained alone with my rag and the sticky floor.

We had three games left; the next two were on the road and the last at home against Bee Tree. That year, the game at Beaucoup, Texas, was the only one for which we traveled east. The others took us deep into the Hill Country. East of Austin the terrain flattens quickly and gnarled cedar gives way to graceful aromatic pine. It's a relaxing drive with the sun at your back in the fall.

Three of us in our conference were regarded as perennial favorites. Both Bee Tree and Bonnet had been ranked higher than Beaucoup at the beginning of the year, but it didn't much matter. I always felt that sportswriters gathered in a sweaty, smoky room in August throwing dice, darts, or crystal balls against the wall to conger their preseason visions. They were no better as seers than the likes of Bud Granger or the Alden brothers.

Bee Tree, the Rodeo, was a true archrival complete with all the good and bad spawned from such artificial love-hate relationships—mostly hate—which simmer in every Texas town of consequence. We'd played them forty-nine times and our record against them read twenty-one wins, twenty-two losses and six ties. On paper, our history against Beaucoup looked equally contentious with Bonnet holding a slim lead in our series of thirty-six games—seventeen, fifteen and two. With Beaucoup, there wasn't the same fierce rivalry, though. They weren't Hill

Country folk. Bonnet playing Bee Tree was Cain versus Abel; we were cut from the same cloth. The Beaucoup Gauchos might as well have been from France or Spain or wherever they have gauchos.

Rivalry or not, every boy on our team knew the stakes. Practice had been sharp and by Friday an air of quiet excitement burbled around school and town and we knew the boys were ready. Outside forces that had worked so hard to pull them apart had lain dormant for two weeks. Two weeks for a high-schooler is as good as never.

What a great game it was. By late October, good football teams play on instinct. Rough edges, mistakes, blown plays, and needless penalties should be demons long past. There were no ghosts on the field that night. Hitting was hard and loud; reverberations pierced our arthritic battle scars sitting in the stands. We saw long runs, short bursts, bombs, quick outs, hanging punts, field goals, and scoring—lots of scoring. Defenses from both benches punished their opponents, missing no tackles, and still the score rose.

Even our cheerleaders' cheers, for once, matched what actually occurred on the field. The game was so good that nobody in earshot or eyeshot sat, pouted, or whined over the absence of Cobus—not even Doug. He might deny it, but he stood, screaming crazy like the rest of us.

With six minutes left in the game, Bonnet was down by eleven—thirty four to twenty-three. Michael Martinez ran a punt back to the fifty. On third down, after two hard-hitting runs by Roy Calbo pushing the ball to the Beaucoup forty-four, Tommy rolled right while Michael streaked down the left sideline. He cut toward the post and Tommy hung a high spiral on the clear October night sky. The ball, Michael, and Beaucoup defender converged on the same point in space as streaks of light racing to fusion; Michael leapt and time stood still. He climbed the air. The ball froze in his fingers. We blinked and the Beaucoup boy lay spread on the ground grasping at Michael's vaporous trail fading to the end zone.

There's no choice at thirty-four to twenty-nine and five minutes remaining; you gotta go for two. What we had going for us was the fact that we had not been in that position all year, so there'd been nothing to scout. Hutch called an end-around. We'd seen it four or five times but not to the right side—Derek Richards's side.

Tommy sprinted right; Roy trailed ready to take a pitch; Michael crossed under the goalpost ready for a pass; the defense swarmed in front of hard-charging Tommy and he handed the ball to Derek.

Lumbering, plodding Derek, begging for every inch of turf to pass under his feet, saliva flying off his tongue, eyes wide with fear—our eyes, not just his—rolled slow motion like a garbage bag full of arms and legs behind Tater Potachnick, our big tackle, with Calbo shoving his butt from behind, into the wall of reeking muscle burgeoning at the goal line. When the referees peeled the grunting bodies off the massive pile-up, Derek lay squashed at the bottom but the score was thirty-one to thirty-four.

Oh, the jubilation his father must have felt. He squealed so loudly—like screeching old brakes on freight cars. He jumped onto the bleacher seat, shrieking, "I told you so! I told you! That's *my* play! Did you see it? Did you see it?"

Of course, we all cheered, even stomped our feet, but Richards's visceral screams unfairly stole the moment. Instead of his boy's fifteen seconds of fame, it had to be his own. Doug and I sat, as did most in our section, out of embarrassment for the fool—for Bonnet. For a long, long minute after we'd hunkered to make ourselves small so the world wouldn't think we were with him, he carried on, high-fiving, chest bumping, and roaring his signature bellow—the hee-haw of a jackass.

He made it easy to reclaim control of our emotions and succumb to the reality that Bonnet still trailed by three and had to kick the ball away. A great deal of football can transpire in four-and-a-half minutes. We held our seats as Beaucoup powered down the field, grinding away the clock; then we held our breath when Bonnet got it back to march in the opposite direction.

They stopped us. Three plays, no gain, and foundering fourth and ten on our own thirty-five. We accepted it. We'd witnessed a Texas high school classic, and—well, it was over. There were still two minutes, but surely we couldn't win. We could have thrown a Hail Mary; Hutch thought it better to kick one. Mary can be such a tease.

Jason Roberts kicked it high so our boys could run under it. They were down the field in time to circle like wolves around the Beaucoup receiver. Certainly, he should have called for the fair catch. He caught it with no hand raised and inexplicably began running up the field. It was such a bad decision.

There are moments on which you look back and, choosing one, realize all that it changed forever. Maybe you don't see it then. It may not sink in for years. But one day you wake and see with bright clarity the long branch of life that began in that instant.

Regrettably, for him, pitiable Derek Richards had two such moments in the span of half a hotdog. Our boy, Jerry Grune, met the Beaucoup runner with a collision that drew a collective gasp and unanimous pained groan from both sides of the field. Grune and the runner dropped in a dazed heap while the ball continued on, bouncing and careening along the turf until, with a last jagged bound, it stuck itself into Derek's outstretched paws.

He had twenty yards to glory. Victory! A lone defender, a mere dot in the distance, having to reverse his course no less, could not catch even stumble-footed Derek. Could he? Every slogging lope of the Bonnet boy was answered with two magnificent thrusts by the Beaucoup flash, each faster than the last, legs whirring like a pinwheel. What if he did catch him? There was time—lots of time. We had the ball! Let him catch Derek. We would score from there! What a beautifully discordant din we few hundred faithful made embracing our so benevolent gift from temptress fate. Derek was caught, of course; the flash closed on him as if snapped by a bungee. In freeze frame, I thought, *fall down Derek, fall down. You've done it boy; we'll carry on from here. Fall, please fall.* As he felt the first touch of the flash, Derek turned and tossed a lateral to nothing but the blackness of night. He had thrown the ball away.

Two Beaucoup boys fell on the ball, their teammates signaling with raised fists of triumph that the game really was over. Sitting stunned while the stands emptied, I saw Hutch walking with his arm around Derek as the team filed from the field. His own father didn't see the coach trying to console the boy. He had beaten a hasty retreat while Beaucoup was burning the last few seconds off the clock. He was many miles down the road before the team was seated on the bus.

Doug and I followed the bus for a while in silence. The first words he spoke were, "What a well-played game."

I was still stroking my misery, dwelling on the catastrophe, feeling that I never wanted to see another game and Doug, as if he were channeling Tildy, sounded downright cheery.

"I suppose," I muttered.

"You'll feel better by breakfast."

It was sage advice from the former Mr. Gloom.

We passed the bus and easily beat it to Bonnet High School. Most of the boys had their own trucks but a few of the parents were waiting in the parking lot for the team's return. Doug and I went to meet Hutch, planning to lure him to the house for beers.

Dragging their gear, they streamed from the bus in silence. Some spoke in whispers. Most tossed their pads and helmet in the bed of a truck and drove away quietly. A few released their anger when they got alone behind the wheel, stripping rubber from their tires and roaring their pickups down the street. When their taillights faded in the distance, the silence returned.

Other than Hutch, one by one the coaches exited the bus and went their own ways as the boys had done. Doug and I stood for over a minute waiting for Hutch, thinking he was the only one left. Finally, Doug stuck his head in the bus door and called out, "Let's go, Coach. Come on."

I didn't hear Hutch answer. Derek Richards climbed down the bus steps and started toward his pickup. Doug had to step aside to let him pass.

We hadn't known Derek was still there and we hadn't known his father was waiting in the shadows. It was dark and we'd paid no attention to whose trucks were still parked on the street.

Baron Richards stepped coldly into his son's path and said, "Get in my truck."

He startled us all. Derek, briefly frozen by the shot of adrenaline, said only, "I have my own," and resumed walking.

His old man didn't budge. He raised his hand like a cop stopping traffic and, placing it open-palmed firmly in Derek's chest, reiterated, "I said, get in my truck, boy. You are going with me tonight."

Derek backed away. "I need some time, Pop. I was thinkin' we might talk about the game in the morning."

"Oh, no. We are talking tonight," hissed the father. "What in Jesus' name were you thinking?"

The kid knew we were there. His embarrassment must have been suffocating.

"Nothing. I was thinkin' nothin'. Now leave me alone."

"Do you know what your stupid move did to me? How do you think this makes me look?"

The dad made no attempt to lower the volume or tenor of his voice.

Hoping his dad would follow suit, Derek answered in hushed tones, "I didn't know it was about you. Can we please talk later?"

"Whether you like it or not, boy, everything you do is about me. You owe me for every stitch of clothing on your back and every bite of food you eat. Without me, you are nothing."

Derek had no response. Lowering head in shame, he veered his course to walk away from his father. The father, so angry that his short spewing breaths could be heard from where we stood a few yards away, jumped in front of his son and grabbed him by the t-shirt.

With a deeper evil in his voice than even he had snarled before, he said, "You will do as I say!"

Hutch had heard enough. He stepped forward into the aura of a streetlight. "Stop! Mr. Richards, let the boy go tonight. You'll both have cooler heads in the morning."

Richards wrenched the t-shirt into a knot and pulled Derek closer. "You keep your sorry excuse for an opinion to yourself, *Coach*." He dragged out the word with as much viciously mocking sarcasm as he could spit.

With that, Doug glided silently through the shadows toward the man and his son, still locked tightly together by the fistful of shirt.

Derek's head popped up. For the first time, he spoke directly into his father's face, loudly with resolve. "You leave him out of it!" With both hands on his father's shoulders, he tried hard to push away.

Baron Richards howled with fury, "I'll teach you to back-talk me!" Holding the shirt tightly, he raised his left hand to strike the boy across the face.

Then came a snap—a ringing crack that echoed from the trees to the brick gym wall and back again. Doug's right fist had exploded out of the darkness and shattered Baron Richards's nose.

Derek's dad never knew what hit him. The ass fell in a heap like a dumped bucket of cow manure. He moaned weakly.

Derek looked at Doug and then to Hutch who was standing as slack-jawed as I. Cocking his head to the side like a puppy watching a red wriggler, he stared for a long minute at his blood-soaked father squirming on the sidewalk and then walked alone to his truck.

"Let's go Hutch," said Doug, flicking his hand to shake off the sting and blood. "Beer's gettin' cold."

Twenty minutes later, we sat in our living room guzzling beer. If it hadn't been for the sadness I felt for the young man Derek, I would have been giddy. Seeing Doug kayo Richards instantly erased the heartache of the loss to Beaucoup; the heartache I felt for the boy wouldn't go away so easily.

"I hope you didn't hurt your golfin' hand on that son of a bitch," I said.

Doug massaged his knuckles with the cold beer bottle.

"Hell, maybe it will help my putting," he said with a wry smile.

"If I recall," I said, leaning back with my feet on the coffee table, "it was in this room, after your last encounter with that jerk, you said you wouldn't really hit him."

"I changed my mind."

Hutch, feigning seriousness, asked, "What hit?" Splattered across the front of his white coaches' shirt was Richards's blood, so it might have been difficult to deny he'd been there.

"It was nothin', Coach," said Doug without emotion. "One of the boys' old man walked into a tree, that's all."

"Too bad," Hutch said, sorrowfully. Then, after a slurp of beer, "How'd the tree fare?"

CHAPTER TWENTY-ONE

IT WAS TO BE an all-golf weekend. After the ebb and flow of adrenaline the evening before, I wanted nothing but sleep on Saturday morning, but I was awake at six. Kjirsten and I had a date to follow Doug to Bee Tree, where he'd registered to play in a one day tournament. He had also invited Tildy to ride along with him in the cart. Tildy and friends had a tee time to play the Bee Tree course on Sunday afternoon. Their showdown with the Bee Tree ladies was a week away.

Kjirsten packed a cooler with chicken and beer. We planned to follow Doug for nine holes and then head out on our own. Tildy would hang out with Doug all day, acting as his personal cheerleader.

On the drive to Bee Tree, I had the pleasure of reliving the previous night's events. Kjirsten had been in Austin for the evening and knew none of it.

She wasn't in my truck long enough for a peck on the cheek, let alone a kiss on the lips, and she asked, "Well, who won the game?"

"We lost," I answered with a sigh.

"No! How close was it?"

I proceeded to tell her all the excruciating details of the loss. As I rambled, I realized how far I had already distanced myself from the game. I felt as though I were retelling folklore.

"That's terrible. Aren't you devastated?" she asked.

"I was. I thought I'd been kicked in the head."

"Your head still looks cute to me."

"Why thanks, babe."

She said, "Well, I have to admit, you're handling it better than I would. I'd be in seclusion all weekend. I wasn't even there and I think I'll bury my head in a sand trap."

"First—and always—I get to be with you."

"Awww."

"Second—things picked up before bedtime."

"Uh-oh."

I was much more animated, taking both hands off the wheel to replay the knockout punch, when I told of the confrontation at the high school after the game. Kjirsten listened wide-eyed to the gory details, responding in the appropriate places with gasps, sighs and "icks."

When I finished she said with a tsk, "Men! Your answer to everything is punctuated with a fist."

Thinking she was disappointed in me, with a tightening in my throat, I said, "I'm pretty sure Doug saved the boy from being hit. I'm not sure what else could have been done."

Smugly, Kjirsten, the love of my life, said, "Well, I would not have resorted to fisticuffs. A swift kick to the groin, maybe, or fingernails to both eyes, but never with fists. That's not ladylike."

The Bee Tree course is a river bottom layout very different from Peach Pit. Peach Pit is high and dry with gentle hills that roll your ball along when you land it in the right place. It stays parched all summer. Bee Tree has plenty of reclaimed water so the fairways and greens are lush, but the lack of air circulation and humidity in the valley renders it unbearable from June through August. Snakes love the soggy lowlands, too, so Bee Tree has never been my favorite course I'll take sun-baked dehydration over sticky and critter-infested any day. Still, in the fall, Bee Tree is a good place to play and would probably be regarded as a step up in quality over Peach Pit if I didn't cringe every time I found myself in their town.

Twenty-four players had signed up for the championship flight. A few were clearly outclassed and should have been in a higher flight; at least two that I saw should have been in a *much* higher flight. Most of Doug's competitors, though, were single-digit handicappers who took their golf seriously.

As far as I knew, Doug had not seen the Bee Tree golf course in years, yet he was even par after six holes. He wasn't the longest driver teeing it up, but his course management was as brilliant as it had always been. It was as though he hadn't missed a week, let alone two decades.

Kjirsten and I strolled along, staying well out of eyesight and earshot. Doug was so good that he was mind-numbing—either that or we were so caught up with each other that we could focus on nothing but ourselves.

A maintenance path ran through the trees from behind the seventh tee. Eyeing it, Kjirsten asked, "Where does this road lead?"

"Beats me," I said. "My guess is that it ends up at the greenskeeper's barn behind the clubhouse."

Tugging at my hand, she whispered, "C'mon, let's go."

She would not have needed the tug; her impish grin had more pull over me than was within my power to resist—not that resisting would have ever crossed my mind.

Tater Potachnick's granddaddy—Pappy—owns five hundred acres on top of Crooked-Saddle Mountain halfway between Bee Tree and Llano. The region is home to some of the best deer hunting in North America. Since the ranchers began following the Texas Parks and Wildlife white-tailed deer management guidelines, the deer have gained 60 percent in weight. Each fall, hunters flock there for the trophies of their dreams. Most are not disappointed.

Any kid who has grown up within fifty miles knows of the deep limestone hole on Pappy's ranch that is fed year-round by a pure artesian well. Even on gray days, the bottom of the rock formation shimmers through thirty feet of clear blue-green water. When the sun shines brightly as it did that Saturday afternoon, the light bounces like ricocheting diamonds through the cold water from ledge to crag to promontory, before escaping back into the sky or disappearing completely in hidden underwater caverns.

In the summer, the kids dive from an outcrop twenty feet above the pool, swim, and have grand parties until the sun sets. Pappy has strict rules about staying after dark. He also makes you pick up your trash or he locks the gate for a couple of weekends until enough kids beg, grovel, and promise to clean up after themselves before he lets them back in.

In autumn, the rules change. First, you have no inclination to swim. Without the hot July sun to warm you, the fifty-five degree pool isn't as inviting. Also, it is hunting season and the doctors and lawyers from Dallas who spend thousands each year to lease the opportunity to bag a big buck don't want hordes of noisy teens tramping through their killin' fields. Not to mention the fact that such tramping presents a real opportunity to get shot.

So Kjirsten and I knocked on Pappy's door to ask his permission to hike down the trail to the pool for our chicken picnic.

"I'll be goddamned," said Pappy through his gap-toothed grin. "Robbie McCheyne. What a sight for my sore ol' eyes."

"Good to see ya, Pappy," I said, extending my hand.

Pappy wiped his on his brown stained overall bib before shaking mine.

He asked, "And who would be this pretty lady?"

Kjirsten shook his hand as unabashedly as I had; a little dried tobacco juice wasn't about to spoil her day. I introduced her and she twisted him around her finger in thirty seconds with her gushing about the ranch, his house and forty-mile views—everything that Pappy held dear. I told him what we wanted—to spend a couple of hours napping on the rocks.

Pappy grabbed a walkie-talkie and radioed, "Base to deer-camp one—come in."

"Let's see where them boys are," he said to us, and then, "Base to deer-camp one...."

His radio crackled, "Deer-camp one, go ahead."

Pappy told them what we wanted. They relayed that they were on the far side of the ranch and had no plans to be near the pool.

He was pleased for us. "He'p yurselfs. It's all yor'n," Pappy said, smiling again—still.

As the afternoon unfolded, I knew that its memory would be a secret retreat where I could find a warm embrace, for as long as I had memories, whenever I needed to hide from the colder discords of reality. More than the memory, the place itself became ours, a thread in the weave of us. Already, I have lost count of the times we have since returned, but that first day has never really ended.

Later that evening, when Doug rolled in and asked me about it, I danced around our afternoon in the trees on rocks above the pool, replying mystically—answering with no answers at all.

There are times that are not meant to be shared with even the closest friend you will ever have.

He asked, "Well? Where'd you two go? I looked for you after nine holes and you were gone."

"You're too good," I replied. "Bored us to tears."

"I bet you went to Laird's barbeque in Llano."

He hadn't known about the picnic cooler. "Nope."

"What'd you do? Go to Fredericksburg?"

I shook my head and lied, "Thought about it, but not for long. My bank account still hasn't recovered from the last time we went antique browsing."

"I give up," he said, furrowing—pausing—thinking I would fill in the gap.

I offered no response along with my best attempts to stare without emotion, knowing—fearing—however, that Doug was most likely watching a full color replay in my eyes.

When he saw only the blank pages that prying further would reveal, he smiled kindly at me and proudly stated, "Okay then, Lochinvar. Ask me about my day."

"Since, instead of sulking, you're strutting around here like a young bull who's just been loosed on the herd, my guess is you won something."

"Yep."

"You won the whole thing, didn't you?"

"Yep."

"Damn! How in hell do you do that? You haven't played a competitive round of golf in half a lifetime and you win on your first time out."

He shrugged, "Well, it wasn't exactly the Texas Open."

"No matter. Those guys play that course every day and know every ant hill that will bounce their ball toward the hole."

With cocky aplomb, he said, "I find that you don't need ant hills from the middle of the fairway."

I had always thought that living with him and my Sisyphean burden of blowing sunshine through his omnipresent cloud of despair was tedious. I had the sudden suspicion that his self-facilitated back-patting might become downright oppressive. I was looking forward to every minute of it.

"And here I am being allowed to stand in the same room with you," I said with insincere humility.

He ignored me while opening a bottle of beer. "I'll tell you, Robbie, it was great. I know those local Bee Tree boys aren't exactly Hooters' tour material, but it felt so good."

Doug pulled a chair and sat, resting his forearms on the kitchen table. "I wasn't sure, you know," he continued. "Doing nothing but hitting balls in the pasture, I had my doubts about moving it back to the course again."

"But you knew you'd try, didn't you?"

"Yeah. Always. I had it in the back of my mind that next year, after Cobus's graduation, would be the time to get serious."

"Tildy changed that."

"You could say she pushed me off the fence but I was going over anyway. It was a matter of time."

I joined him at the table. Seeing him, strong, at peace, looking as young as he had at twenty, was such a contrast to who he had been for so long. How had he ever seen through the shroud of depression and dreamed of this moment? It would be easy to say that Sally leaving had sent him to the abyss, but it started long before that. After she left, when he finally knew that it was for good, I figured he'd stay down for a while and then bounce back. When that didn't happen, after a year or so, I believed his brooding would go on forever. On Saturday night, as we sat guzzling longnecks, it dawned on me that, all of that time, he might have known himself better than I. After the third beer, I couldn't remember that things had ever been any different than they were at that moment.

It was past eight-thirty, so it was surprising when someone banged on the front door. We heard Hutch holler, "Is there a champion here?"

"Coach! Come on in."

Doug had a beer open and sitting in front of a chair for Hutch before the coach was five steps through the door. Hutch strode into the kitchen with hand raised to high-five the man of the hour.

"I want some of what you got to rub off on me," said the coach to a beaming Doug.

"Who told you?"

"Who told me? It's all over town."

"Hah!" spouted the golfer.

Hutch smirked. "Well, maybe not *all* over town. It might have been your caddy who spilled the beans."

Doug squinted quizzically, "My caddy?"

"Yeah. Miss Hannah. Tildy Hannah."

We sat and drank up the instant replay of Doug's entire round again. He wasn't tired of talking about it and I wasn't tired of listening. After he'd holed the winning putt for the third time, he turned to Hutch and said, "I still find it strange that Tildy called you. I mean, it's great. There isn't anyone I'd rather share good news with than you."

Other than with me, I assumed he meant.

Hutch, sheepishly cringing, said, "Miss Hannah may have had another reason to call."

"Aha…the plot thickens," I slurred, placing another beer in front of him.

He inhaled a deep, deep breath and began, "It turns out that she enjoys a measure of influence with a few members of the board of El Paso A&M."

"Uh-oh," I muttered.

"Tildy called me at three o'clock."

Doug said, "That must have been no more than five minutes after I dropped her off."

"Yeah," said Coach. "First thing she told me was about the work of art you sculpted today."

Doug nodded. "No doubt about it; she is my number one fan."

Other than me, I assumed he meant.

Hutch continued, "She was very direct."

"Not Tildy," said Doug, sarcastically, with a chuckle.

"She asked me point blank if I wanted the job in El Paso."

"And?" Doug asked.

"I told her it was what I had always wanted. I have always dreamed of coaching at the college level. A&M is a very good division two school. It would be a great move for my career."

Doug raised his beer bottle as in a toast. "It will be a great move for El Paso A&M."

Feeling the effects of one too many beers, I added nothing.

"Thanks, Doug," Hutch said sincerely. "I was foolish, you know, when I left the University of Texas."

Without thinking, I blurted, "Just like Doug."

If I had uttered such an insensitivity a few weeks earlier, Doug would have glared a white-hot hole through me and retired in silence for the evening. Instead he rolled his eyes and scoffed, "Enough beer for you, pard."

He prodded Hutch to continue—which he did.

"They have a good team. They are used to winning. Their coach is retiring. His two top coordinators are moving up to division one. The AD wouldn't have looked any further if either of them had stayed, but they didn't, and here I am."

I decided on another attempt at salience, "Well. With Tildy on your side, it sounds like you have the inside track. I bet if you win the next two, you'll get the call."

He said, "I did."

"You did what?"

"I got the call. Less than thirty minutes after Tildy hung up, the Athletic Director phoned and offered me the job. He told me how excited he was about the board's vote of approval. I asked him if they shouldn't wait until the end of the season and he cut me off in mid-sentence. They want me."

Doug raised his bottle high. "Here's to dreams come true."

Hutch raised his bottle high. "Here's to dreams come true."

I lifted my empty bottle, not taking my elbow from the table, and eloquently murmured, "Here's two dreams—true."

After Hutch left and I lay alone staring at the spinning ceiling of my bedroom, I reflected on how many good things had befallen us in one afternoon and how strange it was that such bounty wasn't distributed more fairly across time. Such a perfect day. Why then did I have an unrequited gnaw that kept me from sleep? When I closed my eyes and floated along on the lingering ecstasy from my hour in Kjirsten's arms, sleep beckoned. When I thought of Doug winning, finally, sleep nearly came. But then, with Hutch's words echoing, I found myself ceiling staring, wide awake again.

He hadn't mentioned Sally at all; he was probably thinking of Doug's feelings. Surely he had spoken with her before he decided to go. So she would be leaving. Good for them. What if he hadn't told her? What if she didn't want to move five hundred miles away to hot, dry El Paso with no friends, no Cobus, no me? Perhaps she'll find a new hobby. Maybe cooking. What had he said? It *had* been his dream. He didn't actually say it was still his dream. He didn't say he'd told them yes. I must have slept then, because that is the last thought I remember having.

CHAPTER TWENTY-TWO

I FELT SURPRISINGLY GOOD on Sunday, considerin'. By nine I had gourmet coffee brewing, one black skillet for omelets, another for breakfast pork chops, and a pot of boiling grits. The crepes with berries and cream were already on the table. I was playing at chef for breakfast at Sally's.

It was a bit daunting to stand, as I was, the lonely agent for my gender, against three women of intimidating resolve. It was the first time that Kjirsten, Sally, and my mother had been together in an orchestrated gathering and I was hopeful that their individual affections for me would override the innate derision of men that tends to burble with feminine klatches—like wolf-pack frenzy rising. Kjirsten, as always, fit seamlessly. It was I who was nervous.

The girl talk had positively nothing to do with me. I should have been more than content to remain the invisible cook. Retreating to the kitchen table after serving them in the dining room would have been prudent.

The crepes and berries were gone and I was well into my main course. The conversation had worked its way around to gardens, fall flowers, and the women of the town who grew them. Mrs. Hebert had cannas, Milagro Mendoza, roses, and Mother was proud of her mums. Kjirsten and Sally decided they would, together, design a cactus garden for the front of Sally's house. I was chewing pork chop when the notion flitted across my neurons that a cactus garden would require more permanence than Sally had available so that thought wasn't able to escape my mouth. Unfortunately, my tongue was occlusion-free when the talk turned to Tildy's wildflower yard. My train of thought went Tildy, flowers, Tildy, golf, Tildy, Hutch, El Paso A&M, El Paso, Hutch, Sally. I should have stopped the train at flowers.

"Speaking of Tildy," I said obliviously. "What do you think about how she helped Hutch?"

Sally, tilting her head my way with childlike trust, asked, "Helped him with what?"

It was a moment framed by cacophonic silence. The absence of talk, of tableware clinking, or even the sound of breathing grew louder by the half-second as three faces with frozen expression awaited, in all innocence, my response. I realized with lightning acuity that Pandora had never popped the top off a box so calamitously.

I knew the color of my face by the searing heat. "Oh. Nothing, really. She had some advice for him about football."

Backpedaling uphill from the river with a dam bursting behind you has the same finality as a headlong plunge; you will drown in a torrent.

"That's odd," said Kjirsten. "Exactly what did she say to Hutch?"

If only I'd had another bite of pork chop.

"Something about El Paso, I think. Mother, would you pass the orange juice, please?"

The orange juice was not forthcoming.

Animated, Sally stammered, "El Paso. El Paso. What about El Paso?"

Staring with envy at the cool, cool droplets condensed on the decanter of juice, thinking that my lack of eye contact might make the women disappear, I mouthed, "Tildy has friends there with influence, that's all. If he's interested in a job in college, she suggested that they may be able to help."

My supportive, loving mother, sharply said, "Robbie Ian McCheyne. Did you know that when you are avoiding the truth you always look at the floor?"

I snapped my head up to study the crown molding.

"I'm not avoiding the truth! Hutch came by late last night. We had a few beers and he told us they offered him the job. That's all I know—really."

Sally, eyes welling, stated a question, "He's moving to El Paso, isn't he?"

"I don't know. He didn't say that."

With voice breaking and lips trembling she asked me, "Just when was he going to tell me about his big move?"

"Sally," I said, trying my best to look up, "you don't even know that he is moving."

Kjirsten looked daggers through me and then turned to Sally, saying consolingly, "He's right, Sally. We don't know that. Hutch will call today. He would never, ever go without you."

Sally smiled through her tears, "Are you sure? How do you know?"

Kjirsten said, "He is beside himself without you. Every time we see him, you are all he can talk about."

"Really?" she asked.

I said, "Really. Besides if he does go, I know he'll be back for you as soon as he gets established in his new job."

She blurted, "You mean after another year of football!" and ran sobbing from the room.

Kjirsten exclaimed, "Robbie!" For the first time ever, I saw Kjirsten's ire fired my way as she followed Sally.

Mother closed her eyes and shook her head. "Well, Son, that went well."

I slowly began to gather the dishes. She reached out and stopped my hand, saying, "I'll get the dishes," which I decoded as, *you should go home—now!*

I began calling Hutch when I got to my truck. He didn't answer the first three times, so I drove by his house. He wasn't there. He wasn't at the school and he wasn't at the football field. I called a half-dozen more times before one o'clock, when Doug came home from practicing and asked me to go along with him and Tildy's gang for their Sunday afternoon nine. The invitation was a welcome break from my panic. I wouldn't mention Sally in front of Doug, so a ride in his truck with no bull to shoot but golf, football, and old women saved me from my rapidly deteriorating self.

Tildy and her friends were at work on the practice green with Squinty Spencer watching over their putting strokes. Golf gadgets were strewn about. To help her visualize paths to holes, Amanda had snapped lines on the grass with bright orange carpenter's chalk from every imaginable angle.

Hoping to make two-foot putts routine, Inez used a curved board, designed to match the arc of a stroke, over and over and over. She would not have been able to see a putt in excess of two feet drop anyway, so she stayed within her comfort zone.

Macey, loving to hit things hard as she did, putted no putt under the length of fifty feet. She would smack one uphill through the breaks and then waddle her way across the green and smack it back down again. I could not tell if she was actually aiming at anything in particular—like a hole. Usually there would be one in the general vicinity of her ball's final resting place—if general vicinity can be loosely defined as any distance shorter than the length of a school bus.

Tildy practiced alone in a corner of the green with a circle of balls all around the hole, methodically putting one after another like hands on the face of a clock ticking time away.

When we approached, the women, as if on cue, picked the balls that were theirs and marched like nutcracker soldiers to their bags. They bade goodbye to Squinty who was left to clean the green behind them.

I remarked to Doug how serious they seemed. He said, "Now you know why I need you here. Let's see if we can loosen them up."

I wasn't exactly sure how seventy-something loosened women would act or what acceptable loosening stimulation might be. I offered, "Who would like a caddy?"

Inez, unsure of my meaning, averred, "We have electric carts. Mr. Spencer has given us electric carts without charge. Tildy is driving with me. My bag should be on the cart with me."

Amanda added, "She's right. She's right. I am riding with Macey."

Tildy interrupted, "Well, I would like a caddy. Robbie, you can clean my clubs between shots and you can tell my how far it is to the hole. I'd like you to keep my score and the number of putts I take; when we're finished you can carry my clubs to the car."

"Ooh," bubbled Macey, "I want a caddy, too."

"Well! I wish you would have explained that sooner," lamented Amanda.

Doug chuckled, "What about me, Amanda? Will I do? I'll be the caddy for your cart and Robbie will work for Tildy and Inez."

Believing that she had won the caddy lottery, Amanda beamed. "Doug. Yes, Doug. That is wonderful. We get Doug."

I felt like the kid who gets picked last on the playground.

The first hole meanders along a creek on the right; scrub oak and pampas grass interspersed with yucca lines the left. The trouble comes into play from the men's tees, but the angle from the red markers opens up the fairway for the women, so their shot is not as daunting. Inez, hitting last, appeared more nervous than the others and dribbled her tee ball only twenty yards.

Embarrassed, she said, "I'm sorry. I'm sorry."

Doug, seizing a teaching moment, lectured, "Okay. Here's our mantra for today. With apologies to Hollywood, golf means never having to say you're sorry."

Inez started, "I'm sor—", and then caught herself with a smile.

Doug went on, "There's one thing you can do as well as the pros right now. Forget about the last shot and focus on the next."

Inez turned and handed her driver to me and professionally commanded, "Mr. Caddy, will you please give me the proper club for my next shot and lead me to my ball?"

With her fairway club, she swung mechanically like she had done so many times on the practice range and flew the ball eighty yards to the middle of the fairway, near Amanda, short of Tildy, and far short of Macey.

The goal that Doug had set for them was simple. He believed that they should reach the green in par and then allow for three putts. That made sixty-three their virtual par.

I was concerned that the gals would lose too many strokes around the green, but they surprised me. Doug had taught them one swing to use for pitches and chips. They switched clubs, using anything from a five-iron to a wedge, depending on the length of the shot. The swing didn't change—only the club.

All of them equaled or bettered their par-plus-three goal on the first three holes—even Inez. It was clear that sixty-three was not challenging for Tildy. She was one under double-bogey after three, which meant she would have a real chance at a round in the forties. They didn't know how good they were after only eight weeks of practice. They assumed every novice was as skilled.

The tee box for the fourth, a short, picturesque par three, sits above the green by twenty feet in elevation. The shot must carry a small pond with Chinese Pistache trees scattered around the edge. The little creek curls around and well behind the green.

Amanda was nervous about the water. She said, "Inez, this is one time you can be glad you can't see too far."

Tildy snorted and said, "Piffle. Swing like there is no pond."

Doug, chuckling, added, "Another thing you can do is to pick a target that is far in the distance behind the green and imagine you are trying to hit it. I do that when I want to block looming disaster from my mind's eye."

"I was thinking only of a pond," said Amanda, wide-eyed. "Now it's looming disaster!" Then she laughed out loud at herself and hit a fairway club to the middle of the green. She clapped at her achievement as did her friends with accompanying oohs and ahs.

Tildy and Inez also reached the green with their tee shots. They—we—were so excited. Not counting Tildy, it was the first chance that one of them could make a real par. Inez, especially, had only a twenty-foot putt facing her. They appeared about to burst with anticipation. Amanda and Inez stood side by side, hands clasped in front of them, with teeth clenched tightly in wide grins to hold back the squeals.

It was Macey's turn. She announced, "I have chosen the water tower behind the green as my target."

The blue steel mushroom tower on the far horizon was easily five miles away. Squinting, I could barely make it out. It was a distant target as Doug had suggested.

He laughed. "That's perfect, Macey. I might have picked a landmark somewhere on the course, but the water tower it is."

"Oh," she said. "Should I choose something different?"

"No, no," said Doug with broad smile beaming. "The water tower is wonderful. Swing away."

Basking in the spotlight of fun, Macey took her place behind the ball with her five-iron. Even as large as she was, she still looked athletic. She bent at the knees with her backside anchoring her stance like a linebacker waiting to pounce. Macey's arms were big from shoulder to wrist, so the shaft of the club looked like a thin wire protruding. She reached around her bosom squeezing it tightly between her arms until it appeared as if it had melted together with her torso. Nevertheless, when she swung, Macey turned gracefully. Her arms lifted softly as Doug had shown her many weeks before with the axe and log. After the slightest pause with club poised high, her hands dropped in time with the uncoiling of her body and then accelerated the clubhead into the ball with a resonating pop.

Usually, Macey hit low driving shots that rolled on forever. Her tee shot on the fourth soared straight at the water tower, arcing against the Texas blue sky, high over the green, and down to the creek beyond.

"Wow!" I exclaimed. "What a shot."

She said, "Drat."

"Drat?" replied Doug. "That was fabulous."

"But it's in the creek."

"Perhaps, but that was the best swing you have ever made."

Inez, pouting coyly, mewed, "I do wish I could have seen it, Macey."

Amanda was uncharacteristically subdued by awe. "Inez, dear, it was so beautiful. It went high, like Doug's."

"I loved the sound," said Inez.

Tildy added, "I am humbled."

Macey was proud. Invigorated, she directed, "Let's go get it, caddy," as she tossed her club to Doug.

Macey's ball rested on a small island of mud in the middle of the rock-lined creek. The bank was steep, but the water ran clear and looked only a few inches deep.

"I can get it," proclaimed Macey.

"No," Doug said. "We have plenty of balls. It's a red-stake hazard. Drop a ball and chip on."

"I think I can hit it. It's my favorite ball; I drew a butterfly on it."

Amanda pointed out, "Macey, you draw butterflies on all of your golf balls."

"But it's the best shot I ever hit. Doug said so."

Tildy sternly chided, "No, Macey! Leave the ball in the creek, throw a new one down, and hit a nice chip shot like we practiced."

"Oh, okay," she said with a frown and a shrug. She then hit a very nice shot onto the edge of the green with a ball with a butterfly.

"Good one," said Doug.

"Nice," said Amanda.

"See!" said Tildy.

Inez clapped.

I said, "Geeeorgeous."

We turned and walked up the hill to the green—all except Macey. We had taken no more than ten steps when her shocked voice rang out behind us.

"Oh, my. Oh!"

She was stuck in the mud. She had worked her way down the bank of the little stream, navigated the slippery rocks, and stood ankle-deep in brown-red mud.

Doug sprinted toward the water, yelling, "Macey, do not move!"

She moved. She pulled on her right foot and in doing so, shifted her weight to the left. Her left leg sunk halfway up her calf. Reactively, she pulled on the left and her right leg burrowed. By the time Doug reached her, Macey was nearly knee-deep and laughing hysterically.

He leapt from the bank without breaking stride, landed with a splash in the stream and grabbed both of her hands at once.

"Okay, Macey. I've got you now. Don't move at all."

"Oh, my God, I'm so sorry. I'm so stupid." She laughed, talked, and panted rapidly.

"Macey, it's okay. I want you to breathe as slowly as you can, and hold my hands without moving."

Her breaths came quickly. "It's quicksand," she said, without the laughter.

"No, no, no," Doug affirmed loudly. "It's nothing but mud. You won't sink any further. Hold my hands tightly. Look at me, not the mud."

He was trying to relax her. She began laughing again, and then coughing.

I half-slid, half-jumped into the creek and took her right hand from Doug while placing my left on her back for support. Where I stood it was firmer. The mud barely topped my shoelaces. Doug was on rocks. She had managed to find the one sinkhole in a hundred-yard stretch of creek bottom.

Calmly but firmly, he ordered, "Tildy, go to Squinty and get us some help."

Tildy and her cart were already gone from sight.

Inez and Amanda stood together on the bank ashen with fear. Inez asked over and over, "What's happening? What's happening now?"

Amanda answered in short bursts. "She's okay. They're getting her out. She's standing in the mud. She's okay."

After a cough, Macey smiled at Doug and teased, "Fine caddy you are—allowing me to hit my ball into the mud." She tried to laugh, but could only wheeze.

Doug's lips wanted to smile but his eyes betrayed his terror. He rubbed her back as he held her left hand.

A cough spewed followed by two violent gasps. Her right hand ripped from mine and grasped at her chest. Another weak gasp. Then Macey's knees buckled and she collapsed against our arms.

"Get under her! Get under her!"

Both of my feet came out of my shoes in the mud as I struggled to hold her head. I sat down in the creek and straddled her body with my legs. Her calves were still anchored firmly in the mud hole. Doug lowered her head gently onto my lap.

Macey smiled broadly. Between two baby breaths she whispered, "Oh, my. Tell Tildy, I…"

Doug began CPR immediately. He knelt beside her in the cold rippling water while I held her head best I could.

He pushed and pushed. One, two, three, four, five… "Come on, Macey. Stay with me." One, two, three, four, five…

I took her hair from the water, laying it on my leg, and combed it straight with my fingers. "We're here, Macey. Come on, Macey."

Inez and Amanda sat silently on the grass holding hands.

Doug did not vary his rhythm of presses to her breast or kisses of breath until we heard the howl of the siren. The lonely wail rolling across the hills signaled a finality he tried to outrace; he turned up his cadence hoping to bring her back before they arrived.

The Peach Pit volunteer rescue squad drove their ambulance across the course to the fourth tee box, as close as they could get to us. They relieved Doug with their equipment and worked hard for another twenty minutes, but Macey was gone.

Extracting her from the mud was easy with hand shovels. The men placed her on the grass and were preparing the stretcher to carry Macey up the hill when Tildy said, "Wait a minute, please." She bent down to the stream and soaked her towel. She spoke softly while cleaning Macey's legs. "Oh, Macey. You silly girl. I will miss you so."

Amanda took Inez's towel with hers and filled them both with water. They joined Tildy to wash Macey. The softness as they cared for her was beautiful in its delicacy, as if they had been preparing for this their entire lives.

In the frenzy, Macey's butterfly ball from the creek had been thrown onto the bank along with clumps of mud. Tildy found it, wiped it clean, placed it in Macey's palm, and then folded her fingers around it.

Then the men lifted the stretcher and carried Macey away up the hill to the waiting ambulance.

As Doug and I stood back, still dripping wet, I couldn't tell if he was shivering or silently sobbing. I knew why I shook.

CHAPTER TWENTY-THREE

Tildy, Amanda, and Inez rode in the ambulance while I followed in Tildy's Cadillac. On the way, I called Mother and Kjirsten to tell them what had happened. I tried Hutch again with no luck. Kjirsten handled the news like I knew she would. No longer did any of my morning's bumblings matter when considered with Macey's passing. I parked Tildy's car for her at the Bonnet Furniture Mart and Mortuary and then walked home. Doug's truck was parked in front of his grocery store. I peered through the locked front door and could see a light in the back, but I didn't knock.

I'd been in the house for half an hour, wandering from one needless chore to another, when I heard the lawnmower start. Doug was home, but he'd gone to the shed without coming inside and was performing his own needless chore of cutting grass in the remaining hour of daylight.

As I wiped the kitchen table for the third time, Cobus strolled in from his bedroom.

"Hi, Uncle Robbie. What's for supper?" he asked, while peering at the mostly empty shelves of the refrigerator. He sounded surprisingly mellow. For six weeks, every word from his mouth had been served with an edge.

"I don't know, buddy. See what's in the freezer that we can nuke."

Immediately, he questioned, "What's wrong?"

I hadn't realized that my emotions had been that transparent. I said, "Hand me a beer, please," and sat. "I have bad news."

Cobus opened the bottle for me and then stood, arms folded, leaning against the refrigerator door.

"Macey died on the golf course this afternoon."

Unless they've had more heartbreak than their share, eighteen-year-olds aren't supposed to know how to react to death. I was pleased that he worked hard to say the right things.

"Dad's Macey? Macey, the golfer? Miss Hannah's friend?"

"Yep."

I wouldn't have been too critical of him if he had bolted, but he sat at the table with me and measured his words carefully.

"Was Dad there?"

"We both were. He did CPR and I helped as much as I could."

I told him the entire story and he listened intently, interrupting only to ask how his dad was handling things. I didn't have an answer because I hadn't been with Doug since we left Peach Pit.

When he had finished acting at mowing the lawn, Doug came in through the kitchen to where we were. I told him I would fix supper if he'd join us. He looked first at me and then Cobus like he was thinking of turning me down. If Cobus hadn't been there, he would have. Instead, he finally agreed, "Yeah, sure. Let me take a shower. I'll be five minutes."

I thawed a couple quarts of year-old deer chili and divided it between us. For two minutes, we ate without speaking. I was standing to turn on the radio so it would drown out the sounds of three men slurping, when Doug quietly pondered, "It doesn't much matter what you do."

Cobus looked at me as if I might know what his dad meant. I slumped back into my chair knowing from experience it would be fruitless to guess. The descending sallow aura was all too familiar. The man who, twenty-four hours before, had radiated strength, had been Superman, had lit the room, now was weak and gray, withering in our presence. His right hand shook when he lifted his spoon so that he had to steady it with his left. I knew this thief of essence. Perhaps this time there was a valid reason for his intrusion. Perhaps he was only a ghost drifting through, stealing a ride on a wave of grief, and would pass with the night. Perhaps my sudden uncontrollable shiver had nothing to do with ghosts but was only a relic effect of the cold water still drying on my cuffs.

With teeth chattering, I stupidly asked, "Do what?"

He swirled his spoon aimlessly in his chili.

"Anything you ever thought you wanted to do. No matter what path you foolishly choose to hack through the briars, the outcome is the same."

Cobus and I vainly searched each other's face for clues to the meaning of his bramble ramble. He tried to lift his spoon again, but shaking stopped him.

"You end up scratched and bleeding in the middle of a thicket with no way out."

Still choosing to ignore where the trail was headed, I became cowboy Pollyanna on cue, "Yeah, but think of all them blackberries you get to pick on the way."

His only response was finally to will a spoonful of hot chili into his mouth.

With sunken cheeks and hollow eyes, Doug looked toward his son. "God, Cobus, how I wish I was you."

Poignantly, Cobus replied, "No, you don't. Being me isn't so good these days."

Doug snapped back, "It's nothin'. All this shit you been goin' through is nothin'."

"Then why doesn't it feel like nothin'?"

"It's a dirty trick. Being young is a dirty trick. You think everything in your life happens *right now*. You don't know yet that time is clay you can mold any way you like, slowly, carefully carving out your dreams, your friends, your lovers. When you're a young punk, you think time is a cube of ice melting on the hot hood of a fast car and you grasp at the slippery lie clinging to all the wrong people, shouting immoral words, fearing demons who aren't, embracing bogus saviors. By the end of the day everything you thought was real has evaporated with the disappearing sunlight and you're left thirsting in the dark with nothing but your still-shapeless lump of clay."

Cobus, with deeply crinkled forehead, tried to blink away his bewilderment while Doug two-handed another spoonful of chili. With mouth full he rolled on, "They'll try to tell you life goes by so fast. Well, it doesn't! It creeps by, lying, waiting, begging for you to do something with it. And then…and then, when you hit the dead-end and turn around to face the expanse of your wasted hours, is when you know you've been misled by the gods of no time. Funny thing is, there is nothing you can do about it. You can't change it 'cause you don't get to know you have all that time 'til you don't."

Sincerely struggling to remove any hint of sarcasm, hoping he'd know that my tack-on to his train of images was well intended, I cringed and proffered, "And then you're stuck in the middle of the blackberry patch?"

He nodded, "And then you're stuck in the middle of thorns. You can't go back and it's too painful to go on."

"Dad," said the boy, "I'm okay. I'll be okay. Don't worry about me."

All along Cobus thought Doug had been talking about him. Doug would have said he was talking about Cobus, but I knew he wasn't. He was mourning a lot more than Macey.

Doug allowed a thin smile to cross his mood. "That's why I wish I was you."

"Dad, I've been thinking that I would—"

Then the phone rang. Doug was closer, so he stood to answer, saying, "Hold onto that. I'll be right back."

The sheriff was calling and needed to know the details for the record. Cobus and I spoke little, slowly consuming the last of the chili, while we listened to the retelling. When Doug reached the part where they drove away with Macey, Cobus said quietly to me, "I miss my ma."

"Then go see her."

"I will."

"Now. Tonight."

"Maybe."

Once the phone started ringing, it didn't stop. Doug spent the rest of the evening politely reliving Macey's demise with well-intentioned callers. I was overwhelmed by the desire to get out, but I wouldn't leave him alone. Cobus left without saying where he was going.

Round about eight, Kjirsten showed up at the front door to say she'd tried to call for an hour and was afraid the busy signal echoes would haunt her for weeks. She didn't want to be alone, either. She and I sat curled up on the couch while Doug reclined in his space, trying with little success to watch old movies between calls until we fell asleep sometime before midnight. Kjirsten woke at two, kissed me goodnight, wrapped a blanket around me, and drove home. Doug never stirred and slept in his clothes in the chair.

CHAPTER TWENTY-FOUR

I TRIED ALL DAY Monday to find five minutes alone with Hutch.
As soon as I'd throw him a question like, "Where were you
yesterday?" a kid would interrupt with questions of his own about
homework, football, or both, and then the bell would ring and
we'd all be off. After the last class, I ran to the coach's room
hoping to catch him before practice. I found him, squatting with
head buried in locker, rummaging for unnamed junk.

"Coach, it's me."

Without standing, he responded, "Hey Robbie, what's up?"

"Coach, I gotta talk to you. I screwed something up."

"Uh-oh."

"You gotta talk to Sally."

"Oh, that. Heard all about it."

He didn't turn around. I was talking to his back.

"What? I mean, who told you?"

Tommy burst through the door, shouting, "Hey, Coach! Full
pads today?"

"Full pads. Warm 'em up with a couple of laps."

"Yessir!"

I still hadn't seen Hutch's face. Even through my guilt-
induced stupor, I recognized that the absolution I sought would

277

not be granted while surrounded by jock-clad jocks and their whistle-blowing coaches.

I gave up. "Coach, never mind. I'll catch you later."

Finally he stood. He smacked me on the butt with his clipboard as he walked to the door. "It's a busy week," he said. "Don't worry about it. I'll handle it. I'll clear it up this weekend. Lock up for me, will you?" And he was gone to practice.

Oh, that cheered me up. Instead of absolution, I could look forward to the masochistic pleasures of berating myself senseless from Monday 'til Saturday. What did he mean, he'd handle it? Then I knew I'd pushed him off the fence. He'd had no choice but to make up his mind once and for final after I'd thrown him under the bus—under the same bus where I now had permanent residence. I'd done the hard part for him—coldly dumping the news on Sally. It was clear—once he revealed his intentions to leave, Sally wouldn't be speaking to me for the next decade— nor would Kjirsten or Mother. The weekend was six days before the biggest game of the year. God, I hoped he wouldn't tell the kids before they played Bee Tree. If he did, then they'd know all his talk about team, family, football, and camaraderie had meant nothing—nothing at all. If he was planning his big-time announcement for the weekend, it meant he'd be leaving at the semester. He was so cocksure of himself—smug with his clipboard and ball cap and hiding from me in his locker, acting like he was searching for something that wasn't there. Searching for things not there was his theme. I figured it was his way of cruelly severing whatever blessed binds I'd thought had been tied. I was glad I'd told Sally. Better from me than him. The semester was just around the corner. I would wish him luck in El Paso.

CHAPTER TWENTY-FIVE

INSTEAD OF A FUNERAL for Macey in Bonnet, a memorial service was planned for Tuesday afternoon in the Methodist church. Macey was born in Bloomington, Indiana and was one of eight sisters. She had moved to Bonnet in the fifties as a young bride of her husband Woodrow, a war veteran, to raise cattle on their small ranch, which he bought with the GI bill. In eighty-nine, Macey buried him in Bloomington in their family plot in the little cemetery on the hill. Her remaining sister made Macey's final arrangements. On Wednesday morning, they would take her body to Austin for the flight home.

The Methodist church, built in the twenties in the style of the day, was overly ornate with high stained-glass windows—no match for the extremes of Bonnet weather. Those who arrive on Sunday too late to sit near the center aisle, away from windows, shiver in winter and sweat in summer. Gold and chrome icons adorned the sanctuary and altar, where simple wood carvings would have better served a Texas country setting. Still, it was an affectionate gathering place for friends to remember Macey.

We were all there except Hutch, who was at practice. No one questioned, at least not aloud, his absence. After all, he hadn't really known Macey other than as one of the elderly ladies who sat in the front row and cheered his every game. After all, it wouldn't matter after he left town.

Doug sat in the front row with Tildy and friends. Contrasting sharply with the bright flowered dresses of the three women who flanked him, he wore a black suit with bolo tie. He'd said how proud he would be to sit with them; he looked poignantly out of place. He sat rigidly, holding his dress hat on his lap, never crossing his legs, never fidgeting, as if he were eight years old again, afraid of getting thumped if he squirmed. When he rose to sing or pray, he stood as a soldier at attention.

I sat behind them in the second row with Sally, Mother, and Kjirsten. The women attending the service outnumbered men by three to one and the number of those over the age of sixty-five doubled those who weren't. Considering that Bonnet is a small town, I was ashamed at knowing the preponderance of women only as nameless faces. My dereliction of communal acquaintance was surely a direct reflection of the amount of time I never spent in church, which would be the best place to hobnob with the grayer, fairer sex—other than Tildy and her gals, of course, with whom I hobnobbed on a golf range.

Across the aisle in a row alone, sat Galey and Cuthbert Alden in their church-goin' best, which meant they were not in bib overalls. Cuthbert wore a suit coat that was twenty years too small. A curious rustic wooden box sat on the pew between them. The old women afforded them plenty of room, as they were accustomed to doing on the streets. Avoidance of the brothers made sense if perchance you crossed their path downtown after they'd worked a long hot day with their cattle and hogs. We were all thankful for their polished boots. Kjirsten said it was cute how they'd pressed as many wrinkles into their jeans and cotton shirts as they'd ironed out. As always their hair was oily, only this time it was on purpose and combed.

The Methodist preacher, a pale, thin young man, two years out of seminary, spoke first, middle, and last. He hadn't known her well, he said, but had talked with so many who had, that now he thought he did. His cookie-cutter homily was sweet. His proper wife played piano when we all sang together and then he played for her while she sang alone. That was the obligatory, ordinary part. The rest of the service was not so much so.

Tildy ran a slide show. When I'd heard that she planned that, I'd pictured a dusty old projector, often out of focus, with the occasional upside down slide, all narrated with, *And then we went to Rome*, or, *That is Macey by the toe of the Sphinx*, or, *This was Macey and Woodrow at their thirtieth anniversary*. Instead, she presented a laptop and PowerPoint show with background music and a script recorded sometime between Sunday and Tuesday afternoon by our high school choir director. Had any other seventy-something wisp of a woman so quickly orchestrated a similar digital tribute, I might have been incredulously surprised; with Tildy I merely shook my head and was surprised only by my own expectations of anything less.

Sitting through a recitation of eulogies is not easy, I imagine, for even the most pious of souls. For a once-removed cowboy like me, it sits atop a list of pain-producing activities that include weddings, baptisms, and dance recitals. Although I've never been to a dance recital, it remains high on my list.

Tildy's five-minute talk after the slide show was warm and painless. She didn't mention God or Jesus or being in a better place or Macey looking down on us and smiling. It would have been okay if she had, especially since it was in a church, but boy preacher had done that, so she didn't need to repeat it.

She began, "In 1962, Macey said, 'Tomorrow, Woodrow is going to plow me five acres for a garden.' He did, and she worked all spring planting corn and beans and squash. The years before had been wet and she thought it would be the same again. Then it didn't rain in '62 and her garden failed, so in '63 she said, 'Woodrow and I will drill a well near my garden.' They did, and her crops flourished. They grew high and green, and the deer and rabbits loved every bite. The next year she staked an electric fence all around the plot and the varmints stayed away, but the insects had a feast. So, in 1965, Macey spent her time at the county agriculture office learning about bugs. After that she never missed a harvest.

"By 1972, Macey and Woodrow knew there would be no children, so she nurtured ten acres of peach saplings which became the orchard that spawned her blue-ribbon cobblers and pies."

Tildy's quiet style of speech was soothing, hypnotizing in a way that let me drift along on her memories as she spoke, picturing Macey working in the sun or at her stove or waving a towel from her porch as I sped by as a teen in my truck.

"Their house was small and old and very breezy, and Macey's dream was to have a new one, but that was more money than they had available. As she entered her third decade of marriage, she announced to all that she would build it herself; and build it she did—one salvaged, begged, or stolen two-by-four at a time. She pestered all the tradesmen she could corner, until she had taught herself enough to drive every nail, run the wires, and solder plumbing."

Macey had lassoed me as a mule to haul shingles up her rickety piecemeal ladder. She enticed me with food into many things that summer, but I remember most the hauling of shingles in July.

Tildy went on to tell how, after Woodrow died, Macey had sold all but the house and her favorite twenty acres to the Aldens, thus funding her round-the-world adventures, which continued yearly until she died. The reminiscing ended with the beginning of golf with Doug, and Tildy merely said, "Thank you," and sat down.

Then it was Doug's turn to speak. It wasn't right or wrong that Tildy's talk had been all about Macey, and Doug's was more of what she had done for him, but the differences stood out keenly. Tildy spoke of Macey's many simple, hard-earned conquests over life, and we were left on our own for comparisons to our lives or others that we knew. She didn't sprinkle platitudes about fulfillment or her wishes of longing to be like Macey. On the other hand, Doug told us how he'd been going nowhere, how much he admired Macey, and wished that he had done the things she had, and how she had given him, for the first time in many years, a reason to get up in the morning. He thanked her for a few weeks of light. All that he said about her was nice enough and what you would expect to hear in old oaken pews with high colored-glass images of the baby Jesus, or Jesus the healer, or Jesus on the cross listening above with Mary weeping and little lambs kneeling.

After Tildy, I wanted to stand, shout, and run from the church hand in hand with Kjirsten to engage every dream I'd ever dreamed. After Doug, we stood and sang, *The Old Rugged Cross, the emblem of suffering and shame...*

When the skinny preacher announced that the Alden brothers would be next, all heads turned to watch the rustics slide themselves from the pew with their weathered brown box and then jostle down the aisle side by side, cradling the box together as if it were a jewel on satin.

They stood at the front on a carpeted step in front of Tildy rather than behind the pulpit where they wouldn't have fit anyway. When one began to speak, he would hand the box to his brother to hold and then piously take it back when his turn was up. Apparently it was necessary for them, in order to speak, to have arms hanging straight and flaccid at the hip. They worked hard to curtail their customary nervous twitches. The box was the size of a loaf of bread.

Galey started, "You folks will have to excuse I and Cuthbert as how we ain't use to talkin' up front like this; we shoulda done it when Woodrow passed, but we was too scairt and we felt bad ever since."

Galey pivoted smartly and took the box from Cuthbert, who continued, "Galey's right, because we wouldn't be who we was if it weren't for Woodrow and Macey. Our own granddaddy left us the old place next to Woodrow's place and we come here without knowin' much about farmin'. We was gonna sell it off and Woodrow said he'd plant some beans to see if they'd grow along the river."

Cuthbert reached over and took the box back. Galey said, "There was just a shack with a wood stove and a couple of 'lectric lights and Macey brung us food ever' night the first summer we was here. Ever' single night. Them beans growed good and we seen how he'd done it. We bought an old tractor but Woodrow did our combinin' till he died and then Macey give us the combine with the ground she sold us."

Cuthbert interrupted and started talking while still holding the box; Galey had to quickly grab it away from him. It was plain to see that Cuthbert was becoming so feverish about what they were saying that he forgot his box etiquette. "When they told us Macey passed, we wanted to do somethin' for her so we walked to where the old homestead had been and found boards a-layin' on the ground where the walls had used to be. We made this box with them."

Galey held the box up to face-level to show us while Cuthbert continued with his soliloquy. "Then we wanted to put something in the box for Macey to take with her, seein' as how she and Woodrow are goin' to be together now and all."

Galey stepped down to stand in front of Tildy and pulled the top from the box. Cuthbert continued speaking while his brother showed the box to the three women and Doug on the front row. "First, we filt the bottom with dirt from Macey's garden. Then we picked up as many seeds what we could find, some beans and corn, mostly, but we got peach pits, too, and a pecan and then we covered them all up in Macey's dirt."

With that, silent tears began to fall. All the women reached for their tissues; I tried not to move; Doug, for the first time, fidgeted. Kjirsten squeezed my hand tightly. Even Tildy, tough unshakeable Tildy, removed her glasses and brushed one eye and then the other.

Cuthbert said, "When we was walkin' home we found one of Woodrow's rusted branding irons, so we cut the handle off and put it in the box, too."

Galcy took the WM iron from the box and held it high for all to see while the women sobbed aloud. At last he turned to place the box on the step while Cuthbert pulled a small hammer from inside his jacket; they knelt and banged six box nails with echoes ringing in time with our sniffles.

Afterward, we migrated to Fellowship Hall for the food. Every dish was a product of Macey's canning. We stood in gatherings of three or four with little paper plates dolloped with bean casserole, bean dip, or three-bean pie. I dolloped only polite, sociably sized helpings—not because I was particularly polite or sociable; I had seen the desserts and was saving myself for them. Doug stared for a full two minutes at the soup offerings unable to decide if squash bisque, cold beet soup, or potato chowder would best suit his mood. Tildy glided from klatch to klatch, encouraging folks to eat more or to inquire if they were enjoying the food or to thank them for coming.

After thirty minutes, after I had finished peach cobbler and was dissecting a perfectly formed piece of pecan pie, being careful that no cut would upset the symmetry of the nuts remaining, the hall began to empty. Every time I made an orgasmic sound over a mouthful, Kjirsten kicked me under the table, which was after every bite. Doug stood alone nearby, leaning against two walls meeting at the corner.

Tildy, looking tired, looking like one day she could grow old, made her way to him and said, "Thank you so much, Doug, for the kind words."

He sheepishly stood straight, shifting his cup of bisque to his left hand so he could place his right in Tildy's outstretched palms. She clung to him.

With a sigh he said to her, "I didn't say it right, what I felt—what I wish I knew how to say better."

"I believe you did say what you felt," she said ardently. "Thank you for caring."

"Hah. Some days it feels like caring is all I have."

She looked him up and down for a long moment. "You have me."

"Thank *you* for caring."

With a Tildy smirk, she replied, "I mean, you have me to take up your time and hack up your pasture."

Smiling thinly, Doug said, "I'll always have the last eight weeks to remember. Without you, this fall would have been no less dull than the last dozen or so. You got me out of the store. You allowed me to revisit my youth."

Tildy asked, playfully, sarcastically, "You didn't think the last eight weeks were about you, did you?"

He stammered, not fully realizing she was teasing, "I only meant... I mean, I enjoyed every minute and I hope you did, too."

"You can call it enjoyment if you want. It's golf! We are on a mission!"

"You're funny, Tildy. You make me laugh."

"What are you doing tomorrow at noon?" Thinking and talking about golf with Doug animated Tildy. Color flowed over the pallor that had washed her out since Sunday.

"Cutting meat."

"We'll be back from Austin by noon. We want to practice sand shots."

He looked at her quizzically. "I don't understand."

"You know... sand shots. Bunkers, traps, the beach, hazards..."

"I don't know Tildy. I have ignored the store. I've been thinking about expanding."

"Then we want to hit from the high grass—the rough."

"How do you think a full deli would do in Bonnet with fresh salads, hot chicken, and cheese?"

"And the wind. We have never practiced in the wind. What if the wind blows on Sunday?"

"I even thought about a Subway franchise."

She flashed bright red. "A Subway franchise! Have you lost your mind?! This is Bonnet, Texas, not a San Marcos outlet mall. Who will slather mayonnaise when you're off playing in your tournaments?"

He looked away, avoiding eye contact like a kid who'd been caught cheating. "I'm not going to play any more, Tildy. I had fun. I chased an old dream and now its time for me to wake up and go back to work."

Tildy dropped Doug's hand, which she had held until then. She turned as if to walk away and then turned back again, angrily.

"You mean its time for you to go back to sleep."

Doug, looking shocked, blinked. "What?"

"You mean its time for you to go back to sleep. I won't tag along for that. I am an old woman. My friends are old women. It hurts to get out of bed in the morning and walk to the kitchen. On a normal day, it takes fifteen minutes to flex my fingers enough to hold a coffee cup. Yet, every morning for the last eight weeks, we sprang to our feet like bubble-gumming, air-headed teenage girls, knowing we would be with you before the dew dried from your patch of grass. If teaching us the game was only a game, then we have not been part of the same dream. At seventy-four years old, if I could, I would freely drink from whatever fountain of youth would keep me swinging for another seventy-four. You have been a very effective potion, but if you are all dried up, I will do my best to appreciate how arid your life must be. In the meantime, if it is still okay that we play in your pasture, we would like to do that tomorrow."

Doug was stunned. He mumbled, "I'm sorry. It never occurred to me that you still planned on playing."

"It never occurred to me to do anything else. I don't know yet how it will work out playing three against four, but I imagine it's a trivial detail."

He nodded in detached agreement. "Yes, that's trivial. Of course you can use the range." Then, after reflection, he added, "But you don't need me. There's nothing I can say that I haven't before."

I had the impression that if she thought it would help her to reach him, she would flail her feet while prostrate on the floor. She paged through my own playbook of frustrations. It was embarrassing to look in a mirror. It was embarrassing that Doug kept on being Doug and we had to be everything else for him. If Tildy had slogged through all the same fathoms of Doug's morass that I had, she would have known when to give up and drink herself to bed, but bless her heart, she naïvely and stubbornly stood unyielding in the face of his withdrawal to the cozy stagnation of mayonnaise slathering.

"Don't need you? I am scared to death without you. Without you, we fade to dust. Little towns in Texas are dying. Pick any heading and drive. Every bend in the road that once had a movie, a drugstore, a grocery, schools, and churches is painted with a gray shade of aging plywood. Houses that stood colorfully proud, sag now, sadly peeling. But, every now and then you come over the crest of a hill and you find a Bonnet where the yards are still green and the paint is fresh, where there is a store like yours, the churches are full, and the school is just down the street and not on a windswept hill twenty miles away with no identity."

Tildy took him to a place where I had never been. I knew I needed him around. I knew I could never keep myself from returning to prop him up again when there was no good reason. And I knew the harder he pushed away, the tighter we clutched— all of us. I never knew why. In a fury, Tildy had defined it. Whether she had brooded on it at length or whether it was a spontaneous fusion of nostalgia with a Merlinesque vision didn't matter. Without him, there was no us.

Frustrated, trembling, angry, and humbled, he asked, "What do you want from me?"

"I can't answer that. I know a lightning bolt ran through us every time you touched a football when you were young. I can tell you how proud we were to read about you in the paper when you were winning at golf; yet we desperately needed you to return when you did to keep the store open. I see how they still flock to your side at games, on the street, in the café, and how old men hang around the meat counter just to be near you. No matter what standoffish signals you transmit, they are no match for the magnetism that draws us.

"I will cheer for you from afar, as I did before, if you need to leave and chase your youth. It would be harder to watch you age behind a blood-stained apron in the dark behind the pumpernickel and bratwurst. I will weep for you the first time I hear a runny-nosed brat ask, 'Didn't that old guy used to be someone?'

"So, I don't know what is best for you. I only know what you have meant to us—to Bonnet, Texas."

Desperately, he cried, "I never asked for that!"

"I'm sure you didn't," she said. "No one does."

CHAPTER TWENTY-SIX

KJIRSTEN SAID TO ME, "I wouldn't do it."
"Why not?"

"Sally has had a long day, and so have you. Your head is spinning about Doug and she is the last person you can talk to about him."

"I know. I'm worried about her though."

"I know you are, Robbie, but she'll be okay."

"She didn't say two words to me and she left without eating."

"It was a memorial service, sweetie; there was nothing to say. And maybe she wasn't hungry."

"I guess."

"She will be fine. Don't go see her tonight. Wait until the weekend. Everyone will feel better by then. The boys will win on Friday; Saturday will be a good day to celebrate." Then after a smirky pause, "Perhaps you should try your hand at breakfast again."

She kissed me with an evil giggle, hopped out of the truck, and skipped up the walk to her house.

Kjirsten was positively correct. I should not have even driven by Sally's house, let alone slowed to a stop; but it was the shortest route from Kjirsten's to my place, and Mother's Buick was there, so I reasoned I could do no harm by dropping in to say hello. I wanted to make sure she had something to eat.

I wasn't sneaking; I made no effort to be quiet. I clogged up the back steps like always and entered the kitchen door unannounced. That's where I figured they'd be anyway, only they weren't.

Before I could close the door, I could hear them in the bedroom, and I was going to shout out my presence when I heard Sally say, "How could he do this to me?"

Mother replied, consolingly, "He must think it is for the best. Perhaps it is."

Sally was animated. "Are you taking his side?"

"Of course not, honey. But perhaps someday you will look back and realize this was better for all."

"Why do you say that?! Look at me. I am a mess. How will I ever get through this?"

The more Sally's panic crescendoed, the calmer Mother became. Her tone was soothing. "With everyone's help who loves you—me, your friends, your new friend, Kjirsten—even your brother."

"It's his fault this is happening!"

I wanted to dissolve and ooze back over the threshold. It was the most cowardly exit I could envision. I hated the side of my conscience that made me do the right thing. I shut the door with a bang and loudly called, "Halloo, it's me."

Mother came into the kitchen to greet me with a hug and a kiss on the cheek. "Hello, son. What a pleasant surprise."

She stood, politely eyeing me, inviting me to say why I had come, or, as I imagined, inviting me to say when I was leaving.

I lacked the will to hem and haw, so I merely hawed. "I came to see if you'd had anything to eat. Maybe if you wanted to go to the café."

"Oh, honey, that's dear of you, but not tonight. Thank you, anyway."

"Are you sure? I'm buying."

"That is tempting, but really, Sally is not feeling a hundred percent, so we'd better take a rain check."

"Not feeling well? Is she okay? I'll just go in and say hi."

"Shhh," Mother whispered, "she's napping."

Oh, the depravity. My own mother had lied to me. I slinked away. I crawled away. I whimpered away. I took the long way home—through the abysmal shadows of loneliness.

In my house, dark but for a light in the kitchen, I gingerly arranged four bottles in a row on the table, breathing their names one by one—maraschino, bitters, vermouth, and whiskey—aged Kentucky whiskey—and stirred up the first friend who had understood me all day.

CHAPTER TWENTY-SEVEN

O N WEDNESDAY MORNING AT seven-thirty, the only good thing about seeing Doug stagger in, crumpled, still in his church clothes, was that he looked worse than my head felt. I was running late and had downed a jar of tomato juice for breakfast. The counter was a strewn with empty bottles, half-empty bottles, jars, and dirty glasses—all mine.

"My God, look at you," I said, surprised at myself that I wasn't more shocked by his appearance.

"Look at me? Look at this," he said, waving an arm at the mess. "Is there any left for me?"

"Where have you been?"

Doug said, "I slept in my truck," as if that were a perfectly normal thing for a grown man to do alone.

Mimicking his nonchalance, I replied, "Oh. That's all."

"Yeah. I slept at the range."

That made sense since a half-mile would have been too far to drive home.

He opened the pantry, acting out normalcy, and asked, "Is there anything in here to eat?"

I was really late. "Do you want hot or cold?"

"Hot. I've been cold all night."

Served him right.

"Move. Let me look." I grabbed cans of refried beans and Mexican rice and handed them to him in a flurry. "Here," I said, "nuke these. There are eggs, tortillas, and salsa in the fridge. I have to go. I'm late."

"Then go," he said, smiling way more than my frame of mind would tolerate.

As I started the truck, I saw him standing at the door waving for me to roll down the window.

"What is it?" I asked over the rumble of the engine, trying to sound agitated and not at the same time.

Doug shouted, "Thanks for breakfast," and laughed.

How could he be laughing when I felt the way I did, and why was breakfast suddenly so hilarious to everyone but me?

By 9 AM, the rumors were rustling through the faculty room and blew the entire day. Wednesday was school board meeting night, and Baron Richards would be there with serious allegations about Hutch. I tracked down Hutch after lunch; he said he knew. I called Doug; he'd heard while cutting meat. Kjirsten knew and so did everyone else I could think of. Rumors have their way of spreading in a small town.

When Superintendent Zimmer banged the gavel down at seven, the Bonnet High School theater-turned-town-meeting-hall had standing room only. Most of the folks had never attended a school board meeting and were unaware how boring the wheels of a tiny bureaucracy can be. Twenty minutes were spent discussing whether or not starting school bus routes five minutes later in the morning would save fuel since they wouldn't have to sit idling as long for kids who were always late. The discussion was mercifully tabled to a later indeterminate date; I prayed it would be after my retirement. It was eight-fifteen before they had worked their way through the published agenda of budget items, future curriculum ideas, architectural proposals for a new administrative office, and whether or not to remove the Coke machines from the cafeterias because of recent governmental concerns about obesity. Ironically, or maybe not, it was Big Al—three-hundred-pound Big Al—who owned the machines and supplied the drinks, but nobody pointed that out.

The audience had grown more restless with each new discussion—squirming, coughing, leaving for the restrooms, returning from the restrooms, talking—until the superintendent had to peer over his glasses and glare like we were kids in school again and out of control—which we were. The room hushed when he said, "That concludes the scheduled agenda, is there any new business?" at which point the lights in the auditorium came up.

Nobody said a word for an eternal minute until Mickey Thurber blurted out, "How about we vote to put new business first at school board meetings?"

It broke the tension, but only for a second, because Baron Richards stood from where he sat near the front. Aviator sunglasses covered up his black eyes, but they didn't hide the tape holding his nose in place.

"You'll have to excusth the way I thalk," he said, sounding like he had a paper bag over his head—which would have looked better. "As you can thee, I have a thinusth issthue."

I couldn't argue that a gauze-packed nose was not a sinus issue.

His petite wife plainly dressed with hands folded quietly in her lap, hair pulled away from her clean pink face, sat beside where he stood and stared straight ahead.

Superintendent Zimmer announced, "The chair recognizes the gentleman from the audience. Would you state your name for the record, please?"

"I know it might be difficult to recognize me like thisth," he said, presumably believing that mocking himself would be endearing, "but y'all, including the chair, know I'm Baron

Richardth." There was an anonymous snicker. "And the chair alzo knowsth why I'm here."

"Go on, please Mr. Richards."

"I will be brief becausth it hurtsth to thalk. I'm here becausth of how I got the way I am. On Friday after the game, I endured an althercation with a member of the communithy. I do not expect you to deal with him. I will handle that my own way. I am here becausth our illusthrious football coach athith—athith—helped and encouraged the uncalled-for act of violenth and then did nothing to aid me in my hour of need."

The last part worried me. The part about athith—assisting—and encouraging was pure bull, but it was reasonably accurate that we walked away and left him bleeding in the parking lot. I was beginning to feel uneasy about the sticky spot in which the superintendent was about to find himself when I heard a distinctly familiar voice from the back of the auditorium shout, "Hold on there just a minute!"

It was Doug standing, fists on hips, with shoulders wide and proud.

Superintendent Zimmer banged his gavel again and said, firmly, "Now, Doug, you will just have to wait your turn."

Doug, still speaking strongly, said, "I'll gladly wait, but seein' as how I was the chief altercator that ol' dark eyes is referrin' to, I need to remind him how painful it can be to stray from the truth."

The men laughed and the women gasped.

Richards shouted the best he could, "Misther Chairman! Isth he threatening me? I will not sthand for being threatened."

From across the auditorium, a nameless voice yelled, "Then you'd better sit down!"

I liked that. We were not alone. Men and women laughed together.

The superintendent pounded his wooden hammer six times, stood up, and forcefully barked, "I will have order or I will empty this room and call a closed session! Mr. Richards has the floor and he will be allowed to speak."

Smugly, sounding snider than ever with his nasal obstructions, Richards tried again, "Asth you can sthee, Misther Chairman, uncalled-for violence isth unwholesthomely tolerated in thisth town. It isth time we reconsthider inviting men like Misther Hutcheson into our midsth. It stheems that histh off-field passthions are contributing to the unresth of our children."

There was a brief commotion from the back followed by the sound of Doug's boots ringing down the aisle. His clear voice ricocheted from floor to ceiling to beam and back again. "Okay! That's enough!" There was little doubt as to his intent.

Three men sitting near Richards—Amos Swindel, Irwin Criker, and Gator Pickett—stood as if to defend him. Although Gator stood uneasily as if he were just as well standing to leave for the men's room—which would have been a better idea.

Suddenly, every man in the room burst to his feet with spring-loaded auditorium chair flapping behind him. Those nearest the front moved swiftly toward the aisle stepping on or over any woman who sat in their way. They weren't moving to stop Doug; they were moving with him as a mob closing toward the broken-nosed pomposity and his feeble drones. Unfortunately for Richards, he had either forgotten or never understood the one immutable fiber that bound our cores—any man who had grown up with Doug Meadhran would stand with him in the face of Satan himself.

Voice cracking, Zimmer bellowed, "Order!!" His gavel head splintered from its shaft and clattered across the floor.

With men pushing, shoving, and volleying obscenities, their women screamin' at them, and old man Zimmer clamoring for order with his remnant of a gavel handle, the din was tumultuous until young Derek Richards leapt onto the stage. He waved his arms and yelled, "Stop it! Stop it! Stop it!" And we did when we saw his tears shimmering in the haze of the spotlights.

"Stop it," he said again, quieter, when we had all frozen silently where we stood. "I don't know about meetings or what it means to have the floor, but I wanna talk. I wanna say some things."

He looked back at the board members collecting themselves at the table and Superintendent Zimmer, who said, "If you think it will help, son, go ahead."

The boy's dad—shaken, not knowing whether to sit, stand, or run—lowered himself into his seat.

Derek shuffled; he was uneasy standing alone before the madness, but resolute in voice. "My pop is right. The fightin' has gotta stop."

Someone called out, "You're just like your old man."

Carney Jakes hollered, "Shut up and let the boy talk!"

Peering through glistened eyes at his father, the boy said, "Pop, the hittin' has gotta stop," while his mother, appearing smaller than before, looked away.

"I wisht you hadn't got hit the other night, but we know all about hittin' don't we, Pop? If it hadn't been that hit, it would have been another one, wouldn't it? It woulda been a hand on the face, fists later on, and then a belt. We know how the hittin' woulda been. Ma and me know."

No breath could be heard in the room as the last of the men standing melted into their seats. Baron Richards stiffened as if to rise, but his meek wife pinned his arm to the chair and held him. Startled, he looked at her and then grimly settled back.

On the stage, never looking away from his parents, Derek continued, "Coach tried to stop it. He said we should all go home before there was any hittin'. Then, after the hittin', he helped, too, only you don't remember that part, Pop, 'cause you were hurt. I came back with a towel from my truck and told the coach to go on so I could clean you up. I took you home, Pop, only bein' kinda out of it, you don't remember it all. Coach was there for you, Pop—just like he's always there for me. He always is. He believes in me. I ain't too good at football. I know I ain't, but he believes in me when there's some that don't. He wanted to help you and I sent him away because you're my pop and I had to take care of you. Families do that, don't they?"

Baron rose again and the wife wanted to stop him, but he shook her off, slid to the end of the row, and walked up the aisle and away.

It had been so easy to stoke my fury for him when he was all puffed up with artificial threats and paranoia. My scorn followed his broken visage shrinking away naked from the room, trailing pity behind him.

Derek said, "He'll be okay. He'll be home tonight and we'll talk. He'll be okay." Then he left the stage in silence, took the empty seat by his ma, and held her hand.

I saw the boy in a time machine spiraling backward through the generations of his father and grandfather—each of them trapped—thrashing at an invisible webbed prison, vainly tearing at the angry net, dying to escape. I dreamed the gentle gesture of his hand reaching out might one day unravel the mesh.

Finally, superintendent Zimmer cleared his throat and did his best to resume as if nothing had happened. "Principal Wieselmeyer has asked to say a few words this evening." Then, squinting trough the glare, he asked, "Vernon, are you still here?"

"Here I am, Hal," the principal replied firmly, striding to the front.

From the stage, he began, "I want to talk about Coach Hutcheson. I was prepared to speak about him tonight, before the events of the last ten minutes, and nothing that has transpired has changed what I have to say.

"Like it or not, the game of football is important in Bonnet and most other towns in Texas. Everybody wants to win, and fortunately we win more than our share. Sometimes we forget that, but we do better than most. We talk about championships. We dream about them. We believe we should have had one of our own—or maybe more than one. But since no shining trophy is displayed under glass in the hall, or because the town sign doesn't proclaim all the years of our ultimate conquests, we get to feeling like we've been cheated and then we look around hard for someone to blame. That is the sinister lure of championships."

Vernon looked at home on the stage—he would have made a good preacher or politician, only he was more sincere.

Lowering the tenor of his voice and stepping forward to the edge of the footlights to corral our focus, he said, "But championships are no guarantee of champions. Champions are born from a different sort of victory. I'm talking about the victories of courage, morality, and heart we need every day for home, job, friends—life. They have little to do with football and are victories that shine far longer than paint on a sign or luster on a bronze statue.

"Folks, Hutch is molding your boys into champions. In my career, which extends for longer than I want to think about or ever imagined that it would, I have been blessed to work with many winners. I have even held the elusive trophy and tasted the heady spoils of the moment. But in the biggest game of all—the game of character—Hutch Hutcheson is number one in my book. Our kids need him. You need him, and I am proud to have him on my staff."

He started down the stairs to the floor below, then paused and added, "And don't forget that Hutch's team—our team—has won plenty of games… and you never know… we may win it all one year."

It was respectfully quiet while he walked and I figured there were more than a few cowboys in the crowd who considered his talk too corny or soft for their particular brand of toughness, but then, from the right wing, Tommy Jarvis stood up and began a cadenced clap. Then Jason stood, then Michael Martinez, and Roy and Mason. Even Jacob Swindel rose and finally Derek Richards himself. All the boys of the team were there and clapping rhythmically with their fathers beside them. And then we all were standing and applauding—even me, although I knew more than the rest of them about Hutch's future.

At last, Superintendent Zimmer commanded a modicum of attention from us and with stately bearing announced, "We on the school board are not entirely deaf to community rumblings. Aware of certain grievances that were to be raised tonight, we met earlier in private session to discuss our best course of action. You folks have voted us in and we do our best to keep the interests of the community at the front of all considerations. This time is no different; but more than that, tonight we also speak from our own hearts. We drafted a short proclamation, which will be part of the recorded minutes of this meeting."

He pulled a single folded paper from his coat pocket, and read, "We, the undersigned members of the Bonnet, Texas school board, on this day proudly proclaim our support of Coach Samuel 'Hutch' Hutcheson and his contributions to the school, the town of Bonnet, and the students in his trust. It is our intent that he remain an employee of the Bonnet, Texas School District, in his present capacity, for as long as he so desires. As such, we hereby extend our offer to Samuel Hutcheson of a contract that names him as Permanent Football Coach of the Bonnet, Texas Mustangs.

"The draft has been wholeheartedly and unanimously signed by every member of this board."

This time the school board members rose first and applauded and again we followed. I'm certain it appeared as if unbridled adulation was the heart and soul of my ovation.

The boys chanted, "Coach, Coach, Coach."

Zimmer scanned the audience and said, "Coach, if you're here tonight, we'd love to have you come up and say a few words."

From the back row, he answered, "Oh, I'm here. I wouldn't have missed this."

It would have felt good to laugh with them, but I couldn't for choking on the dust of El Paso.

He walked to the front and tried to talk without a microphone from the floor, but Mr. Zimmer wouldn't let him. He goaded him up the stairs and handed him the lapel mic, which Hutch held while he spoke.

"I don't know what to say, really. I've never been confused with one overcome by his own humility, but tonight I am truly humbled. Coaching is all I have ever wanted to do. Even when I was away from it, I thought about little else. I will always be grateful to Vernon Wieselmeyer for the trust he placed in me when he asked me to be your coach. The people of Bonnet have been a second family to me. I could never have dreamed of warmer people, a finer team, or a better place to rebuild my career."

I wondered how long he would speak of us in the past tense before he drove a stake through our hearts, saying he was sorry, it had been swell, but he had to go.

He went on, rubbing his chin, searching for his best least painful way to tell them, "Sometimes the grass really is greener."

I was reasonably certain that there was an underabundance of anything green but cactus in El Paso.

"I have always seen myself as one who carefully considers all opportunities as they are presented," he said, attempting, I imagined, to sound professorial. "I have had a vision shaping my ambitions for some time. Bonnet, Texas has played a big role in that."

All stepping-stones have in common being left behind.

"Four days ago," Hutch said, moving furtively to the recent past tense, ever closer to the vacuous future, "one of the beautiful women of Bonnet brought all my plans into focus. She gave me exactly what I asked for. The rush of emotions I felt at being offered a position as head coach of a college with an excellent football tradition was exhilarating. I want to thank Tildy Hannah for making my dreams come true."

Thanking Tildy for his desertion merely made him look more callous. I guessed she realized earlier than the rest us that severing ties sooner than later was best. There was nothing more I wished to hear, but, after all, he had the floor.

"My dream went: coach and win at a small college, and then, after three or four years, move to a bigger one and then a bigger one, and then, at the end of fame, I saw myself moving to a small Texas town to bask in the glowing memory of all my victories past. Miss Hannah, with a simple phone call, opened the door to all of that. For a full day, I played the dream to its end over and over until I was fast-forwarding over all the smaller schools to the big one, and then, even faster, I skipped right to the victory parade and finally to my little town front porch... right back to Bonnet.

"If it hadn't been for Miss Hannah, I might never have seen that I already am where I want to go. You—we—have a special way of life here. It may not always feel that way when the fence is down or the pot's boiling over, or there's not enough money to buy the kids or yourself all the fancy toys you see on TV, but none of that matters because you have what money can't buy— your own hometown—Bonnet, Texas. I am privileged to be a part of it. I am honored that you have asked me to stay and I am looking forward to many, many years on the greener pasture of the Bonnet High School football field."

I looked around to see how they were taking the bad news, searching for grim faces, but they were all standing again, cheering, stomping and slapping each other on the back. For what? Why was I standing again, too? What had he said? He was staying? I'd known it all along.

When the whooping subsided, Hutch added, "A final thought—a promise—our kids are too important to me to allow any off-field distractions to ever interfere with their potential. As long as I am their coach, they will come first—always."

A final time we stood and hurrahed our support as he returned up the aisle through a gauntlet of high-fives and handshakes. I might have dwelt on Hutch's parting shot about distractions because I knew in my heart that it meant Sally would be off limits, but I stomped a little harder to make myself not think about it.

The superintendent slammed down his gavel head and roared over the hullabaloo, "Meeting adjourned!"

CHAPTER TWENTY-EIGHT

NINE-THIRTY ON A SCHOOL night in Bonnet means streets are empty, stores are dark, and folks are home. After the meeting, Big Al's was ablaze. Men filled more seats than would fit around the table, and all the booths were crammed. Big Al sweated to keep the coffee brewed and poured at the same time until Bud volunteered to waitress, so Big Al only had to sweat over the brewin'.

Hutch was there, and Doug. Hutch talked nothing but football—Texas football, Bonnet football, Pop Warner football—any football we kicked up, and it kept on that way until Cobus came in and walked to us the way he had after the first game all those weeks before, only this time missing his aura of invincibility.

Cobus stood nervously next to Doug, rocking his weight from side to side, working up the nerve to butt in. Bud walked by and handed him a Pepsi without saying a word. Cobus muttered thanks and then murmured hellos to those of us who noticed he was there.

Finally, he bent and asked his dad if they could speak alone, outside. The natural thing would have been to rehash why the boy had left the team and how the outcome of the losses might have been different with him, but it was taboo with Hutch there, so we danced around it and stared at the table. The closest anyone dared to approach the subject was Carney Jakes, who wasn't a round table regular. He was an apt sub for Bud, though, who was still taking his table-waitin' very seriously.

Carney asked Hutch, "Coach, if you wanted to look back on the whole season, which you really can't because it's not been a whole season yet, but if you could, would you do anything different? I mean, do coaches do that—look back and play 'what if' with themselves, thinkin' about what you mighta done if you could do it again?"

Scratching his head in earnest, like he was cogitating real hard, Hutch said, "Hmmm," and after a long pause concluded with, "Nope."

I was careful to time my gulps for fear that such sage utterances would elicit spewed coffee.

Then, showing mercy to Carney, who still squirmed for relevance, Hutch said, "We do get to do it again. We have a game in two days and then the biggest game of the year a week later."

"Yeah," said Carney, "of course, I know that… I mean, there sure has been a lot of things that went on… I mean, it sure has been a different sort of year so far. I was thinkin' if only—"

"If only, if only…" mused Hutch, as if praying to the gods of football, gazing to the heavens, which he couldn't see through the grease-stained ceiling tiles. "If only we could talk about next year. I bet that next year we can win it all."

Overhearing, Bud stopped in his tracks, not fully conscious of the depths of sarcasm to which our oracle had descended.

"I've been thinkin' on that, Coach," he said, setting his pot on the table and stealing Doug's empty chair.

Galey and Cuthbert leaned in with their ears turned forward like donkeys homing to a familiar bray.

Hutch closed his eyes, folded his hands in front, and with a long sigh, said, "Al, what have you got that's stronger than beer?"

Cuthbert snorted, "You was funnin' us all along, Coach. Wasn't you?"

Bud said, "Cuthbert, Cuthbert, Cuthbert. You mean you couldn't tell that," and stood to answer the call of another cup of coffee from a far away booth, which was just as well because Doug came back from the street, expecting, without pause, his chair to be empty.

When he had appropriately situated his posture, Doug said to Hutch, while looking blankly through me, "Cobus wants to speak with you outside, Coach."

Agape and ogling, we followed, with eyes only, the coach striding out in pregnant silence.

Doug broke it by asking, "Hey, Bud, how 'bout another cup over here?"

And the tinkling of spoons on saucers resumed, with dishes ringing in the sink and all of us dribbling on until Hutch stepped back through the door after five minutes and beckoned, "Listen up, folks," when he didn't need to beckon 'cause we would have heard if he had whispered in a pillow.

"I've got a little news and we won't make too much of it. I don't want to hear any gossipin' or speculatin' as to why, or what someone else mighta done, or what should be done. There'll be no unnecessary celebrating either. Young Cobus Meadhran has asked to play in the last two games and I'm pleased to welcome him back to his team. I never took him off the roster. Now you know everything I do. It is what it is and nothin' more."

And then, before turning to leave, "Thanks again, folks, for your support. We'll see you at the game on Friday."

After the door closed, Bud leaned in over the table, balancing with hot coffee pot held wide behind him and with eyebrow crook'd, and said, "I bet there's more to it than that."

Doug winked.

CHAPTER TWENTY-NINE

INALLY, CAME FRIDAY OF the jagged week. Thursday had remained schizophrenic, with the school board meeting high lingering and the kids wanting to congratulate Cobus or needle him, in spite of Coach's admonition, about his return to the team. By the end of Thursday, a humbly retiring smile and shrugged shoulders were permanent physical attributes of the besieged boy. Then, Friday, it was over and all the buzz was football, as it should have been.

A painting of Friday would be a Norman Rockwell American memoir appearing discordantly out of place, hanging with Dali abstractions of all else that transpired around it. If, in my old age, recalling days gone by, I remember only that Friday, I will rock myself to tranquil sleep.

We caravanned into the hills to challenge the Tickle Creek Horns on their home field and won. I can't remember many other times when I felt genuine sadness for an opponent of the Mustangs, but it was tough to watch the end of their era. It was the last game there before Tickle Creek High became a footnote in the records of a unified school without a town. At halftime, all the men who had ever played for the Horns and who could still stand, gathered alongside their old teammates to receive final accolades. Former band members came too and played or banged on what instruments they could scrounge. At the end of the game they massed, one last time near the end zone, with six pipers at the front moaning the last slow hundred-yard march. The bands led, both rusty and shiny, keeping time to the row of drummers thundering out the years of glory. *Rat-atat-atat-atata-boom.* Footballers stepped behind, with old-timers limping on arthritic knees while muscled-up kids held helmets high. Alongside, cheerleaders fluttered pom-poms, shedding streamers in the air. Tickle Creek rippled her folk from the stands to complete the long parade goodbye. We stood for them, saluting, applauding, crying—until the last, a man alone, turned to wave so-long before clearing the gate at the far end. *Rat-atat-atat-atata-boom-boom-boom.*

CHAPTER THIRTY

I COULDN'T SHAKE THE feeling that my Sunday breakfast cooking had poisoned the entire week, and Sally asked me if I'd do it again. She said I'd be cooking for a couple extras without saying who they were. She'd set her table with finer linen than usual and her good china. I questioned nothing, planning instead, to remain mute the entire day.

Quiche required more thought and preparation than frying pork had done six days before. I could have used an extra hand but when Sally asked, cleaver poised to mutilate a couple dozen stalks of asparagus, how long she should boil butter for Hollandaise, I politely encouraged her to leave the kitchen to me. Mother volunteered—the same mother who had warped my truth. I graciously responded, "No, thank you, Mother." My wounded pride was stronger than my immediate need of a juggler. I dropped a tray of strawberries when I dove to catch a bottle of Cold Duck rolling precipitously toward the edge of the refrigerator shelf. While endeavoring to artfully arrange six cups of fruit on the table, I toppled an overstuffed vase of fresh cut flowers.

As I mopped up the mess, Cobus stumbled sleepily from his room.

"Cobus! You're here. Good morning." Nobody had bothered to mention to me that he'd moved back in.

Stealing strawberries on the way to the bathroom, he said "Hi, Uncle Robbie," like he'd never been gone. On his way back I handed him a preemptive plate of jalapeño-jack in order to preserve the balance of fruit and cheese.

Kjirsten arrived, cheery as a puppy, and stood at my side tasting my creations before their unveiling until I felt the urge to slap her hand, which I tactfully stifled.

I heard Cobus call out, "Mom, do I need to dress up?"

"Wear a nice shirt, sweetie," she replied, prompting me to observe Kjirsten and Mother, both looking like they had arrived from church, and then my own Farm Aid '94 faded sweatshirt.

"Sally! You didn't tell me to dress up."

She scrutinized me and weakly affirmed, "Oh, you look fine…" and then over her shoulder, "Cobus, do you have a shirt your uncle can borrow?"

As I changed, worried that my quiche might burn if I weren't there to watch it, I heard the doorbell ring and then Kjirsten say, "Good morning, Hutch. Please come in."

I immediately hoped the quiche was on fire, preferring hysterical panic over all other suddenly looming emotional possibilities. I darted from Cobus's room, jamming shirttail into pants on the run.

"Welcome, Coach. What a surprise," I exclaimed, thrusting my hand toward his. He wore a sport coat and tie.

Kjirsten said, "Hutch, you look great. Winning suits you," while she absentmindedly straightened my collar.

My head was spinning, really, looking for Cobus at all points of the compass. I half-expected to see him driving away in a storm of gravel. He emerged nonchalantly from the kitchen with a glass of chocolate milk.

"Hi, Coach," he said after a swallow.

"Mawnin'," drawled the coach, smiling broadly. "Nice job last night."

"I was pretty rusty, but thanks for gettin' me in the game for a few plays."

"You bet. We need you ready for next week."

"I'll be ready," said Cobus, with more confidence than he'd shown for weeks.

Mother walked out of the kitchen with my quiche and announced, "Welcome, Coach. What perfect timing."

Sally followed with asparagus and sauce.

"Okay! Everybody take a seat. Robbie has fixed a wonderful breakfast. Hutch can sit at the head in honor of last night's win. I'll sit at this end next to the kitchen and everybody else can fill in as they wish."

I thought it better to lie down before the dream ended.

Cobus said, "Asparagus. Uh, do I like asparagus, Mom?"

Hutch answered for her, "Put enough of that lemon-butter sauce on it and it's pretty good."

I was thankful there would be a way for them to gag it down. At least the strawberries were a natural hit, but then, they had required no skill greater than running water.

After the fruit course, Hutch began with small talk, ignoring that I was approaching critical mass for a perplexity melt-down. He asked me, "Hey, Robbie, what did you think of the post-game tribute?"

Cobus jumped in, "You should have seen it, Mom. It was the last game. They are closing the school. The whole town marched down the field with bagpipes and drums."

Mother gasped, "No! Tickle Creek? When I was a girl, it was the place to go."

"Tickle Creek?" Kjirsten asked incredulously.

"Oh, yes. They had the best dance hall. All the good bands came there. Bob Wills, Bill Haley, even ol' Willie Nelson later on."

"Bill Haley?"

"You betcha. His group was the Saddlemen."

"Oh," I said, "a different Bill Haley."

"No, dear, he was the same guy. He swung before he rocked."

Cobus asked, "Who's Bill Haley?"

Evidently he knew who Willie was.

"Early heavy metal," I said.

Mother continued, "I guess, after the dance hall burned down, there was no reason to go there."

Rhetorically, Hutch wondered, "Can the loss of one attraction like that cause the decline of a whole town? Please pass the Hollandaise."

"Here you are, dear," said Mother. "I'm sure there were other reasons, but I suppose once the kids began leaving, they kept on going."

"Can I have more scrambled egg pie?" asked Cobus. Then, "Do you think that could happen here?"

"Quiche," I said.

"What?"

"It's called quiche."

"Oh. Quiche pie. It's good."

Sally said little. Every time I glanced her way, an enigmatic smile had frozen her ability to speak.

Hutch responded to Cobus, "I suppose it could happen anywhere. You can't stay the same. You either grow or shrink, but you can't stay the same."

Finally, Sally jumped in, "That sounds like a football analogy."

"Guilty."

I said, "The kids have to come back to keep a town from ending up like Tickle Creek. They can go away, to college or the Army or to hike across Europe, but they have to come back."

"Like you did," said Kjirsten.

"Yeah, like me. They should be like me."

Kjirsten patted my knee and whispered, "Yes, Robbie—yes, they should."

I finished my last bite of asparagus with no sauce because of the near-quart others had consumed before the boat came round to me, and added, "But today I wish I was like Hutch. If I'd known he was coming, I'd have worn my tie."

"Oh, then you have one," said Kjirsten with smiling eyes.

"Two. I have two. One for funerals and one for wed—"

Why were they staring at me? What sinister smug little evil smile connivance had they plotted? The temperature had just risen thirty degrees and they were so cool in pretty little dresses, brass-buttoned blazers, and Polo shirts. Did they think I wouldn't notice Champagne chilling behind the strawberries, fresh flowers hidden in plain sight on every flat surface, and scented candles out-wafting my quiche pie?

To remain stoically composed, I imagined myself as a Thunderbird flyer with leather jacket, silk scarf, and shades. I was Tom Cruise in *Top Gun* or Tom Hanks in *Apollo 13*. In the laconic vernacular of fighter pilots, I ordered, "Cobus, keys are in the truck. Get me my tie."

"Please," Mother admonished.

"Yeah. Please. And my blue jacket and a shirt. Even better: grab the plastic suit bag. It has everything I need. You can wear the blue jacket."

Cobus looked to Sally and she nodded her snickering permission.

I sprinted to the door in my cross-trainers before he drove off, and I yelled, "Bring my dress boots. Please!"

I turned, horrified to see how they remained mockingly calm with all I had to do.

"Who else is coming?" I asked, while snatching up the serving dishes.

"Pastor Boynton," said Sally. "Now, put that mess in the sink and give me a hug."

She stood and waited until it warmed over me that it was finally her moment and that my own flitting mattered not. I gladly hugged her, Mother, Kjirsten, Sally again, and then I shook Hutch's hand.

"Wow! This is great. I can't believe it. Yes, I can."

Sally, bubbling over, said, "We decided on Sunday and we're getting married today. I've kept it a secret all week, partly out of respect for Macey and because of wagging tongues, but mostly until I was sure Cobus was okay—which he was—sorta. You weren't gone ten minutes last Sunday when Hutch walked in and said, 'Sally, either marry me or I'll drag you to my cave.'"

"Romantic, Coach—romantic," I said.

"Well, when she was finished crying, she made me get on one knee."

"Kjirsten, were you here?"

"Oh, yes. And I took notes."

"And you kept it from me all week?"

"Yes, and you should worry over how easy it was for me to hide it from you and about how much fun I had doing it."

Quite apparently, it had been easy for everyone to hide it from me. I said, "Tuesday, after Macey's service, I came by. Mother said you were sleeping."

"Oh, that. I was panicked and would have ripped the eyes out of the first man I saw. I tried on every stitch I owned and nothing looked good because you told me I needed a new wardrobe."

"Me! That was a year ago. What I said was, you needed something for yourself for a change and you ought to go crazy on a shopping spree."

"I heard you. It felt like you said I was dowdy as a bag lady."

Change trains quickly, Robbie.

"Cobus. What about Cobus? How did you...what did he..."

Sally said, "In a sad way, Macey helped. He was moved by her passing and wanted to be with me Sunday night. We cried together, were angry together, and we laughed together. At last, I told him I was getting married with or without him. I didn't ask his permission or talk about it being off in the future. I said he needed to decide right then if he wanted to waste the next few years of his life mired in bitterness, or if he wanted to share my happiness with me. As tender as the moment was, I'm afraid I was rather forceful."

"You said all that?"

"Yes, I did. The timing was right. He said you told him much the same, and that even his dad tried to get through to him."

"True. I didn't think it stuck."

"Probably not, but the seed was planted."

"What about Coach?" I asked, ignoring that he was standing beside me.

"I kept it simple. I said Hutch wasn't, and didn't want to be, his dad. He wasn't going to be his buddy; he is the other man in my life and nothing more. I told him Hutch is not a replacement; he is a complement."

Hutch said, "Aw, shucks."

She continued, "The more I talked, the more I knew I was doing the right thing, so I took a deep breath and said, 'Hutch is a fine Coach; you're a fine football player. You need to get over it and take your frustration out on the other team instead of your own.'"

"What did he say to that?"

"He said he'd think about it. He got quiet, kissed me on the cheek, went to his own room, and he's been living here since. I didn't know he'd rejoined the team until he came home Thursday night with his practice jersey."

Hutch chimed in, "Wednesday he started to apologize and I let him know it wasn't necessary. He asked if he could suit up with the team for the last two games. He liked it when I told him we hadn't cleaned out his locker. Cobus didn't ask to play; he asked to be with the team. Believe me; he'll be playing on Friday."

"I can't wait."

"Me, either," he said. "To a man, the team welcomed Cobus back. The kids are fired up like it was the first day all over again. We're practicing tomorrow, on Sunday, and I wish it was today."

"Ahem," ruffled Sally, then she whispered, "The wedding. Try not to forget the wedding."

"Yeah, Hutch," I mocked, "what are you thinking?"

"I'm thinking this is the most exciting weekend of my life."

"Nice try."

She kissed him and scolded, "You help Mother finish the dishes. Here comes Cobus. Robbie is going to change. I am going to get ready and Pastor Boynton will be here in twenty minutes."

When Sally returned, she was stunning. I had forgotten how beautiful baby sister was—graceful and lithe. Her charming tendency toward ephemeral reason often disguised her elegance, but her affection always shone.

Not knowing women's attire, as I don't, I'd say she wore a dress down to her knees with a jacket to her Navajo Concha belt. Sally's suit was beige, or tan, or ecru, but the label would have named it flax, fawn, or maple—not saffron because saffron has too much yellow for November. Embroidered orange flowers with brown curling leaves fell along the hems and other right places and Sally looked like a cowgirl hippie all grown-up.

I remembered Sally tagging on to me, swinging on a rope and flailing to the river, hiking up the rocks, learning how to drive, taking out a fence post, going to the prom with Doug, crying over newborn Cobus, crying over Doug, laughing over life, wishing she could cook, fishing, snorkeling, sewing, gardening, golfing, and loving, always loving. I remembered all of that when she danced into the room on a sunbeam and I saw her like it was the first time.

Hutch buckled and sat.

Awe in his eyes, Cobus said, "Mom, you're beautiful!"

She blushed and curtsied to him.

Cobus had Hutch's fancy digital Nikon to keep him busy. I knew he still fought ambiguous feelings even though he hid it well. He began snapping the shutter when she walked in the room and didn't stop until the champagne was gone an hour later. We had to pry the camera from him to get him in a shot or two with the pastor obliging.

Pastor kept it short; the kiss was a peck; Cobus clicked away; Mother cried a little; and Kjirsten squeezed my hand—a lot.

Sally and Hutch were married and away for the night, without saying where, to Fredericksburg or Austin or Marble Falls. Mother watched them drive away with a last blot of her eyes and then cleaned the champagne flutes before leaving the rest to Cobus, Kjirsten, and me.

I asked Cobus what he'd planned for the rest of the weekend.

"Nothing," he said. "Nothing at all. I'll think about homework and probably won't do it. I'll sleep. I'll watch football. I'll drive to Llano to rent a couple movies and get Tommy and Michael to come over and watch them—maybe Derek."

"Good."

Before Kjirsten and I left in search of an afternoon adventure, he shook my hand and said, "Thanks, Uncle Robbie."

"For what?"

"Just thanks."

CHAPTER THIRTY-ONE

TILDY HAD MADE IT perfectly clear that none of us were invited to their first official golf tournament against the Bee Tree women, so I was surprised when Doug wasn't home when I returned from a Saturday night, spur-of-the moment Austin getaway with Kjirsten. I figured Tildy had changed her mind and dragged him along to caddy. I was napping peacefully in his chair with the Dallas Cowboys flickering on the screen when she rang the bell.

"Yoo-hoo," she called out after opening the door a crack. "Anybody home?"

I wiped the drool from my chin, stood up too fast, and promptly sat back down.

"Come in. Come in," I said with as pleasant an utterance as I could gravelly muster.

The three women clamored in, jockeying to be first in the room to twitter their exuberance. Standing again, more slowly, while pulling my hair from my eyes, I happily welcomed the onrush of smothering arms.

"Where's Doug?" asked Inez, gazing at the shadowy images in the room, hoping that one would morph into him.

"I don't know. I thought he was with you."

"Oh, no," said Amanda. "We played all on our own."

"And…how did it go?"

"We're not telling until Doug is here."

Inez made her way to the kitchen door and peered through, still looking for him to materialize.

Tildy said, "Amanda, that's not polite. We can tell Robbie now and then we can tell Doug when he gets home."

They were all dressed alike in their golf uniforms with argyle sweater-vests over long-sleeved white blouses. The ladies' slacks were Bonnet Mustang blue, of course.

"Oh, no," I said. "Telling me now might diminish the fervor. Here's what we'll do. I'll try to raise the missing-in-action on his cell phone. The powder room has clean towels if you wish to freshen up. I'll pour sweet tea and we'll wait together."

"Where do you think he could be?" implored Inez again while shuffling her way to the couch.

Tildy answered, "Don't concern yourself, dear. He isn't far. Robbie is a generous host. Sweet tea sounds wonderful, doesn't it?"

"Of course, of course. I didn't mean to imply that he wasn't. I only wondered where Doug could be. I assumed he would be here when we were finished. Surely, he knew we couldn't wait to tell him about our day."

Amanda snipped, "Oh, Inez, Doug isn't a marionette waiting around on us to twiddle his strings."

"But—"

"But, we'll all be ready for him with freshly powdered noses and tumblers of tea when he returns, won't we?" said Tildy, eyeing Amanda over her spectacles.

"Sweet tea comin' up," I declared, while pointing Amanda to the guest bathroom down the hall.

Doug picked up on the third ring and spoke loudly over the distinct rattle of a diesel engine.

"What?" he said. "The gals are there? How'd they do?"

"Haven't said yet."

"What?"

"We're waiting on you."

"I can't hear you. Have them wait. Fix them tea or something. I'll be there in five minutes."

"Where are you?"

"What?"

In five minutes, I'd filled five Ball jars with chilled tea, hung fresh mint sprigs on each, and arranged them neatly on the old oak plank I called a serving tray. Doug slid his truck to a dusty stop and burst through the kitchen door looking like he'd been drilling for oil in the Sahara desert.

"Hey, pard, get me a clean shirt, will you?"

I set the plank back on the counter.

"Do you think it will help?"

"A hang-up shirt."

"Perhaps one that won't show dirt when it flakes off?"

"That bad, huh?"

"There's the sink."

I returned with an outmoded Hawaiian print and laid it next to where he was mudding up the sink. It would have taken me an hour to shed the Cro-Magnon look; in three minutes with a bar of soap, finger comb, and clean shirt, Doug emerged tall and bright, looking primed to dance away the day.

Inez stood and exclaimed, "Doug, you're here!"

"Howdy, ladies."

He went to shake her hand but she brushed it off and hugged him instead as did her two companions. When they finally let him loose he grabbed a jar and flopped into his chair.

"Well, gals," he said, "fill me in."

"First of all," began Tildy, "don't ask us who won. We didn't really keep score the way you might have. The Bee Tree women were forgiving of so many of our bad shots, that we wore out the eraser."

"I thought you were playing a scramble."

"We did. We did," said Amanda. "And we took turns being Macey, but I'm afraid we still had shots that needed to be forgiven."

"As do we all," I mused.

Doug said, "Tell me about all of your good shots—every one of them. Skip the bad ones. If the Bee Tree squad didn't count 'em, neither will I."

I hadn't seen much of him since the school board meeting. I hadn't been sure if his soul was still as conjoined with Tildy's as it had been before she'd searched it for him at the Methodist church.

She said, "We played only nine holes and Inez sank five putts herself."

"Way to go, Inez!" I said.

"Well, putts are the only shots I can see. I have to do well on those. Amanda was the best in the sand. We did use one of my drives, though."

"Yes," said Tildy. "We used everyone's drive at least once and we had two genuine pars."

"Wow. Two pars. That's tremendous," Doug said, sitting forward in his chair. "Tell me what's next. Do you like golf? Will you keep playing?"

Amanda answered for them all, "Of course! It is such a change from stodgy bridge games with gossiping old ladies. We mean to cause the gossip. Do you know how many exotic golfing places we can visit?"

"I'm afraid I do. It could take you years to get out of Texas."

"Yes, Texas. We joined their league and we'll be playing in Llano, Fredericksburg, Marble Falls, and the like...and Ireland, Hawaii, Australia."

"New Zealand," I added, "I've always wanted to see New Zealand."

Doug grinned, "I don't think you're invited and I doubt the Llano league plays in New Zealand."

Matter-of-factly, Tildy responded, "They will when we get there."

Doug sat back and raised the footrest.

"And we can't forget Bonny Glen," he said with a mysterious gleam.

Reverently, I whispered, "Ahh, Scotland. The homeland of golf."

"Bonnet," he said, before slurping a last gulp of tea.

Tildy said, "I still like Blue Fields."

"Where's that?" I asked.

Stirring ice aimlessly, he replied, "Bonnet... Bonnet... How about Bonny Blue!"

She clapped her hands together sharply and heartily declared, "Yes! Bonny Blue!" Tildy snatched up her jar, sprang to her feet, raised her drink high and sang out, "Here's to Bonny Blue!"

Doug kicked closed the footrest and rose with a swoop. "Here's to Bonny Blue!"

The rest of us rose and toasted, "Bonny Blue!"

I humbly implored, "What's Bonny Blue?"

"The Bonnet golf course," retorted Amanda incredulously, as if I'd questioned my own name.

"Oh. You've christened the driving range. How quaint."

"Not the range," said Tildy. "The golf course. The Bonnet Golf Course—henceforth to be known as Bonny Blue."

When she saw the bewilderment in my gaping eyes, she stated the obvious to Doug, "He doesn't know what we're talking about."

"I haven't seen him since Wednesday," said the mischievous butcher boy.

I sat, folded my arms, and waited.

He sat again, too, slowly levered the footrest into a comfortable position and began, "Well, Robbie ol' boy, Miss Tildy and I have formed an extraordinary partnership, conceived in a dream. On Thursday, at four in the morning, I sat bolt upright in bed with a vision streaming before me clearly as the Llano River in spring. I saw fairways in the hills, bubbling limestone springs, blue granite pools, rolling Bermuda grass greens. I saw a golf course plainly, as if I played it every day. I knew it; but it didn't exist. I walked every hole in my mind's eye. I knew the land, the trees, the streams; but where was it? I started driving at daybreak with no destination in mind. I ended up drinking coffee with Pappy."

"Pappy? Pappy Potachnick?"

"Pappy Potachnick. We walked to the top of his mountain and stood looking over the valley with Bonnet in the distance and Cutter's Creek winding around the western side. Pecans, oaks, and cottonwoods lined her banks with mounded glens carved from cedar overgrowth, and there it was; I saw Bonny Blue for the first time. I handed the binoculars to Pappy and asked him, 'Who owns those little pastures along Cutter's Creek?'"

I knew the answer and Doug did, too, long before he asked Pappy. I swiveled my gaze toward Tildy sitting on the couch to my left. She sat innocently—piously.

"Pappy said, 'Unless she's sold it or give it away, it belongs to Mathilda Hannah.'"

And then Doug said, "Miss Tildy would you like to carry on from here?"

"Well, when I answered my door, Mr. Cool was so addled he could barely babble. Without so much as a hello, he thrust himself inside and, with hat in hand, announced, 'Tildy I want to buy your ranch.' I asked him if he'd like some coffee. He replied he'd already had coffee and then repeated, 'I want to buy your ranch and build a golf course.' I asked him if he'd like a sandwich. He answered, 'No, ma'am. I can't eat. I want to build a golf course for the kids and folks of Bonnet. I want to build a golf team for the school. I want to build the little gem of the hills. I want to buy your ranch.' He followed me to the kitchen, where I poured coffee and made sandwiches. I asked him how much money he had; he said not much. Your friend Douglas, the master developer, guessed he'd find investors tripping all over themselves to build another Horseshoe Bay. Isn't that just what we need in Bonnet—rich Dallas weekend squatters building million dollar monstrosities, running up property taxes and clogging the roads? I told him no and made him eat."

I said, "He must have talked you into it. You've already named it."

"He pouted."

"I did not," he protested. "I was contemplating my options."

"Hah! You don't have many options. I hold the deed to the ranch."

"So you're not selling?" I asked—no less confused than when I'd toasted Bonny Blue.

"Not on your life!"

She sipped her tea, and Amanda said, "Oh, just tell him what you did."

Doug looked smug as a canary who'd poisoned the cat.

"We're getting there. We're getting there. Doug, tell your roommate what you said when I asked about your pro pursuits."

"As much as it pained me, I told her you'd been right from the beginning."

"Me?"

"Yep. You hinted that I may be too old to chase the tour."

"That's not exactly how I remember it, but if it helps for me to be your motivation, that's why I'm here."

"Well, I am too damn old; so what? I'm not too old to redirect the passion. Muscle and nerve might not be what they were twenty years ago, but the fire's still out of control. Forget the tour. I'll find someone to cut meat. I'm building a golf course."

"How?"

"One dump-bucket at a time."

"I mean, how about the land?"

"Ask Tildy."

"The cattle won't be pleased," she said with feigned sympathy. "I leased him the land."

"Leased it?"

Doug leapt back in, "She leased me three hundred acres at a dollar a year for ninety-nine years! I already paid up all ninety-nine. Tell him the rest, Tildy."

"There will be no houses; only Bonny Blue."

"And the camp. Tell him about the camp."

"We'll build a summer camp for kids who can't afford it; they'll come to learn the game. We'll bring them from all corners and they'll never need a dime. Maybe even one day some will return and choose Bonnet as their own hometown."

Doug popped up with the energy of a hummingbird, mimed a golf swing, posed his finish, and said, "Don't forget the championship Bonnet golf team. I have appointed myself the Bonnet golf team coach. Nobody at the school knows it yet—they don't even know they have a team—but I'm the coach, and we're gonna win."

I groped for a tactful way to voice the obvious; conjuring none, I asked "Who's gonna pay for this?"

"Details, details, details," tsked Tildy. "Have you seen the price of oil lately? I'll sell a few thousand barrels of the icky stuff. The write-off will tickle my CPA."

It was Tildy's land, her money, her rules, and Doug's new dream—or maybe the dream had been there all along, only waiting. He was building Bonny Blue.

Doug looked at me and said, "Pard, since you and Cobus are the closest Bonnet's got to green construction experts, I'll keep you plenty busy—on your days off, of course."

I recalled—or didn't—how much I'd earned for the last green we'd tilled, and how long it had taken my back to stop aching. It didn't matter to me a bag of sand. Doug was sticking around. Cobus and his pals would have reason to come home in the summer. I'd be drivin' tractors, 'dozers, big ol' trucks—what could be better'n that?

CHAPTER THIRTY-TWO

ONCE EVERY TWO YEARS, Bonnet suffers a traffic jam. Bee Tree buses follow a constable with strobes piercing ahead of the convoy. The rest of their town rumbles behind, honking down our Main Street for half an hour as each driver waits to file into the stadium lot.

While the Bee Tree faithful park their trucks and Buicks, the entire Bonnet student body, with the exception of the boys on the varsity, which is half the boys, gathers in the gym. We feel the thunder from the drums before we hear them. The tremble rises and the brass ignites the fight song when the throng rounds the corner, tramping up the hill to the gauntlet.

Bing Trundel, lit up like an indigo *Electric Horseman*, reined back his prancing black stallion, while the girls, with standards held high, unfurled their giant scroll. Blue and white streamers fluttered from the masts and five wild Mustangs, charging across the mural, looked too well drawn to shred.

At the opposite end of the field, a yellow and black Bee Tree portal declared, "Ridin' the Rodeo to State." Buff, their old Brahma bull, with billowing plumes of condensation steaming from his nostrils into the November chill, pawed patiently, waiting to lumber down our field before a swarming Bee Tree Rodeo.

They tore through first, trailing yellow crepe and bounding cheerleaders. When they clumped in a great huddle, vibrating up and down to their chant, Kjirsten remarked, "They're like bees in a hive."

Buff was led around the cluster twice, with cowbell dangling, before joggling off to his trailer.

"They can't decide if they're steers or drones," I snidely observed.

Then the Mustangs reared. The paper wall of horses exploded; the boys raced five abreast with Bing on his stallion leading the charge; trumpets blared and we all stood screeching our fanaticism.

Our boys massed in a bounding huddle, too. Kjirsten said, "With their white helmets and blue jerseys, they look like bluebonnets waving in a breeze."

"Let's hope they play like it's a tornado."

The last home game is parents' night. Before the kickoff, senior boys are introduced one at a time by Marvin's voice reverberating from the scratchy PA system. Son presents Mom her bouquet and Dad a jersey signed by the team, and then he escorts both to the center of the field where they stand for cheers and await the rest of the seniors.

It was the last game for Tommy, Michael, Jacob, and Mason as well as Cobus and Derek. I could see Sally's pride from where Kjirsten and I stood. Cobus kissed and hugged her and then handed the jersey to Doug.

Marvin announced, "And here's Cobus Meadhran. Welcome back Cobus. A hand for Cobus's folks, Sally and Doug. It sure looks good to see Doug back on the field. How about it, Doug… does it bring back old memories?"

Doug waved his hat while walking onto the field without turning around.

I had to hand it to Baron Richards for showing up at all. Had I been him, I would have moved to another state, but in the greater Bonnet family, we have been known to forgive. We won't necessarily forget, but forgiveness might find a way to dilute poisons past. Derek's mother held her husband's hand.

The PA crackled, "Last, but not least, is Derek Richards. Thanks for four fine years, Derek. Folks, how about a round of applause for the Richards family? And give it up once more time for all of this year's seniors,"—which we did.

Kjirsten and I started the game sitting where I always had, with Doug, Bud, and the Alden brothers. Big Al merrily deposited himself directly in front of us, rendering it impossible to see past his largeness when he stood unless we stood, too. Big Al stood for the opening kickoff and never sat back down.

It was plain to see that Al was madly in love with Kjirsten because he thoughtfully removed the smoldering cigar from his mouth every time he turned to explain to her what she had just seen. Not that it mattered, because the breeze directed the wisps directly to our faces anyway.

Michael took the opening kickoff on the five, dodged a tackle, and returned to the thirty, where he was smothered in a heap. Big Al turned and said, "Woo-hee, Miss Kjirsten, did you see that? They're hittin' hard tonight."

Kjirsten, who had succumbed at an early age to terminal flirtation, did nothing to discourage his fawning. She said, "Goodness, Al. If they keep that up, we'll have to stand all night."

"I'm afraid we will." He giggled.

I resigned myself to the realization that burning my clothes would be the one best way to purge the redolent tang of Swisher Sweets.

Al was right about the hitting. Tommy handed the first snap to Cobus, who ripped viciously through the line and stood the linebacker up with a loud pop before he received an equally angry blow from their defensive end. Cobus rebounded and jogged back to the huddle like I had seen him do so many times over four years.

The boys ground out two first downs with Cobus carrying the ball four times, before Tommy threw his first pass on third and eight. It fell incomplete, and Bud observed, "Everybody knew it would be a pass."

Al panted smoke and said, "Miss Kjirsten, they'll be punting now."

She said, "Let's hope he can stick it on the two," and then whispered to me, "I heard you say that once."

Jason kicked it through the end zone and Bee Tree came out throwing from the twenty. They completed five sideline passes in a row before their first running play. In three minutes, they ate up forty-four yards of turf before Bud had a chance to say, "Looks like they're moving the ball pretty good on us."

Doug sighed and, making eye contact with no one, sarcastically said, "I guess we'll have to wait 'til next year."

On first and ten from the thirty-six, Cobus, playing outside linebacker, blitzed from the right side and dropped the quarterback for a ten-yard loss.

Al turned to Doug, who had not yet stood, and with a high-pitched squeal, chortled, "Did you see that, Douggy? Did you see that?"

"Gee, Al, no, I didn't. I was obstructed."

Kjirsten said, "Come and sit beside me, Doug. There's room."

He replied, "Thank you, ma'am, but I'll stay here out of the wind."

Al tittered.

Bee Tree ran for a couple and then tried a screen on third and long, which Roy sniffed out and almost intercepted, but didn't. The punter came close to sticking it on the two. Michael stood nonchalantly as if he might let it bound through the end zone or even signal for a fair catch, and then, at the last minute, he brazenly stole it from the sky and took off while we held our breaths—except Al, who puffed on like the Cannonball Express.

Michael streaked across the field against the flow and up the sideline all the way to the fifty. Six hundred in our stands hollered, Kjirsten did a cheerleader imitation with one fist high, and even Doug stood and peered around Al's smoky countenance.

Cuthbert, above the din, shouted to Galey, "Them boys is fired up tonight!"

Galey echoed, "Yes, sir! Fired up."

Bud said, "It's still early."

Doug rolled his eyes and sat.

With five minutes left in the first quarter, Bonnet scored first on Jason's thirty-two yard field goal.

Al lit another cigar.

Galey said, "Scoring first is a real good sign, ain't it, Doug?"

Doug replied, "It's a sign."

Cuthbert nodded in response. "I knew it."

Kjirsten squeezed my hand and whispered with her lips touching my cheek, "Let's go get a hot dog."

When we slid to the aisle, Al, clearly disappointed, cigar hanging from his lower lip, pleaded, "You ain't leaving us, are you, Miss Kjirsten?"

She tweaked his cheek. She tweaked his cheek! With a flip of her ponytail, she replied, "Don't worry, darlin', I'll come back."

If I could have seen the color of his face through the blue haze engulfing his pumpkin head, it would have been red as the glowing ember at the end of his Swisher.

Sally sat in the front row in Macey's old place next to Tildy. We stopped, and they squeezed together to make room for us. Sally made sure she brandished her ring at every opportunity. By that time, everyone in three counties knew she'd married the coach. The Llano paper had even called Hutch and said they were going to run a blurb in the sports section. His only request was that they wait until Saturday, after the last game.

Kjirsten and I sat with the gals for the remainder of the first half and in that time no less than half a dozen women stopped by to hug and squeal over Sally. We hadn't been there long when Derek's mom, neatly dressed in jeans, boots, and Bonnet Blue sweatshirt walked by, and then paused. She turned and courageously stood in front of the bride of the hour. She reached out, with mittens open, inviting Sally to take her hands.

"Mrs. Hutcheson," she said.

It was the first time I had heard those words spoken, and it sounded great. Sally cautiously smiled, unsure of Mrs. Richards's intent. After all, the Richards's household had been a seeping fount of wicked whispers about Little Sister.

"Mrs. Hutcheson, I don't know you well, but Derek idolizes Cobus. We love having him at our house. He is such a gentleman and you are to be congratulated on what a fine person he is."

Sally stammered, "Why…why, thank you. I don't know what to say. It's been an up-and-down season for us and I'm never sure how he does when he's on his own."

Mrs. Richards replied, "He has been a bright spot when he comes around. Derek is better for having him as a friend."

And then, after a moment of reflection, she added, "And congratulations on your wonderful news."

"Thank you, thank you," gushed Sally, warming to her new-found friend.

"I know how hard it must have been to wait so long to have love returned. When I heard, I was giddy all day—for you."

Sally, with eyes welling, hugged Mrs. Richards and asked, "Charlotte, would you please come by one morning next week for coffee?"

"I can't tell you how much that would mean to me," she answered.

Tildy enthusiastically rang in, "May I come?"

Sally clutched Charlotte's arms and, while beaming at her, answered, "Yes. Yes. All us gals. Tuesday at ten o'clock."

I wasn't sure if Charlotte or Sally would be the first to pop from an abundance of warm fuzziness.

Then Amanda yelled, "Get him!"

A Bee Tree tailback had broken free in the open field and was churning toward the goal line.

Sally hollered, "Get him, Cobus, get him!"

Too late. The kid hurtled just inside the end zone pylon, barely out of the reach of a diving Cobus and Roy. After the kick, it was seven to three.

Inez asked, "What happened? How did he get loose?"

With an explanation, the profundity of which would have sufficed had it been Galey, Cuthbert, or Al, I proclaimed, "That's football."

Tildy was more precise. "It was a counter. The left guard pulled and went right, the fullback faked right, and all our defense went with them. Aggression is a good thing, but our boys were overly so. It doesn't take much—one step was all the runner needed with Bonnet leaning the wrong way, and he was gone. You wait, Hutch will talk to them, and the next time they try it, we'll hold our ground and throw them for a loss."

Kjirsten said, "Tildy, you amaze me. How do you know so much about football?"

Tildy said, "You should sit with us, dear; you'd be surprised how clearly you can see things from here."

"Miss Tildy, I believe I will hold you to that."

I contemplated the emotional abuse I would suffer if I abandoned, for the company of beautiful women, my many years' tradition of bonding with my smelly, vulgar, semi-literate stablemates—except for Doug, who was only occasionally some of those things.

Tildy looked at me with feigned disgust—I believe it was feigned—and added, for Kjirsten, "Bring your companion, too; he can sit at the end."

Oh, goody.

With four minutes left in the half, Bonnet commenced a no-huddle claw down the field. Tommy connected on short sideline passes to Michael, and then Derek caught one for a three-yard gain. Cobus banged into both sides of the line. At sixty seconds and third and fifteen from our own forty-five, Michael leapt and made a trademark high-flying acrobatic catch over the top of a Bee-Tree corner for a first down.

Tommy called Cobus's number twice in a row to the left. It was third and seven and we needed another fifteen to reach Jason's field-goal range. Tommy dropped back and faked to Cobus before rolling the play-action to the right. Michael cut across the field; the zone had him sandwiched. Derek was open on the far left. John Elway could have reached him, but Tommy couldn't have without hanging the ball long enough in the air for the entire student body to camp beneath it. Cobus was the third option and Tommy dumped it to him barely two yards over the line. Cobus turned upfield and immediately broke two tackles, high-stepping from the grasp of one kid and leaving him a shoe for a souvenir. A third linebacker grabbed Cobus's jersey and Cobus spun hard, running backwards for three steps before the backer lost his grip and fell with Cobus's knee bouncing off of his helmet. It slowed him enough for the deep corner to jump on his back. Cobus carried the boy seven more yards, dragging, turning, bucking, and stiff-arming one more before four of them ganged him down in a heap. Jason kicked his second field goal of the game and the boys went to the halftime locker room with the score seven to six.

Kjirsten and I hunkered near the warmth of the snack shack to watch the halftime shows. The Bee Tree band members, and much of the rest of their student population, dressed as hillbillies, had scurried across the field to perform in front of us—the home crowd. Each girl paraded her own Ellie Mae Clampett creation with tied-on polka-dot halter tops, while the boys played Uncle Jed. We were stamping our feet and sipping cocoa to stay warm and the high-school girls on the field splayed bare belly buttons.

Kjirsten observed, "Can you imagine how goose-bumpy they must be?"

After solemn consideration, I held forth, "I'm concentrating on the musical intricacies of the orchestration."

They oompah-pahed the chicken dance. Everybody knows the chicken dance. I craned to see if Doug was flapping his wings, toe-scratchin', and bobbin' his beak for corn along with six hundred other peckers, but all I could see was Big Al and a growing evacuation around his polka-wobble, consuming more grandstand turf with each refrain. The other chickens in Al's barnyard looked to be in danger of being either bludgeoned by his rotund flails or buried beneath a catastrophic failure of the bleachers.

Then it was our girls' turn. After the Hatfields and McCoys retreated back across the field, the Bonnet drill squad, clad barely less scantily than the Bee Tree hill-fillies, strutted with poles and flags and pop music blaring.

Kjirsten wondered aloud, "How do they stay warm?"

"Hot blood," I said.

With the exception of Tater Potachnick, the Bonnet band members wore adorned wool uniforms that were considerably more seasonal than the sequined leotards of the drill team. Tater's halftime toils were hectic, if not heroic. He spent five minutes in the locker room absorbing what coaching wisdom he could, and then sprinted back to the field where he stripped to a t-shirt by removing helmet, jersey, and shoulder pads, placing them intact on the bench as a disembodied and faceless footballer bust. Tater was the lone tuba player. The band high-stepped rhythmically in plumed hats. Tater wore cleats, padded football pants, and short sleeves. When the band marched away to their final J. P. Sousa interpretation of the year, Tater slid back into his gear encouraged by the whoops of an adoring cheerleader coven.

Marvin's clear voice blared, "Let's hear it, folks, for Tater and the Bonnet High School Marching Band."

And then, except for eight boys under the age of ten playing water-bottle rugby on the forty, it was still. In the quiet, Bee Tree habitants dreamt a last time about a trip to the state tournament and we Bonnet dwellers plotted the foil. There were twenty-four minutes of football left in the season.

Marvin boomed, "Heeere's the Mustangs."

Kjirsten said, "I have a dilemma. I promised Al I would return, and I believe I committed to Tildy, as well."

"I believe you did."

She said, "How would you feel, if I…"

I completed her thought. "You sit with Tildy and Sally, far, far away from the cigar, and I will do my best to appease Big Al. We'll make it up to him at the café later."

She kissed me quick, for the first time so public, and disappeared in the jumble of fans ambling back into the stands. I climbed to the crow's nest of sages and sat beside Doug, the legend himself.

Al swiveled his head through a 720 degree arc and, unable to disguise his panic, whined, "Where's Miss Kjirsten?"

"She's conflicted," I said.

Jason's kickoff tumbled through the end zone and the Rodeo began on the twenty. Doug was no longer his ordinary, yawning, disinterested self. The endless, mindless stream of our rhetorical babble, which had drifted aimlessly into the ether for the better part of two decades, was finally deemed worthy of his consideration.

Bud thought aloud, "I suppose they'll come out throwin' like they did first half."

Doug, sitting fully upright, wired to every twitch on the field, responded, "Nope. They'll need to establish the run. For Bee Tree to win, they must wear down the right side of our defensive line. We have few good options for substitution there."

Galey, worried, asked, "Do you think they know that?"

The fullback crashed into our right defensive tackle, Mason, and the tailback gained four before the linebackers brought him down.

"I believe they do," said Doug.

Cuthbert, seeking confidence, said, "Hutch will figure it out."

"He already has, but we'll need a break."

Bud asked, "You mean we can't stop them?"

"We'll need a break."

Al blew smoke signals as the fullback bowled Mason over a second time.

For seven minutes, the Rodeo delivered blow after blow. Our slightest shift to the right was answered with response to opposite side for a bigger gain than the one before.

Doug said, "Watch now. We'll suck up the linebackers and they'll throw short passes."

Cobus feinted toward the line; the tight end slid behind him and caught a five-yard jump pass.

"What are we gonna do?" aired Al, with more smoke than voice.

Doug breathed deeply, scratched his chin, and posed, "Hutch is gonna need to get creative. He'll need to come out of the zone defense and go man to man so he can use the linebackers to stop the run."

Now I was concerned. "We don't have anyone fast enough to keep up with that Ingles kid."

Buck Ingles, an early signer with Texas Tech, was Bee Tree's speedster wide receiver, and had remained uncontained all year.

"Sure, we do," said Doug.

"Not Michael," I said. He has to stay deep. He's the last line of defense.

"Joaquin."

"Joaquin? Michael's little brother?"

"How many Joaquins do you know?"

"He's only a freshman. He hasn't played five downs on the varsity all year."

"Yeah, but he's faster than Michael."

"Maybe, but he doesn't weigh 120 pounds."

"Probably not."

Bee Tree ran another play action for a first down and then, from the twelve, the quarterback kept the ball on the option and scored.

Bud said, "That coach had better think of something fast."

Al ground out his Swisher on the bench and suggested, "Maybe you should go tell him your idea, Douggy."

Cuthbert, spiraling into bucolic depression, moaned, "Cain't see how no 120-pound freshman can tackle them big boys."

We got the ball for the first time with five minutes left in the third quarter and we were behind by eight. The clock doesn't stop as often in high school football as it does in the pros or college, so trailing with any amount of time left in the second half engenders a sense of urgency.

Bud said, "It's getting late in the game and we ain't even had the ball."

"Plenty of time. Plenty of time," said Doug.

Tommy began throwing the ball from the first down. He threw to Michael who dove for fingertip, ankle-high snares.

Cobus caught two short passes and punished would-be tacklers with shuddering collisions. Derek dropped one and then caught a short gainer. Tommy threw a screen to Roy, who ran for seven and another first down. The Mustangs flew down the field as if it were a two-minute drill. Michael made another highlight film grab in the back of the end zone to pull within two.

"That was too fast," said Galey. "They should be eatin' time off the clock like them Bee Tree boys."

"We're behind!" yelled Bud.

"But now we gotta give them the ball back," whimpered Cuthbert.

"Not yet," I said. "Now's the time we oughta go for two."

"You got it, pard," said Doug, standing.

Hutch called a pitch-out to Cobus who accelerated around Derek's end, and with Roy blocking ahead of him, finished with a high-reaching dive over the empty grasping arms of three of the enemy. The score was tied with barely a minute left in the third.

Doug pumped his fist once, and said, "Now we gotta give 'em the ball back." Then he sat.

The fourth quarter began as a copy of the third. Bee Tree continued their turf-grinding. The Rodeo chewed up thirty yards without offering a hint as to how they might be stopped.

With great trepidation, like Oz's man behind the curtain, Bud forewarned, "This looks bad."

I sat between Doug and the others; they couldn't hear when, under his breath, he said, "Now, Hutch, now."

On cue, as if Doug possessed a hotline to the coach, young Joaquin was summoned. Hutch stood with his arm around the boy and, with deliberate hand gestures, dictated the kid's rules of engagement. Joaquin nodded, and nodded, and then nodded again; he started onto the field and Hutch called him back. Hutch intensely barked a final order before the wide-eyed freshman sprinted to his place as the right cornerback. Cobus looked at Michael who shrugged with surprise; both of them jogged to the kid and swatted him hard on the butt.

Al wheezed, "Jesus, that boy is tiny."

"Oh, shit," said Bud.

Immediately, Cobus moved three steps closer to the line to stop the run. Bee Tree tried two running plays, like others that had been so successful, and they were stopped cold.

"It's working, ain't it?" said Cuthbert.

"Just like you said, Doug," added Galey.

Al lit a cigar.

"Watch this," Doug said to me, with a sigh of resignation.

Bee Tree ran a wide receiver directly at Joaquin, who peddled backwards quickly. The receiver button-hooked and caught a laser in front of the youngster for a first down on our thirty-eight. Again they backed him up, to the twenty-five and then the twelve.

Bud, the sanguine seer, declared, "It doesn't matter that he's too little; that boy don't get close enough to tackle anyone."

Al blew smoke rings. "What's next, Douggy?"

"Plenty of time," said Cuthbert.

"Plenty of time," aped Galey.

Doug leaned forward with elbows on knees as one of Al's concentrically expanding exhalations corralled his Stetson. Bee Tree's Ingles stood opposite Joaquin. The little boy, determined not to allow another pass to be caught in front of him, shuffled closer to the line with each cadence count. Doug rested his head in his hands. Ingles sprinted at Joaquin and then hesitated, allowing the youngster to close in tight. Had we been watching a Roadrunner cartoon, a blazing path arrowing to the end zone would have trailed Ingles's flame-spitting Nikes as he zipped past Joaquin on the way to an easy reception and touchdown. Point after. Twenty-one, fourteen, Bee Tree.

Bud stood with his hands on his hips and disgustedly pronounced, "Well, that's the shits."

With just over seven minutes left, Galey asked, "There's plenty of time, ain't there?"

Cuthbert replied, "Sure, there is. Ain't there, Doug?"

Doug drew an exasperated breath and Bud cut him off. "Don't ask him. He don't know any more than the rest of us."

The legend laughed and Bud sat back down with a huff.

Joaquin sat dejectedly alone on the end of the bench and the Bonnet varsity began their quest. Shoulder pads cracked; jerseys tore; helmets bounced off one another and a Bee Tree kid broke a bone when he tried to arm tackle Cobus. They carried him off and ferocity carried on. Two-and-a-half minutes vaporized and we had slugged our way to the forty with a mix of short passes and crunching runs. Suddenly, it was third and eight.

Doug stood, as did we all, and, incredulously shaking his head, gave us, "This is Texas football at its best."

"I hope I live through it," gasped Al.

Galey keenly pointed out, "We need a first down."

Bud avowed, "We're in four-down territory."

"No. No. No," fired Doug, staring directly at Bud.

With a scrunched frown, Bud shot back, "Well, I hope you ain't gonna' say there's plenty of time."

Michael and Cobus were covered well. Derek was the third option; he delayed and then released, slanting across the middle from right to left. Tommy hit him in the hands at the same time the Bee Tree corner nailed him in the middle of the back. The ball fell aimlessly to the ground and Derek crumpled. Cobus and Michael each grabbed an arm to pop him back up.

Angrily, Bud said, "He couldn't catch a cold."

I snapped. "Shut up, Bud. Shut the hell up. They're playing as damned hard as they can. He was speared in the back. It's tough to hang on to the ball when your spine goes numb."

On fourth down, Jason punted it into the end zone and Bee Tree got the ball on the twenty. Doug figured they'd need three first downs to run out the clock. Bee Tree wanted three yards and a cloud of dust—ten times in a row.

It didn't work out that way. Bee Tree rolled off two first downs and three minutes and then stalled. On third down, a lineman jumped early and the five-yard penalty gave them a third and nine from their own forty-five with ninety seconds remaining. They had choices. They could run the ball to keep the clock moving and then punt on fourth down, or they could try to pass for one final first down. Hutch sent Joaquin back in the game and the linebackers moved closer to the line to stop the run.

"Here we go," said Al in a bellow.

"You mean here we go, *again*," said Bud. "I can't see why you would put that grade-schooler back in after they already turned him inside-out."

I looked to Doug hoping for an answer, because as much as it pained me to admit it, I was wondering the same thing as Bud. Doug stared on without even a tick of the lip.

Michael trotted over to his little brother, grabbed him by the helmet, and plainly delivered a stern, but brief, admonition. Ingles pointed tauntingly at Joaquin, eight yards away. It began as an instant replay of their previous face off. Ingles confidently sprinted at Joaquin and then stutter-stepped like before only this time the young defender began backpedaling in place instead of rising to the bait. When Ingles lit the after-burners, Joaquin ignited a jet of his own. Stride-by-lightning stride, he mirrored the racer across the field, a mere two steps behind. When the ball was in the air, I could see that two steps were enough for Ingles to make his last catch for Bee Tree. Michael would make the tackle. They would have a first down and their trip to the playoffs.

But then, with a blue-and-white-hot burst that will be relived in Al's hallowed café for as long as Bonnet's erudite gather to imbibe, Joaquin rocketed like a surface-to-air missile, soaring high at the speed of flight, stretching higher than Ingles, higher than Michael, and snatched the spiral from its arc, quick as a swift on a fly.

Our roar was louder than any that had ever risen from old Bonnet stadium. We whooped like kids, standing, stomping, and backslapping. Michael picked up Joaquin and carried him off the field. Hutch gave the kid a congratulatory slap on the helmet and then immediately turned his attention to the offense and a last effort to score.

Bud yelled, "Did you see that, Doug? You're a genius! So is Coach Hutch. So is the kid. You all are!"

"Lucky...damn lucky," said Doug to me.

Galey nodded as if he'd been given an infusion of divine wisdom. "You knowed that was gonna happen all along, didn't ya, Doug?"

"Of course, he did," answered brother Cuthbert. "He told us, didn't he?"

"We still gotta score," reminded Doug.

Al, who, after drawing four inches of ash in thirty seconds, was entirely cocooned in a nauseatingly sweet, smoky cloud, proclaimed, "We will. We will. I can see it comin'," while it stretched credulity to believe he could see anything at all, given the density of his haze.

Man, woman, and child! How right Al was. The Tommy, Michael, and Cobus show scored in five plays. Tommy threw bullets. Michael caught one on the left sideline and then Cobus on the right; both were first downs. Michael received another on a slant across the middle and called time out. On the fourth play, from the fifteen, Tommy rolled right and Michael angled into the end zone from the left. Tommy pump-faked to Michael and then pivoted hard to throw back across the field to Cobus. Tommy's last pass for Bonnet was a perfect strike. Cobus made a simple basket catch and stepped out of bounds at the five. On the scoring play, with twelve seconds left, Cobus took a pitch out to the right and powered through the last Bee Tree hope with a jarring shoulder shot.

We were one down and could have kicked the tying point-after. I asked, "Whatta we do, Doug?"

Bud interrupted. "We'd better kick for one. We'll get 'em in overtime."

Doug, not so confident, replied, "Joaquin hasn't returned to earth yet. I'm not sure we'll stop them again."

"That's right," said Bud, steadfast as ever, "we'd better go for two."

Bonnet broke from the huddle; Cobus lined up on the right.

"They're gonna run the same play," I pointed out.

Doug murmured, "Hmmm."

"Again?" wondered Bud.

Big Al, the shaman, chanted, "If it ain't broke, don't fix it."

"It sure ain't broke," chimed Cuthbert.

Tommy flicked it to Cobus who was confronted immediately by three Bee Tree defenders barreling toward him like stampeding bulls. Calmly, he stopped, stepped, and lobbed the only pass he ever threw for Bonnet. It wasn't a pretty pass. It didn't matter that it fluttered and hung on the air for a lifetime. Derek stood alone and cradled the dying swan in his arms, in the end zone, for two points.

Galey bellowed like a Klaxon. "We won! We won!"

We barely noticed the kickoff to Bee Tree and their feeble attempt to lateral as the clock ran out. We had beaten them and they would have an entire year to mull over what might have been. Bonnet's young and old charged the field to devour the delicious pandemonium.

Bud shouted, "C'mon, boys, let's go pat 'em on the back," and the four tromped down the stairs to join the melee.

The legend and I stayed behind. We sat back and drank it in. The boys took turns lifting each other high to undying cheers—Tommy, Cobus, Michael—one after another. They held Joaquin above their heads and all the girls patted at him like he was a cute little piñata. Tildy, Amanda, and Inez stood applauding on the sidelines, bundled in matching blue and white scarves, knitted berets, and mittens.

Doug said, "At this moment, there is no better place on earth than this."

"None," I replied, with a calm I had not known for a season.

On the field, Sally waited patiently for her man. When he saw her, he squeezed her with a quick one-arm hug and she stayed by his side.

"They're good together," said Doug.

"You okay with that?"

"I love 'em both."

I scanned the stadium for Kjirsten and found her making her way up the steps—waving, smiling—at me.

He said, "I hope you know how lucky you are. If you don't marry her soon, I'll kick your ass."

She sat close and kissed me.

Standing, the legend said, "I'll see you two at Al's."

"Perhaps," she replied.

. . .